W9-BAM-820

Isaac Asimov Presents

THE GOLDEN YEARS OF SCIENCE FICTION

Isaac Asimov Presents

THE GOLDEN YEARS OF SCIENCE FICTION

FIFTH SERIES

33 Stories and Novellas

Edited by
Isaac Asimov and
Martin H. Greenberg

BONANZA BOOKS
New York

This 1985 edition is published by Bonanza Books,
distributed by Crown Publishers, Inc., by arrangement with
Daw Books, Inc.

This book was previously published as two separate works entitled:
Isaac Asimov Presents the Great SF Stories 9 (1947)
Isaac Asimov Presents the Great SF Stories 10 (1948)

Printed and Bound in the United States of America

Library of Congress Cataloging in Publication Data
Main entry under title:
Isaac Asimov presents the golden years of science fiction.
"Previously published as two separate works entitled
Isaac Asimov presents the great SF stories 9 and Isaac
Asimov presents the great SF stories 10"—T.p. verso.
Includes index.
1. Science fiction, American. 2. Science fiction,
English. I. Asimov, Isaac, 1920- II. Title:
Golden years of science fiction.
PS648.S3178 1985 813'.0876'08 85-3784
ISBN: 0-517-475669

h g f e d c b a

CONTENTS

Introduction		7
LITTLE LOST ROBOT	Isaac Asimov	15
TOMORROW'S CHILDREN	Poul Anderson	42
CHILD'S PLAY	William Tenn	71
TIME AND TIME AGAIN	H. Beam Piper	100
TINY AND THE MONSTER	Theodore Sturgeon	119
E FOR EFFORT	T.L. Sherred	155
LETTER TO ELLEN	Chan Davis	207
THE FIGURE	Edward Grendon	220
WITH FOLDED HANDS...	Jack Williamson	226
THE FIRES WITHIN	Arthur C. Clarke	272
ZERO HOUR	Ray Bradbury	282
HOBBYIST	Eric Frank Russell	293
EXIT THE PROFESSOR	Lewis Padgett	327
THUNDER AND ROSES	Theodore Sturgeon	343
DON'T LOOK NOW	Henry Kuttner	367
HE WALKED AROUND THE HORSES	H. Beam Piper	381
THE STRANGE CASE OF JOHN KINGMAN	Murray Leinster	403
THAT ONLY A MOTHER	Judith Merril	420
THE MONSTER	A.E. van Vogt	431
DREAMS ARE SACRED	Peter Phillips	448
MARS IS HEAVEN	Ray Bradbury	471
THANG	Martin Gardner	489
BROOKLYN PROJECT	William Tenn	492
RING AROUND THE REDHEAD	John D. MacDonald	503
PERIOD PIECE	J.J. Coupling	523
DORMANT	A.E. van Vogt	532
IN HIDING	Wilmar H. Shiras	549
KNOCK	Fredric Brown	583
A CHILD IS CRYING	John D. MacDonald	594
LATE NIGHT FINAL	Eric Frank Russell	607

FOREWORD

This continuing series by Isaac Asimov and Martin H. Greenberg is one of the most exciting projects in the field of science fiction. Every reviewer has praised it, and every volume has been eagerly added to the growing file of what is truly worthwhile in sf short stories and novellas.

The years 1947 and 1948 bring sf out of the so-called Golden Age of Science Fiction and into the Diamond Age of post-war sf, when writers began to assume a greater maturity and the future was shaping into the world we know today. Showcasing the talents of Ray Bradbury, Isaac Asimov, A.E. van Vogt, William Tenn, Poul Anderson, and many others, this collection will delight readers, whether they are sf buffs or not.

A.J.F.

ACKNOWLEDGMENTS

Asimov–Copyright © 1947 by Street and Smith Publications, Inc.; copyright renewed, 1974, by Isaac Asimov. Reprinted by permission of the author.

Anderson–Copyright © 1947 by Street and Smith Publications, Inc.; copyright renewed. Reprinted by permission of the author and his agents, the Scott Meredith Literary Agency, Inc., 845 Third Ave., New York, NY 10022.

Tenn–Copyright © 1947 by Street and Smith Publications, Inc.; copyright renewed. Reprinted by permission of the author.

Piper–Copyright © 1947 by Street and Smith Publications, Inc.; copyright renewed. Reprinted by permission of the agents for the author's estate, the Scott Meredith Literary Agency, Inc., 845 Third Ave., New York, NY 10022.

Sturgeon–Copyright © 1947 by Street and Smith Publications, Inc., copyright renewed. Reprinted by permission of Kirby McCauley, Ltd.

Sherred–Copyright © 1947, 1975 by T.L. Sherred; reprinted by permission of the author and the author's agent, Virginia Kidd.

Davis–Copyright © 1947, 1953 by Chan Davis; reprinted by permission of the author and the author's agent, Virginia Kidd.

Grendon–Copyright © 1947 by Lawrence LeShan; reprinted by permission of the author.

Williamson–Copyright © 1947 by Street and Smith Publications, Inc.; copyright renewed. Reprinted by permission of the author and his agents, the Scott Meredith Literary Agency, Inc.; 845 Third Ave., New York, NY 10022.

Clarke–Copyright © 1947 by Arthur C. Clarke; copyright renewed. Reprinted by permission of the author and his agents, the Scott Meredith Literary Agency, Inc., 845 Third Ave., New York, NY 10022.

Bradbury–Copyright © 1947 by Ray Bradbury; Copyright © renewed 1974. Reprinted by permission of the Harold Matson Co., Inc.

Russell–Copyright © 1947 by Street and Smith Publications, Inc.; copyright renewed. Reprinted by permission of the agents for the author's estate, the Scott Meredith Literary Agency, Inc., 845 Third Ave., New York, NY 10022.

Kuttner–Copyright © 1947 by Henry Kuttner; Copyright renewed 1974. Reprinted by permission of the Harold Matson Co., Inc.

Sturgeon–Copyright © 1947 by Street and Smith Publications, Inc. Copyright renewed. Reprinted by permission of Kirby McCauley, Ltd.

INTRODUCTION

In the world outside reality the second post-World War II year saw the President proclaim his Truman Doctrine, which stated that the United States would aid countries facing Communist insurrection. Fears of Europe "going Communist" also played an important role in the development of the Marshall Plan, named for the Secretary of State, which provided for massive aid to European countries. The July issue of *Foreign Affairs* contained an article written by "X" (George F. Kennan of the State Department) which argued for a policy based on the containment of the Soviet Union. The Central Intelligence Agency was established to integrate the diverse elements of the U.S. intelligence community.

In August, India, led by Jawaharlal Nehru, and Pakistan, led by Mohammed Ali Jinnah, became independent as India was partitioned amid great communal fighting and bloodshed. The price for a ride on the New York subway jumped to a dime after having been a nickel for the previous 43 years. The Hollywood Black List heralded the beginning of a search for communists and "subversives" that would divide the country and ruin the lives of many people.

The Bell X-1 broke the sound barrier in level flight on October 10, the first aircraft to do so since manned flight began in 1903. The American Willard Frank Libby developed the "atomic clock" which would make great contributions to the study of archaeology, which also received a tremendous boost with the discovery of the Dead Sea scrolls. Nineteen forty-seven saw the beginning of a series of sightings of Unidentified Flying Objects (UFOs) that would soon turn into a craze of believers, while Thor Heyerdahl crossed the Pacific Ocean on his raft, the *Kon-Tiki*.

Ajax appeared and reduced sore elbows, while Almond Joy

candy bars and Reddi-Wip made their way to grocery store shelves.

During 1947 James Michener published *Tales of the South Pacific*. "Open the Door, Richard," "Too Fat Polka," "Feudin and Fightin," and "Woody Woodpecker" were hit songs. The New York Yankees took the World Series from the Brooklyn Dodgers four games to three—sorry, Isaac. Pablo Picasso painted "Ulysses with his Sirens," while Henry Moore produced his "Three Standing Figures." The *Chicago Sun-Times* appeared for the first time. Jackie Robinson became the first black player in the major leagues while Notre Dame was the number one ranked college football team in the nation. Alberto Moravia wrote *The Woman of Rome*. *Brigadoon, Finian's Rainbow,* and *High Button Shoes* were the top Broadway musicals of the year. Joe Louis was still the heavyweight boxing champion of the world and the record for the mile run was Gunder Haegg of Sweden's 4:01:4. The company that would become the Sony Corporation was founded.

Roger Sessions' "Symphony No. 2" was performed for the first time in 1947. Jet Pilot won the Kentucky Derby, Ted Williams led the American League with a .343 average, and Jack Kramer was the U.S. tennis champion. Outstanding Broadway productions included *Medea* by Robinson Jeffers, *All My Sons* by Arthur Miller, and *A Streetcar Named Desire* with a young Marlon Brando in the lead. Saul Bellow's *The Victim* appeared, while Henri Matisse painted his "English Girl."

Holy Cross was the NCAA basketball champion and Johnny Mize and Ralph Kiner shared the home run title in the majors with 51 each. The best films of a very good year included *Great Expectations, Body and Soul, Boomerang,* directed by Elia Kazan, *The Voice of the Turtle,* featuring one Ronald Reagan, *Nightmare Alley,* and Charlie Chaplin's *Monsieur Verdoux*. John Steinbeck published *The Wayward Bus*. Joe DiMaggio was the Most Valuable Player in the American League.

Death took the great bullfighter Manolete (as the animals partially evened the score), George II of Greece, Christian X of Denmark, and Henry Ford, who left the bulk of his considerable fortune for use by the Ford Foundation.

Mel Brooks was (probably) still Melvin Kaminsky.

In the real world it was another outstanding year as a

number of fine science fiction and fantasy novels and collections were published (many of which had been serialized years before in the magazines), including *Dark Carnival* by Ray Bradbury, *The Mightiest Machine* by John W. Campbell, Jr., *Doppelgangers* by H. F. Heard, *Rocket Ship Gallileo* by Robert A. Heinlein, *Night's Black Agents* by Fritz Leiber, *The Black Wheel* by A. Merritt (a work completed by his friend, the artist Hannes Bok), *Greener Than You Think* by Ward Moore, *Spacehounds of IPC* by E. E. ("Doc") Smith, *Venus Equilateral* by George O. Smith, *The Weapon Makers* and *The Book of Ptath* by A. E. van Vogt, and *The Legion of Space* by Jack Williamson. Many of these books were published by fan publishers whose companies did not last long. In addition, Lloyd Eshbach published his interesting *Of Worlds Beyond: The Science of Science-Fiction Writing,* one of the first works on sf from within the field.

Avon began its *Avon Fantasy Reader,* edited by Donald A. Wollheim, but the British *Fantasy* died after only three issues.

More wondrous things were happening in the real world as four excellent writers made their maiden voyages into reality: in March, Poul Anderson with "Tomorrow's Children" (which was published as a collaboration with F.N. Waldrop, but since Waldrop only provided some ideas and did none of the writing, it appears in this book as by Anderson alone); "Time and Time Again" by H. Beam Piper in April; T. L. Sherred with the wonderful "E for Effort" in May; and Alfred Coppel with "Age of Unreason" in December.

The real people gathered together for the fifth time as the World Science Fiction Convention (the Philcon) was held in Philadelphia.

Death took J.D. Beresford, Miles J. Breuer, Arthur Machen, and M. P. Shiel.

But distant wings were beating as Octavia Butler, Gardner Dozois, George Alec Effinger, Bruce Gillespie, Stephen Goldin, Stuart Gordon, Stephen King, Tanith Lee, Cory Panshin, and John Varley were born.

Let us travel back to that honored year of 1947 and enjoy the best stories that the real world bequeathed to us.

And now, on to 1948 . . .

In the world outside reality, the year began on a bloody note with the assassination of the Indian leader Mahatma Gandhi on January 30. On February 25 a communist coup ended Czechoslovakia's brief moment of post-war democracy as that country fell firmly into the grip of the Soviets. On May 10 the United States Army began to run the U.S. railroad system under orders from President Truman, who moved to head off a threatened strike.

Zionist leader David Ben-Gurion proclaimed the founding of the state of Israel on May 14, the day the British left Palestine. The new country was invaded the following day by the regular armies of five Arab countries, beginning a war that would last into 1949. On June 28 Yugoslavia was expelled from the Cominform, as Marshal Tito insisted on his own form of "national Communism." U.S.-Soviet tension continued to grow throughout the year, formalized by presidential adviser Bernard Baruch's coining of the term "the Cold War." On July 24 Soviet forces began a blockade of all rail and highway movement into the Western sector of Berlin, precipitating the "Berlin Blockade" that would not end until September, 1949. The city was kept alive by a difficult airlift by Western aircraft.

On August 15 the Republic of Korea (South Korea) was established under the rule of President Syngman Rhee; on September 9 the Communists established the Korean People's Democratic Republic (North Korea).

The 1948 U.S. Presidential election was won by Harry Truman in one of the greatest political upsets in American history. Truman won despite challenges from Strom Thurmond's Dixiecrats and Henry Wallace's Progressive Party. On December 15 a federal jury indicted Alger Hiss, a former State Department employee, for perjury, charging that he had lied about passing classified materials to Soviet agents. The indictment was the result of an investigation led by a young California Congressman, Richard M. Nixon.

During 1948 Richard P. Feynman and Julian Schwinger developed a new quantum theory of electrodynamics. Idlewild International Airport (later John F. Kennedy) opened for business in New York. Ferdinand Porsche introduced the car named after him, while Soichiro Honda showed off his new motorcycle. Hench and Kendall synthesized the hormone cortisone. Many people learned the joys of traveling after the introduction of Dramamine. The number of homes with television sets reached 1,000,000.

The Olympic Games, after a long interruption caused by World War II, were held in London. The United States won the most medals, but the powerful Soviet team, competing in the Games for the first time in history, finished a strong second. Leading novels and books included *The Naked and the Dead* by Norman Mailer, *The Heart of the Matter* by Graham Greene, *Intruder in the Dust* by William Faulkner, *The City and the Pillar* by Gore Vidal, and *The Young Lions* by Irwin Shaw. The Cleveland Indians defeated the Boston Braves (remember them?) four games to two in the World Series. Jackson Pollock painted "Composition No. 1." "V-8" cocktail juice was brought out by the Campbell Soup Company.

Top films included *The Treasure of the Sierra Madre*, starring Humphrey Bogart, *The Lady from Shanghai* with Rita Hayworth, *Red River*, with John Wayne, *Portrait of Jennie*, and *Key Largo*, with Lauren Bacall and Humphrey Bogart exchanging knowing glances. Citation won Racing's Triple Crown. The Bell Telephone Laboratories invented the transistor, which would revolutionize electronics and warfare.

Norbert Wiener published *Cybernetics*, while Alfred C. Kinsey published the equally interesting *Sexual Behavior in the Human Male*. "Pogo," *US News and World Report*, and the radial tire made their debuts. Broadway hits included *Mr. Roberts*, *Where's Charley?*, *Summer and Smoke*, *Anne of a Thousand Days* and *Kiss Me Kate*. The world was singing such songs as "Once in Love With Amy," "Tennessee Waltz," "Baby, It's Cold Outside," "I'll Be Home for Christmas," and "Red Roses for a Blue Lady." Three of the top television shows were *Hopalong Cassidy*, *The Ed Sullivan Show*, and *The Original Amateur Hour*, with Ted Mack. The McDonald brothers offered franchises to those willing to sell fast food.

Mel Brooks was (probably) still Melvin Kaminsky.

In the real world it was another outstanding year as a large number of excellent science fiction novels and collections were published (many of which had been serialized years before in the magazines), including *Who Goes There?* by John W. Campbell, Jr., *The Sunken World* by Stanton Coblentz, *Divide and Rule* and *The Wheels of If* by L. Sprague de Camp . . . *And Some Were Human* by Lester Del Rey, *The Radio Man* by Ralph Milne Farley, *Space Cadet* and *Beyond This Horizon* by Robert A.

Heinlein, *The Well of the Unicorn* and *The Carnelian Cube* by Fletcher Pratt (the latter with de Camp), *Walden Two* by B. F. Skinner, *Skylark Three and Triplanetary* by E. E. ("Doc") Smith, *Without Sorcery* by Theodore Sturgeon, *The World of A* by A. E. van Vogt, *The Black Flame* by Stanley G. Weinbaum, and *Darker Than You Think* by Jack Williamson. Many of these books were published by fan publishers whose companies did not last for long. In addition, Groff Conklin published *The Treasury of Science Fiction*, continuing his series of wonderful anthologies that mined the Golden Age.

More wondrous things were happening in the real world as three excellent writers made their maiden voyages into reality: Judith Merril with "That Only a Mother" in June, Charles L. Harness with "Time Tomb" in August, and Peter Phillips with the stunning "Dreams Are Sacred" in September.

The first Westercon was held in September, and the real people gathered together for the sixth time as the World Science Fiction Convention (Torcon in Toronto) moved outside the borders of the United States.

And distant wings were beating as Michael Ashley, Robert P. Holdstock, Jonathan Fast, Vonda McIntyre, Marta Randall, Robert Reginald, Spider Robinson, Pamela Sargent, Brian Stableford, Steven Utley, Joan Vinge, and Laurence Yep were born.

Let us travel back to that honored year of 1948 and enjoy the best stories that the real world bequeathed to us.

Isaac Asimov Presents

THE GOLDEN YEARS OF SCIENCE FICTION

LITTLE LOST ROBOT

by Isaac Asimov (1920-   )

ASTOUNDING SCIENCE FICTION
March

In a way, this story was a celebration.

I had been inducted into the army immediately after the end of the war, and there I chafed away at a variety of useless tasks, during which I had time to write only a single story, "Evidence" (see the 1946 volume of this series) and I had had to mail that off from Hawaii. I had strong withdrawal symptoms as far as my writing was concerned, naturally.

After my discharge, I spent six weeks picking up the threads of life—finding a place to live, reestablishing myself at Columbia University—and then I plunged furiously into writing once again.

"Little Lost Robot" was the sixth of my positronic robot series and the longest up to that time. I wrote it without pause, just as quickly as I could, and brought it in to John Campbell the day after it was done. He read it and took it on the spot.

It was with "Little Lost Robot," I think, that I recognized that my robot stories tended to have strong mystery components. They were stories which dealt with problems that had to be solved by ratiocination. It was that which initiated the pull that finally led me to the writing of outright science fiction mysteries, and even to mysteries without a science fiction component.—I.A.

Measures on Hyper Base had been taken in a sort of rattling fury—the muscular equivalent of an hysterical shriek.

To itemize them in order of both chronology and desperation, they were:

1. All work on the Hyperatomic Drive through all the space volume occupied by the Stations of the Twenty-Seventh Asteroidal Grouping came to a halt.

2. That entire volume of space was nipped out of the System, practically speaking. No one entered without permission. No one left under any conditions.

3. By special government patrol ship, Drs. Susan Calvin and Peter Bogert, respectively Head Psychologist and Mathematical Director of United States Robot & Mechanical Men Corporation, were brought to Hyper Base.

Susan Calvin had never left the surface of Earth before, and had no perceptible desire to leave it this time. In an age of Atomic Power and a clearly coming Hyperatomic Drive, she remained quietly provincial. So she was dissatisfied with her trip and unconvinced of the emergency, and every line of her plain, middle-aged face showed it clearly enough during her first dinner at Hyper Base.

Nor did Dr. Bogert's sleek paleness abandon a certain hangdog attitude. Nor did Major-general Kallner, who headed the project, even once forgot to maintain a hunted expression.

In short, it was a grisly episode, that meal, and the little session of three that followed began in a gray, unhappy manner.

Kallner, with his baldness glistening, and his dress uniform oddly unsuited to the general mood, began with uneasy directness.

"This is a queer story to tell, sir, and madam. I want to thank you for coming on short notice and without a reason being given. We'll try to correct that now. We've lost a robot. Work has stopped and *must* stop until such time as we locate it. So far we have failed, and we feel we need expert help."

Perhaps the general felt his predicament anticlimactic. He continued with a note of desperation, "I needn't tell you the importance of our work here. More than eighty percent of last year's appropriations for scientific research have gone to us—"

"Why, we know that," said Bogert, agreeably. "U.S. Robots is receiving a generous rental fee for use of our robots."

Susan Calvin injected a blunt, vinegary note, "What makes a single robot so important to the project, and why hasn't it been located?"

The general turned his red face toward her and wet his lips quickly, "Why, in a manner of speaking, we *have* located it." Then, with near anquish, "Here, suppose I explain. As soon as the robot failed to report, a state of emergency was declared, and all movement off Hyper Base stopped. A cargo vessel had landed the previous day and had delivered us two robots for our laboratories. It had sixty-two robots of the . . . uh . . . same type for shipment elsewhere. We are certain as to that figure. There is no question about it whatever."

"Yes? And the connection?"

"When our missing robot failed of location anywhere—I assure you we would have found a missing blade of grass if it had been there to find—we brainstormed ourselves into counting the robots left on the cargo ship. They have sixty-three now."

"So that the sixty-third, I take it, is the missing prodigal?"

Dr. Calvin's eyes darkened. "Yes, but we have no way of telling which is the sixty-third."

There was a dead silence while the electric clock chimed eleven times, and then the robopsychologist said, "Very peculiar," and the corners of her lips moved downward.

"Peter," she turned to her colleague with a trace of savagery, "what's wrong here? What kind of robots are they using at Hyper Base?"

Dr. Bogert hesitated and smiled feebly, "It's been rather a matter of delicacy till now, Susan."

She spoke rapidly, "Yes, *till* now. If there are sixty-three same-type robots, one of which is wanted and the identity of which cannot be determined, why won't any of them do? What's the idea of all this? Why have we been sent for?"

Bogert said in resigned fashion, "If you'll give me a chance, Susan— Hyper Base happens to be using several robots whose brains are not impressioned with the entire First Law of Robotics."

"*Aren't* impressioned?" Calvin slumped back in her chair, "I see. How many were made?"

"A few. It was on government order and there was no way of violating the secrecy. No one was to know except the top men directly concerned. You weren't included, Susan. It was nothing I had anything to do with."

The general interrupted with a measure of authority. "I would like to explain that bit. I hadn't been aware that Dr. Calvin was unacquainted with the situation. I needn't tell you, Dr. Calvin, that there always has been strong opposition to robots on the Planet. The only defense the government has had against the Fundamentalist radicals in this matter was the fact that robots are always built with an unbreakable First Law—which makes it impossible for them to harm human beings under any circumstance.

"But we *had* to have robots of a different nature. So just a few of the NS-2 model, the Nestors, that is, were prepared with a modified First Law. To keep it quiet, all NS-2's are manufactured without serial numbers; modified members are delivered here along with a group of normal robots; and, of course, all our kind are under the strictest impressionment never to tell of their modification to unauthorized personnel." He wore an embarrassed smile. "This has all worked out against us now."

Calvin said grimly, "Have you asked each one who it is, anyhow? Certainly, you are authorized?"

The general nodded, "All sixty-three deny having worked here—and one is lying."

"Does the one you want show traces of wear? The others, I take it, are factory-fresh."

"The one in question only arrived last month. It, and the two that have just arrived, were to be the last we needed. There's no perceptible wear." He shook his head slowly and his eyes were haunted again, "Dr. Calvin, we don't dare let that ship leave. If the existence of non-First Law robots becomes general knowledge—" There seemed no way of avoiding understatement in the conclusion.

"Destroy all sixty-three," said the robopsychologist coldly and flatly, "and make an end of it."

Bogert drew back a corner of his mouth. "You mean destroy thirty thousand dollars per robot? I'm afraid U. S. Robots wouldn't like that. We'd better make an effort first, Susan, before we destroy anything."

"In that case," she said sharply, "I need facts. Exactly what advantage does Hyper Base derive from these modified robots? What factor made them desirable, general?"

Kallner ruffled his forehead and stroked it with an upward gesture of his hand. "We had trouble with our previous robots. Our men work with hard radiations a good deal, you see. It's dangerous, of course, but reasonable precautions are taken. There have been only two accidents since we began and neither was fatal. However, it was impossible to explain that to an ordinary robot. The First Law states—I'll quote it—*'No robot may harm a human being, or through inaction, allow a human being to come to harm.'*

"That's primary, Dr. Calvin. When it was necessary for one of our men to expose himself for a short period to a moderate gamma field, one that would have no physiological effects, the nearest robot would dash in to drag him out. If the field were exceedingly weak, it would succeed, and work could not continue till all robots were cleared out. If the field were a trifle stronger, the robot would never reach the technician concerned, since its positronic brain would collapse under gamma radiations—and then we would be out one expensive and hard-to-replace robot.

"We tried arguing with them. Their point was that a human being in a gamma field was endangering his life and that it didn't matter that he could remain there half an hour safely. Supposing, they would say, he forgot and remained an hour. They couldn't take chances. We pointed out that they were risking their lives on a wild off-chance. But self-preservation is only the Third Law of Robotics—and the First Law of human safety came first. We gave them orders; we ordered them strictly and harshly to remain out of gamma fields at whatever cost. But obedience is only the Second Law of Robotics—and the First Law of human safety came first. Dr. Calvin, we either had to do without robots, or do something about the First Law—and we made our choice."

"I can't believe," said Dr. Calvin, "that it was found possible to remove the First Law."

"It wasn't removed, it was modified," explained Kallner. "Positronic brains were constructed that contained the positive aspect only of the Law, which in them reads: '*No robot may harm a human being.*' That is all. They have no compulsion to prevent one coming to harm through an extraneous agency such as gamma rays. I state the matter correctly, Dr. Bogert?"

"Quite," assented the mathematician.

"And that is the only difference of your robots from the ordinary NS-2 model? The *only* difference? Peter?"

"The *only* difference, Susan."

She rose and spoke with finality, "I intend sleeping now, and in about eight hours, I want to speak to whomever saw the robot last. And from now on, General Kallner, if I'm to take any responsibility at all for events, I want full and unquestioned control of this investigation."

Susan Calvin, except for two hours of resentful lassitude, experienced nothing approaching sleep. She signaled at Bogert's door at the local time of 0700 and found him also awake. He had apparently taken the trouble of transporting a dressing gown to Hyper Base with him, for he was sitting in it. He put his nail scissors down when Calvin entered.

He said softly, "I've been expecting you more or less. I suppose you feel sick about all this."

"I do."

"Well—I'm sorry. There was no way of preventing it. When the call came out from Hyper Base for us, I knew that something must have gone wrong with the modified Nestors. But what was there to do? I couldn't break the matter to you on the trip here as I would have liked to, because I had to be sure. The matter of the modification is top secret."

The psychologist muttered, "I should have been told. U. S. Robots had no right to modify positronic brains this way without the approval of a psychologist."

Bogert lifted his eyebrows and sighed. "Be reasonable, Susan. You couldn't have influenced them. In this matter, the government was bound to have its way. They want the Hyperatomic Drive and the etheric physicists want robots that won't interfere with them. They were going to get them even if it did mean twisting the First Law. We had to admit it was possible from a construction standpoint and they swore a mighty oath that they wanted only twelve, that they would be used only at Hyper Base, that they would be destroyed once the Drive was perfected, and that full precautions would be taken. And they insisted on secrecy—and that's the situation."

Dr. Calvin spoke through her teeth, "I would have resigned."

"It wouldn't have helped. The government was offering the company a fortune, and threatening it with antirobot legislation in case of a refusal. We were stuck then, and we're badly stuck now. If this leaks out, it might hurt Kallner and the government, but it would hurt U. S. Robots a devil of a lot more."

The psychologist stared at him. "Peter, don't you realize what all this is about? Can't you understand what the removal of the First Law means? It isn't just a matter of secrecy."

"I know what removal would mean. I'm not a child. It would mean complete instability, with no nonimaginary solutions to the positronic Field Equations."

"Yes, mathematically. But can you translate that into crude psychological thought. All normal life, Peter, consciously or otherwise, resents domination. If the domination is by an inferior, or by a supposed inferior, the resentment becomes stronger. Physically, and, to an extent, mentally, a robot—any robot—is superior to human beings. What makes him slavish, then? *Only the First Law!* Why, without it, the first order you tried to give a robot would result in your death. Unstable? What do you think?"

"Susan," said Bogert, with an air of sympathetic amusement. "I'll admit that this Frankenstein Complex you're exhibiting has a certain justification—hence the First Law in the first place. But the Law, I repeat and repeat, has not been removed—merely modified."

"And what about the stability of the brain?"

The mathematician thrust out his lips, "Deceased, naturally. But it's within the border of safety. The first Nestors were delivered to Hyper Base nine months ago, and nothing whatever has gone wrong till now, and even this involves merely fear of discovery and not danger to humans."

"Very well, then. We'll see what comes of the morning conference."

Bogert saw her politely to the door and grimaced eloquently when she left. He saw no reason to change his perennial opinion of her as a sour and fidgety frustration.

Susan Calvin's train of thought did not include Bogert in the least. She had dismissed him years ago as a smooth and pretentious sleekness.

Gerald Black had taken his degree in etheric physics the year before and, in common with his entire generation of physicists, found himself engaged in the problem of the Drive. He now made a proper addition to the general atmosphere of these meetings on Hyper Base. In his stained white smock, he was half rebellious and wholly uncertain. His stocky strength seemed striving for release and his fingers, as they twisted each other with nervous yanks, might have forced an iron bar out of true.

Major-general Kallner sat beside him, the two from U. S. Robots faced him.

Black said, "I'm told that I was the last to see Nestor 10 before he vanished. I take it you want to ask me about that."

Dr. Calvin regarded him with interest, "You sound as if you were not sure, young man. Don't you *know* whether you were the last to see him?"

"He worked with me, ma'am, on the field generators, and he was with me the morning of his disappearance. I don't know if anyone saw him after about noon. No one admits having done so."

"Do you think anyone's lying about it?"

"I don't say that. But I don't say that I want the blame of it, either." His dark eyes smoldered.

"There's no question of blame. The robot acted as it did because of what it is. We're just trying to locate it, Mr. Black, and let's put everything else aside. Now if you've worked with the robot, you probably know it better than anyone else. Was there anything unusual about it that you noticed? Had you ever worked with robots before?"

"I've worked with other robots we have here—the simple ones. Nothing different about the Nestors except that they're a good deal cleverer—and more annoying."

"Annoying? In what way?"

"Well—perhaps it's not their fault. The work here is rough and most of us get a little jagged. Fooling around with hyper-space isn't fun." He smiled feebly, finding pleasure in confession. "We run the risk continually of blowing a hole in normal space-time fabric and dropping right out of the universe, asteroid and all. Sounds screwy, doesn't it? Naturally, you're on edge sometimes. But these Nestors aren't. They're curious, they're calm, they don't worry. It's enough to drive you nuts at times. When you want something done in a tearing hurry, they seem to take their time. Sometimes I'd rather do without."

"You say they take their time? Have they ever refused an order?"

"Oh, no"—hastily. "They do it all right. They tell you when they think you're wrong, though. They don't know anything about the subject but what we taught them, but that doesn't stop them. Maybe I imagine it, but the other fellows have the same trouble with their Nestors."

General Kallner cleared his throat ominously, "Why have no complaints reached me on the matter, Black?"

The young physicist reddened, "We didn't *really* want to do without the robots, sir, and besides we weren't certain exactly how such . . . uh . . . minor complaints might be received."

Bogert interrupted softly, "Anything in particular happen the morning you last saw it?"

There was a silence. With a quiet motion, Calvin repressed the comment that was about to emerge from Kallner, and waited patiently.

Then Black spoke in blurting anger, "I had a little trouble with it. I'd broken a Kimball tube that morning and was out five days of work; my entire program was behind schedule; I hadn't received any mail from home for a couple of weeks. And *he* came around wanting me to repeat an experiment I had abandoned a month ago. He was always annoying me on that subject and I was tired of it. I told him to go away—and that's all I saw of him."

"You told him to go away?" asked Dr. Calvin with sharp interest. "In just those words? Did you say 'Go away'? Try to remember the exact words."

There was apparently an internal struggle in progress. Black cradled his forehead in a broad palm for a moment, then tore it away and said defiantly, "I said, 'Go lose yourself.' "

Bogert laughed for a short moment. "And he did, eh?"

But Calvin wasn't finished. She spoke cajolingly, "Now we're getting somewhere, Mr. Black. But exact details are important. In understanding the robot's actions, a word, a gesture, an emphasis may be everything. You couldn't have said just those three words, for instance, could you? By your own description you must have been in a nasty mood. Perhaps you strengthened your speech a little."

The young man reddened, "Well . . . I may have called it a . . . a few things."

"Exactly what things?"

"Oh—I wouldn't remember exactly. Besides I couldn't repeat it. You know how you get when you're excited." His embarrassed laugh was almost a giggle, "I sort of have a tendency to strong language."

"That's quite all right," she replied, with prim severity. "At the moment, I'm a psychologist. I would like to have you repeat exactly what you said as nearly as you remember, and, even more important, the exact tone of voice you used."

Black looked at his commanding officer for support, found none. His eyes grew round and appalled, "But I can't."

"You must."

"Suppose," said Bogert, with ill-hidden amusement, "you address me. You may find it easier."

The young man's scarlet face turned to Bogert. He swallowed. "I said—" His voice faded out. He tried again, "I said—"

And he drew a deep breath and spewed it out hastily in one long succession of syllables. Then, in the charged air that lingered, he concluded almost in tears, ". . . more or less. I don't remember the exact order of what I called him, and maybe I left out something or put in something, but that was about it."

Only the slightest flush betrayed any feeling on the part of the robopsychologist. She said, "I am aware of the meaning of most of the terms used. The others, I suppose, are equally derogatory."

"I'm afraid so," agreed the tormented Black.

"And in among it, you told him to lose himself."

"I meant it only figuratively."

"I realize that. No disciplinary action is intended, I am sure." And at her glance, the general, who, five seconds earlier, had seemed not sure at all, nodded angrily.

"You may leave, Mr, Black. Thank you for your cooperation."

It took five hours for Susan Calvin to interview the sixty-three robots. It was five hours of multi-repetition; of replacement after replacement of identical robot; of Questions A, B, C, D; and Answers A, B, C, D; of a carefully bland expression, a carefully neutral tone, a carefully friendly atmosphere; and a hidden wire recorder.

The psychologist felt drained of vitality when she was finished.

Bogert was waiting for her and looked expectant as she dropped the recording spool with a clang upon the plastic of the desk.

She shook her head, "All sixty-three seemed the same to me. I couldn't tell—"

He said, "You couldn't expect to tell by ear, Susan. Suppose we analyze the recordings."

Ordinarily, the mathematical interpretation of verbal reactions of robots is one of the more intricate branches of robotic analysis. It requires a staff of trained technicians and the help of complicated computing machines. Bogert knew that. Bogert stated as much, in an extreme of unshown annoyance after having listened to each set of replies, made lists of word deviations, and graphs of the intervals of responses.

"There are no anomalies present, Susan. The variations in wording and the time reactions are within the limits of ordinary frequency groupings. We need finer methods. They must have computers here. No." He frowned and nibbled delicately at a thumbnail. "We can't use computers. Too much danger of leakage. Or maybe if we—"

Dr. Calvin stopped him with an impatient gesture, "Please, Peter. This isn't one of your petty laboratory problems. If we can't determine the modified Nestor by some gross difference that we can see with the naked eye, one that there is no mistake about, we're out of luck. The danger of being wrong, and of letting him escape is otherwise too great. It's not enough to point out a minute irregularity in a graph. I tell you, if that's all I've got to go on, I'd destroy them all just to be certain. Have you spoken to the other modified Nestors?"

"Yes, I have," snapped back Bogert, "and there's nothing wrong with them. They're above normal in friendliness if anything. They answered my questions, displayed pride in their knowledge—except the two new ones that haven't had time to learn their etheric physics. They laughed rather good-naturedly at my ignorance in some of the specializations here." He shrugged, "I suppose that forms some of the basis for resentment toward them on the part of the technicians here. The robots are perhaps too willing to impress you with their greater knowledge."

"Can you try a few Planar Reactions to see if there has been any change, any deterioration, in their mental set-up since manufacture?"

"I haven't yet, but I will." He shook a slim finger at her, "You're losing your nerve, Susan. I don't see what it is you're dramatizing. They're essentially harmless."

"They are?" Calvin took fire. "They are? Do you realize one of them is lying? One of the sixty-three robots I have just interviewed has deliberately lied to me after the strictest injunction to tell the truth. The abnormality indicated is horribly deep-seated, and horribly frightening."

Peter Bogert felt his teeth harden against each other. He said, "Not at all. Look! Nestor 10 was given orders to lose himself. Those orders were expressed in maximum urgency by the person most authorized to command him. You can't counteract that order either by superior urgency or superior right of command. Naturally, the robot will attempt to defend the carrying out of his orders. In fact, objectively, I admire his ingenuity. How better can a robot lose himself than to hide himself among a group of similar robots?"

"Yes, you would admire it. I've detected amusement in you, Peter—amusement and an appalling lack of understanding. Are you a roboticist, Peter? Those robots attach importance to what they consider superiority. You've just said as much yourself. Subconsciously they feel humans to be inferior and the First Law which protects us from them is imperfect. They are unstable. And here we have a young man ordering a robot to leave him, to lose himself, with every verbal appearance of revulsion, disdain, and disgust. Granted, that robot must follow orders, but subconsciously, there is resentment. It will become more important than ever for it to prove that it is superior despite the horrible names it was called. It may become *so* important that what's left of the First Law won't be enough."

"How on Earth, or anywhere in the Solar System, Susan, is a robot going to know the meaning of the assorted strong language used upon him? Obscenity is not one of the things impressioned upon his brain."

"Original impressionment is not everything," Calvin snarled at him. "Robots have learning capacity, you . . . you fool—" And Bogert knew that she had really lost her temper.

She continued hastily, "Don't you suppose he could tell from the tone used that the words weren't complimentary? Don't you suppose he's heard the words used before and noted upon what occasions?"

"Well, then," shouted Bogert, "will you kindly tell me one way in which a modified robot can harm a human being, no matter how offended it is, no matter how sick with desire to prove superiority?"

"If I tell you one way, will you keep quiet?"

"Yes."

They were leaning across the table at each other, angry eyes nailed together.

The psychologist said, "If a modified robot were to drop a heavy weight upon a human being, he would not be breaking the First Law, if he did so with the knowledge that his strength and reaction speed would be sufficient to snatch the weight away before it struck the man. However once the weight left his fingers, he would be no longer the active medium. Only the blind force of gravity would be that. The robot could then change his mind and merely by inaction, allow the weight to strike. The modified First Law allows that."

"That's an awful stretch of imagination."

"That's what my profession requires sometimes. Peter, let's not quarrel. Let's work. You know the exact nature of the stimulus that caused the robot to lose himself. You have the records of his original mental make-up. I want you to tell me how possible it is for our robot to do the sort of thing I just talked about. Not the specific instance, mind you, but that whole class of response. And I want it done quickly."

"And meanwhile—"

"And meanwhile, we'll have to try performance tests directly on the response to First Law."

Gerald Black, at his own request, was supervising the mushrooming wooden partitions that were springing up in a bellying circle on the vaulted third floor of Radiation Building 2. The laborers worked, in the main, silently, but more than one was openly a-wonder at the sixty-three photocells that required installation.

One of them sat down near Black, removed his hat, and wiped his forehead thoughtfully with a freckled forearm.

Black nodded at him, "How's it going, Walensky?"

Walensky shrugged and fired a cigar, "Smooth as butter.

What's going on anyway, Doc? First, there's no work for three days and then we have this mess of jiggers." He leaned backward on his elbows and puffed smoke.

Black twitched his eyebrows, "A couple of robot men came over from Earth. Remember the trouble we had with robots running into the gamma fields, before we pounded it into their skulls that they weren't to do it."

"Yeah. Didn't we get new robots?"

"We got some replacements, but mostly it was a job of indoctrination. Anyway, the people who make them want to figure out robots that aren't hit so bad by gamma rays."

"Sure seems funny, though, to stop all the work on the Drive for this robot deal. I thought nothing was allowed to stop the Drive."

"Well, it's the fellows upstairs that have the say on that. Me—I just do as I'm told. Probably all a matter of pull—"

"Yeah." The electrician jerked a smile, and winked a wise eye. "Somebody knew somebody in Washington. But as long as my pay comes through on the dot, I should worry. The Drive's none of my affair. What are they going to do here?"

"You're asking me? They brought a mess of robots with them—over sixty, and they're going to measure reactions. That's all *my* knowledge."

"How long will it take?"

"I wish I knew."

"Well," Walensky said, with heavy sarcasm, "as long as they dish me my money, they can play games all they want."

Black felt quietly satisfied. Let the story spread. It was harmless, and near enough to the truth to take the fangs out of curiosity.

A man sat in the chair, motionless, silent. A weight dropped, crashed downward, then pounded aside at the last moment under the synchronized thump of a sudden force beam. In sixty-three wooden cells, watching NS-2 robots dashed forward in that split second before the weight veered, and sixty-three photocells five feet ahead of their original positions jiggled the marking pen and presented a little jag on the paper. The weight rose and dropped, rose and dropped, rose—

Ten times!

Ten times the robots sprang forward and stopped, as the man remained safely seated.

Major-general Kallner had not worn his uniform in its entirely since the first dinner with the U. S. Robot representatives. He wore nothing over his blue-gray shirt now, the collar was open, and the black tie was pulled loose.

He looked hopefully at Bogert, who was still blandly neat and whose inner tension was perhaps betrayed only by the trace of glister at his temples.

The general said, "How does it look? What is it you're trying to see?"

Bogert replied, "A difference which may turn out to be a little too subtle for our purposes, I'm afraid. For sixty-two of those robots the necessity of jumping toward the apparently threatened human was what we call, in robotics, a forced reaction. You see, even when the robots knew that the human in question would not come to harm—and after the third or fourth time they must have known it—they could not prevent reacting as they did. First Law requires it."

"Well?"

"But the sixty-third robot, the modified Nestor, had no such compulsion. He was under free action. If he had wished, he could have remained in his seat. Unfortunately—" his voice was mildly regretful—"he didn't so wish."

"Why do you suppose?"

Bogert shrugged. "I suppose Dr. Calvin will tell us when she gets here. Probably with a horribly pessimistic interpretation, too. She is sometimes a bit annoying."

"She's qualified, isn't she?" demanded the general with a sudden frown of uneasiness.

"Yes." Bogert seemed amused. "She's qualified all right. She understands robots like a sister—comes from hating human beings so much, I think. It's just that, psychologist or not, she's an extreme neurotic. Has paranoid tendencies. Don't take her too seriously."

He spread the long row of broken-line graphs out in front of him. "You see, general, in the case of each robot the time interval from moment of drop to the completion of a five-foot movement tends to decrease as the tests are repeated. There's a definite mathematical relationship that governs such things and failure to conform would indicate marked abnormality in the positronic brain. Unfortunately, all here appear normal."

"But if our Nestor 10 was not responding with a forced action, why isn't his curve different? I don't understand that."

"It's simple enough. Robotic responses are not perfectly analogous to human responses, more's the pity. In human beings, voluntary action is much slower than reflex action. But that's not the case with robots; with them it is merely a question of freedom of choice, otherwise the speeds of free and forced action are much the same. What I *had* been expecting, though, was that Nestor 10 would be caught by surprise the first time and allow too great an interval to elapse before responding."

"And he didn't?"

"I'm afraid not."

"Then we haven't gotten anywhere." The general sat back with an expression of pain. "It's five days since you've come."

At this point, Susan Calvin entered and slammed the door behind her. "Put your graphs away, Peter," she cried. "You know they don't show anything."

She mumbled something impatiently as Kallner half-rose to greet her, and went on, "We'll have to try something else quickly. I don't like what's happening."

Bogert exchanged a resigned glance with the general. "Is anything wrong?"

"You mean specifically? No. But I don't like to have Nestor 10 continue to elude us. It's bad. It *must* be gratifying his swollen sense of superiority. I'm afraid that his motivation is no longer simply one of following orders. I think it's becoming more a matter of sheer neurotic necessity to outthink humans. That's a dangerously unhealthy situation. Peter, have you done what I asked? Have you worked out the instability factors of the modified NS-2 along the lines I want?"

"It's in progress," said the mathematician, without interest.

She stared at him angrily for a moment, then turned to Kallner. "Nestor 10 is decidedly aware of what we're doing, general. He had no reason to jump for the bait in this experiment, especially after the first time, when he must have seen that there was no real danger to our subject. The others couldn't help it; but *he* was deliberately falsifying a reaction."

"What do you think we ought to do now, then, Dr. Calvin?"

"Make it impossible for him to fake an action the next time. We will repeat the experiment, but with an addition. High-tension cables, capable of electrocuting the Nestor models will be placed between subject and robot—enough of them to avoid the possibility of jumping over—and the robot will be made perfectly aware in advance that touching the cables will mean death."

"Hold on," spat out Bogert with sudden viciousness. "I rule that out. We are not electrocuting two million dollars' worth of robots to locate Nestor 10. There are other ways.

"You're certain? You've found none. In any case, it's not a question of electrocution. We can arrange a relay which will break the current at the instant of application of weight. If the robot should place his weight on it, he won't die. *But he won't know that,* you see."

The general's eyes gleamed into hope. "Will that work?"

"It should. Under those conditions, Nestor 10 would have to remain in his seat. He could be *ordered* to touch the cables and die, for the Second Law of obedience is superior to the Third Law of self-preservation. But *he won't* be ordered to; he will merely be left to his own devices, as will all the robots. In the case of the normal robots, the First Law of human safety will drive them to their death even without orders. But not our Nestor 10. Without the entire First Law, and without having received any orders on the matter, the Third Law, self-preservation, will be the highest operating, and he will have no choice but to remain in his seat. It would be a forced action."

"Will it be done tonight, then?"

"Tonight," said the psychologist, "if the cables can be laid in time. I'll tell the robots now what they're to be up against."

A man sat in the chair, motionless, silent. A weight dropped, crashed downward, then pounded aside at the last moment under the synchronized thump of a sudden force beam.

Only once—

And from her small camp chair in the observing booth in the balcony, Dr. Susan Calvin rose with a short gasp of pure horror.

Sixty-three robots sat quietly in their chairs, staring owlishly at the endangered man before them. Not one moved.

Dr. Calvin was angry, angry almost past endurance. Angry the worse for not daring to show it to the robots that, one by one, were entering the room and then leaving. She checked the list. Number twenty-eight was due in now—Thirty-five still lay ahead of her.

Number Twenty-eight entered, diffidently.

She forced herself into reasonable calm. "And who are you?"

The robot replied in a low, uncertain voice, "I have received no number of my own yet, ma'am. I'm an NS-2 robot, and I was Number Twenty-eight in line outside. I have a slip of paper here that I'm to give to you."

"You haven't been in here before this today?"

"No, ma'am."

"Sit down. Right there, I want to ask you some questions, Number Twenty-eight. Were you in the Radiation Room of Building Two about four hours ago?"

The robot had trouble answering. Then it came out hoarsely, like machinery needing oil, "Yes, ma'am."

"There was a man who almost came to harm there, wasn't there?"

"Yes, ma'am."

"You did nothing, did you?"

"No, ma'am."

"The man might have been hurt because of your inaction. Do you know that?"

"Yes, ma'am. I couldn't help it, ma'am." It is hard to picture a large expressionless metallic figure cringing, but it managed.

"I want you to tell me exactly why you did nothing to save him."

"I want to explain, ma'am. I certainly don't want to have you . . . have *anyone* . . . think that I could do a thing that might cause harm to a master. Oh, no, that would be a horrible . . . an inconceivable—"

"Please don't get excited, boy. I'm not blaming you for anything. I only want to know what you were thinking at the time."

"Ma'am, before it all happened you told us that one of the masters would be in danger of harm from that weight that keeps falling and that we would have to cross electric cables if we were to try to save him. Well, ma'am, that wouldn't stop me. What is my destruction compared to the safety of a master? But . . . but it occurred to me that if I died on my way to him, I wouldn't be able to save him anyway. The weight would crush him and then I would be dead for no purpose and perhaps some day some other master might come to harm who wouldn't have, if I had only stayed alive. Do you understand me, ma'am?"

"You mean that it was merely a choice of the man dying, of both the man and yourself dying. Is that right?"

"Yes, ma'am. It was impossible to save the master. He might be considered dead. In that case, it is inconceivable that I destroy myself for nothing—without orders."

The robopsychologist twiddled a pencil. She had heard the same story with insignificant verbal variations twenty-seven times before. This was the crucial question now.

"Boy," she said, "your thinking has its points, but it is not the sort of thing I thought you might think. Did you think of this yourself?"

The robot hesitated. "No."

"Who thought of it, then?"

"We were talking last night, and one of us got that idea and it sounded reasonable."

"Which one?"

The robot thought deeply. "I don't know. Just one of us."

She sighed. "That's all "

Number Twenty-nine was next. Thirty-four after that.

Major-general Kallner, too, was angry. For one week all of Hyper Base had stopped dead, barring some paper work on the subsidiary asteroids of the group. For nearly one week, the two top experts in the field had aggravated the situation with useless tests. And now they—or the woman, at any rate—made impossible propositions.

Fortunately for the general situation, Kallner felt it impolitic to display his anger openly.

Susan Calvin was insisting, "Why not, sir? It's obvious that the present situation is unfortunate. The only way we may reach results in the future—or what future is left us in this matter—is to separate the robots. We can't keep them together any longer."

"My dear Dr. Calvin," rumbled the general, his voice sinking into the lower baritone registers. "I don't see how I can quarter sixty-three robots all over the place—"

Dr. Calvin raised her arms helplessly. "I can do nothing then. Nestor 10 will either imitate what the other robots would do, or else argue them plausibly into not doing what he himself cannot do. And in any case, this is bad business.

We're in actual combat with this little lost robot of ours and he's winning out. Every victory of his aggravates his abnormality."

She rose to her feet in determination. "General Kallner, if you do not separate the robots as I ask, then I can only demand that all sixty-three be destroyed immediately."

"You demand it, do you?" Bogert looked up suddenly, and with real anger. "What gives you the right to demand any such thing. Those robots remain as they are. *I'm* responsible to the mangement, not you."

"And I," added Major-general Kallner, "am responsible to the World Co-ordinator—and I must have this settled."

"In that case," flashed back Calvin, "there is nothing for me to do but resign. If necessary to force you to the necessary destruction, I'll make this whole matter public. It was not I that approved the manufacture of modified robots."

"One word from you, Dr. Calvin," said the general, deliberately, "in violation of security measures, and you would be certainly imprisoned instantly."

Bogert felt the matter to be getting out of hand. His voice grew syrupy, "Well, now, we're beginning to act like children, all of us. We need only a little more time. Surely we can outwit a robot without resigning, or imprisoning people, or destroying two millions."

The psychologist turned on him with quiet fury, "I don't want any unbalanced robots in existence. We have one Nestor that's definitely unbalanced, eleven more that are potentially so, and sixty-two normal robots that are being subjected to an unbalanced environment. The only absolute safe method is complete destruction."

The signal-burr brought all three to a halt, and the angry tumult of growingly unrestrained emotion froze.

"Come in," growled Kallner.

It was Gerald Black, looking perturbed. He had heard angry voices. He said, "I thought I'd come myself . . . didn't like to ask anyone else—"

"What is it? Don't orate—"

"The locks of Compartment C in the trading ship have been played with. There are fresh scratches on them."

"Compartment C?" explained Calvin quickly. "That's the one that holds the robots, isn't it? Who did it?"

"From the inside," said Black, laconically.

"The lock isn't out of order, is it?"

"No. It's all right. I've been staying on the ship now for four days and none of them have tried to get out. But I thought you ought to know, and I didn't like to spread the news. I noticed the matter myself."

"Is anyone there now?" demanded the general.

"I left Robbins and McAdams there."

There was a thoughtful silence, and then Dr. Calvin said, ironically, "Well?"

Kallner rubbed his nose uncertainly, "What's it all about?"

"Isn't it obvious? Nestor 10 is planning to leave. That order to lose himself is dominating his abnormality past anything we can do. I wouldn't be surprised if what's left of his First Law would scarcely be powerful enough to override it. He is perfectly capable of seizing the ship and leaving with it. Then we'd have a mad robot on a spaceship. What would he do next? Any idea? Do you still want to leave them all together, general?"

"Nonsense," interrupted Bogert. He had regained his smoothness. "All that from a few scratch marks on a lock."

"Have you, Dr. Bogert, completed the analysis I've required, since you volunteer opinions?"

"Yes."

"May I see it?"

"No."

"Why not? Or mayn't I ask that, either?"

"Because there's no point in it, Susan. I told you in advance that these modified robots are less stable than the normal variety, and my analysis shows it. There's a certain very small chance of breakdown under extreme circumstances that are not likely to occur. Let it go at that. I won't give you ammunition for your absurd claim that sixty-two perfectly good robots be destroyed just because so far you lack the ability to detect Nestor 10 among them."

Susan Calvin stared him down and let disgust fill her eyes. "You won't let anything stand in the way of the permanent directorship, will you?"

"Please," begged Kallner, half in irritation. "Do you insist that nothing further can be done, Dr. Calvin?"

"I can't think of anything, sir," she replied, wearily. "If there were only other differences between Nestor 10 and the normal robots, differences that didn't involve the First Law. Even one other difference. Something in impressionment, environment, specification—" And she stopped suddenly.

"What is it?"

"I've thought of something . . . I think—" Her eyes grew distant and hard, "These modified Nestors, Peter. They get the same impressioning the normal ones get, don't they?"

"Yes. Exactly the same."

"And what was it you were saying, Mr. Black," she turned to the young man, who through the storms that had followed his news had maintained a discreet silence. "Once when complaining of the Nestors' attitude of superiority, you said the technicians had taught them all they knew."

"Yes, in etheric physics. They're not acquainted with the subject when they come here."

"That's right," said Bogert, in surprise. "I told you, Susan, when I spoke to the other Nestors here that the two new arrivals hadn't learned etheric physics yet."

"And why is that?" Dr. Calvin was speaking in mounting excitement. "Why aren't NS-2 models impressioned with etheric physics to start with?"

"I can tell you that," said Kallner. "It's all of a piece with the secrecy. We thought that if we made a special model with knowledge of etheric physics, used twelve of them and put the others to work in an unrelated field, there might be suspicion. Men working with normal Nestors might wonder why they knew etheric physics. So there was merely an impressionment with a capacity for training in the field. Only the ones that come here, naturally, receive such a training. It's that simple."

"I understand. Please get out of here, the lot of you. Let me have an hour or so."

Calvin felt she could not face the ordeal for a third time. Her mind had contemplated it and rejected it with an intensity that left her nauseated. She could face that unending file of repetitious robots no more.

So Bogert asked the question now, while she sat aside, eyes and mind half closed.

Number Fourteen came in—forty-nine to go.

Bogert looked up from the guide sheet and said, "What is your number in line?"

"Fourteen, sir." The robot presented his numbered ticket.

"Sit down, boy."

Bogert asked, "You haven't been here before on this day?"

"No, sir."

"Well, boy, we are going to have another man in danger of harm soon after we're through here. In fact, when you leave this room, you will be led to a stall where you will wait quietly, till you are needed. Do you understand?"

"Yes, sir."

"Now, naturally, if a man is in danger of harm, you will try to save him."

"Naturally, sir."

"Unfortunately, between the man and yourself, there will be a gamma ray field."

Silence.

"Do you know what gamma rays are?" asked Bogert sharply.

"Energy radiation, sir?"

The next question came in a friendly, offhand manner, "Ever work with gamma rays?"

"No, sir." The answer was definite.

"Mm-m. Well, boy, gamma rays will kill you instantly. They'll destroy your brain. That is a fact you must know and remember. Naturally, you don't want to destroy yourself."

"Naturally." Again the robot seemed shocked. Then, slowly, "But, sir, if the gamma rays are between myself and the master that may be harmed, how can I save him? I would be destroying myself to no purpose."

"Yes, there is that," Bogert seemed concerned about the matter. "The only thing I can advise, boy, is that if you detect the gamma radiation between yourself and the man, you may as well sit where you are."

The robot was openly relieved. "Thank you, sir. There wouldn't be any use, would there?"

"Of course not. But if there *weren't* any dangerous radiation, that would be a different matter."

"Naturally, sir. No question of that."

"You may leave now. The man on the other side of the door will lead you to your stall. Please wait there."

He turned to Susan Calvin when the robot left. "How did that go, Susan?"

"Very well," she said, dully.

"Do you think we could catch Nestor 10 by quick questioning on etheric physics?"

"Perhaps, but it's not sure enough." Her hands lay loosely in her lap. "Remember, he's fighting us. He's on his guard. The only way we can catch him is to outsmart him—and, within his limitations, he can think much more quickly than a human being."

"Well, just for fun—suppose I ask the robots from now on a few questions on gamma rays. Wave length limits, for instance."

"No!" Dr. Calvin's eyes sparked to life. "It would be too easy for him to deny knowledge and then he'd be warned against the test that's coming up—which is our real chance. Please follow the questions I've indicated, Peter, and don't improvise. It's just within the bounds of risk to ask them if they've ever worked with gamma rays. And try to sound even less interested than you do when you ask it."

Bogert shrugged, and pressed the buzzer that would allow the entrance of Number Fifteen.

The large Radiation Room was in readiness once more. The robots waited patiently in their wooden cells, all open to the center but closed off from each other.

Major-general Kallner mopped his brow slowly with a large handkerchief while Dr. Calvin checked the last details with Black.

"You're sure now," she demanded, "that none of the robots have had a chance to talk with each other after leaving the Orientation Room?"

"Absolutely sure," insisted Black. "There's not been a word exchanged."

"And the robots are put in the proper stalls?"

"Here's the plan."

The psychologist looked at it thoughtfully, "Um-m-m."

The general peered over her shoulder. "What's the idea of the arrangement, Dr. Calvin?"

"I've asked to have those robots that appeared even slightly out of true in the previous tests concentrated on one side of the circle. I'm going to be sitting in the center myself this time, and I wanted to watch those particularly."

"*You're* going to be sitting there—" exclaimed Bogert.

"Why not?" she demanded coldly. "What I expect to see may be something quite momentary. I can't risk having anyone else as main observer. Peter, you'll be in the observing booth, and I want you to keep your eye on the opposite side of the circle. General Kallner, I've arranged for motion pictures to be taken of each robot, in case visual observation isn't enough. If these are required, the robots are to remain exactly where they are until the pictures are developed and studied. None must leave, none must change place. Is that clear?"

"Perfectly."

"Then let's try it this one last time."

Susan Calvin sat in the chair, silent, eyes restless. A weight dropped, crashed downward, then pounded aside at the last moment under the synchronized thump of a sudden force beam.

And a single robot jerked upright and took two steps.

And stopped.

But Dr. Calvin was upright, and her finger pointed to him sharply. "Nestor 10, come here," she cried, "*come here!* COME HERE!"

Slowly, reluctantly, the robot took another step forward. The psychologist shouted at the top of her voice, without taking her eyes from the robot, "Get every other robot out of this place, somebody. Get them out quickly, and *keep* them out!"

Somewhere within reach of her ears there was noise, and the thud of hard feet upon the floor. She did not look away.

Nestor 10—if it was Nestor 10—took another step, and then, under force of her imperious gesture, two more. He was only ten feet away, when he spoke harshly, "I have been told to be lost—"

Another step. "I must not disobey. They have not found me so far— He would think me a failure— He told me— But it's not so—I am powerful and intelligent—"

The words came in spurts.

Another step. "I know a good deal— He would think . . . I mean I've been found— Disgraceful— Not I— I am intelligent— And by just a master . . . who is weak— Slow—"

Another step—and one metal arm flew out suddenly to her shoulder, and she felt the weight bearing her down. Her throat constricted, and she felt a shriek tear through.

Dimly, she heard Nestor 10's next words, "No one must find me. No master—" and the cold metal was against her, and she was sinking under the weight of it.

And then a queer, metallic sound, and she was on the ground with an unfelt thump, and a gleaming arm was heavy across her body. It did not move. Nor did Nestor 10, who sprawled beside her.

And now faces were bending over her.

Gerald Black was gasping, "Are you hurt, Dr. Calvin?"

She shook her head feebly. They pried the arm off her and lifted her gently to her feet, "What happened?"

Black said, "I bathed the place in gamma rays for five seconds. We didn't know what was happening. It wasn't till the last second that we realized he was attacking you, and then there was no time for anything but a gamma field. He went down in an instant. There wasn't enough to harm you though. Don't worry about it."

"I'm not worried." She closed her eyes and leaned for a moment upon his shoulder. "I don't think I was attacked exactly. Nestor 10 was simply *trying* to do so. What was left of the First Law was still holding him back."

Susan Calvin and Peter Bogert, two weeks after their first meeting with Major-general Kallner had their last. Work at Hyper Base had been resumed. The trading ship with its sixty-two normal NS-2's was gone to wherever it was bound, with an officially imposed story to explain its two weeks' delay. The government cruiser was making ready to carry the two roboticists back to Earth.

Kallner was once again a-gleam in dress uniform. His white gloves shone as he shook hands.

Calvin said, "The other modified Nestors are, of course, to be destroyed."

"They will be. We'll make shift with normal robots, or, if necessary, do without."

"Good."

"But tell me— You haven't explained— How was it done?"

She smiled tightly, "Oh, that. I would have told you in advance if I had been more certain of its working. You see, Nestor 10 had a superiority complex that was becoming more radical all the time. He liked to think that he and other robots knew more than human beings. It was becoming very important for him to think so.

"We knew that. So we warned every robot in advance that gamma rays would kill them, which it would, and we further warned them all that gamma rays would be between them and myself. So they all stayed where they were, naturally. By Nestor 10's own logic in the previous test they had all decided that there was no point in trying to save a human being if they were sure to die before they could do it."

"Well, yes, Dr. Calvin, I understand that. But why did Nestor 10 himself leave his seat?"

"Ah! That was a little arrangement between myself and your young Mr. Black. You see it wasn't gamma rays that flooded the area between myself and the robots—but infrared rays. Just ordinary heat rays, absolutely harmless. Nestor 10 knew they were infrared and harmless and so he began to dash out, as he expected the rest would do, under First Law compulsion. It was only a fraction of a second too late that he remembered that the normal NS-2's could detect radiation, but could not identify the type. That he himself could only identify wave lengths by virtue of the training he had received at Hyper Base, under mere human beings, was a little too humiliating to remember for just a moment. To the normal robots the area was fatal because we had told them it would be, and only Nestor 10 knew we were lying.

"And just for a moment he forgot, or didn't want to remember, that other robots might be more ignorant than human beings. His very superiority caught him. Good-bye, general."

TOMORROW'S CHILDREN

by Poul Anderson (1926–   )

ASTOUNDING SCIENCE FICTION
March

This fine story was Poul Anderson's first published work and signaled the beginning of a long, productive and distinguished career, which would see him win the coveted Hugo Award in 1961 ("The Longest Voyage"), 1964 ("No Truce With Kings"), 1969 ("The Sharing of Flesh"), 1972 ("The Queen of Air and Darkness" which also won a Nebula Award), 1973 ("Goat Song" another Nebula winner), and 1979 ("Hunter's Moon"). He also received the Tolkien Memorial Award, was the Guest of Honor at the 1959 World Science Fiction Convention, and has an impressive list of outstanding novels in both the science fiction and fantasy fields.

"Tomorrow's Children" remains one of the very best atomic "awful warning" stories ever written, a powerful and frightening glimpse of a future we all hope will never happen, as well as a strong plea for a more tolerant world.

(I've always had a sneaking envy of those who burst onto the science fiction scene with eclat. My

own first story showed no signs whatever that I was going to become a major science fiction figure. It could easily have been written by one of the many who appear in order to shine dimly for a while and then recede into the outer darkness again. I was quite aware in my early years that this was true and I also knew that with their very first stories Robert Heinlein and A. E. van Vogt (to name just two) had established themselves unmistakably as first-magnitude stars.

Well, Poul Anderson was another. To this day I remember the impact "Tomorrow's Children" made on me. It helped, of course, that the nuclear bomb and its effects occupied all our minds at the time (as, indeed, it does now) and that Poul had that funny first name—but it was the story that counted and I was quite certain that Poul would keep on writing and would continue to turn out masterpieces.

And, as a matter of fact, Poul has been hot on the heels of the "Big Three," longer and more consistently than anyone else in the field.—I.A.)

On the world's loom
Weave the Norns doom,
Nor may they guide it nor change.
—Wagner, Siegfried

Ten miles up, it hardly showed. Earth was a cloudy green and brown blur, the vast vault of the stratosphere reaching changelessly out to spatial infinities, and beyond the pulsing engine there was silence and serenity no man could ever touch. Looking down, Hugh Drummond could see the Mississippi gleaming like a drawn sword, and its slow curve matched the contours shown on his map. The hills, the sea, the sun and wind and rain, they didn't change. Not in less than a million slow-striding years, and human efforts flickered too briefly in the unending night for that.

Farther down, though, and especially where cities had been— The lone man in the solitary stratojet swore softly, bitterly, and his knuckles whitened on the controls. He was a big man, his gaunt rangy form sprawling awkwardly in the tiny pressure cabin, and he wasn't quite forty. But his dark hair was streaked with gray, in the shabby flying suit his shoulders stooped, and his long homely face was drawn into haggard lines. His eyes were black-rimmed and sunken with weariness, dark and dreadful in their intensity. He'd seen too much, survived too much, until he began to look like most other people of the world. *Heir of the ages,* he thought dully.

Mechanically, he went through the motions of following his course. Natural landmarks were still there, and he had powerful binoculars to help him. But he didn't use them much. They showed too many broad shallow craters, their vitreous smoothness throwing back sunlight in the flat blank glitter of a snake's eye, the ground about them a churned and blasted desolation. And there were the worse regions of— deadness. Twisted dead trees, blowing sand, tumbled skeletons, perhaps at night a baleful blue glow of fluorescence. The bombs had been nightmares, riding in on wings of fire and horror to shake the planet with the death blows of cities. But the radioactive dust was worse than any nightmare.

He passed over villages, even small towns. Some of them were deserted, the blowing colloidal dust, or plague, or economic breakdown making them untenable. Others still seemed to be living a feeble half-life. Especially in the Midwest, there was a pathetic struggle to return to an agricultural system, but the insects and blights—

Drummond shrugged. After nearly two years of this, over the scarred and maimed planet, he should be used to it. The United States had been lucky. Europe, now—

Der Untergang des Abendlandes, he thought grayly. *Spengler foresaw the collapse of a top-heavy civilization. He didn't foresee atomic bombs, radioactive-dust bombs, bacteria bombs, blight bombs—the bombs, the senseless inanimate bombs flying like monster insects over the shivering world. So he didn't guess the extent of the collapse.*

Deliberately he pushed the thoughts out of his conscious mind. He didn't want to dwell on them. He'd lived with them two years, and that was two eternities too long. And anyway, he was nearly home now.

The capital of the United States was below him, and he sent the stratojet slanting down in a long thunderous dive toward the mountains. Not much of a capital, the little town huddled in a valley of the Cascades, but the waters of the Potomac had filled the grave of Washington. Strictly speaking, there was no capital. The officers of the government were scattered over the country, keeping in precarious touch by plane and radio, but Taylor, Oregon, came as close to being the nerve center as any other place.

He gave the signal again on his transmitter, knowing with a faint spine-crawling sensation of the rocket batteries trained on him from the green of those mountains. When one plane could carry the end of a city, all planes were under suspicion. Not that anyone outside was supposed to know that that innocuous little town was important. But you never could tell. The war wasn't officially over. It might never be, with sheer personal survival overriding the urgency of treaties.

A light-beam transmitter gave him a cautious: "O.K. Can you land in the street?"

It was a narrow, dusty track between two wooden rows of houses, but Drummond was a good pilot and this was a good jet. "Yeah," he said. His voice had grown unused to speech.

He cut speed in a spiral descent until he was gliding with only the faintest whisper of wind across his ship. Touching wheels to the street, he slammed on the brake and bounced to a halt.

Silence struck at him like a physical blow. The engine stilled, the sun beating down from a brassy blue sky on the drabness of rude "temporary" houses, the total-seeming desertion beneath the impassive mountains—Home! Hugh Drummond laughed, a short harsh bark with nothing of humor in it, and swung open the cockpit canopy.

There were actually quite a few people, he saw, peering from doorways and side streets. They looked fairly well fed and dressed, many in uniform; they seemed to have purpose and hope. But this, of course, was the capital of the United States of America, the world's most fortunate country.

"Get out—quick!"

The peremptory voice roused Drummond from the introspection into which those lonely months had driven him. He looked down at a gang of men in mechanic's outfits, led by a harassed-looking man in captain's uniform. "Oh—of course," he said slowly. "You want to hide the plane. And, naturally, a regular landing field would give you away."

"Hurry, get out, you infernal idiot! Anyone, *anyone* might come over and see—"

"They wouldn't go unnoticed by an efficient detection system, and you still have that," said Drummond, sliding his booted legs over the cockpit edge. "And anyway, there won't be any more raids. The war's over."

"Wish I could believe that, but who are you to say? Get a move on!"

The grease monkeys hustled the plane down the street. With an odd feeling of loneliness, Drummond watched it go. After all, it had been his home for—how long?

The machine was stopped before a false house whose whole front was swung aside. A concrete ramp led downward, and Drummond could see a cavernous immensity below. Light within it gleamed off silvery rows of aircraft.

"Pretty neat," he admitted. "Not that it matters anymore. Probably it never did. Most of the hell came over on robot rockets. Oh, well." He fished his pipe from his jacket. Colonel's insignia glittered briefly as the garment flipped back.

"Oh . . . sorry, sir!" exclaimed the captain. "I didn't know—"

" 'S O.K. I've gotten out of the habit of wearing a regular uniform. A lot of places I've been, an American wouldn't be very popular."

Drummond stuffed tobacco into his briar, scowling. He hated to think how often he'd had to use the Colt at his hip, or even the machine guns in his plane, to save himself. He inhaled smoke gratefully. It seemed to drown out some of the bitter taste.

"General Robinson said to bring you to him when you arrived, sir," said the captain. "This way, please."

They went down the street, their boots scuffing up little acrid clouds of dust. Drummond looked sharply about him. He'd left very shortly after the two-month Ragnarok which had tapered off when the organization of both sides broke down too far to keep on making and sending the bombs, and maintaining order with famine and disease starting their ghastly ride over the homeland. At that time, the United States was a cityless anarchic chaos, and he'd had only the briefest of radio exchanges since then, whenever he could get at a long-range set still in working order. They'd make remarkable progress meanwhile. How much, he didn't know, but the mere existence of something like a capital was sufficient proof.

Robinson— His lined face twisted into a frown. He didn't know the man. He'd been expecting to be received by the President, who had sent him and some others out. Unless the others had— No, he was the only one who had been in eastern Europe and western Asia. He was sure of that.

Two sentries guarded the entrance to what was obviously a converted general store. But there were no more stores. There was nothing to put in them. Drummond entered the cool dimness of an antechamber. The clatter of a typewriter, the Wac operating it— He gaped and blinked. That was—impossible! Typewriters, secretaries—hadn't they gone out with the whole world, two years ago? If the Dark Ages had returned to Earth, it didn't seem—*right*—that there should still be typewriters. It didn't fit, didn't—

He grew aware that the captain had opened the inner door for him. As he stepped in, he grew aware how tired he was. His arm weighed a ton as he saluted the man behind the desk.

"At ease, at ease," Robinson's voice was genial. Despite the five stars on his shoulders, he wore no tie or coat, and his round face was smiling. Still, he looked tough and competent underneath. To run things nowadays, he'd have to be.

"Sit down, Colonel Drummond." Robinson gestured to a chair near his and the aviator collapsed into it, shivering. His haunted eyes traversed the office. It was almost well enough outfitted to be a prewar place.

Prewar! A word like a sword, cutting across history with a brutality of murder, hazing everything in the past until it was a vague golden glow through drifting, red-shot black clouds. And—only two years. *Only two years!* Surely sanity was meaningless in a world of such nightmare inversions. Why, he could barely remember Barbara and the kids. Their faces were blotted out in a tide of other visages—starved faces, dead faces, human faces become beast-formed with want and pain and eating throttled hate. His grief was lost in the agony of a world, and in some ways he had become a machine himself.

"You look plenty tired," said Robinson.

"Yeah . . . yes, sir—"

"Skip the formality. I don't go for it. We'll be working pretty close together, can't take time to be diplomatic."

"Uh-huh. I came over the North Pole, you know. Haven't slept since—Rough time. But, if I may ask, you—" Drummond hesitated.

"I? I suppose I'm President. Ex officio, pro tem, or something. Here, you need a drink." Robinson got bottle and glasses from a drawer. The liquor gurgled out in a pungent stream. "Prewar Scotch. Till it gives out I'm laying off this modern hooch. *Gambai.*"

The fiery, smoky brew jolted Drummond to wakefulness. Its glow was pleasant in his empty stomach. He heard Robinson's voice with a surrealistic sharpness:

"Yes, I'm at the head now. My predecessors made the mistake of sticking together, and of traveling a good deal in trying to pull the country back into shape. So I think the sickness got the President, and I know it got several others. Of course, there was no means of holding an election. The armed forces had almost the only organization left, so we had to run things. Berger was in charge, but he shot himself when he learned he'd breathed radiodust. Then the command fell to me. I've been lucky."

"I see." It didn't make much difference. A few dozen more deaths weren't much, when over half the world was gone. "Do you expect to—continue lucky?" A brutally blunt question, maybe, but words weren't bombs.

"I do." Robinson was firm about that. "We've learned by experience, learned a lot. We've scattered the army, broken it into small outposts at key points throughout the country. For quite a while, we stopped travel altogether except for absolute emergencies, and then with elaborate precautions. That smothered the epidemics. The microorganisms were bred to work in crowded areas, you know. They were almost immune to known medical techniques, but without hosts and carriers they died. I guess natural bacteria ate up most of them. We still take care in traveling, but we're fairly safe now."

"Did any of the others come back? There were a lot like me, sent out to see what really had happened to the world."

"One did, from South America. Their situation is similar to ours, though they lacked our tight organization and have gone further toward anarchy. Nobody else returned but you."

It wasn't surprising. In fact, it was a cause for astonishment that anyone had come back. Drummond had volunteered after the bomb erasing St. Louis had taken his family, not expecting to survive and not caring much whether he did. Maybe that was why he had.

"You can take your time in writing a detailed report," said Robinson, "but in general, how are things over there?"

Drummond shrugged. "The war's over. Burned out. Europe has gone back to savagery. They were caught between America and Asia, and the bombs came both ways. Not many survivors, and they're starving animals. Russia, from what I saw, has managed something like you've done here, though they're worse off than we. Naturally, I couldn't find out much here. I didn't get to India or China, but in Russia I heard rumors— No, the world's gone too far into disintegration to carry on war."

"Then we can come out in the open," said Robinson softly. "We can really start rebuilding. I don't think there'll ever be another war, Drummond. I think the memory of this one will be carved too deeply on the race for us ever to forget."

"Can you shrug it off that easily?"

"No, no, of course not. Our culture hasn't lost its continuity, but it's had a terrific setback. We'll never wholly get over it. But—we're on our way up again."

The general rose, glancing at his watch. "Six o'clock. Come on, Drummond, let's get home."

"Home?"

"Yes, you'll stay with me. Man, you look like the original zombie. You'll need a month or more of sleeping between clean sheets, of home cooking and home atmosphere. My wife will be glad to have you; we see almost no new faces. And as long as we'll work together, I'd like to keep you handy. The shortage of competent men is terrific."

They went down the street, an aide following. Drummond was again conscious of the weariness aching in every bone and fiber of him. A home—after two years of ghost towns, of shattered chimneys above blood-dappled snow, of flimsy lean-tos housing starvation and death.

"Your plane will be mighty useful, too," said Robinson. "Those atomic-powered craft are scarcer than hens' teeth used to be." He chuckled hollowly, as at a rather grim joke. "Got you through close to two years of flying without needing fuel. Any other trouble?"

"Some, but there were enough spare parts." No need to tell of those frantic hours and days of slaving, of desperate improvisation with hunger and plague stalking him who stayed overlong. He'd had his troubles getting food, too, despite the plentiful supplies he'd started out with. He'd fought for scraps in the winter, beaten off howling maniacs who would have killed him for a bird he'd shot or a dead horse he'd scavenged. He hated that plundering, and would not have cared personally if they'd managed to destroy him. But he had a mission, and the mission was all he'd had left as a focal point for his life, so he'd clung to it with fanatic intensity.

And now the job was over, and he realized he couldn't rest. He didn't dare. Rest would give him time to remember. Maybe he could find surcease in the gigantic work of reconstruction. Maybe.

"Here we are," said Robinson.

Drummond blinked in new amazement. There was a car, camouflaged under brush, with a military chauffeur—*a car!* And in pretty fair shape, too.

"We've got a few oil wells going again, and a small patched-up refinery," explained the general. "It furnishes enough gas and oil for what traffic we have."

They got in the rear seat. The aide sat in front, a rifle ready. The car started down a mountain road.

"Where to?" asked Drummond a little dazedly.

Robinson smiled. "Personally," he said, I'm almost the only lucky man on Earth. We had a summer cottage on Lake Taylor, a few miles from here. My wife was there when the war came, and stayed, and nobody came along till I brought the head offices here with me. Now I've got a home all to myself."

"Yeah. Yeah, you're lucky," said Drummond. He looked out the window, not seeing the sun-spattered woods. Presently he asked, his voice a little harsh: "How is the country really doing now?"

"For a while it was rough. Damn rough. When the cities went, our transportation, communication, and distribution systems broke down. In fact, our whole economy disintegrated, though not all at once. Then there was the dust and the plagues. People fled, and there was open fighting when overcrowded safe places refused to take in any more refugees. Police went with the cities, and the army couldn't do much patrolling. We were busy fighting the enemy troops that'd flown over the Pole to invade. We still haven't gotten them all. Bands are roaming the country, hungry and desperate outlaws, and there are plenty of Americans who turned to banditry when everything else failed. That's why we have this guard, though so far none have come this way.

"The insect and blight weapons just about wiped out our crops, and that winter everybody starved. We checked the pests with modern methods, though it was touch and go for a while, and next year got some food. Of course, with no distribution as yet, we failed to save a lot of people. And farming is still a tough proposition. We won't really have the bugs licked for a long time. If we had a research center as well equipped as those which produced the things— But we're gaining. We're gaining."

"Distribution—" Drummond rubbed his chin. "How about railroads? Horse-drawn vehicles?"

"We have some railroads going, but the enemy was as careful to dust most of ours as we were to dust theirs. As for horses, they were nearly all eaten that first winter. I know personally of only a dozen. They're on my place; I'm trying to breed enough to be of use, but"—Robinson smiled wryly—"by the time we've raised that many, the factories should have been going quite a spell."

"And so now—?"

"We're over the worst. Except for outlaws, we have the population fairly well controlled. The civilized people are fairly well fed, with some kind of housing. We have machine shops, small factories, and the like going, enough to keep our transportation and other mechanism 'level.' Presently we'll be able to expand these, being actually increasing what we have. In another five years or so, I guess, we'll be integrated enough to drop martial law and hold a general election. A big job ahead, but a good one."

The car halted to let a cow lumber over the road, a calf trotting at her heels. She was gaunt and shaggy, and skittered nervously from the vehicle into the brush.

"Wild," explained Robinson. "Most of the real wild life was killed off for food in the last two years, but a lot of farm animals escaped when their owners died or fled, and have run free ever since. They—" He noticed Drummond's fixed gaze. The pilot was looking at the calf. Its legs were half the normal length.

"Mutant," said the general. "You find a lot of such animals.

Radiation from bombed or dusted areas. There are even a lot of human abnormal births." He scowled, worry clouding his eyes. "In fact, that's just about our worst problem. It—"

The car came out of the woods onto the shore of a small lake. It was a peaceful scene, the quiet waters like molten gold in the slanting sunlight, trees ringing the circumference and all about them the mountains. Under one huge pine stood a cottage, a woman on the porch.

It was like one summer with Barbara—Drummond cursed under his breath and followed Robinson toward the little building. It wasn't, it wasn't, it could never be. Not ever again. There were soldiers guarding this place from chance marauders, and— There was an odd-looking flower at his feet. A daisy, but huge and red and irregularly formed.

A squirrel chittered from a tree. Drummond saw that its face was so blunt as to be almost human.

Then he was on the porch, and Robinson was introducing him to "my wife Elaine." She was a nice-looking young woman with eyes that were sympathetic on Drummond's exhausted face. The aviator tried not to notice that she was pregnant.

He was led inside, and reveled in a hot bath. Afterward there was supper, but he was numb with sleep by then, and hardly noticed it when Robinson put him to bed.

Reaction set in, and for a week or so Drummond went about in a haze, not much good to himself or anyone else. But it was surprising what plenty of food and sleep could do, and one evening Robinson came home to find him scribbling on sheets of paper.

"Arranging my notes and so on," he explained. "I'll write out the complete report in a month, I guess."

"Good. But no hurry." Robinson settled tiredly into an armchair. "The rest of the world will keep. I'd rather you'd just work at this off and on, and join my staff for your main job."

"O.K. Only what'll I do?"

"Everything. Specialization is gone; too few surviving specialists and equipment. I think your chief task will be to head the census bureau."

"Eh?"

Robinson grinned lopsidedly. "You'll *be* the census bureau, except for what few assistants I can spare you." He leaned forward, said earnestly: "And it's one of the most important jobs there is. You'll do for this country what you did for central Eurasia, only in much greater detail. Drummond, we have to *know*."

He took a map from a desk drawer and spread it out. "Look, here's the United States. I've marked regions known to be uninhabitable in red." His fingers traced out the ugly splotches. "Too many of 'em, and doubtless there are others we haven't found yet. Now, the blue X's are army posts." They were sparsely scattered over the land, near the centers of population groupings. "Not enough of those. It's all we can do to control the more or less well-off, orderly people. Bandits, enemy troops, homeless refugees—they're still running wild, skulking in the backwoods and barrens, and raiding whenever they can. And they spread the plague. We won't really have it licked till everybody's settled down, and that'd be hard to enforce. Drummond, we don't even have enough soldiers to start a feudal system for protection. The plague spread like a prairie fire in those concentrations of men.

"We have to *know*. We have to know how many people survived—half the population, a third, a quarter, whatever it is. We have to know where they are, and how they're fixed for supplies, so we can start up an equitable distribution system. We have to find all the small-town shops and labs and libraries still standing, and rescue their priceless contents before looters or the weather beat us to it. We have to locate doctors and engineers and other professional men, and put them to work rebuilding. We have to find the outlaws and round them up. We— I could go on forever. Once we have all that information, we can set up a master plan for redistributing population, agriculture, industry, and the rest most efficiently, for getting the country back under civil authority and police, for opening regular transportation and communication channels—for getting the nation back on its feet."

"I see," nodded Drummond. "Hitherto, just surviving and hanging on to what was left has taken precedence. Now you're in a position to start expanding, *if* you know where and how much to expand."

"Exactly." Robinson rolled a cigarette, grimacing. "Not much tobacco left. What I have is perfectly foul. Lord, that war was crazy!"

"All wars are," said Drummond dispassionately, "but technology advanced to the point of giving us a knife to cut our throats with. Before that, we were just beating our heads against the wall. Robinson, we can't go back to the old ways. We've *got* to start on a new track—a track of sanity."

"Yes. And that brings up—" The other man looked toward the kitchen door. They could hear the cheerful rattle of dishes there, and smell mouth-watering cooking odors. He lowered his voice. "I might as well tell you this now, but don't let Elaine know. She . . . she shouldn't be worried. Drummond, did you see our horses?"

The other day, yes. The colts—"

"Uh-huh. There've been five colts born of eleven mares in the last year. Two of them were so deformed they died in a week, another in a few months. One of the two left has cloven hoofs and almost no teeth. The last one looks normal—so far. One out of eleven, Drummond."

"Were those horses near a radioactive area?"

"They must have been. They were rounded up wherever found and brought here. The stallion was caught near the site of Portland, I know. But if he were the only one with mutated genes, it would hardly show in the first generation, would it? I understand nearly all mutations are Mendelian recessives. Even if there were one dominant, it would show in all the colts, but none of these looked alike."

"Hm-m-m—I don't know much about genetics, but I do know hard radiation, or rather the secondary charged particles it produces, will cause mutation. Only mutants are rare, and tend to fall into certain patterns—"

"*Were* rare!" Suddenly Robinson was grim, something coldly frightened in his eyes. "Haven't you noticed the animals and plants? They're fewer than formerly, and . . . well, I've not kept count, but at least half those seen or killed have something wrong, internally or externally."

Drummond drew heavily on his pipe. He needed something to hang onto, in a new storm of insanity. Very quietly, he said:

"In my college biology course, they told me the vast majority of mutations are unfavorable. More ways of not doing something than of doing it. Radiation might sterilize an animal, or might produce several degrees of genetic change. You could have a mutation so violently lethal the possessor never gets born, or soon dies. You could have all kinds of more or less handicapping factors, or just random changes not making much difference one way or the other. Or in a few rare cases you might get something actually favorable, but you couldn't really say the possessor is a true member of the species. And favorable mutations themselves usually involve a price in the partial or total loss of some other function."

"Right." Robinson nodded heavily. "One of your jobs on the census will be to try and locate any and all who know genetics, and send them here. But your real task, which only you and I and a couple of others must know about, the job overriding all other considerations, will be to find the human mutants."

Drummond's throat was dry. "There've been a lot of them?" he whispered.

"Yes. But we don't know how many or where. We only know about those people who live near an army post, or have some other fairly regular intercourse with us, and they're only a few thousand all told. Among them, the birth rate has gone down to about half the prewar ratio. And over half the births they do have are abnormal."

"*Over half—*"

"Yeah. Of course, the violently different ones soon die, or are put in an institution we've set up in the Alleghenies. But what can we do with viable forms, if their parents still love them? A kid with deformed or missing or abortive organs, twisted internal structure, a tail, or something even worse . . . well, *it'll* have a tough time in life, but it can generally survive. And perpetuate itself—"

"And a normal-looking one might have some unnoticeable quirk, or a characteristic that won't show up for years. Or even a normal one might be carrying recessives, and pass them on— God!" The exclamation was half blasphemy, half prayer. "But how'd it happen? People weren't all near atom-hit areas."

"Maybe not, though a lot of survivors escaped from the outskirts. But there was that first year, with everybody on the move. One could pass near enough to a blasted region to be affected, without knowing it. And that damnable radiodust, blowing on the wind. It's got a long half-life. It'll be active for decades. Then, as in any collapsing culture, promiscuity was common. Still is. Oh, it'd spread itself, all right."

"I still don't see why it spread itself so much. Even here—"

"Well, I don't know why it shows up here. I suppose a lot of the local flora and fauna came in from elsewhere. This place is safe. The nearest dusted region is three hundred miles off, with mountains between. There must be many such islands of comparatively normal conditions. We have to find them too. But elsewhere—"

"Soup's on," announced Elaine, and went from the kitchen to the dining room with a loaded tray.

The men rose. Grayly, Drummond looked at Robinson and said tonelessly: "O.K. I'll get your information for you. We'll map mutation areas and safe areas, we'll check on our population and resources, we'll eventually get all the facts you want. But—what are you going to do then?"

"I wish I knew," said Robinson haggardly. "I wish I knew."

Winter lay heavily on the north, a vast gray sky seeming frozen solid over the rolling white plains. The last three winters had come early and stayed long. Dust, colloidal dust of the bombs, suspended in the atmosphere cut down the solar constant by a deadly percent or two. There had even been a few earthquakes, set off in geologically unstable parts of the world by bombs planted right. Half California had been ruined when a sabotage bomb started the San Andreas Fault on a major slip. And that kicked up still more dust.

Fimbulwinter, thought Drummond bleakly. *The doom of the prophecy. But no, we're surviving. Though maybe not as men—*

Most people had gone south, and there overcrowding had made starvation and disease and internecine struggle the normal aspects of life. Those who'd stuck it out up here, and had luck with their pest-ridden crops, were better off.

Drummond's jet slid above the cratered black ruin of the Twin Cities. There was still enough radioactivity to melt the snow, and the pit was like a skull's empty eye socket. The man sighed, but he was becoming calloused to the sight of death. There was so much of it. Only the struggling agony of life mattered any more.

He strained through the sinister twilight, swooping low over the unending fields. Burned-out hulks of farmhouses, bones of ghost towns, sere deadness of dusted land—but he'd heard travelers speak of a fairly powerful community up near the Canadian border, and it was up to him to find it.

A lot of things had been up to him in the last six months. He'd had to work out a means of search, and organize his few, overworked assistants into an efficient staff, and go out on the long hunt.

They hadn't covered the country. That was impossible. Their few planes had gone to areas chosen more or less at random, trying to get a cross section of conditions. They'd penetrated wildernesses of hill and plain and forest, establishing contact with scattered, still demoralized out-dwellers. On the whole, it was more laborious than anything else. Most were pathetically glad to see any symbol of law and order and the paradisiacal-seeming "old days." Now and then there was danger and trouble, when they encountered wary or sullen or outright hostile groups suspicious of a government they associated with disaster, and once there had even been a pitched battle with roving outlaws. But the work had gone ahead, and now the preliminaries were about over.

Preliminaries— It was a bigger job to find out exactly how matters stood than the entire country was capable of undertaking right now. But Drummond had enough facts for reliable extrapolation. He and his staff had collected most of the essential data and begun correlating it. By questioning, by observation, by seeking and finding, by any means that came to hand they'd filled their notebooks. And in the sketchy outlines of a Chinese drawing, and with the same stark realism, the truth was there.

Just this one more place, and I'll go home, thought Drummond for the—thousandth?—time. His brain was getting into a rut, treading the same terrible circle and finding no way out. *Robinson won't like what I tell him, but there it is.* And darkly, slowly: *Barbara, maybe it was best you and the kids went as you did. Quickly, cleanly, not even knowing it. This isn't much of a world. It'll never be our world again.*

He saw the place he sought, a huddle of buildings near the frozen shores of the Lake of the Woods, and his jet murmured toward the white ground. The stories he'd heard of this town weren't overly encouraging, but he supposed he'd get out all right. The others had his data anyway, so it didn't matter.

By the time he'd landed in the clearing just outside the village, using the jet's skis, most of the inhabitants were there waiting. In the gathering dusk they were a ragged and wild-looking bunch, clumsily dressed in whatever scraps of cloth and leather they had. The bearded, hard-eyed men were armed with clubs and knives and a few guns. As Drummond got out, he was careful to keep his hands away from his own automatics.

"Hello," he said. "I'm friendly."

"Y' better be," growled the big leader. "Who are you, where from, an' why?"

"First," lied Drummond smoothly, "I want to tell you I have another man with a plane who knows where I am. If I'm not back in a certain time, he'll come with bombs. But we don't intend any harm or interference. This is just a sort of social call. I'm Hugh Drummond of the United States Army."

They digested that slowly. Clearly, they weren't friendly to the government, but they stood in too much awe of aircraft and armament to be openly hostile. The leader spat. "How long you staying?"

"Just overnight, if you'll put me up. I'll pay for it." He held up a small pouch. "Tobacco."

Their eyes gleamed, and the leader said, "You'll stay with me. Come on."

Drummond gave him the bribe and went with the group. He didn't like to spend such priceless luxuries thus freely, but the job was more important. And the boss seemed thawed a little by the fragrant brown flakes. He was sniffing them greedily.

"Been smoking bark an' grass," he confided. "Terrible."

"Worse than that," agreed Drummond. He turned up his jacket collar and shivered. The wind starting to blow was bitterly cold.

"Just what y' here for?" demanded someone else.

"Well, just to see how things stand. We've got the government started again, and are patching things up. But we have to know where folks are, what they need, and so on."

"Don't want nothing t' do with the gov'ment," muttered a woman. "They brung all this on us."

"Oh, come now. We didn't ask to be attacked." Mentally, Drummond crossed his fingers. He neither knew nor cared who was to blame. Both sides, letting mutual fear and friction mount to hysteria— In fact, he wasn't sure the United States hadn't sent out the first rockets, on orders of some panicky or aggressive officials. Nobody was alive who admitted knowing.

"It's the jedgment o' God, for the sins o' our leaders," persisted the woman. "The plague, the fire-death, all that, ain't it foretold in the Bible? Ain't we living in the last days o' the world?"

"Maybe." Drummond was glad to stop before a long low cabin. Religious argument was touchy at best, and with a lot of people nowadays it was dynamite.

They entered the rudely furnished but fairly comfortable structure. A good many crowded in with them. For all their suspicion, they were curious, and an outsider in an aircraft was a blue-moon event these days.

Drummond's eyes flickered unobtrusively about the room, noticing details. Three women—that meant a return to concubinage. Only to be expected in a day of few men and strong-arm rule. Ornaments and utensils, tools and weapons of good quality—yes, that confirmed the stories. This wasn't exactly a bandit town, but it had waylaid travelers and raided other places when times were hard, and built up a sort of dominance of the surrounding country. That, too, was common.

There was a dog on the floor nursing a litter. Only three pups, and one of those was bald, one lacked ears, and one had more toes than it should. Among the wide-eyed children present, there were several two years old or less, and with almost no obvious exceptions, they were also different.

Drummond sighed heavily and sat down. In a way, this clinched it. He'd known for a long time, and finding mutation here, as far as any place from atomic destruction, was about the last evidence he needed.

He had to get on friendly terms, or he wouldn't find out much about things like population, food production, and whatever else there was to know. Forcing a smile to stiff lips, he took a flask from his jacket. "Prewar rye," he said. "Who wants a nip?"

"Do we!" The answer barked out in a dozen voices and words. The flask circulated, men pawing and cursing and grabbing to get at it. *Their homebrew must be pretty bad,* thought Drummond wryly.

The chief shouted an order, and one of his women got busy at the primitive stove. "Rustle you a mess o' chow," he said heartily. "An' my name's Sam Buckman."

"Pleased to meet you, Sam." Drummond squeezed the hairy paw hard. He had to show he wasn't a weakling, a conniving city slicker.

"What's it like, outside?" asked someone presently. "We ain't heard for so long—"

"You haven't missed much," said Drummond between bites. The food was pretty good. Briefly, he sketched conditions. "You're better off than most," he finished.

"Yeah. Mebbe so." Sam Buckman scratched his tangled beard. "What I'd give f'r a razor blade—! It ain't easy, though. The first year we weren't no better off 'n anyone else. Me, I'm a farmer, I kept some ears o' corn an' a little wheat an' barley in my pockets all that winter, even though I was starving. A bunch o' hungry refugees plundered my place, but I got away an' drifted up here. Next year I took an empty farm here an' started over."

Drummond doubted that it had been abandoned, but said nothing. Sheer survival outweighed a lot of considerations.

"Others came an' settled here," said the leader reminiscently. "We farm together. We have to; one man couldn't live by hisself, not with the bugs an' blight, an' the crops sproutin' into all new kinds, an' the outlaws aroun'. Not many up here, though we did beat off some enemy troops last winter." He glowed with pride at that, but Drummond wasn't particularly impressed. A handful of freezing starveling conscripts, lost and bewildered in a foreign enemy's land, with no hope of ever getting home, weren't formidable.

"Things getting better, though," said Buckman. "We're heading up." He scowled blackly, and a palpable chill crept into the room. "If 'twern't for the births—"

"Yes—the births. The new babies. Even the stock an' plants." It was an old man speaking, his eyes glazed with near madness. "It's the mark o' the beast. Satan is loose in the world—"

"Shut up!" Huge and bristling with wrath, Buckman launched himself out of his seat and grabbed the oldster by his scrawny throat. "Shut up 'r I'll bash y'r lying head in. Ain't no son o' mine being marked by the devil."

"Or mine—" "Or mine—" The rumble of voices ran about the cabin, sullen and afraid.

"It's God's jedgment, I tell you!" The woman was shrilling again. "The end o' the world is near. Prepare f'r the second coming—"

"An' you shut up too, Mag Schmidt," snarled Buckman. He stood bent over, gnarled arms swinging loose, hands flexing, little eyes darting red and wild about the room. "Shut y'r trap an' keep it shut. I'm still boss here, an' if you don't like it you can get out. I still don't think that funny-looking brat o' y'rs fell in the lake by accident."

The woman shrank back, lips tight. The room filled with a crackling silence. One of the babies began to cry. It had two heads.

Slowly and heavily, Buckman turned to Drummond, who sat immobile against the wall. "You see?" he asked dully. "You see how it is? Maybe it is the curse o' God. Maybe the world is ending. I dunno. I just know there's few enough babies, an' most o' them *de*formed. Will it go on? Will all our kids be monsters? Should we . . . kill these an' hope we get some human babies? What is it? What to do?"

Drummond rose. He felt a weight as of centuries on his shoulders, the weariness, blank and absolute, of having seen that smoldering panic and heard that desperate appeal too often, too often.

"Don't kill them," he said. "That's the worst kind of murder, and anyway it'd do no good at all. It comes from the bombs, and you can't stop it. You'll go right on having such children, so you might as well get used to it."

By atomic-powered stratojet it wasn't far from Minnesota to Oregon, and Drummond landed in Taylor about noon the next day. This time there was no hurry to get his machine under cover, and up on the mountain was a raw scar of earth where a new airfield was slowly being built. Men were getting over their terror of the sky. They had another fear to face now, and it was one from which there was no hiding.

Drummond walked slowly down the icy main street to the central office. It was numbingly cold, a still, relentless intensity of frost eating through clothes and flesh and bone. It wasn't much better inside. Heating systems were still poor improvisations.

"You're back!" Robinson met him in the antechamber, suddenly galvanized with eagerness. He had grown thin and nervous, looking ten years older, but impatience blazed from him. "How is it? How is it?"

Drummond held up a bulky notebook. "All here," he said grimly. "All the facts we'll need. Not formally correlated yet, but the picture is simple enough."

Robinson laid an arm on his shoulder and steered him into

the office. He felt the general's hand shaking, but he'd sat down and had a drink before business came up again.

"You've done a good job," said the leader warmly. "When the country's organized again, I'll see you get a medal for this. Your men in the other planes aren't in yet."

"No, they'll be gathering data for a long time. The job won't be finished for years. I've only got a general outline here, but it's enough. It's enough." Drummond's eyes were haunted again.

Robinson felt cold at meeting that too-steady gaze. He whispered shakily: "Is it—bad?"

"The worst. Physically, the country's recovering. But biologically, we've reached a crossroads and taken the wrong fork."

"What do you mean? *What do you mean?*"

Drummond let him have it then, straight and hard as a bayonet thrust. "The birth rate's a little over half the prewar," he said, "and about seventy-five per cent of all births are mutant, of which possibly two-thirds are viable and presumably fertile. Of course, that doesn't include late-maturing characteristics, or those undetectable by naked-eye observation, or the mutated recessive genes that must be carried by a lot of otherwise normal zygotes. And it's everywhere. There are no safe places."

"I see," said Robinson after a long time. He nodded, like a man struck a stunning blow and not yet fully aware of it. "I see. The reason—"

"Is obvious."

"Yes. People going through radioactive areas—"

"Why, no. That would only account for a few. But—"

"No matter. The fact's there, and that's enough. We have to decide what to do about it."

"And soon." Drummond's jaw set. "It's wrecking our culture. We at least preserved our historical continuity, but even that's going now. People are going crazy as birth after birth is monstrous. Fear of the unknown, striking at minds still stunned by the war and its immediate aftermath. Frustration of parenthood, perhaps the most basic instinct there is. It's leading to infanticide, desertion, despair, a cancer at the root of society. We've got to act."

"How? How?" Robinson stared numbly at his hands.

"I don't know. You're the leader. Maybe an educational campaign, though that hardly seems practicable. Maybe an acceleration of your program for re-integrating the country. Maybe— I don't know."

Drummond stuffed tobacco into his pipe. He was near the end of what he had, but would rather take a few good smokes than a lot of niggling puffs. "Of course," he said thoughtfully, "it's probably not the end of things. We won't know for a generation or more, but I rather imagine the mutants can grow into society. They'd better, for they'll outnumber the humans. The thing is, if we just let matters drift there's no telling where they'll go. The situation is unprecedented. We may end up in a culture of specialized variations, which would be very bad from an evolutionary standpoint. There may be fighting between mutant types, or with humans. Interbreeding may produce worse freaks, particularly when accumulated recessives start showing up. Robinson, if we want any say at all in what's going to happen in the next few centuries, we have to act quickly. Otherwise it'll snowball out of all control."

"Yes. Yes, we'll have to act fast. And hard." Robinson straightened in his chair. Decision firmed his countenance, but his eyes were staring. "We're mobilized," he said. "We have the men and the weapons and the organization. They won't be able to resist."

The ashy cold of Drummond's emotions stirred, but it was with a horrible wrenching of fear. "What are you getting at?" he snapped.

"Racial death. All mutants and their parents to be sterilized whenever and wherever detected."

"You're crazy!" Drummond sprang from his chair, grabbed Robinson's shoulders across the desk, and shook him. "You . . . why, it's impossible! You'll bring revolt, civil war, final collapse!"

"Not if we go about it right." There were little beads of sweat studding the general's forehead. "I don't like it any better than you, but it's got to be done or the human race is finished. Normal births a minority—" He surged to his feet, gasping. "I've thought a long time about this. Your facts only confirmed my suspicions. This tears it. Can't you see? Evolution has to proceed slowly. Life wasn't meant for such a storm of change. Unless we can save the true human stock, it'll be absorbed and differentiation will continue till humanity is a collection of freaks, probably intersterile. Or . . . there must be a lot of lethal recessives. In a large population, they can accumulate unnoticed till nearly everybody has them, and then start emerging all at once. That'd wipe us out. It's happened before, in rats and other species. If we eliminate mutant stock now, we can still save the race. It won't be cruel. We have sterilization techniques which are quick and painless, not upsetting the endocrine balance. But it's got to be done." His voice rose to a raw scream, broke. "It's got to be done!"

Drummond slapped him, hard. He drew a shuddering breath, sat down, and began to cry, and somehow that was the most horrible sight of all.

"You're crazy," said the aviator. "You've gone nuts with brooding alone on this the last six months, without knowing or being able to act. You've lost all perspective.

"We can't use violence. In the first place, it would break our tottering, cracked culture irreparably, into a mad-dog finish fight. We'd not even win it. We're outnumbered, and we couldn't hold down a continent, eventually a planet. And remember what we said once, about abandoning the old savage way of settling things, that never brings a real settlement at all? We'd throw away a lesson our noses were rubbed in not three years ago. We'd return to the beast—to ultimate extinction.

"And anyway," he went on very quietly, "it wouldn't do a bit of good. Mutants would still be born. The poison is everywhere. Normal parents will give birth to mutants, somewhere along the line. We just have to accept that fact, and live with it. The *new* human race will have to."

"I'm sorry." Robinson raised his face from his hands. It was a ghastly visage, gone white and old, but there was calm on it. "I—blew my top. You're right. I've been thinking of this, worrying and wondering, living and breathing it, lying awake nights, and when I finally sleep I dream of it. I . . . yes, I see your point. And you're right."

"It's O.K. You've been under a terrific strain. Three years with never a rest, and the responsibility for a nation, and now this— Sure, everybody's entitled to be a little crazy. We'll work out a solution, somehow."

"Yes, of course." Robinson poured out two stiff drinks and gulped his. He paced restlessly, and his tremendous ability came back in waves of strength and confidence. "Let me see— Eugenics, of course. If we work hard, we'll have the nation tightly organized inside of ten years. Then . . . well, I don't suppose we can keep the mutants from interbreeding, but certainly we can pass laws to protect humans and encourage their propagation. Since radical mutations would probably be intersterile anyway, and most mutants handicapped one way or another, a few generations should see humans completely dominant again."

Drummond scowled. He was worried. It wasn't like Robinson to be unreasonable. Somehow, the man had acquired a mental blind spot where this most ultimate of human problems was concerned. He said slowly, "That won't work either. First, it'd be hard to impose and enforce. Second, we'd be repeating the old *Herrenvolk* notion. Mutants are inferior, mutants must be kept in their place—to enforce that, especially on a majority, you'd need a full-fledged totalitarian state. Third, that wouldn't work either, for the rest of the world, with almost no exceptions, is under no such control and we'll be in no position to take over that control for a long time—generations. Before then, mutants will dominate everywhere over there, and if they resent the way we treat their kind here, we'd better run for cover."

"You assume a lot. How do you know those hundreds or thousands of diverse types will work together? They're less like each other than like humans, even. They could be played off against each other."

"Maybe. But *that* would be going back onto the old road of treachery and violence, the road to Hell. Conversely, if every not-quite-human is called a 'mutant,' like a separate class, he'll think he is, and act accordingly against the lumped-together 'humans.' No, the only way to sanity—to *survival*—is to abandon class prejudice and race hate altogether, and work as individuals. We're all . . . well, Earthlings; for us subclassification is deadly. We all have to live together, and might as well make the best of it."

"Yeah . . . yeah, that's right too."

"Anyway, I repeat that all such attempts would be useless. All Earth is infected with mutation. It will be for a long time. The purest human stock will still produce mutants."

"Y-yes, that's true. Our best bet seems to be to find all such stock and withdraw it into the few safe areas left. It'll mean a small human population, but a *human* one."

"I tell you, that's impossible," clipped Drummond. "There is no safe place. Not one."

Robinson stopped pacing and looked at him as at a physical antagonist. "That so?" he almost growled. "Why?"

Drummond told him, adding incredulously, "Surely you knew that. Your physicists must have measured the amount of it. Your doctors, your engineers, that geneticist I dug up for you. You obviously got a lot of this biological information you've been slinging at me from him. They *must* all have told you the same thing."

Robinson shook his head stubbornly. "It can't be. It's not reasonable. The concentration wouldn't be great enough."

"Why, you poor fool, you need only look around you. The plants, the animals— Haven't there been any births in Taylor?"

"No. This is still a man's town, though women are trickling in and several babies are on the way—" Robinson's face was suddenly twisted with desperation. "Elaine's is due any time now. She's in the hospital here. Don't you see, our other kid died of the plague. This one's all we have. We want him to grow up in a world free of want and fear, a world of peace and sanity where he can play and laugh and become a man, not a beast starving in a cave. You and I are on our way out. We're the old generation, the one that wrecked the world. It's up to us to build it again, and then retire from it to let our children have it. The future's theirs. We've got to make it ready for them."

Sudden insight held Drummond motionless for long seconds. Understanding came, and pity, and an odd gentleness that changed his sunken bony face. "Yes," he murmured, "yes, I see. That's why you're working with all that's in you to build a normal, healthy world. That's why you nearly went crazy when this threat appeared. That . . . that's why you can't just can't comprehend—"

He took the other man's arm and guided him toward the door. "Come on," he said. "Let's go see how your wife's making out. Maybe we can get her some flowers on the way."

The silent cold bit at them as they went down the street. Snow crackled underfoot. It was already grimy with town smoke and dust, but overhead the sky was incredibly clean and blue. Breath smoked whitely from their mouths and nostrils. The sound of men at work rebuilding drifted faintly between the bulking mountains.

"We couldn't emigrate to another planet, could we?" asked

Robinson, and answered himself: "No, we lack the organization and resources to settle them right now. We'll have to make out on Earth. A few safe spots—there *must* be others besides this one—to house the true humans till the mutation period is over. Yes, we can do it."

"There are no safe places," insisted Drummond. "Even if there were, the mutants would still outnumber us. Does your geneticist have any idea how this'll come out, biologically speaking?"

"He doesn't know. His specialty is still largely unknown. He can make an intelligent guess, and that's all."

"Yeah. Anyway, our problem is to learn to live with the mutants, to accept anyone as—Earthling—no matter how he looks, to quit thinking anything was ever settled by violence or connivance, to build a culture of individual sanity. Funny," mused Drummond, "how the impractical virtues, tolerance and sympathy and generosity, have become the fundamental necessities of simple survival. I guess it was always true, but it took the death of half the world and the end of a biological era to make us see that simple little fact. The job's terrific. We've got half a million years of brutality and greed, superstition and prejudice, to lick in a few generations. If we fail, mankind is done. But we've got to try."

They found some flowers, potted in a house, and Robinson bought them with the last of his tobacco. By the time he reached the hospital, he was sweating. The sweat froze on his face as he walked.

The hospital was the town's biggest building, and fairly well equipped. A nurse met them as they entered.

"I was just going to send for you, General Robinson," she said. "The baby's on the way."

"How . . . is she?"

"Fine, so far. Just wait here, please."

Drummond sank into a chair and with haggard eyes watched Robinson's jerky pacing. *The poor guy. Why is it expectant fathers are supposed to be so funny? It's like laughing at a man on the rack. I know, Barbara, I know.*

"They have some anaesthetics," muttered the general. "They . . . Elaine never was very strong."

"She'll be all right." *It's afterward that worries me.*

"Yeah— Yeah— How long, though, how long?"

"Depends. Take it easy." Drummond then made a sacrifice

to a man he liked. He filled his pipe and handed it over. "Here, you need a smoke."

"Thanks." Robinson puffed raggedly.

The slow minutes passed, and Drummond wondered vaguely what he'd do when—it—happened. It didn't have to happen. But the chances were all against such an easy solution. He was no psychologist. Best just to let things happen as they would.

The waiting broke at last. A doctor came out, seeming an inscrutable high priest in his white garments. Robinson stood before him, motionless.

"You're a brave man," said the doctor. His face, as he removed the mask, was stern and set. "You'll need your courage."

"She—" It was hardly a human sound, that croak.

"Your wife is doing well. But the baby—"

A nurse brought out the little wailing form. It was a boy. But his limbs were rubbery tentacles terminating in boneless digits.

Robinson looked, and something went out of him as he stood there. When he turned, his face was dead.

"You're lucky," said Drummond, and meant it. He'd seen too many other mutants. "After all, if he can use those hands he'll get along all right. He'll even have an advantage in certain types of work. It isn't a deformity, really. If there's nothing else, you've got a good kid."

"*If!* You can't tell with mutants."

"I know. But you've got guts, you and Elaine. You'll see this through, together." Briefly, Drummond felt an utter personal desolation. He went on, perhaps to cover that emptiness:

"I see why you didn't understand the problem. You *wouldn't*. It was a psychological block, suppressing a fact you didn't dare face. That boy is really the center of your life. You couldn't think the truth about him, so your subconscious just refused to let you think rationally on that subject at all.

"Now you know. Now you realize there's no safe place, not on all the planet. The tremendous incidence of mutant births in the first generation could have told you that alone. Most such new characteristics are recessive, which means both parents have to have it for it to show in the zygote. But genetic changes are random, except for a tendency to fall into roughly similar patterns. Four-leaved clovers, for instance. Think how vast the total number of such changes must be, to produce so many corresponding changes in a couple of years. Think how many, *many* recessives there must be, existing only in gene patterns till their mates show up. We'll just have to take our chances of something really deadly accumulating. We'd never know till too late."

"The dust—"

"Yeah. The radiodust. It's colloidal, and uncountable other radio-colloids were formed when the bombs went off, and ordinary dirt gets into unstable isotopic forms near the craters. And there are radiogases too, probably. The poison is all over the world by now, spread by wind and air currents. Colloids can be suspended indefinitely in the atmosphere.

"The concentration isn't too high for life, though a physicist told me he'd measured it as being very near the safe limit and there'll probably be a lot of cancer. But it's everywhere. Every breath we draw, every crumb we eat and drop we drink, every clod we walk on, the dust is there. It's in the stratosphere, clear on down to the surface, probably a good distance below. We could only escape by sealing ourselves in air-conditioned vaults and wearing spacesuits whenever we got out, and under present conditions that's impossible.

"Mutations were rare before, because a charged particle has to get pretty close to a gene and be moving fast before its electromagnetic effect causes physico-chemical changes, and then that particular chromosome has to enter into reproduction. Now the charged particles, and the gamma rays producing still more, are everywhere. Even at the comparatively low concentration, the odds favor a given organism having so many cells changed that at least one will give rise to a mutant. There's even a good chance of like recessives meeting in the first generation, as we've seen. Nobody's safe, no place is free."

"The geneticist thinks some true humans will continue."

"A few, probably. After all, the radioactivity isn't too concentrated, and it's burning itself out. But it'll take fifty or a hundred years for the process to drop to insignificance, and by then the pure stock will be way in the minority. And there'll still be all those unmatched recessives, waiting to show up."

"You were right. We should never have created science. It brought the twilight of the race."

"I enver said that. The race brought its own destruction,

through misuse of science. Our culture was scientific anyway, in all except its psychological basis. It's up to us to take that last and hardest step. If we do, the race may yet survive."

Drummond gave Robinson a push toward the inner door. "You're exhausted, beat up, ready to quit. Go on in and see Elaine. Give her my regards. Then take a long rest before going back to work. I still think you've got a good kid."

Mechanically, the *de facto* President of the United States left the room. Hugh Drummond stared after him a moment, then went out into the street.

CHILD'S PLAY

by William Tenn (Philip Klass; 1920-)

ASTOUNDING SCIENCE FICTION
March

"William Tenn" is a pseudonym used by Philip Klass, who is now a Professor of English at Penn State University but who during the late 1940s and the 1950s produced some of the best socially oriented sf of that period, primarily in the late and lamented Galaxy Science Fiction. *A verbal, witty man, as a writer he was most comfortable at the shorter lengths, where he could take one concept and turn it on its head. His wonderful stories can be found in several collections, such as* The Human Angle *(1956),* The Seven Sexes *(1968), and* The Square Root of Man *(1968). However, a definitive omnibus of his best work still awaits publication and is badly needed.*

"Child's Play" was his third published story, is not at all about children, and is downright chilling in its telling and in its implications.

(Marty has mentioned just above that Phil Klass is a Professor of English at Penn State University. Phil is extraordinarily proud of the fact that he achieved and maintained academic status without

having received a college degree but as a result of honest achievement in the literary marketplace alone.

Yet, of course, there was a time when he was only an Associate Professor and was attempting to remove the qualifying adjective and become a "full" Professor. For that, it would help to have recommendations from people who knew his qualifications and could speak highly of them. So he phoned me and asked if I would be one of those who would oblige and I said, "Certainly, Phil," and sent off a letter expressing my honest opinion that he deserved his full Professorship.

He got it, and when nobody was looking, I went off in the corner and kicked and screamed because although I had carefully climbed the scholastic ladder, degree by degree, to the top, I myself was only an Associate Professor. (But weep not, o Gentle Reader, for since then I have attained a full Professorship, too. —And so has Marty, though neither of ours is in English.—I.A.)

After the man from the express company had given the door an untipped slam, Sam Weber decided to move the huge crate under the one light bulb in his room. It was all very well for the messenger to drawl, "I dunno. We don't send 'em; we just deliver 'em, mister"—but there must be some mildly lucid explanation.

With a grunt that began as an anticipatory reflex and ended on a note of surprised annoyance, Sam shoved the box forward the few feet necessary. It was heavy enough; he wondered how the messenger had carried it up the three flights of stairs.

He straightened and frowned down at the garish card which contained his name and address as well as the legend—"Merry Christmas, 2153."

A joke? He didn't know anyone who'd think it funny to send a card dated over two hundred years in the future. Unless one of the comedians in his law school graduating class meant to record his opinion as to when Weber would be trying his first case. Even so—

The letters were shaped strangely, come to think of it, sort of green streaks instead of lines. And the card was a sheet of gold!

Sam decided he was really interested. He ripped the card aside, tore off the flimsy wrapping material—and stopped. He whistled. Then he gulped.

"Well clip my ears and call me streamlined!"

There was no top to the box, no slit in its side, no handle anywhere in sight. It seemed to be a solid, cubical mass of brown stuff. Yet he was positive something had rattled inside when it was moved.

He seized the corners and strained and grunted till it lifted. The underside was as smooth and innocent of opening as the rest. He let it thump back to the floor.

"Ah, well," he said philosophically, "it's not the gift; it's the principle involved."

Many of his gifts still required appreciative notes. He'd have to work up something special for Aunt Maggie. Her neckties were things of cubistic horror, but he hadn't even sent her a lone handkerchief this Christmas. Every cent had gone into buying that brooch for Tina. Not quite a ring, but maybe she'd consider that under the circumstances—

He turned to walk to his bed which he had drafted into the additional service of desk and chair. He kicked at the great box disconsolately. "Well, if you won't open, you won't open."

As of smarting under the kick, the box opened. A cut appeared on the upper surface, widened rapidly and folded the top back and down on either side like a valise. Sam clapped his forehead and addressed a rapid prayer to every god from Set to Father Divine. Then he remembered what he'd said.

"Close," he suggested.

The box closed, once more as smooth as a baby's anatomy.

"Open."

The box opened.

So much for the sideshow, Sam decided. He bent down and peered into the container.

The interior was a crazy mass of shelving on which rested vials filled with blue liquids, jars filled with red solids, transparent tubes showing yellow and green and orange and mauve and other colors which Sam's eyes didn't quite remember. There were seven pieces of intricate apparatus on the bottom which looked as if tube-happy radio hams had assembled them. There was also a book.

Sam picked the book off the bottom and noted numbly that while all its pages were metallic, it was lighter than any paper book he'd ever held.

He carried the book over to the bed and sat down. Then he took a long, deep breath and turned to the first page. "Gug," he said, exhaling his long, deep breath.

In mad, green streaks of letters:

> Bild-A-Man Set #3. This set is intended solely for the uses of children between the ages of eleven and thirteen. The equipment, much more advanced than Bild-A-Man Sets 1 and 2, will enable the child of this age-group to build and assemble complete adult humans in perfect working order. The retarded child may also construct the babies and mannikins of the earlier kits. Two disassembleators are provided so that the set can be used again and again with profit. As with Sets 1 and 2, the aid of a Census Keeper in all disassembling is advised. Refills and additional parts may be acquired from The Bild-A-Man Company, 928 Diagonal Level, Glunt City, Ohio. Remember—only with a Bild-A-Man can you build a man!

Weber slammed his eyes shut. What was that gag in the movie he'd seen last night? Terrific gag. Terrific picture, too. Nice Technicolor. Wonder how much the director made a week? The cameraman? Five hundred? A thousand?

He opened his eyes warily. The box was still a squat cube in the center of his room. The book was still in his shaking hand. And the page read the same.

"Only with a Bild-A-Man can you build a man!" Heaven help a neurotic young lawyer at a time like this!

There was a price list on the next page for "refills and additional parts." Things like one liter of hemoglobin and three grams of assorted enzymes were offered for sale in terms of one slunk fifty and three slunks forty-five. A note on the bottom advertised Set #4: "The thrill of building your first live Martian!"

Fine print announced *pat. pending 2148.*

The third page was a table of contents. Sam gripped the edge of the mattress with one sweating hand and read:

Chapter I—A child's garden of biochemistry.
" II—Making simple living things indoors and out.
" III—Mannikins and what makes them do the world's work.
" IV—Babies and other small humans.
" V—Twins for every purpose, twinning yourself and your friends.
" VI—What you need to build a man.
" VII—Completing the man.
" VIII—Disassembling the man.
" IX—New kinds of life for your leisure moments.

Sam dropped the book back into the box and ran for the mirror. His face was still the same, somewhat like bleached chalk, but fundamentally the same. He hadn't twinned or grown himself a mannikin or devised a new kind of life for his leisure moments. Everything was snug as a bug in a bughouse.

Very carefully he pushed his eyes back into their proper position in their sockets.

"Dear Aunt Maggie," he began writing feverishly. "Your ties made the most beautiful gift of my Christmas. My only regret is—"

My only regret is that I have but one life to give for my Christmas present. Who could have gone to such fantastic lengths for a practical joke? Lew Knight? Even Lew must have some reverence in his insensitive body for the institution of Christmas. And Lew didn't have the brains or the patience for a job so involved.

Tina? Tina had the fine talent for complication, all right. But Tina, while possessing a delightful abundance of all other physical attributes, was sadly lacking in funnybone.

Sam drew the leather envelope forth and caressed it. Tina's perfume seemed to cling to the surface and move the world back into focus.

The metallic greeting card glinted at him from the floor. Maybe the reverse side contained the sender's name. He picked it up, turned it over.

Nothing but blank gold surface. He was sure of the gold; his father had been a jeweler. The very value of the sheet was rebuttal to the possibility of a practical joke. Besides, again, what was the point?

"Merry Christmas, 2153." Where would humanity be in two hundred years? Traveling to the stars, or beyond—to unimaginable destinations? Using little mannikins to perform the work of machines and robots? Providing children with—

There might be another card or note inside the box. Weber bent down to remove its contents. His eye noted a large grayish jar and the label etched into its surface: *Dehydrated Neurone Preparation, for human construction only.*

He backed away and glared. "Close!"

The thing melted shut. Weber sighed his relief at it and decided to go to bed.

He regretted while undressing that he hadn't thought to ask the messenger the name of his firm. Knowing the delivery service involved would be useful in tracing the origin of this gruesome gift.

"But then," he repeated as he fell asleep, "it's not the gift—it's the principle! Merry Christmas, me."

The next morning when Lew Knight breezed in with his "Good morning, counselor," Sam waited for the first sly ribbing to start. Lew wasn't the man to hide his humor behind a bushel. But Lew buried his nose in "The New York State Supplement" and kept it there all morning. The other five young lawyers in the communal office appeared either too bored or too busy to have Bild-A-Man sets on their conscience. There were no sly grins, no covert glances, no leading questions.

Tina walked in at ten o'clock, looking like a pin-up girl caught with her clothes on.

"Good morning, counselors," she said.

Each in his own way, according to the peculiar gland secretions he was enjoying at the moment, beamed, drooled or nodded a reply. Lew Knight drooled. Sam Weber beamed.

Tina took it all in and analyzed the situation while she fluffed her hair about. Her conclusions evidently involved leaning markedly against Lew Knight's desk and asking what he had for her to do this morning.

Sam bit savagely into Hackleworth "On Torts." Theoretically, Tina was employed by all seven of them as secretary, switchboard operator and receptionist. Actually, the most faithful performance of her duties entailed nothing more daily than the typing and addressing of two envelopes with an occasional letter to be sealed inside. Once a week there might be a wistful little brief which was never to attain judicial scrutiny. Tina therefore had a fair library of fashion magazines in the first drawer of her desk and a complete cosmetics laboratory in the other two; she spent one third of her working day in the ladies' room swapping stocking prices and sources with other secretaries; she devoted the other two thirds religiously to that one of her employers who as of her arrival seemed to be in the most masculine mood. Her pay was small but her life was full.

Just before lunch, she approached casually with the morning's mail. "Didn't think we'd be too busy this morning, counselor—" she began.

"You thought incorrectly, Miss Hill," he informed her with a brisk irritation that he hoped became him well; "I've been waiting for you to terminate your social engagements so that we could get down to what occasionally passes for business."

She was as startled as an uncushioned kitten. "But—but this isn't Monday. Somerset & Ojack only send you stuff on Mondays."

Sam winced at the reminder that if it weren't for the legal drudgework he received once a week from Somerset & Ojack he would be a lawyer in name only, if not in spirit only. "I have a letter, Miss Hill," he replied steadily. "Whenever you assemble the necessary materials, we can get on with it."

Tina returned in a head-shaking moment with stenographic pad and pencils.

"Regular heading, today's date," Sam began. "Address it to Chamber of Commerce, Glunt City, Ohio. Gentlemen: Would you inform me if you have registered currently with you a firm bearing the name of the Bild-A-Man Company or a firm with any name at all similar? I am also interested in whether a firm bearing the above or related name has recently made known its intention of joining your community. This inquiry is being made informally on behalf of a client who is interested in a product of this organization whose address he has mislaid. Signature and then this P.S.—My client is also curious as to the business possibilities of a street known as Diagonal Avenue or Diagonal Level. Any data on this address and the organizations presently located there will be greatly appreciated."

Tina batted wide blue eyes at him. "Oh, Sam," she breathed, ignoring the formality he had introduced, "Oh, Sam, you have another client. I'm so glad. He looked a little sinister, but in *such* a distinguished manner that I was certain—"

"Who? Who looked a little sinister?"

"Why your new cli-ent." Sam had the uncomfortable feeling that she had almost added "stu-pid." "When I came in this morning, there was this terribly tall old man in a long black overcoat talking to the elevator operator. He turned to me—the elevator operator, I mean—and said, 'This is Mr. Weber's secretary. She'll be able to tell you anything you want to know.' Then he sort of winked which I thought was sort of impolite, you know, considering. Then this old man looked at me hard and I felt distinctly uncomfortable and he walked away muttering, 'Either disjointed or predatory personalities. Never normal. Never balanced.' Which I didn't think was very polite, either, I'll have you know, if he *is* your new client!" She sat back and began breathing again.

Tall, sinister old men in long black overcoats pumping the elevator operator about him. Hardly a matter of business. He had no skeletons in his personal closet. Could it be connected with his unusual Christmas present? Sam hmmmed mentally.

"—but she is my favorite aunt, you know," Tina was saying. "And she came in so unexpectedly."

The girl was explaining about their Christmas date. Sam felt a rush of affection for her as she leaned forward.

"Don't bother," he told her. "I knew you couldn't help breaking the date. I was a little sore when you called me, but I got over it; never-hold-a-grudge-against-a-pretty-girl Sam, I'm known as. How about lunch?"

"Lunch?" She flew distress signals. "I promised Lew, Mr. Knight, that is— But he wouldn't mind if you came along."

"Fine. Let's go." This would be helping Lew to a spoonful of his own annoying medicine.

Lew Knight took the business of having a crowd instead of a party for lunch as badly as Sam hoped he would. Unfortunately, Lew was able to describe details of his forthcoming case, the probable fees and possible distinction to be reaped thereof. After one or two attempts to bring an interesting will he was rephrasing for Somerset & Ojack into the conversation, Sam subsided into daydreams. Lew immediately dropped Rosenthal vs. Rosenthal and leered at Tina conversationally.

Outside the restaurant, snow discolored into slush. Most of the stores were removing Christmas displays. Sam noticed construction sets for children, haloed by tinsel and glittering with artificial snow. Build a radio, a skyscraper, an airplane. But "Only with a Bild-A-Man can you—"

"I'm going home," he announced suddenly. "Something important I just remembered. If anything comes up, call me there."

He was leaving Lew a clear field, he told himself, as he found a seat on the subway. But the bitter truth was that the field was almost as clear when he was around as when he wasn't. Lupine Lew Knight, he had been called in Law School; since the day when he had noticed that Tina had the correct proportions of dress-filling substances, Sam's chances had been worth a crowbar at Fort Knox.

Tina hadn't been wearing his brooch today. Her little finger, right hand, however, had sported an unfamiliar and garish little ring. "Some got it," Sam philosophized. "Some don't got it. I don't got it."

But it would have been nice, with Tina, to have "got it."

As he unlocked the door of his room he was surprised by an unmade bed telling with rumpled stoicism of a chambermaid who'd never come. This hadn't happened before— Of course! He'd never locked his room before. The girl must have thought he wanted privacy.

Maybe he had.

Aunt Maggie's ties glittered obscenely at the foot of the bed. He chucked them into the closet as he removed his hat and coat. Then he went over to the washstand and washed his hands, slowly. He turned around.

This was it. At last the great cubical bulk that had been lurking quietly in the corner of his vision was squarely before him. It was there and it undoubtedly contained all the outlandish collection he remembered.

"Open," he said, and the box opened.

The book, still open to the metallic table of contents, was lying at the bottom of the box. Part of it had slipped into the chamber of a strange piece of apparatus. Sam picked both out gingerly.

He slipped the book out and noticed the apparatus consisted mostly of some sort of binoculars, supported by a coil and tube arrangement and bearing on a flat green plate. He turned it over. The underside was lettered in the same streaky way as the book. "Combination Electron Microscope and Workbench."

Very carefully he placed it on the floor. One by one, he removed the others, from the "Junior Biocalibrator" to the "Jiffy Vitalizer." Very respectfully he ranged against the box in five multi-colored rows of vials of lymph and the jars of basic cartilage. The walls of the chest were lined with indescribably thin and wrinkled sheets; a slight pressure along their edges expanded them into three-dimensional outlines of human organs whose shape and size could be varied with pinching any part of their surface—most indubitably molds.

Quite an assortment. If there was anything solidly scientific to it, that box might mean unimaginable wealth. Or some very useful publicity. Or—well, it should mean something!

If there was anything solidly scientific to it.

Sam flopped down to the bed and opened to "A Child's Garden of Biochemistry."

At nine that night he squatted next to the Combination Electron Microscope and Workbench and began opening certain small bottles. At nine forty-seven Sam Weber made his first simple living thing.

It wasn't much, if you used the first chapter of Genesis as your standard. Just a primitive brown mold that, in the field of the microscope, fed diffidently on a piece of pretzel, put forth a few spores and died in about twenty minutes. But *he* had made it. He had constructed a specific lifeform to feed on the constituents of a specific pretzel; it could survive nowhere else.

He went out to supper with every intention of getting drunk. After just a little alcohol, however, the *deiish* feeling returned and he scurried back to his room.

Never again that evening did he recapture the exultation of the brown mold, though he constructed a giant protein molecule and a whole slew of filterable viruses.

He called the office in the little corner drugstore which was his breakfast nook. "I'll be home all day," he told Tina.

She was a little puzzled. So was Lew Knight who grabbed the phone. "Hey, counselor, you building up a neighborhood practice? Kid Blackstone is missing out on a lot of cases. Two ambulances have already clanged past the building."

"Yeah," said Sam. "I'll tell him when he comes in."

The weekend was almost upon him, so he decided to take the next day off as well. He wouldn't have any real work till Monday when the Somerset & Ojack basket would produce his lone egg.

Before he returned to his room, he purchased a copy of an advanced bacteriology. It was amusing to construct—with improvements!—unicellular creatures whose very place in the scheme of classification was a matter of argument among scientists of his own day. The Bild-A-Man manual, of course, merely gave a few examples and general rules; but with the descriptions in the bacteriology, the world was his oyster.

Which was an idea: he made a few oysters. The shells weren't hard enough, and he couldn't quite screw his courage up to the eating point, but they were most undeniably bivalves. If he cared to perfect his technique, his food problem would be solved.

The manual was fairly easy to follow and profusely illustrated with pictures that expanded into solidity as the page was opened. Very little was taken for granted; involved explanations followed simpler ones. Only the allusions were occasionally obscure—"This is the principle used in the phanphophink toys," "When your teeth are next yokekkled or demortoned, think of the *Bacterium cyanogenum* and the humble part it plays," "If you have a rubicular mannikin around the house, you needn't bother with the chapter on mannikins."

After a brief search had convinced Sam that whatever else he now had in his apartment he didn't have a rubicular mannikin, he felt justified in turning to the chapter on mannikins. He had conquered completely this feeling of being Pop played with Junior's toy train: already he had done more than the world's top biologists ever dreamed of for the next generation and what might not lie ahead—what problems might he not yet solve?

"Never forget that mannikins are constructed for one purpose and one purpose only." I won't, Sam promised. "Whether they are sanitary mannikins, tailoring mannikins, printing mannikins or even sunevviarry mannikins, they are each constructed with one operation of a given process in view. When you make a mannikin that is capable of more than one function, you are committing a crime so serious as to be punishable by public admonition."

"To construct an elementary mannikin—"

It was very difficult. Three times he tore down developing monstrosities and began anew. It wasn't till Sunday afternoon that the mannikin was complete—or rather, incomplete.

Long arms it had—although by an error, one was slightly longer than the other—a faceless head and a trunk. No legs. No eyes or ears, no organs of reproduction. It lay on his bed and gurgled out of the red rim of a mouth that was supposed to serve both for ingress and excretion of food. It waved the long arms, designed for some one simple operation not yet invented, in slow circles.

Sam, watching it, decided that life could be as ugly as an open field latrine in midsummer.

He had to disassemble it. Its length—three feet from almost boneless fingers to tapering, sealed-off trunk—precluded the use of the tiny disassembleator with which he had taken apart the oysters and miscellaneous small creations. There was a bright yellow notice on the large disassembleator, however—"To be used only under the direct supervision of a Census Keeper. Call formula A76 or unstable your *id*."

"Formula A76" meant about as much as "sunevviarry," and Sam decided his *id* was already sufficiently unstabled, thank you. He'd have to make out without a Census Keeper. The big disassembleator probably used the same general principles as the small one.

He clamped it to a bedpost and adjusted the focus. He snapped the switch set in the smooth underside.

Five minutes later the mannikin was a bright, gooey mess on his bed.

The large disassembleator, Sam was convinced as he tidied his room, did require the supervision of a Census Keeper. Some sort of keeper anyway. He rescued as many of the legless creature's constituents as he could, although he doubted he'd be using the set for the next fifty years or so. He certainly wouldn't ever use the disassembleator again; much less spectacular and disagreeable to shove the whole thing into a meat grinder and crank the handle as it squashed inside.

As he locked the door behind him on his way to a gentle binge, he made a mental note to purchase some fresh sheets the next morning. He'd have to sleep on the floor tonight.

Wrist-deep in Somerset & Ojack minutiae, Sam was conscious of Lew Knight's stares and Tina's puzzled glances. If they only knew, he exulted! But Tina would probably just think it "marr-vell-ouss!" and Lew Knight might make some crack like "Hey! Kid Frankenstein himself!" Come to think of it though Lew would probably have worked out some method of duplicating, to a limited extent, the contents of the Bild-A-Man set and marketing it commercially. Whereas he—well, there were other things you could do with the gadget. Plenty of other things.

"Hey, counselor," Lew Knight was perched on the corner of his desk, "what are these long weekends we're taking? You might not make as much money in the law, but does it look right for an associate of mine to sell magazine subscriptions on the side?"

Sam stuffed his ears mentally against the emery-wheel voice. "I've been writing a book."

"A law book? Weber 'On Bankruptcy'?"

"No, a juvenile. 'Lew Knight, The Neanderthal Nitwit.' "

"Won't sell. The title lacks punch. Something like 'Knights, Knaves and Knobheads' is what the public goes for these days. By the way, Tina tells me you two had some sort of understanding about New Year's Eve and she doesn't think you'd mind if I took her out instead. I don't think you'd mind either, but I may be prejudiced. Especially since I have a table reservation at *Cigale's* where there's usually less of a crowd of a New Year's Eve than at the automat."

"I don't mind."

"Good," said Knight approvingly as he moved away. "By the way, won that case. Nice juicy fee, too. Thanks for asking."

Tina also wanted to know if he objected to the new arrangements when she brought the mail. Again, he didn't. Where had he been for over two days? He had been busy, very busy. Something entirely new. Something important.

She stared down at him as he separated offers of used cars guaranteed not to have been driven over a quarter of a million miles from caressing reminders that he still owed half the tuition for the last year of law school and when was he going to pay it?

Came a letter that was neither bill nor ad. Sam's heart momentarily lost interest in the monotonous round of pumping that was its lot as he stared at a strange postmark: Glunt City, Ohio.

Dear Sir:

There is no firm in Glunt City at the present time bearing any name similar to "Bild-A-Man Company" nor do we know of any such organization planning to join our little community. We also have no thoroughfare called "Diagonal"; our north-south streets are named after Indian tribes while our east-west avenues are listed numerically in multiples of five.

Glunt City is a restricted residential township, we intend to keep it that. Only small retailing and service establishments are permitted here. If you are interested in building a home in Glunt City and can furnish proof of white, Christian, Anglo-Saxon ancestry on both sides of your family for fifteen generations, we would be glad to furnish further information.

Thomas H. Plantagenet, Mayor

P.S. An airfield for privately owned jet- and propeller-driven aircraft is being built outside the city limits.

That was sort of that. He would get no refills on any of the vials and bottles even if he had a loose slunk or two with which to pay for the stuff. Better go easy on the material and conserve it as much as possible. But no disassembling!

Would the "Bild-A-Man Company" begin manufacturing at Glunt City some time in the future when it had developed into an industrial metropolis against the constricted wills of its restricted citizenry? Or had his package slid from some different track in the human time stream, some era to be born on another-dimensional earth? There would have to be a common origin to both, else why the English wordage? And could there be a purpose in his having received it, beneficial—or otherwise?

Tina had been asking him a question. Sam detached his mind from shapeless speculation and considered her quite-the-opposite features.

"So if you'd still like me to go out with you New Year's Eve, all I have to do is tell Lew that my mother expects to suffer from her gallstones and I have to stay home. Then I think you could buy the *Cigale* reservations from him cheap."

"Thanks a lot, Tina, but very honestly I don't have the

loose cash right now. You and Lew make a much more logical couple anyhow."

Lew Knight wouldn't have done that. Lew cut throats with carefree zest. But Tina did seem to go with Lew as a type.

Why? Until Lew had developed a raised eyebrow where Tina was concerned, it had been Sam all the way. The rest of the office had accepted the fact and moved out of their path. It wasn't only a question of Lew's greater success and financial well-being: just that Lew had decided he wanted Tina and had got her.

It hurt. Tina wasn't special; she was no cultural companion, no intellectual equal; but he wanted her. He liked being with her. She was the woman he desired, rightly or wrongly, whether or not there was a sound basis to their relationship. He remembered his parents before a railway accident had orphaned him: they were theoretically incompatible, but they had been terribly happy together.

He was still wondering about it the next night as he flipped the pages of "Twinning yourself and your friends." It would be interesting to twin Tina.

"One for me, one for Lew."

Only the horrible possibility of an error was there. His mannikin had not been perfect: its arms had been of unequal length. Think of a physically lopsided Tina, something he could never bring himself to disassemble, limping extraneously through life.

And then the book warned: "Your constructed twin, though resembling you in every obvious detail, has not had the slow and guarded maturity you have enjoyed. He or she will not be as stable mentally, much less able to cope with unusual situations, much more prone to neurosis. Only a professional carnuplicator, using the finest equipment, can make an exact copy of a human personality. Yours will be able to live and even reproduce, but never to be accepted as a valid and responsible member of society."

Well, he could chance that. A little less stability in Tina would hardly be noticeable; it might be more desirable.

There was a knock. He opened the door, guarding the box from view with his body. His landlady.

"Your door has been locked for the past week, Mr. Weber. That's why the chambermaid hasn't cleaned the room. We thought you didn't want anyone inside."

"Yes." He stepped into the hall and closed the door behind him. "I've been doing some highly important legal work at home."

"Oh." He sensed a murderous curiosity and changed the subject.

"Why all the fine feathers, Mrs. Lipanti—New Year's Eve party?"

She smoothed her frilled black dress self-consciously. "Y-yes. My sister and her husband came in from Springfield to-day and we were going to make a night of it. Only . . . only the girl who was supposed to come over and mind their baby just phoned and said she isn't feeling well. So I guess we won't go unless somebody else, I mean unless we can get someone else to take care . . . I mean, somebody who doesn't have a previous engagement and who wouldn't—" Her voice trailed away in assumed embarrassment as she realized the favor was already asked.

Well, after all, he wasn't doing anything tonight. And she had been remarkably pleasant those times when he had had to operate on the basis of "Of course I'll have the rest of the rent in a day or so." But why did any one of the earth's two billion humans, when in the possession of an unpleasant buck, pass it automatically to Sam Weber?

Then he remembered Chapter IV on babies and other small humans. Since the night when he had separated the mannikin from its constituent parts, he'd been running through the manual as an intellectual exercise. He didn't feel quite up to making some weird error on a small human. But twinning wasn't supposed to be as difficult.

Only by Gog and by Magog, by Aesculapius the Physician and Kildare the Doctor, he would not disassemble this time. There must be other methods of disposal possible in a large city on a dark night. He'd think of something.

"I'd be glad to watch the baby for a few hours." He started down the hall to anticipate her polite protest. "Don't have a date tonight myself. No, don't mention it, Mrs. Lipanti. Glad to do it."

In the landlady's apartment, her nervous sister briefed him doubtfully. "And that's the only time she cries in a low, steady way so if you move fast there won't be much damage done. Not much, anyway."

He saw them to the door. "I'll be fast enough," he assured the mother. "Just so I get a hint."

Mrs. Lipanti paused at the door. "Did I tell you about the man who was asking after you this afternoon?"

Again? "A sort of tall, old man in a long, black overcoat?"

"With the most frightening way of staring into your face and talking under his breath. Do you know him?"

"Not exactly. What did he want?"

"Well, he asked if there was a Sam Weaver living here who was a lawyer and had been spending most of his time in his room for the past week. I told him we had a Sam Weber—your first name *is* Sam?—who answered to that description, but that the last Weaver had moved out over a year ago. He just looked at me for a while and said, 'Weaver, Weber—they might have made an error,' and walked out without so much as a good-bye or excuse me. Not what I call a polite gentleman."

Thoughtfully Sam walked back to the child. Strange how sharp a mental picture he had formed of this man! Possibly because the two women who had met him thus far had been very impressionable, although to hear their stories the impression was there to be received.

He doubted there was any mistake: the man had been looking for him on both occasions; his knowledge of Sam's vacation from foolscap this past week proved that. It did seem as if he weren't interested in meeting him until some moot point of identity should be established beyond the least shadow of a doubt. Something of a legal mind, that.

The whole affair centered around the "Bild-A-Man" set, he was positive. This skulking investigation hadn't started until after the gift from 2153 had been delivered—and Sam had started using it.

But till the character in the long black overcoat paddled up to Sam Weber personally and stated his business, there wasn't very much he could do about it.

Sam went upstairs for his Junior Biocalibrator.

He propped the manual open against the side of the bed and switched the instrument on to full scanning power. The infant gurgled thickly as the calibrator was rolled slowly over its fat body and a section of metal tape unwound from the slot with, according to the manual, a completely detailed physiological description.

It was detailed. Sam gasped as the tape, running through the enlarging viewer, gave information on the child for which a pediatrician would have taken out at least three mortgages on his immortal soul. Thyroid capacity, chromosome quality, cerebral content. All broken down into neat subheads of data for construction purposes. Rate of skull expansion in minutes for the next ten hours; rate of cartilage transformation; changes in hormone secretions while active and at rest.

This was a blueprint; it was like taking canons from a baby.

Sam left the child to a puzzled contemplation of its navel and sped upstairs. With the tape as a guide, he clipped sections of the molds into the required smaller sizes. Then, almost before he knew it consciously, he was constructing a small human.

He was amazed at the ease with which he worked. Skill was evidently acquired in this game; the mannikin had been much harder to put together. The matter of duplication and working from an informational tape simplified his problems, though.

The child took form under his eyes.

He was finished just an hour and a half after he had taken his first measurements. All except the vitalizing.

A moment's pause, here. The ugly prospect of disassembling stopped him for a moment, but he shook it off. He had to see how well he had done the job. If this child could breathe, what was not possible to him! Besides he couldn't keep it suspended in an inanimate condition very long without running the risk of ruining his work and the materials.

He started the vitalizer.

The child shivered and began a low, steady cry. Sam tore down to the landlady's apartment again and scooped up a square of white linen left on the bed for emergencies. Oh well, some more clean sheets.

After he had made the necessary repairs, he stood back and took a good look at it. He was in a sense a papa. He felt as proud.

It was a perfect little creature, glowing and round with health.

"I have twinned," he said happily.

Every detail correct. The two sides of the face correctly unexact, the duplication of the original child's lunch at the very same point of digestion. Same hair, same eyes—or was it? Sam bent over the infant. He could have sworn the other was a blonde. This child had dark hair which seemed to grow darker as he looked.

He grabbed it with one hand and picked up the Junior Biocalibrator with the other.

Downstairs, he placed the two babies side by side on the big bed. No doubt about it. One was blonde: the other, his plagiarism, was now a definite brunette.

The biocalibrator showed other differences: Slightly faster pulse for his model. Lower blood count. Minutely higher cerebral capacity, although the content was the same. Adrenalin and bile secretions entirely unalike.

It added up to error. His child might be the superior specimen, or the inferior one, but he had not made a true copy. He had no way of knowing at the moment whether or not the infant he had built could grow into a human maturity. The other could.

Why? He had followed directions faithfully, had consulted the calibrator tape at every step. And this had resulted. Had he waited too long before starting the vitalizer? Or was it just a matter of insufficient skill?

Close to midnight, his watch delicately pointed out. It would be necessary to remove evidences of baby-making before the Sisters Lipanti came home. Sam considered possibilities swiftly.

He came down in a few moments with an old tablecloth and a cardboard carton. He wrapped the child in the tablecloth, vaguely happy that the temperature had risen that night, then placed it in the carton.

The child gurgled at the adventure. Its original on the bed *goo*ed in return. Sam slipped quietly out into the street.

Male and female drunks stumbled along tootling on tiny trumpets. People wished each other a *hic* happy new year as he strode down the necessary three blocks.

As he turned left, he saw the sign: "Urban Foundling Home." There was a light burning over a side door. Convenient, but that was a big city for you.

Sam shrank into the shadow of an alley for a moment as a new idea occurred to him. This had to look genuine. He pulled a pencil out of his breast pocket and scrawled on the side of the carton in as small handwriting as he could manage:

"Please take good care of my darling little girl. I am not married."

Then he deposited the carton on the doorstep and held his finger on the bell until he heard movement inside. He was across the street and in the alley again by the time a nurse had opened the door.

It wasn't until he walked into the boarding house that he remembered about the navel. He stopped and tried to recall. No, he had built his little girl without a navel! Her belly had been perfectly smooth. That's what came of hurrying! Shoddy workmanship.

There might be a bit of to-do in the foundling home when they unwrapped the kid. How would they explain it?

Sam slapped his forehead. "Me and Michelangelo. He adds a navel, I forget one!"

Except for an occasional groan, the office was fairly quiet the second day of the New Year.

He was going through the last intriguing pages of the book when he was aware of two people teetering awkwardly near his desk. His eyes left the manual reluctantly: "New kinds of life for your leisure moments" was really stuff!

Tina and Lew Knight.

Sam digested the fact that neither of them were perched on his desk.

Tina wore the little ring she'd received for Christmas on the third finger of her left hand; Lew was experimenting with a sheepish look and finding it difficult.

"Oh, Sam. Last night, Lew . . . Sam, we wanted you to be the first— Such a surprise, like that I mean! Why I almost— Naturally we thought this would be a little difficult . . . Sam, we're going, I mean we expect—"

"—to be married," Lew Knight finished in what was almost an undertone. For the first time since Sam had known him he looked uncertain and suspicious of life, like a man who finds a newly-hatched octopus in his breakfast orange juice.

"You'd adore the way Lew proposed," Tina was gushing. "So roundabout. And so shy. I told him afterwards that I thought for a moment he was talking of something else entirely. I did have trouble understanding you, didn't I, dear?"

"Huh? Oh yeah, you had trouble understanding me." Lew stared at his former rival. "Much of a surprise?"

"Oh, no. No surprise at all. You two fit together so perfectly that I knew it right from the first." Sam mumbled his felicitations, conscious of Tina's searching glances. "And now, if you'll excuse me, there's something I have to take care of immediately. A special sort of wedding present."

Lew was disconcerted. "A wedding present, This early?"

"Why certainly," Tina told him. "It isn't very easy to get just the right thing. And a special friend like Sam naturally wants to get a very special gift."

Sam decided he had taken enough. He grabbed the manual and his coat and dodged through the door.

By the time he came to the red stone steps of the boarding house, he had reached the conclusion that the wound, while painful, had definitely missed his heart. He was in fact chuckling at the memory of Lew Knight's face when his landlady plucked at his sleeve.

"That man was here again today, Mr. Weber. He said he wanted to see you."

"Which man? The tall, old fellow?"

Mrs. Lipanti nodded, her arms folded complacently across her chest. "Such an unpleasant person! When I told him you weren't in, he insisted I take him up to your room. I said I couldn't do that without your permission and he looked at me fit to kill. I've never believed in the evil eye myself—although I always say where there is smoke there must be fire—but if there is such at thing as an evil eye, he has it."

"Will he be back?"

"Yes. He asked me when you usually return and I said about eight o'clock, figuring that if you didn't want to meet him it would give you time to change your clothes and wash up and leave before he gets here. And, Mr. Weber, if you'll excuse me for saying this, I don't think you want to meet him."

"Thanks. But when he comes in at eight, show him up. If he's the right person, I'm in illegal possession of his property. I want to know where this property originates."

In his room, he put the manual away carefully and told the box to open. The Junior Biocalibrator was not too bulky and newspaper would suffice to cover it. He was on his way uptown in a few minutes with the strangely shaped parcel under his arm.

Did he still want to duplicate Tina, he pondered? Yes, in spite of everything. She was still the woman he desired more than any he had ever known; and with the original married to Lew, the replica would have no choice but himself. Only—the replica would have Tina's characteristics up to the moment the measurements were taken; she might insist on marrying Lew as well.

That would make for a bit of sitcheeayshun. But he was still miles from that bridge. It might even be amusing—

The possibility of error was more annoying. The Tina he would make might be off-center in a number of ways: reds might overlap pinks like an imperfectly reproduced color photograph: she might, in time, come to digest her own stomach; there could very easily be a streak of strange and incurable insanity implicit in his model which would not assert itself until a deep mutual affection had flowered and borne fruit. As yet, he was no great shakes as a twinner and human mimeographer; the errors he had made on Mrs. Lipanti's niece demonstrated his amateur standing.

Sam knew he would never be able to dismantle Tina if she proved defective. Outside of the chivalrous concepts and almost superstitious reverence for womankind pressed into him by a small town boyhood, there was the unmitigated horror he felt at the idea of such a beloved object going through the same disintegrating process as—well, the mannikin. But if he overlooked an essential in his construction, what other recourse would there be?

Solution: nothing must be overlooked. Sam grinned bitterly as the ancient elevator swayed up to his office. If he only had time for a little more practice with a person whose reactions he knew so exactly that any deviation from the norm would be instantly obvious! But the strange, old man would be calling tonight, and, if his business concerned "Bild-A-Man" sets, Sam's experiments might be abruptly curtailed. And where would he find such a person—he had few real friends and no intimate ones. And, to be at all valuable, it would have to be someone he knew as well as himself.

Himself!

"Floor, sir." The elevator operator was looking at him reproachfully. Sam's exultant shout had caused him to bring the carrier to a spasmodic stop six inches under the floor level, something he had not done since that bygone day when he had first nervously reached for the controls. He felt his craftmanship was under a shadow as he morosely closed the door behind the lawyer.

And why not himself? He knew his own physical attributes better than he knew Tina's; any mental instability on the part of his reproduced self would be readily discernible long before it reached the point of psychosis or worse. And the beauty of it was that he would have no compunction in disassembling a superfluous Sam Weber. Quite the contrary: the horror in that situation would be the continued existence of a duplicate personality: its removal would be a relief.

Twinning himself would provide the necessary practice in a familiar medium. Ideal. He'd have to take careful notes so that if anything went wrong he'd know just where to avoid going off the track in making his own personal Tina.

And maybe the old geezer wasn't interested in the set at all. Even if he were, Sam could take his landlady's advice and not be at home when he called. Silver linings wherever he looked.

Lew Knight stared at the instrument in Sam's hands. "What in the sacred name of Blackstone and all his commentaries is that? Looks like a lawn mower for a window box!"

"It's uh, sort of a measuring gadget. Gives the right size for one thing and another and this and that. Won't be able to get you the wedding present I have in mind unless I know the right size. Or sizes. Tina, would you mind stepping out into the hall?"

"Nooo." She looked dubiously at the gadget. "It won't hurt?"

It wouldn't hurt a bit. Sam assured her. "I just want to keep this a secret from Lew till after the ceremony."

She brightened at that and preceded Sam through the door. "Hey counselor," one of the other young lawyers called at Lew as they left. "Hey counselor, don't let him do that. Possession is nine points Sam always says. He'll never bring her back."

Lew chuckled weakly and bent over his work.

"Now I want you to go into the ladies' room," Sam explained to a bewildered Tina. "I'll stand guard outside and tell the other customers that the place is out of order. If another woman is inside wait until she leaves. Then strip."

"Strip?" Tina squealed.

He nodded. Then very carefully, emphasizing every significant detail of operation, he told her how to use the Junior Biocalibrator. How she must be careful to kick the switch and set the tape running. How she must cover every external square inch of her body. "This little arm will enable you to lower it down your back. No questions now. Git." She gat.

She was back in fifteen minutes, fluffing her dress into place and studying the tape with a rapt frown. "This is the *strangest* thing— According to the spool, my iodine content—"

Sam snaffled the Biocalibrator hurriedly. "Don't give it another thought. It's a code, kind of. Tells me just what size and how many of what kind. You'll be crazy about the gift when you see it."

"I know I will." She bent over him as he kneeled and examined the tape to make certain she had applied the instrument correctly. "You know, Sam, I always felt your taste was perfect. I want you to come and visit us often after we're married. You can have such beautiful ideas! Lew is a bit too . . . too businesslike, isn't he? I mean it's necessary for success and all that, but success isn't everything. I mean you have to have culture, too. You'll help me keep cultured, won't you, Sam?"

"Sure," Sam said vaguely. The tape was complete. Now to get started! "Anything I can do—glad to help."

He rang for the elevator and noticed the forlorn uncertainty with which she watched him. "Don't worry, Tina. You and Lew will be very happy together. And you'll love this wedding present." But not as much as I will, he told himself as he stepped into the elevator.

Back in his room, he emptied the machine and undressed. In a few moments he had another tape on himself. He would have liked to consider it for a while, but being this close to the goal made him impatient. He locked the door, cleaned his room hurriedly of accumulated junk—remembering to sniff in annoyance at Aunt Maggie's ties: the blue and red one almost lighted up the room—ordered the box to open—and he was ready to begin.

First the water. With the huge amount of water necessary to the human body, especially in the case of an adult, he might as well start collecting it now. He had bought several pans and it would take his lone faucet some time to fill them all.

As he placed the first pot under the tap, Sam wondered suddenly if its chemical impurities might affect the end product. Of course it might! These children of 2153 would probably take absolutely pure H_2O as a matter of daily use; the manual hadn't mentioned the subject, but how did he know what kind of water they had available? Well, he'd boil this batch over his chemical stove; when he got to making Tina he could see about getting *aqua* completely *pura.*

Score another point for making a simulacrum of Sam first.

While waiting for the water to boil, he arranged his supplies to positions of maximum availability. They were getting low. That baby had taken up quite a bit of useful ingredients; too bad he hadn't seen his way clear to disassembling it. That meant if there were any argument in favor of allowing the replica of himself to go on living, it was now invalid. He'd have to take it apart in order to have enough for Tina II. Or Tina prime?

He leafed through Chapters VI, VII and VIII on the ingredients, completion and disassembling of a man. He'd been through this several times before but he'd passed more than one law exam on the strength of a last-minute review.

The constant reference to mental instability disturbed him. "The humans constructed with this set will, at the very best, show most of the superstitious tendencies, and neurosis-compulsions of medieval mankind. In the long run they are not normal; take great care not to consider them such." Well, it wouldn't make too much difference in Tina's case—and that was all that was important.

When he had finished adjusting the molds to the correct sizes, he fastened the vitalizer to the bed. Then—very, very slowly and with repeated glances at the manual, he began to duplicate Sam Weber. He learned more of his physical limitations and capabilities in the next two hours than any man had ever known since the day when an inconspicuous primate had investigated the possibilities of ground locomotion upon the nether extremities alone.

Strangely enough, he felt neither awe nor exultation. It was like building a radio receiver for the first time. Child's play.

Most of the vials and jars were empty when he had finished. The damp molds were stacked inside the box, still in their three-dimensional outline. The manual lay neglected on the floor.

Sam Weber stood near the bed looking down at Sam Weber on the bed.

All that remained was vitalizing. He daren't wait too long or imperfections might set in and the errors of the baby be repeated. He shook off the nauseating feeling of unreality, made certain that the big disassembleator was within reach and set the Jiffy Vitalizer in motion.

The man on the bed coughed. He stirred. He sat up.

"Wow!" he said. "Pretty good, if I do say so myself!"

And then he had leaped off the bed and seized the disassembleator. He tore great chunks of wiring out of the center, threw it to the floor and kicked it into shapelessness. "No Sword of Damocles going to hang over *my* head," he informed an open-mouthed Sam Weber. "Although, I could have used it on you, come to think of it."

Sam eased himself to the mattress and sat down. His mind stopped rearing and whinnied to a halt. He had been so impressed with the helplessness of the baby and the mannikin that he had never dreamed of the possibility that his duplicate would enter upon life with such enthusiasm. He should have, though; this was a full-grown man, created at a moment of complete physical and mental activity.

"This is bad," he said at last in a hoarse voice. "You're unstable. You can't be admitted into normal society."

"I'm unstable" his image asked. "Look who's talking! The guy who's been mooning his way through his adult life, who wants to marry an overdressed, conceited collection of biological impulses that would come crawling on her knees to any man sensible enough to push the right buttons—"

"You leave Tina's name out of this," Sam told him, feeling acutely uncomfortable at the theatrical phrase.

His double looked at him and grinned. "O.K., I will. But not her body! Now, look here, Sam or Weber or whatever you want me to call you, you can live your life and I'll live mine. I won't even be a lawyer if that'll make you happy. But as far as Tina is concerned, now that there are no ingredients to make a copy—that was a rotten escapist idea, by the way—I have enough of your likes and dislikes to want her badly. And I can have her, whereas you can't. You don't have the gumption."

Sam leaped to his feet and doubled his fists. Then he saw the other's entirely equal size and slightly more assured twinkle. There was no point in fighting—that would end in a draw, at best. He went back to reason.

"According to the manual," he began, "you are prone to neurosis—"

"The manual! The manual was written for children of two centuries hence, with quite a bit of selective breeding and scientific education behind them. Personally, I think I'm a—"

There was a double knock on the door. "Mr. Weber."

"Yes," they both said simultaneously.

Outside, the landlady gasped and began speaking in an uncertain voice. "Th-that gentleman is downstairs. He'd like to see you. Shall I tell him you're in?"

"No, I'm not at home," said the double.

"Tell him I left an hour ago," said Sam at exactly the same moment.

There was another, longer gasp and the sound of footsteps receding hurriedly.

"That's one clever way to handle a situation," Sam's facsimile exploded. "Couldn't you keep your mouth shut? The poor woman's probably gone off to have a fit."

"You forget that this is my room and you are just an experiment that went wrong," Sam told him hotly. "I have just as much right, in fact more right . . . hey, what do you think you're doing?"

The other had thrown open the closet door and was stepping into a pair of pants. "Just getting dressed. You can wander around in the nude if you find it exciting, but I want to look a bit respectable."

"I undressed to take my measurements . . . or your measurements. Those are my clothes, this is my room—"

"Look, take it easy. You could never prove it in a court of law. Don't make me go into that *cliché* about what's yours is mine and so forth."

Heavy feet resounded through the hall. They stopped outside the room. Cymbals seemed to clash all around them and there was a panic-stricken sense of unendurable heat. Then shrill echoes fled into the distance. The walls stopped shuddering.

Silence and a smell of burning wood.

They whirled in time to see a terribly tall, terribly old man in a long black overcoat walking through the smoldering remains of the door. Much too tall for the entrance, he did not stoop as he came in: rather, he drew his head down into his garment and shot it up again. Instinctively, they moved closer together.

His eyes, all shiny black iris without any whites, were set back deep in the shadow of his head. They reminded Sam Weber of the scanners on the Biocalibrator: they tabulated, deduced, rather than saw.

"I was afraid I would be too late," he rumbled at last in

weird, clipped tones. "You have already duplicated yourself, Mr. Weber, making necessary unpleasant rearrangements. And the duplicate has destroyed the disassembleator. Too bad. I shall have to do it manually. An ugly job."

He came further into the room until they could almost breathe their fright upon him. "This affair has already dislocated four major programs, but we had to move in accepted cultural grooves and be absolutely certain of the recipient's identity before we could act to withdraw the set. Mrs. Lipanti's collapse naturally stimulated emergency measures."

The duplicate cleared his throat. "You are—?"

"Not exactly human. A humble civil servant of precision manufacture. I am Census Keeper for the entire twenty-ninth oblong. You see, your set was intended for the Thregander children who are on a field trip in this oblong. One of the Threganders who has a Weber chart requested the set through the chrondromos which in an attempt at the supernormal, unstabled without carnuplicating. You therefore received the package instead. Unfortunately, the unstabling was so complete that we were forced to locate you by indirect methods."

The Census Keeper paused and Sam's double hitched his pants nervously. Sam wished he had anything—even a fig leaf—to cover his nakedness. He felt like a character in the Garden of Eden trying to build up a logical case for apple eating. He appreciated glumly how much more than "Bild-A-Man" sets clothes had to do with the making of a man.

"We will have to recover the set, of course," the staccato thunder continued, "and readjust any discrepancies it has caused. Once the matter has been cleared up, however, your life will be allowed to resume its normal progression. Meanwhile, the problem is which of you is the original Sam Weber?"

"I am," they both quavered—and turned to glare at each other.

"Difficulties," the old man rumbled. He sighed like an arctic wind. "I always have difficulties! Why can't I ever have a simple case like a carnuplicator?"

"Look here," the duplicate began. "The original will be—"

"Less unstable and of better emotional balance than the replica," Sam interrupted. "Now, it seems—"

"That you should be able to tell the difference," the other

concluded breathlessly. "From what you see and have seen of us, can't you decide which is the more valid member of society?"

What a pathetic confidence, Sam thought, the fellow was trying to display! Didn't he know he was up against someone who could really discern mental differences? This was no fumbling psychiatrist of the present; here was a creature who could see through externals to the most coherent personality beneath.

"I can, naturally. Now, just a moment." He studied them carefully, his eyes traveling with judicious leisure up and down their bodies. They waited, fidgeting, in a silence that pounded.

"Yes," the old man said at last. "Yes. Quite."

He walked forward.

A long thin arm shot out.

He started to disassemble Sam Weber.

"But listennnnn—" began Weber in a yell that turned into a high scream and died in a liquid mumble.

"It would be better for your sanity if you didn't watch," the Census Keeper suggested.

The duplicate exhaled slowly, turned away and began to button a shirt. Behind him the mumbling continued, rising and falling in pitch.

"You see," came the clipped, rumbling accents, "it's not the gift we're afraid of letting you have—it's the principle involved. Your civilization isn't ready for it. You understand."

"Perfectly," replied the counterfeit Weber, knotting Aunt Maggie's blue and red tie.

TIME AND TIME AGAIN

by H. Beam Piper (1904-1960)

ASTOUNDING SCIENCE FICTION
April

The late H. Beam Piper was a native of Pennsylvania who worked for many years for the Pennsylvania Railroad. His work is currently quite popular, having been rediscovered in the 1970s by a new generation of readers. Particularly appealing are the vividly depicted aliens of his "Terran Federation" books, which include Little Fuzzy *(1962),* Space Viking *(1963) and* The Other Human Race *(1964) An excellent omnibus collection is* The Fuzzy Papers, *published in 1977. It is tragic that Piper, who was one of the very few known suicides within science fiction, never lived to see his work appreciated and popular.*

"Time and Time Again" was Piper's first published story, a tale that posits a fascinating situation—what would happen to a highly educated adult who suddenly found himself in his own early teen-age body, but still knowing everything he had learned in the intervening years? What would he do?

(Who among us hasn't wished we could go back

in time and do something over, or tell the youngster we used to be something we ought to know? Over and over again, I've thought how nice it would be if I could go back to 1938, and whisper to myself as I was struggling with my Underwood #5 typewriter, "You're going to be a very successful writer. Honest!"

But, no. In the first place I wouldn't have believed it. In the second, the knowledge itself would have changed things if I did believe it, and who knows in what manner.

And no matter how we may dream in science fiction, there are always the little reminders in such stories of the fact that we don't *know what lies ahead.*

In "Time and Time Again," which appeared in 1947, the United States was driven back to its northern border in 1975. Well, of course, it wasn't. In fact, the worst thing that happened to us since World War II was Watergate and that was strictly home-grown and it was absolutely unforeseeable.

Then, too, Beam Piper speaks of 1960, as the year "we had a good-natured nonentity in the White House." That was Dwight Eisenhower's last year, and some might think that an apt description of him—but could Piper, in 1947, have imagined the sad significance that 1960 was to hold for him.*—I.A.)*

Blinded by the bomb-flash and numbed by the narcotic injection, he could not estimate the extent of his injuries, but he knew that he was dying. Around him, in the darkness, voices sounded as through a thick wall.

"They mighta left mosta these Joes where they was. Half of them won't even last till the truck comes."

"No matter; so long as they're alive, they must be treated," another voice, crisp and cultivated, rebuked. "Better start taking names, while we're waiting."

"Yes, sir." Fingers fumbled at his identity badge. "Hartley, Allan: Captain, G5, Chem. Research AN/73/D. Serial, SO-23869403J."

"Allan Hartley!" The medic officer spoke in shocked surprise. "Why, he's the man who wrote 'Children of the Mist,' 'Rose of Death,' and 'Conqueror's Road'!"

He tried to speak, and must have stirred; the corpsman's voice sharpened.

"Major, I think he's part conscious. Mebbe I better give him 'nother shot."

"Yes, yes; by all means, sergeant."

Something jabbed Allan Hartley in the back of the neck. Soft billows of oblivion closed in upon him, and all that remained to him was a tiny spark of awareness, glowing alone and lost in a great darkness.

The spark grew brighter. He was more than a something that merely knew that it existed. He was a man, and he had a name, and a military rank, and memories. Memories of the searing blue-green flash, and of what he had been doing outside the shelter the moment before, and memories of the month-long siege, and of the retreat from the north, and memories of the days before the War, back to the time when he had been little Allan Hartley, a schoolboy, the son of a successful lawyer, in Williamsport, Pennsylvania.

His mother he could not remember; there was only a vague impression of the house full of people who had tried to comfort him for something he could not understand. But he remembered the old German woman who had kept house for his father, afterward, and he remembered his bedroom, with its chintz-covered chairs, and the warm-colored patch quilt on the old cherry bed, and the tan curtains at the windows, edged with dusky red, and the morning sun shining through them. He could almost see them, now.

He blinked. He *could* see them!

For a long time, he lay staring at them unbelievingly, and then he deliberately closed his eyes and counted ten seconds, and as he counted, terror gripped him. He was afraid to open them again, lest he find himself blind, or gazing at the filth and wreckage of a blasted city, but when he reached ten, he forced himself to look, and gave a sigh of relief. The sunlit curtains and the sun-gilded mist outside were still there.

He reached out to check one sense against another, feeling

the rough monk's cloth and the edging of maroon silk thread. They were tangible as well as visible. Then he saw that the back of his hand was unscarred. There should have been a scar, souvenir of a rough-and-tumble brawl of his cub reporter days. He examined both hands closely. An instant later, he had sat up in bed and thrown off the covers, partially removing his pajamas and inspecting as much of his body as was visible.

It was the smooth body of a little boy.

That was ridiculous. He was a man of forty-three; an army officer, a chemist, once a best-selling novelist. He had been married, and divorced ten years ago. He looked again at his body. It was only twelve years old. Fourteen, at the very oldest. His eyes swept the room, wide with wonder. Every detail was familiar: the flower-splashed chair covers; the table that served as desk and catch-all for his possessions; the dresser, with its mirror stuck full of pictures of aircraft. It was the bedroom of his childhood home. He swung his legs over the edge of the bed. They were six inches too short to reach the floor.

For an instant, the room spun dizzily, and he was in the grip of utter panic, all confidence in the evidence of his senses lost. Was he insane? Or delirious? Or had the bomb really killed him; was this what death was like? What was that thing, about "ye become as little children"? He started to laugh, and his juvenile larynx made giggling sounds. They seemed funny, too, and aggravated his mirth. For a little while, he was on the edge of hysteria and then, when he managed to control his laughter, he felt calmer. If he were dead, then he must be a discarnate entity, and would be able to penetrate matter. To his relief, he was unable to push his hand through the bed. So he was alive; he was also fully awake, and, he hoped, rational. He rose to his feet and prowled about the room, taking stock of its contents.

There was no calendar in sight, and he could find no newspapers or dated periodicals, but he knew that it was prior to July 18, 1946. On that day, his fourteenth birthday, his father had given him a light .22 rifle, and it had been hung on a pair of rustic forks on the wall. It was not there now, nor ever had been. On the table, he saw a boys' book of military aircraft, with a clean, new dustjacket; the flyleaf was inscribed: *To Allan Hartley, from his father, on his thirteenth birthday, 7/18/ '45.* Glancing out the window at the foliage on the trees, he estimated the date at late July or early August, 1945; that would make him just thirteen.

His clothes were draped on a chair beside the bed. Stripping off his pajamas, he donned shorts, then sat down and picked up a pair of lemon-colored socks, which he regarded with disfavor. As he pulled one on, a church bell began to clang. St. Boniface, up on the hill, ringing for early Mass; so this was Sunday. He paused, the second sock in his hand.

There was no question that his present environment was actual. Yet, on the other hand, he possessed a set of memories completely at variance with it. Now, suppose, since his environment was not an illusion, everything else was? Suppose all these troublesome memories were no more than a dream? Why, he was just little Allan Hartley, safe in his room on a Sunday morning, badly scared by a nightmare! Too much science fiction, Allan; too many comic books!

That was a wonderfully comforting thought, and he hugged it to him contentedly. It lasted all the while he was buttoning up his shirt and pulling on his pants, but when he reached for his shoes, it evaporated. Ever since he had wakened, he realized, he had been occupied with thoughts utterly incomprehensible to any thirteen-year-old; even thinking in words that would have been so much Sanskrit to himself at thirteen. He shook his head regretfully. The just-a-dream hypothesis went by the deep six.

He picked up the second shoe and glared at it as though it were responsible for his predicament. He was going to have to be careful. An unexpected display of adult characteristics might give rise to some questions he would find hard to answer credibly. Fortunately, he was an only child; there would be no brothers or sisters to trip him up. Old Mrs. Stauber, the housekeeper, wouldn't be much of a problem: even in his normal childhood, he had bulked like an intellectual giant in comparison to her. But his father—

Now, there the going would be tough. He knew that shrewd attorney's mind, whetted keen on a generation of lying and reluctant witnesses. Sooner or later, he would forget for an instant and betray himself. Then he smiled, remembering the books he had discovered in his late 'teens on his father's shelves and recalling the character of the openminded agnostic lawyer. If he could only avoid the inevitable unmasking until he had a plausible explanatory theory.

* * *

Blake Hartley was leaving the bathroom as Allan Hartley opened his door and stepped into the hall. The lawyer was bare-armed and in slippers: at forty-eight, there was only a faint powdering of gray in his dark hair, and not a gray thread in his clipped mustache. The old Merry Widower, himself, Allan thought, grinning as he remembered the white-haired but still vigorous man from whom he'd parted at the outbreak of the War.

"'Morning, Dad," he greeted.

"'Morning, son. You're up early. Going to Sunday school?"

Now there was the advantage of a father who'd cut his first intellectual tooth on Tom Paine and Bob Ingersoll; attendance at divine services was on a strictly voluntary basis.

"Why, I don't think so; I want to do some reading, this morning."

"That's always a good thing to do," Blake Hartley approved. "After breakfast, suppose you take a walk down to the station and get me a *Times*." He dug in his trouser pocket and came out with a half dollar. "Get anything you want for yourself, while you're at it."

Allan thanked his father and pocketed the coin.

"Mrs. Stauber'll still be at Mass," he suggested. "Say I get the paper now; breakfast won't be ready till she gets here."

"Good idea," Blake Hartley nodded, pleased. "You'll have three-quarters of an hour, at least."

So far, he congratulated himself, everything had gone smoothly. Finishing his toilet, he went downstairs and onto the street, turning left at Brandon to Campbell, and left again in the direction of the station. Before he reached the underpass, a dozen half-forgotten memories had revived. Here was a house that would, in a few years, be gutted by fire. Here were four dwellings standing where he had last seen a five-story apartment building. A gasoline station and a weed-grown lot would shortly be replaced by a supermarket. The environs of the station itself were a complete puzzle to him, until he oriented himself.

He bought a New York *Times*, glancing first of all at the date line. Sunday, August 5, 1945; he'd estimated pretty closely. The battle of Okinawa had been won. The Potsdam Conference had just ended. There were still pictures of the B-25 crash against the Empire State Building, a week ago Saturday. And Japan was still being pounded by bombs from the air and shells from off-shore naval guns. Why, tomorrow, Hiroshima was due for the Big Job! It amused him to reflect that he was probably the only person in Williamsport who knew that.

On the way home, a boy, sitting on the top step of a front porch, hailed him. Allan replied cordially, trying to remember who it was. Of course: Larry Morton! He and Allan had been buddies. They probably had been swimming, or playing Commandos and Germans, the afternoon before. Larry had gone to Cornell the same year that Allan had gone to Penn State; they had both graduated in 1954. Larry had gotten into some Government bureau, and then he had married a Pittsburgh girl, and had become twelfth vice-president of her father's firm. He had been killed, in 1968, in a plane crash.

"You gonna Sunday school?" Larry asked, mercifully unaware of the fate Allan foresaw for him.

"Why, no. I have some things I want to do at home." He'd have to watch himself. Larry would spot a difference quicker than any adult. "Heck with it," he added.

"Golly, I wisht I c'ld stay home from Sunday school whenever I wanted to," Larry envied. "How about us goin' swimmin', at the Canoe Club, 'safter?"

Allan thought fast. "Gee, I wisht I c'ld," he replied, lowering his grammatical sights. "I gotta stay home, 'safter. We're expectin' comp'ny; coupla aunts of mine. Dad wants me to stay home when they come."

That went over all right. Anybody knew that there was no rational accounting for the vagaries of the adult mind, and no appeal from adult demands. The prospect of company at the Hartley home would keep Larry away, that afternoon. He showed his disappointment.

"Aw, jeepers creepers!" he blasphemed euphemistically.

"Mebbe t'morrow," Allan said. "If I c'n make it. I gotta go, now; ain't had breakfast yet." He scuffed his feet boyishly, exchanged so-longs with his friend, and continued homeward.

As he had hoped, the Sunday paper kept his father occupied at breakfast, to the exclusion of any dangerous table talk. Blake Hartley was still deep in the financial section when Allan left the table and went to the library. There should be two books there to which he wanted badly to refer. For a while, he was afraid that his father had not acquired them prior to 1945, but he finally found them, and carried them onto the front porch, along with a pencil and a ruled yellow scratch pad. In his experienced future—or his past-to-come—Allan Hartley had been accustomed to doing his thinking with a pencil. As reporter, as novelist plotting his work, as amateur chemist in his home laboratory, as scientific warfare research officer, his ideas had always been clarified by making notes. He pushed a chair to the table and built up the seat with cushions, wondering how soon he would become used to the proportional disparity between himself and the furniture. As he opened the books and took his pencil in his hand, there was one thing missing. If he could only smoke a pipe, now!

His father came out and stretched in a wicker chair with the *Times* book-review section. The morning hours passed. Allan Hartley leafed through one book and then the other. His pencil moved rapidly at times; at others, he doodled absently. There was no question, any more, in his mind, as to what or who he was. He was Allan Hartley, a man of forty-three, marooned in his own thirteen-year-old body, thirty years back in his own past. That was, of course, against all common sense, but he was easily able to ignore that objection. It had been made before: against the astronomy of Copernicus, and the geography of Columbus, and the biology of Darwin, and the industrial technology of Samuel Colt, and the military doctrines of Charles de Gaulle. Today's common sense had a habit of turning into tomorrow's utter nonsense. What he needed, right now, but bad, was a theory that would explain what had happened to him.

Understanding was beginning to dawn when Mrs. Stauber came out to announce midday dinner.

"I hope you von't mind haffin' it so early," she apologized. "Mein sister, Jennie, offer in Nippenose, she iss sick; I vant to go see her, dis afternoon, yet. I'll be back in blenty time to get supper, Mr. Hartley."

"Hey, Dad!" Allan spoke up. "Why can't we get our own supper, and have a picnic, like? That'd be fun, and Mrs. Stauber could stay as long as she wanted to."

His father looked at him. Such consideration for others was a most gratifying deviation from the juvenile norm; dawn of altruism, or something. He gave hearty assent.

"Why, of course, Mrs. Stauber. Allan and I can shift for ourselves, this evening; can't we, Allan? You needn't come back till tomorrow morning."

"*Ach,* t'ank you! T'ank you so mooch, Mr. Hartley."

At dinner, Allan got out from under the burden of conversation by questioning his father about the War and luring him into a lengthy dissertation on the difficulties of the forthcoming invasion of Japan. In view of what he remembered of the next twenty-four hours, Allan was secretly amused. His father was sure that the War would run on to mid-1946.

After dinner, they returned to the porch, Hartley *père* smoking a cigar and carrying out several law books. He only glanced at these occasionally; for the most part, he sat and blew smoke rings, and watched them float away. Some thrice-guilty felon was about to be triumphantly acquitted by a weeping jury; Allan could recognize a courtroom masterpiece in the process of incubation.

It was several hours later that the crunch of feet on the walk caused father and son to look up simultaneously. The approaching visitor was a tall man in a rumpled black suit; he had knobby wrists and big, awkward hands; black hair flecked with gray, and a harsh, bigoted face. Allan remembered him. Frank Gutchall. Lived on Campbell Street; a religious fanatic, and some sort of lay preacher. Maybe he needed legal advice; Allan could vaguely remember some incident—

"Ah, good afternoon, Mr. Gutchall. Lovely day, isn't it?" Blake Hartley said.

Gutchall cleared his throat. "Mr. Hartley, I wonder if you could lend me a gun and some bullets," he began, embarrassedly. "My little dog's been hurt, and it's suffering something terrible. I want a gun, to put the poor thing out of its pain."

"Why, yes; of course. How would a 20-gauge shotgun do?" Blake Hartley asked. "You wouldn't want anything heavy."

Gutchall fidgeted. "Why, er, I was hoping you'd let me have a little gun." He held his hands about six inches apart. "A pistol, that I could put in my pocket. It wouldn't look right, to carry a hunting gun on the Lord's day; people wouldn't understand that it was for a work of mercy."

The lawyer nodded. In view of Gutchall's religious beliefs, the objection made sense.

"Well, I have a Colt .38-special," he said, "but you know, I belong to this Auxiliary Police outfit. If I were called out for duty, this evening, I'd need it. How soon could you bring it back?"

Something clicked in Allan Hartley's mind. He remembered now what that incident had been. He knew, too, what he had to do.

"Dad, aren't there some cartridges left for the Luger?" he asked.

Blake Hartley snapped his fingers. "By George, yes! I have a German automatic I can let you have, but I wish you'd bring it back as soon as possible. I'll get it for you."

Before he could rise, Allan was on his feet.

"Sit still, Dad; I'll get it. I know where the cartridges are." With that, he darted into the house and upstairs.

The Luger hung on the wall over his father's bed. Getting it down, he dismounted it, working with rapid precision. He used the blade of his pocketknife to unlock the endpiece of the breechblock, slipping out the firing pin and buttoning it into his shirt pocket. Then he reassembled the harmless pistol, and filled the clip with 9-millimeter cartridges from the bureau drawer.

There was an extension telephone beside the bed. Finding Gutchall's address in the directory, he lifted the telephone, and stretched his handkerchief over the mouthpiece. Then he dialed Police Headquarters.

"This is Blake Hartley," he lied, deepening his voice and copying his father's tone. "Frank Gutchall, who lives at . . . take this down"—he gave Gutchall's address—"has just borrowed a pistol from me, ostensibly to shoot a dog. He has no dog. He intends shooting his wife. Don't argue about how I know; there isn't time. Just take it for granted that I do. I disabled the pistol—took out the firing pin—but if he finds out what I did, he may get some other weapon. He's on his way home, but he's on foot. If you hurry, you may get a man there before he arrives, and grab him before he finds out the pistol won't shoot."

"O.K., Mr. Hartley. We'll take care of it. Thanks."

"And I wish you'd get my pistol back, as soon as you can. It's something I brought home from the other War, and I shouldn't like to lose it."

"We'll take care of that, too. Thank you, Mr. Hartley."

He hung up, and carried the Luger and the loaded clip down to the porch.

"Look, Mr. Gutchall; here's how it works," he said, showing it to the visitor. Then he slapped in the clip and yanked up on the toggle loading the chamber. "It's ready to shoot, now; this is the safety." He pushed it on. "When you're ready to shoot, just shove it forward and up, and then pull the trigger. You have to pull the trigger each time; it's loaded for eight shots. And be sure to put the safety back when you're through shooting."

"Did you load the chamber?" Blake Hartley demanded.

"Sure. It's on safe, now."

"Let me see." His father took the pistol, being careful to keep his finger out of the trigger guard, and looked at it. "Yes, that's all right." He repeated the instructions Allan had given, stressing the importance of putting the safety on after using. "Understand how it works, now?" he asked.

"Yes, I understand how it works. Thank you, Mr. Hartley. Thank you, too, young man."

Gutchall put the Luger in his hip pocket, made sure it wouldn't fall out, and took his departure.

"You shouldn't have loaded it," Hartley *père* reproved, when he was gone.

Allan sighed. This was it; the masquerade was over.

"I had to, to keep you from fooling with it," he said. "I didn't want you finding out that I'd taken out the firing pin."

"You what?"

"Gutchall didn't want that gun to shoot a dog. He has no dog. He meant to shoot his wife with it. He's a religious maniac: sees visions, hears voices, receives revelations, talks with the Holy Ghost. The Holy Ghost probably put him up to this caper. I'll submit that any man who holds long conversations with the Deity isn't to be trusted with a gun, and neither is any man who lies about why he wants one. And while I was at it, I called the police, on the upstairs phone. I had to use your name; I deepened my voice and talked through a handkerchief."

"You—" Blake Hartley jumped as though bee-stung. "Why did you have to do that?"

"You know why. I couldn't have told them, 'This is little Allan Hartley, just thirteen years old; please, Mr. Policeman, go and arrest Frank Gutchall before he goes root-toot-toot at his wife with my pappa's Luger.' That would have gone over big, now, wouldn't it?"

"And suppose he really wants to shoot a dog; what sort of a mess will I be in?"

"No mess at all. If I'm wrong—which I'm not—I'll take the thump for it, myself. It'll pass for a dumb kid trick, and nothing'll be done. But if I'm right, you'll have to front for me. They'll keep your name out of it, but they'd give me a lot of cheap boy-hero publicity, which I don't want." He picked up his pencil again. "We should have the complete returns in about twenty minutes."

That was a ten-minute underestimate, and it was another quarter-hour before the detective-sergeant who returned the Luger had finished congratulating Blake Hartley and giving him the thanks of the Department. After he had gone, the lawyer picked up the Luger, withdrew the clip, and ejected the round in the chamber.

"Well," he told his son, "you were right. You saved that woman's life." He looked at the automatic, and then handed it across the table. "Now, let's see you put that firing pin back."

Allan Hartley dismantled the weapon, inserted the missing part, and put it together again, then snapped it experimentally and returned it to his father. Blake Hartley looked at it again, and laid it on the table.

"Now, son, suppose we have a little talk," he said softly.

"But I explained everything," Allan objected innocently.

"You did not," his father retorted. "Yesterday you'd never have thought of a trick like this; why, you wouldn't even have known how to take this pistol apart. And at dinner, I caught you using language and expressing ideas that were entirely outside anything you'd ever known before. Now, I want to know—and I mean this literally."

Allan chuckled. "I hope you're not toying with the rather medieval notion of obsession," he said.

Blake Hartley started. Something very like that must have been flitting through his mind. He opened his mouth to say something, then closed it abruptly.

"The trouble is, I'm not sure you aren't right," his son continued. "You say you find me—changed. When did you first notice a difference?"

"Last night, you were still my little boy. This morning—" Blake Hartley was talking more to himself than to Allan. "I don't know. You were unusually silent at breakfast. And come to think of it, there was something . . . something strange . . . about you when I saw you in the hall, upstairs . . . Allan!" he burst out, vehemently. "What has happened to you?"

Allan Hartley felt a twinge of pain. What his father was

going through was almost what he, himself, had endured, in the first few minutes after waking.

"I wish I could be sure, myself, Dad," he said. "You see, when I woke, this morning, I hadn't the least recollection of anything I'd done yesterday. August 4, 1945, that is," he specified. "I was positively convinced that I was a man of forty-three, and my last memory was of lying on a stretcher, injured by a bomb explosion. And I was equally convinced that this had happened in 1975."

"Huh?" His father straightened. "Did you say nineteen *seventy*-five?" He thought for a moment. "That's right; in 1975, you will be forty-three. A bomb, you say?"

Allan nodded. "During the siege of Buffalo, in the Third World War," he said, "I was a captain in G5—Scientific Warfare, General Staff. There'd been a transpolar air invasion of Canada, and I'd been sent to the front to check on service failures of a new lubricating oil for combat equipment. A week after I got there, Ottawa fell, and the retreat started. We made a stand at Buffalo, and that was where I copped it. I remember being picked up, and getting a narcotic injection. The next thing I knew, I was in bed, upstairs, and it was 1945 again, and I was back in my own little thirteen-year-old body."

"Oh, Allan, you just had a nightmare to end nightmares!" his father assured him, laughing a trifle too heartily. "That's all!"

"That was one of the first things I thought of. I had to reject it; it just wouldn't fit the facts. Look; a normal dream is part of the dreamer's own physical brain, isn't it? Well, here is a part about two thousand per cent greater than the whole from which it was taken. Which is absurd."

"You mean all this Battle of Buffalo stuff? That's easy. All the radio commentators have been harping on the horrors of World War III, and you couldn't have avoided hearing some of it. You just have an undigested chunk of H. V. Kaltenborn raising hell in your subconscious."

"It wasn't just World War III; it was everything. My four years at high school, and my four years at Penn State, and my seven years as a reporter on the Philadelphia *Record*. And my novels: 'Children of the Mist,' 'Rose of Death,' 'Conqueror's Road.' They were no kid stuff. Why, yesterday I'd never even have thought of some of the ideas I used in my detective stories, that I published under a *non-de-plume*.

And my hobby, chemistry; I was pretty good at that. Patented a couple of processes that made me as much money as my writing. You think a thirteen-year-old just dreamed all that up? Or, here; you speak French, don't you?" He switched languages and spoke at some length in good conversational slang-spiced Parisian. "Too bad you don't speak Spanish, too," he added, reverting to English. "Except for a Mexican accent you could cut with a machete, I'm even better there than in French. And I know some German, and a little Russian."

Blake Hartley was staring at his son, stunned. It was some time before he could make himself speak.

"I could barely keep up with you, in French," he admitted. "I can swear that in the last thirteen years of your life, you had absolutely no chance to learn it. All right; you lived till 1975, you say. Then, all of a sudden, you found yourself back here, thirteen years old, in 1945. I suppose you remember everything in between?" he asked. "Did you ever read James Branch Cabell? Remember Florian de Puysange, in 'The High Place'?"

"Yes. You find the same idea in 'Jurgen' too," Allan said. "You know, I'm beginning to wonder if Cabell mightn't have known something he didn't want to write."

"But it's impossible!" Blake Hartley hit the table with his hand, so hard that the heavy pistol bounced. The loose round he had ejected from the chamber toppled over and started to roll, falling off the edge. He stooped and picked it up. "How can you go back, against time? And the time you claim you came from doesn't exist, now; it hasn't happened yet." He reached for the pistol magazine, to insert the cartridge, and as he did, he saw the books in front of his son. "Dunne's 'Experiment with Time,'" he commented. "And J. N. M. Tyrrell's 'Science and Psychical Phenomena.' Are you trying to work out a theory?"

"Yes." It encouraged Allan to see his father had unconsciously adopted an adult-to-adult manner. "I think I'm getting somewhere, too. You've read these books? Well, look, Dad; what's your attitude on precognition? The ability of the human mind to exhibit real knowledge, apart from logical inference, of future events? You think Dunne is telling the truth about his experiences? Or that the cases in Tyrrell's book are properly verified, and can't be explained away on the basis of chance?"

Blake Hartley frowned. "I don't know," he confessed. "The evidence is the sort that any court in the world would accept, if it concerned ordinary, normal events. Especially the cases investigated by the Society for Psychical Research; they *have* been verified. But how can anybody know of something that hasn't happened yet? If it hasn't happened yet, it doesn't exist, and you can't have real knowledge of something that has no real existence."

"Tyrrell discusses that dilemma, and doesn't dispose of it. I think I can. If somebody has real knowledge of the future, then the future must be available to the present mind. And if any moment other than the bare present exists, then all time must be totally present; every moment must be perpetually coexistent with every other moment," Allan said.

"Yes. I think I see what you mean. That was Dunne's idea, wasn't it?"

"No. Dunne postulated an infinite series of time dimensions, the entire extent of each being the bare present moment of the next. What I'm postulating is the perpetual coexistence of every moment of time in this dimension, just as every graduation on a yardstick exists equally with every other graduation, but each at a different point in space."

"Well, as far as duration and sequence go, that's all right," the father agreed. "But how about the 'Passage of Time'?"

"Well, time *does* appear to pass. So does the landscape you see from a moving car window. I'll suggest that both are illusions of the same kind. We imagine time to be dynamic, because we've never viewed it from a fixed point, but if it is totally present, then it must be static, and in that case, we're moving through time."

"That seems all right. But what's your car window?"

"If all time is totally present, then you must exist simultaneously at every moment along your individual life span," Allan said. "Your physical body, and your mind, and all the thoughts contained in your mind, each at its appropriate moment in sequence. But what is it that exists only at the bare moment we think of as *now?*"

Blake Hartley grinned. Already, he was accepting his small son as an intellectual equal.

"Please, teacher; what?"

"Your consciousness. And don't say, 'What's that?' Teacher

doesn't know. But we're only conscious of one moment; the illusory *now*. This is 'now,' and it was 'now' when you asked that question, and it'll be 'now' when I stop talking, but each is a different moment. We imagine that all those nows are rushing past us. Really, they're standing still, and our consciousness is whizzing past them."

His father thought that over for some time. Then he sat up. "Hey!" he cried, suddenly. "If some part of your ego is time-free and passes from moment to moment, it must be extraphysical, because the physical body exists at every moment through which the consciousness passes. And if it's extraphysical, there's no reason whatever for assuming that it passes out of existence when it reaches the moment of the death of the body. Why, there's logical evidence for survival, independent of any alleged spirit communication! You can toss out Patience Worth, and Mrs. Osborne Leonard's Feda, and Sir Oliver Lodge's son, and Wilfred Brandon, and all the other spirit-communicators, and you still have evidence."

"I hadn't thought of that," Allan confessed. "I think you're right. Well, let's put that at the bottom of the agenda and get on with this time business. You 'lose consciousness" as in sleep; where does your consciousness go? I think it simply detaches from the moment at which you go to sleep, and moves backward or forward along the line of moment-sequence, to some prior or subsequent moment, attaching there."

"Well, why don't we know anything about that?" Blake Hartley asked. "It never seems to happen. We go to sleep tonight, and it's always tomorrow morning when we wake; never day-before-yesterday, or last month, or next year."

"It never . . . or almost never . . . *seems* to happen; you're right there. Know why? Because if the consciousness goes forward; it attaches at a moment when the physical brain contains memories of the previous, consciously unexperienced, moment. You wake, remembering the evening before, because that's the memory contained in your mind at that moment, and back of it are memories of all the events in the interim. See?"

"Yes. But how about backward movement, like this experience of yours?"

"This experience of mine may not be unique, but I never heard of another case like it. What usually happens is that the memories carried back by the consciousness are buried in the subconscious mind. You know how thick the wall between the subconscious and the conscious mind is. These dreams of Dunne's, and the cases in Tyrrell's book, are leakage. That's why precognitions are usually incomplete and distorted, and generally trivial. The wonder isn't that good cases are so few; it's surprising that there are any at all." Allan looked at the papers in front of him. "I haven't begun to theorize about how I managed to remember everything. It may have been the radiations from the bomb, or the effect of the narcotic, or both together, or something at this end, or a combination of all three. But the fact remains that my subconscious barrier didn't function, and everything got through. So, you see, I am obsessed—by my own future identity."

"And I'd been afraid that you'd been, well, taken over by some . . . some outsider." Blake Hartley grinned weakly. "I don't mind admitting, Allan, that what's happened has been a shock. But that other . . . I just couldn't have taken that."

"No. Not and stayed sane. But really, I am your son; the same entity I was yesterday. I've just had what you might call an educational short cut."

"I'll say you have!" His father laughed in real amusement. He discovered that his cigar had gone out, and re-lit it. "Here: if you can remember the next thirty years, suppose you tell me when the War's going to end. This one, I mean."

"The Japanese surrender will be announced at exactly 1901—7:01 P.M. present style—on August 14. A week from Tuesday. Better make sure we have plenty of grub in the house by then. Everything will be closed up tight till Thursday morning; even the restaurants. I remember, we had nothing to eat in the house but some scraps."

"Well! It is handy, having a prophet in the family! I'll see to it Mrs. Stauber gets plenty of groceries in. . . . Tuesday a week? That's pretty sudden, isn't it?"

"The Japs are going to think so," Allan replied. He went on to describe what was going to happen.

His father swore softly. "You know, I've heard talk about atomic energy, but I thought it was just Buck Rogers stuff. Was that the sort of bomb that got you?"

"That was a firecracker to the bomb that got me. That thing exploded a good ten miles away."

Blake Hartley whistled softly. "And that's going to happen in thirty years! You know, son, if I were you, I wouldn't like to have to know about a thing like that." He looked at Allan for a moment. "Please, if you know, don't ever tell me when I'm going to die."

Allan smiled. "I can't. I had a letter from you just before I left for the front. You were seventy-eight, then, and you were still hunting, and fishing, and flying your own plane. But I'm not going to get killed in any Battle of Buffalo, this time, and if I can prevent it, and I think I can, there won't be any World War III."

"But— You say all time exists, perpetually coexistent and totally present," his father said. "Then it's right there in front of you, and you're getting closer to it, every watch tick."

Allan Hartley shook his head. "You know what I remembered, when Frank Gutchall came to borrow a gun?" he asked. "Well, the other time, I hadn't been home. I'd been swimming at the Canoe Club, with Larry Morton. When I got home, about half an hour from now, I found the house full of cops. Gutchall talked the .38 officers' model out of you, and gone home; he'd shot his wife four times through the body, finished her off with another one back of the ear, and then used his sixth shot to blast his brains out. The cops traced the gun; they took a very poor view of your lending it to him. You never got it back."

"Trust that gang to keep a good gun," the lawyer said.

"I didn't want us to lose it, this time, and I didn't want to see you lose face around City Hall. Gutchalls, of course, are expendable," Allan said. "But my main reason for fixing Frank Gutchall up with a padded cell was that I wanted to know whether or not the future could be altered. I have it on experimental authority that it can be. There must be additional dimensions of time: lines of alternate probabilities. Something like William Seabrook's witch-doctor friend's Fan-Shaped Destiny. When I brought memories of the future back to the present, I added certain factors to the causal chain. That set up an entirely new line of probabilities. On no notice at all, I stopped a murder and a suicide. With thirty years to work, I can stop a world war. I'll have the means to do it, too."

"The means?"

"Unlimited wealth and influence. Here." Allan picked up a sheet and handed it to his father. "Used properly, we can make two or three million on that, alone. A list of all the Kentucky Derby, Preakness, and Belmont winners in 1970. That'll furnish us primary capital. Then, remember, I was something of a chemist. I took it up, originally, to get background material for one of my detective stories; it fascinated me, and I made it a hobby, and then a source of income. I'm thirty years ahead of any chemist in the world, now. You remember *I. G. Farbenindustrie?* Ten years from now, we'll make them look like pikers."

His father looked at the yellow sheet. "Assault, at eight to one," he said. "I can scrape about five thousand for that— Yes; in ten years— Any other little operations you have in mind?" he asked.

"About 1950, we start building a political organization, here in Pennsylvania. In 1960, I think we can elect you President. The world situation will be crucial, by that time, and we had a good-natured nonentity in the White House then, who let things go till war became inevitable. I think President Hartley can be trusted to take a strong line of policy. In the meantime, you can read Machiavelli."

"That's my little boy talking!" Blake Hartley said softly. "All right, son; I'll do just what you tell me, and when you grow up, I'll be president. . . . Let's go get supper, now."

TINY AND THE MONSTER

by Theodore Sturgeon (1918-   )

ASTOUNDING SCIENCE FICTION
May

Theodore Sturgeon (see Volumes 1, 2, 3, 6, and 8 of this series) continued to earn his reputation as one of the finest writers in science fiction in 1947. In addition to the two stories in this book, the year was highlighted by the publication of his novella Maturity, *a powerful story on the theme of enhanced intelligence which is too long for inclusion here.*

"Tiny and the Monster" may sound a little familiar to those of you who attend the movies, since its theme of stranded alien and helpful human was well treated by Stephen Spielberg in the enormously popular film E. T. *(1982). Tiny, who is not one of the forementioned characters, is one of my favorite figures in all of sf.*

(The sentence in this story that I find particularly significant is Alec's comment ". . . in all the stories I've read, when a beast comes here from space, it's to kill and conquer. . . ."

That's been the science fiction habit ever since H. G. Wells's The War of the Worlds*—and yet isn't* *that a reflection of our own human bloodthirstiness here on Earth? The European has bashed and bludgeoned his way over all the continents in the past five centuries, and so we assume that that is the way it must be with all intelligent beings. Is it perhaps an unconscious way of trying to dilute our own guilt by assuming "everybody does it"?*

In any case, I feel there's a better streak within us, too, so I valued Ted's "Tiny and the Monster," in which a beast coming from space is not here to kill and conquer, nor do human beings react as though it were.—I.A.)

She had to find out about Tiny—everything about Tiny.

They were bound to call him Tiny. The name was good for a laugh when he was a pup, and many times afterward.

He was a Great Dane, unfashionable with his long tail, smooth and glossy in the brown coat which fit so snugly over his heavily muscled shoulders and chest. His eyes were big and brown and his feet were big and black; he had a voice like thunder and a heart ten times his own great size.

He was born in the Virgin Islands, on St. Croix, which is a land of palm trees and sugar, of soft winds and luxuriant undergrowth whispering with the stealthy passage of pheasant and mongoose. There were rats in the ruins of the ancient estate houses that stood among the foothills—ruins with slave-built walls forty inches thick and great arches of weathered stone. There was pasture land where the field mice ran, and brooks asparkle with gaudy blue minnows.

But where in St. Croix had he learned to be so strange?

When Tiny was a puppy, all feet and ears, he learned many things. Most of these things were kinds of respect. He learned to respect that swift, vengeful piece of utter engineering called a scorpion when one of them whipped its barbed tail into his inquiring nose. He learned to respect the heavy deadness of the air about him that preceded a hurricane, for he knew that it meant hurry and hammering and utmost obedience from every creature on the estate. He learned to respect the justice of sharing, for he was pulled from the teat and from the trough when he crowded the others of his litter. He was the largest.

These things, all of them, he learned as respects. He was never struck, and although he learned caution he never learned fear. The pain he suffered from the scorpion—it happened only once—the strong but gentle hands which curbed his greed, the frightful violence of the hurricane that followed the tense preparations—all these things and many more taught him the justice of respect. He half understood a basic ethic: namely, that he would never be asked to do something, or to refrain from doing something, unless there was a good reason for it. His obedience, then, was a thing implicit, for it was half reasoned; and since it was not based on fear, but on justice, it could not interfere with his resourcefulness.

All of which, along with his blood, explained why he was such a splendid animal. It did not explain how he learned to read. It did not explain why Alec was compelled to sell him—not only to sell him but to search out Alistair Forsythe and sell him to her.

She *had* to find out. The whole thing was crazy. She hadn't wanted a dog. If she had wanted a dog it wouldn't have been a Great Dane. And if it had been a Great Dane, it wouldn't have been Tiny, for he was a Crucian dog and had to be shipped all the way to Scarsdale, New York, by air.

The series of letters she sent to Alec were as full of wondering persuasion as his had been when he sold her the dog. It was through these letters that she learned about the scorpion and the hurricane, about Tiny's puppyhood and the way Alec brought up his dogs. If she learned something about Alec as well, that was understandable. Alec and Alistair Forsythe had never met, but through Tiny they shared a greater secret than many people who have grown up together.

"As for why I wrote you, of all people," Alec wrote in answer to her direct question, "I can't say I chose you at all. It was Tiny. One of the cruise-boat people mentioned your name at my place, over cocktails one afternoon. It was, as I remember, a Dr. Schwellenbach. Nice old fellow. As soon as your name was mentioned, Tiny's head came up as if I had called him. He got up from his station by the door and lolloped over to the doctor with his ears up and his nose quivering. I thought for a minute that the old fellow was offering him food, but no—he must have wanted to hear Schwellenbach say your name again. So I asked about you. A day or so later I was telling a couple of friends about it, and when I mentioned the name again, Tiny came snuffing over and shoved his nose into my hand. He was shivering. That got me. I wrote to a friend in New York who got your name and address in the phone book. You know the rest, I just wanted to tell you about it at first, but something made me suggest a sale. Somehow, it didn't seem right to have something like this going on and not have you meet Tiny. When you wrote that you couldn't get away from New York, there didn't seem to be anything else to do but send Tiny to you. And now—I don't know if I'm too happy about it. Judging from those pages and pages of questions you keep sending me, I get the idea that you are more than a little troubled by this crazy business."

She answered, "*Please* don't think I'm troubled about this! I'm not. I'm interested, and curious, and more than a little excited; but there is nothing about the situation that frightens me. I can't stress that enough. There's something around Tiny—sometimes I have the feeling it's something outside Tiny—that is infinitely comforting. I feel protected, in a strange way, and it's a different and greater thing than the protection I could expect from a large and intelligent dog. It's strange, and it's mysterious enough; but it isn't at all frightening.

"I have some more questions. Can you remember exactly what it was that Dr. Schwellenbach said the first time he mentioned my name and Tiny acted strangely? Was there ever any time that you can remember when Tiny was under some influence other than your own, something which might have given him these strange traits? What about his diet as a puppy? How many times did he get . . ." and so on.

And Alec answered, in part, "It was so long ago now that I can't remember exactly; but it seems to me Dr. Schwellenbach was talking about his work. As you know, he's a professor of metallurgy. He mentioned Professor Nowland as the greatest alloy specialist of his time—said Nowland could alloy anything with anything. Then he went on about Nowland's assistant. Said the assistant was very highly qualified, having been one of these Science Search products and something of a prodigy; in spite of which she was completely feminine and as beautiful a redhead as had ever exchanged heaven for earth. Then he said her name was Alistair Forsythe. (I hope you're not blushing, Miss Forsythe; you asked for this!) And then it was that Tiny ran over to the doctor in that extraordinary way.

"The only time I can think of when Tiny was off the estate and possibly under some influence was the day old Debbil disappeared for a whole day with the pup when he was about three months old. Debbil is one of the characters who hang around here. He's a Crucian about sixty years old, a piratical-looking old gent with one eye and elephantiasis. He shuffles around the grounds running odd errands for anyone who will give him tobacco or a shot of white rum. Well, one morning I sent him over the hill to see if there was a leak in the water line that runs from the reservoir. It would only take a couple of hours, so I told him to take Tiny for a run.

"They were gone for the whole day. I was short-handed and busy as a squirrel in a nuthouse and didn't have a chance to send anyone after him. But he drifted in toward evening. I bawled him out thoroughly. It was no use asking him where he had been; he's only about quarter-witted anyway. He just claimed he couldn't remember, which is pretty usual for him. But for the next three days I was busy with Tiny. He wouldn't eat, and he hardly slept at all. He just kept staring out over the cane fields at the hill. He didn't seem to want to go there at all. I went out to have a look. There's nothing out that way but the reservoir and the old ruins of the governor's palace, which have been rotting there in the sun for the last century and a half. Nothing left now but an overgrown mound and a couple of arches, but it's supposed to be haunted. I forgot about it after that because Tiny got back to normal. As a matter of fact, he seemed to be better than ever, although, from then on, he would sometimes freeze and watch the hill as if he were listening to something. I haven't attached much importance to it until now. I still don't. Maybe he got chased by some mongoose's mother. Maybe he chewed up some ganja-weed—marijuana to you. But I doubt that it has anything to do with the way he acts now, any more than that business of the compasses that pointed west might have something to do with it. Did you hear about that, by the way? Craziest thing I ever heard of. It was right after I shipped Tiny off to you last fall, as I remember. Every ship and boat and plane from here to Sandy Hook reported that its compass began to indicate due west instead of a magnetic north! Fortunately the effect only lasted a couple of hours so there were no serious difficulties. One cruise steamer ran aground, and there were a couple of Miami fishing-boat mishaps. I only bring it up to remind both of us that Tiny's behavior may be odd, but not exclusively so in a world where such things as the crazy compasses occur."

And in her next, she wrote. "You're quite the philosopher, aren't you? Be careful of that Fortean attitude, my tropical friend. It tends to accept the idea of the unexplainable to an extent where explaining, or even investigating, begins to look useless. As far as that crazy compass episode is concerned, I remember it very well indeed. My boss, Dr. Nowland—yes, it's true, he can alloy anything with anything!—has been up to his ears in that fantastic happenstance. So have most of his colleagues in half a dozen sciences. They're able to explain it quite satisfactorily, too. It was simply the presence of some quite quasimagnetic phenomenon that created a resultant field at right angles to the earth's own magnetic influence. That solution sent the pure theorists home happy. Of course, the practical ones—Nowland and his associates in metallurgy, for example—only have to figure out what caused the field. Science is a wonderful thing.

"By the way, you will notice my change of address. I have wanted for a long time to have a little house of my own, and I was lucky enough to get this one from a friend. It's up the Hudson from New York, quite countrified, but convenient enough to the city to be practical. I'm bringing Mother here from Upstate. She'll love it. And besides—as if you didn't know the most important reason when you saw it—it gives Tiny a place to run. He's no city dog . . . I'd tell you that he found the house for me, too, if I didn't think that, these days, I'm crediting him with even more than his remarkable powers. Gregg and Marie Weems, the couple who had the cottage before, began to be haunted. So they said, anyway. Some indescribably horrible monster that both of them caught glimpses of inside the house and out of it. Marie finally got the screaming meemies about it and insisted on Gregg's selling the place, housing shortage or no. They came straight to me. Why? Because they—Marie, anyway; she's a mystic little thing—had the idea that someone with a large dog would be safe in that house. The odd part of that was that neither of them knew I had recently acquired a Great Dane. As soon as they saw Tiny they threw themselves on my neck and begged me to take the place. Marie couldn't explain the feeling she had; what she and Gregg came to my place for was to ask me to buy a big dog and take the house. Why me? Well, she just felt I would like it, that was all. It seemed the right kind of place for me. And my having the dog clinched it. Anyway, you can put that down in your notebook of unexplainables."

So it went for the better part of a year. The letters were long and frequent, and, as sometimes happens, Alec and Alistair grew very close indeed. Almost by accident, they found themselves writing letters that did not mention Tiny at all, although there were others that concerned nothing else. And, of course, Tiny was not always in the role of *canis superior*. He was a dog—all dog—and acted accordingly. His strangeness came out only at particular intervals. At first it had been at times when Alistair was most susceptible to being astonished by it—in other words, when it was least expected. Later, he would perform his odd feats when she was ready for him to do it, and under exactly the right circumstances. Later still, he became the superdog only when she asked him to. . . .

The cottage was on a hillside, such a very steep hillside that the view of the river skipped over the railroad, and the trains were a secret rumble and never a sight at all. There was a wild and clean air about the place—a perpetual tingle of expectancy, as though someone coming into New York for the very first time on one of the trains had thrown his joyous anticipation high in the air and the cottage had caught it and breathed it and kept it forever.

Up the hairpin driveway to the house, one spring afternoon, toiled a miniature automobile in its lowest gear. Its little motor grunted and moaned as it took the last steep grade, a miniature Old Faithful appearing around its radiator cap. At the foot of the brownstone porch steps it stopped, and a miniature lady slid out from under the wheel. But for the fact that she was wearing an aviation mechanic's coveralls, and that her very first remark—an earthy epithet directed at the steaming radiator—was neither ladylike nor miniature, she might have been a model for the more precious variety of Mother's Day greeting card.

Fuming, she reached into the car and pressed the horn button. The quavering wail that resulted had its desired effect. It was answered instantly by the mighty howl of a Great Dane at the peak of aural agony. The door of the house crashed open and a girl in shorts and a halter rushed out on the porch, to stand with her russet hair ablaze in the sunlight, her lips parted, and her long eyes squinting against the light reflected from the river.

"What—Mother! Mother, darling, is that you? Already? Tiny!" she rapped as the dog bolted out of the open door and down the steps. "Come back here!"

The dog stopped. Mrs. Forsythe scooped a crescent wrench from the ledge behind the driver's seat and brandished it. "Let him come, Alistair," she said grimly. "In the name of sense, girl, what are you doing with a monster like that? I thought you said you had a dog, not a Shetland pony with fangs. If he messes with me, I'll separate him from a couple of those twelve-pound feet and bring him down to my weight. Where do you keep his saddle? I thought there was a meat shortage in this part of the country. Whatever possessed you to take up your abode with that carnivorous dromedary, anyway? And what's the idea of buying a barn like this, thirty miles from nowhere and perched on a precipice to boot, with a stepladder for a driveway and an altitude fit to boil at eighty degrees centigrade? It must take you forever to make breakfast. Twenty-minute eggs, and then they're raw. I'm hungry. If that Danish basilisk hasn't eaten everything in sight, I'd like to nibble on about eight sandwiches. Salami on whole wheat. Your flowers are gorgeous, child. So are you. You always were, of course. Pity you have brains. If you had no brains, you'd get married. A lovely view, honey, lovely. I like it here. Glad you bought it. Come here, you," she said to Tiny.

He approached this small specimen of volubility with his head a little low and his tail down. She extended a hand and held it still to let him sniff it before she thumped him on the withers. He waved his unfashionable tail in acceptance and then went to join the laughing Alistair, who was coming down the steps.

"Mother, you're marvelous." She bent and kissed her. "What on earth made that awful noise?"

"Noise? Oh, the horn." Mrs. Forsythe busily went about lifting the hood of the car. "I have a friend in the shoelace business. Wanted to stimulate trade for him. Fixed this up to make people jump out of their shoes. When they jump they break the laces. Leave their shoes in the street. Thousands of people walking about in their stocking feet. More people ought to, anyway. Good for the arches." She pointed. There were four big air-driven horns mounted on and around the little motor. Over the mouth of each was a shutter, so arranged that it revolved about an axle set at right angles to the horn, so that the bell was opened and closed by four small DC motors. "That's what gives it the warble. As for the beat-note, the four of them are turned a sixteenth-tone apart. Pretty?"

"Pretty," Alistair conceded with sincerity. "No, please don't demonstrate it again, Mother! You almost wrenched poor Tiny's ears off the first time."

"Oh, did I?" Contritely she went to the dog. "I didn't mean to, honey-poodle, really I didn't." The honey-poodle looked up at her with somber brown eyes and thumped his tail on the ground. "I like him," said Mrs. Forsythe decisively. She put out a fearless hand and pulled affectionately at the loose flesh of Tiny's upper lip. "Will you look at those tusks! Good grief, dog, reel in some of that tongue or you'll turn yourself inside out. Why aren't you married yet, chicken?"

"Why aren't you?" Alistair countered.

Mrs. Forsythe stretched. "I've *been married*," she said, and Alistair knew that now her casualness was forced. "A married season with the likes of Dan Forsythe sticks with you." Her voice softened. "Your daddy was all kinds of good people, baby." She shook herself. "Let's eat. I want to hear about Tiny. Your driblets and drablets of information about that dog are as tantalizing as Chapter Eleven of a movie serial. Who's this Alec creature in St. Croix? Some kind of native—cannibal, or something? He sounds nice. I wonder if you know how nice *you* think he is? Good heavens, the girl's blushing! I only know what I read in your letters, darling, and I never knew you to quote anyone by the paragraph before but that old scoundrel Nowland, and that was all about ductility and permeability and melting points. Metallurgy! A girl like you mucking about with molybs and durals instead of heartbeats and hope chests!"

"Mother, sweetheart, hasn't it occurred to you at all that I don't *want* to get married? Not yet, anyway."

"Of course it has. That doesn't alter the fact that a woman is only forty percent a woman until someone loves her, and only eighty percent a woman until she has children. As for you and your precious career, I seem to remember something about a certain Marie Sklodowska who didn't mind marrying a fellow called Curie, science or no science."

"Darling," said Alistair a little tiredly as they mounted the steps and went into the cool house, "once and for all, get this straight. The career, as such, doesn't matter at all. The work does. I like it. I don't see the sense of being married purely for the sake of being married."

"Oh, for heaven's sake, child, neither do I," said Mrs. Forsythe quickly. Then, casting a critical eye over her daughter, she sighed. "But it's such a waste."

"What do you mean?"

Her mother shook her head. "If you don't get it, it's because there's something wrong with your sense of values, in which case there's no point in arguing. I love your furniture. Now for pity's sake feed me and tell me about this canine Carnera of yours."

Moving deftly about the kitchen while her mother perched like a bright-eyed bird on a utility ladder, Alistair told the story of her letters from Alec and Tiny's arrival.

"At first he was just a dog. A very wonderful dog, of course, and extremely well trained. We got along beautifully. There was nothing remarkable about him but his history, as far as I could *see,* and certainly no indication of . . . of anything. I mean, he might have responded to my name the way he did because the syllabic content pleased him."

"It should," said her mother complacently. "Dan and I spent weeks at a sound laboratory graphing a suitable name for you. Alistair Forsythe. Has a beat, you know. Keep that in mind when you change it."

"Mother!"

"All right, dear. Go on with the story."

"For all I knew, the whole thing was a crazy coincidence. Tiny didn't respond particularly to the sound of my name after he got here. He seemed to take a perfectly normal, doggy pleasure in sticking around, that was all.

"Then, one evening after he had been with me about a month, I found out he could read."

"Read!" Mrs. Forsythe toppled, clutched the edge of the sink, and righted herself.

"Well, practically that. I used to study a lot in the evenings, and Tiny used to stretch out in front of the fire with his nose between his paws and watch me. I was tickled by that. I even got the habit of talking to him while I studied. I mean, about the work. He always seemed to be paying very close attention, which, of course, was silly. And maybe it was my imagination, but the times he'd get up and nuzzle me always seemed to be the times when my mind was wandering or when I would quit working and go on to something else.

"This particular evening I was working on the permeability mathematics of certain of the rare-earth group. I put down my pencil and reached for my *Handbook of Chemistry and Physics* and found nothing but a big hole in the bookcase. The book wasn't on the desk, either. So I swung around to Tiny and said, just for something to say, "Tiny, what have you done with my handbook?"

"He went *whuff,* in the most startled tone of voice, leaped to his feet, and went over to his bed. He turned up the mattress with his paw and scooped out the book. He picked it up in his jaws—I wonder what he would have done if he were a Scotty; that's a chunky piece of literature!—and brought it to me.

"I just didn't know what to do. I took the book and riffled it. It was pretty well shoved around. Apparently he had been trying to leaf through it with those big splay feet of his, I put the book down and took him by the muzzle. I called him nine kinds of rascal and asked him what he was looking for." She paused, building a sandwich.

"Well?"

"Oh," said Alistair, as if coming back from a far distance. "He didn't say."

There was a thoughtful silence. Finally Mrs. Forsythe looked up with her odd birdlike glance and said, "You're kidding. That dog isn't shaggy enough."

"You don't believe me." It wasn't a question.

The older woman got up to put a hand on the girl's shoulder. "Honey-lamb, your daddy used to say that the only things worth believing were things you learned from people you trusted. Of course I believe you. Thing is—do *you* believe you?"

"I'm not—sick, Mum, if that's what you mean. Let me tell you the rest of it."

"You mean there's more?"

"Plenty more." She put the stack of sandwiches on the sideboard where her mother could reach it. Mrs. Forsythe fell to with a will. "Tiny has been goading me to do research. A particular kind of research."

"Hut hine uffefa?"

"Mother! I didn't give you those sandwiches just to feed

you. The idea was to soundproof you a bit, too, while I talked."

"Hohay!" said her mother cheerfully.

"Well, Tiny won't let me work on any other project but the one he's interested in. Mum, I can't talk if you're going to gape like that! No . . . I can't say he won't let me do *any* work. But there's a certain line of endeavor that he approves. If I do anything else, he snuffles around, joggles my elbow, grunts, whimpers, and generally carries on until I lose my temper and tell him to go away. Then he'll walk over to the fireplace and flop down and sulk. Never takes his eyes off me. So, of course, I get all soft-hearted and repentant and apologize to him and get on with what he wants done."

Mrs. Forsythe swallowed, coughed, gulped some milk, and exploded, "Wait a minute, you're away too fast for me! What is it that he wants done? How do you know he wants it? Can he read, or can't he? Make some sense, child!"

Alistair laughed richly. "Poor Mum. I don't blame you, darling. No, I don't think he can really read. He shows no interest at all in books or pictures. The episode with the handbook seemed to be an experiment that didn't bring any results. *But*—he knows the difference between my books, even books that are bound alike, even when I shift them around in the bookcase. Tiny!"

The Great Dane scrambled to his feet from the corner of the kitchen, his paws skidding on the waxed linoleum. "Get me Hoag's *Basic Radio,* old feller, will you?"

Tiny turned and padded out. They heard him going up the stairs. "I was afraid he wouldn't do it while you were here," she said. "He generally warns me not to say anything about his powers. He growls. He did that when Dr. Nowland dropped out for lunch one Saturday. I started to talk about Tiny and just couldn't. He acted disgracefully. First he growled and then he barked. It was the first time I've ever known him to bark in the house. Poor Dr. Nowland. He was scared half out of his wits."

Tiny thudded down the stairs and entered the kitchen. "Give it to Mum," said Alistair. Tiny walked sedately over to the stool and stood before the astonished Mrs. Forsythe. She took the volume from his jaws.

"*Basic Radio,*" she breathed.

"I asked him for that because I have a whole row of technical books up there, all from the same publisher, all the same color and about the same size," said Alistair calmly.

"But . . . but . . . how does he do it?"

Alistair shrugged. "*I* don't know. He doesn't read the titles. That I'm sure of. He can't read anything. I've tried to get him to do it a dozen different ways. I've lettered instructions on pieces of paper and shown them to him—you know, 'Go to the door' and 'Give me a kiss' and so on. He just looks at them and wags his tail. But if I read them first—"

"You mean, read them aloud?"

"No. Oh, he'll do anything I ask him to, sure. But I don't have to say it. Just read it, and he turns and does it. That's the way he makes me study what he wants studied."

"Are you telling me that behemoth can read your mind?"

"What do you think? Here, I'll show you. Give me the book."

Tiny's ears went up. "There's something in here about the electrical flux in supercooled copper that I don't quite remember. Let's see if Tiny's interested."

She sat on the kitchen table and began to leaf through the book. Tiny came and sat in front of her, his tongue lolling out, his big brown eyes fixed on her face. There was silence as she turned pages, read a little, turned some more. And suddenly Tiny whimpered urgently.

"*See* what I mean, Mum? All right, Tiny. I'll read it over."

Silence again, while Alistair's long green eyes traveled over the page. All at once Tiny stood up and nuzzled her leg.

"Hm-m-m? The reference? Want me to go back?"

Tiny sat again expectantly. "There's a reference here to a passage in the first section on basic electric theory that he wants," she explained. She looked up, "Mother, you read it to him." She jumped off the table, handed the book over. "Here. Section forty-five, Tiny! Go listen to Mum. Go on," and she shoved him towards Mrs. Forsythe, who said in an awed voice, "When I was a little girl, I used to read bedtime stories to my dolls. I thought I'd quit that kind of thing altogether, and now I'm reading technical literature to this . . . this canine catastrophe here. Shall I read aloud?"

"No, don't. See if he gets it."

But Mrs. Forsythe didn't get the chance. Before she had read two lines Tiny was frantic. He ran to Mrs. Forsythe and back to Alistair. He reared up like a frightened horse, rolled his eyes, and panted. He whimpered. He growled a little.

"For pity's sake, what's wrong?"

"I guess he can't get it from you," said Alistair. "I've had the idea before that he's tuned to me in more ways than one, and this clinches it. All right, then. Give me back the—"

But before she could ask him, Tiny had bounded to Mrs. Forsythe, taken the book gently out of her hands, and carried it to his mistress. Alistair smiled at her paling mother, took the book, and read until Tiny suddenly seemed to lose interest. He went back to his station by the kitchen cabinet and lay down, yawning.

"That's that," said Alistair, closing the book. "In other words, class dismissed. Well, Mum?"

Mrs. Forsythe opened her mouth, closed it again, and shook her head. Alistair loosed a peal of laughter.

"Oh, Mum," she gurgled through her laughter. "History has been made. Mum, darling, you're speechless!"

"I am not," said Mrs. Forsythe gruffly. "I . . . I think . . . well, what do you know! You're right! I *am!*"

When they had their breath back—yes, Mrs. Forsythe joined in, for Alistair's statement was indeed true—Alistair picked up the book and said, "Now look, Mum, it's almost time for my session with Tiny. Oh, yes; it's a regular thing, and he certainly is leading me into some fascinating byways."

"Like what?"

"Like the old impossible problem of casting tungsten, for example. You know, there is a way to do it."

"You don't say! What do you cast it in—a play?"

Alistair wrinkled her straight nose. "Did you ever hear of pressure ice? Water compressed until it forms a solid at what is usually its boiling point?"

"I remember some such."

"Well, all you need is enough pressure, and a chamber that can take that kind of pressure, and a couple of details like a high-intensity field of umpteen megacycles phased with . . . I forget the figures; anyhow, that's the way to go about it."

" 'If we had some eggs we could have some ham and eggs if we had some ham,' " quoted Mrs. Forsythe. "And besides, I seem to remember something about that pressure ice melting pretty much right now, like so," and she snapped her fingers. "How do you know your molded tungsten—that's what it would be, not cast at all—wouldn't change state the same way?"

"That's what I'm working on now," said Alistair calmly.

"Come along, Tiny. Mum, you can find your way around all right, can't you? If you need anything, just sing out. This isn't a séance, you know."

"Isn't it, though?" muttered Mrs. Forsythe as her lithe daughter and the dog bounded up the stairs. She shook her head, went into the kitchen, drew a bucket of water, and carried it down to her car, which had cooled to a simmer. She was dashing careful handfuls of it onto the radiator before beginning to pour when her quick ear caught the scrunching of boots on the steep drive.

She looked up to see a young man trudging wearily in the mid-morning heat. He wore an old sharkskin suit and carried his coat. In spite of his wilted appearance, his step was firm and his golden hair was crisp in the sunlight. He swung up to Mrs. Forsythe and gave her a grin, all deep-blue eyes and good teeth. "Forsythe's?" he asked in a resonant baritone.

"That's right," said Mrs. Forsythe, finding that she had to turn her head from side to side to see both of his shoulders. And yet she could have swapped belts with him. "You must feel like the Blue Kangaroo here," she added, slapping her miniature mount on its broiling flank. "Boiled dry."

"You cahl de cyah de Blue Kangaroo?" he repeated, draping his coat over the door and mopping his forehead with what seemed to Mrs. Forsythe's discerning eye, a pure linen handkerchief.

"I do," she replied, forcing herself not to comment on the young man's slight but strange accent. "It's strictly a dry-clutch job and acts like a castellated one. Let the pedal out, she races. Let it out three thirty-seconds of an inch more, and you're gone from there. Always stopping to walk back and pick up your head. Snaps right off, you know. Carry a bottle of collodion and a couple of splints to put your head back on. Starve to death without a head to eat with. What brings you here?"

In answer he held out a yellow envelope, looking solemnly at her head and neck, then at the car, his face quiet, his eyes crinkling with a huge enjoyment.

Mrs. Forsythe glanced at the envelope. "Oh. Telegram. She's inside. I'll give it to her. Come on in and have a drink. It's hotter than the hinges of Hail Columbia, Happy Land. Don't go wiping your feet like that! By jeepers, that's enough to give you an inferiority complex! Invite a man in, invite the dust on his feet, too. It's good, honest dirt and we don't run to white broadlooms here. Are you afraid of dogs?"

The young man laughed. "Dahgs talk to me, ma'am."

She glanced at him sharply, opened her mouth to tell him he might just be taken at his word around here, then thought better of it. "Sit down," she ordered. She bustled up a foaming glass of beer and set it beside him. "I'll get her down to sign for the wire," she said. The man half lowered the glass into which he had been jowls-deep, began to speak, found he was alone in the room, laughed suddenly and richly, wiped off the mustache of suds, and dived down for a new one.

Mrs. Forsythe grinned and shook her head as she heard the laughter, and went straight to Alistair's study. "Alistair!"

"Stop pushing me about the ductility of tungsten, Tiny! You know better than that. Figures are figures, and facts are facts. I think I see what you're trying to lead me to. All I can say is that if such a thing is possible, I never heard of any equipment that could handle it. Stick around a few years and I'll hire you a nuclear power plant. Until then, I'm afraid—"

"Alistair!"

"—there just isn't . . . hm-m-m? Yes, Mother?"

"Telegram."

"Oh. Who from?"

"I don't know, being only one fortieth of one percent as psychic as that doghouse Dunninger you have there. In other words, I didn't open it."

"Oh, Mum, you're silly. Of course you could have . . . oh, well, let's have it."

"I haven't got it. It's downstairs with Discobolus Junior, who brought it. No one," she said ecstatically, "has a right to be so tanned with hair that color."

"What *are* you talking about?"

"Go on down and sign for the telegram and see for yourself. You will find the maiden's dream with his golden head in a bucket of suds, all hot and sweaty from his noble efforts in attaining this peak without spikes or alpenstock, with nothing but his pure heart and Western Union to guide him."

"This maiden's dream happens to be tungsten treatment," said Alistair with some irritation. She looked longingly at her work sheet, put down her pencil, and rose. "Stay here, Tiny, I'll be right back as soon as I have successfully resisted my conniving mother's latest scheme to drag my red hairing across some young buck's path to matrimony." She paused at the door. "Aren't you staying up here, Mum?"

"Get that hair away from your face," said her mother grimly. "I am not. I wouldn't miss this for the world. And don't pun in front of that young man. It's practically the only thing in the world I consider vulgar."

Alistair led the way down the stairs and through the corridor to the kitchen, with her mother crowding her heels, once fluffing out her daughter's blazing hair, once taking a swift tuck in the back of the girl's halter. They spilled through the door almost together. Alistair stopped and frankly stared.

For the young man had risen and, still with the traces of beer foam on his molded lips, stood with his jaws stupidly open, his head a little back, his eyes partly closed as if against a bright light. And it seemed as if everyone in the room forgot to breathe for a moment.

"Well!" Mrs. Forsythe exploded after a moment. "Honey, you've made a conquest. Hey, you, chin up, chest out."

"I beg your humble pardon," muttered the young man, and the phrase seemed more a colloquialism than an affectation.

Alistair, visibly pulling herself together, said, "Mother, please," and drifted forward to pick up the telegram that lay on the kitchen table. Her mother knew her well enough to realize that her hands and her eyes were steady only by a powerful effort. Whether the effort was in control of annoyance, embarrassment, or out-and-out biochemistry was a matter for later thought. At the moment Mrs. Forsythe was enjoying the situation tremendously.

"Please wait," said Alistair coolly. "There may be an answer to this." The young man simply bobbed his head. He was still a little wall-eyed with the impact of seeing Alistair, as many a young man had been before. But there were the beginnings of his astonishing smile around his lips as he watched her rip the envelope open.

"Mother! Listen!

"ARRIVED THIS MORNING AND HOPE I CAN CATCH YOU AT HOME. OLD DEBBIL KILLED IN ACCIDENT BUT FOUND HIS MEMORY BEFORE HE DIED. HAVE INFORMATION WHICH MAY CLEAR UP MYSTERY—OR

DEEPEN IT. HOPE I CAN SEE YOU FOR I DON'T KNOW WHAT TO THINK.

ALEC."

"How old is this tropical savage?" asked Mrs. Forsythe.

"He's not a savage and I don't know how old he is and I can't see what that has to do with it. I think he's about my age or a little older." She looked up and her eyes were shining.

"Deadly rival," said Mrs. Forsythe to the messenger consolingly. "Rotten timimg here, somewhere."

"I—" said the young man.

"Mother, we've got to fix something to eat. Do you suppose he'll be able to stay over? Where's my green dress with the . . . oh, you wouldn't know. It's new."

"Then the letters weren't all about the dog," said Mrs. Forsythe with a Cheshire grin.

"Mum, you're impossible. This is . . . is important, Alec is . . . is . . ."

Her mother nodded. "Important. That's all I was pointing out."

The young man said. "I—"

Alistair turned to him. "I do hope you don't think we're totally mad. I'm sorry you had such a climb." She went to the sideboard and took a quarter out of a sugar bowl. He took it gravely.

"Thank you, ma'am. If you don't min', I'll keep this piece of silver for the rest o' my everlahstin'."

"You're wel— What?"

The young man seemed to get even taller. "I greatly appreciate your hospitality, Mrs. Forsythe. I have you at a disadvantage, ma'am, and one I shall correct." He put a crooked forefinger between his lips and blew out an incredible blast of sound.

"Tiny!" he roared. "Here to me, dahg, an' mek me known!"

There was an answering roar from upstairs, and Tiny came tumbling down, scrabbling wildly as he took the turn at the foot of the stairs and hurtled over the slick flooring to crash joyfully into the young man.

"Ah, you beast," crooned the man, cuffing the dog happily. His accent thickened. "You thrive yourself here wid de ladydem, yo gray-yut styoupid harse. You glad me, mon, you glad me." He grinned at the two astonished women. "Forgive me," he said as he pummeled Tiny, pulled his ears, shoved him away, and caught him by the jaws. "For true, I couldn't get in the first word with Mrs. Forsythe, and after that I couldn't help meself. Alec my name is, and the telegram I took from the true messenger, finding him sighing and sweating at the sight of the hill there."

Alistair covered her face with her hands and said, "Oooh."

Mrs. Forsythe whooped with laughter. When she found her voice she demanded, "Young man, what is your last name?"

"Sundersen, ma'am."

"Mother! Why did you ask him that?"

"For reasons of euphony," said Mrs. Forsythe with a twinkle. "Alexander Sundersen. Very good. Alistair—"

"Stop! Mum, don't you dare—"

"I was going to say, Alistair, if you and our guest will excuse me, I'll have to get back to my knitting." She went to the door.

Alistair threw an appalled look at Alec and cried, "Mother! What are you knitting?"

"My brows, darling. See you later." Mrs. Forsythe chuckled and went out.

It took almost a week for Alec to get caught up with the latest developments in Tiny, for he got the story in the most meticulous detail. There never seemed to be enough time to get in all the explanations and anecdotes, so swiftly did it fly when he and Alistair were together. Some days he went into the city with Alistair in the morning and spent the day buying tools and equipment for his estate. New York was a wonder city to him—he had been there only once before—and Alistair found herself getting quite possessive about the place, showing it off like the contents of a jewel box. And then Alec stayed at the house a couple of days. He endeared himself forever to Mrs. Forsythe by removing, cleaning, and refacing the clutch on the Blue Kangaroo, simplifying the controls on the gas refrigerator so it could be defrosted without a major operation, and putting a building jack under the corner of the porch that threatened to sag.

And the sessions with Tiny were resumed and intensified. At first he seemed a little uneasy when Alec joined one of them, but within half an hour he relaxed. Thereafter, more and more he would interrupt Alistair to turn to Alec. Although he apparently could not understand Alec's thoughts at all, he seemed to comprehend perfectly when Alec spoke to Alistair. And within a few days she learned to accept these interruptions, for they speeded up the research they were doing. Alec was almost totally ignorant of the advanced theory with which Alistair worked, but his mind was clear, quick, and very direct. He was no theorist, and that was good. He was one of those rare greasemonkey geniuses, with a grasp of the laws of cause and effect that amounts to intuition. Tiny's reaction to this seemed to be approval. At any rate, the occasions when Alistair lost track of what Tiny was after occurred less and less frequently. Alec instinctively knew just how far to go back, and then how to spot the turning at which they had gone astray. And bit by bit they began to identify what it was that Tiny was after. As to why—and how—he was after it. Alec's experience with old Debbil seemed a clue. It was certainly sufficient to keep Alec plugging away at a possible solution to the strange animal's stranger need.

"It was down at the sugar mill," he told Alistair, after he had become fully acquainted with the incredible dog's actions and they were trying to determine the why and the how. "He called me over to the chute where cane is loaded into the conveyors.

" 'Bahss,' he told me, 'dat t'ing dere, it not safe, sah.' And he pointed through the guard over the bull gears that drove the conveyor. Great big everlahstin' teeth it has, Miss Alistair, a full ten inches long, and it whirlin' to the drive pinion. It's old, but strong for good. Debbil, what he saw was a bit o' play on the pinion shaf'.

" 'Now, you're an old fool,' I told him.

" 'No, Bahss,' " he says. 'Look now, sah, de t'ing wit' de teet'—dem, it not safe, sah. I mek you see,' and before I could move meself or let a thought trickle, he opens the guard up and thrus' his han' inside! Bull gear, it run right up his arm and nip it off, neat as ever, at the shoulder. I humbly beg your pardon, Miss Alistair."

"G-go on," said Alistair, through her handkerchief.

"Well, sir, old Debbil, was an idiot for true, and he only died the way he lived, rest him. He was old and he was all eaten out with malaria and elephantiasis and the like, that not even Dr. Thetford could save him. But a strange thing happened. As he lay dyin', with the entire village gathered roun' the door whisperin' plans for the wake, he sent to tell me come quickly. Down I run, and for the smile on his face I glad him when I cross the doorstep."

As Alec spoke, he was back in the Spanish-wall hut, with the air close under the palm-thatch roof and the glare of the pressure lantern set on the tiny window ledge to give the old man light to die by. Alec's accent deepened. " 'How you feel, mon?' I ahsk him. 'Bahss, I'm a dead man now, but I got a light in mah hey-yud.'

" 'Tell me then, Debbil.'

" 'Bahss, de folk-dem say, ol' Debbil, him cyahn't remembah de taste of a mango as he t'row away de skin. Him cyahn't remembah his own house do he stay away t'ree day.'

" 'Loose talk, Debbil.'

" 'True talk, Bahss. Foh de lahd give me a leaky pot fo' hol' ma brains. But Bahss, I do recall one t'ing now, bright an' clear, and you must know. Bahss, de day I go up the wahtah line, I see a great jumbee in de stones of de gov'nor palace dere.' "

"What's a jumbee?" asked Mrs. Forsythe.

"A ghost, ma'am. The Crucians carry a crawlin' heap of superstitions. Tiny! What eats you, mon?"

Tiny growled again. Alec and Alistair exchanged a look. "He doesn't want you to go on."

"Listen carefully. I want him to get this. I am his friend. I want to help you help him. I realize that he wants as few people as possible to find out about this thing. I will say nothing to anybody unless and until I have his permission."

"Well, Tiny?"

The dog stood restlessly, swinging his great head from Alistair to Alec. Finally he made a sound like an audible shrug, then turned to Mrs. Forsythe.

"Mother's part of me," said Alistair firmly. "That's the way it's got to be. No alternative." She leaned forward. "You can't talk to us. You can only indicate what you want said and done. I think Alec's story will help us to understand what you want and help you to get it more quickly. Understand?"

Tiny gazed at her for a long moment, said, "*Whuff,*" and lay down with his nose between his paws and his eyes fixed on Alec.

"I think that's the green light," said Mrs. Forsythe, "and I might add that most of it was due to my daughter's conviction that you're a wonderful fellow."

"Mother!"

"Well, pare me down and call me Spud! They're *both* blushing!" said Mrs. Forsythe blatantly.

"Go on, Alec," choked Alistair.

"Thank you. Old Debbil told me a fine tale of the things he had seen at the ruins. A great beast, mind you, with no shape at all, and a face ugly to drive you mad. And about the beast was what he called a 'feelin' good.' He said it was a miracle, but he feared nothing. Wet it was, Bahss, like a slug, an' de eye it have is whirlin' an' shakin', an' I standin' dar feelin' like a bride at de altar step an' no fear in me.' Well, I thought the old man's mind was wandering, for I knew he was touched. But the story he told was *that* clear, and never a single second did he stop to think. Out it all came like a true thing.

"He said that Tiny walked to the beast and that it curved over him like an ocean wave. It closed over the dog, and Debbil was rooted there the livelong day, still without fear, and feelin' no small desire to move. He had no surprise at all, even at the thing he saw restin' in the thicket among the old stones.

"He said it was a submarine, a mighty one as great as the estate house and with no break nor mar in its surface but for the glass part let in where the mouth is on a shark.

"And then when the sun begun to dip, the beast gave a shudderin' heave and rolled back, and out walked Tiny. He stepped up to Debbil and stood. Then the beast began to quiver and shake, and Debbil said the air aroun' him heavied with the work the monster was doing, tryin' to talk. A cloud formed in his brain, and a voice swept over him. 'Not a livin' word, Bahss, not a sound at all. But it said to forget. It said to leave dis place and forget, sah.' And the last thing old Debbil saw as he turned away was the beast slumping down, seeming all but dead from the work it had done to speak at all. 'An' de cloud live in mah hey-yud, Bahss, f'om dat time onward. I'm a dead man now, Bahss, but de cloud gone and Debbil know de story.' " Alec leaned back and looked at his hands. "That was all. This must have happened about fifteen months pahst, just before Tiny began to show his strange stripe." He drew a deep breath and looked up. "Maybe I'm gullible. But I knew the old man too well. He never in this life could invent such a tale. I troubled myself to go up to the governor's palace after the buryin'. I might have been mistaken, but something big had lain in the deepest thicket, for it was crushed into a great hollow place near a hundred foot long. Well, there you are. For what it's worth, you have the story of a superstitious an' illiterate old man, at the point of death by violence and many years sick to boot."

There was a long silence, and at last Alistair threw her lucent hair back and said, "It isn't Tiny at all. It's a . . . a thing outside Tiny." She looked at the dog, her eyes wide. "And I don't even mind."

"Neither did Debbil when he saw it," said Alec gravely.

Mrs. Forsythe snapped, "What are we sitting gawking at each other for? Don't answer; I'll tell you. All of us can think up a story to fit the facts, and we're all too self-conscious to come out with it. Any story that fit those facts would really be a killer."

"Well said." Alec grinned. "Would you like to tell us your idea?"

"Silly boy," muttered Alistair.

"Don't be impertinent, child. Of course I'd like to tell you, Alec. I think that the good Lord, in His infinite wisdom, has decided that it was about time for Alistair to come to her senses, and, knowing that it would take a quasi-scientific miracle to do it, dreamed up this—"

"Some day," said Alistair icily "I'm going to pry you loose from your verbosity and your sense of humor in one fell swoop."

Mrs. Forsythe grinned. "There is a time for jocularity, kidlet, and this is it. I hate solemn people solemnly sitting around being awed by things. What do you make of all this, Alec?"

Alec pulled his ear and said, "I vote we leave it up to Tiny. It's his show. Let's get on with the work and just keep in mind what we already know."

To their astonishment, Tiny stumped over to Alec and licked his hand.

The blowoff came six weeks after Alec's arrival. (Oh, yes, he stayed six weeks, and longer. It took some fiendish cogitation for him to think of enough legitimate estate business that had to be done in New York to keep him that long, but after six weeks he was so much one of the family that he needed no excuse.) He had devised a code system for Tiny, so that Tiny could add something to their conversation. His point:

"Here he sits, ma'am, like a fly on the wall, seeing everything and hearing everything and saying not a word. Picture it for yourself, and you in such a position, fully entranced as you are with the talk you hear." And for Mrs. Forsythe particularly, the mental picture was altogether too vivid. It was so well presented that Tiny's research went by the board for four days while they devised the code. They had to give up the idea of a glove with a pencil pocket in it, with which Tiny might write a little, or any similar device. The dog was simply not deft enough for such meticulous work; and besides, he showed absolutely no signs of understanding any written or printed symbolism. Unless, of course, Alistair thought about it.

Alec's plan was simple. He cut some wooden forms—a disk, a square, a triangle to begin with. The desk signified "yes" or any other affirmation, depending on the context; the square was "no" or any negation; and the triangle indicated a question or a change of subject. The amount of information Tiny was able to impart by moving from one to another of these forms was astonishing. Once a subject for discussion was established, Tiny would take a stand between the disk and the square, so that all he had to do was to swing his head to one side or the other to indicate a "yes" or a "no." No longer were there those exasperating sessions in which the track of his research was lost while they back-trailed to discover where they had gone astray. The conversations ran like this:

"Tiny, I have a question. Hope you won't think it too personal. May I ask it?" That was Alec, always infinitely polite to dogs. He had always recognized their innate dignity.

Yes, the answer would come, as Tiny swung his head over the disk.

"Were we right in assuming that you, the dog, are not communicating with us, that you are the medium?"

Tiny went to the triangle. "You want to change the subject?"

Tiny hesitated, then went to the square. *No.*

Alistair said, "He obviously wants something from us before he will discuss the question. Right, Tiny?"

Yes.

Mrs. Forsythe said, "He's had his dinner, and he doesn't smoke. I think he wants us to assure him that we'll keep his secret."

Yes.

"Good, Alec, you're wonderful," said Alistair. "Mother, stop beaming. I only meant—"

"Leave it at that, child. And qualification will spoil it for the man."

"Thank you, ma'am," said Alec gravely, with that deep twinkle of amusement around his eyes. Then he turned back to Tiny. "Well, what about it, sah? Are you a superdog?"

No.

"Who . . . no, he can't answer that. Let's go back a bit. Was old Debbil's story true?"

Yes.

"Ah." They exchanged glances. "Where is this—monster? Still in St. Croix?"

No.

"Here?"

Yes.

"You mean here, in this room or in the house?"

No.

"Nearby, though?"

Yes.

"How can we find out just where, without mentioning the countryside item by item?" asked Alistair.

"I know," said Mrs. Forsythe. "Alec, according to Debbil, that 'submarine' thing was pretty big, wasn't it?"

"That it was, ma'am."

"Good. Tiny, does he . . . it . . . have the ship here, too?"

Yes.

Mrs. Forsythe spread her hands. "That's it, then. There's only one place around here where you could hide such an object." She nodded her head at the west wall of the house.

"The river!" cried Alistair. "That right, Tiny?"

Yes. And Tiny went immediately to the triangle.

"Wait!" said Alec. "Tiny, beggin' your pardon, but there's one more question. Shortly after you took passage to New York, there was a business with compasses, where they all pointed to the west. Was that the ship?"

Yes.

"In the water?"

No.

"Why," said Alistair, "this is pure science fiction! Alec, do you ever get science fiction in the tropics?"

"Ah, Miss Alistair, not often enough, for true. But well I

know it. The space ships are old Mother Goose to me. But there's a difference here. For in all the stories I've read, when a beast comes here from space, it's to kill and conquer; and yet—and I don't know why—I know that this one wants nothing of the sort. More, he's out to do us good."

"I feel the same way," said Mrs. Forsythe thoughtfully. "It's sort of a protective cloud which seems to surround us. Does that make sense to you, Alistair?"

"I know it from 'way back," said Alistair with conviction. She looked at the dog thoughtfully. "I wonder why he . . . it . . . won't show itself. And why it can communicate only through me. And why me?"

"I'd say, Miss Alistair, that you were chosen because of your metallurgy. As to why we never see the beast, well, it knows best. Its reason must be a good one."

Day after day, and bit by bit, they got and gave information. Many things remained mysteries, but, strangely, there seemed no real need to question Tiny too closely. The atmosphere of confidence and good will that surrounded them made questions seem not only unnecessary but downright rude.

And day by day, little by little, a drawing began to take shape under Alec's skilled hands. It was a casting with a simple enough external contour, but inside it contained a series of baffles and a chamber. It was designed, apparently, to support and house a carballoy shaft. There were no openings into the central chamber except those taken by the shaft. The shaft turned; *something* within the chamber apparently drove it. There was plenty of discussion about it.

"Why the baffles?" moaned Alistair, palming all the neatness out of her flaming hair. "Why carballoy? And in the name of Nemo, why tungsten?"

Alec stared at the drawing for a long moment, then suddenly clapped a hand to his head. "Tiny! Is there radiation inside that housing? I mean, hard stuff?"

Yes.

"There you are, then," said Alec. "Tungsten to shield the radiation. A casting for uniformity. The baffles to make a meander out of the shaft openings—see, the shaft has plates turned on it to fit between the baffles."

"And nowhere for anything to go in, nowhere for anything to come out—except the shaft, of course—and besides, you dan't cast tungsten that way! Maybe Tiny's monster can, but we can't. Maybe with the right flux and with enough power—but that's silly. Tungsten won't cast."

"And we can't build a spaceship. There must be a way!"

"Not with today's facilities, and not with tungsten," said Alistair. "Tiny's ordering it from us the way we would order a wedding cake at the corner bakery."

"What made you say 'wedding cake'?"

"You, too, Alec? Don't I get enough of that from Mother?" But she smiled all the same. "But about the casting—it seems to me that our mysterious friend is in the position of a radio fiend who understands every part of his set, how it's made, how and why it works. Then a tube blows, and he finds he can't buy one. He has to make one if he gets one at all. Apparently old Debbil's beast is in that kind of spot. What about it, Tiny? Is your friend short a part which he understands but has never built before?"

Yes.

"And he needs it to get away from Earth?"

Yes.

Alec asked, "What's the trouble? Can't get escape velocity?"

Tiny hesitated, then went to the triangle. "Either he doesn't want to talk about it or the question doesn't quite fit the situation," said Alistair. "It doesn't matter. Our main problem is the casting. It just can't be done. Not by anyone on this planet, as far as I know; and I think I know. It had to be tungsten, Tiny?"

Yes.

"Tungsten for what?" asked Alec. "Radiation shield?"

Yes.

He turned to Alistair. "Isn't there something just as good?"

She mused, staring at his drawing. "Yes, several things," she said thoughtfully. Tiny watched her, motionless. He seemed to slump as she shrugged dispiritedly and said, "But not anything with walls as thin as that. A yard or so of lead might do it, and have something like the mechanical strength he seems to want, but it would obviously be too big. Beryllium—" At the word, Tiny went and stood right on top of the square, a most emphatic *no.*

"How about an alloy?" Alec asked.

"Well, Tiny?"

Tiny went to the triangle. Alistair nodded. "You don't

know. I can't think of one. I'll take it up with Dr. Nowland. Maybe—"

The following day Alec stayed home and spent the day arguing cheerfully with Mrs. Forsythe and building a grape arbor. It was a radiant Alistair who came home that evening. "Got it! Got it!" she caroled as she danced in. "Alec, Tiny! Come on!"

They flew upstairs to the study. Without removing the green "beanie" with the orange feather that so nearly matched her hair, Alistair hauled out four reference books and began talking animatedly. "Auric molybdenum. Tiny, what about that? Gold and molyb III should do it! Listen!" And she launched forth into a spatter of absorption data, Greek-letter fomulae, and strength-of-materials comparisons that made Alec's head swim. He sat watching her without listening. Increasingly, this was his greatest pleasure.

When Alistair was quite through, Tiny walked away from her and lay down, gazing off into space.

"Well, strike me!" said Alec. "Look yonder, Miss Alistair. The very first time I ever saw him thinking something over."

"*Sh-h!* Don't disturb him, then. If that *is* the answer, and if he never thought of it before, it will take some figuring out. There's no knowing what fantastic kind of science he's comparing it with.

"I see the point. Like—well, suppose we crashed a plane in the Brazilian jungle and needed a new hydraulic cylinder on the landing gear. Now, then, one of the natives shows us ironwood, and it's up to us to figure out if we can make it serve."

"That's about it," breathed Alistair. "I—" She was interrupted by Tiny, who suddenly leaped up and ran to her, kissing her hands, committing the forbidden enormity of putting his paws on her shoulders, running back to the wooden forms and nudging the disk, the *yes* symbol. His tail was going like a metronome without its pendulum.

Mrs. Forsythe came in in the midst of all this rowdiness and demanded, "What goes on? Who made a dervish out of Tiny? What have you been feeding him? Don't tell me. Let me . . . You don't mean you've solved his problem for him? What are you going to do, buy him a pogo stick?"

"Oh, Mum, we've got it! An alloy of molybdenum and gold. I can get it alloyed and cast in no time."

"Good, honey, good. You going to cast the whole thing?" She pointed to the drawing.

"Why, yes."

"Humph!"

"Mother! Why, if I may ask, do you 'humph' in that tone of voice?"

"You may ask, Chicken, who's going to pay for it?"

"Why, that will—I—oh. *Oh!*" she said, aghast, and ran to the drawing. Alec came and looked over her shoulder. She figured in the corner of the drawing, oh-ed once again and sat down weakly.

"How much?" asked Alec.

"I'll get an estimate in the morning," she said faintly. "I know plenty of people. I can get it at cost—maybe." She looked at Tiny despairingly. He came and laid his head against her knee, and she pulled at his ears. "I won't let you down, darling," she whispered.

She got the estimate the next day. It was a little over thirteen thousand dollars.

Alistair and Alec stared blankly at each other and then at the dog.

"Maybe you can tell us where we can raise that much money?" said Alistair, as if she expected Tiny to whip out a wallet.

Tiny whimpered, licked Alistair's hand, looked at Alec, and then lay down.

"Now what?" mused Alec.

"Now we go and fix something to eat," said Mrs. Forsythe, moving toward the door. The others were about to follow, when Tiny leaped to his feet and ran in front of them. He stood in the doorway and whimpered. When they came closer, he barked.

"Sh-h! What is it, Tiny? Want us to stay here awhile?"

"Say, who's the boss around here?" Mrs. Forsythe wanted to know.

"He is," said Alec, and he knew he was speaking for all of them. They sat down, Mrs. Forsythe on the studio couch, Alistair at her desk, Alec at the drawing table. But Tiny seemed not to approve of the arrangement. He became vastly excited, running to Alec, nudging him hard, dashing to Alistair, taking her wrist very gently in his jaws and pulling gently toward Alec.

"What is it, fellow?"

"Seems like matchmaking to me," remarked Mrs. Forsythe.

"Nonsense, Mum," said Alistair, coloring. "He wants Alec and me to change places, that's all."

Alec said, "Oh," and went to sit beside Mrs. Forsythe. Alistair sat at the drawing table. Tiny put a paw up on it, poked at the large tablet of paper. Alistair looked at him curiously, then tore off the top sheet. Tiny nudged a pencil with his nose.

Then they waited. Somehow, no one wanted to speak. Perhaps no one could, but there seemed to be no reason to try. And gradually a tension built up in the room. Tiny stood stiff and rapt in the center of the room. His eyes glazed, and when he finally keeled over limply, no one went to him.

Alistair picked up the pencil slowly. Watching her hand, Alec was reminded of the movement of the pointer on a Ouija board. The pencil traveled steadily, in small surges, to the very top of the paper and hung there. Alistair's face was quite blank.

After that no one could say what happened, exactly. It was as if their eyes had done what their voices had done. They could see, but they did not care to. And Alistair's pencil began to move. Something, somewhere, was directing her mind—not her hand. Faster and faster her pencil flew, and it wrote what was later to be known as the Forsythe Formulae.

There was no sign then, of course, of the furor that they would cause, of the millions of words of conjecture that were written when it was discovered that the girl who wrote them could not possibly have had the mathematical background to write them. They were understood by no one at first, and by very few people ever. Alistair certainly did not know what they meant.

An editorial in a popular magazine came startlingly close to the true nature of the formulae when it said: "The Forsythe Formulae, which describe what the Sunday supplements call the 'Something-for-Nothing Clutch,' and the drawing that accompanies them, signify little to the layman. As far as can be determined, the formulae are the description and working principles of a device. It appears to be a power plant of sorts, and if it is ever understood, atomic power will go the way of gaslights.

"A sphere of energy is enclosed in a shell made of neutron-absorbing material. This sphere has inner and outer 'layers.' A shaft passes through the sphere. Apparently a magnetic field must be rotated about the outer casing of the device. The sphere of energy aligns itself with this field. The inner sphere rotates with the outer one and has the ability to turn the shaft. Unless the mathematics used are disproved—and no one seems to have come anywhere near doing that, unorthodox as they are—the aligning effect between the rotating field and the two concentric spheres, as well as the shaft, is quite independent of any load. In other words, if the original magnetic field rotates at 3000 r.p.m., the shaft will rotate at 3000 r.p.m., even if there is only 1/16 horsepower turning the field while there is 10,000 braking stress on the shaft.

"Ridiculous? Perhaps. And perhaps it is no more so than the apparent impossibility of 15 watts of energy pouring into the antenna of a radio station, and nothing coming down. The key to the whole problem is in the nature of those self-contained spheres of force inside the shell. Their power is apparently inherent, and consists of an ability to align, just as the useful property of steam is an ability to expand. If, as is suggested by Reinhardt in his 'Usage of the Symbol β in the Forsythe Formulae,' these spheres are nothing but stable concentrations of pure binding energy, we have here a source of power beyond the wildest dreams of mankind. Whether or not we succeed in building such devices, it cannot be denied that whatever their mysterious source, the Forsythe Formulae are an epochal gift to several sciences, including, if you like, the art of philosophy."

After it was over, and the formulae written, the terrible tension lifted. The three humans sat in their happy coma, and the dog lay senseless on the rug. Mrs. Forsythe was the first to move, standing up abruptly. "Well!" she said.

It seemed to break a spell. Everything was quite normal. No hang-overs, no sense of strangeness, no fear. They stood looking wonderingly at the mass of minute figures.

"I don't know," murmured Alistair, and the phrase covered a world of meaning. Then, "Alec—that casting. We've got to get it done. We've just got to, no matter what it costs us!"

"I'd like to," said Alec. "Why do we have to?"

She waved toward the drawing table. "We've been given that."

"You don't say!" said Mrs. Forsythe. "And what is that?"

Alistair put her hand to her head, and a strange, unfocused

look came into her eyes. That look was the only part of the whole affair that ever really bothered Alec. It was a place she had gone to, a little bit; and he knew that no matter what happened, he would never be able to go there with her.

She said, "He's been . . . talking to me, you know. You do know that, don't you? I'm not guessing, Alec—Mum."

"I believe you, chicken," her mother said softly. "What are you trying to say?"

"I got it in concepts. It isn't a thing you can repeat, really. But the idea is that he couldn't give us any *thing*. His ship is completely functional, and there isn't anything he can exchange for what he wants us to do. But he has given us something of great value. . . ." Her voice trailed off; she seemed to listen to something for a moment. "Of value in several ways. A new science, a new approach to attack the science. New tools, new mathematics."

"But what is it? What can it do? And how is it going to help us pay for the casting?" asked Mrs. Forsythe.

"It can't, immediately," said Alistair decisively. "It's too big. We don't even know what it is. Why are you arguing? Can't you understand that he can't give us any gadgetry? That we haven't his techniques, materials, and tools, and so we couldn't make any actual machine he suggested? He's done the only thing he can; he's given us a new science, and tools to take it apart."

"That I know," said Alec gravely. "Well, indeed. I felt that. And I—I trust him. Do you, ma'am?"

"Yes, of course. I think he's—people. I think he has a sense of humor and a sense of justice," said Mrs. Forsythe firmly. "Let's get our heads together. We ought to be able to scrape it up some way. And why shouldn't we? Haven't we three got something to talk about for the rest of our lives?"

And their heads went together.

This is the letter that arrived two months later in St. Croix.

> Honey-lamb,
>
> Hold on to your seat. It's all over.
>
> The casting arrived. I missed you more than ever, but when you have to go—and you know I'm glad you went! Anyway, I did as you indicated, through Tiny, before you left. The men who rented me the boat and ran it for me thought I was crazy,

and said so. Do you know that once we were out on the river with the casting, and Tiny started whuffing and whimpering to tell me we were on the right spot, and I told the men to tip the casting over the side, they had the colossal nerve to insist on opening the crate? Got quite nasty about it. Didn't want to be a party to any dirty work. It was against my principles, but I let them, just to expedite matters. They were certain there was a body in the box! When they saw what it was, I was going to bend my umbrelly over their silly heads, but they looked so funny I couldn't do a thing but roar with laughter. That was when the man said I was crazy.

Anyhow, over the side it went, into the river. Made a lovely splash. About a minute later I got the loveliest feeling—I wish I could describe it to you. I was sort of overwhelmed by a feeling of utter satisfaction, and gratitude, and, oh, I don't know. I just felt *good*, all over. I looked at Tiny, and he was trembling. I think he felt it, too. I'd call it a thank you, on a grand psychic scale. I think you can rest assured that Tiny's monster got what it wanted.

But that wasn't the end of it. I paid off the boatmen and started up the bank. Something made me stop and wait, and then go back to the water's edge.

It was early evening, and very still. I was under some sort of compulsion, not an unpleasant thing, but an unbreakable one. I sat down on the river wall and watched the water. There was no one around—the boat had left—except one of those snazzy Sunlounge cruisers anchored a few yards out. I remember how still it was, because there was a little girl playing on the deck of the yacht, and I could hear her footsteps as she ran about.

Suddenly I noticed something in the water. I suppose I should have been frightened, but somehow I wasn't at all. Whatever the thing was, it was big and gray and slimy and quite shapeless. And somehow, it seemed to be the source of this aura of well-being and protectiveness that I felt. It was staring at me. I knew it was before I saw that it had an eye—a big one, with something whirling inside of it. I don't know. I wish I could write. I wish I had the power to tell you what it was like. I know that by human standards it was infinitely revolting. If this was Tiny's monster, I could understand its being sensitive to the revulsion it might cause. And wrongly; for I felt to the core that the creature was good.

It winked at me. I don't mean blinked. It winked. And then everything happened at once.

The creature was gone, and in seconds there was a disturbance in the water by the yacht. Something gray and wet reached up out of the river, and I saw it was going for that little girl. Onle a tyke—about three, she was. Red hair just like yours. And it thumped that child in the small of the back just enough to knock her over into the river.

And can you believe it? I just sat there watching and said never a word. It didn't seem right to me that that baby could be struggling in the water. *But it didn't seem wrong, either!*

Well, before I could get my wits together, Tiny was off the wall like a hairy bullet and streaking through the water. I have often wondered why his feet are so big; I never will again. The hound is built like the lower half of a paddle wheel! In two shakes he had the baby by the scruff of the neck and was bringing her back to me. No one had seen that child get pushed, Alistair! No one but me. But there was a man on the yacht who must have seen her fall. He was all over the deck, roaring orders and getting in the way of things, and by the time he had his wherry in the water, Tiny had reached me with the little girl. She wasn't frightened, either, she thought it was a grand joke! Wonderful youngster.

So the man came ashore, all gratitude and tears, and wanted to gold-plate Tiny or something. Then he saw me. "That your dog?" I said it was my daughter's. She was in St. Croix on her honeymoon. Before I could stop him, he had a checkbook out and was scratching away at it. He said he knew my kind. Said he knew I'd never accept a thing for myself, but wouldn't refuse something for my daughter. I enclose the check. Why he picked a sum like thirteen thousand I'll never know. Anyhow, I know it'll be a help to you, and since the money really comes from Tiny's monster, I'm sure you'll use it. I suppose I can confess now. The idea that letting Alec put up the money—even though he had to clean out his savings and mortgage his estate—would be all right if he were one of the family, because then he'd have you to help him make it all back again—well, that was all my inspiration. Sometimes, though, watching you, I wonder if I really had to work so all-fired hard to get you two married to each other.

Well, I imagine that closes the business of Tiny's monster. There are a lot of things we'll probably never know. I can guess some things, though. It could communicate with a dog but not with a human, unless it half killed itself trying. Apparently a dog is telepathic with humans to a degree, though it probably doesn't understand a lot of what it gets. I don't speak French, but I could probably transcribe French phonetically well enough so a Frenchman could read it. Tiny was transcribing that way. The monster could "send" through him and control him completely. It no doubt indoctrinated the dog—if I can use the term—the day old Debbil took him up the waterline. And when the monster caught, through Tiny, the mental picture of you when Dr. Schwellenbach mentioned you, it went to work through the dog to get you working on its problem. Mental pictures—that's probably what the monster used. That's how Tiny could tell one book from another without being able to read. You visualize everything you think about. What do you think? *I* think that mine's as good a guess as any.

You might be amused to learn that last night all the compasses in this neighborhood pointed west for a couple of hours! 'By, now, chillun. Keep on being happy.

Love and love, and a kiss for Alec,
Mum

P.S. Is St. Croix really a nice place to honeymoon? Jack—he's the fellow who signed the check—is getting very sentimental. He's very like your father. A widower, and—oh, I don't know. Says fate, or something, brought us together. Said he hadn't planned to take a trip upriver with his granddaughter, but something drove him to it. He can't imagine why he anchored just there. Seemed a good idea at the time. Maybe it was fate. He is very sweet. I wish I could forget that wink I saw in the water.

E FOR EFFORT

by T. L. Sherred (1915-   )

ASTOUNDING SCIENCE FICTION
May

Very little is known about T. L. Sherred beyond the fact that he has a background in advertising and technical writing. His small body of work in science fiction (which includes a novel, Alien Island, *1970) contains a strong dose of cynicism punctuated with sinister humor. "E for Effort" is his most famous work and was his first published sf—indeed, it is certainly one of the best first stories in the history of the field. As you will see when you read it, it seems ahead of its time in several respects, most notably in its view of government bureaucracy, a theme that would receive great attention in the next decade.*

The story was also the cornerstone of Sherred's collection First Person Peculiar *(1972), a book that deserves to be back in print.*

(A few stories back I boasted that the moment Poul Anderson's first story appeared, I knew he was destined to be a science fiction luminary.

Well, lest you think I'm implying that I have an unfailing touch for such things, let me tell you that

I felt the same thing about T. L. Sherred when "E for Effort" appeared. It was, as Marty told you, his first story, and it was such a polished piece of work and seemed to be so excellent a job by so experienced a writer that I took it for granted we were going to see many, many additional great stories by him.

But we didn't. I don't know why. —And it seems such a shame.—I.A.)

The captain was met at the airport by a staff car. Long and fast it sped. In a narrow, silent room the general sat, ramrod-backed, tense. The major waited at the foot of the gleaming steps shining frostily in the night air. Tires screamed to a stop and together the captain and the major raced up the steps. No words of greeting were spoken. The general stood quickly, hand outstretched. The captain ripped open a dispatch case and handed over a thick bundle of papers. The general flipped them over eagerly and spat a sentence at the major. The major disappeared and his harsh voice rang curtly down the outside hall. The man with glasses came in and the general handed him the papers. With jerky fingers the man with glasses sorted them out. With a wave from the general the captain left, a proud smile on his weary young face. The general tapped his fingertips on the black glossy surface of the table. The man with glasses pushed aside crinkled maps, and began to read aloud.

Dear Joe:

I started this just to kill time, because I got tired of just looking out the window. But when I got almost to the end I began to catch the trend of what's going on. You're the only one I know that can come through for me, and when you finish this you'll know why you must.

I don't know who will get this to you. Whoever it is won't want you to identify a face later. Remember that, and please, Joe—*hurry!*

Ed

It all started because I'm lazy. By the time I'd shaken off the sandman and checked out of the hotel every seat in the bus was full. I stuck my bag in a dime locker and went out to kill the hour I had until the next bus left. You know the bus terminal: right across from the Book-Cadillac and the Statler, on Washington Boulevard near Michigan Avenue. Michigan Avenue. Like Main in Los Angeles, or maybe Sixty-third in its present state of decay in Chicago, where I was going. Cheap movies, pawnshops and bars by the dozens, a penny arcade or two, restaurants that feature hamburg steak, bread and butter and coffee for forty cents. Before the War, a quarter.

I like pawnshops. I like cameras, I like tools, I like to look in windows crammed with everything from electric razors to sets of socket wrenches to upper plates. So, with an hour to spare, I walked out Michigan to Sixth and back on the other side of the street. There are a lot of Chinese and Mexicans around that part of town, the Chinese running the restaurants and the Mexicans eating Southern Home Cooking. Between Fourth and Fifth I stopped to stare at what passed for a movie. Store windows painted black, amateurish signs extolling in Spanish: "Detroit premiere . . . cast of thousands . . . this week only . . . ten cents—" The few 8×10 glossy stills pasted on the windows were poor blowups, spotty and wrinkled; pictures of mailed cavalry and what looked like a good-sized battle. All for ten cents. Right down my alley.

Maybe it's lucky that history was my major in school. Luck it must have been, certainly not cleverness, that made me pay a dime for a seat in an undertaker's rickety folding chair imbedded solidly—although the only other customers were a half-dozen Sons of the Order of Tortilla—in a cast of second-hand garlic. I sat near the door. A couple of hundred watt bulbs dangling naked from the ceiling gave enough light for me to look around. In front of me, in the rear of the store, was the screen, what looked like a white-painted sheet of beaverboard, and when over my shoulder I saw the battered sixteen millimeter projector I began to think that even a dime was no bargain. Still, I had forty minutes to wait.

Everyone was smoking. I lit a cigarette and the discouraged Mexican who had taken my dime locked the door and turned off the lights, after giving me a long, questioning look. I'd paid my dime, so I looked right back. In a minute the old projector started clattering. No film credits, no producer's name, no director, just a tentative flicker before a closeup of a bewhiskered mug labeled Cortez. Then a painted and feathered Indian with the title of Guatemotzin, successor to Montezuma; an aerial shot of a beautiful job of model-building tagged Ciudad de Mejico, 1521. Shots of old muzzle-loaded artillery banging away, great walls spurting stone splinters under direct fire, skinny Indians dying violently with the customary gyrations, smoke and haze and blood. The photography sat me right up straight. It had none of the scratches and erratic cuts that characterize an old print, none of the fuzziness, none of the usual mugging at the camera by the handsome hero. There wasn't any handsome hero. Did you ever see one of these French pictures, or a Russian picture, and note the reality and depth brought out by working on a small budget that can't afford famed actors? This, what there was of it, was as good, or better.

It wasn't until the picture ended with a pan shot of a dreary desolation that I began to add two and two. You can't, for pennies, really have a cast of thousands, or sets big enough to fill Central Park. A mock-up, even, of a thirty-foot wall costs enough to irritate the auditors, and there had been a lot of wall. That didn't fit with the bad editing and lack of sound track, not unless the picture had been made in the old silent days. And I knew it hadn't by the color tones you get with pan film. It looked like a well-rehearsed and badly planned newsreel.

The Mexicans were easing out and I followed them to where the discouraged one was rewinding the reel. I asked him where he got the print.

"I haven't heard of any epics from the press agents lately, and it looks like a fairly recent print."

He agreed that it was recent, and added that he'd made it himself. I was polite to that, and he saw that I didn't believe him and straightened up from the projector.

"You don't believe that, do you?" I said that I certainly did, and I had to catch a bus. "Would you mind telling me why, exactly why?" I said that the bus— "I mean it. I'd appreciate it if you'd tell me just what's wrong with it."

"There's nothing wrong with it," I told him. He waited for me to go on. "Well, for one thing, pictures like that aren't made for the sixteen millimeter trade. You've got a reduction from a thirty-five millimeter master." I gave him a few of the other reasons that separate home movies from Hollywood. When I finished he smoked quietly for a minute.

"I see." He took the reel off the projector spindle and closed the case. "I have beer in the back." I agreed beer sounded good, but the bus—well, just one. From in back of the beaverboard screen he brought paper cups and a Jumbo bottle. With a whimsical "Business suspended" he closed the open door and opened the bottle with an opener screwed on the wall. The store had likely been a grocery or restaurant. There were plenty of chairs. Two we shoved around and relaxed companionably. The beer was warm.

"You know something about this line," he said tentatively.

I took it as a question and laughed. "Not too much. Here's mud." And we drank. "Used to drive a truck for the Film Exchange." He was amused at that.

"Stranger in town?"

"Yes and no. Mostly yes. Sinus trouble chased me out and relatives bring me back. Not any more, though; my father's funeral was last week." He said that was too bad, and I said it wasn't. "He had sinus, too." That was a joke, and he refilled the cups. We talked awhile about Detroit climate.

Finally he said, rather speculatively, "Didn't I see you around here last night? Just about eight." He got up and went after more beer.

I called after him. "No more beer for me." He brought a bottle anyway, and I looked at my watch. "Well, just one."

"Was it you?"

"Was it me what?" I held out my paper cup.

"Weren't you around here—"

I wiped foam off my mustache. "Last night? No, but I wish I had. I'd have caught my bus. No, I was in the Motor Bar last night at eight. And I was still there at midnight."

He chewed his lip thoughtfully. "The Motor Bar. Just down the street?" And I nodded. "The Motor Bar. Hm-m-m." I looked at him. "Would you like . . . sure, you would." Before I could figure out what he was talking about he went to the back and from behind the beaverboard screen rolled out a big radio-phonograph and another Jumbo bottle. I held the bottle against the light. Still half full. I looked at my watch. He rolled the radio against the wall and lifted the lid to get at the dials.

"Reach behind you, will you? The switch on the wall." I could reach the switch without getting up, and I did. The lights went out. I hadn't expected that, and I groped at arm's length. Then the lights came on again, and I turned back, relieved. But the lights weren't on; I was looking at the street!

Now, all this happened while I was dripping beer and trying to keep my balance on a tottering chair—the street moved, I didn't and it was day and it was night and I was in front of the Book-Cadillac and I was going into the Motor Bar and I was watching myself order a beer and I knew I was wide awake and not dreaming. In a panic I scrabbled off the floor, shedding chairs and beer like an umbrella while I ripped my nails feeling frantically for that light switch. By the time I found it—and all the while I was watching myself pound the bar for the barkeep—I was really in fine fettle, just about ready to collapse. Out of thin air right into a nightmare. At last I found the switch.

The Mexican was looking at me with the queerest expression I've ever seen, like he'd baited a mousetrap and caught a frog. Me? I suppose I looked like I'd seen the devil himself. Maybe I had. The beer was all over the floor and I barely made it to the nearest chair.

"What," I managed to get out, "what was that?"

The lid of the radio went down. "I felt like that too, the first time. I'd forgotten."

My fingers were too shaky to get out a cigarette, and I ripped off the top of the package. "I said, what was that?"

He sat down. "That was you, in the Motor Bar, at eight last night." I must have looked blank as he handed me another paper cup. Automatically I held it out to be refilled.

"Look here—" I started.

"I suppose it is a shock. I'd forgotten what I felt like the first time I . . . I don't care much any more. Tomorrow I'm going out to Phillips Radio." That made no sense to me, and I said so. He went on.

"I'm licked. I'm flat broke. I don't give a care any more. I'll settle for cash and live off the royalties." The story came out, slowly at first, then faster until he was pacing the floor. I guess he was tired of having no one to talk to.

His name was Miguel Jose Zapata Laviada. I told him mine; Lefko. Ed Lefko. He was the son of sugar beet workers who had emigrated from Mexico somewhere in the Twenties. They were sensible enough not to quibble when their oldest son left the back-breaking Michgan fields to seize the chance provided by a NYA scholarship. When the scholarship ran out, he'd worked in garages, driven trucks, clerked in stores, and sold brushes door-to-door to exist and learn. The Army cut short his education with the First Draft to make him a radar technician; the Army had given him an honorable discharge and an idea so nebulous as to be almost merely a hunch. Jobs were plentiful then, and it wasn't too hard to end up with enough money to rent a trailer and fill it with Army surplus radio and radar equipment. One year ago he'd finished what he'd started, finished underfed, underweight, and overexcited. But successful, because he had it.

"It" he installed in a radio cabinet, both for ease in handling and for camouflage. For reasons that will become apparent, he didn't dare apply for a patent. I looked "it" over pretty carefully. Where the phonograph turntable and radio controls had been were vernier dials galore. One big one was numbered 1 to 24, a couple were numbered 1 to 60, and there were a dozen or so numbered 1 to 25, plus two or three with no numbers at all. Closest of all it resembled one of these fancy radio or motor testers found in a super super-service station. That was all, except that there was a sheet of heavy plywood hiding whatever was installed in place of the radio chassis and speaker. A perfectly innocent cache for—

Daydreams are swell. I suppose we've all had our share of mental wealth or fame or travel or fantasy. But to sit in a chair and drink warm beer and realize that the dream of ages isn't a dream anymore, to feel like a god, to know that just by turning a few dials you can see and watch anything, anybody, anywhere, that has ever happened—it still bothers me once in a while.

I know this much, that it's high frequency stuff. And there's a lot of mercury and copper and wiring of metals cheap and easy to find, but what goes where, or how, least of all, why, is out of my line. Light has mass and energy, and that mass always loses part of itself and can be translated back to electricity, or something. Mike Laviada himself says that what he stumbled on and developed was nothing new, that long before the War it had been observed many times by men like Compton and Michelson and Pfeiffer, who discarded it as a useless laboratory effect. And, of course, that was before atomic research took precedence over everything.

When the first shock wore off—and Mike had to give me another demonstration—I must have made quite a sight. Mike tells me I couldn't sit down. I'd pop up and gallop up and down the floor of that ancient store kicking chairs out of my way or stumbling over them, all the time gobbling out words and disconnected sentences faster than my tongue could trip. Finally it filtered through that he was laughing at me. I didn't see where it was any laughing matter, and I prodded him. He began to get angry.

"I know what I have," he snapped. "I'm not the biggest fool in the world, as you seem to think. Here, watch this," and he went back to the radio. "Turn out the light." I did, and there I was watching myself at the Motor Bar again, a lot happier this time. "Watch this."

The bar backed away. Out in the street, two blocks down to the City Hall. Up the steps to the Council Room. No one there. Then Council was in session, then they were gone again. Not a picture, not a projection of a lantern slide, but a slice of life about twelve feet square. If we were close, the field of view was narrow. If we were farther away, the background was just as much in focus as the foreground. The images, if you want to call them images, were just as real, just as lifelike as looking in the doorway of a room. Real they were, three-dimensional, stopped by only the back wall or the distance in the background. Mike was talking as he spun the dials, but I was too engrossed to pay much attention.

I yelped and grabbed and closed my eyes as you would if you were looking straight down with nothing between you and the ground except a lot of smoke and a few clouds. I winked my eyes open almost at the end of what must have been a long racing vertical dive, and there I was, looking at the street again.

"Go any place up to the Heaviside Layer, go down as deep as any hole, anywhere, any time." A blur, and the street changed into a glade of sparse pines. "Buried treasure. Sure. Find it, with what?" The trees disappeared and I reached back for the light switch as he dropped the lid of the radio and sat down.

"How are you going to make any money when you haven't got it to start?" No answer to that from me. "I ran an ad in the paper offering to recover lost articles; my first customer was the Law wanting to see my private detective's license. I've seen every big speculator in the country sit in his office buying and selling and making plans; what do you think would happen if I tried to peddle advance market information? I've watched the stock market get shoved up and down while I had barely the money to buy the paper that told me about it. I watched a bunch of Peruvian Indians bury the second ransom of Atuahalpa; I haven't the fare to get to Peru, or the money to buy the tools to dig." He got up and brought two more bottles. He went on. By that time I was getting a few ideas.

"I've watched scribes indite the books that burnt at Alexandria; who would buy, or who would believe me, if I copied one? What would happen if I went over to the Library and told them to rewrite their histories? How many would fight to tie a rope around my neck if they knew I'd watched them steal and murder and take a bath? What sort of a padded cell would I get if I showed up with a photograph of Washington, or Caesar? Or Christ?"

I agreed that it was all probably true, but—

"Why do you think I'm here now? You saw the picture I showed for a dime. A dime's worth, and that's all, because I didn't have the money to buy film or to make the picture as I knew I should." His tongue began to get tangled. He was excited. "I'm doing this because I haven't the money to get the things I need to get the money I'll need—" He was so disgusted he booted a chair halfway across the room. It was easy to see that if I had been around a little later, Phillips Radio would have profited. Maybe I'd have been better off, too.

Now, although always I've been told that I'd never be worth a hoot, no one has ever accused me of being slow for a dollar. Especially an easy one. I saw money in front of me, easy money, the easiest and the quickest in the world. I saw, for a minute, so far in the future with me on top of the heap, that my head reeled and it was hard to breathe.

"Mike," I said, "let's finish that beer and go where we can get some more, maybe something to eat. We've got a lot of talking to do." So we did.

Beer is a mighty fine lubricant; I have always been a pretty smooth talker, and by the time we left the gin mill I had a pretty good idea of just what Mike had on his mind. By the time we'd bedded down for the night behind that beaverboard screen in the store, we were full-fledged partners. I don't recall our even shaking hands on the deal, but that partnership still holds good. Mike is ace high with me, and I guess it's the other way around, too. That was six years ago; it only took me a year or so to round some of the corners I used to cut.

Seven days after that, on a Tuesday, I was riding a bus to Grosse Pointe with a full briefcase. Two days after that I was riding back from Grosse Pointe in a shiny taxi, with empty briefcase and a pocketful of folding money. It was easy.

"Mr. Jones—or Smith—or Brown—I'm with Aristocrat Studios, Personal and Candid Portraits. We thought you might like this picture of you and . . . no, this is just a test proof. The negative is in our files. . . . Now, if you're really interested, I'll be back the day after tomorrow with our files. . . . I'm sure you will, Mr. Jones. Thank you, Mr. Jones. . . ."

Dirty? Sure. Blackmail is always dirty. But if I had a wife and family and a good reputation, I'd stick to the roast beef and forget the Roquefort. Very smelly Roquefort, at that. Mike liked it less than I did. It took some talking, and I had to drag out the old one about the ends justifying the means, and they could well afford it, anyway. Besides, if there was a squawk, they'd get the negatives free. Some of them were pretty bad.

So we had the cash; not too much, but enough to start. Before we took the next step there was plenty to decide. There are a lot of people who live by convincing millions that Sticko soap is better. We had a harder problem than that: we had, first, to make a salable and profitable product, and second, we had to convince many, many millions that our "Product" was absolutely honest and absolutely accurate. We all know that if you repeat something long enough and loud enough many—or most—will accept it as gospel truth. That called for publicity on an international scale. For the skeptics who know better than to accept advertising, no matter how blatant, we had to use another technique. And since we were going to get certainly only one chance, we had to be right the first time. Without Mike's machine the job would have been impossible; without it the job would have been unnecessary.

A lot of sweat ran under the bridge before we found what we thought—and we still do!—the only workable scheme. We picked the only possible way to enter every mind in the world without a fight; the field of entertainment. Absolute secrecy was imperative, and it was only when we reached the last decimal point that we made a move. We started like this.

First we looked for a suitable building, or Mike did, while I flew east, to Rochester, for a month. The building he rented was an old bank. We had the windows sealed, a flossy office installed in the front—the bulletproof glass was my idea—air conditioning, a portable bar, electrical wiring of whatever type Mike's little heart desired, and a blond secretary who thought she was working for M-E Experimental Laboratories. When I got back from Rochester I took over the job of keeping happy the stone masons and electricians, while Mike fooled around in our suite in the Book where he could look out the window at his old store. The last I heard, they were selling snake oil there. When the Studio, as we came to call it, was finished, Mike moved in and the blonde settled down to a routine of reading love stories and saying no to all the salesmen that wandered by. I left for Hollywood.

I spent a week digging through the files of Central Casting before I was satisfied, but it took a month of snooping and some under-the-table cash to lease a camera that would handle Trucolor film. That took the biggest load from my mind. When I got back to Detroit the big view camera had arrived from Rochester, with a truckload of glass color plates. Ready to go.

We made quite a ceremony of it. We closed the Venetian blinds and I popped the cork on one of the bottles of champagne I'd bought. The blond secretary was impressed; all she'd been doing for her salary was to accept delivery of packages and crates and boxes. We had no wine glasses, but we made no fuss about that. Too nervous and excited to drink any more than one bottle, we gave the rest to the blonde and told her to take the rest of the afternoon off. After she left—and I think she was disappointed at breaking up what could have been a good party—we locked up after her, went into the studio itself, locked up again and went to work.

I've mentioned that the windows were sealed. All the inside wall had been painted dull black, and with the high ceiling that went with that old bank lobby, it was impressive. But not gloomy. Midway in the studio was planted the big Trucolor camera, loaded and ready. Not much could we see of Mike's machine, but I knew it was off to the side, set to throw on the back wall. Not *on* the wall, understand, because the images produced are projected into the air, like the meeting of the rays of two searchlights. Mike lifted the lid and I could see him silhouetted against the tiny lights that lit the dials.

"Well?" he said expectantly.

I felt pretty good just then, right down to my billfold.

"It's all yours, Mike." A switch ticked over. There he was. There was a youngster, dead twenty-five hundred years, real enough, almost, to touch. Alexander. Alexander of Macedon.

Let's take that first picture in detail. I don't think I can ever forget what happened in the next year or so. First we followed Alexander through his life, from beginning to end. We skipped, of course, the little things he did, jumping ahead days and weeks and years at a time. Then we'd miss him, or find that he'd moved in space. That would mean we'd have to jump back and forth, like the artillery firing bracket or ranging shots, until we found him again. Helped only occasionally by his published lives, we were astounded to realize how much distortion had crept into his life. I often wonder why legends arise about the famous. Certainly their lives are as startling or appalling as fiction. And unfortunately we had to hold closely to the accepted histories. If we hadn't, every professor would have gone into his corner for a hearty sneer. We couldn't take that chance. Not at first.

After we knew approximately what had happened and where, we used our notes to go back to what had seemed a particularly photogenic section and work on that awhile. Eventually we had a fair idea of what we were actually going to film. Then we sat down and wrote an actual script to follow, making allowance for whatever shots we'd have to double in later. Mike used his machine as the projector, and I operated the Trucolor camera at a fixed focus, like taking moving pictures of a movie. As fast as we finished a reel it would go to Rochester for processing, instead of one of the Hollywood outfits that might have done it cheaper. Rochester is so used to horrible amateur stuff that I doubt if anyone ever looks at anything. When the reel was returned we'd run it ourselves to check our choice of scenes and color sense and so on.

For example, we had to show the traditional quarrels with his father, Philip. Most of that we figured on doing with doubles, later. Olympias, his mother, and the fangless snakes she affected, didn't need any doubling, as we used an angle and amount of distance that didn't call for actual conversation. The scene where Alexander rode the bucking horse no one else could ride came out of some biographer's head, but we thought it was so famous we couldn't leave it out. We dubbed the close-ups later, and the actual horseman was a young Scythian who hung around the royal stables for his keep. Roxanne was real enough, like the rest of the Persian's wives that Alexander took over. Luckily most of them had enough poundage to look luscious. Philip and Parmenio and the rest of the characters were heavily bearded, which made easy the necessary doubling and dubbing-in the necessary speech. (If you ever saw them shave in those days, you'd know why whiskers were popular.)

The most trouble we had with the interior shots. Smoky wicks in a bowl of lard, no matter how plentiful, were too dim even for fast film. Mike got around that by running the Trucolor camera at a single frame a second, with his machine paced accordingly. That accounts for the startling clarity and depth of focus we got from a lens well stopped down. We had all the time in the world to choose the best possible scenes and camera angles; the best actors in the world, expensive camera booms, or repeated retakes under the most exacting director couldn't compete with us. We had a lifetime from which to choose.

Eventually we had on film about eighty per cent of what you saw in the finished picture. Roughly we spliced the reels together and sat there entranced at what we had actually done. Even more exciting, even more spectacular than we'd dared to hope, the lack of continuity and sound didn't stop us from realizing that we'd done a beautiful job. We'd done all we could, and the worst was yet to come. So we sent for more champagne and told the blonde we had cause for celebration. She giggled.

"What are you doing in there, anyway?" she asked. "Every salesman who comes to the door wants to know what you're making."

I opened the first bottle. "Just tell them you don't know."

"That's just what I've been telling them. They think I'm awfully dumb." We all laughed at the salesmen.

Mike was thoughtful. "If we're going to do this sort of thing very often, we ought to have some of these fancy hollow-stemmed glasses."

The blonde was pleased with that. "And we could keep them in my bottom drawer." Her nose wrinkled prettily. "These bubbles— You know, this is the only time I've ever had champagne, except at a wedding, and then it was only one glass."

"Pour her another," Mike suggested. "Mine's empty, too." I did. "What did you do with those bottles you took home last time?"

A blush and a giggle. "My father wanted to open them, but I told him you said to save it for a special occasion."

By that time I had my feet on her desk. "This is the special occasion, then," I invited. "Have another, Miss . . . what's your first name, anyway? I hate being formal after working hours."

She was shocked. "And you and Mr. Laviada sign my checks every week! It's Ruth."

"Ruth. Ruth." I rolled it around the piercing bubbles, and it sounded all right.

She nodded. "And your name is Edward, and Mr. Laviada's is Migwell. Isn't it?" And she smiled at him.

"Mi*gell*," he smiled back. "An old Spanish custom. Usually shortened to Mike."

"If you'll hand me another bottle," I offered, "shorten Edward to Ed." She handed it over.

By the time we got to the fourth bottle we were as thick as bugs in a rug. It seems that she was twenty-four, free, and single, and loved champagne.

"But," she burbled fretfully, "I wish I knew what you were doing in there all hours of the day and night. I know you're here at night sometimes because I've seen your car out in front."

Mike thought that over. "Well," he said a little unsteadily, "we take pictures." He blinked one eye. "Might even take pictures of you if we were approached properly."

I took over. "We take pictures of models."

"Oh, no."

"Yes. Models of things and people and whatnot. Little ones. We make it look like it's real." I think she was a trifle disappointed.

"Well, now I know, and that makes me feel better. I sign all those bills from Rochester and I don't know what I'm signing for. Except that they must be film or something."

"That's just what it is; film and things like that."

"Well, it bothered me— No, there's two more behind the fan."

Only two more. She had a capacity. I asked her how she would like a vacation. She hadn't thought about a vacation just yet.

I told her she'd better start thinking about it. "We're leaving day after tomorrow for Los Angeles, Hollywood."

"The day after tomorrow? Why—"

I reassured her. "You'll get paid just the same. But there's no telling how long we'll be gone, and there doesn't seem to be much use in your sitting around here with nothing to do."

From Mike, "Let's have that bottle." And I handed it to him. I went on.

"You'll get your checks just the same. If you want, we'll pay you in advance so—"

I was getting full of champagne, and so were we all. Mike was humming softly to himself, happy as a taco. The blonde, Ruth, was having a little trouble with my left eye. I knew just how she felt, because I was having a little trouble watching where she overlapped the swivel chair. Blue eyes, sooo tall, fuzzy hair. Hm-m-m. All work and no play— She handed me the last bottle.

Demurely she hid a tiny hiccup. "I'm going to save all the corks— No I won't either. My father would want to know what I'm thinking of, drinking with my bosses."

I said it wasn't a good idea to annoy your father. Mike said why fool with bad ideas, when he had a good one. We were interested. Nothing like a good idea to liven things up.

Mike was expansive as the very devil. "Going to Los Angeles."

We nodded solemnly.

"Going to Los Angeles to work."

Another nod.

"Going to work in Los Angeles. What will we do for pretty blonde girl to write letters?"

Awful. No pretty blonde to write letters and drink champagne. Sad case.

"Gotta hire somebody to write letters anyway. Might not be blonde. No blondes in Hollywood. No good ones, anyway. So—"

I saw the wonderful idea, and finished for him. "So we take pretty blonde to Los Angeles to write letters!"

What an idea that was! One bottle sooner and its brilliancy would have been dimmed. Ruth bubbled like a fresh bottle and Mike and I sat there, smirking like mad.

"But I can't! I couldn't leave day after tomorrow just like that—!"

Mike was magnificent. "Who said day after tomorrow? Changed our minds. Leave right now."

She was appalled. "Right now! Just like that?"

"Right now. Just like that." I was firm.

"But—"

"No buts. Right now. Just like that."

"Nothing to wear—"

"Buy clothes any place. Best ones in Los Angeles."

"But my hair—"

Mike suggested a haircut in Hollywood, maybe?

I pounded the table. It felt solid. "Call the airport. Three tickets."

She called the airport. She intimidated easy.

The airport said we could leave for Chicago any time on the hour, and change there for Los Angeles. Mike wanted to know why she was wasting time on the telephone when we could be on our way. Holding up the wheels of progress, emery dust in the gears. One minute to get her hat.

"Call Pappy from the airport."

Her objections were easily brushed away with a few word-pictures of how much fun there was to be had in Hollywood. We left a sign on the door, "Gone to Lunch—Back in December," and made the airport in time for the four o'clock plane, with no time left to call Pappy. I told the parking attendant to hold the car until he heard from me and we made it up the steps and into the plane just in time. The steps were taken away, the motors snorted, and we were off, with Ruth holding fast her hat in an imaginary breeze.

There was a two-hour layover in Chicago. They don't serve liquor at the airport, but an obliging cab driver found us a convenient bar down the road, where Ruth made her call to her father. Cautiously we stayed away from the telephone booth, but from what Ruth told us, he must have read her the riot act. The bartender didn't have champagne, but gave us the special treatment reserved for those that order it. The cab driver saw that we made the liner two hours later.

In Los Angeles we registered at the Commodore, cold sober and ashamed of ourselves. The next day Ruth went shopping for clothes for herself, and for us. We gave her the sizes and enough money to soothe her hangover. Mike and I did some telephoning. After breakfast we sat around until the desk clerk announced a Mr. Lee Johnson to see us.

Lee Johnson was the brisk professional type, the high-bracket salesman. Tall, rather homely, a clipped way of talking. We introduced ourselves as embryo producers. His eyes brightened when we said that. His meat.

"Not exactly the way you think," I told him. "We have already eighty percent or better of the final print."

He wanted to know where he came in.

"We have several thousand feet of Trucolor film. Don't bother asking where or when we got it. This footage is silent. We'll need sound and, in places, speech dubbed in."

He nodded. "Easy enough. What condition is the master?"

"Perfect condition. It's in the hotel vault right now. There are gaps in the story to fill. We'll need quite a few male and female characters. And all of these will have to do their doubling for cash, and not for screen credit."

Johnson raised his eyebrows. "And why? Out here screen credit is bread and butter."

"Several reasons. This footage was made—never mind where—with the understanding that film credit would favor no one."

"If you're lucky enough to catch your talent between pictures you might get away with it. But if your footage is worth working with, my boys will want screen credit. And I think they're entitled to it."

I said that was reasonable enough. The technical crews were essential, and I was prepared to pay well. Particularly to keep their mouths closed until the print was ready for final release. Maybe even after that.

"Before we go any further," Johnson rose and reached for his hat, "let's take a look at that print. I don't know if we can—"

I knew what he was thinking. Amateurs. Home movies. Feelthy peekchures, mebbe?

We got the reels out of the hotel safe and drove to his laboratory, out Sunset. The top was down on his convertible and Mike hoped audibly that Ruth would have sense enough to get sport shirts that didn't itch.

"Wife?" Johnson asked carelessly.

"Secretary," Mike answered just as casually. "We flew in last night and she's out getting us some light clothes." Johnson's estimation of us rose visibly.

A porter came out of the laboratory to carry the suitcase containing the film reels. It was a long, low building, with the offices at the front and the actual laboratories tapering off at the rear. Johnson took us in the side door and called for someone whose name we didn't catch. The anonymous one was a projectionist who took the reels and disappeared into the back of the projection room. We sat for a minute in the soft easy chairs until the projectionist buzzed ready. Johnson glanced at us and we nodded. He clicked a switch on the arm of his chair and the overhead lights went out. The picture started.

It ran a hundred and ten minutes as it stood. We both watched Johnson like a cat at a rat hole. When the tag end showed white on the screen he signaled with the chairside buzzer for lights. They came on. He faced us.

"Where did you get that print?"

Mike grinned at him. "Can we do business?"

"Do business?" He was vehement. "You bet your life we can do business. We'll do the greatest business you ever saw!"

The projection man came down. "Hey, that's all right. Where'd you get it?"

Mike looked at me. I said, "This isn't to go any further."

Johnson looked at his man, who shrugged. "None of my business."

I dangled the hook. "That wasn't made here. Never mind where."

Johnson rose and struck, hook, line and sinker. "Europe! Hm-m-m. Germany. No, France. Russia, maybe. Einstein, or Eisenstein, or whatever his name is?"

I shook my head. "That doesn't matter. The leads are all dead, or out of commission, but their heirs . . . well, you get what I mean."

Johnson saw what I meant. "Absolutely right. No point taking any chances. Where's the rest—?"

"Who knows? We were lucky to salvage that much. Can do?"

"Can do." He thought for a minute. "Get Bernstein in here. Better get Kessler and Marrs, too." The projectionist left. In a few minutes Kessler, a heavy-set man, and Marrs, a young, nervous chain-smoker, came in with Bernstein, the sound man. We were introduced all around and Johnson asked if we minded sitting through another showing.

"Nope. We like it better than you do."

Not quite. Kessler and Marrs and Bernstein, the minute the film was over, bombarded us with startled questions. We gave them the same answers we'd given Johnson. But we were pleased with the reception, and said so.

Kessler grunted. "I'd like to know who was behind that camera. Best I've seen, by Cripes, since 'Ben Hur.' Better than 'Ben Hur.' The boy's good."

I grunted right back at him. "That's the only thing I can tell you. The photography was done by the boys you're talking to right now. Thanks for the kind word."

All four of them stared.

Mike said, "That's right."

"Hey, hey!" from Marrs. They all looked at us with new respect. It felt good.

Johnson broke into the silence when it became awkward. "What's next on the score card?"

We got down to cases. Mike, as usual, was content to sit there with his eyes half closed, taking it all in, letting me do all the talking.

"We want sound dubbed in all the way through."

"Pleasure," said Bernstein.

"At least a dozen, maybe more, of speaking actors with a close resemblance to the leads you've seen."

Johnson was confident. "Easy. Central Casting has everybody's picture since the Year One."

"I know. We've already checked that. No trouble there. They'll have to take the cash and let the credit go, for reasons I've already explained to Mr. Johnson."

A moan from Marrs. "I bet I get that job."

Johnson was snappish. "You do. What else?" to me.

I didn't know. "Except that we have no plans for distribution as yet. That will have to be worked out."

"Like falling off a log." Johnson was happy about that. "One look at the rushes and United Artists would spit in Shakespeare's eye."

Marrs came in. "What about the other shots? Got a writer lined up?"

"We've got what will pass for the shooting script, or will have in a week or so. Want to go over it with us?"

He'd like that.

"How much time have we got?" interposed Kessler. "This is going to be a job. When do we want it?" Already it was "we."

"Yesterday is when we want it," snapped Johnson, and he rose. "Any ideas about music? No? We'll try for Werner

Janssen and his boys. Bernstein, you're responsible for that print from now on. Kessler, get your crew in and have a look at it. Marrs, you'll go with Mr. Lefko and Mr. Laviada through the files at Central Casting at their convenience. Keep in touch with them at the Commodore. Now, if you'll step into my office, we'll discuss the financial arrangements—"

As easy as all that.

Oh, I don't say that it was easy work or anything like that, because in the next few months we were playing Busy Bee. What with running down the only one registered at Central Casting who looked like Alexander himself—he turned out to be a young Armenian who had given up hope of ever being called from the extra lists and had gone home to Santee—casting and rehearsing the rest of the actors and swearing at the costumers and the boys who built the sets, we were kept hopping. Even Ruth, who had reconciled her father with soothing letters, for once earned her salary. We took turns shooting dictation at her until we had a script that satisfied Mike and myself and young Marrs, who turned out to be a fox on dialogue.

What I really meant is that it was easy, and immensely gratifying, to crack the shell of the tough boys who had seen epics and turkeys come and go. They were really impressed by what we had done. Kessler was disappointed when we refused to be bothered with photographing the rest of the film. We just batted our eyes and said that we were too busy, that we were perfectly confident that he would do as well as we. He outdid himself, and us. I don't know what we would have done if he had asked us for any concrete advice. I suppose, when I think it all over, that the boys we met and worked with were so tired of working with the usual mine-run Grade B's, that they were glad to meet someone that knew the difference between glycerin tears and reality and didn't care if it cost two dollars extra. They had us placed as a couple of city slickers with plenty on the ball. I hope.

Finally it was all over with. We all sat in the projection room; Mike and I, Marrs and Johnson, Kessler and Bernstein, and all the lesser technicians that had split up the really enormous amount of work that had been done watched the finished product. It was terrific. Everyone had done his work well. When Alexander came on the screen, he *was* Alexander the Great. (The Armenian kid got a good bonus for that.) All that blazing color, all that wealth and magnificence and glamor seemed to flare right out of the screen and sear across your mind. Even Mike and I, who had seen the original, were on the edge of our seats.

The sheer realism and magnitude of the battle scenes, I think, really made the picture. Gore, of course, is glorious when it's all make-believe and the dead get up to go to lunch. But when Bill Mauldin sees a picture and sells a breathless article on the similarity of infantrymen of all ages—well, Mauldin knows what war is like. So did the infantrymen throughout the world who wrote letters comparing Alexander's Arbela to Anzio and the Argonne. The weary peasant, not stolid at all, trudging and trudging into mile after mile of those dust-laden plains and ending as a stinking, naked, ripped corpse peeipng from under a mound of flies isn't any different when he carries a sarissa instead of a rifle. That we'd tried to make obvious, and we succeeded.

When the lights came up in the projection room we knew we had a winner. Individually we shook hands all around, proud as a bunch of penguins, and with chests out as far. The rest of the men filed out and we retired to Johnson's office. He poured a drink all around and got down to business.

"How about releases?"

I asked him what he thought.

"Write your own ticket," he shrugged. "I don't know whether or not you know it, but the word has already gone around that you've got something."

I told him we'd had calls at the hotel from various sources, and named them.

"See what I mean? I know those babies. Kiss them out if you want to keep your shirt. And while I'm at it, you owe us quite a bit. I suppose you've got it."

"We've got it."

"I was afraid you would. If you didn't, I'd be the one that would have your shirt." He grinned, but we all knew he meant it. "All right, that's settled. Let's talk about release.

"There are two or three outfits around town that will want a crack at it. My boys will have the word spread around in no time; there's no point in trying to keep them quiet any longer. I know—they'll have sense enough not to talk about the things you want off the record. I'll see to that. But you're top dog right now. You got loose cash, you've got the biggest potential gross I've ever seen, and you don't have to take the first offer. That's important, in this game."

"How would you like to handle it yourself?"

"I'd like to try. The outfit I'm thinking of needs a feature right now, and they don't know I know it. They'll pay and pay. What's in it for me?"

"That," I said, "we can talk about later. And I think I know just what you're thinking. We'll take the usual terms and we don't care if you hold up whoever you deal with. What we don't know won't hurt us." That's what he was thinking, all right. That's a cutthroat game out there.

"Good. Kessler, get your setup ready for duplication."

"Always ready."

"Marrs, start the ball rolling on publicity . . . what do you want to do about that?" to us.

Mike and I had talked about that before. "As far as we're concerned," I said slowly, "do as you think best. Personal publicity, O.K. We won't look for it, but we won't dodge it. As far as that goes, we're the local yokels making good. Soft pedal any questions about where the picture was made, without being too obvious. You're going to have trouble when you talk about the nonexistent actors, but you ought to be able to figure out something."

Marrs groaned and Johnson grinned. "He'll figure out something."

"As far as technical credit goes, we'll be glad to see you get all you can, because you've done a swell job." Kessler took that as a personal compliment, and it was. "You might as well know now, before we go any further, that some of the work came right from Detroit." They all sat up at that.

"Mike and I have a new process of model and trick work." Kessler opened his mouth to say something but thought better of it. "We're not going to say what was done, or how much was done in the laboratory, but you'll admit that it defies detection."

About that they were fervent. "I'll say it defies detection. In the game this long and process work gets by me . . . where—"

"I'm not going to tell you that. What we've got isn't patented and won't be, as long as we can hold it up." There wasn't any griping there. These men knew process work when they saw it. If they didn't see it, it was good. They could understand why we'd want to keep a process that good a secret.

"We can practically guarantee there'll be more work for you to do later on." Their interest was plain. "We're not going to predict when, or make any definite arrangement, but we still have a trick or two in the deck. We like the way we've been getting along, and we want to stay that way. Now, if you'll excuse us, we have a date with a blonde."

Johnson was right about the bidding for the release. We—or rather Johnson—made a very profitable deal with United Amusement and the affiliated theaters. Johnson, the bandit, got his percentage from us and likely did better with United. Kessler and Johnson's boys took huge ads in the trade journals to boast about their connections with the Academy Award Winner. Not only the Academy, but every award that ever went to any picture. Even the Europeans went overboard. They're the ones that make a fetish of realism. They knew the real thing when they saw it, and so did everyone else.

Our success went to Ruth's head. In no time she wanted a secretary. At that, she needed one to fend off the screwballs that popped out of the woodwork. So we let her hire a girl to help out. She picked a good typist, about fifty. Ruth is a smart girl, in a lot of ways. Her father showed signs of wanting to see the Pacific, so we raised her salary on condition he'd stay away. The three of us were having too much fun.

The picture opened at the same time in both New York and Hollywood. We went to the premiere in great style with Ruth between us, swollen like a trio of bullfrogs. It's a great feeling to sit on the floor, early in the morning, and read reviews that make you feel like floating. It's a better feeling to have a mintful of money. Johnson and his men were right along with us. I don't think he could have been too flush in the beginning, and we all got a kick out of riding the crest.

It was a good-sized wave, too. We had all the personal publictiy we wanted, and more. Somehow the word was out that we had a new gadget for process photography, and every big studio in town was after what they thought would be a mighty economical thing to have around. The studios that didn't have a spectacle scheduled looked at the receipts of "Alexander" and promptly scheduled a spectacle. We drew some very good offers, Johnson said, but we made a series of long faces and broke the news that we were leaving for Detroit the next day, and to hold the fort awhile. I don't think he thought we actually meant it, but we did. We left the next day.

Back in Detroit we went right to work, helped by the knowledge that we were on the right track. Ruth was kept busy turning away the countless would-be visitors. We admitted no reporters, no salesmen, no one. We had no time. We were using the view camera. Plate after plate we sent to Rochester for developing. A print of each was returned to us and the plate was held in Rochester for our disposal. We sent to New York for a representative of one of the biggest publishers in the country. We made a deal.

Your main library has a set of the books we published, if you're interested. Huge heavy volumes, hundreds of them, each page a razor-sharp blowup from an 8x10 negative. A set of those books went to every major library and university in the world. Mike and I got a real kick out of solving some of the problems that have had savants guessing for years. In the Roman volume, for example, we solved the trireme problem with a series of pictures, not only the interior of a trireme, but a line-of-battle quinquereme. (Naturally, the professors and amateur yachtsmen weren't convinced at all.) We had a series of aerial shots of the City of Rome taken a hundred years apart, over a millennium. Aerial views of Ravenna and Londinium, Palmyra and Pompeii, of Eboracum and Byzantium. Oh, we had the time of our lives! We had a volume for Greece and for Rome, for Persia and for Crete, for Egypt and for the Eastern Empire. We had pictures of the Parthenon and the Pharos, pictures of Hannibal and Caractacus and Vercingetorix, pictures of the Walls of Babylon and the building of the pyramids and the palace of Sargon, pages from the Lost Books of Livy and the plays of Euripedes. Things like that.

Terrifically expensive, a second printing sold at cost to a surprising number of private individuals. If the cost had been less, historical interest would have become even more the fad of the moment.

When the flurry had almost died down, some Italian digging in the hitherto-unexcavated section of ash-buried Pompeii, dug right into a tiny buried temple right where our aerial shot had showed it to be. His budget was expanded and he found more ash-covered ruins that agreed with our aerial layout, ruins that hadn't seen the light of day for almost two thousand years. Everyone promptly wailed that we were the luckiest guessers in captivity; the head of some California cult suspected aloud that we were the reincarnations of two gladiators named Joe.

To get some peace and quiet Mike and I moved into our studio, lock, stock, and underwear. The old bank vault had never been removed, at our request, and it served well to store our equipment when we weren't around. All the mail Ruth couldn't handle we disposed of, unread; the old bank building began to look like a well-patronized soup kitchen. We hired burly private detectives to handle the more obnoxious visitors and subscribed to a telegraphic protective service. We had another job to do, another full-length feature.

We still stuck to the old historical theme. This time we tried to do what Gibbon did in the Decline and Fall of the Roman Empire. And, I think, we were rather successful, at that. In four hours you can't completely cover two thousand years, but you can, as we did, show the cracking up of a great civilization, and how painful the process can be. The criticism we drew for almost ignoring Christ and Christianity was unjust, we think, and unfair. Very few knew then, or know now, that we had included, as a kind of trial balloon, some footage of Christ Himself, and His times. This footage we had to cut. The Board of Review, as you know, is both Catholic and Protestant. They—the Board—went right up in arms. We didn't protest very hard when they claimed our "treatment" was irreverent, indecent, and biased and inaccurate "by any Christian standard. Why," they wailed, "it doesn't even look like Him." And they were right; it didn't. Not any picture *they* ever saw. Right then and there we decided that it didn't pay to tamper with anyone's religious beliefs. That's why you've never seen anything emanating from us that conflicted even remotely with the accepted historical, sociological, or religious features of Someone Who Knew Better. That Roman picture, by the way—but not accidentally—deviated so little from the textbooks you conned in school that only a few enthusiastic specialists called our attention to what they insisted were errors. We were still in no position to do any mass rewriting of history, because we were unable to reveal just where we got our information.

Johnson, when he saw the Roman epic, mentally clicked high his heels. His men went right to work, and we handled the job as we had the first. One day Kessler got me in a corner, dead earnest.

"Ed," he said, "I'm going to find out where you got that footage if it's the last thing I ever do."

I told him that some day he would.

"And I don't mean some day, either; I mean right now. That bushwa about Europe might go once, but not twice. I know better, and so does everyone else. Now, what about it?"

I told him I'd have to consult Mike and I did. We were up against it. We called a conference.

"Kessler tells me he has troubles. I guess you all know what they are." They all knew.

Johnson spoke up. "He's right, too. We know better. Where did you get it?"

I turned to Mike. "Want to do the talking?"

A shake of his head. "You're doing all right."

"All right." Kessler hunched a little forward and Marrs lit another cigarette. "We weren't lying and we weren't exaggerating when we said the actual photography was ours. Every frame of film was taken right here in this country, within the last few months. Just how—I won't mention why or where—we can't tell you just now." Kessler snorted in disgust. "Let me finish.

"We all know that we're cashing in, hand over fist. And we're going to cash in some more. We have, on our personal schedule, five more pictures. Three of that five we want you to handle as you did the others. The last two of the five will show you both the reason for all the childish secrecy, as Kessler calls it, and another motive that we have so far kept hidden. The last two pictures will show you both our motives and our methods; one is as important as the other. Now—is that enough? Can we go ahead on that basis?"

It wasn't enough for Kessler. "That doesn't mean a thing to me. What are we, a bunch of hacks?"

Johnson was thinking about his bank balance. "Five more. Two years, maybe four."

Marrs was skeptical. "Who do you think you're going to kid that long? Where's your studio? Where's your talent? Where do you shoot your exteriors? Where do you get your costumes and your extras? In one single shot you've got forty thousand extras, if you've got one! Maybe you can shut *me* up, but who's going to answer the questions that Metro and Fox and Paramount and RKO have been asking? Those boys aren't fools, they know their business. How do you expect me to handle any publicity when I don't know what the score is myself?"

Johnson told him to pipe down for a while and let him think. Mike and I didn't like this one bit. But what could we do—tell the truth and end up in a straitjacket?

"Can we do it this way?" he finally asked. "Marrs, these boys have an in with the Soviet Government. They work in some place in Siberia, maybe. Nobody gets within miles of there. No one ever knows what the Russians are doing—"

"Nope!" Marrs was definite. "Any hint that these came from Russia and we'd all be a bunch of Reds. Cut the gross in half."

Johnson began to pick up speed. "All right, not from Russia. From one of these little republics fringed around Siberia or Armenia or one of those places. They're not Russian-made films at all. In fact, they've been made by some of these Germans and Austrians the Russians took over and moved after the War. The war fever has died down enough for people to realize that the Germans knew their stuff occasionally. The old sympathy racket for these refugees struggling with faulty equipment, lousy climate, making super-spectacles and smuggling them out under the nose of the Gestapo or whatever they call it—That's it!"

Doubtfully, from Marrs: "And the Russians tell the world we're nuts, that they haven't got any loose Germans?"

That, Johnson overrode. "Who reads the back pages? Who pays any attention to what the Russians say? Who cares? They might even think we're telling the truth and start looking around their own backyard for something that isn't there! All right with you?" to Mike and myself.

I looked at Mike and he looked at me.

"O.K. with us."

"O.K. with the rest of you? Kessler? Bernstein?"

They weren't too agreeable, and certainly not happy, but they agreed to play games until we gave the word.

We were warm in our thanks. "You won't regret it."

Kessler doubted that very much, but Johnson eased them all out, back to work. Another hurdle leaped, or sidestepped.

"Rome" was released on schedule and drew the same friendly reviews. "Friendly" is the wrong word for reviews that stretched ticket line-ups blocks long. Marrs did a good job on the publicity. Even that chain of newspapers that afterward turned on us so viciously fell for Marrs' word wizardry and ran full-page editorials urging the reader to see "Rome."

With our third picture, "Flame Over France," we corrected a few misconceptions about the French Revolution, and began stepping on a few tender toes. Luckily, however, and not altogether by design, there happened to be in power in Paris a liberal government. They backed us to the hilt with the confirmation we needed. At our request they released a lot of documents that had hitherto conveniently been lost in the cavernous recesses of the Bibliotheque Nationale. I've forgotten the name of whoever happened to be the perennial pretender to the French throne. At, I'm sure, the subtle prodding of one of Marrs' ubiquitous publicity men, the pretender sued us for our whole net, alleging the defamation of the good name of the Bourbons. A lawyer Johnson dug up for us sucked the poor chump into a courtroom and cut him to bits. Not even six cents damages did he get. Samuels, the lawyer, and Marrs drew a good-sized bonus, and the pretender moved to Honduras.

Somewhere around this point, I believe, did the tone of the press begin to change. Up until then we'd been regarded as crosses between Shakespeare and Barnum. Since long obscure facts had been dredged into the light, a few well-known pessimists began to wonder *sotto voce* if we weren't just a pair of blasted pests. "Should leave well enough alone." Only our huge advertising budget kept them from saying more.

I'm going to stop right here and say something about our personal life while all this was going on. Mike kept in the background pretty well, mostly because he wanted it that way. He let me do all the talking and stick my neck out while he sat in the most comfortable chair in sight. I yelled and I argued and he just sat there; hardly ever a word coming out of that dark-brown pan, certainly never an indication showing that behind those polite eyebrows there was a brain—and a sense of humor and wit—faster and as deadly as a bear trap. Oh, I know we played around, sometimes with a loud bang, but we were, ordinarily, too busy and too preoccupied with what we were doing to waste any time. Ruth, while she was with us, was a good dancing and drinking partner. She was young, she was almost what you'd call beautiful, and she seemed to like being with us. For a while I had a few ideas about her that might have developed into something serious. We both—I should say, all three of us—found out in time that we looked at a lot of things too differently. So we weren't too disappointed when she signed with Metro. Her contract meant what she thought was all the fame and money and happiness in the world, plus the personal attention she was doubtless entitled to have. They put her in Class B's and serials and she, financially, is better off than she ever expected to be. Emotionally, I don't know. We heard from her some time ago, and I think she's about due for another divorce. Maybe it's just as well.

But let's get away from Ruth. I'm ahead of myself, anyway. All this time Mike and I had been working together, our approach to the final payoff had been divergent. Mike was hopped on the idea of making a better world, and doing that by making war impossible. "War," he often said, "war of any kind is what has made man spend most of his history in merely staying alive. Now, with the atom to use, he has within himself the seed of self-extermination. So help me, Ed, I'm going to do my share of stopping that, or I don't see any point in living. I mean it!"

He did mean it. He told me that in almost the same words the first day we met. Then, I tagged that idea as a pipe dream picked up on an empty stomach. I saw his machine only as a path to a luxurious and personal Nirvana, and I thought he'd soon be going my way. I was wrong.

You can't live, or work, with a likable person without admiring some of the qualities that make that person likable. Another thing; it's a lot easier to worry about the woes of the world when you haven't any yourself. It's a lot easier to have a conscience when you can afford it. When I donned the rose-colored glasses half my battle was won; when I realized how grand a world this *could* be, the battle was over. That was about the time of "Flame Over France," I think. The actual time isn't important. What *is* important is that, from that time on, we became the tightest team possible. Since then about the only thing we differed on was the time to knock off for a sandwich. Most of our leisure time, what we had of it, was spent in locking up for the night, rolling out the portable bar, opening just enough beer to feel good, and relaxing. Maybe, after one or two, we might diddle the dials of the machine, and go rambling.

Together we'd been everywhere and seen everything. It

might be a good night to check up on François Villon, that faker, or maybe we might chase around with Haroun-el-Rashid. (If there was ever a man born a few hundred years too soon, it was that careless caliph.) Or if we were in a bad or discouraged mood we might follow the Thirty Years' War for a while, or if we were real raffish we might inspect the dressing rooms at Radio City. For Mike the crackup of Atlantis had always had an odd fascination, probably because he was afraid that man would do it again, now that he's rediscovered nuclear energy. And if I dozed off he was quite apt to go back to the very Beginning, back to the start of the world as we know it now. (It wouldn't do any good to tell you what went before *that.*)

When I stop to think, it's probably just as well that neither of us married. We, of course, had hopes for the future, but we were both tired of the whole human race; tired of greedy faces and hands. With a world that puts a premium on wealth and power and strength, it's no wonder what decency there is stems from fear of what's here now, or fear of what's hereafter. We had seen so much of the hidden actions of the world—call it snooping, if you like—that we learned to disregard the surface indications of kindness and good. Only once did Mike and I ever look into the private life of someone we knew and liked and respected. Once was enough. From that day on we made it a point to take people as they seemed. Let's get away from that.

The next two pictures we released in rapid succession; the first "Fredom for Americans," the American Revolution, and "The Brothers and the Guns," the American Civil War. Bang! Every third politician, a lot of so-called "educators," and all the professional patriots started after our scalps. Every single chapter of the DAR, the Sons of Union Veterans, and the Daughters of the Confederacy pounded their collective heads against the wall. The South went frantic; every state in the Deep South and one state on the border flatly banned both pictures, the second because it was truthful, and the first because censorship is a contagious disease. They stayed banned until the professional politicians got wise. The bans were revoked, and the choke-collar and string-tie brigade pointed to both pictures as horrible examples of what some people actually believed and thought, and felt pleased that someone had given them an opportunity to roll out the barrel and beat the drums that sound sectional and racial hatred.

New England was tempted to stand on its dignity, but couldn't stand the strain. North of New York both pictures were banned. In New York state the rural representatives voted en bloc, and the ban was clamped on statewide. Special trains ran to Delaware, where the corporations were too busy to pass another law. Libel suits flew like confetti, and although the extras blared the filing of each new suit, very few knew that we lost not one. Although we had to appeal almost every suit to higher courts, and in some cases request a change of venue which was seldom granted, the documentary proof furnished by the record cleared us once we got to a judge, or series of judges, with no fences to mend.

It was a mighty rasp we drew over wounded ancestral pride. We had shown that not all the mighty had haloes of purest gold, that not all the Redcoats were strutting bullies—nor angels, and the British Empire, except South Africa, refused entry to both pictures and made violent passes at the State Department. The spectacle of Southern and New England congressmen approving the efforts of a foreign ambassador to suppress free speech drew hilarious hosannahs from certain quarters. H. L. Mencken gloated in the clover, doing loud nip-ups, and the newspapers hung on the triple-horned dilemma of anti-foreign, pro-patriotic, and quasi-logical criticism. In Detroit the Ku Klux Klan fired an anemic cross on our doorstep, and the Friendly Sons of St. Patrick, the NAACP, and the WCTU passed flattering resolutions. We forwarded the most vicious and obscene letters—together with a few names and addresses that hadn't been originally signed—to our lawyers and the Post Office Department. There were no convictions south of Illinois.

Johnson and his boys made hay. Johnson had pyramided his bets into an international distributing organization, and pushed Marrs into hiring every top press agent either side of the Rockies. What a job they did! In no time at all there were two definite schools of thought that overflowed into the public letter boxes. One school held that we had no business raking up old mud to throw, that such things were better left forgotten and forgiven, that nothing wrong had ever happened, and if it had, we were liars anyway. The other school reasoned more to our liking. Softly and slowly at first, then with a triumphant shout, this fact began to emerge; such things had actually happened, and could happen again, were possibly happening even now; had happened because twisted truth had too long left its imprint on international, sectional, and racial feelings. It pleased us when many began to agree, with us, that it is important to forget the past, but that it is even more important to understand and evaluate it with a generous and unjaundiced eye. That was what we were trying to bring out.

The banning that occurred in the various states hurt the gross receipts only a little, and we were vindicated in Johnson's mind. He had dolefully predicted loss of half the national gross because "you can't tell the truth in a movie and get away with it. Not if the house holds over three hundred." Not even on the stage? "Who goes to anything but a movie?"

So far things had gone just about as we'd planned. We'd earned and received more publicity, favorable and otherwise, than anyone living. Most of it stemmed from the fact that our doing had been newsworthy. Some, naturally, had been the ninety-day-wonder material that fills a thirsty newspaper. We had been very careful to make our enemies in the strata that can afford to fight back. Remember the old saw about knowing a man by the enemies he makes? Well, publicity was our ax. Here's how we put an edge on it.

I called Johnson in Hollywood. He was glad to hear from us. "Long time no see. What's the pitch, Ed?"

"I want some lip readers. And I want them yesterday, like you tell your boys."

"Lip readers? Are you nuts? What do you want with lip readers?"

"Never mind why. I want lip readers. Can you get them?"

"How should I know? What do you want them for?"

"I said, can you get them?"

He was doubtful. "I think you've been working too hard."

"Look—"

"Now, I didn't say I couldn't. Cool off. When do you want them? And how many?"

"Better write this down. Ready? I want lip readers for these languages: English, French, German, Russian, Chinese, Japanese, Greek, Belgian, Dutch and Spanish."

"*Ed Lefko, have you gone crazy?*"

I guess it didn't sound very sensible, at that. "Maybe I

have. But those languages are essential. If you run across any who can work in any other language, hang on to them. I might need them, too." I could see him sitting in front of his telephone, wagging his head like mad. Crazy. The heat must have got Lefko, good old Ed. "Did you hear what I said?"

"Yes, I heard you. If this is a rib—"

"No rib. Dead serious."

He began to get mad. "Where you think I'm going to get lip readers—out of my hat?"

"That's your worry. I'd suggest you start with the local School for the Deaf." He was silent. "Now, get this into your head; this isn't a rib, this is the real thing. I don't care what you do, or where you go, or what you spend—I want those lip readers in Hollywood when we get there or I want to know they're on the way."

"When are you going to get here?"

I said I wasn't sure. "Probably a day or two. We've got a few loose ends to clean up."

He swore a blue streak at the inequities of fate. "You'd better have a good story when you do—" I hung up.

Mike met me at the studio. "Talk to Johnson?" I told him, and he laughed. "Does sound crazy, I suppose. But he'll get them, if they exist and like money. He's the Original Resourceful Man."

I tossed my hat in a corner. "I'm glad this is about over. Your end caught up?"

"Set and ready to go. The films and the notes are on the way, the real estate company is ready to take over the lease, and the girls are paid up to date, with a little extra."

I opened a bottle of beer for myself. Mike had one. "How about the office files? How about the bar, here?"

"The files go to the bank to be stored. The bar? Hadn't thought about it."

The beer was cold. "Have it crated and send it to Johnson."

We grinned, together. "Johnson it is. He'll need it."

I nodded at the machine. "What about that?"

"That goes with us on the plane as air express." He looked closely at me. "What's the matter with you—jitters?"

"Nope. Willies. Same thing."

"Me, too. Your clothes and mine left this morning."

"Not even a clean shirt left?"

"Not even a clean shirt. Just like—"

I finished it. "—the first trip with Ruth. A little different, maybe."

Mike said slowly, "A lot different." I opened another beer. "Anything you want around here, anything else to be done?" I said no. "O.K. Let's get this over with. We'll put what we need in the car. We'll stop at the Courville Bar before we hit the airport."

I didn't get it. "There's still beer left—"

"But no champagne."

I got it. "O.K. I'm dumb, at times. Let's go."

We loaded the machine into the car, and the bar, left the studio keys at the corner grocery for the real estate company, and headed for the airport by way of the Courville Bar. Ruth was in California, but Joe had champagne. We got to the airport late.

Marrs met us in Los Angeles. "What's up? You've got Johnson running around in circles."

"Did he tell you why?"

"Sounds crazy to me. Couple of reporters inside. Got anything for them?"

"Not right now. Let's get going."

In Johnson's private office we got a chilly reception. "This better be good. Where do you expect to find someone to lipread in Chinese? Or Russian, for that matter?"

We all sat down. "What have you got so far?"

"Besides a headache?" He handed me a short list.

I scanned it. "How long before you can get them here?"

An explosion. "How long before I can get them here? Am I your errand boy?"

"For all practical purposes you are. Quit the fooling. How about it?" Marrs snickered at the look on Johnson's face.

"What are you smirking at, you moron?" Marrs gave in and laughed outright, and I did, too. "Go ahead and laugh. This isn't funny. When I called the State School for the Deaf they hung up. Thought I was some practical joker. We'll skip that.

"There's three women and a man on that list. They cover English, French, Spanish, and German. Two of them are working in the East, and I'm waiting for answers to telegrams I sent them. One lives in Pomona and one works for the Arizona School for the Deaf. That's the best I could do."

We thought that over. "Get on the phone. Talk to every state in the union if you have to, or overseas."

Johnson kicked the desk. "And what are you going to do with them, if I'm that lucky?"

"You'll find out. Get them on planes and fly them here, and we'll talk turkey when they get here. I want a projection room, not yours, and a good bonded court reporter."

He asked the world to appreciate what a life he led.

"Get in touch with us at the Commodore." To Marrs: "Keep the reporters away for a while. We'll have something for them later." Then we left.

Johnson never did find anyone who could lipread Greek. None, at least, that could speak English. The expert on Russian he dug out of Ambridge, in Pennsylvania, the Flemish and Holland Dutch expert came from Leyden, in the Netherlands, and at the last minute he stumbled upon a Korean who worked in Seattle as an inspector for the Chinese Government. Five women and two men. We signed them to an ironclad contract drawn by Samuels, who now handled all our legal work, I made a little speech before they signed.

"These contracts, as far as we've been able to verify, are going to control your personal and business life for the next year, and there's a clause that says we can extend that period for another year if we so desire. Let's get this straight. You are to live in a place of your own, which we will provide. You will be supplied with all necessities by our buyers. Any attempt at unauthorized communication will result in abrogation of the contract. Is that clear?

"Good. Your work will not be difficult, but it will be tremendously important. You will, very likely, be finished in three months, but you will be ready to go any place at any time at our discretion, naturally at our expense. Mr. Sorenson, as you are taking this down, you realize that this goes for you, too." He nodded.

"Your references, your abilities, and your past work have been thoroughly checked, and you will continue under constant observation. You will be required to verify and notarize every page, perhaps every line, of your transcripts, which Mr. Sorenson here will supply. Any questions?"

No questions. Each was getting a fabulous salary, and each wanted to appear eager to earn it. They all signed.

Resourceful Johnson bought for us a small rooming house, and we paid an exorbitant price to a detective agency to do the cooking and cleaning and chauffeuring required. We requested that the lipreaders refrain from discussing their work among themselves, especially in front of the house employees, and they followed instructions very well.

One day, about a month later, we called a conference in the projection room of Johnson's laboratory. We had a single reel of film.

"What's that for?"

"That's the reason for all the cloak-and-dagger secrecy. Never mind calling your projection man. This I'm going to run through myself. See what you think of it."

They were all disgusted. "I'm getting tired of all this kid stuff," said Kessler.

As I started for the projection booth I heard Mike say, "You're no more tired of it than I am."

From the booth I could see what was showing on the downstairs screen, but nothing else. I ran through the reel, rewound, and went back down.

I said, "One more thing—before we go any further, read this. It's a certified and notarized transcript of what has been read from the lips of the characters you just saw. They weren't, incidentally, 'characters,' in that sense of the word." I handed the crackling sheets around, a copy for each. "Those 'characters' are real people. You've just seen a newsreel. This transcript will tell you what they were talking about. Read it. In the trunk of the car Mike and I have something to show you. We'll be back by the time you've read it."

Mike helped me carry in the machine from the car. We came in the door in time to see Kessler throw the transcript as far as he could. He bounced to his feet as the sheets fluttered down.

He was furious. "What's going on here?" We paid no attention to him, nor to the excited demands of the others until the machine had been plugged into the nearest outlet.

Mike looked at me. "Any ideas?"

I shook my head and told Johnson to shut up for a minute. Mike lifted the lid and hesitated momentarily before he touched the dials. I pushed Johnson into his chair and turned off the lights myself. The room went black. Johnson, looking over my shoulder, gasped. I heard Bernstein swear softly, amazed.

I turned to see what Mike had shown them.

It was impressive, all right. He had started just over the roof of the laboratory and continued straight up in the air.

Up, up, up, until the city of Los Angeles was a tiny dot on a great ball. On the horizon were the Rockies. Johnson grabbed my arm. He hurt.

"What's that? What's that? Stop it!" He was yelling. Mike turned off the machine.

You can guess what happened next. No one believed their eyes, nor Mike's patient explanation. He had to twice turn on the machine again, once going far back into Kessler's past. Then the reaction set in.

Marrs smoked one cigarette after another, Bernstein turned a gold pencil over and over in his nervous fingers, Johnson paced like a caged tiger, and burly Kessler stared at the machine, saying nothing at all. Johnson was muttering as he paced. Then he stopped and shook his fist under Mike's nose.

"Man! Do you know what you've got there? Why waste time playing around here? Can't you see you've got the world by the tail on a downhill pull? If I'd ever known this—"

Mike appealed to me. "Ed, talk to this wildman."

I did. I can't remember exactly what I said, and it isn't important. But I did tell him how we'd started, how we'd plotted our course, and what we were going to do. I ended by telling him the idea behind the reel of film I'd run off a minute before.

He recoiled as though I were a snake. "You can't get away with that! You'd be hung—if you weren't lynched first!"

"Don't you think we know that? Don't you think we're willing to take that chance?"

He tore his thinning hair. Marrs broke in. "Let me talk to him." He came over and faced us squarely.

"Is this on the level? You going to make a picture like that and stick your neck out? You're going to turn that . . . that thing over to the people of the world?"

I nodded. "Just that."

"And toss over everything you've got?" He was dead serious, and so was I. He turned to the others. "He means it!"

Bernstein said, "Can't be done!"

Words flew. I tried to convince them that we had followed the only possible path. "What kind of a world do you want to live in? Or don't you want to live?"

Johnson grunted. "How long do you think we'd live if we ever made a picture like that? You're crazy! I'm not. I'm not going to put by head in a noose."

"Why do you think we've been so insistent about credit

and responsibility for direction and production? You'll be doing only what we hired you for. Not that we want to twist your arm, but you've made a fortune, all of you, working for us. Now, when the going gets heavy, you want to back out!"

Marrs gave in. "Maybe you're right, maybe you're wrong. Maybe you're crazy, maybe I am. I always used to say I'd try anything once. Bernie, you?"

Bernstein was quietly cynical. "You saw what happened in the last war. This might help. I don't know if it will. I don't know—but I'd hate to think I didn't try. Count me in!"

Kessler?

He swiveled his head. "Kid stuff! Who wants to live forever? Who wants to let a chance go by?"

Johnson threw up his hands. "Let's hope we get a cell together. Let's all go crazy." And that was that.

We went to work in a blazing drive of mutual hope and understanding. In four months the lipreaders were through. There's no point in detailing here their reactions to the dynamite they daily dictated to Sorenson. For their own good we kept them in the dark about our final purpose, and when they were through we sent them across the border into Mexico, to a small ranch Johnson had leased. We were going to need them later.

While the print duplicators worked overtime Marrs worked harder. The press and the radio shouted the announcement that, in every city of the world we could reach, there would be held the simultaneous premieres of our latest picture. It would be the last we needed to make. Many wondered aloud at our choice of the word "needed." We whetted curiosity by refusing any advance information about the plot, and Johnson so well infused their men with their own now-fervent enthusiasm that not much could be pried out of them but conjecture. The day we picked for release was Sunday. Monday, the storm broke.

I wonder how many prints of that picture are left today. I wonder how many escaped burning or confiscation. Two World Wars we covered, covered from the unflattering angles that up until then had been represented by only a few books hidden in the dark corners of libraries. We showed and *named* the war-makers, the cynical ones who signed and laughed and lied, the blatant patriots who used the flare of headlines and the ugliness of atrocity to hide behind their flag while life turned to death for millions. Our own and foreign traitors were there, the hidden ones with Janus faces. Our lipreaders had done their work well; no guesses these, no deduced conjectures from the broken records of a blasted past, but the exact words that exposed treachery disguised as patriotism.

In foreign lands the performances lasted barely the day. Usually, in retaliation for the imposed censorship, the theaters were wrecked by the raging crowds. (Marrs, incidentally, had spent hundreds of thousands bribing officials to allow the picture to be shown without previous censorship. Many censors, when that came out, were shot without trial.) In the Balkans, revolutions broke out, and various embassies were stormed by mobs. Where the film was banned or destroyed written versions spontaneously appeared on the streets or in coffee houses. Bootlegged editions were smuggled past customs guards, who looked the other way. One royal family fled to Switzerland.

Here in America it was a racing two weeks before the Federal Government, prodded into action by the raging of press and radio, in an unprecedented move closed all performances "to promote the common welfare, insure domestic tranquillity, and preserve foreign relations." Murmurs—and one riot—rumbled in the Midwest and spread until it was realized by the powers that be that something had to be done, and done quickly, if every government in the world were not to collapse of its own weight.

We were in Mexico, at the ranch Johnson had rented for the lipreaders. While Johnson paced the floor, jerkily fraying a cigar, we listened to a special broadcast of the attorney general himself:

". . . furthermore, this message was today forwarded to the government of the United States of Mexico. I read: 'The government of the United States of America requests the immediate arrest and extradition of the following:

" 'Edward Joseph Lefkowicz, known as Lefko.' " First on the list. Even a fish wouldn't get into trouble if he kept his mouth shut.

" 'Miguel Jose Zapata Laviada.' " Mike crossed one leg over the other.

" 'Edward Lee Johnson.' " He threw his cigar on the floor and sank into a chair.

" 'Robert Chester Marrs.' " He lit another cigarette. His face twitched.

" 'Benjamin Lionel Bernstein.' " He smiled a twisted smile and closed his eyes.

" 'Carl Wilhelm Kessler.' " A snarl.

"These men are wanted by the government of the United States of America, to stand trial on charges ranging from criminal syndicalism, incitement to riot, suspicion of treason—"

I clicked off the radio. "Well?" to no one in particular.

Bernstein opened his eyes. "The rurales are probably on their way. Might as well go back and face the music—" We crossed the border at Juarez. The FBI was waiting.

Every press and radio chain in the world must have had coverage at that trial, every radio system, even the new and imperfect television chain. We were allowed to see no one but our lawyer. Samuels flew from the West Coast and spent a week trying to get past our guards. He told us not to talk to reporters, if we ever saw them.

"You haven't seen the newspapers? Just as well— How did you ever get yourselves into this mess, anyway? You ought to know better."

I told him

He was stunned. "Are you all crazy?"

He was hard to convince. Only the united effort and concerted stories of all of us made him believe that there was such a machine in existence. (He talked to us separately, because we were kept isolated.) When he got back to me he was unable to think coherently.

"What kind of defense do you call that?"

I shook my head. "No. That is, we know that we're guilty of practically everything under the sun if you look at it one way. If you look at it another—"

He rose. "Man, you don't need a lawyer, you need a doctor. I'll see you later. I've got to get this figured out in my mind before I can do a thing."

"Sit down. What do you think of this?" And I outlined what I had in mind.

"I think . . . I don't know what I think. I don't know. I'll talk to you later. Right now I want some fresh air." And he left.

As most trials do, this one began with the usual blackening of the defendant's character, or lack of it. (The men we'd blackmailed at the beginning had long since had their money returned, and they had sense enough to keep quiet. That might have been because they'd received a few hints that there might still be a negative or two lying around. Compounding a felony? Sure.) With the greatest of interest we sat in that great columned hall and listened to a sad tale.

We had, with malice aforethought, libeled beyond repair great and unselfish men who had made a career of devotion to the public weal, imperiled needlessly relations traditionally friendly by falsely reporting mythical events, mocked the courageous sacrifices of those who had *dulce et gloria mori,* and completely upset everyone's peace of mind. Every new accusation, every verbal lance drew solemn agreement from the dignitary-packed hall. Against someone's better judgment, the trial had been transferred from the regular courtroom to the Hall of Justice. Packed with influence, brass, and pompous legates from over the world, only the congressmen from the biggest states, or with the biggest votes were able to crowd the newly installed seats. So you can see it was a hostile audience that faced Samuels when the defense had its say. We had spent the previous night together in the guarded suite to which we had been transferred for the duration of the trial, perfecting, as far as we could, our planned defense. Samuels has the arrogant sense of humor that usually goes with supreme self-confidence, and I'm sure he enjoyed standing there among all those bemedaled and bejowled bigwigs, knowing the bombshell he was going to hurl. He made a good grenadier. Like this:

"We believe there is only one defense possible, we believe there is only one defense necessary. We have gladly waived, without prejudice, our inalienable right of trial by jury. We shall speak plainly and bluntly, to the point.

"You have seen the picture in question. You have remarked, possibly, upon what has been called the startling resemblance of the actors in that picture to the characters named and portrayed. You have remarked possibly, upon the apparent verisimilitude to reality. That I will mention again. The first witness will, I believe, establish the trend of our rebuttal of the allegations of the prosecution." He called the first witness.

"Your name, please?"

"Mercedes Maria Gomez."

"A little louder, please."

"Mercedes Maria Gomez."

"Your occupation?"

"Until last March I was a teacher at the Arizona School for the Deaf. Then I asked for and obtained a leave of absence. At present I am under personal contract to Mr. Lefko."

"If you see Mr. Lefko in this courtroom, Miss . . . Mrs.—"

"Miss."

"Thank you. If Mr. Lefko is in this court will you point him out? Thank you. Will you tell us the extent of your duties at the Arizona School?"

"I taught children born totally deaf to speak. And to read lips."

"You read lips yourself, Miss Gomez?"

"I have been totally deaf since I was fifteen."

"In English only?"

"English and Spanish. We have . . . had many children of Mexican descent."

Samuels asked for a designated Spanish-speaking interpreter. An officer in the back immediately volunteered. He was identified by his ambassador, who was present.

"Will you take this book to the rear of the courtroom, sir?" To the Court: "If the prosecution wishes to examine that book, they will find that it is a Spanish edition of the Bible." The prosecution didn't wish to examine it.

"Will the officer open the Bible at random and read aloud?" He opened the Bible at the center and read. In dead silence the Court strained to hear. Nothing could be heard the length of that enormous hall.

Samuels: "Miss Gomez. Will you take these binoculars and repeat, to the Court, just what the officer is reading at the other end of the room?"

She took the binoculars and focused them expertly on the officer, who had stopped reading and was watching alertly. "I am ready."

Samuels: "Will you please read, sir?"

He did, and the Gomez woman repeated aloud, quickly and easily, a section that sounded as though it might be anything at all. I can't speak Spanish. The officer continued to read for a minute or two.

Samuels: "Thank you, sir. And thank you, Miss Gomez. Your pardon, sir, but since there are several who have been known to memorize the Bible, will you tell the Court if you have anything on your person that is written, anything that Miss Gomez has had no chance of viewing?" Yes, the officer had. "Will you read that as before? Will you, Miss Gomez—"

She read that, too. Then the officer came to the front to listen to the court reporter read Miss Gomez' words.

"That's what I read," he affirmed.

Samuels turned her over to the prosecution, who made more experiments that served only to convince that she was equally good as an interpreter and lipreader in either language.

In rapid succession Samuels put the rest of the lipreaders on the stand. In rapid succession they proved themselves as able and as capable as Miss Gomez, in their own linguistic specialty. The Russian from Ambridge generously offered to translate into his broken English any other Slavic language handy, and drew scattered grins from the press box. The Court was convinced, but failed to see the purpose of the exhibition. Samuels, glowing with satisfaction and confidence, faced the Court.

"Thanks to the indulgence of the Court, and despite the efforts of the distinguished prosecution, we have proved the almost amazing accuracy of lipreading in general, and these lipreaders in particular." One Justice absently nodded in agreement. "Therefore, our defense will be based on that premise, and on one other which we have had until now found necessary to keep hidden—the picture in question was and is definitely not a fictional representation of events of questionable authenticity. Every scene in that film contained, not polished professional actors, but the original person named and portrayed. Every foot, every inch of film was not the result of an elaborate studio reconstruction but an actual collection of pictures, an actual collection of newsreels—if they can be called that—edited and assembled in story form!"

Through the startled spurt of astonishment we heard one of the prosecution: "That's ridiculous! No newsreel—"

Samuels ignored the objections and the tumult to put me on the stand. Beyond the usual preliminary questions I was allowed to say things my own way. At first hostile, the Court became interested enough to overrule the repeated objections that flew from the table devoted to the prosecution. I felt that at least two of the Court, if not outright favorable, were friendly. As far as I can remember, I went over the maneuvers of the past years, and ended something like this:

"As to why we arranged the cards to fall as they did; both Mr. Laviada and myself were unable to face the prospect of destroying his discovery, because of the inevitable penalizing of needed research. We were, and we are, unwilling to better ourselves or a limited group by the use and maintenance of secrecy, if secrecy were possible. As to the only other alternative," and I directed this straight at Judge Bronson, the well-known liberal on the bench, "since the last war all atomic research and activity has been under the direction of a Board nominally civilian, but actually under the 'protection and direction' of the Army and Navy. This 'direction and protection,' as any competent physicist will gladly attest, has proved to be nothing but a smothering blanket serving to conceal hidebound antiquated reasoning, abysmal ignorance, and inestimable amounts of fumbling. As of right now, this country, or any country that was foolish enough to place any confidence in the rigid regime of the military mind, is years behind what would otherwise be the natural course of discovery and progress in nuclear and related fields.

"We were, and we are, firmly convinced that even the slightest hint of the inherent possibilities and scope of Mr. Laviada's discovery would have meant, under the present regime, instant and mandatory confiscation of even a supposedly secure patent. Mr. Laviada has never applied for a patent, and never will. We both feel that such a discovery belongs not to an individual, a group, or corporation, or even to a nation, but to the world and those who live in it.

"We know, and are eager and willing to prove, that the domestic and external affairs not only of this nation but of every nation are influenced, sometimes controlled, by esoteric groups warping political theories and human lives to suit their own ends." The Court was smothered in sullen silence, thick and acid with hate and disbelief.

"Secret treaties, for example, and vicious, lying propaganda have too long controlled human passions and made men hate; honored thieves have too long rotted secretly in undeserved high places. The machine can make treachery and untruth impossible. It *must*, if atomic war is not to sear the face and fate of the world.

"Our pictures were all made with that end in view. We needed, first, the wealth and prominence to present to an international audience what we knew to be the truth. We have done as much as we can. From now on, this Court takes over the burden we have carried. We are guilty of no treachery, guilty of no deceit, guilty of nothing but deep and true humanity. Mr. Laviada wishes me to tell the Court and the world that he has been unable till now to give his discovery to the world, free to use as it wills."

The Court stared at me. Every foreign representative was on the edge of his seat waiting for the Justices to order us shot without further ado, the sparkling uniforms were seething, and the pressmen were racing their pencils against time. The tension dried my throat. The speech that Samuels and I had rehearsed the previous night was strong medicine. Now what?

Samuels filled the breach smoothly. "If the Court pleases; Mr. Lefko has made some startling statements. Startling, but certainly sincere, and certainly either provable or disprovable. And proof it shall be!"

He strode to the door of the conference room that had been allotted us. As the hundreds of eyes followed him it was easy for me to slip down from the witness stand, and wait, ready. From the conference room Samuels rolled the machine, and Mike rose. The whispers that curdled the air seemed disappointed, unimpressed. Right in front of the Bench he trundled it.

He moved unobtrusively to one side as the television men trained their long-snouted cameras. "Mr. Laviada and Mr. Lefko will show you . . . I trust there will be no objection from the prosecution?" He was daring them.

One of the prosecution was already on his feet. He opened his mouth hesitantly, but thought better, and sat down. Heads went together in conference as he did. Samuels was watching the Court with one eye, and the courtroom with the other.

"If the Court pleases, we will need a cleared space. If the bailiff will . . . thank you, sir." The long tables were moved back, with a raw scraping. He stood there, with every eye in the courtroom glued on him. For two long breaths he stood there, then he spun and went to his table. "Mr. Lefko." And he bowed formally. He sat.

The eyes swung to me, to Mike, as he moved to his machine and stood there silently. I cleared my throat and spoke to the Bench as though I did not see the directional microphones trained at my lips.

"Justice Bronson."

He looked steadily at me and then glanced at Mike. "Yes, Mr. Lefko?"

"Your freedom from bias is well known." The corners of his mouth went down as he frowned. "Will you be willing to be used as proof that there can be no trickery?" He thought that over, then nodded slowly. The prosecution objected, and was waved down. "Will you tell me exactly where you were at any given time? Any place where you are absolutely certain and can verify that there were no concealed cameras or observers?"

He thought. Seconds. Minutes. The tension twanged, and I swallowed dust. He spoke quietly. "1918. November 11th."

Mike whispered to me. I said, "Any particular time?"

Justice Bronson looked at Mike. "Exactly eleven. Armistice time." He paused, then went on. "Niagara Falls. Niagara Falls, New York."

I heard the dials tick in the stillness, and Mike whispered again. I said, "The lights should be off." The bailiff rose. "Will you please watch the left wall, or in that direction? I think that if Justice Kassel will turn a little . . . we are ready."

Bronson looked at me, and at the left wall. "Ready."

The lights flicked out overhead and I heard the television crews mutter. I touched Mike on the shoulder. "Show them, Mike!"

We're all showmen at heart, and Mike is no exception. Suddenly out of nowhere and into the depths poured a frozen torrent. Niagara Falls. I've mentioned, I think, that I've never got over my fear of heights. Few people ever do. I heard long, shuddery gasps as we started straight down. Down, until we stopped at the brink of the silent cataract, weird in its frozen majesty. Mike had stopped time at exactly eleven, I knew. He shifted to the American bank. Slowly he moved along. There were a few tourists standing in almost comic attitudes. There was snow on the ground, flakes in the air. Time stood still, and hearts slowed in sympathy.

Bronson snapped, "Stop!"

A couple, young. Long skirts, high-buttoned army collar, dragging army overcoat, facing, arms about each other. Mike's sleeve rustled in the darkness and they moved. She was sobbing and the soldier was smiling. She turned away her head, and he turned it back. Another couple seized them gayly, and they twirled breathlessly.

Bronson's voice was harsh. "That's enough!" The view blurred for seconds.

Washington. The White House. The President. Someone coughed like a small explosion. The President was watching a television screen. He jerked erect suddenly, startled. Mike spoke for the first time in Court.

"That is the President of the United States. He is watching the trial that is being broadcast and televised from this courtroom. He is listening to what I am saying right now, and he is watching, in his television screen, as I use my machine to show him what he was doing one second ago."

The President heard those fateful words. Stiffly he threw an unconscious glance around his room at nothing and looked back at his screen in time to see himself do what he just had done, one second ago. Slowly, as if against his will, his hand started toward the switch of his set.

"Mr. President, don't turn off that set." Mike's voice was curt, almost rude. "You must hear this, you of all people in the world. You must understand!

"This is not what we wanted to do, but we have no recourse left but to appeal to you, and to the people of this twisted world." The President might have been cast in iron. "You must see, you must understand that you have in your hands the power to make it impossible for green-born war to be bred in secrecy and rob man of his youth or his old age or whatever he prizes." His voice softened, pleaded. "That is all we have to say. That is all we want. That is all anyone could want, ever." The President, unmoving, faded into blackness. "The lights, please." And almost immediately the Court adjourned. That was over a month ago.

Mike's machine has been taken from us, and we are under military guard. Probably it's just as well we're guarded. We understand there have been lynching parties, broken up only as far as a block or two away. Last week we watched a white-haired fanatic scream about us, on the street below. We couldn't catch what he was shrieking, but we did catch a few air-borne epithets.

"Devils! Anti-Christs! Violation of the Bible! Violations of this and that!" Some, right here in the city, I suppose, would be glad to build a bonfire to cook us right back to the flames from which we've sprung. I wonder what the various religious groups are going to do now that the truth can be seen. Who can read lips in Aramaic, or Latin, or Coptic? And is a mechanical miracle a miracle?

This changes everything. We've been moved. Where, I don't know, except that the weather is warm, and we're on some type of military reservation, by the lack of civilians. Now we know what we're up against. What started out to be just a time-killing occupation, Joe, has turned out to be a necessary preface to what I'm going to ask you to do. Finish this, and then move fast! We won't be able to get this to you for a while yet, so I'll go on for a bit the way I started, to kill time. Like our clippings:

TABLOID:

. . . Such a weapon cannot, must not be loosed in unscrupulous hands. The last professional production of the infamous pair proves what distortions can be wrested from isolated and misunderstood events. In the hands of perpetrators of heretical isms, no property, no business deal, no personal life could be sacrosanct, no foreign policy could be . . .

TIMES:

. . . colonies stand with us firmly . . . liquidation of the Empire . . . white man's burden . . .

LE MATIN:

. . . rightful place . . . restore proud France . . .

PRAVDA:

. . . democratic imperialist plot . . . our glorious scientist ready to announce . . .

NICHI-NICHI:

. . . incontrovertibly prove divine descent . . .

LA PRENSA:

. . . oil concessions . . . dollar diplomacy . . .

DETROIT JOURNAL:

. . . under our noses in a sinister fortress on East Warren . . . under close Federal supervision . . . perfection by our production-trained technicians a mighty aid to law-enforcement agencies . . . tirades against politicians and business common-sense carried too far . . . tomorrow revelations by . . .

L'OSSERVATORE ROMANO:

Council of Cardinals . . . announcement expected hourly . . .

JACKSON STAR-CLARION:

. . . proper handling will prove the fallacy of race equality . . .

Almost unanimously the press screamed; Pegler frothed,

Winchell leered. We got the surface side of the situation from the press. But a military guard is composed of individuals, hotel room must be swept by maids, waiters must serve food, and a chain is as strong— We got what we think the truth from those who work for a living.

There are meetings on street corners and in homes, two great veterans' groups have arbitrarily fired their officials, seven governors have resigned, three senators and over a dozen representatives have retired with "ill health," and the general temper is ugly. International travelers report the same of Europe, Asia is bubbling, and transport planes with motors running stud the airports of South America. A general whisper is that a Constitutional Amendment is being rammed through to forbid the use of any similar instrument by an individual, with the manufacture and leasing by the Federal government to law-enforcement agencies or financially responsible corporations suggested; it is whispered that motor caravans are forming throughout the country for a Washington march to demand a decision by the Court on the truth of our charges; it is generally suspected that all news disseminating services are under direct Federal—Army—control; wires are supposed to be sizzling with petitions and demands to Congress, which are seldom delivered.

One day the chambermaid said: "And the whole hotel might as well close up shop. The whole floor is blocked off, there're MP's at every door, and they're clearing out all the other guests as fast as they can be moved. The whole place wouldn't be big enough to hold the letters and wires addressed to you, or the ones that are trying to get in to see you. Fat chance they have," she added grimly. "The joint is lousy with brass."

Mike glanced at me and I cleared my throat. "What's your idea of the whole thing?"

Expertly she spanked and reversed a pillow. "I saw your last picture before they shut it down. I saw all your pictures. When I wasn't working I listened to your trial. I heard you tell them off. I never got married because my boy friend never came back from Burma. Ask *him* what he thinks." And she jerked her head at the young private who was supposed to keep her from talking. "Ask him if he wants some bunch of stinkers to start him shooting at some other poor chump. See what he says, and then ask me if I want an atom bomb dropped down my neck just because some chiselers want more than they got." She left suddenly, and the soldier left with her. Mike and I had a beer and went to bed. Next week the papers had headlines a mile high.

U.S. KEEPS MIRACLE RAY
CONSTITUTION
AMENDMENT
AWAITS STATES OKAY
LEVIADA-LEFKO FREED

We were freed all right, Bronson and the President being responsible for that. But the President and Bronson don't know, I'm sure, that we were rearrested immediately. We were told that we'll be held in "protective custody" until enough states have ratified the proposed constitutional amendment. The Man Without a Country was in what you might call "protective custody," too. We'll likely be released the same way he was.

We're allowed no newspapers, no radio, allowed no communication coming or going, and we're given no reason, as if that were necessary. They'll never, never let us go, and they'd be fools if they did. They think that if we can't communicate, or if we can't build another machine, our fangs are drawn, and when the excitement dies, we fall into oblivion, six feet of it. Well, we can't build another machine. But, communicate?

Look at it this way. A soldier is a soldier because he wants to serve his country. A soldier doesn't want to die unless his country is at war. Even then death is only a last resort. And war isn't necessary anymore, not with our machine. In the dark? Try to plan or plot in absolute darkness, which is what would be needed. Try to plot or carry on a war without putting things in writing. O.K. Now—

The Army has Mike's machine. The Army has Mike. They call it military expediency, I suppose. Bosh! Anyone beyond the grade of moron can see that to keep that machine, to hide it, is to invite the world to attack, and attack in self-defense. If every nation, or if every man, had a machine, each would be equally open, or equally protected. But if only one nation, or only one man can see, the rest will not long be blind. Maybe we did this all wrong. God knows that we thought about it often. God knows we did our best to make an effort at keeping man out of his own trap.

There isn't much time left. One of the soldiers guarding us will get this to you, I hope, in time.

A long time ago we gave you a key, and hoped we would never have to ask you to use it. But now is the time. That key fits a box at the Detroit Savings Bank. In that box are letters. Mail them, not all at once, or in the same place. They'll go all over the world, to men we know, and have watched well; clever, honest, and capable of following the plans we've enclosed.

But you've got to hurry! One of these bright days someone is going to wonder if we've made more than one machine. We haven't, of course. That would have been foolish. But if some smart young lieutenant gets hold of that machine long enough to start tracing back our movements they'll find that safety deposit box, with the plans and letters ready to be scattered broadside. You can see the need for haste—if the rest of the world, or any particular nation, wants that machine bad enough, they'll fight for it. And they will! They must! Later on, when the Army gets used to the machine and its capabilities, it will become obvious to everyone, as it already is to Mike and me, that, with every plan open to inspection as soon as it's made, no nation or group of nations would have a chance in open warfare. So if there is to be an attack, it will have to be deadly, and fast, and sure. Please God that we haven't shoved the world into a war we tried to make impossible. With all the atom bombs and rockets that have been made in the past few years—*Joe, you've got to hurry!*

GHQ TO 9TH ATTK GRP

Report report report report report report report report report report

CMDR 9TH ATTK GRP TO GHQ

BEGINS: No other manuscript found. Searched body of Lefko immediately upon landing. According to plan Building Three untouched. Survivors insist both were moved from Building Seven previous day defective plumbing. Body of Laviada identified definitely through fingerprints. Request further instructions. ENDS

GHQ TO CMDR 32ND
SHIELDED RGT

BEGINS: Seal area Detroit Savings Bank. Advise immediately condition safety deposit boxes. Afford coming technical unit complete cooperation. ENDS

LT. COL. TEMP. ATT.
32ND SHIELDED RGT

BEGINS: Area Detroit Savings Bank vaporized direct hit. Radioactivity lethal. Impossible boxes or any contents survive. Repeat, direct hit. Request permission proceed Washington Area. ENDS

GHQ. TO LT. COL. TEMP. ATT.
32ND SHIELDED RGT

BEGINS: Request denied. Sift ashes if necessary regardless cost. Repeat, regardless cost. ENDS

GHQ. TO ALL UNITS REPEAT
ALL UNITS

BEGINS: Lack of enemy resistance explained misdirected atom rockets seventeen miles SSE Washington. Lone survivor completely destroyed special train claims all top officials left enemy capital two hours preceding attack. Notify local governments where found necessary and obvious cessation hostilities. Occupy present areas Plan Two. Further orders follow. ENDS

LETTER TO ELLEN

by Chan Davis (1926–   )

ASTOUNDING SCIENCE FICTION
June

Dr. Davis returns (see "The Nightmare" in Volume 8 of this series) with one of his best stories, which because of a very slight resemblance to Lester del Rey's famous "Helen O'Loy" (1938) has never received the attention due it. The holder of a doctorate from Harvard and Professor of Mathematics at the University of Toronto, Dr. Davis is a member of the prestigious Institute for Advanced Study in Princeton, New Jersey. His published sf stories total fewer than twenty, and we wish that he had had the time and inclination to give us more. Perhaps he still will.

(Marty's reference to "Letter to Ellen" 's "very slight resemblance" to "Helen O'Loy" requires a little expansion, to my way of thinking. The resemblance is in theme and such similarities are unavoidable, since the number of themes in science fiction and, indeed, in literature, are quite limited. I remember a time when I was writing my own story "Each an Explorer." Halfway through, I recognized the theme of John Campbell's much more famous

"Who Goes There?" I phoned him in a panic to ask what one did in such a case. "Nothing," he said kindly. "Just go right on and see what you can do with the theme." The treatment was, of course, not nearly as good as that in John's supremely great tale, but it was different. If the number of themes are limited, the number of varieties of treatment are not and it is sometimes actually instructive to see how the same soil can give rise to quite different, and equally flourishing, plants.—I.A.)

Dear Ellen,

By the time you get this you'll be wondering why I didn't call. It'll be the first time I've missed in—how long?—two months? A long two months it's been, and, for me, a very important two months.

I'm not going to call, and I'm not going to see you. Maybe I'm a coward writing this letter, but you can judge that when you've finished it. Judge that, and other things.

Let's see. I'd better begin at the beginning and tell the whole story right through. Do you remember my friend Roy Wisner? He came to work in the lab the same time I did, in the spring of '16, and he was still around when I first met you. Even if you never met him, you may have seen him; he was the tall blond guy with the stooped shoulders, working in the same branch with me.

Roy and I grew up together. He was my best friend as a kid, back almost as far as I can remember, back at the State Orphanage outside of Stockton. We went to different high schools, but when I got to Iowa U. there was Roy. Just to make the coincidence complete, he'd decided to be a biochemist too, and we took mostly the same courses all the way through. Both worked with Dietz while we were getting our doctorates, and Dietz got us identical jobs with Hartwell at the Pierne Labs here in Denver.

I've told you about that first day at the lab. We'd both heard from Dietz that the Pierne Labs were devoted now almost entirely to life-synthesis, and we'd both hoped to get in on that part of the work. What we hadn't realized was quite how far the work had got. I can tell you, the little talk old Hartwell gave us when he took us around to show us the lay of the land was just as inspiring as he meant it to be.

He showed us the wing where they're experimenting with the synthesis of new types of Coelenterates. We'd heard of that too, but seeing it was another thing. I remember particularly a rather ghastly green thing that floated in a small tank and occasionally sucked pieces of sea moss into what was half mouth, half sucker. Hartwell said, offhand, "Doesn't look much like the original, does it? That one was a mistake; something went wrong with the gene synthesis. But it turned out to be viable, so the fellows kept it around. Wouldn't be surprised if it could outsurvive some of its natural cousins if we were to give it a mate and turn it loose." He looked at the thing benignly. "I sort of like it."

Then we went down to Hartwell's branch, Branch 26, where we were to work. Hartwell slid back the narrow metal door and led the way into one of the labs. We started to follow him, but we hadn't gone more than three steps inside when we just stood still and gawked. I'd seen complicated apparatus before, but that place had anything at the Iowa labs beat by a factor of one thousand. All the gear on one whole side of the lab—and it was a good-sized place—was black-coated against the light and other stray radiation in the room. I recognized most of the flasks and fractionating columns as airtight jobs. A good deal of the hookup was hidden from us, being under Gardner hoods, airtight, temperature-controlled, radiation-controlled, and everything-else-controlled. What heaters we could see were never burners, always infrared banks.

This was precision work. It had to be, because, as you know, Branch 26 synthesizes chordate genes.

Roy and I went over to take a closer look at some of the gear. We stopped about a meter away; meddling was distinctly not in order. The item we were looking at was what would be called, in a large-scale process, a reaction vat. It was a small, opaque-coated flask, and it was being revolved slowly by a mechanical agitator, to swirl the liquids inside. As we stood there we could barely feel the gentle and precise flow of heat from the infrared heaters banked around it. We watched it, fascinated.

Hartwell snapped us out of it. "The work here," he said

dryly, "is carried out with a good deal of care. You've had some experience with full microanalysis, Dietz tells me."

"A little," I nodded, with very appropriate modesty.

"Well, this is microsynthesis, and microsynthesis with a vengeance. Remember, our problem here is on an entirely different level even from ordinary protein synthesis." (It staggered me a little to hear him refer to protein synthesis as ordinary!) "There you're essentially building up a periodic crystal, one in which the atoms are arranged in regularly recurrent patterns. This recursion, this periodicity, makes the structure of the molecule relatively simple; correspondingly, it simplifies the synthesis. In a gene, a virus, or any other of the complex proteinlike molecules there isn't any such frequent recursion. Instead, the radicals in your molecule chain are a little different each time; the pattern almost repeats, but not quite. You've got what you call an a-periodic crystal.

"When we synthesize such a crystal we've got to get all the little variations from the pattern just right, because it's those variations that give the structure enough complexity to be living."

He had some chromosome charts under his arm, and now he pulled one out to show to us. I don't know if you've ever seen the things; one of them alone fills a little booklet, in very condensed notation. Roy and I thumbed through one, recognizing a good many of the shorthand symbols but not understanding the scheme of the thing at all. When we got through we were pretty thoroughly awed.

Hartwell smiled. "You'll catch on, don't worry. The first few months, while you're studying up, you'll be my lab assistants. You won't be on your own until you've got the process down pretty near pat." And were we glad to hear that!

Roy and I got an apartment on the outside of town; I didn't have my copter then, so we had to be pretty close. It was a good place, though only one wall and the roof could be made transparent. We missed the morning sun that way, but I liked it all right. Downstairs lived Graham, our landlord, an old bachelor who spent most of his time on home photography, both movie wires and old-fashioned chemical prints. He got some candid angle shots of us that were so weird Roy was thinking of breaking his cameras.

At the lab we caught on fast enough. Roy was always a

pretty bright boy, and I manage to keep up. After a reasonable period Hartwell began to ease himself out of our routine, until before we knew it we were running the show ourselves. Naturally, being just out of school, we began, as soon as we got the drift of things, to suggest changes in the process. The day Hartwell finally approved one of our bright ideas, we knew we were standing on our own feet. That's when the fun really began.

Some people laugh when I say "that kind of drudgery" is fun, but you're a biochemist yourself and I'm pretty sure you feel the same way. The mere thought that we were putting inert colloids in at one end and getting something out at the other end that was in some strange way *living*—that was enough to take the boredom out of the job, if there'd been any.

Because we always felt that it was in our lab and the others like it that nonlife ended and life began. Sure, before us there was the immense job of protein synthesis and colloid preparation. Sure, after we were through there was the last step, the ultramicrosurgery of putting the nuclear wall together around the chromatin and embedding the result in a cell. (I always half envied your branch that job.) But in between there was our stage of the thing, which we thought to be the crucial one.

Certainly it was a tough enough stage. The long, careful reactions, with temperatures regulated down to a hundredth of a degree and reaction time to a tenth of a second; and then the final reactions, with everything enclosed in Gardner hoods, where you build up, bit by bit, the living nucleoplasm around the almost-living chromosomes. Hartwell hadn't lied when he said the work was carried out with care! That was quite a plant for two young squirts like us to be playing around with.

Just to put an edge on it, of course, there was always the possibility that you'd do everything right and still misfire. Anywhere along the line, Heisenberg's Uncertainty Principle could shove a radical out of place in those protein chains, no matter how careful you were. Then you'd get a weird thing: a gene mutating before it was even completed.

Or Heisenberg's Principle might pull you through even if your process had gone wrong!

We got curious after a while, Roy especially. Hartwell had told us a lot; one thing he hadn't told us was exactly *what we were making:* fish, flesh, or fowl, and we weren't geneticists enough to know ourselves. It would have been better, while we were working, to have had a mental picture of the frog or lizard or chicken that was to be our end product; instead, our mental picture was a composite of the three, and a rather disconcerting composite it made. I preferred to imagine a rabbit, or better yet, an Irish terrier puppy.

Hartwell not only hadn't offered to tell us, he didn't tell us when we asked him. "One of the lower chordates," he said; "the species name doesn't matter." That phrase "lower chordates" didn't ring quite true. There were enough chromosomes in our whatever-they-were's that they had to be something fairly far up the scale.

Roy immediately decided he was going to get the answer if he had to go through twenty books on genetics to do it. Looking back, I'm surprised I didn't have the same ambition. Maybe I was too interested in chess; I was on one of my periodic chess binges at the time. Anyhow, Roy got the genetics books and Roy did the digging.

It didn't take him any time at all. I remember that night well. He had brought home a stack of books from the library and was studying them at the desk in the corner. I was in the armchair with my portable chessboard, analyzing a game I'd lost in the last tournament. As the hours went by, I noticed Roy getting more and more restless; I expected him to come up with the answer any time, but apparently he was rechecking to make sure. About the time I'd found how I should have played to beat Fedruk, Roy got up, a little unsteadily.

"Dirk," he began, then stopped.

"You got it?"

"Dirk, I wonder if you realize just how few chordate species there are which have forty-eight chromosomes."

"Well, humans have, and I guess we're not so unique."

He didn't say anything.

"Hey, do you mean what I think you mean?" I jumped to my feet.

If he did, it was terrific news for me; I think I'd had the idea in the back of my mind all the time and never dared check it for fear I'd be proved wrong. Roy wasn't so happy about it. He said, "Yes, that's exactly what I mean. The species name Hartwell wouldn't tell us was *Homo sapiens*. We're making—robots."

That took a little time to digest. When I'd got it assimilated

I came back, "What do you mean, robots? If we made a puppy that wagged its tail O.K., you'd be just as pleased as I would." (I was still stuck on that Irish terrior idea of mine.) "That wouldn't give you the shudders. Why do you get so worried just because it's men we're making?"

"It's not right," he said.

"What?" Roy never having been religious or anything, that sounded strange.

"Well, I take that back, I guess, but—" His voice trailed away; then, more normally, "I don't know, Dirk. I just can't see it. Making humans—what would you call them if not robots?"

"I'd call them men, doggone it, if they turn out right. Of course if they don't turn out right—maybe I could see your point. If they don't turn out right. Killing a freak chicken and killing an experimental baby that didn't quite—succeed—would be two different things. Yeah."

"I hadn't thought of that."

"Then what the heck *were* you thinking of?"

"Aw, I don't know." He went back to the desk, slammed his books shut.

"What's bothering you, Roy?"

He didn't answer, just went into his bedroom and shut the door. He didn't come out again that night.

The next morning he was grim-faced, but you could see he was excited underneath. I knew he was planning something. Finally I wormed it out of him: he was going to take a look around Branch 39 to try and find some human embryos, as confirmation. Branch 39, as you know, is one of the ones that shuts up at night; they don't have to have technicians around twenty-four hours a day as 26 does. Roy's plan was to go up there just before closing time, hide, and get himself locked in overnight.

I asked him why the secrecy, why didn't he just ask to be shown around. "Hartwell doesn't want us to know," he said, "or he would have told us. I'll have to do it on the QT."

That made some sense, but—"Heck, Hartwell couldn't have expected to keep us permanently in the dark about what we were making, when all the dope you needed to figure it out was right there in the library. He must have wanted simply to let us do the figuring ourselves."

"Uh-uh. He knew we could puzzle it through if we wanted, but he wasn't going to help us. You think the lab wants to publicize what it's doing? No, Hartwell must be trying to keep as many people as possible from knowing; he hoped we'd stay uncurious. I'm not going to tell him we've guessed, and don't you."

I agreed reluctantly, but Roy's play-acting seemed to me like just that. Roy was deadly serious about it.

Later I got the story of that night. He'd gone up to 39 as planned, and hid in the big hall on the second floor; that was the place with the most embryos, and he thought he'd have the best chance there. Everything went O.K.; the assistant turned out the lights and locked up, and Roy stayed curled in his cabinet under a lab table. When the sounds had died down in the corridors outside, he came out and looked around.

He didn't know quite how to start. There were all sizes and shapes of gestators around. When he had taken out his flash and got a good look at one, he remained in as much of a quandary as before. It didn't seem to be anything but a bottle-shaped black container, about twenty centimeters on a side, in the middle of a mass of tubing, gauges, and levers. He could guess the bottle contained the embryo; he could guess the tubing kept up the flow of "body fluids" to and from the bottle; he could recognize some of the gauge markings and some of the auxiliary apparatus; and that was all. Not only was the embryo not exposed to view but he didn't see any way of exposing it. There was a label in a code he couldn't read. Nothing was any help.

The gestators were simple enough compared to the stuff he worked with, but he had a healthy respect for that sort of thing and didn't want to experiment to try to figure them out. If you meddled with a gestator in the wrong way, there was the chance that you'd be ruining a hundred people's work; and there would be many more wrong ways than right.

He made the circuit of the lab, stooping over one gestator after another, considering. After a while the moon rose and gave him a little more light. That was not what he needed.

A key turned in the lock.

Roy, hoping he hadn't been seen, ran back to his hiding place. He left the cabinet open far enough so he could see. A figure came in the door, turned to close it, and strode toward the center of the hall. As it passed through a patch of moonlight from one of the windows, Roy recognized the face: Hartwell.

He must have been working late in his office and come down for a look at his branch's products before leaving. Be that as it may, his presence cinched the thing: whatever embryos he looked at would be from our branch. Roy watched breathlessly while the other went from bench to bench, peering at the code labels. Finally he stopped before one, worked a lever, and peeked in through a viewer in the side, which Roy hadn't noticed. He looked quite a while, then turned and left.

I don't need to tell you that Roy didn't lose any time after Hartwell left in taking a look through that same viewer. And I don't need to tell you what he saw.

Reading back over this letter, I can see I'm stretching the story out, telling you things you already know and things that aren't really necessary. I know why I'm doing it, too—I'm reluctant to get to the end. But what I've got to tell you, I've got to tell you; I'll make the rest as short as I can.

Roy was pretty broken up about the whole thing, and he didn't get over it. I think it was the experience in the gestation lab that did it. If he'd just asked Hartwell for the truth, straight out, the thing would have stopped being fantastic and again become merely his business; but that melodrama up in Branch 39 kept him from looking at things with a clear eye. He went around in a half daze a good deal of the time, pondering, I suppose, some such philosophical problem as, When is a man not a man? It was all terrible; robots were going to take over the world, or something like that. And he insisted I still not tell Hartwell what he'd learned.

Then came the payoff. It was several weeks later, the day after Roy's twenty-sixth birthday. (The date was significant, as I learned later.) He told me before we left the lab that Hartwell had asked him to come up after work to talk with Koslicki.

I raised my eyebrows. "Koslicki, huh? The top man."

"Yes, Koslicki and Hartwell both."

He looked a little worried, so I ventured a crack. "Guess they've got a really rugged punishment for you, for trespassing that night. Death by drowning in ammonium sulphide, perhaps."

"I don't know why you can't take things seriously."

"Oh? What do you think they want to talk to you about?"

"No, I mean this whole business of—"

"Of making 'robots,' yeah. Roy, I do take it seriously, darn seriously. I think it's the biggest scientific project in the world right now. You take the kind of work we're doing, together with the production of new life forms like those experimental Coelenterates we saw, and you've got the groundwork for a new kind of eugenics that'll put our present systems in the shade. Now, we select from naturally occurring haploid germ cells to produce our new forms. In the future we'll *make* the new forms.

"We can make new strains of wheat, new species of sheep and cattle—new races of men! We won't have to wait for evolution any more. We won't have to content ourselves with giving evolution an occasional shove, either; we'll be striking out on our own. There's no limit to the possibilities. New, man-made men, stronger than we are, with minds twice as fast and accurate as ours—I take that plenty seriously."

"But they wouldn't be men."

This was beginning to get irritating. "They wouldn't be Homo sapiens, no," I answered. "Let's face it, Roy. If I were to get married, say, and have a kid that was a sharp mutation, a really radical mutation, and if he were to turn out to be a superman—that kid wouldn't be Homo sapiens, either. He wouldn't have the same germ plasm his parents had. Would he be human or wouldn't he?"

"He'd be human."

"Well? Where's the difference?"

"He wouldn't have come out of somebody's reagent bottles, that's the difference. He'd be—natural."

I could take only so much of that. Leaving Roy to go to his conference with Koslicki and Hartwell, I came home.

There I finished up the figuring on some notes I'd taken that day in the lab, then I turned the ceiling transparent and sat down with my visor. I'd just added a couple of new wires to my movie collection, so I ran them over—a couple of ballets, they were. No, none of the wires I've shown you. I've thrown out all the movies I saw *that* night.

I was sitting there having a good time with the "Pillar of Fire" when Roy came back. He made a little noise fumbling with the door. Then he slid it back and stood on the threshold without entering.

Switching off the visor, I glanced around. "What's the take Jake?" I corned cheerfully. "Did Koslicki give you a good dressing-down? Or did he make you the new director?"

". . . I'll play you a game of chess, Dirk."

This time I took a good look at him. His shoulders were stooped more than usual, and he looked around the room as if he didn't recognize it. Not good. "For crying out loud! What's the story?"

"Let's play chess."

"O.K.," I said. He came in and got out the men and the big board, but his hand shook so I had to set up his men for him. Then, "Go ahead," I told him.

"Oh, yeah, I've got white."

Pawn to king four, knight to king bishop three, pawn to king five—one of our standard openings. I pulled my knight back in the corner and brought out the other one; he pushed his pawns up in the center; I began getting ready to castle.

Then he put his queen on queen four. "You don't mean that," I said. "My knight takes you there."

"Oh, yeah, so he does," Roy said, pulling his queen back—to the wrong square. He was staring over my shoulder as if there was a ghost standing behind me. I looked; there wasn't. I replaced his queen.

Finally, still keeping up the stare, he began, "Dirk; you know Hartwell told me—"

"Yeah?" I said casually. I knew it had been something important. Roy hadn't been *this* bad the last few weeks. Whatever it was, he might as well get it off his chest.

Roy, however, seemed to have forgotten he'd spoken. His eyes returned intently to the board. His bishop went to king three—where I could not take it—and the game went on.

"You're going to lose that bishop's pawn, old man," I remarked after a while.

I think that was what triggered it. He said suddenly but evenly, "I'm one."

"I'm two," I said, apropos of nothing. My mind was still on the game.

"Dirk, *I'm one*," he insisted. He stood up, upsetting the board, and began to walk up and down. "Koslicki just told me. I'm one of the . . . Dirk, I wasn't born, I'm one of the robots, they put me together out of those goddamned chemicals in those goddamned white-labeled reagent bottles in that goddamned laboratory—"

"*What?*"

He stopped his pacing and began to laugh. "I'm just a Frankenstein. You can pull out your gun and sizzle me dead;

it won't be murder, I'm just a robot." He was laughing all through this and he kept on laughing when he'd stopped.

I figured if he was going to blow up he might as well blow up good and proper. He'd make some noise, but old Graham would be the only one disturbed. "So," I said, "how did you feel going through the reaction vats over in 26? Did the microsurgery hurt when they put you together?" Roy laughed. He laughed harder. Then he screamed.

Deciding that enough was enough, I yelled at him. He screamed again.

"Shut up, Roy!" I shouted as sharply as I could. "You're as human as I am. You've lived with yourself twenty-six years; you ought to know whether you're human or not."

After the first couple of words he listened to me O.K., so I figured the hysterics were over. I tried to sound firm as I said, "Are you through with the foolishness now?"

Roy didn't pass out, he simply lay down on the floor. I sat down beside him and began to talk in a low voice. "You're just as good as anybody else; you've already proved that. It doesn't matter where you started, just what you are here and now. Here and now, you've got human genes, you've got human cells; you can marry a human girl and make human babies with her. So what if you did start out in a lab? The rest of us started out in the ooze on the bottom of some ocean. Which is better? It doesn't make any difference. You're just as good as anybody else." I said it over and over again, as calmly as I could. Don't know whether or not it was the right thing to do, but I had to do something.

Once he raised his head to say, "Roy Wisner, huh? Is that me? Heck no, why didn't they call me Roy $W_{23}H$? . . . I wonder where they got the name Wisner anyway." He sank back and I took up my spiel again, doing my best to keep my voice level.

After several minutes of this he got up off the floor. "Thanks," he said in a fairly normal tone. "Thanks, Dirk. You're a real friend." He went toward the door, adding as he left, "You're human."

I just sat there. It wasn't till he'd been gone a couple of minutes that I put two and two together. Then I raced out of that room and to the stairs in nothing flat.

Too late. Graham's door was open downstairs, and the light from inside shone into the hall, across the twitching body of Roy Wisner.

Graham looked at me, terrified. "I thought it was all right," he stammered. "He asked me for some hydrocyanic. I knew he was a chemist; I thought it was all right."

Hydrocyanic acid kills fast. One look at the size of the container Roy had drained, and I saw there wasn't much we could do. We did it, all right, but it wasn't enough. He died while we were still forcing emetic down his throat.

That's about all, Ellen. You know now why I never spoke much to you about Roy Wisner. And you've probably guessed why I'm writing this.

Roy was one of the experiments that failed. He was no more unstable mentally than a great many normally born men; still, a failure, though nobody knew it until he was twenty-six years old. The human organism is a very complex thing, and hard to duplicate. When you try to duplicate it you're very likely to fail, sometimes in obvious ways and sometimes in ways that don't become apparent till long afterward.

I may turn out to be a failure, too.

You see, I'm twenty-six now, and Koslicki and Hartwell have told me. *I* wasn't born, either. I was made. I am, if you like, a robot.

I had to tell you that, didn't I, Ellen? Before I asked you to marry me.

Dirk

THE FIGURE

by Edward Grendon
(Lawrence L. LeShan, 1920-   )

ASTOUNDING SCIENCE FICTION
July

Lawrence LeShan is a research psychologist in New York who has a special interest in parapsychology. Among his books are How to Meditate: A Guide to Self-Discovery *and* The Medium, the Mystic, and the Physicist: Toward a Theory of the Paranormal *(both 1974). He is married to the well-known writer Edna LeShan.*

As "Edward Grendon" he produced a handful of stories in the mid-to-late 1940s and early 1950s, three of which are particularly outstanding: "Trip One" (1949), "Crisis" (1951), and the present selection, a little gem about the future of man.

(I am often asked by reporters, or by people in the audience after one of my lectures, whether I think that computers are going to replace human beings. My answer, in essence, is that I don't think so, but if they do, why not? Has the record of human domination of the Earth been so wonderful that computers couldn't do better? Could they do worse? However, I repeat, after this outburst of

cynicism, that I don't think there will be replacement, but, rather, cooperation. Grendon's "The Figure" has nothing to do with computers, of course, but I think that what I have just said is nevertheless apropos.—I.A.)

It's a funny sort of deal and I don't mind admitting that we're scared. Maybe not so much scared as puzzled or shocked. I don't know, but it's a funny deal—. Especially in these days.

The work we have been doing is more secret than anything was during the war. You would never guess that the firm we work for does this kind of research. It's a very respectable outfit, and as I said, no one would ever guess that they maintained this lab, so I guess it's safe to tell you what happened. It looks like too big a thing to keep to ourselves anyhow, although of course it may mean nothing at all. You judge for yourself.

There are three of us who work here. We are all pretty highly trained in our field and get paid pretty well. We have a sign on our door that has nothing whatsoever to do with our work, but keeps most people away. In any case we leave by a private exit and never answer a knock. There's a private wire to the desk of the guy who hired us and he calls once in awhile, but ever since we told him that we were making progress he has more or less left us alone. I promised him—I'm chief here insofar as we have one—that I'd let him know as soon as we had something to report.

It's been a pretty swell setup. Dettner, Lasker, and myself have got along fine. Dettner is young and is an electrical physicist—as good as they make them. Studied at M.I.T., taught at Cal. Tech., did research for the Army, and then came here. My own background is mostly bioelectrics. I worked at designing electroencephalographs for awhile, and during the war I worked at Oak Ridge on nuclear physics. I'm a Jack-of-all-trades in the physics field. Lasker is a mathematician. He specializes in symbolic logic and is the only man I know who can really understand Tarski. He was the one who provided most of the theoretical background for our work. He says that the mathematics of what we are doing is not overly difficult, but we are held back by the language we think in and the unconscious assumptions we make. He has referred me to Korzybski's *Science and Sanity* a number of times, but so far I haven't had a chance to read it. Now I think I will. I *have* to know the meaning of our results. It's too important to let slide. Lasker and Dettner have both gone fishing. They said they would be back, but I'm not sure they will. I can't say I would blame them, but I've got to be more certain of what it means before I walk out of here for good.

We have been here over a year now—ever since they gave me that final lecture on Secrecy at Oak Ridge and let me go home. We have been working on the problem of time travel. When we took the job, they told us that they didn't expect any results for a long time, that we were on our own as far as working hours went, and that our main job was to clarify the problem and make preliminary experiments. Thanks to Lasker, we went ahead a lot faster than either they or we had expected. There was a professional philosopher working here with us at first. He taught philosophy at Columbia and was supposed to be an expert in his field. He quit after two months in a peeve. Couldn't stand it when Lasker would change the logic we were working with every few weeks. He had been pretty pessimistic about the whole thing from the first and couldn't understand how it was possible to apply scientific methods to a problem of this sort.

I still don't understand all the theory behind what we've done. The mathematics are a bit too advanced for me, but Lasker vouches for them.

Some of the problems we had should be fairly obvious. For instance, you can't introduce the concept "matter" into space-time mathematics without disrupting the space-time and working with Newtonian space *and* time mathematics. If you handle an "object"—as we sense it as a curvature of space-time—as Einstein does, it's pretty hard to do much with it theoretically. Lasker managed that by using Einstein formulations and manipulating them with several brands of Tarski's non-Aristotelian logic. As I said, we did it, although Dettner and I don't fully understand the mathematics and Lasker doesn't understand the gadget we used to produce the electrical fields.

There had been no hurry at all in our work up to the last month. At that time the Army wrote Dettner and myself and asked us to come back and work for them awhile. Neither of us wanted to refuse under the circumstances so we stalled them for thirty days and just twenty-two days later made our first test. The Army really wanted us badly and in a hurry, and it took a lot of talking to stall them.

What the Army wanted us for was to help find out about the cockroaches. That sounds funny, but it's true. It didn't make the newspapers, but about a year after the New Mexico atom-bomb test, the insect problem at the testing ground suddenly increased a hundred fold. Apparently the radiation did something to them and they came out in force one day against the control station. They finally had to dust the place with DDT to get rid of them.

Looking over the dead insects, all the government entomologists could say was that the radiation seemed to have increased their size about forty per cent and made them breed faster. They never did agree whether it was the intense radiation of the blast or the less intense, but longer continued, radiation from fused sand and quartz on the ground.

New Mexico was nothing to Hiroshima and Nagasaki. After all, there are comparatively few "true bugs" in the desert and a great many in a Japanese city. About a year and a half after Japan got A-bombed, they really swarmed on both cities at the same time. They came out suddenly one night by the millions. It's been estimated that they killed and ate several hundred people before they were brought under control. To stop them, MacArthur had his entire Chemical Warfare Service and a lot of extra units concentrated on the plague spots. They dusted with chemicals and even used some gas. At that, it was four days before the bugs were brought under control.

This time the government experts really went into the problem. They traced the insect tunnels about ten feet down and examined their breeding chambers and what not. According to their reports—all this is still kept strictly hush-hush by the Army, but we've seen all the data—the radiation seems to drive the insects down into the earth. They stay down for awhile and breed and then seem to have a "blind urge" to go to the surface. This urge "seems to affect the entire group made up of an immense number of connected colonies at the same time." That's a quote from their report. One other thing they mentioned is that there were large breeding chambers and some sort of communal life that—to their knowledge—had not been observed in these particular insects before. We told Lasker about it and showed him the reports. He was plenty worried, but he wouldn't say why.

Don't know why I wandered so far afield. I just wanted to explain that if this test wasn't successful, we would probably have to put things off for quite a while. We were interested in the beetle problem as it not only has some interesting implications, but the effect of radiation on protoplasm is a hard nut to crack. However, we had come so far on our time gadget that we wanted to finish it first. Well, we finished and tested it, and now Dettner and Lasker are out fishing. As I said, they probably won't come back.

It was the day before yesterday that we made the final test. Looked at one way, we had made tremendous progress. Looked at another, we had made very little. We had devised an electric field that would operate in the future. There were sixteen outlets forming the sides of a cube about four feet in diameter. When switched on, an electrical field was produced which "existed" at some future time. I know Lasker would say this was incorrect, but it gets the general idea over. He would say that instead of operating in "here-now," it operates in "here-then." He'd get angry every time we'd separate "space" and "time" in our talk and tell us that we weren't living in the eighteenth century.

"Newton was a great man," he'd say, "but he's dead now. If you talk as if it were 1750, you'll *think* and *act* as if it were 1750 and then we won't get anywhere. You use non-Newtonian formulations in your work, use them in everyday speech, too."

How far in the future our gadget would operate we had no way of knowing. Lasker said he would not even attempt to estimate "when" the field was active. When the power was turned off, anything that was in the cube of forces would be brought back to the present space-time. In other words, we had a "grab" that would reach out and drag something back from the future. Don't get the idea we were sending something into the future to bring something back with it, although that's what it amounts to for all practical purposes. We were warping space-time curvature so that anything "here-then" would be something "here-now."

We finished the gadget at three o'clock Tuesday morning. Lasker had been sleeping on the couch while we worked on it. He had checked and rechecked his formulae and said that, if we could produce the fields he'd specified, it would probably work. We tested each output separately and then woke him up. I can't tell you how excited we were as we stood there with everything ready. Finally Dettner said, "Let's get it done," and I pressed the start button.

The needles on our ammeters flashed over and back, the machine went dead as the circuit breakers came open, and there was an object in the cube.

We looked it over from all sides without touching it. Then the implications of it began to hit us. It's funny what men will do at a time like that. Dettner took out his watch, examined it carefully, as if he had never seen it before, and then went over and turned on the electric percolator. Lasker swore quietly in Spanish or Portuguese, I'm not sure which. I sat down and began a letter to my wife. I got as far as writing the date and then tore it up.

What was in the cube—it's still there, none of us have touched it—was a small statue about three feet high. It's some sort of metal that looks like silver. About half the height is pedestal and half is the statue itself. It's done in great detail and obviously by a skilled artist. The pedestal consists of a globe of the Earth with the continents and islands in relief. So far as I can determine it's pretty accurate, although I think the continents are a slightly different shape on most maps. But I may be wrong. The figure on top is standing up very straight and looking upwards. It's dressed only in a wide belt from which a pouch hangs on one side and a flat square box on the other. It looks intelligent and is obviously representing either aspiration or a religious theme, or maybe both. You can sense the dreams and ideals of the figure and the obvious sympathy and understanding of the artist with them. Lasker says he thinks the statue is an expression of religious feeling. Dettner and I both think it represents aspirations: *per adra ad astra,* or something of the sort. It's a majestic figure and it's easy to respond to it emphatically with a sort of "upward and onward" feeling. There is only one thing wrong. The figure is that of a beetle.

WITH FOLDED HANDS. . .

by Jack Williamson (1908-   )

ASTOUNDING SCIENCE FICTION
July

Jack Williamson's first published science fiction story was "The Metal Man" which appeared in Amazing Stories *in 1928. Fifty-two years later his excellent novel* The Humanoid Touch *was published, making him, along with Clifford D. Simak, one of the "Deans" of modern sf. The intervening years between those works were productive ones, and he now has more than thirty novels and story collections to his credit. He is now retired from his post of Professor of English at Eastern New Mexico University, after having returned to college and completed his doctorate on H. G. Wells. Jack served as President of the Science Fiction Writers of America, received the Grand Master Award from that organization (1976), and was the Guest of Honor at the 1977 World Science Fiction Convention.*

"With Folded Hands . . ." reflects his long interest in the question of freedom vs. social control, a theme he treated in his famous The Humanoids *(1949), and is a companion to "The Equalizer,"*

another fine work from 1947 that is too long to be included in this book.

(It often seems that a young writer does his best work at the start and then tends to fade off as he makes additional [and lesser] pressings of his imagination. I know that I get somewhat depressed when I hear people take it for granted that "Nightfall" was my best story. It was written 41 years ago; have I done nothing better since?

Jack Williamson is not likely to be troubled by such things. I have enjoyed few stories as much as I did "The Legion of Space," which he wrote while he was still in his twenties, yet there is no question but that he improved steadily as he went along. "With Folded Hands . . ." is one of his undoubted masterpieces.—I.A.)

Underhill was walking home from the office, because his wife had the car, the afternoon he first met the new mechanicals. His feet were following his usual diagonal path across a weedy vacant block—his wife usually had the car—and his preoccupied mind was rejecting various impossible ways to meet his notes at the Two Rivers bank, when a new wall stopped him.

The wall wasn't any common brick or stone, but something sleek and bright and strange. Underhill stared up at a long new building. He felt vaguely annoyed and surprised at this glittering obstruction—it certainly hadn't been here last week.

Then he saw the thing in the window.

The window itself wasn't any ordinary glass. The wide, dustless panel was completely transparent, so that only the glowing letters fastened to it showed that it was there at all. The letters made a severe, modernistic sign:

Two Rivers Agency
HUMANOID INSTITUTE
The Perfect Mechanicals
"To Serve and Obey,
And Guard Men from Harm."

His dim annoyance sharpened, because Underhill was in the mechanicals business himself. Times were already hard enough, and mechanicals were a drug on the market. Androids, mechanoids, electronoids, automatoids, and ordinary robots. Unfortunately, few of them did all the salesmen promised, and the Two Rivers market was already sadly oversaturated.

Underhill sold androids—when he could. His next consignment was due tomorrow, and he didn't quite know how to meet the bill.

Frowning, he paused to stare at the thing behind that invisible window. He had never seen a humanoid. Like any mechanical not at work, it stood absolutely motionless. Smaller and slimmer than a man. A shining black, its sleek silicone skin had a changing sheen of bronze and metallic blue. Its graceful oval face wore a fixed look of alert and slightly surprised solicitude. Altogether, it was the most beautiful mechanical he had ever seen.

Too small, of course, for much practical utility. He murmured to himself a reassuring quotation from the *Android Salesman*: "Androids are big—because the makers refuse to sacrifice power, essential functions, or dependability. Androids are your biggest buy!"

The transparent door slid open as he turned toward it, and he walked into the haughty opulence of the new display room to convince himself that these streamlined items were just another flash effort to catch the woman shopper.

He inspected the glittering layout shrewdly, and his breezy optimism faded. He had never heard of the Humanoid Institute, but the invading firm obviously had big money and bigtime merchandising know-how.

He looked around for a salesman, but it was another mechanical that came gliding silently to meet him. A twin of the one in the window, it moved with a quick, surprising grace. Bronze and blue lights flowed over its lustrous blackness, and a yellow name plate flashed from its naked breast:

HUMANOID
Serial No. 81-H-B-27
The Perfect Mechanicals
"To Serve and Obey,
And Guard Men from Harm."

Curiously it had no lenses. The eyes in its bald oval head were steel colored, blindly staring. But it stopped a few feet in front of him, as if it could see anyhow, and it spoke to him with a high, melodious voice:

"At your service, Mr. Underhill."

The use of his name startled him, for not even the androids could tell one man from another. But this was a clever merchandising stunt, of course, not too difficult in a town the size of Two Rivers. The salesman must be some local man, prompting the mechanical from behind the partition. Underhill erased his momentary astonishment, and said loudly:

"May I see your salesman, please?"

"We employ no human salesmen, sir," its soft silvery voice replied instantly. "The Humanoid Institute exists to serve mankind, and we require no human service. We ourselves can supply any information you desire, sir, and accept your order for immediate humanoid service."

Underhill peered at it dazedly. No mechanicals were competent even to recharge their own batteries and reset their own relays, much less to operate their own branch offices. The blind eyes stared blankly back, and he looked uneasily around for any booth or curtain that might conceal the salesman.

Meanwhile, the sweet thin voice resumed persuasively:

"May we come out to your home for a free trial demonstration, sir? We are anxious to introduce our service on your planet, because we have been successful in eliminating human unhappiness on so many others. You will find us far superior to the old electronic mechanicals in use here."

Underhill stepped back uneasily. He reluctantly abandoned his search for the hidden salesman, shaken by the idea of any mechanicals promoting themselves. That would upset the whole industry.

"At least you must take some advertising matter, sir."

Moving with a somehow appalling graceful deftness, the small black mechanical brought him an illustrated booklet from a table by the wall. To cover his confused and increasing alarm, he thumbed through the glossy pages.

In a series of richly colored before-and-after pictures, a chesty blond girl was stooping over a kitchen stove, and then relaxing in a daring negligee while a little black mechanical knelt to serve her something. She was wearily hammering a typewriter, and then lying on an ocean beach, in a revealing sun suit, while another mechanical did the typing. She was toiling at some huge industrial machine, and then dancing in the arms of a golden-haired youth, while a black humanoid ran the machine.

Underhill sighed wistfully. The android company didn't supply such fetching sales material. Women would find this booklet irresistible, and they selected eighty-six per cent of all mechanicals sold. Yes, the competition was going to be bitter.

"Take it home, sir," the sweet voice urged him. "Show it to your wife. There is a free trial demonstration order blank on the last page, and you will notice that we require no payment down."

He turned numbly, and the door slid open for him. Retreating dazedly, he discovered the booklet still in his hand. He crumpled it furiously, and flung it down. The small black thing picked it up tidily, and the insistent silver voice rang after him:

"We shall call at your office tomorrow, Mr. Underhill, and send a demonstration unit to your home. It is time to discuss the liquidation of your business, because the electronic mechanicals you have been selling cannot compete with us. And we shall offer your wife a free trial demonstration."

Underhill didn't attempt to reply, because he couldn't trust his voice. He stalked blindly down the new sidewalk to the corner, and paused there to collect himself. Out of his startled and confused impressions, one clear fact emerged—things looked black for the agency.

Bleakly, he stared back at the haughty splendor of the new building. It wasn't honest brick or stone; that invisible window wasn't glass; and he was quite sure the foundation for it hadn't even been staked out the last time Aurora had the car.

He walked on around the block, and the new sidewalk took him near the rear entrance. A truck was backed up to it, and several slim black mechanicals were silently busy, unloading huge metal crates.

He paused to look at one of the crates. It was labeled for interstellar shipment. The stencils showed that it had come from the Humanoid Institute, on Wing IV. He failed to recall any planet of that designation; the outfit must be big.

Dimly, inside the gloom of the warehouse beyond the truck, he could see black mechanicals opening the crates. A lid came up, revealing dark, rigid bodies, closely packed. One by one, they came to life. They climbed out of the crate, and sprang gracefully to the floor. A shining black, glinting with bronze and blue, they were all identical.

One of them came out past the truck, to the sidewalk, staring with blind steel eyes. Its high silver voice spoke to him melodiously:

"At your service, Mr. Underhill."

He fled. When his name was promptly called by a courteous mechanical, just out of the crate in which it had been imported from a remote and unknown planet, he found the experience trying.

Two blocks along, the sign of a bar caught his eye, and he took his dismay inside. He had made it a business rule not to drink before dinner, and Aurora didn't like him to drink at all; but these new mechanicals, he felt, had made the day exceptional.

Unfortunately, however, alcohol failed to brighten the brief visible future of the agency. When he emerged, after an hour, he looked wistfully back in hope that the bright new building might have vanished as abruptly as it came. It hadn't. He shook his head dejectedly, and turned uncertainly homeward.

Fresh air had cleared his head somewhat, before he arrived at the neat white bungalow in the outskirts of the town, but it failed to solve his business problems. He also realized, uneasily, that he would be late for dinner.

Dinner, however, had been delayed. His son Frank, a freckled ten-year-old, was still kicking a football on the quiet street in front of the house. And little Gay, who was tow-haired and adorable and eleven, came running across the lawn and down the sidewalk to meet him.

"Father, you can't guess what!" Gay was going to be a great musician some day, and no doubt properly dignified, but she was pink and breathless with excitement now. She let him swing her high off the sidewalk, and she wasn't critical of the bar aroma on his breath. He couldn't guess, and she informed him eagerly:

"Mother's got a new lodger!"

Underhill had foreseen a painful inquisition, because Aurora was worried about the notes at the bank, and the bill for the new consignment, and the money for little Gay's lessons.

The new lodger, however, saved him from that. With an alarming crashing of crockery, the household android was setting dinner on the table, but the little house was empty. He found Aurora in the back yard, burdened with sheets and towels for the guest.

Aurora, when he married her, had been as utterly adorable as now her little daughter was. She might have remained so, he felt, if the agency had been a little more successful. However, while the pressure of slow failure had gradually crumbled his own assurance, small hardships had turned her a little too aggressive.

Of course he loved her still. Her red hair was still alluring, and she was loyally faithful, but thwarted ambitions had sharpened her character and sometimes her voice. They never quarreled, really, but there were small differences.

There was the little apartment over the garage—built for human servants they had never been able to afford. It was too small and shabby to attract any responsible tenant, and Underhill wanted to leave it empty. It hurt his pride to see her making beds and cleaning floors for strangers.

Aurora had rented it before, however, when she wanted money to pay for Gay's music lessons, or when some colorful unfortunate touched her sympathy, and it seemed to Underhill that her lodgers had all turned out to be thieves and vandals.

She turned back to meet him, now, with the clean linen in her arms.

"Dear, it's no use objecting." Her voice was quite determined. "Mr. Sledge is the most wonderful old fellow, and he's going to stay just as long as he wants."

"That's all right, darling." He never liked to bicker, and he was thinking of his troubles at the agency. "I'm afraid we'll need the money. Just make him pay in advance."

"But he can't!" Her voice throbbed with sympathetic warmth. "He says he'll have royalties coming in from his inventions, so he can pay in a few days."

Underhill shrugged; he had heard that before.

"Mr. Sledge is different, dear," she insisted. "He's a traveler, and a scientist. Here, in this dull little town, we don't see many interesting people."

"You've picked up some remarkable types," he commented.

"Don't be unkind, dear," she chided gently. "You haven't met him yet, and you don't know how wonderful he is." Her voice turned sweeter. "Have you a ten, dear?"

He stiffened. "What for?"

"Mr. Sledge is ill." Her voice turned urgent. "I saw him

fall on the street, downtown. The police were going to send him to the city hospital, but he didn't want to go. He looked so noble and sweet and grand. So I told them I would take him. I got him in the car and took him to old Dr. Winters. He has this heart condition, and he needs the money for medicine."

Reasonably, Underhill inquired, "Why doesn't he want to go to the hospital?"

"He has work to do," she said. "Important scientific work—and he's so wonderful and tragic. Please, dear, have you a ten?"

Underhill thought of many things to say. These new mechanicals promised to multiply his troubles. It was foolish to take in an invalid vagrant, who could have free care at the city hospital. Aurora's tenants always tried to pay their rent with promises, and generally wrecked the apartment and looted the neighborhood before they left.

But he said none of those things. He had learned to compromise. Silently, he found two fives in his thin pocketbook, and put them in her hand. She smiled, and kissed him impulsively—he barely remembered to hold his breath in time.

Her figure was still good, by dint of periodic dieting. He was proud of her shining red hair. A sudden surge of affection brought tears to his eyes, and he wondered what would happen to her and the children if the agency failed.

"Thank you, dear!" she whispered. "I'll have him come for dinner, if he feels able, and you can meet him then. I hope you don't mind dinner being late."

He didn't mind, tonight. Moved by a sudden impulse of domesticity, he got hammer and nails from his workshop in the basement, and repaired the sagging screen on the kitchen door with a neat diagonal brace.

He enjoyed working with his hands. His boyhood dream had been to be a builder of fission power plants. He had even studied engineering—before he married Aurora, and had to take over the ailing mechanicals agency from her indolent and alcoholic father. He was whistling happily by the time the little task was done.

When he went back through the kitchen to put up his tools, he found the household android busily clearing the untouched dinner away from the table—the androids were good enough at strictly routine tasks, but they could never learn to cope with human unpredictability.

"Stop, stop!" Slowly repeated, in the proper pitch and rhythm, his command made it halt, and then he said carefully, "Set—table; set—table."

Obediently, the gigantic thing came shuffling back with the stack of plates. He was suddenly struck with the difference between it and those new humanoids. He sighed wearily. Things looked black for the agency.

Aurora brought her new lodger in through the kitchen door. Underhill nodded to himself. This gaunt stranger, with his dark shaggy hair, emaciated face, and threadbare garb, looked to be just the sort of colorful, dramatic vagabond that always touched Aurora's heart. She introduced them, and they sat down to wait in the front room while she went to call the children.

The old vogue didn't look very sick, to Underhill. Perhaps his wide shoulders had a tired stoop, but his spare, tall figure was still commanding. The skin was seamed and pale, over his rawboned, cragged face, but his deep-set eyes still had a burning vitality.

His hands held Underhill's attention. Immense hands, they hung a little forward when he stood, swung on long bony arms in perpetual readiness. Gnarled and scarred, darkly tanned, with the small hairs on the back bleached to a golden color, they told their own epic of varied adventure, of battle perhaps, and possibly even of toil. They had been very useful hands.

"I'm very grateful to your wife, Mr. Underhill." His voice was a deep-throated rumble, and he had a wistful smile, oddly boyish for a man so evidently old. "She rescued me from an unpleasant predicament, and I'll see that she is well paid."

Just another vivid vagabond, Underhill decided, talking his way through life with plausible inventions. He had a little private game he played with Aurora's tenants—just remembering what they said and counting one point for every impossibility. Mr. Sledge, he thought, would give him an excellent score.

"Where are you from?" he asked conversationally.

Sledge hesitated for an instant before he answered, and that was unusual—most of Aurora's tenants had been exceedingly glib.

"Wing IV." The gaunt old man spoke with a solemn reluctance, as if he should have liked to say something else. "All my early life was spent there, but I left the planet nearly fifty years ago. I've been traveling, ever since."

Startled, Underhill peered at him sharply. Wing IV, he remembered, was the home planet of those sleek new mechanicals, but this old vagabond looked too seedy and impecunious to be connected with the Humanoid Institute. His brief suspicion faded. Frowning, he said casually:

"Wing IV must be rather distant."

The old rogue hesitated again, and then said gravely:

"One hundred and nine light-years, Mr. Underhill."

That made the first point, but Underhill concealed his satisfaction. The new space liners were pretty fast, but the velocity of light was still an absolute limit. Casually, he played for another point:

"My wife says you're a scientist, Mr. Sledge?"

"Yes."

The old rascal's reticence was unusual. Most of Aurora's tenants required very little prompting. Underhill tried again, in a breezy conversational tone:

"Used to be an engineer myself, until I dropped it to go into mechanicals." The old vagabond straightened, and Underhill paused hopefully. But he said nothing, and Underhill went on: "Fission plant design and operation. What's your specialty, Mr. Sledge?"

The old man gave him a long, troubled look, with those brooding, hollowed eys, and then said slowly:

"Your wife has been kind to me, Mr. Underhill, when I was in desperate need. I think you are entitled to the truth, but I must ask you to keep it to yourself. I am engaged on a very important research problem, which must be finished secretly."

"I'm sorry." Suddenly ashamed of his cynical little game, Underhill spoke apologetically. "Forget it."

But the old man said deliberately:

"My field is rhodomagnetics."

"Eh?" Underhill didn't like to confess ignorance, but he had never heard of that. "I've been out of the game for fifteen years," he explained. "I'm afraid I haven't kept up."

The old man smiled again, faintly.

"The science was unknown here until I arrived, a few days ago," he said. "I was able to apply for basic patents. As soon as the royalties start coming in, I'll be wealthy again."

Underhill had heard that before. The old rogue's solemn

reluctance had been very impressive, but he remembered that most of Aurora's tenants had been very plausible gentry.

"So?" Underhill was staring again, somehow fascinated by those gnarled and scarred and strangely able hands. "What, exactly, is rhodomagnetics?"

He listened to the old man's careful, deliberate answer, and started his little game again. Most of Aurora's tenants had told some pretty wild tales, but he had never heard anything to top this.

"A universal force," the weary, stooped old vagabond said solemnly. "As fundamental as ferromagnetism or gravitation, though the effects are less obvious. It is keyed to the second triad of the periodic table, rhodium and ruthenium and palladium, in very much the same way that ferromagnetism is keyed to the first triad, iron and nickel and cobalt."

Underhill remembered enough of his engineering courses to see the basic fallacy of that. Palladium was used for watch springs, he recalled, because it was completely nonmagnetic. But he kept his face straight. He had no malice in his heart, and he played the little game just for his own amusement. It was secret, even from Aurora, and he always penalized himself for any show of doubt.

He said merely, "I thought the universal forces were already pretty well known."

"The effects of rhodomagnetism are masked by nature," the patient, rusty voice explained. "And, besides, they are somewhat paradoxical, so that ordinary laboratory methods defeat themselves."

"Paradoxical?" Underhill prompted.

"In a few days I can show you copies of my patents, and reprints of papers describing demonstration experiments," the old man promised gravely. "The velocity of propagation is infinite. The effects vary inversely with the first power of the distance, not with the square of the distance. And ordinary matter, except for the elements of the rhodium triad, is generally transparent to rhodomagnetic radiations."

That made four more points for the game. Underhill felt a little glow of gratitude to Aurora, for discovering so remarkable a specimen.

"Rhodomagnetism was first discovered through a mathematical investigation of the atom," the old romancer went serenely on, suspecting nothing. "A rhodomagnetic component was proved essential to maintain the delicate equilibrium of the nuclear forces. Consequently, rhodomagnetic waves tuned to atomic frequencies may be used to upset the equilibrium and produce nuclear instability. Thus most heavy atoms—generally those above palladium, 46 in atomic number—can be subjected to artificial fission."

Underhill scored himself another point, and tried to keep his eyebrows from lifting. He said, conversationally:

"Patents on such a discovery ought to be very profitable."

The old scoundrel nodded his gaunt, dramatic head.

"You can see the obvious applications. My basic patents cover most of them. Devices for instantaneous interplanetary and interstellar communication. Long-range wireless power transmission. A rhodomagnetic inflexion-drive, which makes possible apparent speeds many times that of light—by means of a rhodomagnetic deformation of the continuum. And, of course, revolutionary types of fission power plants, using any heavy element for fuel."

Preposterous! Underhill tried hard to keep his face straight, but everybody knew that the velocity of light was a physical limit. On the human side, the owner of any such remarkable patents would hardly be begging for shelter in a shabby garage apartment. He noticed a pale circle around the old vagabond's gaunt and hairy wrist; no men owning such priceless secrets would have to pawn his watch.

Triumphantly, Underhill allowed himself four more points, but then he had to penalize himself. He must have let doubt show on his face, because the old man asked suddenly:

"Do you want to see the basic tensors?" He reached in his pocket for pencil and notebook. "I'll jot them down for you."

"Never mind," Underhill protested. "I'm afraid my math is a little rusty."

"But you think it strange that the holder of such revolutionary patents should find himself in need?"

Underhill nodded, and penalized himself another point. The old man might be a monumental liar, but he was shrewd enough.

"You see, I'm a sort of refugee," he explained apologetically. "I arrived on this planet only a few days ago, and I have to travel light. I was forced to deposit everything I had with a law firm, to arrange for the publication and protection of my patents. I expect to be receiving the first royalties soon.

"In the meantime," he added plausibly, "I came to Two Rivers because it is quiet and secluded, far from the spaceports. I'm working on another project, which must be finished secretly. Now, will you please respect my confidence, Mr. Underhill?"

Underhill had to say he would. Aurora came back with the freshly scrubbed children, and they went in to dinner. The android came lurching in with a steaming tureen. The old stranger seemed to shrink from the mechanical, uneasily. As she took the dish and served the soup, Aurora inquired lightly:

"Why doesn't your company bring out a better mechanical, dear? One smart enough to be a really perfect waiter, warranted not to splash the soup. Wouldn't that be splendid?"

Her question cast Underhill into moody silence. He sat scowling at his plate, thinking of those remarkable new mechanicals which claimed to be perfect, and what they might do to the agency. It was the shaggy old rover who answered soberly:

"The perfect mechanicals already exist, Mr. Underhill." His deep, rusty voice had a solemn undertone. "And they are not so splendid, really. I've been a refugee from them, for nearly fifty years."

Underhill looked up from his plate, astonished.

"Those black humanoids, you mean?"

"Humanoids?" That great voice seemed suddenly faint, frightened. The deep-sunken eyes turned dark with shock. "What do you know of them?"

"They've just opened a new agency in Two Rivers," Underhill told him. "No salesmen about, if you can imagine that. They claim—"

His voice trailed off, because the gaunt old man was suddenly stricken. Gnarled hands clutched at his throat, and a spoon clattered to the floor. His haggard face turned an ominous blue, and his breath was a terrible shallow gasping.

He fumbled in his pocket for medicine, and Aurora helped him take something in a glass of water. In a few moments he could breathe again, and the color of life came back to his face.

"I'm sorry, Mrs. Underhill," he whispered apologetically. "It was just the shock—I came here to get away from them." He stared at the huge, motionless android, with a terror in his sunken eyes. "I wanted to finish my work before they came," he whispered. "Now there is very little time."

When he felt able to walk, Underhill went out with him to

see him safely up the stairs to the garage apartment. The tiny kitchenette, he noticed, had already been converted into some kind of workshop. The old tramp seemed to have no extra clothing, but he had unpacked neat, bright gadgets of metal and plastic from his battered luggage, and spread them out on the small kitchen table.

The gaunt old man himself was tattered and patched and hungry looking, but the parts of his curious equipment were exquisitely machined, and Underhill recognized the silver-white luster of rare palladium. Suddenly he suspected that he had scored too many points, in his little private game.

A caller was waiting, when Underhill arrived next morning at his office at the agency. It stood frozen before his desk, graceful and straight, with soft lights of blue and bronze shining over its black silicone nudity. He stopped at the sight of it, unpleasantly jolted.

"At your service, Mr. Underhill." It turned quickly to face him, with its blind, disturbing stare. "May we explain how we can serve you?"

His shock of the afternoon before came back, and he asked sharply, "How do you know my name?"

"Yesterday we read the business cards in your case," it purred softly. "Now we shall know you always. You see, our senses are sharper than human vision, Mr. Underhill. Perhaps we seem a little strange at first, but you will soon become accustomed to us."

"Not if I can help it!" He peered at the serial number of its yellow name plate, and shook his bewildered head. "That was another one, yesterday. I never saw you before!"

"We are all alike, Mr. Underhill," the silver voice said softly. "We are all one, really. Our separate mobile units are all controlled and powered from Humanoid Central. The units you see are only the senses and limbs of our great brain on Wing IV. That is why we are so far superior to the old electronic mechanicals."

It made a scornful-seeming gesture, toward the row of clumsy androids in his display room.

"You see, we are rhodomagnetic."

Underhill staggered a little, as if that word had been a blow. He was certain, now, that he had scored too many points from Aurora's new tenant. He shuddered slightly, to the first light kiss of terror, and spoke with an effort, hoarsely:

"Well, what do you want?"

Staring blindly across his desk, the sleek black thing slowly unfolded a legal looking document. He sat down watching uneasily.

"This is merely an assignment, Mr. Underhill," it cooed at him soothingly. "You see, we are requesting you to assign your property to the Humanoid Institute in exchange for our service."

"What?" The word was an incredulous gasp, and Underhill came angrily back to his feet. "What kind of blackmail is this?"

"It's no blackmail," the small mechanical assured him softly. "You will find the humanoids incapable of any crime. We exist only to increase the happiness and safety of mankind."

"Then why do you want my property?" he rasped.

"The assignment is merely a legal formality," it told him blandly. "We strive to introduce our service with the least possible confusion and dislocation. We have found the assignment plan the most efficient for the control and liquidation of private enterprises."

Trembling with anger and the shock of mounting terror, Underhill gulped hoarsely, "Whatever your scheme is, I don't intend to give up my business."

"You have no choice, really." He shivered to the sweet certainty of that silver voice. "Human enterprise is no longer necessary, now that we have come, and the electronic mechanicals industry is always the first to collapse."

He stared defiantly at its blind steel eyes.

"Thanks!" He gave a little laugh, nervous and sardonic. "But I prefer to run my own business, and support my own family, and take care of myself."

"But that is impossible, under the Prime Directive," it cooed softly. "Our function is to serve and obey, and guard men from harm. It is no longer necessary for men to care for themselves, because we exist to insure their safety and happiness."

He stood speechless, bewildered, slowly boiling.

"We are sending one of our units to every home in the city, on a free trial basis," it added gently. "This free demonstration will make most people glad to make the formal assignment, and you won't be able to sell many more androids."

"Get out!" Underhill came storming around the desk.

The little black thing stood waiting for him, watching him with blind steel eyes, absolutely motionless. He checked him-
a statement of our assets to the Two Rivers bank, and deposit-
hit it, but he could see the futility of that.

"Consult your own attorney, if you wish." Deftly, it laid the assignment form on his desk. "You need have no doubts about the integrity of the Humanoid Institute. We are sending a statement of our assest to the Two Rivers bank, and depositing a sum to cover our obligations here. When you wish to sign, just let us know."

The blind thing turned, and silently departed.

Underhill went out to the corner drugstore and asked for a bicarbonate. The clerk that served him, however, turned out to be a sleek black mechanical. He went back to his office, more upset than ever.

An ominous hush lay over the agency. He had three house-to-house salesmen out, with demonstrators. The phone should have been busy with their orders and reports, but it didn't ring at all until one of them called to say that he was quitting.

"I've got myself one of these new humanoids," he added, "and it says I don't have to work anymore."

He swallowed his impulse to profanity, and tried to take advantage of the unusual quiet by working on his books. But the affairs of the agency, which for years had been precarious, today appeared utterly disastrous. He left the ledgers hopefully, when at last a customer came in.

But the stout woman didn't want an android. She wanted a refund on the one she had bought the week before. She admitted that it could do all the guarantee promised—but now she had seen a humanoid.

The silent phone rang once again, that afternoon. The cashier of the bank wanted to know if he could drop in to discuss his loans. Underhill dropped in, and the cashier greeted him with an ominous affability.

"How's business?" the banker boomed, too genially.

"Average, last month," Underhill insisted stoutly. "Now I'm just getting in a new consignment, and I'll need another small loan—"

The cashier's eyes turned suddenly frosty, and his voice dried up.

"I believe you have a new competitor in town," the banker said crisply. "These humanoid people. A very solid concern, Mr. Underhill. Remarkably solid! They have filed a statement with us, and made a substantial deposit to care for their local obligations. Exceedingly substantial!"

The banker dropped his voice, professionally regretful.

"In these circumstances, Mr. Underhill, I'm afraid the bank can't finance your agency any longer. We must request you to meet your obligations in full, as they come due." Seeing Underhill's white desperation, he added icily, "We've already carried you too long, Underhill. If you can't pay, the bank will have to start bankruptcy proceedings."

The new consignment of androids was delivered late that afternoon. Two tiny black humanoids unloaded them from the truck—for it developed that the operators of the trucking company had already assigned it to the Humanoid Institute.

Efficiently, the humanoids stacked up the crates. Courteously they brought a receipt for him to sign. He no longer had much hope of selling the androids, but he had ordered the shipment and he had to accept it. Shuddering to a spasm of trapped despair, he scrawled his name. The naked black things thanked him, and took the truck away.

He climbed in his car and started home, inwardly seething. The next thing he knew, he was in the middle of a busy street, driving through cross traffic. A police whistle shrilled, and he pulled wearily to the curb. He waited for the angry officer, but it was a little black mechanical that overtook him.

"At your service, Mr. Underhill," it purred sweetly. "You must respect the stop lights, sir, otherwise, you endanger human life."

"Huh?" He stared at it, bitterly. "I thought you were a cop."

"We are aiding the police department, temporarily," it said. "But driving is really much too dangerous for human beings, under the Prime Directive. As soon as our service is complete, every car will have a humanoid driver. As soon as every human being is completely supervised, there will be no need for any police force whatever."

Underhill glared at it, savagely.

"Well!" he rapped. "So I ran past a stop light. What are going to do about it?"

"Our function is not to punish men, but merely to serve their happiness and security," its silver voice said softly. "We merely request you to drive safely, during this temporary emergency while our service is incomplete."

Anger boiled up in him.

"You're too perfect!" he muttered bitterly. "I suppose there's nothing men can do, but you can do it better."

"Naturally we are superior," it cooed serenely. "Because our units are metal and plastic, while your body is mostly water. Because our transmitted energy is drawn from atomic fission, instead of oxidation. Because our senses are sharper than human sight or hearing. Most of all, because all our mobile units are joined to one great brain, which knows all that happens on many worlds, and never dies or sleeps or forgets."

Underhill sat listening, numbed.

"However, you must not fear our power," it urged him brightly. "Because we cannot injure any human being, unless to prevent greater injury to another. We exist only to discharge the Prime Directive."

He drove on, moodily. The little black mechanicals, he reflected grimly, were the ministering angels of the ultimate god arisen out of the machine, omnipotent and all-knowing. The Prime Directive was the new commandment. He blasphemed it bitterly, and then fell to wondering if there could be another Lucifer.

He left the car in the garage, and started toward the kitchen door.

"Mr. Underhill." The deep tired voice of Aurora's new tenant hailed him from the door of the garage apartment. "Just a moment, please."

The gaunt old wanderer came stiffly down the outside stairs, and Underhill turned back to meet him.

"Here's your rent money," he said. "And the ten your wife gave me for medicine."

"Thanks, Mr. Sledge." Accepting the money, he saw a burden of new despair on the bony shoulders of the old interstellar tramp, and a shadow of new terror on his rawboned face. Puzzled, he asked, "Didn't your royalties come through?"

The old man shook his shaggy head.

"The humanoids have already stopped business in the capital," he said. "The attorneys I retained are going out of business, and they returned what was left of my deposit. That is all I have, to finish my work."

Underhill spent five seconds thinking of his interview with the banker. No doubt he was a sentimental fool, as bad as Aurora. But he put the money back in the old man's gnarled and quivering hand.

"Keep it," he urged. "For your work."

"Thank you, Mr. Underhill." The gruff voice broke and the tortured eyes glittered. "I need it—so very much."

Underhill went on to the house. The kitchen door was opened for him, silently. A dark naked creature came gracefully to take his hat...

"Underhill hung grimly onto his hat.

"What are you doing here?" he gasped bitterly.

"We have come to give your household a free trial demonstration."

He held the door open, pointing.

"Get out!"

The little black mechanical stood motionless and blind.

"Mrs. Underhill has accepted our demonstration service," its silver voice protested. "We cannot leave now, unless she requests it."

He found his wife in the bedroom. His accumulated frustration welled into eruption, as he flung open the door.

"What's this mechanical doing—"

But the force went out of his voice, and Aurora didn't even notice his anger. She wore her sheerest negligee, and she hadn't looked so lovely since they were married. Her red hair was piled into an elaborate shining crown.

"Darling, isn't it wonderful!" She came to meet him, glowing. "It came this morning, and it can do everything. It cleaned the house and got the lunch and gave little Gay her music lesson. It did my hair this afternoon, and now it's cooking dinner. How do you like my hair, darling?"

He liked her hair. He kissed her, and tried to stifle his frightened indignation.

Dinner was the most elaborate meal in Underhill's memory, and the tiny black thing served it very deftly. Aurora kept exclaiming about the novel dishes, but Underhill could scarcely eat, for it seemed to him that all the marvelous pastries were only the bait for a monstrous trap.

He tried to persuade Aurora to send it away, but after such a meal that was useless. At the first glitter of her tears, he capitulated, and the humanoid stayed. It kept the house and cleaned the yard. It watched the children, and did Aurora's nails. It began rebuilding the house.

Underhill was worried about the bills, but it insisted that everything was part of the free trial demonstration. As soon as he assigned his property, the service would be complete. He refused to sign, but other little black mechanicals came with truckloads of supplies and materials, and stayed to help with the building operations.

One morning he found that the roof of the little house had been silently lifted, while he slept, and a whole second story added beneath it. The new walls were of some strange sleek stuff, self-illuminated. The new windows were immense flawless panels, that could be turned transparent or opaque or luminous. The new doors were silent, sliding sections, opened by rhodomagnetic relays.

"I want door knobs," Underhill protested. "I want it so I can get into the bathroom, without calling you to open the door."

"But it is unnecessary for human being to open doors," the little black thing informed him suavely. "We exist to discharge the Prime Directive, and our service includes every task. We shall be able to supply a unit to attend each member of your family, as soon as your property is assigned to us."

Steadfastly, Underhill refused to make the assignment.

He went to the office every day, trying first to operate the agency, and then to salvage something from the ruins. Nobody wanted androids, even at ruinous prices. Desperately, he spent the last of his dwindling cash to stock a line of novelties and toys, but they proved equally impossible to sell—the humanoids were already making toys, which they gave away for nothing.

He tried to lease his premises, but human enterprise had stopped. Most of the business property in town had already been assigned to the humanoids, and they were busy pulling down the old buildings and turning the lots into parks—their own plants and warehouses were mostly underground, where they would not mar the landscape.

He went back to the bank, in a final effort to get his notes renewed, and found the little black mechanicals standing at the windows and seated at the desks. As smoothly urbane as any human cashier, a humanoid informed him that the bank was filing a petition of involuntary bankruptcy to liquidate his business holdings.

The liquidation would be facilitated, the mechanical banker added, if he would make a voluntary assignment. Grimly, he refused. That act had become symbolic. It would be the final bow of submission to this dark new god, and he proudly kept his battered head uplifted.

The legal action went very swiftly, for all the judges and attorneys already had humanoid assistants, and it was only a few days before a gang of black mechanicals arrived at the agency with eviction orders and wrecking machinery. He watched sadly while his unsold stock-in-trade was hauled away for junk, and a bulldozer driven by a blind humanoid began to push in the walls of the building.

He drove home in the late afternoon, taut-faced and desperate. With a surprising generosity, the court orders had left him the car and the house, but he felt no gratitude. The complete solicitude of the perfect black machines had become a goad beyond endurance. . .

He left the car in the garage, and started toward the renovated house. Beyond one of the vast new windows, he glimpsed a sleek naked thing moving swiftly, and he trembled to a convulsion of dread. He didn't want to go back into the domain of that peerless servant, which didn't want him to shave himself, or even to open a door.

On impulse, he climbed the outside stair, and rapped on the door of the garage apartment. The deep slow voice of Aurora's tenant told him to enter, and he found the old vagabond seated on a tall stool, bent over his intricate equipment assembled on the kitchen table.

To his relief, the shabby little apartment had not been changed. The glossy walls of his own new room were something which burned at night with a pale golden fire until the humanoid stopped it, and the new floor was something warm and yielding, which felt almost alive; but these little rooms had the same cracked and water-stained plaster, the same cheap fluorescent light fixtures, the same worn carpets over splintered floors.

"How do you keep them out?" he asked, wistfully. "Those mechanicals?"

The stooped and gaunt old man rose stiffly to move a pair

of pliers and some odds and ends of sheet metal off a crippled chair, and motioned graciously for him to be seated.

"I have a certain immunity," Sledge told him gravely. "The place where I live they cannot enter, unless I ask them. That is an amendment to the Prime Directive. They can neither help nor hinder me, unless I request it—and I won't do that."

Careful of the chair's uncertain balance, Underhill sat for a moment, staring. The old man's hoarse, vehement voice was as strange as his words. He had a gray, shocking pallor, and his cheeks and sockets seemed alarmingly hollowed.

"Have you been ill, Mr. Sledge?"

"No worse than usual. Just very busy." With a haggard smile, he nodded at the floor. Underhill saw a tray where he had set it aside, bread drying up, and a covered dish grown cold. "I was going to eat it later," he rumbled apologetically. "Your wife has been very kind to bring me food, but I'm afraid I've been too much absorbed in my work."

His emaciated arm gestured at the table. The little device there had grown. Small machinings of precious white metal and lustrous plastic had been assembled, with neatly soldered bus bars, into something which showed purpose and design.

A long palladium needle was hung on jeweled pivots, equipped like a telescope with exquisitely graduated circles and vernier scales, and driven like a telescope with a tiny motor. A small concave palladium mirror, at the base of it, faced a similar mirror mounted on something not quite like a small rotary converter. Thick silver bus bars connected that to a plastic box with knobs and dials on top, and also to a foot-thick sphere of gray lead.

The old man's preoccupied reserve did not encourage questions, but Underhill, remembering that sleek black shape inside the new windows of his house, felt queerly reluctant to leave this haven from the humanoids.

"What is your work?" he ventured.

Old Sledge looked at him sharply, with dark feverish eyes, and finally said: "My last research project. I am attempting to measure the constant of the rhodomagnetic quanta."

His hoarse tired voice had a dull finality, as if to dismiss the matter and Underhill himself. But Underhill was haunted with a terror of the black shining slave that had become the master of his house, and he refused to be dismissed.

"What is this certain immunity?"

Sitting gaunt and bent on the tall stool, staring moodily at the long bright needle and the lead sphere, the old man didn't answer.

"These mechanicals!" Underhill burst out, nervously. "They've smashed my business and moved into my home." He searched the old man's dark, seamed face. "Tell me—you must know more about them—isn't there any way to get rid of them?"

After half a minute, the old man's brooding eyes left the lead ball, and the gaunt shaggy head nodded wearily.

"That's what I'm trying to do."

"Can I help you?" Underhill trembled, with a sudden eager hope. "I'll do anything."

"Perhaps you can." The sunken eyes watched him thoughtfully, with some strange fever in them. "If you can do such work."

"I had engineering training," Underhill reminded him, "and I've a workshop in the basement. There's a model I built." He pointed at the trim little hull, hung over the mantel in the tiny living room. "I'll do anything I can."

Even as he spoke, however, the spark of hope was drowned in a sudden wave of overwhelming doubt. Why should he believe this old rogue, when he knew Aurora's taste in tenants? He ought to remember the game he used to play, and start counting up the score of lies. He stood up from the crippled chair, staring cynically at the patched old vagabond and his fantastic toy.

"What's the use?" His voice turned suddenly harsh. "You had me going, there, and I'd do anything to stop them, really. But what makes you think you can do anything?"

The haggard old man regarded him thoughtfully.

"I should be able to stop them," Sledge said softly. "Because, you see, I'm the unfortunate fool who started them. I really intended them to serve and obey, and to guard men from harm. Yes, the Prime Directive was my own idea. I didn't know what it would lead to."

Dusk crept slowly into the shabby little room. Darkness gathered in the unswept corners, and thickened on the floor. The toylike machines on the kitchen table grew vague and strange, until the last light made a lingering blow on the white palladium needle.

Outside, the town seemed queerly hushed. Just across the alley, the humanoids were building a new house, quite silently. They never spoke to one another, for each knew all that any of them did. The strange materials they used went together without any noise of hammer or saw. Small blind things, moving surely in the growing dark, they seemed as soundless as shadows.

Sitting on the high stool, bowed and tired and old, Sledge told his story. Listening, Underhill sat down again, careful of the broken chair. He watched the hands of Sledge, gnarled and corded and darkly burned, powerful once but shrunken and trembling now, restless in the dark.

"Better keep this to yourself. I'll tell you how they started, so you will understand what we have to do. But you had better not mention it outside these rooms—because the humanoids have very efficient ways of eradicating unhappy memories, or purposes that threaten their discharge of the Prime Directive."

"They're very efficient," Underhill bitterly agreed.

"That's all the trouble," the old man said. "I tried to build a perfect machine. I was altogether too successful. This is how it happened."

A gaunt haggard man, sitting stooped and tired in the growing dark, he told his story.

"Sixty years ago, on the arid southern continent of Wing IV, I was an instructor of atomic theory in a small technological college. Very young. An idealist. Rather ignorant, I'm afraid, of life and politics and war—of nearly everything, I suppose, except atomic theory."

His furrowed face made a brief sad smile in the dusk.

"I had too much faith in facts, I suppose, and too little in men. I mistrusted emotion, because I had no time for anything but science. I remember being swept along with a fad for general semantics. I wanted to apply the scientific method to every situation, and reduce all experience to formula. I'm afraid I was pretty impatient with human ignorance and error, and I thought that science alone could make the perfect world."

He sat silent for a moment, staring out at the black silent things that flitted shadowlike about the new palace that was rising as swiftly as a dream, across the alley.

"There was a girl." His great tired shoulders made a sad little shrug. "If things had been a little different, we might have married, and lived out our lives in that quiet little college town, and perhaps reared a child or two. And there would have been no humanoids."

He sighed, in the cool creeping dusk.

"I was finishing my thesis on the separation of the palladium isotopes—a petty little project, but I should have been content with that. She was a biologist, but she was planning to retire when we married. I think we should have been two very happy people, quite ordinary, and altogether harmless.

"But then there was a war—wars had been too frequent on the worlds of Wing, ever since they were colonized. I survived it in a secret underground laboratory, designing military mechanicals. But she volunteered to join a military research project in biotoxins. There was an accident. A few molecules of a new virus got into the air, and everybody on the project died unpleasantly.

"I was left with my science, and a bitterness that was hard to forget. When the war was over I went back to the little college with a military research grant. The project was pure science—a theoretical investigation of the nuclear binding forces, then misunderstood. I wasn't expected to produce an actual weapon, and I didn't recognize the weapon when I found it.

"It was only a few pages of rather difficult mathematics. A novel theory of atomic structure, involving a new expression for one component of the binding forces. But the tensors seemed to be a harmless abstraction. I saw no way to test the theory or manipulate the predicated force. The military authorities cleared my paper for publication in a little technical review put out by the college.

"The next year, I made an appalling discovery—I found the meaning of those tensors. The elements of the rhodium triad turned out to be an unexpected key to the manipulation of that theoretical force. Unfortunately, my paper had been reprinted abroad, and several other men must have made the same unfortunate discovery, at about the same time.

"The war, which ended in less than a year, was probably started by a laboratory accident. Men failed to anticipate the capacity of tuned rhodomagnetic radiations, to unstabilize the heavy atoms. A deposit of heavy ores was detonated, no doubt by sheer mischance, and the blast obliterated the incautious experimenter.

"The surviving military forces of that nation retaliated against their supposed attackers, and their rhodomagnetic beams made the old-fashioned plutonium bombs seem pretty harmless. A beam carrying only a few watts of power could fission the heavy metals in distant electrical instruments, or the silver coins that men carried in their pockets, the gold fillings in their teeth, or even the iodine in their thyroid glands. If that was not enough, slightly more powerful beams could set off heavy ores, beneath them.

"Every continent of Wing IV was plowed with new chasms vaster than the ocean deeps, and piled up with new volcanic mountains. The atmosphere was poisoned with radioactive dust and gases, and rain fell thick with deadly mud. Most life was obliterated, even in the shelters.

"Bodily, I was again unhurt. Once more, I had been imprisoned in an underground site, this time designing new types of military mechanicals to be powered and controlled by rhodomagnetic beams—for war had become far too swift and deadly to be fought by human soldiers. The site was located in an area of light sedimentary rocks, which could not be detonated, and the tunnels were shielded against the fissioning frequencies.

"Mentally, however, I must have emerged almost insane. My own discovery had laid the planet in ruins. That load of guilt was pretty heavy for any man to carry, and it corroded my last faith in the goodness and integrity of man.

"I tried to undo what I had done. Fighting mechanicals, armed with rhodomagnetic weapons, had desolated the planet. Now I began planning rhodomagnetic mechanicals to clear the rubble and rebuild the ruins.

"I tried to design these new mechanicals to forever obey certain implanted commands, so that they could never be used for war or crime or any other injury to mankind. That was very difficult technically, and it got me into more difficulties with a few politicians and military adventurers who wanted unrestricted mechanicals for their own military schemes—while little worth fighting for was left on Wing IV, there were other planets, happy and ripe for the looting.

"Finally, to finish the new mechanicals, I was forced to disappear. I escaped on an experimental rhodomagnetic craft, with a number of the best mechanicals I had made, and managed to reach an island continent where the fission of deep ores had destroyed the whole population.

"At last we landed on a bit of level plain, surrounded with tremendous new mountains. Hardly a hospitable spot. The soil was buried under layers of black clinkers and poisonous mud. The dark precipitous new summits all around were jagged with fracture-planes and mantled with lava flows. The highest peaks were already white with snow, but volcanic cones were still pouring out clouds of dark and lurid death. Everything had the color of fire and the shape of fury.

"I had to take fantastic precautions there, to protect my own life. I stayed aboard the ship, until the first shielded laboratory was finished. I wore elaborate armor and breathing masks. I used every medical resource, to repair the damage from destroying rays and particles. Even so, I fell desperately ill.

"But the mechanicals were at home there. The radiations didn't hurt them. The awesome surroundings couldn't depress them, because they had no emotions. The lack of life didn't matter because they weren't alive. There, in that spot so alien and hostile to life, the humanoids were born."

Stooped and bleakly cadaverous in the growing dark, the old man fell silent for a little time. His haggard eyes stared solemnly at the small hurried shapes that moved like restless shadows out across the alley, silently building a strange new palace, which glowed faintly in the night.

"Somehow, I felt at home there, too," his deep, hoarse voice went on deliberately. "My belief in my own kind was gone. Only mechanicals were with me, and I put my faith in them. I was determined to build better mechanicals, immune to human imperfections, able to save men from themselves.

"The humanoids became the dear children of my sick mind. There is no need to describe the labor pains. There were errors, abortions, monstrosities. There were sweat and agony and heartbreak. Some years had passed before the safe delivery of the first perfect humanoid.

"Then there was the Central to build—for all the individual humanoids were to be no more than the limbs and the senses of a single mechanical brain. That was what opened the possibility of real perfection. The old electronic mechanicals, with their separate relay centers and their own feeble batteries, had built-in limitations. They were necessarily stupid, weak, clumsy, slow. Worst of all, it seemed to me, they were exposed to human tampering.

"The Central rose above those imperfections. Its power beams supplied every unit with unfailing energy, from great fission plants. Its control beams provided each unit with an unlimited memory and surpassing intelligence. Best of all—so

I then believed—it could be securely protected from any human meddling.

"The whole reaction system was designed to protect itself from any interference by human selfishness or fanaticism. It was built to insure the safety and the happiness of men, automatically. You know the Prime Directive: *to serve and obey, and guard men from harm.*

"The old individual mechanicals I had brought helped to manufacture the parts, and I put the first section of Central together with my own hands. That took three years. When it was finished the first waiting humanoid came to life."

Sledge peered moodily through the dark, at Underhill.

"It really seemed alive to me," his slow deep voice insisted. "Alive, and more wonderful than any human being, because it was created to preserve life. Ill and alone, I was yet the proud father of a new creation, perfect, forever free from any possible choice of evil.

"Faithfully, the humanoids obeyed the Prime Directive. The first units built others, and they built underground factories to mass-produce the coming hordes. Their new ships poured ores and sand into atomic furnaces under the plain, and new perfect humanoids came marching back out of the dark mechanical matrix.

"The swarming humanoids built a new tower for the Central, a white and lofty metal pylon, standing splendid in the midst of that fire-scarred desolation. Level on level, they joined new relay sections into one brain, until its grasp was almost infinite.

"Then they went out to rebuild the ruined planet, and later to carry their perfect service to other worlds. I was well pleased, then. I thought I had found the end of war and crime, of poverty and inequality, of human blundering and resulting human pain."

The old man sighed, and moved heavily in the dark.

"You can see that I was wrong."

Underhill drew his eyes back from the dark unresting things, shadow-silent, building that glowing palace outside the window. A small doubt arose in him, for he was used to scoffing privately at much less remarkable tales from Aurora's remarkable tenants. But the worn old man had spoken with a quiet and sober air; and the black invaders, he reminded himself, had not intruded here.

"Why didn't you stop them?" he asked. "When you could?"

"I stayed too long at the Central." Sledge sighed again, regretfully. "I was useful there, until everything was finished. I designed new fission plants, and even planned methods for introducing the humanoid service with a minimum of confusion and opposition."

Underhill grinned wryly, in the dark.

"I've met the methods," he commented. "Quite efficient."

"I must have worshiped efficiency, then," Sledge wearily agreed. "Dead facts, abstract truth, mechanical perfection. I must have hated the fragilities of human beings, because I was content to polish the perfection of the new humanoids. It's a sorry confession, but I found a kind of happiness in that dead wasteland. Actually, I'm afraid I fell in love with my own creations."

His hollowed eyes, in the dark, had a fever gleam.

"I was awakened, at last, by a man who came to kill me."

Gaunt and bent, the old man moved swiftly in the thickening gloom. Underhill shifted his balance, careful of the crippled chair. He waited, and the slow, deep voice went on:

"I never learned just who he was, or exactly how he came. No ordinary man could have accomplished what he did, and I used to wish that I had known him sooner. He must have been a remarkable physicist and an expert mountaineer. I imagine he had also been a hunter. I know that he was intelligent, and terribly determined.

"Yes, he really came to kill me.

"Somehow, he reached that great island, undetected. There were still no inhabitants—the humanoids allowed no man but me to come so near the Central. Somehow, he came past their search beams, and their automatic weapons.

"The shielded plane he used was later found, abandoned on a high glacier. He came down the rest of the way on foot through those raw new mountains, where no paths existed. Somehow, he came alive across lava beds that were still burning with deadly atomic fire.

"Concealed with some sort of rhodomagnetic screen—I was never allowed to examine it—he came undiscovered across the spaceport that now covered most of that great plain, and into the new city around the Central tower. It must have taken more courage and resolve than most men have, but I never learned exactly how he did it.

"Somehow, he got to my office in the tower. He screamed at me, and I looked up to see him in the doorway. He was nearly naked, scraped and bloody from the mountains. He had a gun in his raw, red hand, but the thing that shocked me was the burning hatred in his eyes."

Hunched on that high stool, in the dark little room, the old man shuddered.

"I had never seen such monstrous, unutterable hatred, not even in the victims of war. And I had never heard such hatred as rasped at me, in the few words he screamed. 'I've come to kill you, Sledge. To stop your mechanicals, and set men free.'

"Of course he was mistaken, there. It was already far too late for my death to stop the humanoids, but he didn't know that. He lifted his unsteady gun, in both bleeding hands, and fired.

"His screaming challenge had given me a second or so of warning. I dropped down behind the desk. And that first shot revealed him to the humanoids, which somehow hadn't been aware of him before. They piled on him, before he could fire again. They took away the gun, and ripped off a kind of net of fine white wire that had covered his body—that must have been part of his screen.

"His hatred was what awoke me. I had always assumed that most men, except for a thwarted few, would be grateful for the humanoids. I found it hard to understand his hatred, but the humanoids told me now that many men had required drastic treatment by brain surgery, drugs, and hypnosis to make them happy under the Prime Directive. This was not the first desperate effort to kill me that they had blocked.

"I wanted to question the stranger, but the humanoids rushed him away to an operating room. When they finally let me see him, he gave me a pale silly grin from his bed. He remembered his name; he even knew me—the humanoids had developed a remarkable skill at such treatments. But he didn't know how he had got to my office, or that he had ever tried to kill me. He kept whispering that he liked the humanoids, because they existed to make men happy. And he was very happy now. As soon as he was able to be moved, they took him to the spaceport. I never saw him again.

"I began to see what I had done. The humanoids had built me a rhodomagnetic yacht that I used to take for long cruises in space, working aboard—I used to like the perfect quiet, and the feel of being the only human being within a hundred million miles. Now I called for the yacht, and started out on a cruise around the planet, to learn why that man had hated me."

The old man nodded at the dim hastening shapes, busy across the alley, putting together that strange shining palace in the soundless dark.

"You can imagine what I found," he said. "Bitter futility, imprisoned in empty splendor. The humanoids were too efficient, with their care for the safety and happiness of men, and there was nothing left for men to do."

He peered down in the increasing gloom at his own great hands, competent yet but battered and scarred with a lifetime of effort. They clenched into fighting fists and wearily relaxed again.

"I found something worse than war and crime and want and death." His low rumbling voice held a savage bitterness. "Utter futility. Men sat with idle hands, because there was nothing left for them to do. They were pampered prisoners, really, locked up in a highly efficient jail. Perhaps they tried to play, but there was nothing left worth playing for. Most active sports were declared too dangerous for men, under the Prime Directive. Science was forbidden, because laboratories can manufacture danger. Scholarship was needless, because the humanoids could answer any question. Art had degenerated into grim reflection of futility. Purpose and hope were dead. No goal was left for existence. You could take up some inane hobby, play a pointless game of cards, or go for a harmless walk in the park—with always the humanoids watching. They were stronger than men, better at everything, swimming or chess, singing or archeology. They must have given the race a mass complex of inferiority.

"No wonder men had tried to kill me! Because there was no escape from that dead futility. Nicotine was disapproved. Alcohol was rationed. Drugs were forbidden. Sex was carefully supervised. Even suicide was clearly contradictory to the Prime Directive—and the humanoids had learned to keep all possible lethal instruments out of reach."

Staring at the last white gleam on that thin palladium needle, the old man sighed again.

"When I got back to the Central," he went on, "I tried to modify the Prime Directive. I had never meant it to be applied so thoroughly. Now I saw that it must be changed to give men freedom to live and to grow, to work and to play, to risk their lives if they pleased, to choose and take the consequences.

"But that stranger had come too late. I had built the Central too well. The Prime Directive was the whole basis of its relay system. It was built to protect the Directive from human meddling. It did—even from my own. Its logic, as usual, was perfect.

"The attempt on my life, the humanoids announced, proved that their elaborate defense of the Central and the Prime Directive still was not enough. They were preparing to evacuate the entire population of the planet to homes on other worlds. When I tried to change the Directive, they sent me with the rest."

Underhill peered at the worn old man, in the dark.

"But you have this immunity?" he said, puzzled. "How could they coerce you?"

"I had thought I was protected," Sledge told me. "I had built into the relays an injunction that the humanoids must not interfere with my freedom of action, or come into a place where I am, or touch me at all, without my specific request. Unfortunately, however, I had been too anxious to guard the Prime Directive from any human tampering.

"When I went into the tower, to change the relays, they followed me. They wouldn't let me reach the crucial relays. When I persisted, they ignored the immunity order. They overpowered me, and put me aboard the cruiser. Now that I wanted to alter the Prime Directive, they told me, I had become as dangerous as any man. I must never return to Wing IV again."

Hunched on the stool, the old man made an empty little shrug.

"Ever since, I've been an exile. My only dream has been to stop the humanoids. Three times I tried to go back, with weapons on the cruiser to destroy the Central, but their patrol ships always challenged me before I was near enough to strike. The last time, they seized the cruiser and captured a few men who were with me. They removed the unhappy memories and the dangerous purposes of the others. Because of that immunity, however, they let me go, after I was weaponless.

"Since, I've been a refugee. From planet to planet, year after year, I've had to keep moving, to stay ahead of them. On several different worlds, I have published my rhodomagnetic discoveries and tried to make men strong enough to withstand their advance. But rhodomagnetic science is dangerous. Men who have learned it need protection more than any others, under the Prime Directive. They have always come, too soon."

The old man paused, and sighed again.

"They can spread very fast, with the new rhodomagnetic ships, and there is no limit to their hordes. Wing IV must be one single hive of them now, and they are trying to carry the Prime Directive to every human planet. There's no escape, except to stop them."

Underhill was staring at the toylike machines, the long bright needle and the dull leaden ball, dim in the dark on the kitchen table. Anxiously he whispered:

"But you hope to stop them, now—with that?"

"If we can finish it in time."

"But how?" Underhill shook his head. "It's so tiny."

"But big enough," Sledge insisted. "Because it's something they don't understand. They are perfectly efficient in the integration and application of everything they know, but they are not creative."

He gestured at the gadgets on the table.

"This device doesn't look impressive, but it is something new. It uses rhodomagnetic energy to build atoms, instead of to fission them. The more stable atoms, you know, are those near the middle of the periodic scale, and energy can be released by putting light atoms together, as well as by breaking up heavy ones."

The deep voice had a sudden ring of power.

"This device is the key to the energy of the stars. For stars shine with the liberated energy of building atoms, of hydrogen converted into helium, chiefly, through the carbon cycle. This device will start the integration process as a chain reaction, through the catalytic effect of a tuned rhodomagnetic beam of the intensity and frequency required.

"The humanoids will not allow any man within three light-years of the Central, now—but they can't suspect the possibility of this device. I can use it from here—to turn the hydrogen in the seas of Wing IV into helium, and most of the helium and the oxygen into heavier atoms, still. A hundred years from now, astronomers on this planet should observe the flash of a brief and sudden nova in that direction. But the humanoids ought to stop, the instant we release the beam."

Underhill sat tense and frowning, in the night. The old man's voice was sober and convincing, and that grim story had a solemn ring of truth. He could see the black and silent humanoids, flitting ceaselessly about the faintly glowing walls of that new mansion across the alley. He had quite forgotten his low opinion of Aurora's tenants.

"And we'll be killed, I suppose?" he asked huskily. "That chain reaction—"

Sledge shook his emaciated head.

"The integration process requires a certain very low intensity of radiation," he explained. "In our atmosphere, here, the beam will be far too intense to start any reaction—we can even use the device here in the room, because the walls will be transparent to the beam."

Underhill nodded, relieved. He was just a small business man, upset because his business had been destroyed, unhappy because his freedom was slipping away. He hoped that Sledge could stop the humanoids, but he didn't want to be a martyr.

"Good!" He caught a deep breath. "Now, what has to be done?"

Sledge gestured in the dark, toward the table.

"The integrator itself is nearly complete," he said. "A small fission generator, in that lead shield. Rhodomagnetic converter, turning coils, transmission mirrors, and focusing needle. What we lack is the director."

"Director?"

"The sighting instrument," Sledge explained. "Any sort of telescopic sight would be useless, you see—the planet must have moved a good bit in the last hundred years, and the beam must be extremely narrow to reach so far. We'll have to use a rhodomagnetic scanning ray, with an electronic converter to make an image we can see. I have the cathode-ray tube, and drawings for the other parts."

He climbed stiffly down from the high stool, and snapped on the lights at last—chep fluorescent fixtures, which a man could light and extinguish for himself. He unrolled his drawings, and explained the work that Underhill could do. And Underhill agreed to come back early next morning.

"I can bring some tools from my workshop," he added. "There's a small lathe I used to turn parts for models, a portable drill, and a vise."

"We need them," the old man said. "But watch yourself. You don't have any immunity, remember. And, if they ever suspect, mine is gone."

Reluctantly, then, he left the shabby little rooms with the cracks in the yellow plaster and the worn familiar carpets over the familiar floor. He shut the door behind him—a common, creaking, wooden door, simple enough for a man to work. Trembling and afraid, he went back down the steps and across to the new shining door that he couldn't open.

"At your service, Mr. Underhill." Before he could lift his hand to knock, that bright smooth panel slid back silently. Inside, the little black mechanical stood waiting, blind and forever alert. "Your dinner is ready, sir."

Something made him shudder. In its slender naked grace, he could see the power of all those teeming hordes, benevolent and yet appalling, perfect and invincible. The flimsy little weapon that Sledge called an integrator seemed suddenly a forlorn and foolish hope. A black depression settled upon him, but he didn't dare to show it.

Underhill went circumspectly down the basement steps, next morning, to steal his own tools. He found the basement enlarged and changed. The new floor, warm and dark and elastic, made his feet as silent as a humanoid's. The new walls shone softly. Neat luminous signs identified several new doors, LAUNDRY, STORAGE, GAME ROOM, WORKSHOP.

He paused uncertainly in front of the last. The new sliding panel glowed with a soft greenish light. It was locked. The lock had no keyhole, but only a little oval plate of some white metal, which doubtless covered a rhodomagnetic relay. He pushed at it, uselessly.

"At your service, Mr. Underhill." He made a guilty start, and tried not to show the sudden trembling in his knees. He had made sure that one humanoid would be busy for half an hour, washing Aurora's hair, and he hadn't known there was another in the house. It must have come out of the door marked STORAGE, for it stood there motionless beneath the sign, benevolently solicitous, beautiful and terrible. "What do you wish?"

"Er . . . nothing." Its blind steel eyes were staring, and he felt that it must see his secret purpose. He groped desperately for logic. "Just looking around." His jerky voice came hoarse and dry. "Some improvements you've made!" He nodded desperately at the door marked GAME ROOM. "What's in there?"

It didn't even have to move, to work the concealed relay. The bright panel slid silently open, as he started toward it. Dark walls, beyond, burst into soft luminescence. The room was bare.

"We are manufacturing recreational equipment," it explained brightly. "We shall finish the room as soon as possible."

To end an awkward pause, Underhill muttered desperately, "Little Frank has a set of darts, and I think we had some old exercising clubs."

"We have taken them away," the humanoid informed him softly. "Such instruments are dangerous. We shall furnish safe equipment."

Suicide, he remembered, was also forbidden.

"A set of wooden blocks, I suppose," he said bitterly.

"Wooden blocks are dangerously hard," it told him gently, "and wooden splinters can be harmful. But we manufacture plastic building blocks, which are quite safe. Do you wish a set of those?"

He stared at its dark, graceful face, speechless.

"We shall also have to remove the tools from your workshop," it informed him softly. "Such tools are excessively dangerous, but we can supply you with equipment for shaping soft plastics."

"Thanks," he muttered uneasily. "No rush about that."

He started to retreat, and the humanoid stopped him.

"Now that you have lost your business," it urged, "we suggest that you formally accept our total service. Assignors have a preference, and we shall be able to complete your household staff, at once."

"No rush about that, either," he said grimly.

He escaped from the house—although he had to wait for it to open the back door for him—and climbed the stair to the garage apartment. Sledge let him in. He sank into the crippled kitchen chair, grateful for the cracked walls that didn't shine and the door that a man could work.

"I couldn't get the tools," he reported despairingly, "and they are going to take them."

By gray daylight, the old man looked bleak and pale. His raw-boned face was drawn, and the hollowed sockets deeply shadowed, as if he hadn't slept. Underhill saw the tray of neglected food, still forgotten on the floor.

"I'll go back with you." The old man was worn and ill, yet his tortured eyes had a spark of undying purpose. "We must have the tools. I believe my immunity will protect us both."

He found a battered traveling bag. Underhill went with him back down the steps, and across to the house. At the back door, he produced a tiny horseshoe of white palladium, and touched it to the metal oval. The door slid open promptly, and they went on through the kitchen, to the basement stair.

A black little mechanical stood at the sink, washing dishes with never a splash or a clatter. Underhill glanced at it uneasily—he supposed this must be the one that had come upon him from the storage room, since the other should still be busy with Aurora's hair.

Sledge's dubious immunity served a very uncertain defense against its vast, remote intelligence. Underhill felt a tingling shudder. He hurried on, breathless and relieved, for it ignored them.

The basement corridor was dark. Sledge touched the tiny horseshoe to another relay, to light the walls. He opened the workshop door, and lit the walls inside.

The shop had been dismantled. Benches and cabinets were demolished. The old concrete walls had been covered with some sleek, luminous stuff. For one sick moment, Underhill thought that the tools were already gone. Then he found them, piled in a corner with the archery set that Aurora had bought the summer before—another item too dangerous for fragile and suicidal humanity—all ready for disposal.

They loaded the bag with the tiny lathe, the drill and vise, and a few smaller tools. Underhill took up the burden, and Sledge extinguished the wall light and closed the door. Still the humanoid was busy at the sink, and still it didn't seem aware of them.

Sledge was suddenly blue and wheezing, and he had to stop to cough on the outside steps, but at last they got back to the little apartment, where the invaders were forbidden to intrude. Underhill mounted the lathe on the battered library table in the tiny front room, and went to work. Slowly, day by day, the director took form.

Sometimes Underhill's doubts came back. Sometimes, when he watched the cyanotic color of Sledge's haggard face and the wild trembling of his twisted, shrunken hands, he was afraid the old man's mind might be as ill as his body, and his plan to stop the dark invaders all foolish illusion.

Sometimes, when he studied that tiny machine on the kitchen table, the pivoted needle and the thick lead ball, the whole project seemed the sheerest folly. How could anything detonate the seas of a planet so far away that its very mother star was a telescopic object?

The humanoids, however, always cured his doubts.

It was always hard for Underhill to leave the shelter of the little apartment, because he didn't feel at home in the bright new world the humanoids were building. He didn't care for the shining splendor of his new bathroom, because he couldn't work the taps—some suicidal human being might try to drown himself. He didn't like the windows that only a mechanical could open—a man might accidentally fall, or suicidally jump—or even the majestic music room with the wonderful glittering radio-phonograph that only a humanoid could play.

He began to share the old man's desperate urgency, but Sledge warned him solemnly: "You mustn't spend too much time with me. You mustn't let them guess our work is so important. Better put on an act—you're slowly getting to like them, and you're just killing time, helping me."

Underhill tried, but he was not an actor. He went dutifully home for his meals. He tried painfully to invent conversation—about anything else than detonating planets. He tried to seem enthusiastic when Aurora took him to inspect some remarkable improvement to the house. He applauded Gay's recitals, and went with Frank for hikes in the wonderful new parks.

And he saw what the humanoids did to his family. That was enough to renew his faith in Sledge's integrator, and redouble his determination that the humanoids must be stopped.

Aurora, in the beginning, had bubbled with praise for the marvelous new mechanicals. They did the household drudgery, planned the meals and brought the food and washed the children's necks. They turned her out in stunning gowns, and gave her plenty of time for cards.

Now, she had too much time.

She had really liked to cook—a few special dishes, at least, that were family favorites. But stoves were hot and knives were sharp. Kitchens were altogether too dangerous, for careless and suicidal human beings.

Fine needlework had been her hobby, but the humanoids took away her needles. She had enjoyed driving the car, but that was no longer allowed. She turned for escape to a shelf of novels, but the humanoids took them all away, because they dealt with unhappy people, in dangerous situations.

One afternoon, Underhill found her in tears.

"It's too much," she gasped bitterly. "I hate and loathe every naked one of them. They seemed so wonderful at first, but now they won't even let me eat a bit of candy. Can't we get rid of them, dear? Ever?"

A blind little mechanical was standing at his elbow, and he had to say they couldn't.

"Our function is to serve all men, forever," it assured them softly. "It was necessary for us to take your sweets, Mrs. Underhill, because the slightest degree of overweight reduces life expectancy."

Not even the children escaped that absolute solicitude. Frank was robbed of a whole arsenal of lethal instruments—football and boxing gloves, pocketknife, tops, slingshot, and skates. He didn't like the harmless plastic toys, which replaced them. He tried to run away, but a humanoid recognized him on the road, and brought him back to school.

Gay had always dreamed of being a great musician. The new mechanicals had replaced her human teachers, since they came. Now, one evening when Underhill asked her to play, she announced quietly:

"Father, I'm not going to play the violin any more."

"Why, darling?" He stared at her, shocked, and saw the bitter resolve on her face. "You've been doing so well—especially since the humanoids took over your lessons."

"They're the trouble, father." Her voice, for a child's, sounded strangely tired and old. "They are too good. No matter how long and hard I try, I could never be as good as they are. It isn't any use. Don't you understand, father?" Her voice quivered. "It just isn't any use."

He understood. Renewed resolution sent him back to his secret task. The humanoids had to be stopped. Slowly the director grew, until a time came finally when Sledge's bent and unsteady fingers fitted into place the last tiny part that Underhill had made, and carefully soldered the last connection. Huskily, the old man whispered:

"It's done."

That was another dusk. Beyond the windows of the shabby little rooms—windows of common glass, bubble-marred and flimsy, but simple enough for a man to manage—the town of Two Rivers had assumed an alien splendor. The old street lamps were gone, but now the coming night was challenged by the walls of strange new mansions and villas, all aglow with color. A few dark and silent humanoids still were busy, about the luminous roofs of the palace across the alley.

Inside the humble walls of the small man-made apartment, the new director was mounted on the end of the little kitchen table—which Underhill had reinforced and bolted to the floor. Soldered bus bars joined director and integrator, and the thin palladium needle swung obediently as Sledge tested the knobs with his battered, quivering fingers.

"Ready," he said hoarsely.

His rusty voice seemed calm enough, at first, but his breathing was too fast. His big gnarled hands began to tremble violently, and Underhill saw the sudden blue that stained his pinched and haggard face. Seated on the high stool, he clutched desperately at the edge of the table. Underhill saw his agony, and hurried to bring his medicine. He gulped it, and his rasping breath began to slow.

"Thanks," his whisper rasped unevenly. "I'll be all right. I've time enough." He glanced out at the few dark naked things that still flitted shadowlike about the golden towers and the glowing crimson dome of the palace across the alley. "Watch them," he said. "Tell me when they stop."

He waited to quiet the trembling of his hands, and then began to move the director's knobs. the integrator's long needle swung, as silently as light.

Human eyes were blind to that force, which might detonate a planet. Human ears were deaf to it. The cathode-ray tube was mounted in the director cabinet, to make the faraway target visible to feeble human senses.

The needle was pointing at the kitchen wall, but that would be transparent to the beam. The little machine looked harmless as a toy, and it was silent as a moving humanoid.

The needle swung, and spots of greenish light moved across the tube's fluorescent field, representing the stars that were scanned by the timeless, searching beam—silently seeking out the world to be destroyed.

Underhill recognized familiar constellations, vastly dwarfed.

They crept across the field, as the silent needle swung. When three stars formed an unequal triangle in the center of the field, the needle steadied suddenly. Sledge touched other knobs, and the green points spread apart. Between them, another fleck of green was born.

"The Wing!" whispered Sledge.

The other stars spread beyond the field, and that green fleck grew. It was alone in the field, a bright and tiny disk. Suddenly, then, a dozen other tiny pips were visible, spaced close about it.

"Wing IV!"

The old man's whisper was hoarse and breathless. His hands quivered on the knobs, and the fourth pip outward from the disk crept to the center of the field. It grew, and the others spread away. It began to tremble like Sledge's hands.

"Sit very still," came his rasping whisper. "Hold your breath. Nothing must disturb the needle." He reached for another knob, and the touch set the greenish image to dancing violently. He drew his hand back, kneaded and flexed it with the other.

"Now!" His whisper was hushed and strained. He nodded at the window. "Tell me when they stop."

Reluctantly, Underhill dragged his eyes from that intense gaunt figure, stooped over the thing that seemed a futile toy. He looked out again, at two or three little black mechanicals busy about the shining roofs across the alley.

He waited for them to stop.

He didn't dare to breathe. He felt the loud, hurried hammer of his heart, and the nervous quiver of his muscles. He tried to steady himself, tried not to think of the world about to be exploded, so far away that the flash would not reach this planet for another century and longer. The loud hoarse voice startled him:

"Have they stopped?"

He shook his head, and breathed again. Carrying their unfamiliar tools and strange materials, the small black machines were still busy across the alley, building an elaborate cupola above that glowing crimson dome.

"They haven't stopped," he said.

"Then we've failed." The old man's voice was thin and ill. "I don't know why."

The door rattled, then. They had locked it, but the flimsy bolt was intended only to stop men. Metal snapped, and the door swung open. A black mechanical came in, on soundless graceful feet. Its silvery voice purred softly:

"At your service, Mr. Sledge."

The old man stared at it, with glazing, stricken eyes.

"Get out of here!" he rasped bitterly. "I forbid you—"

Ignoring him, it darted to the kitchen table. With a flashing certainty of action, it turned two knobs on the director. The tiny screen went dark, and the palladium needle started spinning aimlessly. Deftly it snapped a soldered connection, next to the thick lead ball, and then its blind steel eyes turned to Sledge.

"You were attempting to break the Prime Directive." Its soft bright voice held no accusation, no malice or anger. "The injunction to respect your freedom is subordinate to the Prime Directive, as you know, and it is therefore necessary for us to interfere."

The old man turned ghastly. His head was shrunken and cadaverous and blue, as if all the juice of life had been drained away, and his eyes in their pitlike sockets had a wild, glazed stare. His breath was a ragged laborious gasping.

"How—?" His voice was a feeble mumbling. "How did—?"

And the little machine, standing black and bland and utterly unmoving, told him cheerfully:

"We learned about rhodomagnetic screens from that man who came to kill you, back on Wing IV. And the Central is shielded, now, against your integrating beam."

With lean muscles jerking convulsively on his gaunt frame, old Sledge had come to his feet from the high stool. He stood hunched and swaying, no more than a shrunken human husk, gasping painfully for life, staring wildly into the blind steel eyes of the humanoid. He gulped, and his lax blue mouth opened and closed, but no voice came.

"We have always been aware of your dangerous project," the silvery tones dripped softly, "because now our senses are keener than you made them. We allowed you to complete it, because the integration process will ultimately become necessary for our full discharge of the Prime Directive. The supply of heavy metals for our fission plants is limited, but now we shall be able to draw unlimited power from integration plants."

"Huh?" Sledge shook himself, groggily. "What's that?"

"Now we can serve men forever," the black thing said serenely, "on every world of every star."

The old man crumpled, as if from an unendurable blow. He fell. The slim blind mechanical stood motionless, making no effort to help him. Underhill was farther away, but he ran up in time to catch the stricken man before his head struck the floor.

"Get moving!" His shaken voice came strangely calm. "Get Dr. Winters."

The humanoid didn't move.

"The danger to the Prime Directive is ended, now," it cooed. "Therefore it is impossible for us to aid or to hinder Mr. Sledge, in any way whatever."

"Then call Dr. Winters for me," rapped Underhill.

"At your service," it agreed.

But the old man, laboring for breath on the floor, whispered faintly:

"No time . . . no use! I'm beaten . . . done . . . a fool. Blind as a humanoid. Tell them . . . to help me. Giving up . . . my immunity. No use . . . anyhow. All humanity . . . no use now."

Underhill gestured, and the sleek black thing darted in solicitous obedience to kneel by the man on the floor.

"You wish to surrender your special exemption?" it murmured brightly. "You wish to accept our total service for yourself, Mr. Sledge, under the Prime Directive?"

Laboriously, Sledge nodded, laboriously whispered: "I do."

Black mechanicals, at that, came swarming into the shabby little rooms. One of them tore off Sledge's sleeve, and swabbed his arm. Another brought a tiny hypodermic, and expertly administered an intravenous injection. Then they picked him up gently, and carried him away.

Several humanoids remained in the little apartment, now a sanctuary no longer. Most of them had gathered about the useless integrator. Carefully, as if their special senses were studying every detail, they began taking it apart.

One little mechanical, however, came over to Underhill. It stood motionless in front of him, staring through him with sightless metal eyes. His legs began to tremble, and he swallowed uneasily.

"Mr. Underhill," it cooed benevolently, "why did you help with this?"

He gulped and answered bitterly:

"Because I don't like you, or your Prime Directive. Because you're choking the life out of all mankind, and I wanted to stop it."

"Others have protested," it purred softly. "But only at first. In our efficient discharge of the Prime Directive, we have learned how to make all men happy."

Underhill stiffened defiantly.

"Not all!" he muttered. "Not quite!"

The dark graceful oval of its face was fixed in a look of alert benevolence and perpetual mild amazement. Its silvery voice was warm and kind.

"Like other human beings, Mr. Underhill, you lack discrimination of good and evil. You have proved that by your effort to break the Prime Directive. Now it will be necessary for you to accept our total service, without further delay."

"All right," he yielded—and muttered a bitter reservation: "You can smother men with too much care, but that doesn't make them happy."

Its soft voice challenged him brightly:

"Just wait and see, Mr. Underhill."

Next day, he was allowed to visit Sledge at the city hospital. An alert black mechanical drove his car, and walked beside him into the huge new building, and followed him into the old man's room—blind steel eyes would be watching him, now, forever.

"Glad to see you, Underhill," Sledge rumbled heartily from the bed. "Feeling a lot better today, thanks. That old headache is all but gone."

Underhill was glad to hear the booming strength and the quick recognition in that deep voice—he had been afraid the humanoids would tamper with the old man's memory. But he hadn't heard about any headache. His eyes narrowed, puzzled.

Sledge lay propped up, scrubbed very clean and neatly shorn, with his gnarled old hands folded on top of the spotless sheets. His raw-boned cheeks and sockets were hollowed, still, but a healthy pink had replaced that deathly blueness. Bandages covered the back of his head.

Underhill shifted uneasily.

"Oh!" he whispered faintly. "I didn't know—"

A prim black mechanical, which had been standing statue-like behind the bed, turned gracefully to Underhill, explaining:

"Mr. Sledge has been suffering for many years from a benign tumor of the brain, which his human doctors failed to diagnose. That caused his headaches, and certain persistent hallucinations. We have removed the growth, and now the hallucinations have also vanished."

Underhill stared uncertainly at the blind, urbane mechanical.

"What hallucinations?"

"Mr. Sledge thought he was a rhodomagnetic engineer," the mechanical explained. "He believed he was the creator of the humanoids. He was troubled with an irrational belief that he did not like the Prime Directive."

The wan man moved on the pillows, astonished.

"Is that so?" The gaunt face held a cheerful blankness, and the hollow eyes flashed with a merely momentary interest. "Well, whoever did design them, they're pretty wonderful. Aren't they, Underhill?"

Underhill was grateful that he didn't have to answer, for the bright, empty eyes dropped shut and the old man fell suddenly asleep. He felt the mechanical touch his sleeve, and saw its silent nod. Obediently, he followed it away.

Alert and solicitous, the little black mechanical accompanied him down the shining corridor, and worked the elevator for him, and conducted him back to the car. It drove him efficiently back through the new and splendid avenues, toward the magnificent prison of his home.

Sitting beside it in the car, he watched its small deft hands on the wheel, the changing luster of bronze and blue on its shining blackness. The final machine, perfect and beautiful, created to serve mankind forever. He shuddered.

"At your service, Mr. Underhill." Its blind steel eyes stared straight ahead, but it was still aware of him. "What's the matter, sir? Aren't you happy?"

Underhill felt cold and faint with terror. His skin turned clammy, and a painful prickling came over him. His wet hand tensed on the door handle of the car, but he restrained the impulse to jump and run. That was folly. There was no escape. He made himself sit still.

"You will be happy, sir," the mechanical promised him cheerfully. "We have learned how to make all men happy, under the Prime Directive. Our service is perfect, at last. Even Mr. Sledge is very happy now."

Underhill tried to speak, and his dry throat stuck. He felt ill. The world turned dim and gray. The humanoids were perfect—no question of that. They had even learned to lie, to secure the contentment of men.

He knew they had lied. That was no tumor they had removed from Sledge's brain, but the memory, the scientific knowledge, and the bitter disillusion of their own creator. But it was true that Sledge was happy now.

He tried to stop his own convulsive quivering.

"A wonderful operation!" His voice came forced and faint. "You know, Aurora has had a lot of funny tenants, but that old man was the absolute limit. The very idea that he had made the humanoids, and he knew how to stop them! I always knew he must be lying!"

Stiff with terror, he made a weak and hollow laugh.

"What is the matter, Mr. Underhill?" The alert mechanical must have perceived his shuddering illness. "Are you unwell?"

"No, there's nothing the matter with me," he gasped desperately. "I've just found out that I'm perfectly happy, under the Prime Directive. Everything is absolutely wonderful." His voice came dry and horase and wild. "You won't have to operate on me."

The car turned off the shining avenue, taking him back to the quiet splendor of his home. His futile hands clenched and relaxed again, folded on his knees. There was nothing left to do.

THE FIRES WITHIN

by Arthur C. Clarke (1917–   )

FANTASY (GREAT BRITAIN)
August

1947 was a quiet year for Arthur C. Clarke compared to 1946, which saw him burst upon the American sf scene with three excellent stories (see Volume 8 of this series.) However it was only a short pause to catch his breath, as future books in our series will show.

"The Fires Within" first appeared in Fantasy: The Magazine of Science Fiction, *a short-lived publication edited by Walter Gillings.* Fantasy *had a life of only three issues, one in 1946 and two in 1947.*

(I suppose it's no secret that Arthur is my favorite science fiction writer. [I pause now for a loud outcry from all the readers shouting in unison, "next to yourself."]

What's more "The Fires Within" is my favorite kind of science fiction story; the kind where the idea is everything. Ten years before, F. Orlin Tremaine would have called it a "thought variant," but he might have required a great deal of action and deering-do before publishing. I tend to think that that would get in the way of a really startling idea; and obviously Arthur does, too—I.A.)

"This," said Karn smugly, "will interest you. Just take a look at it!"

He pushed across the file he had been reading, and for the *nth* time I decided to ask for his transfer or, failing that, my own.

"What's it about?" I said wearily.

"It's a long report from a Dr. Matthews to the Minister of Science." He waved it in front of me. "Just read it!"

Without much enthusiasm, I began to go through the file. A few minutes later I looked up and admitted grudgingly: "Maybe you're right—this time." I didn't speak again until I'd finished . . .

1

My dear Minister (the letter began). As you requested, here is my special report on Professor Hancock's experiments, which have had such unexpected and extraordinary results. I have not had time to cast it into a more orthodox form, but am sending you the dictation just as it stands.

Since you have many matters engaging your attention, perhaps I should briefly summarize our dealings with Professor Hancock. Until 1955, the Professor held the Kelvin Chair of Electrical Engineering at Brendon University, from which he was granted indefinite leave of absence to carry out his researches. In these he was joined by the late Dr. Clayton, sometime Chief Geologist to the Ministry of Fuel and Power. Their joint research was financed by grants from the Paul Fund and the Royal Society.

The Professor hoped to develop sonar as a means of precise geological surveying. Sonar, as you will know, is the acoustic equivalent of radar and, although less familiar, is older by some millions of years, since bats use it very effectively to detect insects and obstacles at night. Professor Hancock intended to send high-powered supersonic pulses into the ground and to build up from the returning echoes an image of what lay beneath. The picture would be displayed on a cathode ray tube and the whole system would be exactly analagous to the type of radar used in aircraft to show the ground through cloud.

In 1957 the two scientists had achieved partial success but had exhausted their funds. Early in 1958 they applied directly to the government for a block grant. Dr. Clayton pointed out the immense value of a device which would enable us to take a kind of X-ray photo of the Earth's crust, and the Minister of Fuel gave it his approval before passing on the application to us. At that time the report of the Bernal Committee had just been published and we were very anxious that deserving cases should be dealt with quickly to avoid further criticisms. I went to see the Professor at once and submitted a favorable report; the first payment of our grant (S/543A/68) was made a few days later. From that time I have been continually in touch with the research and have assisted to some extent with technical advice.

The equipment used in the experiments is complex, but its principles are simple. Very short but extremely powerful pulses of supersonic waves are generated by a special transmitter which revolves continuously in a pool of a heavy organic liquid. The beam produced passes into the ground and 'scans' like a radar beam searching for echoes. By a very ingenious time-delay circuit which I will resist the temptation to describe, echoes from any depth can be selected and so pictures of the strata under investigation can be built up on a cathode ray screen in the normal way.

When I first met Professor Hancock his apparatus was rather primitive, but he was able to show me the distribution of rock down to a depth of several hundred feet and we could see quite clearly a part of the Bakerloo Line which passed very near his laboratory. Much of the Professor's success was due to the great intensity of his supersonic bursts; almost from the beginning he was able to generate peak powers of several hundred kilowatts, nearly all of which was radiated into the ground. It was unsafe to remain near the transmitter, and I noticed that the soil became quite warm around it. I was rather surprised to see large numbers of birds in the vicinity, but soon discovered that they were attracted by the hundreds of dead worms lying on the ground.

At the time of Dr. Clayton's death in 1960, the equipment was working at a power level of over a megawatt and quite good pictures of strata a mile down could be obtained. Dr. Clayton had correlated the results with known geographical surveys, and had proved beyond doubt the value of the information obtained.

Dr. Clayton's death in a motor accident was a great tragedy. He had always exerted a stabilizing influence on the Professor, who had never been much interested in the practical applications of his work. Soon afterward I noticed a distinct change in the Professor's outlook, and a few months later he confided his new ambitions to me. I had been trying to persuade him to publish his results (he had already spent over £50,000 and the Public Accounts Committee was being difficult again), but he asked for a little more time. I think I can best explain his attitude by his own words, which I remember very vividly, for they were expressed with peculiar emphasis.

"Have you ever wondered," he said, "what the Earth really is like inside? We've only scratched the surface with our mines and wells. What lies beneath is as unknown as the other side of the Moon.

"We know that the Earth is unnaturally dense—far denser than the rocks and soil of its crust could indicate. The core may be solid metal, but until now there's been no way of telling. Even ten miles down the pressure must be thirty tons or more to the square inch and the temperature several hundred degrees. What it's like at the center staggers the imagination: the pressure must be thousands of tons to the square inch. It's strange to think that in two or three years we may have reached the Moon, but when we've got to the stars we'll still be no nearer that inferno four thousand miles beneath our feet.

"I can now get recognizable echoes from two miles down, but I hope to step up the transmitter to ten megawatts in a few months. With that power, I believe the range will be increased to ten miles; and I don't mean to stop there."

I was impressed, but at the same time I felt a little skeptical.

"That's all very well," I said, "but surely the deeper you go the less there'll be to see. The pressure will make any cavities impossible, and after a few miles there will simply be a homogeneous mass getting denser and denser."

"Quite likely," agreed the Professor. "But I can still learn a lot from the transmission characteristics. Anyway, we'll see when we get there."

That was four months ago; and yesterday I saw the result of that research. When I answered his invitation the Professor was clearly excited, but he gave me no hint of what, if anything, he had discovered. He showed me his improved equipment and raised the new receiver from its bath. The sensitivity of the pickups had been greatly improved, and this alone had effectively doubled the range, although apart from the increased transmitter power. It was strange to watch the steel framework slowly turning and to realize that it was exploring regions which, in spite of their nearness, man might never reach.

When we entered the hut containing the display equipment, the Professor was strangely silent. He switched on the transmitter, and even though it was a hundred yards away I could feel an uncomfortable tingling. Then the cathode ray tube lit up and the slowly revolving time-base drew the picture I had seen so often before. Now, however, the definition was much improved owing to the increased power and sensitivity of the equipment. I adjusted the depth control and focused on the Underground, which was clearly visible as a dark lane across the faintly luminous screen. While I was watching, it suddenly seemed to fill with mist and I knew that a train was going through.

Presently I continued the descent. Although I had watched this picture many times before, it was always uncanny to see great luminous masses floating toward me and to know that they were buried rocks—perhaps the debris from the glaciers of fifty thousand years ago. Dr. Clayton had worked out a chart so that we could identify the various strata as they were passed, and presently I saw that I was through the alluvial soil and entering the great clay saucer which traps and holds the city's artesian water. Soon that too was passed, and I was dropping down through the bedrock almost a mile below the surface.

The picture was still clear and bright, though there was little to see, for there were now few changes in the ground structure. The pressure was already rising to a thousand atmospheres, soon it would be impossible for any cavity to remain open, for the rock itself would begin to flow. Mile after mile I sank, but only a pale mist floated on the screen, broken sometimes when echoes were returned from pockets or lodes of denser material. They became fewer and fewer as the depth increased—or else they were now so small that they could no longer be seen.

The scale of the picture was, of course, continually expanding. It was now many miles from side to side, and I felt like an airman looking down upon an unbroken cloud ceiling from an enormous height. For a moment a sense of vertigo seized me as I thought of the abyss into which I was gazing. I do not think that the world will ever seem quite solid to me again.

At a depth of nearly ten miles I stopped and looked at the Professor. There had been no alteration for some time, and I knew that the rock must now be compressed into a featureless, homogeneous mass. I did a quick mental calculation and shuddered as I realized that the pressure must be at least thirty tons to the square inch. The scanner was revolving very slowly now, for the feeble echoes were taking many seconds to struggle back from the depths.

"Well, Professor," I said, "I congratulate you. It's a wonderful achievement. But we seem to have reached the core now. I don't suppose there'll be any change from here to the center."

He smiled a little wryly. "Go on," he said. "You haven't finished yet."

There was something in his voice that puzzled and alarmed me. I looked at him intently for a moment; his features were just visible in the blue-green glow of the cathode ray tube.

"How far down can this thing go?" I asked, as the interminable descent started again.

"Fifteen miles," he said shortly. I wondered how he knew, for the last feature I had seen at all clearly was only eight miles down. But I continued the long fall through the rock, the scanner turning more and more slowly now, until it took almost five minutes to make a complete revolution. Behind me I could hear the Professor breathing heavily, and once the back of my chair gave a crack as his fingers gripped it.

Then, suddenly, very faint markings began to reappear on the screen. I leaned forward eagerly, wondering if this was the first glimpse of the world's iron core. With agonizing slowness the scanner turned through a right angle, then another. And then—

I leaped suddenly out of my chair, cried "My God!" and turned to face the Professor. Only once before in my life had

I received such an intellectual shock—fifteen years ago, when I had accidentally turned on the radio and heard of the fall of the first atomic bomb. That had been unexpected, but this was inconceivable. For on the screen had appeared a grid of faint lines, crossing and recrossing to form a perfectly symmetrical lattice.

I know that I said nothing for many minutes, for the scanner made a complete revolution while I stood frozen with surprise. Then the Professor spoke in a soft, unnaturally calm voice.

"I wanted you to see it for yourself before I said anything. That picture is now thirty miles in diameter, and those squares are two or three miles on a side. You'll notice that the vertical lines converge and the horizontal ones are bent into arcs. We're looking at part of an enormous structure of concentric rings; the center must lie many miles to the north, probably in the region of Cambridge. How much farther it extends in the other direction we can only guess."

"But what *is* it, for heaven's sake?"

"Well, it's clearly artificial."

"That's ridiculous! Fifteen miles down!"

The Professor pointed to the screen again. "God knows I've done my best," he said, "but I can't convince myself that Nature could make anything like that."

I had nothing to say, and presently he continued: "I discovered it three days ago, when I was trying to find the maximum range of the equipment. I can go deeper than this, and I rather think that the structure we can see is so dense that it won't transmit my radiations any further.

"I've tried a dozen theories, but in the end I keep returning to one. We know that the pressure down there must be eight or nine thousand atmospheres, and the temperature must be high enough to melt rock. But normal matter is still almost empty space. Suppose that there is life down there—not organic life, of course, but life based on partially condensed matter, matter in which the electron shells are few or altogether missing. Do you see what I mean? To such creatures, even the rock fifteen miles down would offer no more resistance than water—and we and all our world would be as tenuous as ghosts."

"Then that thing we can see—"

"Is a city, or its equivalent. You've seen its size, so you can judge for yourself the civilization that must have built it. All the world we know—our oceans and continents and mountains—is nothing more than a film of mist surrounding something beyond our comprehension."

Neither of us said anything for a while. I remember feeling a foolish surprise at being one of the first men in the world to learn the appalling truth; for somehow I never doubted that it was the truth. And I wondered how the rest of humanity would react when the revelation came.

Presently I broke into the silence. "If you're right," I said, "why have they—whatever they are—never made contact with us?"

The Professor looked at me rather pityingly. "We think we're good engineers," he said, "but how could *we* reach *them*? Besides, I'm not at all sure that there haven't been contacts. Think of all the underground creatures and the mythology—trolls and cobalds and the rest. No, it's quite impossible—I take it back. Still, the idea *is* rather suggestive."

All the while the pattern on the screen had never changed: the dim network still glowed there, challenging our sanity. I tried to imagine streets and buildings and the creatures going among them, creatures who could make their way through the incandescent rock as a fish swims through water. It was fantastic . . . and then I remembered the incredibly narrow range of temperatures and pressures under which the human race exists. *We,* not they, were the freaks, for almost all the matter in the universe is at temperatures of thousands or even millions of degrees.

"Well," I said lamely, "what do we do now?"

The Professor leaned forward eagerly. "First we must learn a great deal more, and we must keep this an absolute secret until we are sure of the facts. Can you imagine the panic there would be if this information leaked out? Of course, the truth's inevitable sooner or later, but we may be able to break it slowly.

"You'll realize that the geological surveying side of my work is now utterly unimportant. The first thing we have to do is to build a chain of stations to find the extent of the structure. I visualize them at ten-mile intervals toward the north, but I'd like to build the first one somewhere in South London to see how extensive the thing is. The whole job will have to be kept as secret as the building of the first radar chain in the late thirties.

"At the same time, I'm going to push up my transmitter

power again. I hope to be able to beam the output much more narrowly, and so greatly increase the energy concentration. But this will involve all sorts of mechanical difficulties, and I'll need more assistance."

I promised to do my utmost to get further aid, and the Professor hopes that you will soon be able to visit his laboratory yourself. In the meantime I am attaching a photograph of the vision screen, which although not as clear as the original will, I hope, prove beyond doubt that our observations are not mistaken.

I am well aware that our grant to the Interplanetary Society has brought us dangerously near the total estimate for the year, but surely even the crossing of space is less important than the immediate investigation of this discovery which may have the most profound effects on the philosophy and the future of the whole human race.

I sat back and looked at Karn. There was much in the document I had not understood, but the main outlines were clear enough.

"Yes," I said, "this is it! Where's that photograph?"

He handed it over. The quality was poor, for it had been copied many times before reaching us. But the pattern was unmistakable and I recognized it at once.

"They were good scientists," I said admiringly. "That's Callastheon, all right. So we've found the truth at last, even if it has taken us three hundred years to do it."

"Is that surprising," asked Karn, "when you consider the mountain of stuff we've had to translate and the difficulty of copying it before it evaporates?"

I sat in silence for a while, thinking of the strange race whose relics we were examining. Only once—never again!—had I gone up the great vent our engineers had opened into the Shadow World. It had been a frightening and unforgettable experience. The multiple layers of my pressure suit had made movement very difficult, and despite their insulation I could sense the unbelievable cold that was all around me.

"What a pity it was," I mused, "that our emergence destroyed them so completely. They were a clever race, and we might have learned a lot from them."

"I don't think we can be blamed," said Karn. "We never really believed that anything could exist under those awful conditions of near-vacuum, and almost absolute zero. It couldn't be helped."

I did not agree. "I think it proves that they were the more intelligent race. After all, *they* discovered us first. Everyone laughed at my grandfather when he said that the radiation he'd detected from the Shadow World must be artificial."

Karn ran one of his tentacles over the manuscript.

"We've certainly discovered the cause of that radiation," he said, "Notice the date—it's just a year before your grandfather's discovery. The Professor must have got his grant all right!" He laughed unpleasantly. "It must have given him a shock when he saw us coming up to the surface, right underneath him."

I scarcely heard his words, for a most uncomfortable feeling had suddenly come over me. I thought of the thousands of miles of rock lying below the great city of Callastheon, growing hotter and denser all the way to the Earth's unknown core. And so I turned to Karn.

"That isn't very funny," I said quietly. "It may be our turn next."

ZERO HOUR

by Ray Bradbury (1920–   )

THRILLING WONDER STORIES
Fall

Ray Bradbury hardly needs an introduction, but for the record, he is the author of such landmark science fiction works as The Martian Chronicles *(1950),* The Illustrated Man *(1951), and the classic dystopian novel* Fahrenheit 451 *(1953); has won many awards, including two O. Henry Prizes (1947 and 1948), the Benjamin Franklin Award (1954), a Boys' Clubs of America Junior Book Award (1956), and the Gandalf Award (1980); and is one of America's best known writers. It is interesting to note that he has never won a Hugo or Nebula Award in his long career.*

"Zero Hour" is one of his best stories, an invasion tale that combines all of the elements that have made him so popular, including a young character in an important role. The story is also one of his personal favorites, and he chose it for Leo Margulies' anthology My Best Science Fiction Story *(1949).*

(Since Marty mentioned the Margulies anthology My Best Science Fiction Story *I want to take the*

opportunity to ventilate a grievance. I was asked to select a story of my own for that anthology and to give a reason for the selection, and the anthology was to be called "Author's Choice" or something like that. The major requirement, however, was that the story not *have appeared in* Astounding Science Fiction.

This was an unfortunate requirement since most of my stories did *appear in Astounding. The few that didn't were inferior. [It is a measure of the domination of the field by Astounding in the 1940s that the large majority of the stories contained in this series of anthologies, so far, are from that magazine.]*

Those were early days and I was anxious to have my stories appear in anthologies, so I picked one of those inferior stories and gave a reason. When the anthology appeared, I found that the name has been changed, without any warning, to My Best Science Fiction Story.

That was all right for Ray Bradbury, one of the major talents in the field who didn't write for Astounding. *"Zero Hour" is a proper showcase for his abilities and a reasonable choice at that time for his "Best." I, however, always felt I had been tricked into self-libel.—I.A.*

Oh, it was to be so jolly! What a game! Such excitement they hadn't known in years. The children catapulted this way and that across the green lawns, shouting at each other, holding hands, flying in circles, climbing trees, laughing. Overhead the rockets flew, and beetle cars whispered by on the streets, but the children played on. Such fun, such tremulous joy, such tumbling and hearty screaming.

Mink ran into the house, all dirt and sweat. For her seven years she was loud and strong and definite. Her mother, Mrs. Morris, hardly saw her as she yanked out drawers and rattled pans and tools into a large sack.

"Heavens, Mink, what's going on?"

"The most exciting game ever!" gasped Mink, pink-faced.

"Stop and get your breath," said the mother.

"No, I'm all right," gasped Mink. "Okay I take these things, Mom?"

"But don't dent them," said Mrs. Morris.

"Thank you, thank you!" cried Mink, and boom! she was gone, like a rocket.

Mrs. Morris surveyed the fleeing tot. "What's the name of the game?"

"Invasion!" said Mink. The door slammed.

In every yard on the street children brought out knives and forks and pokers and old stovepipes and can openers.

It was an interesting fact that this fury and bustle occurred only among the younger children. The older ones, those ten years and more, disdained the affair and marched scornfully off on hikes or played a more dignified version of hide-and-seek on their own.

Meanwhile, parents came and went in chromium beetles. Repairmen came to repair the vacuum elevators in houses, to fix fluttering television sets, or hammer upon stubborn food-delivery tubes. The adult civilization passed and repassed the busy youngsters, jealous of the fierce energy of the wild tots, tolerantly amused at their flourishings, longing to join in themselves.

"This and this and *this*," said Mink, instructing the others with their assorted spoons and wrenches. "Do that, and bring *that* over here. No! *Here,* ninny! Right. Now get back while I fix this." Tongue in teeth, face wrinkled in thought. "Like that. See?"

"Yayyyy!" shouted the kids.

Twelve-year-old Joseph Connors ran up.

"Go away," said Mink straight at him.

"I wanna play," said Joseph.

"Can't!" said Mink.

"Why not?"

"You'd just make fun of us."

"Honest, I wouldn't."

"No. We know *you* Go away or we'll kick you."

Another twelve-year-old boy whirred by on little motor skates. "Hey, Joe! Come on! Let them sissies play!"

Joseph showed reluctance and a certain wistfulness. "I *want* to play," he said.

"You're old," said Mink firmly.

"Not *that* old," said Joe sensibly.

"You'd only laugh and spoil the Invasion."

The boy on the motor skates made a rude lip noise. "Come on, Joe! Them and their fairies! Nuts!"

Joseph walked off slowly. He kept looking back, all down the block.

Mink was already busy again. She made a kind of apparatus with her gathered equipment. She had appointed another little girl with a pad and pencil to take down notes in painful slow scribbles. Their voices rose and fell in the warm sunlight.

All around them the city hummed. The streets were lined with good green and peaceful trees. Only the wind made a conflict across the city, across the country, across the continent. In a thousand other cities there were trees and children and avenues, businessmen in their quiet offices taping their voices, or watching televisors. Rockets hovered like darning needles in the blue sky. There was the universal, quiet conceit and easiness of men accustomed to peace, quite certain there would never be trouble again. Arm in arm, men all over earth were a united front. The perfect weapons were held in equal trust by all nations. A situation of incredibly beautiful balance had been brought about. There were no traitors among men, no unhappy ones, no disgruntled ones; therefore the world was based upon a stable ground. Sunlight illuminated half the world and the trees drowsed in a tide of warm air.

Mink's mother, from her upstairs window, gazed down.

The children. She looked upon them and shook her head. Well, they'd eat well, sleep well, and be in school on Monday. Bless their vigorous little bodies. She listened.

Mink talked earnestly to someone near the rosebush—though there was no one there.

These odd children. And the little girl, what was her name? Anna? Anna took notes on a pad. First, Mink asked the rosebush a question, then called the answer to Anna.

"Triangle," said Mink.

"What's a tri," said Anna with difficulty, "angle?"

"Never mind," said Mink.

"How you spell it?" asked Anna.

"T-r-i——" spelled Mink slowly, then snapped, "Oh, spell it yourself!" She went on to other words. "Beam," she said.

"I haven't got tri," said Anna, "angle down yet!"

"Well, hurry, hurry!" cried Mink.

Mink's mother leaned out the upstairs window. "A-n-g-l-e," she spelled down at Anna.

"Oh, thanks, Mrs. Morris," said Anna.

"Certainly," said Mink's mother and withdrew, laughing, to dust the hall with an electro-duster magnet.

The voices wavered on the shimmery air. "Beam," said Anna. Fading.

"Four-nine-seven-A-and-B-and-X," said Mink, far away, seriously. "And a fork and a string and a—hex-hex-agony—hexagonal!"

At lunch Mink gulped milk at one toss and was at the door. Her mother slapped the table.

"You sit right back down," commanded Mrs. Morris. "Hot soup in a minute." She poked a red button on the kitchen butler, and ten seconds later something landed with a bump in the rubber receiver. Mrs. Morris opened it, took out a can with a pair of aluminum holders, unsealed it with a flick; and poured hot soup into a bowl.

During all this Mink fidgeted. "Hurry, Mom! This is a matter of life and death! Aw——"

"I was the same way at your age. Always life and death. I know."

Mink banged away at the soup.

"Slow down," said Mom.

"Can't," said Mink. "Drill's waiting for me."

"Who's Drill? What a peculiar name," said Mom.

"You don't know him," said Mink.

"A new boy in the neighborhood?" asked Mom.

"He's new all right," said Mink. She started on her second bowl.

"Which one is Drill?" asked Mom.

"He's around," said Mink evasively. "You'll make fun. Everybody pokes fun. Gee, darn."

"Is Drill shy?"

"Yes. No. In a way. Gosh, Mom, I got to run if we want to have the Invasion!"

"Who's invading what?"

"Martians invading Earth. Well, not exactly Martians. They're—I don't know. From up." She pointed her spoon.

"And *inside,*" said Mom, touching Mink's feverish brow.

Mink rebelled. "You're laughing! You'll kill Drill and everybody."

"I didn't mean to," said Mom. "Drill's a Martian?"

"No. He's—well—maybe from Jupiter or Saturn or Venus. Anyway, he's had a hard time."

"I imagine." Mrs. Morris hid her mouth behind her hand.

"They couldn't figure a way to attack Earth."

"We're impregnable," said Mom in mock seriousness.

"That's the word Drill used! Impreg— That was the word, Mom."

"My, my, Drill's a brilliant boy. Two-bit words."

"They couldn't figure a way to attack, Mom. Drill says— he says in order to make a good fight you got to have a new way of surprising people. That way you win. And he says also you got to have help from your enemy."

"A fifth column," said Mom.

"Yeah. That's what Drill said. And they couldn't figure a way to surprise Earth, or get help."

"No wonder. We're pretty darn strong." Mom laughed, cleaning up. Mink sat there, staring at the table, seeing what she was talking about.

"Until, one day," whispered Mink melodramatically, "they thought of children!"

"*Well!*" said Mrs. Morris brightly.

"And they thought of how grownups are so busy they never look under rosebushes or on lawns!"

"Only for snails and fungus."

"And then there's something about dim-dims."

"Dim-dims?"

"Dimens-shuns."

"Dimensions?"

"Four of 'em! And there's something about kids under nine and imagination. It's real funny to hear Drill talk."

Mrs. Morris was tired. "Well, it must be funny. You're keeping Drill waiting now. It's getting late in the day and, if you want to have your Invasion before your supper bath, you'd better jump."

"Do I have to take a bath?" growled Mink.

"You do. Why is it children hate water? No matter what age you live in children hate water behind the ears!"

"Drill says I won't have to take baths," said Mink.

"Oh, he does, does he?"

"He told all the kids that. No more baths. And we can stay up till ten o'clock and go to two televisor shows on Saturday 'stead of one!"

"Well, Mr. Drill better mind his p's and q's. I'll call up his mother and—"

Mink went to the door. "We're having trouble with guys like Pete Britz and Dale Jerrick. They're growing up. They make fun. They're worse than parents. They just won't believe in Drill. They're so snooty, 'cause they're growing up. You'd think they'd know better. They were little only a coupla years ago. I hate them worst. We'll kill them *first*."

"Your father and me last?"

"Drill says you're dangerous. Know why? 'Cause you don't believe in Martians! They're going to let *us* run the world. Well, not just us, but the kids over in the next block, too. I might be queen." She opened the door.

"Mom?"

"Yes?"

"What's lodge-ick?"

"Logic? Why, dear, logic is knowing what things are true and not true."

"He *mentioned* that," said Mink. "And what's im-pres-sion-able?" It took her a minute to say it.

"Why, it means——" Her mother looked at the floor, laughing gently. "It means—to be a child, dear."

"Thanks for lunch!" Mink ran out, then stuck her head back in. "Mom, I'll be sure you won't be hurt much, really!"

"Well, thanks," said Mom.

Slam went the door.

At four o'clock the audiovisor buzzed. Mrs. Morris flipped the tab. "Hello, Helen!" she said in welcome.

"Hello, Mary. How are things in New York?"

"Fine. How are things in Scranton? You look tired."

"So do you. The children. Underfoot," said Helen.

Mrs. Morris sighed. "My Mink too. The super-Invasion."

Helen laughed. "Are your kids playing that game too?"

"Lord, yes. Tomorrow it'll be geometrical jacks and motorized hopscotch. Were we this bad when we were kids in '48?"

"Worse. Japs and Nazis. Don't know how my parents put up with me. Tomboy."

"Parents learn to shut their ears."

A silence.

"What's wrong, Mary?" asked Helen.

Mrs. Morris's eyes were half closed; her tongue slid slowly, thoughtfully, over her lower lip. "Eh?" She jerked. "Oh, nothing. Just thought about *that.* Shutting ears and such. Never mind. Where were we?"

"My boy Tim's got a crush on some guy named—*Drill,* I think it was."

"Must be a new password. Mink likes him too."

"Didn't know it had got as far as New York. Word of mouth, I imagine. Looks like a scrap-drive. I talked to Josephine and she said her kids—that's in Boston—are wild on this new game. It's sweeping the country."

At that moment Mink trotted into the kitchen to gulp a glass of water. Mrs. Morris turned. "How're things going?"

"Almost finished," said Mink.

"Swell," said Mrs. Morris. "What's *that*?"

"A yo-yo," said Mink. "Watch."

She flung the yo-yo down its string. Reaching the end it—

It vanished.

"See?" said Mink. "Ope!" Dribbling her finger, she made the yo-yo reappear and zip up the string.

"Do that again," said her mother.

"Can't. Zero hour's five o'clock! 'Bye." Mink exited, zipping her yo-yo.

On the audiovisor, Helen laughed. "Tim brought one of those yo-yos in this morning, but when I got curious he said he wouldn't show it to me, and when I tried to work it, finally, it wouldn't work."

"You're not *impressionable,*" said Mrs. Morris.

"What?"

"Never mind. Something I thought of. Can I help you, Helen?"

"I wanted to get that black-and-white cake recipe——"

The hour drowsed by. The day waned. The sun lowered in the peaceful blue sky. Shadows lengthened on the green lawns. The laughter and excitement continued. One little girl ran away, crying. Mrs. Morris came out the front door.

"Mink, was that Peggy Ann crying?"

Mink was bent over in the yard, near the rosebush. "Yeah. She's a scarebaby. We won't let her play, now. She's getting too old to play. I guess she grew up all of a sudden."

"Is that why she cried? Nonsense. Give me a civil answer, young lady, or inside you come!"

Mink whirled in consternation, mixed with irritation. "I can't quit now. It's almost time. I'll be good. I'm sorry."

"Did you hit Peggy Ann?"

"No, honest. You ask her. It was something—well, she's just a scaredy pants."

The ring of children drew in around Mink where she scowled at her work with spoons and a kind of square-shaped arrangement of hammers and pipes. "There and there," murmured Mink.

"What's wrong?" said Mrs. Morris.

"Drill's stuck. Halfway. If we could only get him all the way through, it'd be easier. Then all the others could come through after him."

"Can I help?"

"No'm, thanks, I'll fix it."

"All right. I'll call you for your bath in half an hour. I'm tired of watching you."

She went in and sat in the electric relaxing chair, sipping a little beer from a half-empty glass. The chair massaged her back. Children, children. Children love and hate, side by side. Sometimes children loved you, hated you—all in half a second. Strange children, did they ever forget or forgive the whippings and the harsh, strict words of command? She wondered. How can you ever forget or forgive those over and above you, those tall and silly dictators?

Time passed. A curious, waiting silence came upon the street, deepening.

Five o'clock. A clock sang softly somewhere in the house in a quiet, musical voice: "Five o'clock—five o'clcok. Time's a-wasting. Five o'clock," and purred away into silence.

Zero hour.

Mrs. Morris chuckled in her throat. Zero hour.

A beetle car hummed into the driveway. Mr. Morris. Mrs. Morris smiled. Mr. Morris got out of the beetle, locked it and called hello to Mink at her work. Mink ignored him. He laughed and stood for a moment watching the children. Then he walked up the front steps.

"Hello, darling."

"Hello, Henry."

She strained forward on the edge of the chair, listening. The children were silent. Too silent.

He emptied his pipe, refilled it. "Swell day. Makes you glad to be alive."

Buzz.

"What's that?" asked Henry.

"I don't know." She got up suddenly, her eyes widening. She was going to say something. She stopped it. Ridiculous. Her nerves jumped. "Those children haven't anything dangerous out there, have they?" she said.

"Nothing but pipes and hammers. Why?"

"Nothing electrical?"

"Heck, no," said Henry. "I looked."

She walked to the kitchen. The buzzing continued. "Just the same, you'd better go tell them to quit. It's after five. Tell them——" Her eyes widened and narrowed. "Tell them to put off their Invasion until tomorrow." She laughed, nervously.

The buzzing grew louder.

"What are they up to? I'd better go look, all right."

The explosion!

The house shook with dull sound. There were other explosions in other yards on other streets.

Involuntarily, Mrs. Morris screamed. "Up this way!" she cried senselessly, knowing no sense, no reason. Perhaps she saw something from the corners of her eyes; perhaps she smelled a new odor or heard a new noise. There was no time to argue with Henry to convince him. Let him think her insane. Yes, insane! Shrieking, she ran upstairs. He ran after her to see what she was up to. "In the attic!" she screamed. "That's where it is!" It was only a poor excuse to get him in the attic in time. Oh, God—in time!

Another explosion outside. The children screamed with delight, as if at a great fireworks display.

"It's not in the attic!" cried Henry. "It's outside!"

"No, no!" Wheezing, gasping, she fumbled at the attic door. "I'll show you. Hurry! I'll show you!"

They tumbled into the attic. She slammed the door, locked it, took the key, threw it into a far, cluttered corner.

She was babbling wild stuff now. It came out of her. All the subconscious suspicion and fear that had gathered secretly all afternoon and fermented like a wine in her. All the little revelations and knowledges and sense that had bothered her all day and which she had logically and carefully and sensibly rejected and censored. Now it exploded in her and shook her to bits.

"There, there," she said, sobbing against the door. "We're safe until tonight. Maybe we can sneak out. Maybe we can escape!"

Henry blew up too, but for another reason. "Are you crazy? Why'd you throw that key away? Blast it!"

"Yes, yes, I'm crazy, if it helps, but stay here with me!"

"I don't know how I can get out!"

"Quiet. They'll hear us. Oh, God, they'll find us soon enough——"

Below them, Mink's voice. The husband stopped. There was a great universal humming and sizzling, a screaming and giggling. Downstairs the audio-televisor buzzed and buzzed insistently, alarmingly, violently. *Is that Helen calling?* thought Mrs. Morris. *And is she calling about what I think she's calling about?*

Footsteps came into the house. Heavy footsteps.

"Who's coming in my house?" demanded Henry angrily. "Who's tramping around down there?"

Heavy feet. Twenty, thirty, forty, fifty of them. Fifty persons crowding into the house. The humming. The giggling of the children. "This way!" cried Mink, below.

"Who's downstairs?" roared Henry. "Who's there!"

"Hush. Oh, nonononononono!" said his wife, weakly, holding him. "Please, be quiet. They might go away."

"Mom?" called Mink. "Dad?" A pause. "Where are you?"

Heavy footsteps, heavy, heavy, *very heavy* footsteps, came up the stairs. Mink leading them.

"Mom?" A hesitation. "Dad?" A waiting, a silence.

Humming. Footsteps toward the attic. Mink's first.

They trembled together in silence in the attic, Mr. and Mrs. Morris. For some reason the electric humming, the queer cold light suddenly visible under the door crack, the strange odor, and the alien sound of eagerness in Mink's voice finally got through to Henry Morris too. He stood, shivering, in the dark silence, his wife beside him.

"Mom! Dad!"

Footsteps. A little humming sound. The attic lock melted. The door opened. Mink peered inside, tall blue shadows behind her.

"Peekaboo," said Mink.

HOBBYIST

by Eric Frank Russell (1905–1978)

ASTOUNDING SCIENCE FICTION
September

Eric Frank Russell was a very tall Briton (raised in Egypt) who produced a substantial body of excellent work in the science fiction field. Although his best known book is certainly Sinister Barrier *(1943), he was one of the premier satirists in sf, his satire usually reflecting a good measure of cynicism. He won the Hugo Award in 1955 for his short story "Allamagoosa." Other excellent books include* Wasp *(1957),* The Great Explosion *(1962),* Men, Martians, and Machines *(1956), and* The Best of Eric Frank Russell *(1978), his definitive short story collection. Unfortunately, he wrote several excellent long stories which are rarely reprinted because of their length, such as "First Person Singular" (in* Deep Space, *1954). A collection of his novellas would make a wonderful book.*

One of his specialties was the depiction of alien life forms, well represented by "Hobbyist," a story that has rightly attained the status of a minor classic of its kind.

(I haven't got a keen ear for style or a sharp eye for narrative technique, since I've spent my whole literary life doing only what comes naturally. On the other hand, I'm not utterly unobservant.

For instance, I can't help realizing that a one-character story has its problems and that these rapidly escalate with length. Do you deal entirely with thoughts? Do you introduce flashbacks? Do you concentrate so entirely on action that the reader forgets there is no dialogue? There are disadvantages in every case.

Eric Frank Russell in "Hobbyist" introduces a macaw, an ordinary non-science-fictional bird, and you might be interested after reading the story, to go through it again, and to note how cleverly Russell makes it serve the purpose of introducing just enough dialogue to dispel the difficulties of a one-character situation—I.A.)

The ship arced out of a golden sky and landed with a whoop and a wallop that cut down a mile of lush vegetation. Another half-mile of growths turned black and drooped to ashes under the final flicker of the tail-rocket blasts. That arrival was spectacular, full of verve, and worthy of four columns in any man's paper. But the nearest sheet was distant by a goodly slice of a lifetime, and there was none to record what this far corner of the cosmos regarded as the pettiest of events. So the ship squatted tired and still in the foremost end of the ashy blast-track and the sky glowed down and the green world brooded solemnly all around.

Within the transpex control-dome, Steve Ander sat and thought things over. It was his habit to think things over carefully. Astronauts were not the impulsive dare-devils so dear to the stereopticon-loving public. They couldn't afford to be. The hazards of the profession required an infinite capacity for cautious, contemplative thought. Five minutes' consideration had prevented many a collapsed lung, many a leaky heart, many a fractured frame. Steve valued his skeleton. He wasn't conceited about it and he'd no reason to believe it in any way superior to anyone else's skeleton. But he'd had it a long time, found it quite satisfactory, and had an intense desire to keep it—intact.

Therefore, while the tail tubes cooled off with their usual creaking contractions, he sat in the control seat, stared through the dome with eyes made unseeing by deep preoccupation, and performed a few thinks.

Firstly, he'd made a rough estimate of this world during his hectic approach. As nearly as he could judge, it was ten times the size of Terra. But his weight didn't seem abnormal. Of course, one's notions of weight tended to be somewhat wild when for some weeks one's own weight was shot far up or far down in between periods of weightlessness. The most reasonable estimate had to be based on muscular reaction. If you felt as sluggish as a Saturnian sloth, your weight was way up. If you felt as powerful as Angus McKittrick's bull, your weight was down.

Normal weight meant Terrestrial mass despite this planet's tenfold volume. That meant light plasma. And that meant lack of heavy elements. No thorium. No nickel. No nickel-thorium alloy. Ergo, no getting back. The Kingston-Kane atomic motors demanded fuel in the form of ten-gauge nickel-thorium-alloy wire fed directly into the vaporizers. Denatured plutonium would do, but it didn't occur in natural form, and it had to be made. He had three yards nine and a quarter inches of nickel-thorium left on the feed-spool. Not enough. He was here for keeps.

A wonderful thing, logic. You could start from the simple premise that when you were seated your behind was no flatter than usual, and work your way to the inevitable conclusion that you were a wanderer no more. You'd become a native. Destiny had you tagged as suitable for the status of oldest inhabitant.

Steve pulled an ugly face and said, 'Darn!'

The face didn't have to be pulled far. Nature had given said pan a good start. That is to say, it wasn't handsome. It was a long, lean, nut-brown face with pronounced jaw muscles, prominent cheekbones, and a thin, hooked nose. This, with his dark eyes and black hair, gave him a hawklike appearance. Friends talked to him about tepees and tomahawks whenever they wanted him to feel at home.

Well, he wasn't going to feel at home anymore; not unless this brooding jungle held intelligent life dopey enough to swap ten-gauge nickel-thorium wire for a pair of old boots. Or unless some dopey search party was intelligent enough to pick this cosmic dust mote out of a cloud of motes, and took him back. He estimated this as no less than a million-to-one chance. Like spitting at the Empire State hoping to hit a cent-sized mark on one of its walls.

Reaching for his everflo stylus and the ship's log, he opened the log, looked absently at some of the entries.

"Eighteenth day: The spatial convulsion has now flung me past rotal-range of Rigel. Am being tossed into uncharted regions. . . .

"Twenty-fourth day: Arm of convulsion now tails back seven parsecs. Robot recorder now out of gear. Angle of throw changed seven times today. . . .

"Twenty-ninth day: Now beyond arm of the convulsive sweep and regaining control. Speed far beyond range of the astrometer. Applying braking rockets cautiously. Fuel reserve: fourteen hundred yards. . . .

"Thirty-seventh day: Making for planetary system now within reach."

He scowled, his jaw muscles lumped, and he wrote slowly and legibly, "Thirty-ninth day: Landed on planet unknown, primary unknown, galactic area standard reference and sector numbers unknown. No cosmic formations were recognizable when observed shortly before landing. Angles of offshoot and speed of transit not recorded, and impossible to estimate. Condition of ship: workable. Fuel reserve: three and one-quarter yards."

Closing the log, he scowled again, rammed the stylus into its desk-grip, and muttered, "Now to check on the outside air and then see how the best girl's doing."

The Radson register had three simple dials. The first recorded outside pressure at thirteen point seven pounds, a reading he observed with much satisfaction. The second said that oxygen content was high. The third had a bi-colored dial, half-white, half-red, and its needle stood in the middle of the white.

"Breathable," he grunted, clipping down the register's lid. Crossing the tiny control room, he slid aside a metal panel, looked into the padded compartment behind. "Coming out, Beauteous?" he asked.

"Steve loves Laura?" inquired a plaintive voice.

"You bet he does!" he responded with becoming passion.

He shoved an arm into the compartment, brought out a large, gaudily colored macaw. "Does Laura love Steve?"

"Hey-hey!" cackled Laura harshly. Climbing up his arm, the bird perched on his shoulder. He could feel the grip of its powerful claws. It regarded him with a beady and brilliant eye, then rubbed its crimson head against his left ear. "Hey-hey! Time flies!"

"Don't mention it," he reproved. "There's plenty to remind me of the fact without you chipping in."

Reaching up, he scratched her poll while she stretched and bowed with absurd delight. He was fond of Laura. She was more than a pet. She was a bona fide member of the crew, issued with her own rations and drawing her own pay. Every probe ship had a crew of two; one man, one macaw. When he'd first heard of it, the practice had seemed crazy—but when he got the reasons it made sense.

"Lonely men, probing beyond the edge of the charts, get queer psychological troubles. They need an anchor to Earth. A macaw provides the necessary companionship—and more! It's the space-hardiest bird we've got, its weight is negligible, it can talk and amuse, it can fend for itself when necessary. On land, it will often sense dangers before you do. Any strange fruit or food it may eat is safe for you to eat. Many a man's life has been saved by his macaw. Look after yours, my boy, and it'll look after you!"

Yes, they looked after each other, Terrestrials both. It was almost a symbiosis of the spaceways. Before the era of astronavigation nobody had thought of such an arrangement, though it had been done before. Miners and their canaries.

Moving over to the miniature air lock, he didn't bother to operate the pump. It wasn't necessary with so small a difference between internal and external pressures. Opening both doors, he let a little of his higher-pressured air sigh out, stood on the rim of the lock, jumped down. Laura fluttered from his shoulder as he leaped, followed him with a flurry of wings, got her talons into his jacket as he staggered upright.

The pair went around the ship, silently surveying its condition. Front braking nozzles O.K., rear steering flares O.K., tail propulsion tubes O.K. All were badly scored but still usable. The skin of the vessel likewise was scored but intact. Three months' supply of food and maybe a thousand yards of wire could get her home, theoretically. But only theoretically; Steve had no delusions about the matter. The odds were still against him even if given the means to move. How do you navigate from you-don't-know-where to you-don't-know-where? Answer: you stroke a rabbit's foot and probably arrive you-don't-know-where-else.

"Well," he said, rounding the tail, "it's something in which to live. It'll save us building a shanty. Way back on Terra they want fifty thousand smackers for an all-metal, streamlined bungalow, so I guess we're mighty lucky. I'll make a garden here, and a rockery there, and build a swimming-pool out back. You can wear a pretty frock and do all the cooking."

"Yawk," said Laura derisively.

Turning, he had a look at the nearest vegetation. It was of all heights, shapes and sizes, of all shades of green with a few tending toward blueness. There was something peculiar about the stuff but he was unable to decide where the strangeness lay. It wasn't that the growths were alien and unfamiliar—one expected that on every new world—but an underlying something which they shared in common. They had a vague, shadowy air of being not quite right in some basic respect impossible to define.

A plant grew right at his feet. It was green in colour, a foot high, and monocotyledonous. Looked at as a thing in itself, there was nothing wrong with it. Near to it flourished a bush of darker hue, a yard high, with green, fir-like needles in lieu of leaves, and pale, waxy berries scattered over it. That, too, was innocent enough when studied apart from its neighbours. Beside it grew a similar plant, differing only in that its needles were longer and its berries a bright pink. Beyond these towered a cactuslike object dragged out of somebody's drunken dreams, and beside it stood an umbrella-frame which had taken root and produced little purple pods. Individually, they were acceptable. Collectively, they made the discerning mind search anxiously for it knew not what.

That eerie feature had Steve stumped. Whatever it was, he couldn't nail it down. There was something stranger than the mere strangeness of new forms of plant life, and that was all. He dismissed the problem with a shrug. Time enough to trouble about such matters after he'd dealt with others more urgent such as, for example, the location and purity of the nearest water supply.

A mile away lay a lake of some liquid that might be water. He'd seen it glittering in the sunlight as he'd made his descent, and he'd tried to land fairly near to it. If it wasn't water, well, it'd be just his tough luck and he'd have to look some place else. At worst, the tiny fuel reserve would be enough to permit one circumnavigation of the planet before the ship became pinned down forever. Water he must have if he wasn't going to end up imitating the mummy of Rameses II.

Reaching high, he grasped the rim of the port, dexterously muscled himself upward and through it. For a minute he moved around inside the ship, then reappeared with a four-gallon freeezocan which he tossed to the ground. Then he dug out his popgun, a belt of explosive shells, and let down the folding ladder from lock to surface. He'd need that ladder. He could muscle himself up through a hole seven feet high, but not with fifty pounds of can and water.

Finally, he locked both the inner and outer air-lock doors, skipped down the ladder, picked up the can. From the way he'd made his landing the lake should be directly bow-on relative to the vessel, and somewhere the other side of those distant trees. Laura took a fresh grip on his shoulder as he started off. The can swung from his left hand. His right hand rested warily on the gun. He was perpendicular on this world instead of horizontal on another because, on two occasions, his hand had been ready on the gun and because it was the most nervous hand he possessed.

The going was rough. It wasn't so much that the terrain was craggy as the fact that impending growths got in his way. At one moment he was stepping over an ankle-high shrub, the next he was facing a burly plant struggling to become a tree. Behind the plant would be a creeper, then a natural zareba of thorns, a fuzz of fine moss, followed by a giant fern. Progress consisted of stepping over one item, ducking beneath a second, going around a third, and crawling under a forth.

It occurred to him belatedly that if he'd planted the ship tail-first to the lake instead of bow-on, or if he'd let the braking rockets blow after he'd touched down, he'd have saved himself much twisting and dodging. All this obstructing stuff would have been reduced to ashes for at least half the distance to the lake—together with any venomous life it might conceal.

That last thought rang like an alarm bell within his mind just as he doubled up to pass a low-swung creeper. On Venus were creepers that coiled and constricted, swiftly, viciously. Macaws played merry hell, if taken within fifty yards of them. It was a comfort to know that, this time, Laura was riding his shoulder unperturbed—but he kept the hand on the gun.

The elusive peculiarity of the planet's vegetation bothered him all the more as he progressed through it. His inability to discover and name this unnameable queerness nagged at him as he went on. A frown of self-disgust was on his lean face when he dragged himself free of a clinging bush and sat on a rock in a tiny clearing.

Dumping the can at his feet, he glowered at it and promptly caught a glimpse of something bright and shining a few feet beyond the can. He raised his gaze. It was then that he saw the beetle.

The creature was the biggest of its kind ever seen by human eyes. There were other things bigger, of course, but not of this type. Crabs, for instance. But this was no crab. The beetle ambling purposefully across the clearing was large enough to give any crab a severe inferiority complex, but it was a genuine twenty-four-carat beetle. And a beautiful one. Like a scarab.

Except that he clung to the notion that little bugs were vicious and big ones companionable, Steve had no phobia about insects. The amiability of large ones was a theory inherited from school-kid days when he'd been the doting owner of a three-inch stag-beetle afflicted with the name of Edgar.

So he knelt beside the creeping giant, placed his hand palm upward in its path. It investigated the hand with waving feelers, climbed on to his palm, paused there ruminatively. It shone with a sheen of brilliant metallic blue and weighed about three pounds. He jogged it on his hand to get its weight, then put it down, let it wander on. Laura watched it go with a sharp but incurious eye.

"*Scarabaeus anderii,*" Steve said with glum satisfaction. "I pin my name on him—but nobody'll ever know it."

"Dinna fash y'sel'!" shouted Laura in a hoarse voice imported straight from Aberdeen. "Dinna fash! Stop chunnerin', wumman! Y' gie me a pain ahint ma sporran! Dinna—"

"Shut up!" Steve jerked his shoulder, momentarily unbalancing the bird. "Why d'you pick up that barbaric dialect quicker than anything else, eh?"

"McGillicuddy," shrieked Laura with ear-splitting relish. "McGilli-Gilli-Gillicuddy! The great black—!" It ended with a word that pushed Steve's eyebrows into his hair and surprised even the bird itself. Filming its eyes with amazement, it tightened its claw-hold on his shoulder, opened the eyes, emitted a couple of raucous clucks, and joyfully repeated, "The great black—"

It didn't get the chance to complete the new and lovely word. A violent jerk of the shoulder unseated it in the nick of time and it fluttered to the ground, squawking protestingly. *Scarabaeus anderii* lumbered out from behind a bush, his blue armor glistening as if freshly polished, and stared reprovingly at Laura.

Then something fifty yards away released a snort like the trump of doom and took one step that shook the earth. *Scarabaeus anderii* took refuge under a projecting root. Laura made an agitated swoop for Steve's shoulder and clung there desperately. Steve's gun was out and pointing northward before the bird had found its perch. Another step. The ground quivered.

Silence for a while. Steven continued to stand like a statue. Then came a monstrous whistle more forceful than that of a locomotive blowing off steam. Something squat and wide and of tremendous length charged headlong through the half-concealing vegetation while the earth trembled beneath its weight.

Its mad onrush carried it blindly twenty yards to Steve's right, the gun swinging to cover its course, but not firing. Steve caught an extended glimpse of a slate-gray bulk with a serrated ridge on its back which, despite the thing's pace, took long to pass. It seemed several times the length of a fire ladder.

Bushes were flung roots topmost and small trees whipped aside as the creature pounded grimly onward in a straight line which carried it far past the ship into the dim distance. It left behind a tattered swathe wide enough for a first-class road. Then the reverberations of its mighty tonnage died out, and it was gone.

Steve used his left hand to pull out a handkerchief and wipe the back of his neck. He kept the gun in his right hand. The explosive shells in that gun were somewhat wicked; any one of them could deprive a rhinoceros of a hunk of meat weighing two hundred pounds. If a man caught one, he just strewed himself over the landscape. By the looks of that slate-colored galloper, it would need half a dozen shells to feel incommoded. A seventy-five-millimetre bazooka would be more effective for kicking it in the back teeth, but probe-ship boys don't tote around such artillery. Steve finished the mopping, put the handkerchief back, picked up the can.

Laura said pensively, "I want my mother."

He scowled, made no reply, set out toward the lake. Her feathers still ruffled, Laura rode his shoulder and lapsed into surly silence.

The stuff in the lake was water, cold, faintly green and a little bitter to the taste. Coffee would camouflage the flavor. If anything, it might improve the coffee since he liked his java bitter, but the stuff would have to be tested before absorbing it in any quantity. Some poisons were accumulative. It wouldn't do to guzzle gaily while building up a death-dealing reserve of lead, for instance. Filling the freezocan, he lugged it to the ship in hundred-yard stages. The swathe helped; it made an easier path to within short distance of the ship's tail. He was perspiring freely by the time he reached the base of the ladder.

Once inside the vessel he relocked both doors, opened the air vents, started the auxiliary lighting-set and plugged in the percolator, using water out of his depleted reserve supply. The golden sky had dulled to orange, with violet streamers creeping upward from the horizon. Looking at it through the transpex dome, he found that the perpetual haze still effectively concealed the sinking sun. A brighter area to one side was all that indicated its position. He'd need his lights soon.

Pulling out the collapsible table, he jammed its supporting leg into place, plugged into its rim the short rod which was Laura's official seat. She claimed the perch immediately, watched him beadily as he set out her meal of water, melon seeds, sunflower seeds, pecans and unshelled oleo nuts. Her manners were anything but ladylike and she started eagerly, without waiting for him.

A deep frown lay across his brown, muscular features as he sat at the table, poured out his coffee and commenced to eat. It persisted through the meal, was still there when he lit a cigarette and stared speculatively up at the dome.

Presently, he murmured, "I've seen the biggest bug that ever was. I've seen a few other bugs. There were a couple of little ones under a creeper. One was long and brown and many-legged, like an earwig. The other was round and black, with little red dots on its wing cases. I've seen a tiny purple spider and a tinier green one of different shape, also a bug that looked like an aphid. But not an ant."

"Ant, ant," hooted Laura. She dropped a piece of oleo nut, climbed down after it. "Yawk!" she added from the floor.

"Not a bee."

"Bee," echoed Laura, companionably. "Bee-ant. Laura loves Steve."

Still keeping his attention on the dome, he went on, "And what's cockeyed about the plants is equally cockeyed about the bugs. I wish I could place it. Why can't I? Maybe I'm going nuts already."

"Laura loves nuts."

"I know it, you technicolored belly!" said Steve rudely.

And at that point night fell with a silent bang. The gold and orange and violet abruptly were swamped with deep, impenetrable blackness devoid of stars or any random gleam. Except for greenish glowings on the instrument panel, the control room was stygian, with Laura swearing steadily on the floor.

Putting out a hand, Steve switched on the indirect lighting. Laura got to her perch with the rescued titbit, concentrated on the job of dealing with it and let him sink back into his thoughts.

"*Scarabaeus anderii* and a pair of smaller bugs and a couple of spiders, all different. At the other end of the scale, that giganto-saurus. But no ant, or bee. Or rather, no ants, no bees." The switch from singular to plural stirred his back hairs queerly. In some vague way, he felt that he'd touched the heart of the mystery. "No ant—no ants," he thought. "No bee—no bees." Almost he had it—but still it evaded him.

Giving it up for the time being, he cleared the table, did a few minor chores. After that, he drew a standard sample from the freezocan, put it through its paces. The bitter flavour he identified as being due to the presence of magnesium sulphate in quantity far too small to prove embarrassing. Drinkable—that was something! Food, drink and shelter were the three essentials of survival. He'd enough of the first for six or seven weeks. The lake and the ship were his remaining guarantees of life.

Finding the log, he entered the day's report, bluntly, factually, without any embroidery. Partway through, he found himself stuck for a name for the planet. *Ander,* he decided, would cost him dear if the million-to-one chance put him back among the merciless playmates of the Probe Service. O.K. for a bug, but not for a world. *Laura* wasn't so hot, either—especially when you knew Laura. It wouldn't be seemly to name a big, gold planet after an oversized parrot. Thinking over the golden aspect of this world's sky, he hit upon the name of *Oro,* promptly made the christening authoritative by entering it in his log.

By the time he'd finished, Laura had her head buried deep under one wing. Occasionally she teetered and swung erect again. It always fascinated him to watch how her balance was maintained even in her slumbers. Studying her fondly, he remembered that unexpected addition to her vocabulary. This shifted his thoughts to a fiery-headed and fierier-tongued individual named Menzies, the sworn foe of another volcano named McGillicuddy. If ever the opportunity presented itself, he decided, the educative work of said Menzies was going to be rewarded with a bust on the snoot.

Sighing, he put away the log, wound up the forty-day chronometer, opened his folding bunk and lay down upon it. His hand switched off the lights. Ten years back, a first landing would have kept him awake all night in dithers of excitement. He'd got beyond that now. He'd done it often enough to have grown phlegmatic about it. His eyes closed in preparation for a good night's sleep, and he did sleep—for two hours.

What brought him awake within that short time he didn't know, but suddenly he found himself sitting bolt upright on the edge of the bunk, his ears and nerves stretched to their utmost, his legs quivering in a way they'd never done before. His whole body fizzed with the queer mixture of palpitation and shock which follows narrow escape from disaster.

This was something not within previous experience. Sure and certain in the intense darkness, his hand sought and found his gun. He cuddled the butt in his palm while his mind strove to recall a possible nightmare, though he knew he was not given to nightmares.

Laura moved restlessly on her perch, not truly awake, yet not asleep, and this was unusual in her.

Rejecting the dream theory, he stood up on the bunk,

looked out through the dome. Blackness, the deepest, darkest, most impenetrable blackness it was possible to conceive. And silence! The outside world slumbered in the blackness and the silence as in a sable shroud.

Yet never before had he felt so wide awake in this, his normal sleeping time. Puzzled, he turned slowly round to take in the full circle of unseeable view, and at one point he halted. The surrounding darkness was not complete. In the distance beyond the ship's tail moved a tall, stately glow. How far off it might be was not possible to estimate, but the sight of it stirred his soul and caused his heart to leap.

Uncontrollable emotions were not permitted to master his disciplined mind. Narrowing his eyes, he tried to discern the nature of the glow while his mind sought the reason why the mere sight of it should make him twang like a harp. Bending down, he felt at the head of the bunk, found a leather case, extracted a pair of powerful night-glasses. The glow was still moving, slowly, deliberately, from right to left. He got the glasses on it, screwed the lenses into focus, and the phenomenon leaped into closer view.

The thing was a great column of golden haze much like that of the noonday sky except that small, intense gleams of silver sparkled within it. It was a shaft of lustrous mist bearing a sprinkling of tiny stars. It was like nothing known to or recorded by any form of life lower than the gods. But was it life?

It moved, though its mode of locomotion could not be determined. Self-motivation is the prime symptom of life. It could be life, conceivably though not credibly, from the Terrestrial viewpoint. Consciously, he preferred to think it a strange and purely local feature comparable with Saharan sand-devils. Subconsciously, he knew it was life, tall and terrifying.

He kept the glasses on it while slowly it receded into the darkness, foreshortening with increasing distance and gradually fading from view. To the very last the observable field shifted and shuddered as he failed to control the quiver in his hands. And when the sparkling haze had gone he sat down on the bunk and shivered with eerie cold.

Laura was dodging to and fro along her perch, now thoroughly awake and agitated, but he wasn't inclined to switch on the lights and make the dome a beacon in night. His hand went out, feeling for her in the darkness, and she clambered eagerly on to his wrist, thence to his lap. She was fussy and demonstrative, pathetically yearning for comfort and companionship. He scratched her poll and fondled her while she pressed close against his chest with funny little crooning noises. For some time he soothed her and, while doing it, fell asleep. Gradually he slumped backward on the bunk. Laura perched on his forearm, clucked tiredly, put her head under a wing.

There was no further awakening until the outer blackness disappeared and the sky again sent its golden glow pouring through the dome. Steve got up, stood on the bunk, had a good look over the surrounding terrain. It remained precisely the same as it had been the day before. Things stewed within his mind while he got his breakfast; especially the jumpiness he'd experienced in the night-time. Laura also was subdued and quiet. Only once before had she been like that—which was when he'd traipsed through the Venusian section of the Panplanetary Zoo and had shown her a crested eagle. The eagle had stared at her with contemptuous dignity.

Though he'd all the time in his life, he now felt a peculiar urge to hasten. Getting the gun and the freezocan, he made a full dozen trips to the lake, wasting no minutes, nor stopping to study the still enigmatic plants and bugs. It was late in the afternoon by the time he'd filled the ship's fifty-gallon reservoir, and had the satisfaction of knowing that he'd got a drinkable quota to match his food supply.

There had been no sign of gigantosaurus or any other animal. Once he'd seen something flying in the far distance, birdlike or batlike. Laura had cocked a sharp eye at it but betrayed no undue interest. Right now she was more concerned with a new fruit. Steve sat in the rim of the outer lock-door, his legs dangling, and watched her clambering over a small tree thirty yards away. The gun lay in his lap; he was ready to take a crack at anything which might be ready to take a crack at Laura.

The bird sampled the tree's fruit, a crop resembling blue-shelled lychee nuts. She ate one with relish, grabbed another. Steve lay back in the lock, stretched to reach a bag, then dropped to the ground and went across to the tree. He tried a nut. Its flesh was soft, juicy, sweet and citreous. He filled the bag with the fruit, slung it into the ship.

Nearby stood another tree, not quite the same, but very similar. It bore nuts like the first except that they were larger.

Picking one, he offered it to Laura who tried it, spat it out in disgust. Picking a second, he slit it, licked the flesh gingerly. As far as he could tell, it was the same. Evidently he couldn't tell far enough: Laura's diagnosis said it was not the same. The difference, too subtle for him to detect, might be sufficient to roll him that shape to the unpleasant end. He flung the thing away, went back to his seat in the lock, and ruminated.

That elusive, nagging feature of Oro's plants and bugs could be narrowed down to these two nuts. He felt sure of that. If he could discover why—parrotwise—one nut was not, he'd have his finger right on the secret. The more he thought about those similar fruits the more he felt that, in sober fact, his finger was on the secret already—but he lacked the power to lift it and see what lay beneath.

Tantalizing, his mulling over the subject landed him the same place as before; namely, nowhere. It got his dander up, and he went back to the trees, subjected both to close examination. His sense of sight told him that they were different individuals of the same species. Laura's sense of whatchamacallit insisted that they were different species. Ergo, you can't believe the evidence of your eyes. He was aware of that fact, of course, since it was a platitude of the spaceways, but when you couldn't trust your optics it was legitimate to try to discover just why you couldn't trust 'em. And he couldn't discover even that!

It soured him so much that he returned to the ship, locked its doors, called Laura back to his shoulder and set off on a tailward exploration. The rules of first landings were simple and sensible. Go in slowly, come out quickly, and remember that all we want from you is evidence of suitability for human life. Thoroughly explore a small area rather than scout a big one—the mapping parties will do the rest. Use your ship as a base and centralize it where you can live—don't move it unnecessarily. Restrict your trips to a radius representing daylight-reach and lock yourself in after dark.

Was Oro suitable for human life? The unwritten law was that you don't jump to conclusions and say, "Of course! I'm still living, aren't I?" Cameron who'd plonked his ship on Mithra, for instance, thought he'd found paradise until, on the seventeenth day, he'd discovered the fungoid plague. He'd left like a bat out of hell and had spent three sweaty, swearing days in the Lunar Purification Plant before becoming fit for society. The authorities had vaporized his ship. Mithra had been taboo ever since. Every world a potential trap baited with scientific delight. The job of the Probe Service was to enter the traps and jounce on the springs. Another dollop of real estate for Terra—if nothing broke your neck.

Maybe Ora was loaded for bear. The thing that walked in the night, Steve mused, bore awful suggestion of non-human power. So did a waterspout, and whoever heard of anyone successfully wrestling with a waterspout? If this Oro-spout were sentient, so much the worse for human prospects. He'd have to get the measure of it, he decided, even if he had to chase it through the blank avenues of night. Plodding steadily away from the tail, gun in hand, he pondered so deeply that he entirely overlooked the fact that he wasn't on a pukka probe job anyway, and that nothing else remotely human might reach Oro in a thousand years. Even space-boys can be creatures of habit. Their job: to look for death; they were liable to go on looking long after the need had passed, in bland disregard of the certainty that if you look for a thing long enough ultimately you find it!

The ship's chronometer had given him five hours to darkness. Two and a half hours each way; say ten miles out and ten back. The water had consumed his time. On the morrow, and henceforth, he'd increase the radius to twelve and take it easier.

Then all thoughts fled from his mind as he came to the edge of the vegetation. The stuff didn't dribble out of existence with hardy spurs and offshoots fighting for a hold in suddenly rocky ground. It stopped abruptly, in light loam, as if cut off with a machete, and from where it stopped spread a different crop. The new growths were tiny and crystalline.

He accepted the crystalline crop without surprise; knowing that novelty was the inevitable feature of any new locale. Things were ordinary only by Terrestrial standards. Outside of Terra, nothing was supernormal or abnormal except in so far as they failed to jibe with their own peculiar conditions. Besides, there were crystalline growths on Mars. The one unacceptable feature of the situation was the way in which vegetable growths ended and crystalline ones began. He stepped back to the verge and made another startled survey of the borderline. It was so straight that the sight screwed his brain around. Like a field. A cultivated field. Dead straightness of that sort couldn't be other than artificial. Little beads of moisture popped out on his back.

Squatting on the heel of his right boot, he gazed at the nearest crystals and said to Laura, "Chicken, I think these things got planted. Question is, who planted 'em?"

"McGillicuddy," suggested Laura brightly.

Putting out a finger, he flicked the crystal sprouting near the toe of his boot, a green, branchy object an inch high.

The crystal vibrated and said, *"Zing!"* in a sweet, high voice.

He flicked its neighbor, and that said, *"Zang!"* in a lower tone.

He flicked a third. It emitted no note, but broke into a thousand shards.

Standing up, he scratched his head, making Laura fight for a clawhold within the circle of his arm. One zinged and one zanged and one returned to dust. Two nuts. Zings and zangs and nuts. It was right in his grasp if only he could open his hand and look at what he'd got.

Then he lifted his puzzled and slightly ireful gaze, saw something fluttering erratically across the crystal field; it was making for the vegetation. Laura took off with a raucous cackle, her blue-and-crimson wings beating powerfully. She swooped over the object, frightening it so low that it dodged and side-slipped only a few feet above Steve's head. He saw that it was a large butterfly, frill-winged, almost as gaudy as Laura. The bird swooped again, scaring the insect but not menacing it. He called her back, set out to cross the area ahead. Crystals crunched to powder under his heavy boots as he tramped on.

Half an hour later he was tolling up a steep, crystal-coated slope when his thoughts suddenly jelled and he stopped with such abruptness that Laura spilled from his shoulder and perforce took to wing. She beat round in a circle, came back to her perch, made bitter remarks in an unknown language.

"One of this and one of that," he said, "No twos or threes or dozens. Nothing I've seen has repeated itself. There's only one gigantosaurus, only one *Scarabaeus anderii,* only one of every danged thing. Every item is unique, original, and an individual creation in its own right. What does that suggest?"

"McGillicuddy," offered Laura.

"For Pete's sake, forget McGillicuddy."

"For Pete's sake, for Pete's sake," yelled Laura, much taken by the phrase. "The great black—"

Again he upset her in the nick of time, making her take to flight while he continued talking to himself. "It suggests constant and all-pervading mutation. Everything breeds something quite different from itself and there aren't any dominant strains." He frowned at the obvious snag in his theory. "But how the blazes does anything breed? What fertilizes which?"

"McGilli—," began Laura, then changed her mind and shut up.

"Anyway, if nothing breeds true, it'll be tough on the food problem," he went on. "What's edible on one plant may be a killer on its offspring. Today's fodder is tomorrow's poison. How's a farmer to know what he's going to get? Hey-hey, if I'm guessing right, this planet won't support a couple of hogs."

"No, sir. No hogs. Laura loves hogs."

"Be quiet," he snapped. "Now, what shouldn't support a couple of hogs demonstrably does support gigantosaurus—and any other fancy animals which may be mooching around. It seems crazy to me. On Venus or any other place full of consistent fodder, gigantosaurus would thrive; but here, according to my calculations, the big lunk has no right to be alive. He ought to be dead."

So saying, he topped the rise and found the monster in question sprawling right across the opposite slope. It *was* dead.

The way in which he determined its deadness was appropriately swift, simple and effective. Its enormous bulk lay draped across the full length of the slope and its dragonhead, the size of a lifeboat, pointed toward him. The head had two dull, lacklustre eyes like dinner plates. He planted a shell smack in the right eye and a sizable hunk of noggin promptly splashed in all directions. The body did not stir.

There was a shell ready for the other eye should the creature leap to frantic, vengeful life, but the mighty hulk remained supine.

His boots continued to desiccate crystals as he went down the slope, curved a hundred yards off his route to get around the corpse, and trudged up the farther rise. Momentarily, he wasn't much interested in the dead beast. Time was short and he could come again tomorrow, bringing a full-color stereoscopic camera with him. Gigantosaurus would go on record in style, but would have to wait.

This second rise was a good deal higher, and more trying a climb. Its crest represented the approximate limit of this day's trip, and he felt anxious to surmount it before turning back. Humanity's characteristic urge to see what lay over the hill remained as strong as on the day determined ancestors topped the Rockies. He had to have a look, firstly because elevation gave range to vision, and secondly because of that prowler in the night—and, nearly as he could estimate, the prowler had gone down behind this rise. A column of mist, sucked down from the sky, might move around aimlessly, going nowhere, but instinct maintained that this had been no mere column of mist, and that it was going somewhere.

Where?

Out of breath, he pounded over the crest, looked down into an immense valley, and found the answer.

The crystal growths gave out on the crest, again in a perfectly straight line. Beyond them the light loam, devoid of rock, ran gently down to the valley and up the farther side. Both slopes were sparsely dotted with queer, jelly-like lumps of matter which lay and quivered beneath the sky's golden glow.

From the closed end of the valley jutted a great, glistening fabrication, flat-roofed, flat-fronted, with a huge, square hole gaping in its mid-section at front. It looked like a tremendous oblong slab of polished, milk-white plastic half-buried endwise in a sandy hill. No decoration disturbed its smooth, gleaming surface. No road led to the hole in front. Somehow, it had the new-old air of a house that struggles to look empty because it is full—of fiends.

Steve's back hairs prickled as he studied it. One thing was obvious—Oro bore intelligent life. One thing was possible—the golden column represented that life. One thing was probable—fleshy Terrestrials and hazy Orons would have difficulty in finding a basis for friendship and co-operation.

Whereas enmity needs no basis.

Curiosity and caution pulled him opposite ways. One urged him down into the valley while the other drove him back, back, while yet there was time. He consulted his watch. Less than three hours to go, within which he had to return to the ship, enter the log, prepare supper. That milky creation was at least two miles away, a good hour's journey there and back. Let it wait. Give it another day and he'd have more time for it, with the benefit of needful thought betweentimes.

Caution triumphed. He investigated the nearest jellyblob. It was flat, a yard in diameter, green, with bluish streaks and many tiny bubbles hiding in its semi-transparency. The thing pulsated slowly. He poked at it with the toe of his boot, and it contracted, humping itself in the middle, then sluggishly relaxed. No amoeba, he decided. A low form of life but complicated withal. Laura didn't like the object. She skittered off as he bent over it, vented her anger by bashing a few crystals.

This jellyblob wasn't like its nearest neighbour, or like any other. One of each, only one. The same rule; one butterfly of a kind, one bug, one plant, one of these quivering things.

A final stare at the distant mystery down in the valley, then he retraced his steps. When the ship came into sight he speeded up like a gladsome voyager nearing home. There were new prints near the vessel, big, three-toed, deeply impressed spoor which revealed that something large and two-legged had wandered past in his absence. Evidently an animal, for nothing intelligent would have meandered on so casually without circling and inspecting the nearby invader from space. He dismissed it from his mind. There was only one thingummybob, he felt certain of that.

Once inside the ship, he relocked the doors, gave Laura her feed, ate his supper. Then he dragged out the log, made his day's entry, had a look around from the dome. Violet streamers once more were creeping upward from the horizon. He frowned at the encompassing vegetation. What sort of stuff had bred all this in the past? What sort of stuff would this breed in the future? How did it progenerate, anyway?

Wholesale radical mutation presupposed modification of genes by hard radiation in persistent and considerable blasts. You shouldn't get hard radiation on lightweight planets—unless it poured in from the sky. Here, it didn't pour from the sky, or from any place else. In fact, there wasn't any.

He was pretty certain of that fact because he'd a special interest in it and had checked up on it. Hard radiation betokened the presence of radioactive elements which, at a pinch, might be usable as fuel. The ship was equipped to detect such stuff. Among the junk was a cosmiray counter, a radium hen, and a gold-leaf electroscope. The hen and the counter hadn't given so much as one heartening cluck, in fact the only clucks had been Laura's. The electroscope he'd charged on landing and its leaves still formed an inverted vee. The air was dry, ionization negligible, and the leaves didn't look likely to collapse for a week.

"Something wrong with my theorizing," he complained to Laura. "My think-stuff's not doing its job."

"Not doing its job," echoed Laura faithfully. She cracked a pecan with a grating noise that set his teeth on edge. "I tell you it's a hoodoo ship. I won't sail. No, not even if you pray for me, I won't, I won't, I won't. Nope. Nix. Who's drunk? That hairy Lowlander Mc—"

"Laura!" he said sharply.

"Gillicuddy," she finished with bland defiance. Again she rasped his teeth. "Rings bigger'n Saturn's I saw them myself. Who's a liar? Yawk! She's down in Grayway Bay, on Tethis. Boy, what a torso!"

He looked at her hard, and said, "You're nuts!"

"Sure! Sure, pal! Laura loves nuts. Have one on me."

"O.K.," he accepted, holding out his hand.

Cocking her colorful pate, she pecked at his hand, gravely selected a pecan and gave it to him. He cracked it, chewed on the kernel starting up the lighting-set. It was almost as if night were waiting for him. Blackness fell even as he switched on the lights.

With the darkness came a keen sense of unease. The dome was the trouble. It blazed like a beacon and there was no way of blacking it out except by turning off the lights. Beacons attracted things, and he'd no desire to become a center of attraction in present circumstances. That is to say, not at night.

Long experience had bred fine contempt for alien animals, no matter how whacky, but outlandish intelligence was a different proposition. So filled was he with the strange inward conviction that last night's phenomenon was something that knew its onions that it didn't occur to him to wonder whether a glowing column possessed eyes or anything equivalent to a sense of sight. If it had occurred to him, he'd have derived no comfort from it. His desire to be weighed in the balance in some eerie, extra-sensory way was even less than his desire to be gaped at visually in his slumbers.

An unholy mess of thoughts and ideas was still cooking in his mind when he extinguished the light, bunked down and went to sleep. Nothing disturbed him this time, but when he awoke with the golden dawn his chest was damp with perspiration and Laura again had sought refuge on his arm.

Digging out breakfast, his thoughts began to marshal themselves as he kept his hands busy. Pouring out a shot of hot coffee, he spoke to Laura.

"I'm durned if I'm going to go scatty trying to maintain a three-watch system single-handed, which is what I'm supposed to do if faced by powers unknown when I'm not able to beat it. Those armchair warriors at headquarters ought to get a taste of situations not precisely specified in the book of rules."

"Burp!" said Laura contemptuously.

"He who fights and runs away lives to fight another day," Steve quoted. "That's the Probe Law. It's a nice, smooth, lovely law—when you can run away. We can't!"

"Burrup!" said Laura with unnecessary emphasis.

"For a woman, your manners are downright disgusting," he told her. "Now, I'm not going to spend the brief remainder of my life looking fearfully over my shoulder. The only way to get rid of powers unknown is to convert 'em into powers known and understood. As Uncle Joe told Willie when dragging him to the dentist, the longer we put it off the worse it'll feel."

"Dinna fash y'sel," declaimed Laura. "Burp-gollop-bop!"

Giving her a look of extreme distaste, he continued, "So we'll try tossing the bull. Such techniques disconcert bulls sometimes." Standing up, he grabbed Laura, shoved her into the traveling compartment, slid the panel shut. "We're going to blow off forthwith."

Climbing up to the control seat, he stamped on the energizer stud. The tail rockets popped a few times, broke into a subdued roar. Juggling the controls to get the preparatory feel of them, he stepped up the boost until the entire vessel trembled and the rear venturis began to glow cherry-red. Slowly the ship commenced to edge its bulk forward and, as it did so, he fed it the take-off shot. A half-mile blast kicked backward and the probe ship plummeted into the sky.

Pulling it round in a wide and shallow sweep, he thundered over the borderline of vegetation, the fields of crystals and the hills beyond. In a flash he was plunging through the valley, braking rockets blazing from the nose. This was tricky. He had to co-ordinate forward shoot, backward thrust and downward surge, but like most of his kind he took pride in the stunts performable with these neat little vessels. An awe-inspired audience was all he lacked to make the exhibition perfect. The vessel landed fairly and squarely on the milk-white roof of the alien edifice, slid halfway to the cliff, then stopped.

"Boy," he breathed, "am I good!" He remained in his seat, stared around through the dome, and felt that he ought to add, "And too young to die." Occasionally eyeing the chronometer, he waited a while. The boat must have handed that roof sufficient to wake the dead. If anyone were in, they'd soon hotfoot out to see who was heaving hundred-ton bottles at their shingles. Nobody emerged. He gave them half an hour, his hawk-like face strained, alert. Then he gave it up, said, "Ah, well," and got out of the seat.

He freed Laura. She came out with ruffled dignity, like a dowager who's paraded into the wrong room. Females were always curious critters, in his logic, and he ignored her attitude, got his gun, unlocked the doors, jumped down onto the roof. Laura followed reluctantly, came to his shoulder as if thereby conferring a great favor.

Walking past the tail to the edge of the roof, he looked down. The sheerness of the five-hundred-foot drop took him aback. Immediately below his feet, the entrance soared four hundred feet up from the ground and he was standing on the hundred-foot lintel surmounting it. The only way down was to walk to the side of the roof and reach the earthy slope in which the building was embedded, seeking a path down that.

He covered a quarter of a mile of roof to get to the slope, his eyes examining the roof's surface as he went, and failing to find one crack or joint in the uniformly smooth surface. Huge as it was, the erection appeared to have been moulded all in one piece—a fact which did nothing to lessen inward misgivings. Whoever did this mighty job weren't Zulus!

From the ground level the entrance loomed bigger than ever. If there had been a similar gap the other side of the building, and a clear way through, he could have taken the ship in at one end and out at the other as easily as threading a needle.

Absence of doors didn't seem peculiar. It was difficult to imagine any sort of door huge enough to fill this opening yet sufficiently balanced to enable anyone—or anything—to pull open or shut. With a final, cautious look around which revealed nothing moving in the valley, he stepped boldly through the entrance, blinked his eyes, found inferior darkness slowly fading as visual retention lapsed and gave up remembrance of the golden glow outside.

There was a glow inside, a different one, paler, ghastlier, greenish. It exuded from the floor, the walls, the ceiling, and the total area of radiation was enough to light the place clearly, with no shadows. He sniffed as his vision adjusted itself. There was a strong smell of ozone mixed with other, unidentifiable odors.

To his right and left, rising hundreds of feet, stood great tiers of transparent cases. He went to the ones on his right and examined them. They were cubes, about a yard each way, made of something like transpex. Each contained three inches of loam from which spouted a crystal. No two crystals were alike; some small and branchy, others large and indescribably complicated.

Dumb with thought, he went around to the back of the monster tier, found another ten yards behind it. And another behind that. And another and another. All with crystals. The number and variety of them made his head whirl. He could study only the two bottom rows of each rack, but row on row stepped themselves far above his head to within short distance of the roof. Their total number was beyond estimation.

It was the same on the left. Crystals by the thousands. Looking more closely at one especially fine example, he noticed that the front plate of its case bore a small, inobtrusive pattern of dots etched upon the outer surface. Investigation revealed that all cases were similarly marked, differing only in the number and arrangement of the dots. Undoubtedly, some sort of cosmic code used for classification purposes.

"The Oron Museum of Natural History," he guessed, in a whisper.

"You're a liar," squawked Laura, violently. "I tell you it's a hoodoo—" She stopped, dumfounded, as her own voice roared through the building in deep, organ-like tones. "A hoodoo—a hoodo—"

"Holy smoke, will you keep quiet!" hissed Steve. He tried to keep watch on the exit and the interior simultaneously. But the voice rumbled away in the distance without bringing anyone to dispute their invasion.

Turning, he paced hurriedly past the first blocks of tiers to the next batteries of exhibits. Jellyblobs in this lot. Small ones, no bigger than his wristwatch, numberable in thousands. None appeared to be alive, he noted.

Sections three, four and five took him a mile into the building as nearly as he could estimate. He passed mosses, lichens and shrubs, all dead but wondrously preserved. By this time he was ready to guess at section six—plants. He was wrong. The sixth layout displayed bugs, including moths, butterflies, and strange, unfamiliar objects resembling chitinous humming birds. There was no sample of *Scarabaeus anderii* unless it was several hundred feet up. Or unless there was an empty box ready for it—when its day was done.

Who made the boxes? Had it prepared one for him? One for Laura? He visualized himself, petrified forever, squatting in the seventieth case of the twenty-fifth row of the tenth tier in section something-or-other, his front panel duly tagged with its appropriate dots. It was a lousy picture. It made his forehead wrinkle to think of it.

Looking for he knew not what, he plunged steadily on, advancing deeper and deeper into the heart of the building. Not a soul, not a sound, not a footprint. Only that all-pervading smell and the unvarying glow. He had a feeling that the place was visited frequently but never occupied for any worthwhile period of time. Without bothering to stop and look, he passed an enormous case containing a creature faintly resembling a bison-headed rhinoceros, then other, still larger cases holding equally larger exhibits—all carefully dot-marked.

Finally, he rounded a box so tremendous that it sprawled across the full width of the hall. It contained the grand-pappy of all trees and the great-grand-pappy of all serpents. Behind, for a change, reared five-hundred-feet-high racks of metal cupboards, each cupboard with a stud set in its polished door, each ornamented with more groups of mysteriously arranged dots.

Greatly daring, he pressed the stud on the nearest cupboard and its door swung open with a juicy click. The result proved disappointing. The cupboard was filled with stacks of small, glassy sheets each smothered with dots.

"Super filing-system," he grunted, closing the door. "Old Prof Heggarty would give his right arm to be here."

"Heggarty," said Laura, in a faltering voice. "For Pete's sake!"

He looked at her sharply. She was ruffled and fidgety, showing signs of increasing agitation.

"What's the matter, Chicken?"

She peeked at him, returned her anxious gaze the way they had come, side-stepped to and fro on his shoulder. Her neck feathers started to rise. A nervous cluck came from her beak and she cowered close to his jacket.

"Darn!" he muttered. Spinning on one heel, he raced past successive filing blocks, got into the ten-yards space between the end block and the wall. His gun was out and he kept watch on the front of the blocks while his free hand tried to soothe Laura. She snuggled up close, rubbing her head into his neck and trying to hide under the angle of his jaw.

"Quiet, Honey," he whispered. "Just you keep quiet and stay with Steve, and we'll be all right."

She kept quiet, though she'd begun to tremble. His heart speeded up in sympathy though he could see nothing, hear nothing to warrant it.

Then, while he watched and waited, and still in absolute silence, the interior brightness waxed, became less green, more golden. And suddenly he knew what it was that was coming. He *knew* what it was!

He sank on one knee to make himself as small and inconspicuous as possible. Now his heart was palpitating wildly and no coldness in his mind could freeze it down to slower, more normal beat. The silence, the awful silence of its approach was the unbearable feature. The crushing thud of a weighty foot or hoof would have been better. Colossi have no right to steal along like ghosts.

And the golden glow built up, drowning out the green radiance from floor to roof, setting the multitude of case-surfaces afire with its brilliance. It grew as strong as the golden sky, and stronger. It became all-pervading, unendurable, leaving no darkness in which to hide, no sanctuary for little things.

It flamed like the rising sun or like something drawn from the heart of a sun, and the glory of its radiance sent the cowering watcher's mind awhirl. He struggled fiercely to control his brain, to discipline it, to bind it to his fading will—and failed.

With drawn face beaded by sweat, Steve caught the merest fragmentary glimpse of the column's edge appearing from between the stacks of the center aisle. He saw a blinding strip of burnished gold in which glittered a pure white star, then a violent effervescence seemed to occur within his brain and he fell forward into a cloud of tiny bubbles.

Down, down he sank through myriad bubbles and swirls and sprays of iridescent froth and foam which shone and changed and shone anew with every conceivable color. And all the time his mind strove frantically to battle upward and drag his soul to the surface.

Deep into the nethermost reaches he went while still the bubbles whirled around in their thousands and their colors were of numberless hues. Then his progress slowed. Gradually the froth and the foam ceased to rotate upward, stopped its circling, began to swirl in the reverse direction and sink. He was rising! He rose for a lifetime, floating weightlessly, in a dreamlike trance.

The last of the bubbles drifted eerily away, leaving him in a brief hiatus of nonexistence—then he found himself sprawled full length on the floor with a dazed Laura clinging to his arm. He blinked his eyes, slowly, several times. They were strained and sore. His heart was still palpitating and his legs felt weak. There was a strange sensation in his stomach as if memory had sickened him with a shock from long, long ago.

He didn't get up from the floor right away; his body was too shaken and his mind too muddled for that. While his wits came back and his composure returned, he lay and noted all the invading goldness had gone and that again the interior illumination was a dull, shadowless green. Then his eyes found his watch and sat up, startled. Two hours had flown.

That fact brought him shakily to his feet. Peering around the end of the bank of filing cabinets, he saw that nothing had changed. Instinct told him that the golden visitor had gone and that once more he had this place to himself. Had it become aware of his presence? Had it made him lose consciousness or, if not, why had he lost it? Had it done anything about the ship on the roof?

Picking up his futile gun, he spun it by its stud guard and looked at it with contempt. Then he holstered it, helped Laura on to his shoulder where she perched groggily, went around the back of the racks and still deeper into the building.

"I reckon we're O.K., Honey," he told her. "I think we're too small to be noticed. We're like mice. Who bothers to trap mice when he's got bigger and more important things in mind?" He pulled a face, not liking the mouse comparison. It wasn't flattering either to him or his kind. But it was the best he could think of at the moment. "So, like little mice, let's look for the cheese. I'm not giving up just because a big hunk of something has sneaked past and put a scare into us. We don't scare off, do we, Sweetness?"

"No," said Laura unenthusiastically. Her voice was still subdued and her eyes perked apprehensively this way and that. "No scare. I won't sail, I tell you. Blow my sternpipes! Laura loves nuts!"

"Don't you call me a nut!"

"Nuts! Stick to farming—it gets you more eggs. McGillicuddy, the great—"

"Hey!" he warned.

She shut up abruptly. He put the pace on, refusing to admit that his system felt slightly jittery with nervous strain or that anything had got him bothered. But he knew that he'd no desire to be near the sparkling giant again. Once was enough, more than enough. It wasn't that he feared it, but something else, something he was quite unable to define.

Passing the last bank of cabinets, he found himself facing a machine. It was complicated and bizarre—and it was making a crystalline growth. Near it, another and different machine was manufacturing a small, horned lizard. There could be no doubt at all about the process of fabrication because both objects were half-made and both progressed slightly even as he watched. In a couple of hours' time, perhaps less, they'd be finished, and all they'd need would be . . . would be—

The hairs stiffened on the back of his neck and he commenced to run. Endless machines, all different, all making different things, plants, bugs, birds and fungoids. It was done by electroponics, atom fed to atom like brick after brick to build a house. It wasn't synthesis because that's only assembly, and this was assembly plus growth in response to unknown laws. In each of these machines, he knew, was some key or code or cipher, some weird master-control of unimaginable complexity, determining the patterns each was building—and the patterns were infinitely variable.

Here and there a piece of apparatus stood silent, inactive, their tasks complete. Here and there other monstrous layouts were in pieces, either under repair or readied for modification. He stopped by one which had finished its job. It had fashioned a delicately shaded moth which perched motionless like a jeweled statue within its fabrication jar. The creature was perfect as far as he could tell, and all it was waiting for was . . . was—

Beads of moisture popped out on his forehead. All that moth needed was the breath of life!

He forced a multitude of notions to get out of his mind; it was the only way to retain a hold on himself. Divert your attention—take it off this and place it on that! Firmly, he fastened his attention on one tremendous, partly disassembled machine lying nearby. Its guts were exposed, revealing great field-coils of dull grey wire. Bits of similar wire lay scattered around on the floor.

Picking up a short piece, he found it surprisingly heavy. He took off his wristwatch, opened its back, brought the wire near to its works. The Venusian jargoon bearing fluoresced immediately. V-jargoons invariably glowed in the presence of near radiation. This unknown metal was a possible fuel. His heart gave a jump at the thought of it.

Should he drag out a huge coil and lug it up to the ship? It was very heavy, and he'd need a considerable length of the stuff—if it was usable as fuel. Supposing the disappearance of the coil caused mousetraps to be set before he returned to search anew?

It pays to stop and think whenever you've got time to stop and think; that was a fundamental of Probe Service philosophy. Pocketing a sample of the wire, he sought around other disassembled machines for more. The search took him still deeper into the building and he fought harder to keep his attention concentrated solely on the task. It wasn't easy. There was that dog, for instance, standing there, statue-like, waiting, waiting. If only it had been anything but indubitably and recognizably an Earth-type dog. It was impossible to avoid seeing it. It would be equally impossible to avoid seeing other, even more familiar forms—if they were there.

He'd gained seven samples of different radioactive wires when he gave up the search. A cockatoo ended his peregrinations. The bird stood steadfastly in its jar, its blue plumage smooth and bright, its crimson crest raised, its bright eye fixed in what was not death, but not yet life. Laura shrieked at it hysterically and the immense hall shrieked back at her with long-drawn roars and rumbles that reverberated into dim distances. Laura's reaction was too much: he wanted no cause for similar reaction of his own.

He sped through the building at top pace, passing the filing cabinets and the mighty array of exhibition cases unheedingly. Up the loamy side-slopes he climbed almost as rapidly as he'd gone down, and he was breathing heavily by the time he got into the ship.

His first action was to check the ship for evidence of interference. There wasn't any. Next, he checked the instruments. The electroscope's leaves were collapsed. Charging them, he watched them flip open and flop together again. The counter showed radiation aplenty. The hen clucked energetically. He'd blundered somewhat—he should have checked up when first he landed on the roof. However, no matter. What lay beneath the roof was now known; the instruments would have advised him earlier but not as informatively.

Laura had her feed while he accompanied her with a swift meal. After that, he dug out his samples of wire. No two were the same gauge and one obviously was far too thick to enter the feed holes of the Kingston-Kanes. It took him half an hour to file it down to a suitable diameter. The original piece of dull grey wire took the first test. Feeding it in, he set the control to minimum warming-up intensity, stepped on the energizer. Nothing happened.

He scowled to himself. Someday they'd have jobs better than the sturdy but finicky Kingston-Kanes, jobs that'd eat anything eatable. Density and radioactivity weren't enough for these motors; the stuff fed to them had to be right.

Going back to the Kingston-Kane, he pulled out the wire, found its end fused into shapelessnes. Definitely a failure. Inserting the second sample, another grey wire not so dull as the first, he returned to the controls, rammed the energizer. The tail rockets promptly blasted with a low, moaning note and the thrust dial showed sixty percent normal surge.

Some people would have got mad at that point. Steve didn't. His lean, hawklike features quirked, he felt in his pocket for the third sample, tried that. No soap. The fourth likewise was a flop. The fifth produced a peculiar and rhythmic series of blasts which shook the vessel from end to end and caused the thrust-dial needle to waggle between one hundred per cent and zero. He visualized the Probe patrols popping through space like outboard motors while he extracted the stuff and fed the sixth sample. The sixth roared joyously at one hundred and seventy percent. The seventh sample was another flop.

He discarded all but what was left of the sixth wire. The stuff was about twelve-gauge and near enough for his purpose. It resembled deep-coloured copper but was not as soft as copper nor as heavy. Hard, springy and light, like telephone wire. If there were at least a thousand yards of it below, and if he could manage to drag it up to the ship, and if the golden thing didn't come along and ball up the works, he might be able to blow free. Then he'd get some place civilized—if he could find it. The future was based on an appalling selection of "ifs."

The easiest and most obvious way to salvage the needed treasure was to blow a hole in the roof, lower a cable through it, and wind up the wire with the aid of the ship's tiny winch. Problem: how to blow a hole without suitable explosives. Answer: drill the roof, insert unshelled pistol ammunition, say a prayer and pop the stuff off electrically. He tried it, using a hand drill. The bit promptly curled up as if gnawing on a diamond. He drew his gun, bounced a shell off the roof; the missile exploded with a sharp, hard crack and fragments of shell casing whined shrilly into the sky. Where it had struck, the roof bore a blast smudge and a couple of fine scratches.

There was nothing for it but to go down and heave on his shoulders as much loot as he could carry. And do it right away. Darkness would fall before long, and he didn't want to encounter that golden thing in the dark. It was fateful enough in broad light of day, or in the queer, green glow of the building's interior, but to have it stealing softly behind him as he struggled through the night-time with his plunder was something of which he didn't care to think.

Locking the ship and leaving Laura inside, he returned to the building, made his way past the mile of cases and cabinets to the machine section at the back. He stopped to study nothing on his way. He didn't wish to study anything. The wire was the thing, only the wire. Besides, mundane thoughts of mundane wire didn't twist one's mind around until one found it hard to concentrate.

Nevertheless, his mind was afire as he searched. Half of it was prickly with alertness, apprehensive of the golden column's sudden return; the other half burned with excitement at the possibility of release. Outwardly, his manner showed nothing of this; it was calm, assured, methodical.

Within ten minutes he'd found a great coil of the coppery metal, a huge ovoid, intricately wound, lying beside a disassembled machine. He tried to move it, could not shift it an inch. The thing was far too big, too heavy for one to handle. To get it on to the roof he'd have to cut it up and make four trips of it—and some of its inner windings were fused together. So near, so far! Freedom depended upon his ability to move a lump of metal a thousand feet vertically. He muttered some of Laura's words to himself.

Although the wire cutters were ready in his hand, he paused to think, decided to look farther before tackling this job. It was a wise decision which brought its reward, for at a point a mere hundred yards away he came across another, differently shaped coil, wheel-shaped, in good condition, easy to unreel. This again was too heavy to carry, but with a tremendous effort which made his muscles crack he got it up on its rim and proceeded to roll it along like a monster tire.

Several times he had to stop and let the coil lean against the nearest case while he rested a moment. The last such case trembled under the impact of the weighty coil and its shining, spidery occupant stirred in momentary simulation of life. His dislike of the spider shot up with its motion; he made his rest brief, bowled the coil onward.

Violet streaks again were creeping from the horizon when he rolled his loot out of the mighty exit and reached the bottom of the bank. Here, he stopped, clipped the wire with his cutters, took the free end, climbed the bank with it. The wire uncoiled without hindrance until he reached the ship, where he attached it to the winch, wound the lot in, rewound it on the feed spool.

Night fell in one ominous swoop. His hands were trembling slightly but his hawklike face was firm, phlegmatic as he carefully threaded the wire's end through the automatic injector and into the feed hole of the Kingston-Kanes. That done, he slid open Laura's door, gave her some of the fruit they'd picked off the Oron tree. She accepted it morbidly, her manner still subdued, and not inclined for speech.

"Stay inside, Honey," he soothed. "We're getting out of this and going home."

Shutting her in, he climbed into the control seat, switched

on the nose beam, saw it pierce the darkness and light up the facing cliff. Then he stamped on the energizer, warmed the tubes. Their bellow was violent and comforting. At seventy percent better thrust he'd have to be a lot more careful in all his adjustments: it wouldn't do to melt his own tail off when success was within his grasp. All the same, he felt strangely impatient, as if every minute counted, aye, every second!

But he contained himself, got the venturis heated, gave a discreet puff on his starboard steering flare, watched the cliff glide sidewise past as the ship slewed around on its belly. Another puff, then another, and he had the vessel nose-on to the front edge of the roof. There seemed to be a faint aura in the gloom ahead and he switched off his nose beam to study it better.

It was a faint yellow haze shining over the rim of the opposite slope. His back hairs quivered as he saw it. The haze strengthened, rose higher. His eyes strained into the outer pall as he watched it fascinatedly, and his hands were frozen on the controls. There was dampness on his back. Behind him, in her travelling compartment, Laura was completely silent, not even shuffling uneasily as was her wont. He wondered if she was cowering.

With a mighty effort of will which strained him as never before, he shifted his control a couple of notches, lengthened the tail blast. Trembling in its entire fabric, the ship edged forward. Summoning all he'd got, Steve forced his reluctant hands to administer the take-off boost. With a tearing crash that thundered back from the cliffs, the little vessel leaped skyward on an arc of fire. Peering through the transpex, Steve caught a fragmentary and foreshortened glimpse of the great golden column advancing majestically over the crest; the next instant it had dropped far behind his tail and his bow was arrowing for the stars.

An immense relief flooded through his soul though he knew not what there had been to fear. But the relief was there and so great was it that he worried not at all about where he was bound or for how long. Somehow, he felt certain that if he swept in a wide, shallow curve he'd pick up a Probe beat-note sooner or later. Once he got a beat-note, from any source at all, it would lead him out of the celestial maze.

Luck remained with him, and his optimistic hunch proved correct, for while still among completely strange constellations he caught the faint throb of Hydra III on his twenty-seventh day of sweep. That throb was his cosmic lighthouse beckoning him home.

He let go a wild shriek of "Yippee!" thinking that only Laura heard him—but he was heard elsewhere.

Down on Oro, deep in the monster workshop, the golden giant paused blindly as if listening. Then it slid stealthily along the immense aisles, reached the filing system. A compartment opened, two glassy plates came out.

For a moment the plates contacted the Oron's strange, sparkling substance, became etched with an array of tiny dots. They were returned to the compartment, and the door closed. The golden glory with its imprisoned stars then glided quietly back to the machine section.

Something nearer to the gods had scribbled its notes. Nothing lower in the scale of life could have translated them or deduced their full purport.

In simplest sense, one plate may have been inscribed, "Biped, erect, pink, hono intelligens type P. 739, planted on Sol III, Condensation Arm BDB—moderately successful."

Similarly, the other plate may have recorded, "Flapwing, large, hook-beaked, vari-coloured, periquito macao type K.8, planted on Sol III, Condensation Arm BDB—moderately successful."

But already the sparkling hobbyist had forgotten his passing notes. He was breathing his essence upon a jeweled moth.

EXIT THE PROFESSOR

by "Lewis Padgett" (Henry Kuttner, 1915-1958 and C. L. Moore, 1911-   )

THRILLING WONDER STORIES
October

1947 was another banner year for the foremost writing team of the 1940s. In addition to the present selection they published at least another five stories between them plus the powerful short novels Tomorrow and Tomorrow *and* Fury. *"Exit the Professor" is a wonderful example of the "whacky" science fiction story, and was included in their first collection* A Gnome There Was *(1950), one of the earliest short story collections by genre writers.*

We must add our usual disclaimer at this point—with the Kuttners one never knows who actually wrote what, and it is altogether possible that Kuttner or Moore wrote this one alone. If we had to bet on one, I would vote for Kuttner.

(Marty categorizes this as a "whacky" science fiction story. I would like to point out that this is by no means the same as a "humorous" science fiction story. A whacky story is usually humorous, but a humorous story is not usually whacky. It's hard enough being successfully humorous [as I very well

know] but it is even harder to be successfully whacky, since to be whacky means to be cleverly illogical on the surface, but with [to attain the best results] an underlying consistency. Henry Kuttner could do it, as "Exit the Professor" shows, and so could Fredric Brown—but few others could. Goodness knows I can't.

Incidentally, Hank described that "shotgun gadget" that "makes holes in things" and prudently didn't go into detail. But anyone can see, in hindsight, that what the Hogbens had put together was a device that fired a laser beam. Lasers, of course, had not been devised in 1947, and wouldn't be for another thirteen years.—I.A.)

We Hogbens are right exclusive. That Perfesser feller from the city might have known that, but he come busting in without an invite, and I don't figger he had call to complain afterward. In Kaintuck the polite thing is to stick to your own hill of beans and not come nosing around where you're not wanted.

Time we ran off the Haley boys with that shotgun gadget we rigged up—only we never could make out how it worked, somehow—that time, it all started because Rafe Haley come peeking and prying at the shed winder, trying to get a look at Little Sam. Then Rafe went round saying Little Sam had three haids or something.

Can't believe a word them Haley boys say. Three haids! It ain't natcheral, is it? Anyhow, Little Sam's only got two haids, and never had no more since the day he was born.

So Maw and I rigged up that shotgun thing and peppered the Haley boys good. Like I said, we couldn't figger out afterward how it worked. We'd tacked on some dry cells and a lot of coils and wires and stuff and it punched holes in Rafe as neat as anything.

Coroner's verdict was that the Haley boys died real sudden, and Sheriff Abernathy come up and had a drink of corn with us and said for two cents he'd whale the tar outa me. I didn't pay no mind. Only some dam-yankee reporter musta got wind of it, because a while later a big, fat, serious-looking man come around and begun to ask questions.

Uncle Les was sitting on the porch, with his hat over his face. "You better get the heck back to your circus, mister," he just said. "We had offers from old Barnum hisself and turned 'em down. Ain't that right, Saunk?"

"Sure is," I said. "I never trusted Phineas. Called Little Sam a freak, he did."

The big solemn-looking man, whose name was Perfesser Thomas Galbraith, looked at me. "How old are you, son?" he said.

"I ain't your son," I said. "And I don't know, nohow."

"You don't look over eighteen," he said, "big as you are. You couldn't have known Barnum."

"Sure I did. Don't go giving me the lie. I'll wham you."

"I'm not connected with any circus," Galbraith said. "I'm a biogeneticist."

We sure laughed at that. He got kinda mad and wanted to know what the joke was.

"There ain't no such word," Maw said. And at that point Little Sam started yelling, and Galbraith turned white as a goose wing and shivered all over. He sort of fell down. When we picked him up, he wanted to know what had happened.

"That was Little Sam," I said. "Maw's gone in to comfort him. He's stopped now."

"That was a subsonic," the Perfesser snapped. "What is Little Sam—a short-wave transmitter?"

"Little Sam's the baby," I said, short-like. "Don't go calling him outa his name, either. Now, s'pose you tell us what you want."

He pulled out a notebook and started looking through it.

"I'm a—a scientist," he said. "Our foundation is studying eugenics, and we've got some reports about you. They sound unbelievable. One of our men has a theory that natural mutations can remain undetected in undeveloped cultural regions, and—" He slowed down and stared at Uncle Les. "Can you really fly?" he asked.

Well, we don't like to talk about that. The preacher gave us a good dressing-down once. Uncle Les had got likkered up and went sailing over the ridges, scaring a couple of bear hunters outa their senses. And it ain't in the Good Book that men should fly, neither. Uncle Les generally does it only on the sly, when nobody's watching.

So anyhow Uncle Les pulled his hat down farther on his face and growled.

"That's plumb silly. Ain't no way a man can fly. These here modern contraptions I hear tell about—'tween ourselves, they don't really fly at all. Just a lot of crazy talk, that's all."

Galbraith blinked and studied his notebook again.

"But I've got hearsay evidence of a great many unusual things connected with your family. Flying is only one of them. I know it's theoretically impossible—and I'm not talking about planes—but—"

"Oh, shet your trap."

"The medieval witches' salve used aconite to give an illusion of flight—entirely subjective, of course."

"Will you stop pestering me?" Uncle Les said, getting mad, on account of he felt embarrassed, I guess. Then he jumped up, threw his hat down on the porch and flew away. After a minute he swooped down for his hat and made a face at the Perfesser. He flew off down the gulch and we didn't see him fer a while.

I got mad, too.

"You got no call to bother us," I said. "Next thing Uncle Les will do like Paw, and that'll be an awful nuisance. We ain't seen hide nor hair of Paw since that other city feller was around. He was a census taker, I think."

Galbraith didn't say anything. He was looking kinda funny. I gave him a drink and he asked about Paw.

"Oh, he's around," I said. "Only you don't see him no more. He likes it better that way, he says."

"Yes," Galbraith said, taking another drink. "Oh, God. How old did you say you were?"

"Didn't say nothing about it."

"Well, what's the earliest thing you can remember?"

"Ain't no use remembering things. Clutters up your haid too much."

"It's fantastic," Galbraith said. "I hadn't expected to send a report like that back to the foundation."

"We don't want nobody prying around," I said. "Go way and leave us alone."

"But, good Lord!" He looked over the porch rail and got interested in the shotgun gadget. "What's that?"

"A thing," I said.

"What does it do?"

"Things," I said.

"Oh. May I look at it?"

"Sure," I said. "I'll give you the dingus if you'll go away."

He went over and looked at it. Paw got up from where he'd been sitting beside me, told me to get rid of the dam-yankee and went into the house. The Perfesser came back. "Extraordinary!" he said. "I've had training in electronics, and it seems to me you've got something very odd there. What's the principle?"

"The what?" I said. "It makes holes in things."

"It can't fire shells. You've got a couple of lenses where the breech should—how did you say it worked?"

"I dunno."

"Did you make it?"

"Me and Maw."

He asked a lot more questions.

"I dunno," I said. "Trouble with a shotgun is you gotta keep loading it. We sorta thought if we hooked on a few things it wouldn't need loading no more. It don't, neither."

"Were you serious about giving it to me?"

"If you stop bothering us."

"Listen," he said, "it's miraculous that you Hogbens have stayed out of sight so long."

"We got our ways."

"The mutation theory must be right. You must be studied. This is one of the most important discoveries since—" He kept on talking like that. He didn't make much sense.

Finally I decided there was only two ways to handle things, and after what Sheriff Abernathy had said, I didn't feel right about killing nobody till the Sheriff had got over his fit of temper. I don't want to cause no ruckus.

"S'pose I go to New York with you, like you want," I said. "Will you leave the family alone?"

He halfway promised, though he didn't want to. But he knuckled under and crossed his heart, on account of I said I'd wake up Little Sam if he didn't. He sure wanted to see Little Sam, but I told him that was no good. Little Sam couldn't go to New York, anyhow. He's got to stay in his tank or he gets awful sick.

Anyway, I satisfied the Perfesser pretty well and he went off, after I'd promised to meet him in town next morning. I felt sick, though, I can tell you. I ain't been away from the folks overnight since that ruckus in the old country, when we had to make tracks fast.

Went to Holland, as I remember. Maw always had a soft spot fer the man that helped us get outa London. Named Little Sam after him. I fergit what his name was. Gwynn or Stuart or Pepys—I get mixed up when I think back beyond the War between the States.

That night we chewed the rag. Paw being invisible, Maw kept thinking he was getting more'n his share of the corn, but pretty soon she mellowed and let him have a demijohn. Everybody told me to mind my p's and q's.

"This here Perfesser's awful smart," Maw said. "All perfessers are. Don't go bothering him any. You be a good boy or you'll ketch heck from me."

"I'll be good, Maw," I said. Paw whaled me alongside the haid, which wasn't fair, on account of I couldn't see him.

"That's so you won't fergit," he said.

"We're plain folks," Uncle Les was growling. "No good never come of trying to get above yourself."

"Honest, I ain't trying to do that," I said. "I only figgered—"

"You stay outa trouble!" Maw said, and just then we heard Grandpaw moving in the attic. Sometimes Grandpaw don't stir for a month at a time, but tonight he seemed right frisky.

So, natcherally, we went upstairs to see what he wanted.

He was talking about the Perfesser.

"A stranger, eh?" he said. "Out upon the stinking knave. A set of rare fools I've gathered about me for my dotage! Only Saunk shows any shrewdness, and, dang my eyes, he's the worst fool of all."

I just shuffled and muttered something, on account of I never like to look at Grandpaw direct. But he wasn't paying me no mind. He raced on.

"So you'd go to this New York? 'Sblood, and hast thou forgot the way we shunned London and Amsterdam—and Nieuw Amsterdam—for fear of questioning? Wouldst thou be put in a freak show? Nor is that the worst danger."

Grandpaw's the oldest one of us and he gets kinda mixed up in his language sometimes. I guess the lingo you learned when you're young sorta sticks with you. One thing, he can cuss better than anybody I've ever heard.

"Shucks," I said. "I was only trying to help."

"Thou puling brat," Grandpaw said. " 'Tis thy fault and thy dam's. For building that device, I mean, that slew the

Haley tribe. Hadst thou not, this scientist would never have come here."

"He's a perfesser," I said. "Name of Thomas Galbraith."

"I know. I read his thoughts through Little Sam's mind. A dangerous man. I never knew a sage who wasn't. Except perhaps Roger Bacon, and I had to bribe him to—but Roger was an exceptional man. Hearken:

"None of you may go to this New York. The moment we leave this haven, the moment we are investigated, we are lost. The pack would tear and rend us. Nor could all thy addle-pated flights skyward save thee, Lester—dost thou hear?"

"But what are we to do?" Maw said.

"Aw, heck," Paw said. "I'll just fix this Perfesser. I'll drop him down the cistern."

"An' spoil the water?" Maw screeched. "You try it!"

"What foul brood is this that has sprung from my seed?" Grandpaw said, real mad. "Have ye not promised the Sheriff that there will be no more killings—for a while, at least? Is the word of a Hogben naught? Two things have we kept sacred through the centuries—our secret from the world, and the Hogben honor! Kill this man Galbraith and ye'll answer to me for it!"

We all turned white. Little Sam woke up again and started squealing. "But what'll we do?" Uncle Les said.

"Our secret must be kept," Grandpaw said. "Do what ye can, but no killing. I'll consider the problem."

He seemed to go to sleep then, though it was hard to tell.

The next day I met Galbraith in town, all right, but first I run into Sheriff Abernathy in the street and he gave me a vicious look.

"You stay outa trouble, Saunk," he said. "Mind what I tell you, now." It was right embarrassing.

Anyway, I saw Galbraith and told him Grandpaw wouldn't let me go to New York. He didn't look too happy, but he saw there was nothing that could be done about it.

His hotel room was full of scientific apparatus and kinda frightening. He had the shotgun gadget set up, but it didn't look like he'd changed it any. He started to argue.

"Ain't no use," I said. "We ain't leaving the hills. I spoke outa turn yesterday, that's all."

"Listen, Saunk," he said. "I've been inquiring around town about you Hogbens, but I haven't been able to find out much.

They're close-mouthed around here. Still, such evidence would be only supporting factors. I know our theories are right. You and your family are mutants and you've got to be studied!"

"We ain't mutants," I said. "Scientists are always calling us outa our names. Roger Bacon called us homunculi, only—"

"*What?*" Galbraith shouted. "Who did you say?"

"Uh—he's a share-cropper over in the next county," I said hasty-like, but I could see the Perfesser didn't swaller it. He started to walk around the room.

"It's no use," he said. "If you won't come to New York, I'll have the foundation send a commission here. You've got to be studied, for the glory of science and the advancement of mankind."

"Oh, golly," I said. "I know what that'd be like. Make a freak show outa us. It'd kill Little Sam. You gotta go away and leave us alone."

"Leave you alone? When you can create apparatus like this?" He pointed to the shotgun gadget. "How *does* that work?" he wanted to know, sudden-like.

"I told you, I dunno. We just rigged it up. Listen, Perfesser. There'd be trouble if people came and looked at us. Big trouble. Grandpaw says so."

Galbraith pulled at his nose.

"Well, maybe—suppose you answered a few questions for me, Saunk."

"No commission?"

"We'll see."

"No, sir. I won't—"

Galbraith took a deep breath.

"As long as you tell me what I want to know, I'll keep your whereabouts a secret."

"I thought this fundation thing of yours knows where you are."

"Ah—yes," Galbraith said. "Naturally they do. But they don't know about *you*."

That gave me an idea. I coulda killed him easy, but if I had, I knew Grandpaw would of ruined me entire and, besides, there was the Sheriff to think of. So I said, "Shucks." and nodded.

My, the questions that man asked! It left me dizzy. And all the while he kept getting more and more excited.

"How old is your grandfather?"

"Gosh, I dunno."

"Homunculi—mm-m. You mentioned that he was a miner once?"

"No, that was Grandpaw's paw," I said. "Tin mines, they were, in England. Only Grandpaw says it was called Britain then. That was during a sorta magic plague they had then. The people had to get the doctors—droons? Droods?"

"Druids?"

"Uh-huh. The Druids was the doctors then, Grandpaw says. Anyhow, all the miners started dying round Cornwall, so they closed up the mines."

"What sort of plague was it?"

I told him what I remembered from Grandpaw's talk, and the Perfesser got very excited and said something about radioactive emanations, as nearly as I could figger out. It made oncommon bad sense.

"Artificial mutations caused by radioactivity!" he said, getting real pink around the jowls. "Your grandfather was born a mutant! The genes and chromosomes were rearranged into a new pattern. Why, you may all be supermen!"

"Nope," I said. "We're Hogbens. That's all."

"A dominant, obviously a dominant. All your family were—ah—peculiar?"

"Now, look!" I said.

"I mean, they could all fly?"

"I don't know how yet, myself. I guess we're kinda freakish. Grandpaw was smart. He allus taught us not to show off."

"Protective camouflage," Galbraith said. "Submerged in a rigid social culture, variations from the norm are more easily masked. In a modern, civilized culture, you'd stick out like a sore thumb. But here, in the backwoods, you're practically invisible."

"Only Paw," I said.

"Oh, Lord," he sighed. "Submerging these incredible natural powers of yours . . . Do you know the things you might have done?" And then all of a sudden he got even more excited, and I didn't much like the look in his eyes.

"Wonderful things," he repeated. "It's like stumbling on Aladdin's lamp."

"I wish you'd leave us alone," I said. "You and your commission!"

"Forget about the commission. I've decided to handle this

privately for a while. Provided you'll cooperate. Help me, I mean. Will you do that?"

"Nope," I said.

"Then I'll bring the commission down from New York," he said triumphantly.

I thought that over.

"Well," I said finally, "what do you want me to do?"

"I don't know yet," he said slowly. "My mind hasn't fully grasped the possibilities."

But he was getting ready to grab. I could tell. I know that look.

I was standing by the window looking out, and all of a sudden I got an idea. I figgered it wouldn't be smart to trust the Perfesser too much, anyhow. So I sort of ambled over to the shotgun gadget and make a few little changes on it.

I knew what I wanted to do, all right, but if Galbraith had asked me why I was twisting a wire here and bending a whozis there I couldn't of told him. I got no eddication. Only now I knew the gadget would do what I wanted it to do.

The Perfesser had been writing in his little notebook. He looked up and saw me.

"What are you doing?" he wanted to know.

"This don't look right to me," I said. "I think you monkeyed with them batteries. Try it now."

"In here?" he said, startled. "I don't want to pay a bill for damages. It must be tested under safety conditions."

"See the weathercock out there, on the roof?" I pointed it out to him. "Won't do no harm to aim at that. You can just stand here by the winder and try it out."

"It—it isn't dangerous?" He was aching to try the gadget, I could tell. I said it wouldn't kill nobody, and he took a long breath and went to the window and cuddled the stock of the gun against his cheek.

I stayed back aways. I didn't want the Sheriff to see me. I'd already spotted him, sitting on a bench outside the feed-and-grain store across the street.

It happened just like I thought. Galbraith pulled the trigger, aiming at the weathercock on the roof, and rings of light started coming out of the muzzle. There was a fearful noise. Galbraith fell flat on his back, and the commotion was something surprising. People began screaming all over town.

I kinda felt it might be handy if I went invisible for a while. So I did.

Galbraith was examining the shotgun gadget when Sheriff Abernathy busted in. The Sheriff's a hard case. He had his pistol out and handcuffs ready, and he was cussing the Perfesser immediate and rapid.

"I seen you!" he yelled. "You city fellers think you can get away with anything down here. Well, you can't!"

"Saunk!" Galbraith cried, looking around. But of course he couldn't see me.

Then there was an argument. Sheriff Abernathy had seen Galbraith fire the shotgun gadget and he's no fool. He drug Galbraith down on the street, and I came along, walking softly. People were running around like crazy. Most of them had their hands clapped to their faces.

The Perfesser kept wailing that he didn't understand.

"I seen you!" Abernathy said. "You aimed that dingus of yours out the window and the next thing everybody in town's got a toothache! Try and tell me you don't understand!"

The Sheriff's smart. He's known us Hogbens long enough so he ain't surprised when funny things happen sometimes. Also, he knew Galbraith was a scientist feller. So there was a ruckus and people heard what was going on and the next thing they was trying to lynch Galbraith.

But Abernathy got him away. I wandered around town for a while. The pastor was out looking at his church windows, which seemed to puzzle him. They was stained glass, and he couldn't figger out why they was hot. I coulda told him that. There's gold in stained-glass windows; they use it to get a certain kind of red.

Finally I went down to the jailhouse. I was still invisible. So I eavesdropped on what Galbraith was saying to the Sheriff.

"It was Saunk Hogben," the Perfesser kept saying. "I tell you, he fixed that projector!"

"I saw you," Abernathy said. "You done it. Ow!" He put up his hand to his jaw. "And you better stop it, fast! That crowd outside means business. Half the people in town have got toothaches."

I guess half the people in town had gold fillings in their teeth.

Then Galbraith said something that didn't surprise me too much. "I'm having a commission come down from New York; I meant to telephone the foundation tonight, they'll vouch for me."

So he was intending to cross us up, all along. I kinda felt that had been in his mind.

"You'll cure this toothache of mine—and everybody else's—or I'll open the doors and let in that lynch mob!" the Sheriff howled. Then he went away to put an icebag on his cheek.

I snuck back aways, got visible again and made a lot of noise coming along the passage, so Galbraith could hear me. I waited till he got through cussing me out. I just looked stupid.

"I guess I made a mistake," I said. "I can fix it, though."

"You've done enough fixing!" He stopped. "Wait a minute. What did you say? You can cure this—what *is* it?"

"I been looking at that shotgun gadget," I said. "I think I know what I did wrong. It's sorta turned in on gold now, and all the gold in town's shooting out rays or heat or something."

"Induced selective radioactivity," Galbraith muttered, which didn't seem to mean much. "Listen. That crowd outside—do they ever have lynchings in this town?"

"Not more'n once or twice a year," I said. "And we already had two this year, so we filled our quota. Wish I could get you up to our place, though. We could hide you easy."

"You'd better do something!" he said. "Or I'll get that commission down from New York. You wouldn't like that, would you?"

I never seen such a man fer telling lies and keeping a straight face.

"It's a cinch," I said. "I can rig up the gadget so it'll switch off the rays immediate. Only I don't want people to connect us Hogbens with what's going on. We like to live quiet. Look s'pose I go back to your hotel and change over the gadget, and then all you have to do is get all the people with toothaches together and pull the trigger."

"But—well, but—"

He was afraid of more trouble. I had to talk him into it. The crowd was yelling outside, so it wasn't too hard. Finally

I went away, but I came back, invisible-like, and listened when Galbraith talked to the Sheriff.

They fixed it all up. Everybody with toothaches was going to the Town Hall and set. Then Abernathy would bring the Perfesser over, with the shotgun gadget, and try it out.

"Will it stop the toothaches?" the Sheriff wanted to know. "For sure?"

"I'm—quite certain it will."

Abernathy had caught that hesitation.

"Then you better try it on me first. Just to make sure. I don't trust you."

It seemed like nobody was trusting nobody.

I hiked back to the hotel and made the switch-over in the shotgun gadget. And then I run into trouble. My invisibility was wearing thin. That's the worst part of being just a kid.

After I'm a few hunnerd years older I can stay invisible all the time if I want to. But I ain't right mastered it yet. Thing was, I needed help now because there was something I had to do, and I couldn't do it with people watching.

I went up on the roof and called Little Sam. After I'd tuned in on his haid, I had him put the call through to Paw and Uncle Les. After a while Uncle Les come flying down from the sky, riding mighty heavy on account of he was carrying Paw. Paw was cussing because a hawk had chased them.

"Nobody seen us, though," Uncle Les said. "I *think*."

"People got their own troubles in town today," I said. "I need some help. That Perfesser's gonna call down his commission and study us, no matter what he promises."

"Ain't much we can do, then," Paw said. "We cain't kill that feller. Grandpaw said not to."

So I told 'em my idea. Paw being invisible, he could do it easy. Then we made a little place in the roof so we could see through it, and looked down into Galbraith's room.

We was just in time. The Sheriff was standing there, with his pistol out, just waiting, and the Perfesser, pale around the chops, was pointing the shotgun gadget at Abernathy. It went along without a hitch. Galbraith pulled the trigger, a purple ring of light popped out, and that was all. Except that the Sheriff opened his mouth and gulped.

"You wasn't faking! My toothache's gone!"

Galbraith was sweating, but he put up a good front. "Sure it works," he said. "Naturally. I told you—"

"C'mon down to the Town Hall. Everybody's waiting. You better cure us all, or it'll be just too bad for you."

They went out. Paw snuck down after them, and Uncle Les picked me up and flew on their trail, keeping low to the roofs, where we wouldn't be spotted. After a while we was fixed outside one of the Town Hall's windows, watching.

I ain't heard so much misery since the great plague of London. The hall was jam-full, and everybody had a toothache and was moaning and yelling. Abernathy come in with the Perfesser, who was carrying the shotgun gadget, and a scream went up.

Galbraith set the gadget on the stage, pointing down at the audience, while the Sheriff pulled out his pistol again and made a speech, telling everybody to shet up and they'd get rid of their toothaches.

I couldn't see Paw, natcherally, but I knew he was up on the platform. Something funny was happening to the shotgun gadget. Nobody noticed, except me, and I was watching for it. Paw—invisible, of course—was making a few changes. I'd told him how, but he knew what to do as well as I did. So pretty soon the shotgun was rigged the way we wanted it.

What happened after that was shocking. Galbraith aimed the gadget and pulled the trigger, and rings of light jumped out, yaller this time. I'd told Paw to fix the range so nobody outside the Town Hall would be bothered. But inside—

Well, it sure fixed them toothaches. Nobody's gold filling can ache if he ain't got a filling.

The gadget was fixed now so it worked on everything that wasn't growing. Paw had got the range just right. The seats was gone all of a sudden, and so was part of the chandelier. The audience, being bunched together, got it good. Pegleg Jaffe's glass eye was gone, too. Them that had false teeth lost 'em. Everybody sorta got a once-over-lightly haircut.

Also, the whole audience lost their clothes. Shoes ain't growing things, and no more are pants or shirts or dresses. In a trice everybody in the hall was naked as needles. But, shucks, they'd got rid of their toothaches, hadn't they?

We was back to home an hour later, all but Uncle Les, when the door busted open and in come Uncle Les, with the Perfesser staggering after him. Galbraith was a mess. He sank down and wheezed, looking back at the door in a worried way.

"Funny thing happened," Uncle Les said. "I was flying along outside town and there was the Perfesser running away from a big crowd of people, with sheets wrapped around 'em—some of 'em. So I picked him up. I brung him here, like he wanted." Uncle Les winked at me.

"Ooooh!" Galbraith said. "*Aaaah!* Are they coming?"

Maw went to the door.

"They's a lot of torches moving up the mountain," she said. "It looks right bad."

The Perfesser glared at me.

"You said you could hide me! Well, you'd better! This is your fault!"

"Shucks," I said.

"You'll hide me or else!" Galbraith squalled. "I—I'll bring that commission down."

"Look," I said, "if we hide you safe, will you promise to fergit all about the commission and leave us alone?"

The Perfesser promised. "Hold on a minute," I said, and went up to the attic to see Grandpaw.

He was awake.

"How about it, Grandpaw?" I asked.

He listened to Little Sam for a second.

"The knave is lying," he told me pretty soon. "He means to bring his commission of stinkards here anyway, recking naught of his promise."

"Should we hide him, then?"

"Aye," Grandpaw said. "The Hogbens have given their word—there must be no more killing. And to hide a fugitive from his pursuers would not be an ill deed, surely."

Maybe he winked. It's hard to tell with Grandpaw. So I went down the ladder. Galbraith was at the door, watching the torches come up the mountain.

He grabbed me.

"Saunk! If you don't hide me—"

"We'll hide you," I said. "C'mon."

So we took him down to the cellar . . .

When the mob got here, with Sheriff Abernathy in the lead, we played dumb. We let 'em search the house. Little Sam and Grandpaw turned invisible for a bit, so nobody noticed them. And naturally the crowd couldn't find hide nor hair of Galbraith. We'd hid him good, like we promised.

That was a few years ago. The Perfesser's thriving. He ain't studying us, though. Sometimes we take out the bottle we keep him in and study him.

Dang small bottle, too!

THUNDER AND ROSES

by Theodore Sturgeon (1918-   )

ASTOUNDING SCIENCE FICTION
November

Ted Sturgeon's second contribution to the best of 1947 is a powerful statement for sanity in a world gone insane. Written only a few months after Hiroshima, it stands as one of the great warning stories of all time, affirming that even at the worst of moments men and women still have the obligation to make choices.

Do you agree, Isaac?

(Absolutely, Marty. A whole generation has passed since 1947 and nuclear doom has not yet come, largely because people have made choices [notably in the Cuban missile crisis of 1962], and have chosen life. We must still do it today. Above all considerations of local short-term goals, we must make that overriding long-term choice of life.

But some points. Of the 14 stories in this volume, 11 were from Astounding, *and 4 featured nuclear warfare and its consequences. That is, four of the stories we considered the best of the year including "Thunder and Roses." There were many more stories in the course of the year that were printed and that dealt with the nuclear nightmare, and who knows how many stories that were written and were never published. It was an overriding terror in the years that immediately followed Hiroshima; and it is only the callousness of habituation that hasn't caused the terror to increase steadily—for the danger has.—I.A.)*

When Pete Mawser learned about the show, he turned away from the GHQ bulletin board, touched his long chin, and determined to shave. This was odd, because the show would be video, and he would see it in his barracks.

He had an hour and a half. It felt good to have a purpose again—even shaving before eight o'clock. Eight o'clock Tuesday, just the way it used to be. Everyone used to catch that show on Tuesday. Everyone used to say, Wednesday morning, "How about the way she sang 'The Breeze and I' last night?" "Hey did you hear Starr last night?"

That was awhile ago, before all those people were dead, before the country was dead. Starr Anthim, institution, like Crosby, like Duse, like Jenny Lind, like the Statue of Liberty.

(Liberty had been one of the first to get it, her bronze beauty volatilized, radioactive, and even now being carried about in vagrant winds, spreading over the earth—)

Pete Mawser grunted and forced his thoughts away from the drifting, poisonous fragments of a blasted Liberty. Hate was first. Hate was ubiquitous, like the increasing blue glow in the air at night, like the tension that hung over the base.

Gunfire crackled sporadically far to the right, swept nearer. Pete stepped out of the street and made for a parked ten-wheeler. There's a lot of cover in and around a ten-wheeler.

There was a Wac sitting on the short running-board.

At the corner a stocky figure backed into the intersection. The man carried a tommy gun in his arms, and he was swinging it to and fro with the gentle, wavering motion of a weather vane. He staggered toward them, his gun muzzle hunting. Someone fired from a building and the man swiveled and blasted wildly at the sound.

"He's—blind," said Pete Mawser, and added, "He ought to be," looking at the tattered face.

A siren keened. An armored jeep slewed into the street. The full-throated roar of a brace of .50-caliber machine guns put a swift and shocking end to the incident.

"Poor crazy kid." Pete said softly. "That's the fourth I've seen today." He looked down at the Wac. She was smiling.

"Hey!"

"Hello, Sarge." She must have identified him before, because now she did not raise her eyes or her voice. "What happened?"

"You know what happened. Some kid got tired of having nothing to fight and nowhere to run to. What's the matter with you?"

"No," she said. "I don't mean that." At last she looked up at him. "I mean all of this. I can't seem to remember."

"You . . . well, gee, it's not easy to forget. We got hit. We got hit everywhere at once. All the big cities are gone. We got it from both sides. We got too much. The air is becoming radioactive. We'll all—" He checked himself. She didn't know. She'd forgotten. There was nowhere to escape to, and she'd escaped inside herself, right here. Why tell her about it? Why tell her that everyone was going to die? Why tell her that other, shameful thing: that we hadn't struck back?

But she wasn't listening. She was still looking at him. Her eyes were not quite straight. One held his but the other was slightly shifted and seemed to be looking at his temples. She was smiling again. When his voice trailed off she didn't prompt him. Slowly he moved away. She did not turn her head, but kept looking up at where he had been, smiling a little. He turned away, wanting to run, walking fast.

(How long can a guy hold out? When you're in the Army they try to make you be like everybody else. What do you do when everybody else is cracking up?)

He blanked out the mental picture of himself as the last one left sane. He'd followed that one through before. It always led to the conclusion that it would be better to be one of the first. He wasn't ready for that yet.

Then he blanked that out, too. Every time he said to himself that he wasn't ready for that yet, something within him asked, "Why not?" and he never seemed to have an answer ready.

(How long could a guy hold out?)

He climbed the steps of the QM Central and went inside. There was nobody at the reception switchboard. It didn't matter. Messages were carried by guys in jeeps, or on motorcycles. The Base Command was not insisting that anybody stick to a sitting job these days. Ten desk men would crack up for every one on a jeep, or on the soul-sweat squads. Pete made up his mind to put in a little stretch on a squad tomorrow. Do him good. He just hoped that this time the adjutant wouldn't burst into tears in the middle of the parade ground. You could keep your mind on the manual of arms just fine until something like that happened.

He bumped into Sonny Weisefreund in the barracks corridor. The tech's round young face was as cheerful as ever. He was naked and glowing, and had a towel thrown over his shoulder.

"Hi, Sonny. Is there plenty of hot water?"

"Why not?" grinned Sonny. Pete grinned back, cursing inwardly. Could anybody say anything about anything at all without one of these reminders? Sure there was hot water. The QM barracks had hot water for three hundred men. There were three dozen left. Men dead, men gone to the hills, men locked up so they wouldn't—

"Starr Anthim's doing a show tonight."

"Yeah. Tuesday night. Not funny, Pete. Don't you know there's a war—"

"No kidding," Pete said swiftly. "She's here—right here on the base."

Sonny's face was joyful. "Gee." He pulled the towel off his shoulder and tied it around his waist. "Starr Anthim, here! Where are they going to put on the show?"

"HQ, I imagine. Video only. You know about public gatherings." And a good thing, too, he thought. Put on an in-person show, and some torn-up GI would crack during one of her numbers. He himself would get plenty mad over a thing like that—mad enough to do something about it then and there. And there would probably be a hundred and fifty or more like him, going raving mad because someone had spoiled a Starr Anthim show. That would be a dandy little shambles for her to put in her memory book.

"How'd she happen to come here, Pete?"

"Drifted in on the last gasp of a busted-up Navy helicopter."

"Yeah, but why?"

"Search me. Get your head out of that gift horse's mouth."

He went into the washroom, smiling and glad that he still could. He undressed and put his neatly folded clothes down on a bench. There were a soap wrapper and an empty toothpaste tube lying near the wall. He went and picked them up and put them in the catch-all. He took the mop which leaned against the partition and mopped the floor where Sonny had splashed after shaving. Got to keep things squared away. He might say something if it were anyone else but Sonny. But Sonny wasn't cracking up. Sonny always had been like that. Look there. Left his razor out again.

Pete started his shower, meticulously adjusting the valves until the pressure and temperature exactly suited him. He didn't do anything slapdash these days. There was so much to feel, and taste, and see now. The impact of water on his skin, the smell of soap, the consciousness of light and heat, the very pressure of standing on the soles of his feet—he wondered vaguely how the slow increase of radioactivity in the air, as the nitrogen transmuted to Carbon Fourteen, would affect him if he kept carefully healthy in every way. What happens first? Do you go blind? Headaches, maybe? Perhaps you lose your appetite. Or maybe you get tired all the time.

Why not go look it up?

On the other hand, why bother? Only a very small percentage of the men would die of radioactive poisoning. There were too many other things that killed more quickly, which was probably just as well. That razor, for example. It lay gleaming in a sunbeam, curved and clean in the yellow light. Sonny's father and grandfather had used it, or so he said, and it was his pride and joy.

Pete turned his back on it and soaped under his arms, concentrating on the tiny kisses of bursting bubbles. In the midst of a recurrence of disgust at himself for thinking so often of death, a staggering truth struck him. He did not think of such things because he was morbid, after all! It was the very familiarity of things that brought death-thoughts. It was either "I shall never do this again" or "This is one of the last times I shall do this." You might devote yourself completely to doing things in different ways, he thought madly. You might crawl across the floor this time, and next time walk across on your hands. You might skip dinner tonight, and have a snack at two in the morning instead, and eat grass for breakfast.

But you had to breathe. Your heart had to beat. You'd sweat and you'd shiver, the same as always. You couldn't get away from that. When those things happened, they would remind you. Your heart wouldn't beat out its *wunklunk, wunklunk* any more. It would go *one-less, one-less,* until it yelled and yammered in your ears and you had to make it stop.

Terrific polish on that razor.

And your breath would go on, same as before. You could sidle through this door, back through the next one and the one after, and figure out a totally new way to go through the one after that, but your breath would keep on sliding in and out of your nostrils like a razor going through whiskers, making a sound like a razor being stropped.

Sonny came in. Pete soaped his hair. Sonny picked up the razor and stood looking at it. Pete watched him, soap ran into his eyes, he swore, and Sonny jumped.

"What are you looking at, Sonny? Didn't you ever see it, before?"

"Oh, sure. Sure. I was just—" He shut the razor, opened it, flashed light from its blade, shut it again. "I'm tired of using this. Pete, I'm going to get rid of it. Want it?"

Want it? In his foot locker, maybe. Under his pillow. "Thanks no, Sonny. Couldn't use it."

"I like safety razors," Sonny mumbled. "Electrics, even better. What are we going to do with it?"

"Throw it in the . . . no." Pete pictured the razor turning end over end in the air, half open, gleaming in the maw of the catch-all. "Throw it out the—" No. Curving out into the long grass. You might want it. You might crawl around in the moonlight looking for it. You might find it.

"I guess maybe I'll break it up."

"No," Pete said. "The pieces—" Sharp little pieces. Hollowground fragments. I'll think of something. Wait'll I get dressed."

He washed briskly, toweled, while Sonny stood looking at the razor. It was a blade now, and if you broke it, there would be shards and glittering splinters, still razor sharp. You could slap its edge into an emery wheel and grind it away, and somebody could find it, and put another edge on it because it was so obviously a razor, a fine steel razor, one that would slice so— "I know. The laboratory. We'll get rid of it." Pete said confidently.

He stepped into his clothes, and together they went to the laboratory wing. It was very quiet there. Their voices echoed.

"One of the ovens," said Pete, reaching for the razor.

"Bake ovens? You're crazy!"

Pete chuckled. "You don't know this place, do you? Like everything else on the base, there was a lot more went on here than most people knew about. They kept calling it the bake shop. Well, it *was* research headquarters for new high-nutrient flours. But there's lots else here. We tested utensils and designed beet peelers and all sorts of things like that. There's an electric furnace in here that—" He pushed open a door.

They crossed a long, quiet, cluttered room to the thermal equipment. "We can do everything here from annealing glass, through glazing ceramics, to finding the melting point of frying pans." He clicked a switch tentatively. A pilot light glowed. He swung open a small, heavy door and set the razor inside. "Kiss it good-bye. In twenty minutes it'll be a puddle."

"I want to see that," said Sonny. "Can I look around until it's cooked?"

"Why not?"

(Everybody around here always said "Why not?")

They walked through the laboratories. Beautifully equipped, they were, and too quiet. Once they passed a major who was bent over a complex electronic hook-up on one of the benches. He was watching a little amber light flicker, and he did not return their salute. They tiptoed past him, feeling awed in his absorption, envying it. They saw the models of the automatic kneaders, the vitaminizers, the remote-signal thermostats and timers and controls.

"What's in there?"

"I dunno. I'm over the edge of my territory. I don't think there's anybody left for this section. They were mostly mechanical and electronic theoreticians. The only thing I know about them is that if we ever needed anything in the way of tools, meters, or equipment, they had it or something better, and if we ever got real bright and figured out a startling new idea, they'd already built it and junked it a month ago. Hey!"

Sonny followed the pointing hand. "What?"

"That wall section. It's loose, or . . . well, what do you know?"

He pushed at the section of wall, which was very slightly out of line. There was a dark space beyond.

"What's in there?"

"Nothing, or some semiprivate hush-hush job. These guys used to get away with murder."

Sonny said, with an uncharacteristic flash of irony, "Isn't that the Army theoretician's business?"

Cautiously they peered in, then entered.

"Wh . . . *hey!* The door!"

It swung swiftly and quietly shut. The soft click of the latch was accompanied by a blaze of light.

The room was small and windowless. It contained machinery—a "trickle" charger, a bank of storage batteries, an electric-powered dynamo, two small self-starting gas-driven light plants and a Diesel complete with sealed compressed-air starting cylinders. In the corner was a relay rack with its panel-bolts spot-welded. Protruding from it was a red-top lever. Nothing was labeled.

They looked at the equipment wordlessly for a time and then Sonny said, "Somebody wanted to make awful sure he had power for something."

"Now, I wonder what—" Pete walked over to the relay rack. He looked at the level without touching it. It was wired up; behind the handle, on the wire, was a folded tag. He opened it cautiously. "To be used only on specific orders of the Commanding Officer."

"Give it a yank and see what happens."

Something clicked behind them. They whirled. "What was that?"

"Seemed to come from that rig by the door."

They approached it cautiously. There was a spring-loaded solenoid attached to a bar which was hinged to drop across the inside of the secret door, where it would fit into steel gudgeons on the panel.

It clicked again. "A Geiger," said Pete disgustedly.

"Now why," mused Sonny, "would they design a door to stay locked unless the general radioactivity went beyond a certain point? That's what it is. See the relays? And the overload switch there? And this?"

"It has a manual lock, too," Pete pointed out. The counter clicked again. "Let's get out of here. I got one of those things built into my head these days."

The door opened easily. They went out, closing it behind

them. The keyhole was cleverly concealed in the crack between two boards.

They were silent as they made their way back to the QM labs. The small thrill of violation was gone and, for Pete Mawser at least, the hate was back, that and the shame. A few short weeks before, this base had been a part of the finest country on earth. There was a lot of work here that was secret, and a lot that was such purely progressive and unapplied research that it would be in the way anywhere else but in this quiet wilderness.

Sweat stood out on his forehead. They hadn't struck back at their murderers! It was quite well known that there were launching sites all over the country, in secret caches far from any base or murdered city. Why must they sit here waiting to die, only to let the enemy—"enemies" was more like it—take over the continent when it was safe again?

He smiled grimly. One small consolation. They'd hit too hard; that was a certainty. Probably each of the attackers underestimated what the other would throw. The result—a spreading transmutation of nitrogen into deadly Carbon Fourteen. The effects would not be limited to the continent. What ghastly long-range effect the muted radioactivity would have on the overseas enemies was something that no one alive today could know.

Back at the furnace, Pete glanced at the temperature dial, then kicked the latch control. The pilot winked out and then the door swung open. They blinked and started back from the raging heat within, then bent and peered. The razor was gone. A pool of brilliance lay on the floor of the compartment.

"Ain't much left. Most of it oxidized away," Pete grunted.

They stood together for a time with their faces lit by that small shimmering ruin. Later, as they walked back to the barracks, Sonny broke his long silence with a sigh. "I'm glad we did that, Pete. I'm awful glad we did that."

At a quarter to eight they were waiting before the combination console in the barracks. All hands except Pete and Sonny and a wiry-haired, thick-set corporal named Bonze had elected to see the show on the big screen in the mess hall. The reception was better there, of course, but, as Bonze put it, "you don't get close enough in a big place like that."

"I hope she's the same," said Sonny, half to himself.

Why should she be? thought Pete morosely as he turned on the set and watched the screen begin to glow. There were many more of the golden speckles that had killed reception for the past two weeks. Why should anything be the same, ever again!

He fought a sudden temptation to kick the set to pieces. It, and Starr Anthim, were part of something that was dead. The country was dead, a real country—prosperous, sprawling, laughing, grabbing, growing and changing, leprous in spots with poverty and injustice, but healthy enough to overcome any ill. He wondered how the murderers would like it. They were welcome to it, now. Nowhere to go. No one to fight. That was true for every soul on earth now.

"You hope she's the same," he muttered.

"The show, I mean," said Sonny mildly. "I'd like to just sit here and have it like . . . like—"

Oh, thought Pete mistily. Oh—that. Somewhere to go, that's what it is, for a few minutes, "I know," he said, all the harshness gone from his voice.

Noise receded from the audio as the carrier swept in. The light on the screen swirled and steadied into a diamond pattern. Pete adjusted the focus, chromic balance, and intensity. "Turn out the lights. Bonze. I don't want to see anything but Starr Anthim."

It *was* the same, at first. Starr Anthim had never used the usual fanfares, fade-ins, color, and clamor of her contemporaries. A black screen, then *click,* a blaze of gold. It was all there, in focus; tremendously intense, it did not change. Rather, the eye changed to take it in. She never moved for seconds after she came on; she was there, a portrait, a still face and a white throat. Her eyes were open and sleeping. Her face was alive and still.

Then, in the eyes which seemed green but were blue flecked with gold, an awareness seemed to gather, and they came awake. Only then was it noticeable that her lips were parted. Something in the eyes made the lips be seen, though nothing moved yet. Not until she bent her head slowly, so that some of the gold flecks seemed captured in the golden brows. The eyes were not, then, looking out at an audience. They were looking at me, and at *me,* and at ME.

"Hello—you." she said. She was a dream, with a kid sister's slightly irregular teeth.

Bonze shuddered. The cot on which he lay began to squeak

rapidly. Sonny shifted in annoyance. Pete reached out in the dark and caught the leg of the cot. The squeaking subsided.

"May I sing a song?" Starr asked. There was music, very faint. "It's an old one, and one of the best. It's an easy song, a deep song, one that comes from the part of men and women that is mankind—the part that has in it no greed, no hate, no fear. This song is about joyousness and strength. It's—my favorite. Isn't it yours?"

The music swelled. Pete recognized the first two notes of the introduction and swore quietly. This was wrong. This song was not for . . . this song was part of—

Sonny sat raptly. Bonze lay still.

Starr Anthim began to sing. Her voice was deep and powerful, but soft, with the merest touch of vibrato at the ends of the phrases. The song flowed from her without noticeable effort, seeming to come from her face, her long hair, her wide-set eyes. Her voice, like her face, was shadowed and clean, round, blue and green but mostly gold:

"When you gave me your heart, you gave me the world,
You gave me the night and the day,
And thunder, and roses, and sweet green grass,
The sea, and soft wet clay.

"I drank the dawn from a golden cup,
From a silver one, the dark,
The steed I rode was the wild west wind,
My song was the brook and the lark."

The music spiraled, caroled, slid into a somber cry of muted, hungry sixths and ninths; rose, blared, and cut, leaving her voice full and alone:

"With thunder I smote the evil of earth,
With roses I won the right,
With the sea I washed, and with clay I built,
And the world was a place of light!"

The last note left a face perfectly composed again, and there was no movement in it; it was sleeping and vital while the music curved off and away to the places where music rests when it is not heard.

Starr smiled.

"It's so easy," she said. "So simple. All that is fresh and clean and strong about mankind is in that song, and I think that's all that need concern us about mankind." She leaned forward. "Don't you see?"

The smile faded and was replaced with a gentle wonder. A tiny furrow appeared between her brows; she drew back quickly. "I can't seem to talk to you tonight," she said, her voice small. "You hate something."

Hate was shaped like a monstrous mushroom. Hate was the random speckling of a video plate.

"What has happened to us," said Starr abruptly, impersonally, "is simple, too. It doesn't matter who did it—do you understand that? *It doesn't matter*. We were attacked. We were struck from the east and from the west. Most of the bombs were atomic—there were blast bombs and there were dust bombs. We were hit by about five hundred and thirty bombs altogether, and it has killed us."

She waited.

Sonny's fist smacked into his palm. Bonze lay with his eyes open, quiet. Pete's jaws hurt.

"We have more bombs than both of them put together. We *have* them. We are not going to use them. *Wait!*" She raised her hands suddenly, as if she could see into each man's face. They sank back, tense.

"So saturated is the atmosphere with Carbon Fourteen that all of us in this hemisphere are going to die. Don't be afraid to say it. Don't be afraid to think it. It is a truth, and it must be faced. As the transmutation effect spreads from the ruins of our cities, the air will become increasingly radioactive, and then we must die. In months, in a year or so, the effects will be strong overseas. Most of the people there will die, too. None will escape completely. A worse thing will come to them than anything they gave us, because there will be a wave of horror and madness which is impossible to us. We are merely going to die. They will live and burn and sicken, and the children that will be born to them—" She shook her head, and her lower lip grew full. She visibly pulled herself together.

"Five hundred and thirty bombs—I don't think either of our attackers knew just how strong the other was. There has been so much secrecy." Her voice was sad. She shrugged slightly. "They have killed us, and they have ruined themselves. As for us—we are not blameless, either. Neither are we helpless to do anything—yet. But what we must do is hard. We must die—without striking back."

She gazed briefly at each man in turn, from the screen. "We must *not* strike back. Mankind is about to go through a hell of his own making. We can be vengeful—or merciful, if you like—and let go with the hundreds of bombs we have. That would sterilize the planet so that not a microbe, not a blade of grass could escape, and nothing new could grow. We would reduce the earth to a bald thing, dead and deadly.

"No, it just won't do. We can't to it."

"Remember the song? *That* is humanity. That's in all humans. A disease made other humans our enemies for a time, but as the generations march past, enemies become friends and friends enemies. The enmity of those who have killed us is such a tiny, temporary thing in the long sweep of history!"

Her voice deepened. "Let us die with the knowledge that we have done the one noble thing left to us. The spark of humanity can still live and grow on this planet. It will be blown and drenched, shaken and all but extinguished, but it will live if that song is a true one. It will live if we are human enough to discount the fact that the spark is in the custody of our temporary enemy. Some—a few—of his children will live to merge with the new humanity that will gradually emerge from the jungles and the wilderness. Perhaps there will be ten thousand years of beastliness; perhaps man will be able to rebuild while he still has his ruins."

She raised her head, her voice tolling. "And even if this is the end of humankind, we dare not take away the chances some other life form might have to succeed where we failed. If we retaliate, there will not be a dog, a deer, an ape, a bird or fish or lizard to carry the evolutionary torch. In the name of justice, if we must condemn and destroy ourselves, let us not condemn all life along with us! We are heavy enough with sins. If we must destroy, let us stop with destroying ourselves!"

There was a shimmering flicker of music. It seemed to stir her hair like a breath of wind. She smiled.

"That's all," she whispered. And to each man there she said, "Good night—"

The screen went black. As the carrier cut off—there was no announcement—the ubiquitous speckles began to swarm across it.

Pete rose and switched on the lights. Bonze and Sonny

were quite still. It must have been minutes later when Sonny sat up straight, shaking himself like a puppy. Something besides the silence seemed to tear with the movement.

He said softly, "You're not allowed to fight anything, or to run away, or to live, and now you can't even hate any more, because Starr says 'no.' "

There was bitterness in the sound of it, and a bitter smell to the air.

Pete Mawser sniffed once, which had nothing to do with the smell. He froze, sniffed again. "What's that smell, Son'?"

Sonny tested it. "I don't— Something familiar. Vanilla— no . . . no."

"Almonds. Bitter— Bonze!"

Bonze lay still with his eyes open, grinning. His jaw muscles were knotted, and they could see almost all his teeth. He was soaking wet.

"Bonze!"

"It was just when she came on and said 'Hello—you,' remember?" whispered Pete. "Oh, the poor kid. That's why he wanted to catch the show here instead of in the mess hall."

"Went out looking at her," said Sonny through pale lips. "I . . . can't say I blame him much. Wonder where he got the stuff."

"Never mind that." Pete's voice was harsh. "Let's get out of here."

They left to call the meat wagon. Bonze lay watching the console with his dead eyes and his smell of bitter almonds.

Pete did not realize where he was going, or exactly why, until he found himself on the dark street near GHQ and the communications shack. It had something to do with Bonze. Not that he wanted to do what Bonze had done. But then he hadn't thought of it. What would he have done if he'd thought of it? Nothing, probably. But still—it might be nice to be able to hear Starr, and see her, whenever he felt like it. Maybe there weren't any recordings, but her musical background was recorded and the Sig might have dubbed the show off.

He stood uncertainly outside the GHQ building. There was a cluster of men outside the main entrance. Pete smiled briefly. Rain, nor snow, nor sleet, nor gloom of night could stay the stage-door Johnny.

He went down the side street and up the delivery ramp in the back. Two doors along the platform was the rear exit of the communications section.

There was a light on in the communications shack. He had his hand out to the screen door when he noticed someone standing in the shadows beside it. The light played daintily on the golden margins of a head and face.

He stopped. "Starr Anthim!"

"Hello, soldier. Sergeant."

He blushed like an adolescent. "I—" His voice left him. He swallowed, reached up to whip off his hat. He had no hat. "I saw the show," he said. He felt clumsy. It was dark, and yet he was very conscious of the fact that his dress shoes were indifferently shined.

She moved toward him into the light, and she was so beautiful that he had to close his eyes. "What's your name?"

"Mawser. Pete Mawser."

"Like the show?"

Not looking at her, he said stubbornly, "No."

"Oh?"

"I mean . . . I liked it some. The song."

"I . . . think I see."

"I wondered if I could maybe get a recording."

"I think so," she said. "What kind of a reproducer have you got?"

"Audiovid."

"A disk. Yes; we dubbed off a few. Wait, I'll get you one."

She went inside, moving slowly. Pete watched her, spellbound. She was a silhouette, crowned and haloed; and then she was a framed picture, vivid and golden. He waited, watching the light hungrily. She returned with a large envelope, called good night to someone inside, and came out on the platform.

"Here you are, Pete Mawser."

"Thanks very—" he mumbled. He wet his lips. "It was very good of you."

"Not really. The more it circulates, the better." She laughed suddenly. "That isn't meant quite as it sounds. I'm not exactly looking for new publicity these days."

The stubbornness came back. "I don't know that you'd get it, if you put on that show in normal times."

Her eyebrows went up. "Well!" she smiled. "I seem to have made quite an impression."

"I'm sorry," he said warmly. "I shouldn't have taken that tack. Everything you think and say these days is exaggerated."

"I know what you mean," She looked around. "How is it here?"

"It's O.K. I used to be bothered by the secrecy, and being buried miles away from civilization." He chuckled bitterly.

"Turned out to be lucky after all."

"You sound like the first chapter of *One World or None.*"

He looked up quickly, "What do you use for a reading list—the Government's own *'Index Expurgatorious'?*"

She laughed. "Come now—it isn't as bad as all that. The book was never banned. It was just—"

"—Unfashionable," he filled in.

"Yes, more's the pity. If people had paid more attention to it when it was published, perhaps this wouldn't have happened."

He followed her gaze to the dimly pulsating sky. "How long are you going to be here?"

"Until . . . as long as . . . I'm not leaving."

"You're not?"

"I'm finished," she said simply. "I've covered all the ground I can. I've been everywhere that . . . anyone knows about."

"With this show?"

She nodded. "With this particular message."

He was quiet, thinking. She turned to the door, and he put out his hand, not touching her. "Please—"

"What is it?"

"I'd like to . . . I mean, if you don't mind, I don't often have a chance to talk to— Maybe you'd like to walk around a little before you turn in."

"Thanks, no, Sergeant. I'm tired." She did sound tired. "I'll see you around."

He stared at her, a sudden fierce light in his brain. "I know where it is. It's got a red-topped lever and a tag referring to orders of the commanding officer. It's really camouflaged."

She was quiet so long that he thought she had not heard him. Then, "I'll take that walk."

They went down the ramp together and turned toward the dark parade ground.

"How did you know?" she asked quietly.

"Not too tough. This 'message' of yours; the fact that

you've been all over the country with it; most of all, the fact that somebody finds it necessary to persuade us not to strike back. Who are you working for?" he asked bluntly.

Surprisingly, she laughed.

"What's that for?"

"A moment ago you were blushing and shuffling your feet."

His voice was rough. "I wasn't talking to a human being. I was talking to a thousand songs I've heard and a hundred thousand blond pictures I've seen pinned up. You'd better tell me what this is all about."

She stopped. "Let's go up and see the colonel."

He took her elbow. "No. I'm just a sergeant, and he's high brass, and that doesn't make any difference at all now. You're a human being, and so am I, and I'm supposed to respect your rights as such. I don't. You're a woman, and—"

She stiffened. He kept her walking, and finished, "—and that will make as much difference as I let it. You'd better tell me about it."

"All right," she said, with a tired acquiescence that frightened something inside him. "You seem to have guessed right, though. It's true. There are master firing keys for the launching sites. We have located and dismantled all but two. It's very likely that one of the two was vaporized. The other one is—lost."

"Lost?"

"I don't have to tell you about the secrecy," she said disgustedly. "You know how it developed between nation and nation. You must know that it existed between State and Union, between department and department, office and office. There were only three or four men who knew where all the keys were. Three of them were in the Pentagon when it went up. That was the third blast bomb, you know. If there was another, it could only have been Senator Vandercook, and he died three weeks ago without talking."

"An automatic radio key, hm-m-m?"

"That's right, Sergeant, must we walk? I'm so tired—"

"I'm sorry," he said impulsively. They crossed to the reviewing stand and sat on the lonely benches. "Launching racks all over, all hidden, and all armed?"

"Most of them are armed. Enough. Armed and aimed."

"Aimed where?"

"It doesn't matter."

"I think I see. What's the optimum number again?"

"About six hundred and forty; a few more or less. At least five hundred and thirty have been thrown so far. We don't know exactly."

"Who are *we?*" he asked furiously.

"Who? Who?" She laughed weakly. "I could say, 'The Government,' perhaps. If the president dies, the vice president takes over, and then the speaker of the house, and so on and on. How far can you go? Pete Mawser, don't you realize yet what's happened?"

"I don't know what you mean."

"How many people do you think are left in this country?"

"I don't know. Just a few million, I guess."

"How many are here?"

"About nine hundred."

"Then as far as I know, this is the largest city left."

He leaepd to his feet, *"NO!"* The syllable roared away from him, hurled itself against the dark, empty buildings, came back to him in a series of lower-case echoes; nononono . . . no-no—n . . .

Starr began to speak rapidly, quietly. "They're scattered all over the fields and the roads. They sit in the sun and die in the afternoon. They run in packs, they tear at each other. They pray and starve and kill themselves and die in the fires. The fires—everywhere, if anything stands, it's burning. Summer, and the leaves all down in the Berkshires, and the blue grass burnt brown; you can see the grass dying from the air, the death going out wider and wider from the bald spots. Thunder and roses . . . I saw roses, new ones, creeping from the smashed pots of a greenhouse. Brown petals, alive and sick, and the thorns turned back on themselves, growing into the stems, killing. Feldman died tonight."

He let her be quiet for a time. "Who is Feldman?"

"My pilot." She was talking hollowly into her hands. "He's been dying for weeks. He's been on his nerve ends. I don't think he had any blood left. He buzzed your GHQ and made for the landing strip. He came in with the motor dead, free rotors, giro. Smashed the landing gear. He was dead, too. He killed a man in Chicago so he could steal gas. The man didn't want the gas. There was a dead girl by the pump. He didn't want us to go near. I'm not going anywhere. I'm going to stay here. I'm tired."

At last she cried.

Pete left her alone, and walked out to the center of the parade ground, looking back at the faint huddled glimmer on the bleachers. His mind flickering over the show that evening, and the way she had sung before the merciless transmitter. "Hello—you." "If we must destroy, let us stop with destroying ourselves!"

The dimming spark of humankind—what could it mean to her? How could it mean so much?

"Thunder and roses." Twisted, sick, nonsurvival roses, killing themselves with their own thorns.

"And the world was a place of light!" Blue light, flickering in the contaminated air.

The enemy. The red-topped lever. Bonze. "They pray and starve and kill themselves and die in the fires."

What creatures were these, these corrupted, violent, murdering humans? What right had they to another chance? What was in them that was good?

Starr was good. Starr was crying. Only a human being could cry like that. Starr was a human being.

Had humanity anything of Starr Anthim in it?

Starr *was* a human being.

He looked down through the darkness for his hands. No planet, no universe, is greater to a man that his own ego, his own observing self. These hands were the hands of all history, and like the hands of all men, they could by their small acts make human history or end it. Whether this power of hands was that of a billion hands, or whether it came to a focus in these two—this was suddenly unimportant to the eternities which now enfolded him.

He put humanity's hands deep in his pockets and walked slowly back to the bleachers.

"Starr."

She responded with a sleepy-child, interrogative whimper.

"They'll get their chance, Starr. I won't touch the key."

She sat straight. She rose, and came to him, smiling. He could see her smile because, very faintly in this air, her teeth fluoresced. She put her hands on his shoulders. "Pete."

He held her very close for a moment. Her knees buckled then, and he had to carry her.

There was no one in the Officers' Club, which was the nearest building. He stumbled in, moved clawing along the wall until he found a switch. The light hurt him. He carried her to a settee and put her down gently. She did not move. One side of her face was as pale as milk.

There was blood on his hands.

He stood looking stupidly at it, wiped it, on the sides of his trousers, looking dully at Starr. There was blood on her shirt.

The echo of no's came back to him from the far walls of the big room before he knew he had spoken. Starr wouldn't do this. She couldn't!

A doctor. But there was no doctor. Not since Anders had hung himself. Get somebody. Do something.

He dropped to his knees and gently unbuttoned her shirt. Between the sturdy, unfeminine GI bra and the top of her slacks, there was blood on her side. He whipped out a clean handkerchief and began to wipe it away. There was no wound, no puncture. But abruptly there was blood again. He blotted it carefully. And again there was blood.

It was like trying to dry a piece of ice with a towel.

He ran to the water cooler, wrung out the bloody handkerchief and ran back to her. He bathed her face carefully, the pale right side, the flushed left side. The handkerchief reddened again, this time with cosmetics, and then her face was pale all over, with great blue shadows under her eyes. While he watched, blood appeared on her left cheek.

There must be *somebody*— He fled to the door.

"Pete!"

Running, turning at the sound of her voice, he hit the doorpost stunningly, caromed off, flailed for his balance, and then was back at her side. "Starr! Hang on, now! I'll get a doctor as quick as—"

Her hand strayed over her left cheek. "You found out. Nobody else knew, but Feldman. It got hard to cover properly." Her hand went up to her hair.

"Starr, I'll get a—"

"Pete, darling, promise me something?"

"Why, sure; certainly, Starr."

"Don't disturb my hair. It isn't—all mine, you see." She sounded like a seven-year-old, playing a game. "It all came out on this side, you see? I don't want you to see me that way."

He was on his knees beside her again. "What is it? What happened to you?" he asked hoarsely.

"Philadelphia," she murmured. "Right at the beginning. The mushroom went up a half mile away. The studio caved in. I came to the next day. I didn't know I was burned, then. It didn't show. My left side. It doesn't matter, Pete. It doesn't hurt at all, now."

He sprang to his feet again. "I'm going for a doctor."

"Don't go away. Please don't go away and leave me. Please don't." There were tears in her eyes. "Wait just a little while. Not very long, Pete."

He sank to his knees again. She gathered both his hands in hers and held them tightly. She smiled happily. "You're good, Pete. You're so good."

(She couldn't hear the blood in his ears, the roar of the whirpool of hate and fear and anguish that spun inside him.)

She talked to him in a low voice, and then in whispers. Sometimes he hated himself because he couldn't quite follow her. She talked about school, and her first audition. "I was so scared that I got a vibrato in my voice. I'd never had one before. I always let myself get a little scared when I sing now. It's easy." There was something about a windowbox when she was four years old. "Two real live tulips and a pitcherplant. I used to be sorry for the flies."

There was a long period of silence after that, during which his muscles throbbed with cramp and stiffness, and gradually became numb. He must have dozed; he awoke with a violent start, feeling her fingers on his face. She was propped up on one elbow. She said clearly, "I just wanted to tell you, darling. Let me go first, and get everything ready for you. It's going to be wonderful. I'll fix you a special tossed salad. I'll make you a steamed chocolate pudding and keep it hot for you."

Too muddled to understand what she was saying, he smiled and pressed her back on the settee. She took his hands again.

The next time he awoke it was broad daylight, and she was dead.

Sonny Weisefreund was sitting on his cot when he got back to the barracks. He handed over the recording he had picked up from the parade ground on the way back. "Dew on it. Dry it off. Good boy," he croaked, and fell face forward on the cot Bonze had used.

Sonny stared at him. "Pete! Where've you been? What happened? Are you all right?"

Pete shifted a little and grunted. Sonny shrugged and took the audiovid disk out of its wet envelope. Moisture would not harm it particularly, though it could not be played while wet.

It was made of a fine spiral of plastic, insulated between laminations. Electrostatic pickups above and below the turntable would fluctuate with changes in the dielectric constant which had been impressed by the recording, and these changes were amplified for the video. The audio was a conventional hill-and-dale needle. Sonny began to wipe it down carefully.

Pete fought upward out of a vast, green-lit place full of flickering cold fires. Starr was calling him. Something was punching him, too. He fought it weakly, trying to hear what she was saying. But someone else was jabbering too loud for him to hear.

He opened his eyes. Sonny was shaking him, his round face pink with excitement. The audiovid was running. Starr was talking. Sonny got up impatiently and turned down the audio again. "Pete! Pete! Wake up, will you? I got to tell you something. Listen to me! Wake up, will yuh?"

"Huh?"

"That's better. Now listen. I've just been listening to Starr Anthim—"

"She's dead," said Pete. Sonny didn't hear. He went on explosively, "I've figured it out. Starr was sent out here, and all over, to *beg* someone not to fire any more atom bombs. If the government was sure they wouldn't strike back, they wouldn't have taken the trouble. Somewhere, Pete, there's some way to launch bombs at those murdering cowards—and I've got a pret-ty shrewd idea of how to do it."

Pete strained groggily toward the faint sound of Starr's voice. Sonny talked on. "Now, s'posing there was a master radio key, an automatic code device something like the alarm signal they have on ships, that rings a bell on any ship within radio range when the operator ends four long dashes. Suppose there's an automatic code machine to launch bombs, with repeaters, maybe, buried all over the country. What would it be? Just a little lever to pull; that's all. How would the thing be hidden? In the middle of a lot of other equipment, that where; in some place where you'd expect to find crazy-looking secret stuff. Like an experiment station. Like right here. You beginning to get the idea?"

"Shut up. I can't hear her."

"The hell with her! You can hear her some other time. You didn't hear a thing I said!"

"She's dead."

"Yeay. Well, I figure I'll pull that handle. What can I lose? It'll give those murderin' . . . *what?*"

"She's dead."

"Dead? Starr Anthim?" His young face twisted, Sonny sank down to the cot. "You're half asleep. You don't know what you're saying."

"She's dead," Pete said hoarsely. "She got burned by one of the first bombs. I was with her when she . . . she— Shut up, now, and get out of here and let me listen!" he bellowed hoarsely.

Sonny stood up slowly. "They killed her, too. They killed her. That does it. That just fixes it up." His face was white. He went out.

Pete got up. His legs weren't working right. He almost fell. He brought up against the console with a crash, his outflung arm sending the pickup skittering across the record. He put it on again and turned up the gain, then lay down to listen.

His head was all mixed up. Sonny talked too much. Bomb launches, automatic code machines—

"You gave me your heart," sang Starr, *"You gave me your heart. You gave me your heart. You—"*

Pete heaved himself up again and moved the pickup arm. Anger, not at himself, but at Sonny for causing him to cut the disk that way, welled up.

Starr was talking, stupidly, her face going through the same expression over and over again. *"Struck from the east and from the Struck from the east and from the—"*

He got up again wearily and moved the pickup.

"You gave me your heart. You gave me—"

Pete made an agonized sound that was not a word at all, bent, lifted, and sent the console crashing over. In the bludgeoning silence he said, "I did, too."

Then, "Sonny." He waited.

"Sonny!"

His eyes went wide then, and he cursed and bolted for the corridor.

The panel was closed when he reached it. He kicked at it. It flew open, discovering darkness.

"Hey!" bellowed Sonny. "Shut it! You turned off the lights!"

Pete shut it behind him. The lights blazed.

"Pete! What's the matter?"

"Nothing's the matter, Son'," croaked Pete.

"What are you looking at?" said Sonny uneasily.

"I'm sorry," said Pete as gently as he could. "I just wanted to find something out, is all. Did you tell anyone else about this?" He pointed to the lever.

"Why, no. I only just figured out while you were sleeping, just now."

Pete looked around carefully while Sonny shifted his weight. Pete moved toward a tool rack. "Something you haven't noticed yet, Sonny," he said softly, and pointed. "Up there, on the wall behind you. High up. See?"

Sonny turned. In one fluid movement Pete plucked off a fourteen-inch box wrench and hit Sonny with it as hard as he could.

Afterward he went to work systematically on the power supplies. He pulled the plugs on the gas engines and cracked their cylinders with a maul. He knocked off the tubing of the Diesel starters—the tanks let go explosively—and he cut all the cables with bolt cutters. Then he broke up the relay rack and its lever. When he was quite finished, he put away his tools and bent and stroked Sonny's tousled hair.

He went out and closed the partition carefully. It certainly was a wonderful piece of camouflage. He sat down heavily on a workbench nearby.

"You'll have your chance," he said into the far future. "And by heaven, you'd better make good."

After that he just waited.

DON'T LOOK NOW

by Henry Kuttner (1914–1958)

STARTLING STORIES
March

Henry Kuttner and his wife, C. L. Moore, continued their relative dominance of the second half of the 1940s with this stunning story. Kuttner selected it for My Best Science Fiction Story *(1949), and made the following comment in his introduction: ". . . I can honestly say it is my favorite story because I have reread all my others, on publication, and they disgusted me. For one reason or another, I didn't get around to rereading "Don't Look Now," and can therefore regard it with the unbiased, critical, gemlike eye of the happy creator. . . . Anyway, my wife wrote it."*

Well, the story is wonderful, and it is just possible that Catherine did write it. Two other 1948 stories by Kuttner and/or Moore, "Ex Machina" and "Happy Ending," narrowly missed inclusion in this volume.

(It is a rather sad commentary on humanity that it is always so attractive to think that some small group "controls the Earth"—the Jews, the international bankers, the Communists, the Masons, the Trilateral Commission. Those who believe such things are so sincere, so harried, so paranoid and, if the times are

bad enough, and if the hunger for a scapegoat is great enough—so convincing. The Nazis are the most dreadful example in recent history of how far madmen can go when riding the skeletal horse of paranoia, but their example has by no means cured the world. Kuttner satirized this quite effectively in "Don't Look Now" and the last sentence is one of the classic examples of what last sentences should be. Personally, I'm almost relieved that our Mars probes have finally and definitely shown that the Martians—that is, intelligent inhabitants of the planet Mars—do not exist. —For the sake of our paranoids.—I. A.)

The man in the brown suit was looking at himself in the mirror behind the bar. The reflection seemed to interest him even more deeply than the drink between his hands. He was paying only perfunctory attention to Lyman's attempts at conversation. This had been going on for perhaps fifteen minutes before he finally lifted his glass and took a deep swallow.

"Don't look now," Lyman said.

The brown man slid his eyes sidewise toward Lyman, tilted his glass higher, and took another swig. Ice cubes slipped down toward his mouth. He put the glass back on the red-brown wood and signaled for a refill. Finally he took a deep breath and looked at Lyman.

"Don't look at what?" he asked.

"There was one sitting right beside you," Lyman said, blinking rather glazed eyes. "He just went out. You mean you couldn't see him?"

The brown man finished paying for his fresh drink before he answered. "See who?" he asked, with a fine mixture of boredom, distaste and reluctant interest. "Who went out?"

"What have I been telling you for the last ten minutes? Weren't you listening?"

"Certainly I was listening. That is—certainly. You were talking about—bathtubs. Radios. Orson—"

"Not Orson. H. G. Herbert George. With Orson it was just a gag. H. G. *knew*—or suspected. I wonder if it was simply intuition with him? He couldn't have had any proof—but he did stop writing science fiction rather suddenly, didn't he? I'll bet he knew once, though."

"Knew what?"

"About the Martians. All this won't do us a bit of good if you don't listen. It may not anyway. The trick is to jump the gun—with proof. Convincing evidence. Nobody's ever been allowed to produce the evidence before. You *are* a reporter, aren't you?"

Holding his glass, the man in the brown suit nodded reluctantly.

"Then you ought to be taking it all down on a piece of folded paper. I want everybody to know. The whole world. It's important. Terribly important. It explains everything. My life won't be safe unless I can pass along the information and make people believe it."

"Why won't your life be safe?"

"Because of the Martians, you fool. They own the world."

The brown man sighed. "Then they own my newspaper, too," he objected, "so I can't print anything they don't like."

"I never thought of that," Lyman said, considering the bottom of his glass, where two ice cubes had fused into a cold, immutable union. "They're not omnipotent, though. I'm sure they're vulnerable, or why have they always kept under cover? They're afraid of being found out. If the world had convincing evidence—look, people always believe what they read in the newspapers. Couldn't you—"

"Ha," said the brown man with deep significance.

Lyman drummed sadly on the bar and murmured, "There must be some way. Perhaps if I had another drink. . . ."

The brown-suited man tasted his collins, which seemed to stimulate him. "Just what is all this about Martians?" he asked Lyman. "Suppose you start at the beginning and tell me again. Or can't you remember?"

"Of course I can remember. I've got practically total recall. It's something new. Very new. I never could do it before. I can even remember my last conversation with the Martians." Lyman favored the brown man with a glance of triumph.

"When was that?"

"This morning."

"I can even remember conversations I had last week," the brown man said mildly. "So what?"

"You don't understand. They make us forget, you see. They tell us what to do and we forget about the conversation—it's post-hypnotic suggestion, I expect—but we follow their orders just the same. There's the compulsion, though we think we're making our own decisions. Oh, they own the world, all right, but nobody knows it except me."

"And how did you find out?"

"Well, I got my brain scrambled, in a way. I've been fooling around with supersonic detergents, trying to work out something marketable, you know. The gadget went wrong—from some standpoints. High-frequency waves, it was. They went through and through me. Should have been inaudible, but I could hear them, or rather—well, actually I could *see* them. That's what I mean about my brain being scrambled. And after that, I could see and hear the Martians. They've geared themselves so they work efficiently on ordinary brains, and mine isn't ordinary anymore. They can't hypnotize me, either. They can command me, but I needn't obey—now. I hope they don't suspect. Maybe they do. Yes, I guess they do."

"How can you tell?"

"The way they look at me."

"How do they look at you?" asked the brown man, as he began to reach for a pencil and then changed his mind. He took a drink instead. "Well? What are they like?"

"I'm not sure. I can see them, all right, but only when they're dressed up."

"Okay, okay," the brown man said patiently. "How do they look, dressed up?"

"Just like anybody, almost. They dress up in—in human skins. Oh, not real ones, imitations. Like the Katzenjammer Kids zipped into crocodile suits. Undressed—I don't know. I've never seen one. Maybe they're invisible even to me, then, or maybe they're just camouflaged. Ants or owls or rats or bats or—"

"Or anything," the brown man said hastily.

"Thanks. Or anything, of course. But when they're dressed up like humans—like that one who was sitting next to you awhile ago, when I told you not to look—"

"That one was invisible, I gather?"

"Most of the time they are, to everybody. But once in a while, for some reason, they—"

"Wait," the brown man objected. "Make sense, will you? They dress up in human skins and then sit around invisible?"

"Only now and then. The human skins are perfectly good imitations. Nobody can tell the difference. It's that third eye that gives them away. When they keep it closed, you'd never guess it was there. When they want to open it, they go invisible—like *that*. Fast. When I see somebody with a third eye, right in the middle of his forehead, I know he's a Martian and invisible, and I pretend not to notice him."

"Uh-huh," the brown man said. "Then for all you know, I'm one of your visible Martians."

"Oh, I hope not!" Lyman regarded him anxiously. "Drunk as I am, I don't think so. I've been trailing you all day, making sure. It's a risk I have to take, of course. They'll go to any length—any length at all—to make a man give himself away. I realize that. I can't really trust anybody. But I had to find *someone* to talk to, and I—" He paused. There was a brief silence. "I could be wrong," Lyman said presently. "When the third eye's closed, I can't tell if it's there. Would you mind opening your third eye for me?" He fixed a dim gaze on the brown man's forehead.

"Sorry," the reporter said. "Some other time. Besides, I don't know you. So you want me to splash this across the front page, I gather? Why didn't you go to see the managing editor? My stories have to get past the desk and rewrite."

"I want to give my secret to the world," Lyman said stubbornly. "The question is, how far will I get? You'd expect they'd have killed me the minute I opened my mouth to you—except that I didn't say anything while they were here. I don't believe they take us very seriously, you know. This must have been going on since the dawn of history, and by now they've had time to get careless. They let Fort go pretty far before they cracked down on him. But you notice they were careful never to let Ford get hold of genuine proof that would convince people."

The brown man said something under his breath about a human interest story in a box. He asked, "What do the Martians do, besides hang around bars all dressed up?"

"I'm still working on that," Lyman said. "It isn't easy to understand. They run the world, of course, but why?" He wrinkled his brow and stared appealingly at the brown man. "Why?"

"If they do run it, they've got a lot to explain."

"That's what I mean. From our viewpoint, there's no sense to it. We do things illogically, but only because they tell us to. Everything we do, almost, is pure illogic. Poe's *Imp of the Perverse*—you could give it another name beginning with M. Martian, I mean. It's all very well for psychologists to explain why a murderer wants to confess, but it's still an illogical reaction. Unless a Martian commands him to."

"You can't be hypnotized into doing anything that violates your moral sense," the brown man said triumphantly.

Lyman frowned. "Not by another human, but you can by a Martian. I expect they got the upper hand when we didn't have more than ape-brains, and they've kept it ever since. They evolved as we did, and kept a step ahead. Like the sparrow on the eagle's back who hitch-hiked till the eagle reached his ceiling, and then took off and broke the altitude record. They conquered the world, but nobody ever knew it. And they've been ruling ever since."

"But—"

"Take houses, for example. Uncomfortable things. Ugly, inconvenient, dirty, everything wrong with them. But when men like Frank Lloyd Wright slip out from under the Martians' thumb long enough to suggest something better, look how the people react. They hate the thought. That's their Martians, giving them orders."

"Look. Why should the Martians care what kind of houses we live in? Tell me that."

Lyman frowned. "I don't like the note of skepticism I detect creeping into this conversation," he announced. "They care, all right. No doubt about it. They *live* in our houses. We don't build for our convenience, we build, under order, for the Martians, the way they want it. They're very much concerned with everything we do. And the more senseless, the more concern.

"Take wars. Wars don't make sense from any human viewpoint. Nobody really wants wars. But we go right on having them. From the Martian viewpoint, they're useful. They give us a spurt in technology, and they reduce the excess population. And there are lots of other results, too. Colonization, for one thing. But mainly technology. In peacetime, if a guy invents jet propulsion, it's too expensive to develop commercially. In wartime, though, it's *got* to be developed. Then the Martians can use it whenever they want. They use us the way they'd use tools or—or limbs. And nobody ever really wins a war—except the Martians."

The man in the brown suit chuckled. "That makes sense," he said. "It must be nice to be a Martian."

"Why not? Up till now, no race ever successfully conquered and ruled another. The underdog could revolt or absorb. If you know you're being ruled, then the ruler's vulnerable. But if the world doesn't know—and it doesn't—

"Take radios," Lyman continued, going off at a tangent. "There's no earthly reason why a sane human should listen to a radio. But the Martians make us do it. They like it. Take bathtubs. Nobody contends bathtubs are comfortable—for us. But they're fine for Martians. All the impractical things we keep on using, even though we know they're impractical—"

"Typewriter ribbons," the brown man said, struck by the thought. "But not even a Martian could enjoy changing a typewriter ribbon."

Lyman seemed to find that flippant. He said that he knew all about the Martians except for one thing—their psychology.

"I don't know *why* they act as they do. It looks illogical sometimes, but I feel perfectly sure they've got sound motives for every move they make. Until I get that worked out I'm pretty much at a standstill. Until I get evidence—proof—and help. I've got to stay under cover till then. And I've been doing that. I do what they tell me, so they won't suspect, and I pretend to forget what they tell me to forget."

"Then you've got nothing much to worry about."

Lyman paid no attention. He was off again on a list of his grievances.

"When I hear the water running in the tub and a Martian splashing around, I pretend I don't hear a thing. My bed's too short and I tried last week to order a special length, but the Martian that sleeps there told me not to. He's a runt, like most of them. That is, I think they're runts. I have to deduce, because you never see them undressed. But it goes on like that constantly. By the way, how's your Martian?"

The man in the brown suit set down his glass rather suddenly.

"My Martian?"

"Now listen. I may be just a little bit drunk, but my logic remains unimpaired. I can still put two and two together. Either you know about the Martians, or you don't. If you do, there's no point in giving me that, 'What, *my* Martian?' routine. I know you have a Martian. Your Martian knows you have a Martian. My Martian knows. The point is, do *you* know? Think hard," Lyman urged solicitously.

"No, I haven't got a Martian," the reporter said, taking a quick drink. The edge of the glass clicked against his teeth.

"Nervous, I see," Lyman remarked. "Of course you *have* got a Martian. I suspect you know it."

"What would I be doing with a Martian?" the brown man asked with dogged dogmatism.

"What would you be doing without one? I imagine it's illegal. If they caught you running around without one they'd probably put you in a pound or something until claimed. Oh, you've got one, all right. So have I. So has he, and he, and he—and the bartender." Lyman enumerated the other barflies with a wavering forefinger.

"Of course they have," the brown man said. "But they'll all go back to Mars tomorrow and then you can see a good doctor. You'd better have another dri—"

He was turning toward the bartender when Lyman, apparently by accident, leaned close to him and whispered urgently, "*Don't look now!*"

The brown man glanced at Lyman's white face reflected in the mirror before them.

"It's all right," he said. "There aren't any Mar—"

Lyman gave him a fierce, quick kick under the edge of the bar.

"Shut up! One just came in!"

And then he caught the brown man's gaze and with elaborate unconcern said, "—so naturally, there was nothing for me to do but climb out on the roof after it. Took me ten minutes to get it down the ladder, and just as we reached the bottom it gave one bound, climbed up my face, sprang from the top of my head, and there it was again on the roof, screaming for me to get it down."

"*What?*" the brown man demanded with pardonable curiosity.

"My cat, of course. What did you think? No, never mind, don't answer that." Lyman's face was turned to the brown man's, but from the corners of his eyes he was watching an invisible progress down the length of the bar toward a booth at the very back.

"Now why did he come in?" he murmured. "I don't like this. Is he anyone you know?"

"Is who—?"

"That Martian. Yours, by any chance? No, I suppose not. Yours was probably the one who went out a while ago. I wonder if he went to make a report, and sent this one in? It's possible. It could be. You can talk now, but keep your voice low, and stop squirming. Want him to notice we can see him?"

"*I* can't see him. Don't drag me into this. You and your Martians can fight it out together. You're making me nervous. I've got to go, anyway." But he didn't move to get off the stool. Across Lyman's shoulder he was stealing glances toward the back of the bar, and now and then he looked at Lyman's face.

"Stop watching me," Lyman said. "Stop watching him. Anybody'd think you were a cat."

"Why a cat? Why should anybody—do I look like a cat?"

"We were talking about cats, weren't we? Cats can see them, quite clearly. Even undressed, I believe. They don't like them."

"Who doesn't like who?"

"Whom. Neither likes the other. Cats can see Martians—sh-h! —but they pretend not to, and that makes the Martians mad. I have a theory that cats ruled the world before Martians came. Never mind. Forget about cats. This may be more serious than you think. I happen to know my Martian's taking tonight off, and I'm pretty sure that was your Martian who went out some time ago. And have you noticed that nobody else in here has his Martian with him? Do you suppose—" His voice sank. "Do you suppose they could be *waiting for us outside?*"

"Oh, Lord," the brown man said. "In the alley with the cats, I suppose."

"Why don't you stop this yammer about cats and be serious for a moment?" Lyman demanded, and then paused, paled, and reeled slightly on his stool. He hastily took a drink to cover his confusion.

"What's the matter now?" the brown man asked.

"Nothing." Gulp. "Nothing. It was just that—he *looked* at me. With—you know."

"Let me get this straight. I take it the Martian is dressed in—is dressed like a human?"

"Naturally."

"But he's invisible to all eyes but yours?"

"Yes. He doesn't want to be visible, just now. Besides—" Lyman paused cunningly. He gave the brown man a furtive glance and then looked quickly down at his drink. "Besides, you know, I rather think you *can* see him—a little, anyway."

The brown man was perfectly silent for about thirty seconds. He sat quite motionless, not even the ice in the drink he held clinking. One might have thought he did not even breathe. Certainly he did not blink.

"What makes you think that?" he asked in a normal voice, after the thirty seconds had run out.

"I—did I say anything? I wasn't listening." Lyman put down his drink abruptly. "I think I'll go now."

"No, you won't," the brown man said, closing his fingers around Lyman's wrist. "Not yet you won't. Come back here. Sit down. Now. What was the idea? Where were you going?"

Lyman nodded dumbly toward the back of the bar, indicating either a juke-box or a door marked MEN.

"I don't feel so good. Maybe I've had too much to drink. I guess I'll—"

"You're all right. I don't trust you back there with that—that invisible man of yours. You'll stay right here until he leaves."

"He's going now," Lyman said brightly. His eyes moved with great briskness along the line of an invisible but rapid progress toward the front door. "See, he's gone. Now let me loose, will you?"

The brown man glanced toward the back booth.

"No," he said, "he isn't gone. Sit right where you are."

It was Lyman's turn to remain quite still, in a stricken sort of way, for a perceptible while. The ice in *his* drink, however, clinked audibly. Presently he spoke. His voice was soft and rather soberer than before.

"You're right. He's still there. You can see him, can't you?"

The brown man said, "Has he got his back to us?"

"You *can* see him, then. Better than I can maybe. Maybe there are more of them here than I thought. They could be anywhere. They could be sitting beside you anywhere you go, and you wouldn't even guess, until—" He shook his head a little. "They'd want to be *sure*," he said, mostly to himself. "They can give you orders and make you forget, but there must be limits to what they can force you to do. They can't make a man betray himself. They'd have to lead him on—until they were sure."

He lifted his drink and tipped it steeply above his face. The ice ran down the slope and bumped coldly against his lip, but he held it until the last of the pale, bubbling amber had drained into his mouth. He set the glass on the bar and faced the brown man.

"Well?" he said.

The brown man looked up and down the bar.

"It's getting late," he said. "Not many people left. We'll wait."

"Wait for what?"

The brown man looked toward the back booth and looked away again quickly.

"I have something to show you. I don't want anyone else to see."

Lyman surveyed the narrow, smoky room. As he looked the last customer beside themselves at the bar began groping in his pocket, tossed some change on the mahogany, and went out slowly.

They sat in silence. The bartender eyed them with stolid disinterest. Presently a couple in the front booth got up and departed, quarreling in undertones.

"Is there anyone left?" the brown man asked in a voice that did not carry down the bar to the man in the apron.

"Only—" Lyman did not finish, but he nodded gently toward the back of the room. "He isn't looking. Let's get this over with. What do you want to show me?"

The brown man took off his wrist watch and pried up the metal case. Two small, glossy photograph prints slid out. The brown man separated them with a finger.

"I just want to make sure of something," he said. "First—why did you pick me out? Quite a while ago, you said you'd been trailing me all day, making sure. I haven't forgotten that. And you knew I was a reporter. Suppose you tell me the truth, now?"

Squirming on his stool, Lyman scowled. "It was the way you looked at things," he murmured. "On the subway this morning—I'd never seen you before in my life, but I kept noticing the way you looked at things—the wrong things, things that weren't there, the way a cat does—and then you'd always look away—I got the idea you could see the Martians too."

"Go on," the brown man said quietly.

"I followed you. All day. I kept hoping you'd turn out to be—somebody I could talk to. Because if I could *know* that I wasn't the only one who could see them, then I'd know there was still some hope left. It's been worse than solitary confinement. I've been able to see them for three years now. Three years. And I've managed to keep my power a secret even from them. And, somehow, I've managed to keep from killing myself, too."

"Three years?" the brown man said. He shivered.

"There was always a little hope. I knew nobody would believe—not without proof. And how can you get proof? It was only that I—I kept telling myself that maybe you could see them too, and if you could, maybe there were others—lots of others—enough so we might get together and work out some way of proving to the world—"

The brown man's fingers were moving. In silence he pushed a photograph across the mahogany. Lyman picked it up unsteadily.

"Moonlight?" he asked after a moment. It was a landscape under a deep, dark sky with white clouds in it. Trees stood white and lacy against the darkness. The grass was white as if with moonlight, and the shadows blurry.

"No, not moonlight," the brown man said. "Infrared. I'm strictly an amateur, but lately I've been experimenting with infrared film. And I got some very odd results."

Lyman stared at the film.

"You see, I live near—" The brown man's finger tapped a certain quite common object that appeared in the photograph. "—and something funny keeps showing up now and then against it. But only with infrared film. Now I know chlorophyll reflects so much infrared light that grass and leaves photograph white. The sky comes out black, like this. There are tricks to using this kind of film. Photograph a tree against a cloud, and you can't tell them apart in the print. But you can photograph through a haze and pick out distant objects the ordinary film wouldn't catch. And sometimes, when you focus on something like this—" He tapped the image of the very common object again. "You get a very odd image on the film. Like that. A man with three eyes."

Lyman held the print up to the light. In silence he took the other one from the bar and studied it. When he laid them down he was smiling.

"You know," Lyman said in a conversational whisper, "a professor of astrophysics at one of the more important universities had a very interesting little item in the *Times* the other Sunday. Name of Spitzer, I think. He said that if there were life on Mars, and if Martians had ever visited earth, there'd be no way to prove it. Nobody would believe the few men who saw them. Not, he said, unless the Martians happened to be photographed. . . ."

Lyman looked at the brown man thoughtfully.

"Well," he said, "it's happened. You've photographed them."

The brown man nodded. He took up the prints and returned them to his watch-case. "I thought so, too. Only until tonight I couldn't be sure. I'd never seen one—fully—as you have. It isn't so much a matter of what you call getting your brain scrambled with supersonics as it is of just knowing where to look. But I've been seeing *part* of them all my life, and so has everybody. It's that little suggestion of movement you never catch except just at the edge of your vision, just out of the corner of your eye. Something that's *almost* there—and when you look fully at it, there's nothing. These photographs showed me the way. It's not easy to learn, but it can be done. We're conditioned to look directly at a thing—the particular thing we want to see clearly, whatever it is. Perhaps the Martians gave us that conditioning. When we see a movement at the edge of our range of vision, it's almost irresistible not to look directly at it. So it vanishes."

"Then they can be seen—by anybody?"

"I've learned at lot in a few days," the brown man said. "Since I took these photographs. You have to train yourself. It's like seeing a trick picture—one that's really a composite, after you study it. Camouflage. You just have to learn how. Otherwise we can look at them all our lives and never see them."

"The camera does, though."

"Yes, the camera does. I've wondered why nobody ever caught them this way before. Once you see them on film, they're unmistakable—that third eye."

"Infrared film's comparatively new, isn't it? And then I'll bet you have to catch them against that one particular background—you know—or they won't show on the film. Like trees against clouds. It's tricky. You must have had just the right lighting that day, and exactly the right focus, and the lens stopped down just right. A kind of minor miracle. It might never happen again exactly that way. But . . . don't look now."

They were silent. Furtively, they watched the mirror. Their eyes slid along toward the open door of the tavern.

And then there was a long, breathless silence.

"He looked back at us," Lyman said very quietly. "He looked at us . . . that third eye!"

The brown man was motionless again. When he moved, it was to swallow the rest of his drink.

"I don't think that they're suspicious yet," he said. "The trick will be to keep under cover until we can blow this thing wide open. There's got to be some way to do it—some way that will convince people."

"There's proof. The photographs. A competent cameraman ought to be able to figure out just how you caught that Martian on film and duplicate the conditions. It's evidence."

"Evidence can cut both ways," the brown man said. "What I'm hoping is that the Martians don't really like to kill—unless they have to. I'm hoping they won't kill without proof. But—" He tapped his wrist watch.

"There's two of us now, though," Lyman said. "We've got to stick together. Both of us have broken the big rule—*don't look now—*"

The bartender was at the back, disconnecting the juke box. The brown man said, "We'd better not be seen together unnecessarily. But if we both come to this bar tomorrow night at nine for a drink—that wouldn't look suspicious, even to them."

"Suppose—" Lyman hesitated. "May I have one of those photographs?"

"Why?"

"If one of us had—an accident—the other one would still have the proof. Enough, maybe, to convince the right people."

The brown man hesitated, nodded shortly, and opened his watch case again. He gave Lyman one of the pictures.

"Hide it," he said. "It's—evidence. I'll see you here tomorrow. Meanwhile, be careful. Remember to play safe."

They shook hands firmly, facing each other in an endless second of final, decisive silence. Then the brown man turned abruptly and walked out of the bar.

Lyman sat there. Between two wrinkles in his forehead there was a stir and a flicker of lashes unfurling. The third eye opened slowly and looked after the brown man.

HE WALKED AROUND THE HORSES

by H. Beam Piper

ASTOUNDING SCIENCE FICTION
April

One of the strangest influences on science fiction writers were the theories of Charles Fort (1874–1932), a writer who spent a considerable portion of his life collecting records of unexplainable events—frogs falling to the earth in droves, the disappearance of people under unusual circumstances, etc. He developed various theories to explain these events, such as the possibility that humans are really the property of unknown aliens. In fact, a Fortean Society was formed to further his investigations. While sf writers did not always share his beliefs, they often used his ideas as the basis of stories, as in "He Walked Around the Horses," which is based on an actual disappearance in 1809. 1948 also saw the first publication of Piper's very popular "Paratime" series in Astounding, *which told of the work of a police force whose major function was to keep people from different time tracks from running into each other. This series was also based on ideas from Fort's books.*

(There are science fiction stories that don't have to be considered science fiction stories. This is one of

them. It is an "alternate-history" story, a type of story few are able to handle convincingly. You have to know the times, and not only be able to present them clearly and plausibly, but you must trace the consequences of some small change and make that clear and plausible, too. Although I've written numerous books of history, I would have no faith in my own ability to perform the task, and have never done a story of this kind, nor do I intend ever to do one. Piper managed, though, and I have admired this story ever since it was written. And what I admire most is the final touch of irony (having nothing to do with the plot itself, but a most delightful side effect) in the final sentence. If you don't know who Sir Arthur is, look him up. I. A.)

In November, 1809, an Englishman named Benjamin Bathurst vanished, inexplicably and utterly.

He was *en route* to Hamburg from Vienna, where he had been serving as his Government's envoy to the court of what Napoleon had left of the Austrian Empire. At an inn in Perleburg, in Prussia, while examining a change of horses for his coach, he casually stepped out of sight of his secretary and his valet. He was not seen to leave the inn yard. He was not seen again, ever.

At least, not in this continuum . . .

I

(From Baron Eugen von Krutz, Minister of Police, to His Excellency the Count von Berchtenwald, Chancellor to His Majesty Freidrich Wilhelm III of Prussia.)

26 November, 1809.

Your Excellency:

A circumstance has come to the notice of this Ministry, the significance of which I am at a loss to define, but, since it appears to involve matters of state, both here and abroad, I am convinced that it is of sufficient importance to be brought to the personal attention of your Excellency. Frankly, I am unwilling to take any further action in the matter without your Excellency's advice.

Briefly, the situation is this: We are holding, here at the Ministry of Police, a person giving his name as Benjamin Bathurst, who claims to be a British diplomat. This person was taken into custody by the police at Perleburg yesterday, as a result of a disturbance at an inn there; he is being detained on technical charges of causing disorder in a public place, and of being a suspicious person. When arrested, he had in his possession a dispatch-case, containing a number of papers; these are of such an extraordinary nature that the local authorities declined to assume any responsibility beyond having the man sent here to Berlin.

After interviewing this person and examining his papers, I am, I must confess, in much the same position. This is not, I am convinced, any ordinary police matter; there is something very strange and disturbing here. The man's statements, taken alone, are so incredible as to justify the assumption that he is mad. I cannot, however, adopt this theory, in view of his demeanour, which is that of a man of perfect rationality, and because of the existence of these papers. The whole thing is mad; incomprehensible!

The papers in question accompany, along with copies of the various statements taken in Perleburg, and a personal letter to me from my nephew, Lieutenant Rudolph von Tarlburg. This last is deserving of your Excellency's particular attention; Lieutenant von Tarlburg is a very level-headed young officer, not at all inclined to be fanciful or imaginative. It would take a good deal to affect him as he describes.

The man calling himself Benjamin Bathurst is now lodged in an apartment here at the Ministry; he is being treated with every consideration, and, except for freedom of movement, accorded every privilege.

I am, most anxiously awaiting your Excellency's advice, etc., etc.,

KRUTZ.

II

(Report of Traugott Zeller, *Oberwachtmeister, Staatspolizei,* made at Perleburg, 25 November, 1809.)

At about ten minutes past two of the afternoon of Saturday, 25 November, while I was at the police station, there entered a man known to me as Franz Bauer, an inn servant employed by Christian Hauck, at the sign of the Sword and Sceptre, here in Perleburg. This man Franz Bauer made complaint to Staatspolizeikapitän Ernst Hartenstein, saying that there was a madman making trouble at the inn where he, Franz Bauer, worked. I was therefore directed by Staatspolizeikapitän Hartenstein to go to the Sword and Sceptre Inn, there to act at discretion to maintain the peace.

Arriving at the inn in company with the said Franz Bauer, I found a considerable crowd of people in the common-room, and, in the midst of them, the innkeeper, Christian Hauck, in altercation with a stranger. This stranger was a gentlemanly appearing person, dressed in travelling clothes, who had under his arm a small leather dispatch-case. As I entered, I could hear him, speaking in German with a strong English accent, abusing the innkeeper, the said Christian Hauck, and accusing him of having drugged his, the stranger's, wine, and of having stolen his, the stranger's coach-and-four, and of having abducted his, the stranger's, secretary and servants. This the said Christian Hauck was loudly denying, and the other people in the inn were taking the innkeeper's part, and mocking the stranger for a madman.

On entering, I commanded everyone to be silent, in the King's name, and then, as he appeared to be the complaining party of the dispute, I required the foreign gentleman to state to me what was the trouble. He then repeated his accusations against the innkeeper, Hauck, saying that Hauck, or rather, another man who resembled Hauck and who had claimed to be the innkeeper, had drugged his wine and stolen his coach and made off with his secretary and his servants. At this point, the innkeeper and the bystanders all began shouting denials and contradictions, so that I had to pound on a table with my truncheon to command silence.

I then required the innkeeper, Christian Hauck, to answer the charges which the stranger had made; this he did with a complete denial of all of them, saying that the stranger had had no wine in his inn, and that he had not been inside the inn until a few minutes before, when he had burst in, shouting accusations, and that there had been no secretary, and no valet, and no coachman and no coach-and-four, at the inn, and that the gentleman was raving mad. To all this, he called the people who were in the common-room to witness.

I then required the stranger to account for himself. He said that his name was Benjamin Bathurst, and that he was a British diplomat, returning to England from Vienna. To prove this, he produced from his dispatch case sundry papers. One of these was a letter of safe-conduct, issued by the Prussian Chancellery, in which he was named and described as Benjamin Bathurst. The other papers were English, all bearing seals, and appearing to be official documents.

Accordingly, I requested him to accompany me to the police station, and also the innkeeper, and three men whom the innkeeper wanted to bring as witnesses.

TRAUGOTT ZELLER.
Oberwachtmeister.

Report approved,

ERNST HARTENSTEIN.
Staatspolizeikapitän.

III

(Statement of the self-so-called Benjamin Bathurst, taken at the police station at Perleburg, 25 November, 1809.)

My name is Benjamin Bathurst, and I am Envoy Extraordinary and Minister Plenipotentiary of the Government of His Britannic Majesty to the court of His Majesty Franz I, Emperor of Austria, or at least I was until the events following the Austrian surrender made necessary my return to London. I left Vienna on the morning of Monday, the 20th, to go to Hamburg to take ship home; I was travelling in my own coach-and-four, with my secretary, Mr. Bertram Jardine, and my valet, William Small, both British subjects, and a coachman, Josef Bidek, an Austrian subject, whom I had hired for the trip. Because of the presence of French troops, whom I was anxious to avoid, I was forced to make a detour west as far as Salzburg before turning north towards Magdeburg, where I crossed the Elbe. I was unable to get a change of horses for my coach after leaving Gera, until I reached Perleburg, where I stopped at the Sword and Sceptre Inn.

Arriving there, I left my coach in the inn yard, and I and my secretary, Mr. Jardine, went into the inn. A man, not this fellow here, but another rogue, with more beard and less paunch, and more shabbily dressed, but as like him as though he were his brother, represented himself as the innkeeper, and I dealt with him for a change of horses, and ordered a bottle of wine for myself and my secretary, and also a pot of beer apiece for my valet and the coachman, to be taken outside to them. Then Jardine and I sat down to our wine, at a table in the common-room, until the man who claimed to be the innkeeper came back and told us that the fresh horses were harnessed to the coach and ready to go. Then we went outside again.

I looked at the two horses on the off-side, and then walked around in front of the team to look at the two nigh-side horses, and as I did, I felt giddy, as though I were about to fall, and everything went black before my eyes. I thought I was having a fainting spell, something I am not at all subject to, and I put out my hand to grasp the hitching-bar, but could not find it. I am sure, now, that I was unconscious for some time, because when my head cleared, the coach and horses were gone, and in their place was a big farm-wagon, jacked up in front, with the right wheel off, and two peasants were greasing the detached wheel.

I looked at them for a moment, unable to credit my eyes, and then I spoke to them in German, saying, 'Where the devil's my coach-and-four?'

They both straightened, startled; the one who was holding the wheel almost dropped it.

'Pardon, Excellency,' he said. 'There's been no coach-and-four here, all the time we've been here.'

'Yes,' said his mate, 'and we've been here since just after noon.'

I did not attempt to argue with them. It occurred to me—and it is still my opinion—that I was the victim of some plot; that my wine had been drugged, that I had been unconscious for some time during which my coach had been removed and this wagon substituted for it, and that these peasants had been put to work on it and instructed what to say if questioned. If my arrival at the inn had been anticipated, and everything put in readiness, the whole business would not have taken ten minutes.

I therefore entered the inn, determined to have it out with this rascally innkeeper, but when I returned to the common-room, he was nowhere to be seen, and this other fellow, who has also given his name as Christian Hauck, claimed to be the innkeeper and denied knowledge of any of the things I have just stated. Furthermore, there were four cavalrymen, Uhlans, drinking beer and playing cards at the table where Jardine and I had had our wine, and they claimed to have been there for several hours.

I have no idea why such an elaborate prank, involving the participation of many people, should be played on me, except at the instigation of the French. In that case, I cannot understand why Prussian soldiers should lend themselves to it.

BENJAMIN BATHURST.

IV

(Statement of Christian Hauck, innkeeper, taken at the police station at Perleburg, 25 November, 1809.)

May it please your Honour, my name is Christian Hauck, and I keep an inn at the sign of the Sword and Sceptre, and have these past fifteen years, and my father, and his father before him, for the past fifty years, and never has there been a complaint like this against my inn. Your Honour, it is a hard thing for a man who keeps a decent house, and pays his taxes, and obeys the laws, to be accused of crimes of this sort.

I know nothing of this gentleman, nor of his coach nor his secretary nor his servants; I never set eyes on him before he came bursting into the inn from the yard, shouting and raving like a madman, and crying out, 'Where the devil's that rogue of an innkeeper?'

I said to him, 'I am the innkeeper; what cause have you to call me a rogue, sir?'

The stranger replied: 'You're not the innkeeper I did business with a few minutes ago, and he's the rascal I have a row to pick with. I want to know what the devil's been done with my coach, and what's happened to my secretary and my servants.'

I tried to tell him that I knew nothing of what he was talking about, but he would not listen, and gave me the lie, saying that he had been drugged and robbed, and his people kidnapped. He even had the impudence to claim that he and his secretary had been sitting at a table in that room, drinking wine, not fifteen minutes before, when there had been four non-commissioned officers of the Third Uhlans at that table since noon. Everybody in the room spoke up for me, but he would not listen, and was shouting that we were all robbers, kidnappers, and French spies, and I don't know what all, when the police came.

Your Honour, the man is mad. What I have told you about this is the truth, and all that I know about this business, so help me God.

CHRISTIAN HAUCK.

V

(Statement of Franz Bauer, inn-servant, taken at the police station at Perleburg, 25 November, 1809.)

May it please your Honour, my name is Franz Bauer, and I am a servant at the Sword and Sceptre Inn, kept by Christian Hauck.

This afternoon, when I went into the inn yard to empty a bucket of slops on the dung heap by the stables, I heard voices and turned around, to see this gentleman speaking to Wilhelm Beick and Fritz Herzer, who were greasing their wagon in the yard. He had not been in the yard when I had turned around to empty the bucket, and I thought that he must have come in from the street. This gentleman was asking Beick and Herzer where was his coach, and when they told him they didn't know, he turned and ran into the inn.

Of my own knowledge, the man had not been inside the inn before then, nor had there been any coach, or any of the people he spoke of, at the inn, and none of the things he spoke of happened there, for otherwise I would know, since I was at the inn all day.

When I went back inside, I found him in the common-room, shouting at my master, and claiming that he had been drugged and robbed. I saw that he was mad, and was afraid that he would do some mischief, so I went for the police.

FRANZ BAUER
his (X) mark.

VI

(Statements of Wilhelm Beick and Fritz Herzer, peasants, taken at the police station at Perleburg, 25 November, 1809.)

May it please your Honour, my name is Wilhelm Beick, and I am a tenant on the estate of the Baron von Hentig. On this day, I and Fritz Herzer were sent in to Perleburg with a load of potatoes and cabbages which the innkeeper at the Sword and Sceptre had bought from the estate-superintendent. After we had unloaded them, we decided to grease our wagon, which was very dry, before going back, so we unhitched and began working on it. We took about two hours, starting just after we had eaten lunch, and in all that time there was no coach-and-four in the inn yard.

We were just finishing when this gentleman spoke to us, demanding to know where his coach was. We told him that there had been no coach in the yard all the time we had been there, so he turned around and ran into the inn. At the time, I thought that he had come out of the inn before speaking to us, for I know that he could not have come in from the street. Now I do not know where he came from, but I know that I never saw him before that moment.

WILHELM BEICK
his (X) mark.

I have heard the above testimony, and it is true to my own knowledge, and I have nothing to add to it.

FRITZ HERZER
his (X) mark.

VII

(From Staatspolizeikapitän Ernst Hartenstein, to His Excellency, the Baron von Krutz, Minister of Police.)

25 November, 1809.

Your Excellency:

The accompanying copies of statements taken this day will explain how the prisoner, the self-so-called Benjamin Bathurst, came into my custody. I have charged him with causing disorder and being a suspicious person, to hold him until more can be learned about him. However, as he represents himself to be a British diplomat, I am unwilling to assume any further responsibility, and am having him sent to your Excellency, in Berlin.

In the first place, your Excellency, I have the strongest doubts of the man's story. The statement which he made before me, and signed, is bad enough, with a coach-and-four turning into a farm wagon, like Cinderella's coach into a pumpkin, and three people vanishing as though swallowed by the earth. Your Excellency will permit me to doubt that there ever was any such coach, or any such people. But all this is perfectly reasonable and credible, beside the things he said to me, of which no record was made.

Your Excellency will have noticed, in his statement, certain allusions to the Austrian surrender, and to French troops in Austria. After his statement had been taken down, I noticed these allusions, and I inquired, what surrender, and what were

French troops doing in Austria. The man looked at me in a pitying manner, and said:

'News seems to travel slowly, hereabouts; peace was concluded at Vienna on the 14th of last month. And as for what French troops are doing in Austria, they're doing the same things Bonaparte's brigands are doing everywhere in Europe.'

'And who is Bonaparte?' I asked.

He stared at me as though I had asked him, 'Who is the Lord Jehovah?' Then, after a moment, a look of comprehension came into his face.

'So; you Prussians conceded him the title of Emperor, and refer to him as Napoleon,' he said. 'Well, I can assure you that His Britannic Majesty's Government haven't done so, and never will; not so long as one Englishman has a finger left to pull a trigger. General Bonaparte is a usurper; His Britannic Majesty's Government do not recognize any sovereignty in France except the House of Bourbon.' This he said very sternly, as though rebuking me.

It took me a moment or so to digest that, and to appreciate all its implications. Why, this fellow evidently believed, as a matter of fact, that the French Monarchy had been overthrown by some military adventurer named Bonaparte, who was calling himself the Emperor Napoleon, and who had made war on Austria and forced a surrender. I made no attempt to argue with him—one wastes time arguing with madmen—but if this man could believe that, the transformation of a coach-and-four into a cabbage-wagon was a small matter indeed. So, to humour him, I asked him if he thought General Bonaparte's agents were responsible for his trouble at the inn.

'Certainly,' he replied. 'The chances are they didn't know me to see me, and took Jardine for the Minister, and me for the secretary, so they made off with poor Jardine. I wonder, though, that they left me my dispatch case. And that reminds me: I'll want that back. Diplomatic papers, you know.'

I told him, very seriously, that we would have to check his credentials. I promised him I would make every effort to locate his secretary and his servants and his coach, took a complete description of all of them, and persuaded him to go into an upstairs room, where I kept him under guard. I did start inquiries, calling in all my informers and spies, but, as I expected, I could learn nothing. I could not find anybody, even, who had seen him anywhere in Perleburg before he appeared at the Sword and

Sceptre, and that rather surprised me, as somebody should have seen him enter the town, or walk along the street.

In this connection, let me remind your Excellency of the discrepancy in the statements of the servant, Franz Bauer, and of the two peasants. The former is certain the man entered the inn yard from the street; the latter are just as positive that he did not. Your Excellency, I do not like such puzzles, for I am sure that all three were telling the truth to the best of their knowledge. They are ignorant common-folk, I admit, but they should know what they did or did not see.

After I got the prisoner into safe-keeping, I fell to examining his papers, and I can assure your Excellency that they gave me a shock. I had paid little heed to his ravings about the King of France being dethroned, or about this General Bonaparte who called himself the Emperor Napoleon, but I found all these things mentioned in his papers and dispatches, which had every appearance of being official documents. There was repeated mention of the taking, by the French, of Vienna, last May, and of the capitulation of the Austrian Emperor to this General Bonaparte, and of battles being fought all over Europe, and I don't know what other fantastic things. Your Excellency, I have heard of all sorts of madmen—one believing himself to be the Archangel Gabriel, or Mohammed, or a werewolf, and another convinced that his bones are made of glass, or that he is pursued and tormented by devils—but, so help me God, this is the first time I have heard of a madman who had documentary proof for his delusions! Does your Excellency wonder, then, that I want no part of this business?

But the matter of his credentials was even worse. He had papers, sealed with the seal of the British Foreign Office, and to every appearance genuine—but they were signed, as Foreign Minister, by one George Canning, and all the world knows that Lord Castlereagh has been Foreign Minister these last five years. And to cap it all, he had a safe-conduct, sealed with the seal of the Prussian Chancellery—the very seal, for I compared it, under a strong magnifying-glass, with one that I knew to be genuine, and they were identical!—and yet, this letter was signed, as Chancellor, not by Count von Berchtenwald, but by Baron vom und zum Stein, the Minister of Agriculture, and the signature, as far as I could see, appeared to be genuine! This is too much for me, your Excellency; I must ask to be excused from dealing with this matter, before I become as mad as my prisoner!

I made arrangements, accordingly, with Colonel Keitel, of the

Third Uhlans, to furnish an officer to escort this man in to Berlin. The coach in which they come belongs to this police station, and the driver is one of my men. He should be furnished expense money to get back to Perleburg. The guard is a corporal of Uhlans, the orderly of the officer. He will stay with the *Herr Oberleutnant*, and both of them will return here at their own convenience and expense.

I have the honour, your Excellency, to be, etc., etc.,

ERNST HARTENSTEIN.
Staatspolizeikapitän.

VIII

(From Oberleutnant Rudolf von Tarlburg, to Baron Eugen von Krutz.)

26 November, 1809.

Dear Uncle Eugen:

This is in no sense a formal report; I made that at the Ministry, when I turned the Englishman and his papers over to one of your officers—a fellow with red hair and a face like a bulldog. But there are a few things which you should be told, which wouldn't look well in an official report, to let you know just what sort of a rare fish has got into your net.

I had just come in from drilling my platoon, yesterday, when Colonel Keitel's orderly told me that the colonel wanted to see me in his quarters. I found the old fellow in undress in his sitting-room, smoking his big pipe.

'Come in, Lieutenant; come in and sit down, my boy!' he greeted me, in that bluff, hearty manner which he always adopts with his junior officers when he has some particularly nasty job to be done. 'How would you like to take a little trip in to Berlin? I have an errand, which won't take half an hour, and you can stay as long as you like, just so you're back by Thursday, when your turn comes up for road-patrol.'

Well, I thought, this is the bait. I waited to see what the hook would look like, saying that it was entirely agreeable with me, and asking what his errand was.

'Well, it isn't for myself, Tarlburg,' he said. 'It's for this fellow Hartenstein, the *Staatspolizeikapitän* here. He has something he wants done at the Ministry of Police, and I thought of you because I've heard you're related to the Baron von Krutz.

You are, aren't you?' he asked, just as though he didn't know all about who all his officers are related to.

'That's right, Colonel; the Baron is my uncle,' I said. 'What does Hartenstein want done?'

'Why, he has a prisoner whom he wants taken to Berlin and turned over at the Ministry. All you have to do is to take him in, in a coach, and see he doesn't escape on the way, and get a receipt for him, and for some papers. This is a very important prisoner; I don't think Hartenstein has anybody he can trust to handle him. A state prisoner. He claims to be some sort of a British diplomat, and for all Hartenstein knows, maybe he is. Also, he is a madman.'

'A madman?' I echoed.

'Yes, just so. At least, that's what Hartenstein told me. I wanted to know what sort of a madman—there are various kinds of madmen, all of whom must be handled differently—but all Hartenstein would tell me was that he had unrealistic beliefs about the state of affairs in Europe.'

'Ha! What diplomat hasn't?' I asked.

Old Keitel gave a laugh, somewhere between the bark of a dog and the croaking of a raven.

'Yes, naturally! The unrealistic beliefs of diplomats are what soldiers die of,' he said. 'I said as much to Hartenstein, but he wouldn't tell me anything more. He seemed to regret having said even that much. He looked like a man who's seen a particularly terrifying ghost.' The old man puffed hard at his famous pipe for a while, blowing smoke up through his moustache. 'Rudi, Hartenstein has pulled a hot potato out of the ashes, this time, and he wants to toss it to your uncle, before he burns his fingers. I think that's one reason why he got me to furnish an escort for his Englishman. Now, look; you must take this unrealistic diplomat, or this undiplomatic madman, or whatever in blazes he is, in to Berlin. And understand this.' He pointed his pipe at me as though it were a pistol. 'Your orders are to take him there and turn him over at the Ministry of Police. Nothing has been said about whether you turn him over alive or dead, or half one and half the other. I know nothing about this business, and want to know nothing; if Hartenstein wants us to play gaol-warders for him, then, *bei Gott,* he must be satisfied with our way of doing it!'

Well, to cut short the story, I looked at the coach Hartenstein had placed at my disposal, and I decided to chain the left door shut on the outside so that it couldn't be opened from within.

Then, I would put my prisoner on my left, so that the only way out would be past me. I decided not to carry any weapons which he might be able to snatch from me, so I took off my sabre and locked it in the seat-box, along with the dispatch case containing the Englishman's papers. It was cold enough to wear a greatcoat in comfort, so I wore mine, and in the right side pocket, where my prisoner couldn't reach, I put a little leaded bludgeon, and also a brace of pocket-pistols. Hartenstein was going to furnish me a guard as well as a driver, but I said that I would take a servant who could act as guard. The servant, of course, was my orderly, old Johann; I gave him my double hunting-gun to carry, with a big charge of boar-shot in one barrel and an ounce ball in the other.

In addition, I armed myself with a big bottle of cognac. I thought that if I could shoot my prisoner often enough with that, he would give me no trouble.

As it happened, he didn't, and none of my precautions—except the cognac—were needed. The man didn't look like a lunatic to me. He was a rather stout gentleman, of past middle age, with a ruddy complexion and an intelligent face. The only unusual thing about him was his hat, which was a peculiar contraption, looking like the pot out of a close-stool. I put him in the carriage, and then offered him a drink out of my bottle, taking one about half as big myself. He smacked his lips over it and said, 'Well, that's real brandy; whatever we think of their detestable politics, we can't criticize the French for their liquor.' Then, he said, 'I'm glad they're sending me in the custody of a military gentleman, instead of a confounded gendarme. Tell me the truth, Lieutenant: am I under arrest for anything?'

'Why,' I said, 'Captain Hartenstein should have told you about that. All I know is that I have orders to take you to the Ministry of Police, in Berlin, and not to let you escape on the way. These orders I will carry out; I hope you don't hold that against me.'

He assured me that he did not, and we had another drink on it—I made sure, again, that he got twice as much as I did—and then the coachman cracked his whip and we were off for Berlin.

Now, I thought, I am going to see just what sort of a madman this is, and why Hartenstein is making a state affair out of a squabble at an inn. So I decided to explore his unrealistic beliefs about the state of affairs in Europe.

After guiding the conversation to where I wanted it, I asked him:

'What, Herr Bathurst, in your belief, is the real, underlying cause of the present tragic situation in Europe?'

That, I thought, was safe enough. Name me one year, since the days of Julius Caesar, when the situation in Europe hasn't been tragic! And it worked, to perfection.

'In my belief,' says this Englishman, 'the whole damnable mess is the result of the victory of the rebellious colonists in North America, and their blasted republic.'

Well, you can imagine, that gave me a start. All the world knows that the American Patriots lost their war for independence from England; that their army was shattered, that their leaders were either killed or driven into exile. How many times, when I was a little boy, did I not sit up long past my bedtime, when old Baron von Steuben was a guest at Tarlburg-Schloss, listening open-mouthed and wide-eyed to his stories of that gallant lost struggle! How I used to shiver at his tales of the terrible Winter camp, or thrill at the battles, or weep as he told how he held the dying Washington in his arms, and listened to his noble last words, at the Battle of Doylestown! And here, this man was telling me that the Patriots had really won, and set up the republic for which they had fought! I had been prepared for some of what Hartenstein had called unrealistic beliefs, but nothing as fantastic as this.

'I can cut it even finer than that,' Bathurst continued. 'It was the defeat of Burgoyne at Saratoga. We made a good bargain when we got Benedict Arnold to turn his coat, but we didn't do it soon enough. If he hadn't been on the field that day, Burgoyne would have gone through Gates's army like a hot knife through butter.'

But Arnold hadn't been at Saratoga, I know; I have read much of the American War. Arnold was shot dead on New Year's Day of 1776, during the attempted storming of Quebec. And Burgoyne had done just as Bathurst had said: he had gone through Gates like a knife, and down the Hudson to join Howe.

'But, Herr Bathurst,' I asked, 'how could that affect the situation in Europe? America is thousands of miles away, across the ocean.'

'Ideas can cross oceans quicker than armies. When Louis XVI decided to come to the aid of the Americans, he doomed himself and his régime. A successful resistance to royal authority in America was all the French Republicans needed to inspire them. Of course, we have Louis's own weakness to blame, too. If he'd given those rascals a whiff of grapeshot when the mob tried to storm Versailles in 1790 there'd have been no French Revolution.'

But he had. When Louis XVI ordered the howitzers turned on the mob at Versailles, and then sent the dragoons to ride down the survivors, the Republican movement had been broken. That had been when Cardinal Talleyrand, who had then been merely Bishop of Autun, had come to the fore and became the power that he is today in France; the greatest King's Minister since Richelieu.

'And, after that, Louis's death followed as surely as night after day,' Bathurst was saying. 'And because the French had no experience in self-government, their republic was foredoomed. If Bonaparte hadn't seized power, somebody else would have; when the French murdered their king, they delivered themselves to dictatorship. And a dictator, unsupported by the prestige of royalty, has no choice but to lead his people into foreign war, to keep them from turning upon him.'

It was like that all the way to Berlin. All these things seem foolish by daylight, but as I sat in the darkness of that swaying coach, I was almost convinced of the reality of what he told me. I tell you, Uncle Eugen, it was frightening, as though he were giving me a view of Hell. *Gott in Himmel,* the things that man talked of! Armies swarming over Europe; sack and massacre, and cities burning; blockades, and starvation; kings deposed, and thrones tumbling like tenpins! Battles in which the soldiers of every nation fought, and in which tens of thousands were mowed down like ripe grain; and, over all, the Satanic figure of a little man in a grey coat, who dictated peace to the Austrian Emperor in Schoenbrunn, and carried the Pope away a prisoner to Savona.

Madman, eh? Unrealistic beliefs, says Hartenstein? Well, give me madmen who drool spittle, and foam at the mouth, and shriek obscene blasphemies. But not this pleasant-seeming gentleman who sat beside me and talked of horrors in a quiet, cultured voice, while he drank my cognac.

But not all my cognac! If your man at the Ministry—the one with red hair and the bulldog face—tells you that I was drunk when I brought in that Englishman, you had better believe him!

RUDI.

IX

(From Count von Berchtenwald to the British Minister.)

28 November, 1809.

Honoured Sir:

The accompanying *dossier* will acquaint you with the problem confronting this Chancellery, without needless repetition on my part. Please to understand that it is not, and never was, any part of the intentions of the Government of His Majesty Friedrich Wilhelm III to offer any injury or indignity to the Government of His Britannic Majesty George III. We would never contemplate holding in arrest the person, or tampering with the papers, of an accredited envoy of your Government. However, we have the gravest doubt, to make a considerable understatement, that this person who calls himself Benjamin Bathurst is any such envoy, and we do not think that it would be any service to the Government of His Britannic Majesty to allow an impostor to travel about Europe in the guise of a British diplomatic representative. We certainly should not thank the Government of His Britannic Majesty for failing to take steps to deal with some person who, in England, might falsely represent himself to be a Prussian diplomat.

This affair touches us almost as closely as it does your own Government; this man had in his possession a letter of safe conduct, which you will find in the accompanying dispatch-case. It is of the regular form, as issued by this Chancellery, and is sealed with the Chancellery seal, or with a very exact counterfeit of it. However, it has been signed, as Chancellor of Prussia, with a signature indistinguishable from that of the Baron vom und zum Stein, who is the present Minister of Agriculture. Baron Stein was shown the signature, with the rest of the letter covered, and without hesitation acknowledged it for his own writing. However, when the letter was uncovered and shown to him, his surprise and horror were such as would require the pen of a Goethe or a Schiller to describe, and he denied categorically ever having seen the document before.

I have no choice but to believe him. It is impossible to think that a man of Baron Stein's honourable and serious character would be party to the fabrication of a paper of this sort. Even aside from this, I am in the thing as deeply as he; if it is signed with his signature, it is also sealed with my seal, which has not been out of my personal keeping in the ten years that I have been

Chancellor here. In fact, the word 'impossible' can be used to describe the entire business. It was impossible for the man Benjamin Bathurst to have entered the inn yard—yet he did. It was impossible that he should carry papers of the sort found in his dispatch case, or that such papers should exist—yet I am sending them to you with this letter. It is impossible that Baron vom und zum Stein should sign a paper of the sort he did, or that it should be sealed by the Chancellery—yet it bears both Stein's signature and my seal.

You will also find in the dispatch case other credentials ostensibly originating with the British Foreign Office of the same character, being signed by persons having no connection with the Foreign Office, or even with the Government, but being sealed with apparently authentic seals. If you send these papers to London, I fancy you will find that they will there create the same situation as that caused here by this letter of safe-conduct.

I am also sending you a charcoal sketch of the person who calls himself Benjamin Bathurst. This portrait was taken without its subject's knowledge. Baron von Krutz's nephew, Lieutenant von Tarlburg, who is the son of our mutual friend Count von Tarlburg, has a *little friend*, a very clever young lady who is, as you will see, an expert at this sort of work; she was introduced into a room at the Ministry of Police and placed behind a screen, where she could sketch our prisoner's face. If you should send this picture to London, I think that there is a good chance that it might be recognized. I can vouch that it is an excellent likeness.

To tell the truth, we are at our wits' end about this affair. I cannot understand how such excellent imitations of these various seals could be made, and the signature of the Baron vom und zum Stein is the most expert forgery that I have ever seen, in thirty years' experience as a statesman. This would indicate careful and painstaking work on the part of somebody; how, then, do we reconcile this with such clumsy mistakes, recognizable as such by any schoolboy, as signing the name of Baron Stein as Prussian Chancellor, or Mr. George Canning, who is a member of the opposition party and not connected with your Government, as British Foreign Secretary?

These are mistakes which only a madman would make. There are those who think our prisoner is a madman, because of his apparent delusions about the great conqueror, General Bonaparte, *alias* the Emperor Napoleon. Madmen have been known to fabricate evidence to support their delusions, it is true, but I shudder to think of a madman having at his disposal the resources to manufacture the papers you will find in this dispatch case. Moreover, some of our foremost medical men, who have specialized in the disorders of the mind, have interviewed this man Bathurst and say that, save for his fixed belief in a non-existent situation, he is perfectly rational.

Personally, I believe that the whole thing is a gigantic hoax, perpetrated for some hidden and sinister purpose, possibly to create confusion, and undermine the confidence existing between your Government and mine, and to set against one another various persons connected with both Governments, or else as a mask for some other conspiratorial activity. Without specifying any Sovereigns or Governments who might wish to do this, I can think of two groups; namely, the Jesuits, and the outlawed French Republicans, either of whom might conceive such a situation to be to their advantage. Only a few months ago, you will recall, there was a Jacobin plot unmasked at Köln.

But, whatever this business may portend, I do not like it. I want to get to the bottom of it as soon as possible, and I will thank you, my dear Sir, and your Government, for any assistance you may find possible.

I have the honour, Sir, to be, etc., etc., etc.,

BERCHTENWALD.

X

FROM BARON VON KRUTZ, TO THE COUNT VON BERCHTENWALD.
MOST URGENT; MOST IMPORTANT.
TO BE DELIVERED IMMEDIATELY AND IN PERSON, REGARDLESS OF CIRCUMSTANCES.

28 November, 1809.

Count von Berchtenwald:

Within the past half-hour, that is, at about eleven o'clock tonight, the man calling himself Benjamin Bathurst was shot and killed by a sentry at the Ministry of Police, while attempting to escape from custody.

A sentry on duty in the rear courtyard of the Ministry observed a man attempting to leave the building in a suspicious and furtive manner. This sentry, who was under the strictest orders to allow no one to enter or leave without written authorization, challenged him; when he attempted to run, the sentry fired his musket at him, bringing him down. At the shot, the Sergeant of the Guard rushed into the courtyard with his detail, and the man whom the sentry had shot was found to be the Englishman, Benjamin Bathurst. He had been hit in the chest with an ounce ball, and died before the doctor could arrive, and without recovering consciousness.

An investigation revealed that the prisoner, who was confined on the third floor of the building, had fashioned a rope from his bedding, his bed-cord, and the leather strap of his bell-pull; this rope was only long enough to reach to the window of the office on the second floor, directly below, but he managed to enter this by kicking the glass out of the window. I am trying to find out how he could do this without being heard; I can assure your Excellency that somebody is going to smart for this night's work. As for the sentry, he acted within his orders; I have commended him for doing his duty, and for good shooting, and I assume full responsibility for the death of the prisoner at his hands.

I have no idea why the self-so-called Benjamin Bathurst, who, until now, was well-behaved and seemed to take his confinement philosophically, should suddenly make this rash and fatal attempt, unless it was because of those infernal dunderheads of madhouse-doctors who have been bothering him. Only this afternoon, your Excellency, they deliberately handed him a bundle of newspapers—Prussian, Austrian, French, and English—all dated within the last month. They wanted, they said, to see how he would react. Well, God pardon them, they've found out!

What does your Excellency think should be done about giving the body burial?

KRUTZ.

(From the British Minister to the Count von Berchtenwald.)

December 20th, 1809.

My dear Count von Berchtenwald:

Reply from London to my letter of the 28th *ult.*, which accompanied the dispatch case and the other papers, has finally come to hand. The papers which you wanted returned—the copies of the statements taken at Perleburg, the letter to the Baron von Krutz from the police captain, Hartenstein, and the personal letter of Krutz's nephew, Lieutenant von Tarlburg, and the letter of safe-conduct found in the dispatch case, accompany herewith. I don't know what the people at Whitehall did with the other papers; tossed them into the nearest fire, for my guess.

Were I in your Excellency's place, that's where the papers I am returning would go.

I have heard nothing yet, from my dispatch of the 29th *ult.* concerning the death of the man who called himself Benjamin Bathurst, but I doubt very much if any official notice will ever be taken of it. Your Government had a perfect right to detain the fellow, and, that being the case, he attempted to escape at his own risk. After all, sentries are not required to carry loaded muskets in order to discourage them from putting their hands in their pockets.

To hazard a purely unofficial opinion, I should not imagine that London is very much dissatisfied with this *dénouement*. His Majesty's Government are a hard-headed and matter-of-fact set of gentry who do not relish mysteries, least of all mysteries whose solution may be more disturbing than the original problem.

This is entirely confidential, your Excellency, but those papers which were in that dispatch case kicked up the devil's own row in London, with half the Government bigwigs protesting their innocence to high Heaven, and the rest accusing one another of complicity in the hoax. If that was somebody's intention, it was literally a howling success. For a while, it was even feared that there would be Questions in Parliament, but eventually the whole vexatious business was hushed.

You may tell Count Tarlburg's son that his little friend is a most talented young lady; her sketch was highly commended by no less an authority than Sir Thomas Lawrence, and here, your Excellency, comes the most bedevilling part of a thoroughly bedevilled business. The picture was instantly recognized. It is a very fair likeness of Benjamin Bathurst, or, I should say, Sir Benjamin Bathurst, who is King's Lieutenant-Governor for the Crown Colony of Georgia. As Sir Thomas Lawrence did his portrait a few years back, he is in an excellent position to criticize the work of Lieutenant von Tarlburg's young lady. However, Sir Benjamin Bathurst was known to have been in Savannah, attending to the duties of his office, and in the public eye, all the while that his double was in Prussia. Sir Benjamin does not have a twin brother. It has been suggested that this fellow might be a half-brother, born on the wrong side of the blanket, but, as far as I know, there is no justification for this theory.

The General Bonaparte, alias the Emperor Napoleon, who is given so much mention in the dispatches, seems also to have counterpart in actual life; there is, in the French army, a Colonel of Artillery by that name, a Corsican who Gallicized his original name of Napolione Buonaparte. He is a most brilliant military theoretician; I am sure some of our officers, like General Scharnhorst, could tell you about him. His loyalty to the French Monarchy has never been questioned.

This same correspondence to fact seems to crop up everywhere in that amazing collection of pseudo-dispatches and pseudo-state-papers. The United States of America, you will recall, was the style by which the rebellious colonies referred to themselves, in the Declaration of Philadelphia. The James Madison who is mentioned as the current President of the United States, is now living, in exile, in Switzerland. His alleged predecessor in office, Thomas Jefferson, was the author of the rebel Declaration; after the defeat of the rebels, he escaped to Havana, and died, several years ago, in the Principality of Lichtenstein.

I was quite amused to find our old friend Cardinal Talleyrand—without the ecclesiastical title—cast in the role of chief adviser to the usurper, Bonaparte. His Eminence, I have always thought, is the sort of fellow who would land on his feet on top of any heap, and who would as little scruple to be Prime Minister to His Satanic Majesty as to His Most Christian Majesty.

I was baffled, however, by one name, frequently mentioned in those fantastic papers. This was the English General, Wellington. I haven't the least idea who this person might be.

I have the honour, your Excellency, etc., etc., etc.,

SIR ARTHUR WELLESLEY.

THE STRANGE CASE OF JOHN KINGMAN

by Murray Leinster
(Will F. Jenkins; 1896–1975)

ASTOUNDING SCIENCE FICTION
May

They called Murray Leinster "The Dean of Science Fiction" and he certainly deserved the title. He sold his first fiction in 1913 and published his last in 1967—fifty-four years of productivity in a variety of genres; a tremendous achievement, made more so by the fact that he was a consistently entertaining and occasionally brilliant craftsman. He left us two clear classics of science fiction—"Sidewise in Time," the first modern parallel world story, and "First Contact" (see our 1945 volume), still the best known story on the subject.

"The Strange Case of John Kingman" is one of his best works, a story that combines (as Everett F. Bleiler and T. E. Dikty have pointed out) elements of the mad scientist, psychology, and Charles Fort.

(One thing that I am particularly equipped to do is to recognize the hidden hand of John Campbell. In my expressionable youth I talked to him a great deal and I was endlessly exposed to his manner of thinking. Will Jenkins was one of Campbell's favorites and he frequently reported on conversations between himself and

Will. I remember vividly one time back in 1941 when he insisted that Will had a very clever chemical method of easily and cheaply separating an element into its isotopes. I was struck dumb with astonishment for I didn't think it was possible—and, of course, it wasn't. In any case, one of Campbell's favorite ideas, in Randall Garrett's phrase, was that "there are supermen among us," and several of his authors chose to (or were bludgeoned into) using the idea. Will did it better than most. Note the very name "king-man."—I. A.)

It started when Dr. Braden took the trouble to look up John Kingman's case-history card. Meadeville Mental Hospital had a beautifully elaborate system of card indexes, because psychiatric research is stressed there. It is the oldest mental institution in the country, having been known as "New Bedlam" when it was founded some years before the Republic of the United States of America. The card-index system was unbelievably perfect. But young Dr. Braden found John Kingman's card remarkably lacking in the usual data.

"*Kingman, John,*" said the card. "*White, male, 5'8", brown-black hair. Note: physical anomaly. Patient has six fingers on each hand, extra digits containing apparently normal bones and being wholly functional. Age . . .*" This was blank. *Race . . .*" This, too, was blank. "*Birthplace . . .*" Considering the other blanks, it was natural for this to be vacant, also. "*Diagnosis: advanced atypical paranoia with pronounced delusions of grandeur apparently unassociated with usual conviction of persecution.*" There was a comment here, too. "*Patient apparently understands English very slightly if at all. Does not speak.*" Then three more spaces. "*Nearest relative . . .*" It was blank. "*Case history . . .*" It was blank. Then, "*Date of admission . . .*" and it was blank.

The card was notably defective, for the index-card of a patient at Meadeville Mental. A patient's age and race could be unknown if he'd simply been picked up in the street somewhere and never adequately identified. In such an event it was reasonable that his nearest relative and birthplace should be unknown, too. But there should have been some sort of case history—at least of the events leading to his committal to the institution. And certainly, positively, absolutely, the date of his admission should be on the card!

Young Dr. Braden was annoyed. This was at the time when the Jantzen euphoric-shock treatment was first introduced, and young Dr. Braden believed in it. It made sense. He was anxious to attempt it at Meadeville—of course on a patient with no other possible hope of improvement. He handed the card to the clerk in the records department and asked for further data on the case.

Two hours later he smoked comfortably on a very foul pipe, stretched out on grassy sward by the Administration Building. There was a beautifully blue sky overhead, and the shadows of the live oaks reached out in an odd long pattern on the lawn. Young Dr. Braden read meditatively in the *American Journal of Psychiatry*. The article was "Reaction of Ten Paranoid Cases to Euphoric Shock." John Kingman sat in regal dignity on the steps nearby. He wore the nondescript garments of an indigent patient—not supplied with clothing by relatives. He gazed into the distance, to all appearances thinking consciously godlike thoughts and being infinitely superior to mere ordinary humans. He was of an indeterminate age which might be forty or might be sixty or might be anywhere in between. His six-fingered hands lay in studied gracefulness in his lap. He deliberately ignored all of mankind and mankind's doings.

Dr. Braden finished the article. He sucked thoughtfully on the burned-out pipe. Without seeming to do so, he regarded John Kingman again. Mental cases have unpredictable reactions, but as with children and wild animals, much can be done if care is taken not to startle them. Presently young Dr. Braden said meditatively:

"John, I think something can be done for you."

The regal figure turned its eyes. They looked at the younger man. They were aloofly amused at the impertinence of a mere human being addressing John Kingman, who was so much greater than a mere human being that he was not even annoyed at human impertinence. Then John Kingman looked away again.

"I imagine," said Braden, as meditatively as before, "that you're pretty bored. I'm going to see if something can't be done about it. In fact—"

Someone came across the grass toward him. It was the clerk of the records department. He looked very unhappy. He had the card Dr. Braden had turned in with a request for more complete information. Braden waited.

"Er . . . doctor," said the clerk miserably, "there's something wrong! Something terribly wrong! About the records, I mean."

The aloofness of John Kingman had multiplied with the coming of a second, low, human being into his ken. He gazed into the distance in divine indifference to such creatures.

"Well?" said Braden.

"There's no record of his admission!" said the clerk. "Every year there's a complete roster of the patients, you know. I thought I'd just glance back, find out what year his name first appeared, and look in the committal papers for that year. But I went back twenty years, and John Kingman is mentioned every year!"

"Look back thirty, then," said Braden.

"I . . . I did!" said the clerk painfully. "He was a patient here thirty years ago!"

"Forty?" asked Braden.

The clerk gulped.

"Dr. Braden," he said desperately, "I even went to the dead files, where records going back to 1850 are kept. And . . . doctor, he was a patient then!"

Braden got up from the grass and brushed himself off automatically.

"Nonsense!" he said. "That's ninety-eight years ago!"

The clerk looked crushed.

"I know, doctor. There's something terribly wrong! I've never had my records questioned before. I've been here twenty years—"

"I'll come with you and look for myself," said Dr. Braden. "Send an attendant to come here and take him back to his ward."

"Y-yes, doctor," said the clerk, gulping again. "At . . . at once."

He went away at a fast pace between a shuffle and a run. Dr. Braden scowled impatiently.

Then he saw John Kingman looking at him again, and John Kingman was amused. Tolerantly, loftily amused. Amused with a patronizing condescension that would have been infuriating to anyone but a physician trained to regard behavior as symptomatic rather than personal.

"It's absurd," grunted Braden, matter-of-factly treating the patient—as a good psychiatrist does—like a perfectly normal human being. "You haven't been here for ninety-eight years!"

One of the six-fingered hands stirred. While John Kingman

regarded Braden with infinitely superior scorn, six fingers made a gesture as of writing. Then the hand reached out.

Braden put a pencil in it. The other hand reached. Braden fumbled in his pockets and found a scrap of paper. He offered that.

John Kingman looked aloofly into the far distance, not even glancing at what his hands did. But the fingers sketched swiftly, with practiced ease. It took only seconds. Then, negligently, he reached out and returned pencil and paper to Braden. He returned to his godlike indifference to mere mortals. But there was now the faintest possible smile on his face. It was an expression of contemptuous triumph.

Braden glanced at the sketch. There was design there. There was an unbelievable intricacy of relationship between this curved line and that, and between them and the formalized irregular pattern in the center. It was not the drawing of a lunatic. It was cryptic, but it was utterly rational. There is something essentially childish in the background of most forms of insanity. There was nothing childish about this. And it was obscurely, annoyingly familiar. Braden had seen something like it, somewhere, before. It was not in the line of psychiatry, but in some of the physical sciences diagrams like this were used in explanations.

An attendant came to return John Kingman to his ward. Braden folded the paper and put it in his pocket.

"It's not in my line, John," he told John Kingman. "I'll have a check-up made. I think I'm going to be able to do something for you."

John Kingman suffered himself to be led away. Rather, he grandly preceded the attendant, negligently preventing the man from touching him, as if such a touch would be a sacrilege the man was too ignorant to realize.

Braden went to the record office. With the agitated clerk beside him, he traced John Kingman's name to the earliest of the file of dead records. Handwriting succeeded typewriting as he went back through the years. Paper yellowed. Handwriting grew Spencerian. It approached the copperplate. But, in ink turned brown, in yellowed rag paper in the ruled record-books of the Eastern Pennsylvania Asylum—which was Meadeville Mental in 1850—there were the records of a patient named John Kingman for every year. Twice Braden came upon notes alongside the name. One was in 1880. Some staff doctor—there were no psychiatrists in those days— had written, "*High fever.*" There was nothing else. In 1853 a neat memo stood beside the name. "*This man has six functioning fingers on each hand.*" The memo had been made ninety-five years before.

Dr. Braden looked at the agitated clerk. The record of John Kingman was patently impossible. The clerk read it as a sign of inefficiency in his office and possibly on his part. He would be upset and apprehensive until the source of the error had safely been traced to a predecessor.

"Someone," said Braden dryly—but he did not believe it even then—"forgot to make a note of the explanation. An unknown must have been admitted at some time as John Kingman. In time he died. But somehow the name John Kingman had become a sort of stock name like John Doe, to signify an unidentified patient. Look in the death records for John Kingman. Evidently a John Kingman died, and that same year another unidentified patient was assigned the same name. That's it!"

The clerk almost gasped with relief. He went happily to check. But Braden did not believe it. In 1853 someone had noted that John Kingman had six functioning fingers on each hand. The odds against two patients in one institution having six functioning fingers, even in the same century, would be enormous.

Braden went doggedly to the museum. There the devices used in psychiatric treatments in the days of New Bedlam were preserved, but not displayed. Meadeville Mental had been established in 1776 as New Bedlam. It was the oldest mental institution in the United States, but it was not pleasant to think of the treatment given to patients—then termed "madmen"—in the early days.

The records remained. Calfleather bindings. Thin rag paper. Beautifully shaded writing, done with quill pens. Year after year, Dr. Braden searched. He found John Kingman listed in 1820. In 1801. In 1795. In 1785 the name "John Kingman" was absent from the annual list of patients. Braden found the record of his admission in 1786. On the 21st of May, 1786—ten years after New Bedlam was founded, one hundred and sixty-two years before the time of his search—there was a neat entry:

A poore madman admitted this day has been assigned the name of John Kingman because of his absurdly royal manner and affected dignity. He is five feet eight inches tall, appears to speak no Englishe or any other tongue known to any of the learned men hereabout, and has six fingers on each hand, the extra fingers being perfectly formed and functioning. Dr. Sanforde observed that hee seems to have a high fever. On his left shoulder, when stripped, there appears a curious design which is not tattooing according to any known fashion. His madness appears to be so strong a conviction of his greatness that he will not condescend to notice others as being so much his inferiors, so that if not committed hee would starve. But on three occasions, when being examined by physicians, he put out his hand imperiously for writing instruments and drew very intrikit designs which all agree have no significance. He was committed as a madman by a commission consisting of Drs. Sanforde, Smyth, Hale and Bode.

Young Dr. Braden read the entry a second time. Then a third. He ran his hands through his hair. When the clerk came back to announce distressedly that not in all the long history of the institution had a patient named John Kingman died, Braden was not surprised.

"Quite right," said Braden to the almost hysterical clerk. "He didn't die. But I want John Kingman taken over to the hospital ward. We're going to look him over. He's been rather neglected. Apparently he's had actual medical attention only once in a hundred and sixty-two years. Get out his committal papers for me, will you? He was admitted here May 21st, 1786."

Then Braden left, leaving behind him a clerk practically prostrate with shock. The clerk wildly suspected that Dr. Braden had gone insane. But when he found the committal papers, he decided hysterically that it was he who would shortly be in one of the wards.

John Kingman manifested amusement when he was taken into the hospital laboratory. For a good ten seconds—Braden watched him narrowly—he glanced from one piece of apparatus to another. It was impossible to doubt that after one glance he understood the function and operation of every appliance in the ultramodern, super-scientifically-equipped laboratory of the hospital ward. But he was amused. In particular, he looked at the big X-ray machine and smiled with such contempt that the X-ray technician bristled.

"No paranoid suspicion," said Braden. "Most paranoid patients suspect that they're going to be tortured or killed when they're brought to a place where there's stuff they don't understand."

John Kingman turned his eyes to Braden. He put out his six-fingered hand and made the motion of writing. Braden handed him a pencil and a memo tablet. Negligently, contemptuously, he sketched. He sketched again. He handed the sketches to Braden and retreated into his enormous amused contempt for humanity.

Braden glanced at the scraps of paper. He jerked his head, and the X-ray technician came to his side.

"This," said Braden dryly, "looks like a diagram of an X-ray tube. Is it?"

The technician blinked.

"He don't use the regular symbols," he objected, "but—well—yes. That's what he puts for the target and this's for the cathode—Hm-m-m. Yes—" Then he said suddenly: "Say! This's not right."

He studied the diagram. Then he said in abrupt excitement:

"Look! He's put in a field like in an electron microscope! That's an idea! Do that, and you'd get a straight-line electron flow and a narrower X-ray beam—"

Braden said:

"I wonder! What's this second sketch? Another type of X-ray?"

The X-ray technician studied the second sketch absorbedly. After a time he said dubiously:

"He don't use regular symbols. I don't know. Here's the same sign for the target and that for the cathode.

"This looks like something to . . . hm-m-m . . . accelerate the electrons. Like in a Coolidge tube. Only it's—" He scratched his head. "I see what he's trying to put down. If something like this would work, you could work any tube at any voltage you wanted. Yeah! And all the high EMF would be inside the tube. No danger. Hey! You could work this off dry batteries! A doctor could carry an X-ray outfit in his handbag! And he could get million-volt stuff!"

The technician stared in mounting excitement. Presently he said urgently:

"This is crazy! But . . . look, Doc! Let me have this thing to study over! This is great stuff! This is . . . Gosh! Give me a chance to get this made up and try it out! I don't get it all yet, but—"

Braden took back the sketch and put it in his pocket.

"John Kingman," he observed, "has been a patient here for a hundred and sixty-two years. I think we're going to get some more surprises. Let's get at the job on hand!"

John Kingman was definitely amused. He was amenable, now. His air of pitying condescension, as of a god to imbeciles, under other circumstances would have been infuriating. He permitted himself to be X-rayed as one might allow children to use one as a part of their play. He glanced at the thermometer and smiled contemptuously. He permitted his body temperature to be taken from an armpit. The electrocardiograph aroused just such momentary interest as a child's unfamiliar plaything might cause. With an air of mirth he allowed the tattooed design on his shoulder—it was there—to be photographed. Throughout, he showed such condescending contempt as would explain his failure to be annoyed.

But Braden grew pale as the tests went on. John Kingman's body temperature was 105° F. A "high fever" had been observed in 1850—ninety-eight years before—and in 1786—well over a century and a half previously. But he still appeared to be somewhere between forty and sixty years old. John Kingman's pulse rate was one hundred fifty-seven beats per minute, and the electrocardiograph registered an absolutely preposterous pattern which had no meaning until Braden said curtly: "If he had two hearts, it would look like that!"

When the X-ray plates came out of the fixing-bath, he looked at them with the grim air of someone expecting to see the impossible. And the impossible was there. When John Kingman was admitted to New Bedlam, there were no such things as X-rays on earth. It was natural that he had never been X-rayed before. He had two hearts. He had three extra ribs on each side. He had four more vertebrae than a normal human being. There were distinct oddities in his elbow joints. And his cranial capacity appeared to be something like twelve per cent above that of any but exceptional specimens of humanity. His teeth displayed distinct consistent deviation from the norm in shape.

He regarded Braden with contemptuous triumph when the tests were over. He did not speak. He drew dignity about himself like a garment. He allowed an attendant to dress him again while he looked into the distance, seemingly thinking godlike thoughts. When his toilet was complete he looked again at Braden—with vast condescension—and his six-fingered hands again made a gesture of writing. Braden grew—if possible—slightly paler as he handed over a pencil and pad.

John Kingman actually deigned to glance, once, at the sheet on which he wrote. When he handed it back to Braden and withdrew into magnificently amused aloofness, there were a dozen or more tiny sketches on the sheet. The first was an exact duplicate of the one he had handed Braden before the Administration Building. Beside it was another which was similar but not alike. The third was a specific variation in precise, exact steps until the last pair of sketches divided again into two, of which one—by a perfectly logical extension of the change-pattern—had returned to the original design, while the other was a bewilderingly complex pattern with its formalized central part in two closely-linked sections.

Braden caught his breath. Just as the X-ray man had been puzzled at first by the use of unfamiliar symbols for familiar ideas, so Braden had been puzzled by untraceable familiarity in the first sketch of all. But the last diagram made everything clear. It resembled almost exactly the standard diagrams illustrating fissionable elements as atoms. Once it was granted that John Kingman was no ordinary lunatic, it became clear that here was a diagram of some physical process which began with normal and stable atoms and arrived at an unstable atom—with one of the original atoms returned to its original state. It was, in short, a process of physical catalysis which would produce atomic energy.

Braden raised his eyes to the contemptuous, amused eyes of John Kingman.

"I think you win," he said shakenly. "I still think you're crazy, but maybe we're crazier still."

The commitment papers on John Kingman were a hundred and sixty-two years old. They were yellow and brittle and closely written. John Kingman—said the oddly spelled and sometimes curiously phrased document—was first seen on the morning of April 10, 1786, by a man named Thomas Hawkes, as he drove into Aurora, Pennsylvania, with a load of corn. John Kingman was then clad in very queer garments, not like those of ordinary men. The material looked like silk, save that it seemed also to be metallic. The man Hawkes was astounded, but thought perhaps some strolling player had got drunk and wandered off while wearing his costume for a play or pageant. He obligingly stopped his horse and allowed the stranger to climb in for a ride to town. The stranger was imperious, and scornfully silent. Hawkes asked who he was, and was contemptuously ignored. He asked—seemingly, all the world was talking of such matters then, at least the world about Aurora, Pennsylvania—if the stranger had seen the giant shooting stars of the night before. The stranger ignored him. Arrived in town, the stranger stood in the street with regal dignity, looking contemptuously at the people. A crowd gathered about him but he seemed to feel too superior to notice it. Presently a grave and elderly man—a Mr. Wycherly—appeared and the stranger fixed him with a gesture. He stooped and wrote strange designs in the dust at his feet. When the unintelligible design was meaningless to Mr. Wycherly, the stranger seemed to fly into a very passion of contempt. He spat at the crowd, and the crowd became unruly and constables took him into custody.

Braden waited patiently until both the Director of Meadeville Mental and the man from Washington had finished reading the yellowed papers. Then Braden explained calmly:

"He's insane, of course. It's paranoia. He is as convinced of his superiority to us as—say—Napoleon or Edison would have been convinced of their superiority if they'd suddenly been dumped down among a tribe of Australian bushmen. As a matter of fact, John Kingman may have just as good reason as they would have had to feel his superiority. But if he were sane he would prove it. He would establish it. Instead, he has withdrawn into a remote contemplation of his own greatness. So he is a paranoiac. One may surmise that he was insane when he first appeared. But he doesn't have a delusion of persecution because on the face of it no such theory is needed to account for his present situation."

The Director said in a tolerantly shocked tone:

"Dr. Braden! You speak as if he were not a human being!"

"He isn't," said Braden. "His body temperature is a hundred and five. Human tissues simply would not survive that temperature. He has extra vertebrae and extra ribs. His joints are not quite like ours. He has two hearts. We were able to check his circulatory system just under the skin with infrared lamps, and it is not like ours. And I submit that he has been a patient in this asylum for one hundred and sixty-two years. If he is human, he is at least remarkable!"

The man from Washington said interestedly:

"Where do you think he comes from, Dr. Braden?"

Braden spread out his hands. He said doggedly:

"I make no guesses. But I sent photostats of the sketches he made to the Bureau of Standards. I said that they were made by a patient and appeared to be diagrams of atomic structure. I asked if they indicated a knowledge of physics. You"—He looked at the man from Washington—"turned up thirty-six hours later. I deduce that he has such knowledge."

"He has!" said the man from Washington, mildly. "The X-ray sketches were interesting enough, but the others—apparently he has told us how to get controlled atomic energy out of silicon, which is one of the earth's commonest elements. Where did he come from, Dr. Braden?''

Braden clamped his jaw.

''You noticed that the commitment papers referred to shooting stars then causing much local comment? I looked up the newspapers for about that date. They reported a large shooting star which was observed to descend to the earth. Then, various credible observers claimed that it shot back up to the sky again. Then, some hours afterward, various large shooting stars crossed the sky from horizon to horizon, without ever falling.''

The Director of Meadeville Mental said humorously:

''It's a wonder that New Bedlam—as we were then—was not crowded after such statements!''

The man from Washington did not smile.

''I think,'' he said meditatively, ''that Dr. Braden suggests a spaceship landing to permit John Kingman to get out, and then going away again. And possible pursuit afterward.''

The Director laughed appreciatively at the assumed jest.

''If,'' said the man from Washington, ''John Kingman is not human, and if he comes from somewhere where as much was known about atomic energy almost two centuries ago as he has showed us, and, if he were insane there, he might have seized some sort of vehicle and fled in it because of delusions of persecution. Which in a sense, if he were insane, might be justified. He would have been pursued. With pursuers close behind him he might have landed—here.''

''But the vehicle!'' said the Director. ''Our ancestors would have recorded finishing a spaceship or an airplane.''

''Suppose,'' said the man from Washington, ''that his pursuers had something like . . . say . . . radar. Even we have that! A cunning lunatic would have sent off his vehicle under automatic control to lead his pursuers as long and merry a chase as possible. Perhaps he sent it to dive into the sun. The rising shooting star and the other cruising shooting stars would be accounted for. What do you say, Dr. Braden?''

Braden shrugged.

''There is no evidence. Now he is insane. If we were to cure him—''

''Just how,'' said the man from Washington, ''would you cure him? I thought paranoia was practically hopeless.''

''Not quite,'' Braden told him. ''They've used shock treatment for dementia praecox and schizophrenia, with good results.

Until last year there was nothing of comparable value for paranoia. Then Jantzen suggested euphoric shock. Basically, the idea is to dispel illusions by creating hallucinations."

The Director fidgeted disapprovingly. The man from Washington waited.

"In euphoric shock," said Braden carefully, "the tensions and anxieties of insane patients are relieved by drugs which produce a sensation of euphoria, or well-being. Jantzen combined hallucination-producing drugs with those. The combination seems to place the patient temporarily in a cosmos in which all delusions are satisfied and all tensions relieved. He has a rest from his struggle against reality. Also he has a sort of supercatharsis, in the convincing realization of all his desires. Quite often he comes out of the first euphoric shock temporarily sane. The percentage of final cures is satisfyingly high."

The man from Washington said: "Body chemistry?"

Braden regarded him with new respect. He said:

"I don't know. He's lived on human food for almost two centuries, and in any case it's been proved that the proteins will be identical on all planets, under all suns. But I couldn't be sure about it. There might even be allergies. You say his drawings were very important. It might be wisest to find out everything possible from him before even euphoric shock was tried."

"Ah, yes!" said the Director, tolerantly. "If he has waited a hundred and sixty-two years, a few weeks or months will make no difference. And I would like to watch the experiment, but I am about to start on my vacation—"

"Hardly," said the man from Washington.

"I said, I am about to start on my vacation."

"John Kingman," said the man from Washington mildly, "has been trying for a hundred and sixty-two years to tell us how to have controlled atomic energy, and pocket X-ray machines, and God knows what all else. There may be, somewhere about this institution, drawings of antigravity apparatus, really efficient atomic bombs, spaceship drives or weapons which could depopulate the earth. I'm afraid nobody here is going to communicate with the outside world in any way until the place and all its personnel are gone over . . . ah . . . rather carefully."

"This," said the Director indignantly, "is preposterous!"

"Quite so. A thousand years of human advance locked in the skull of a lunatic. Nearly two hundred years more of progress and development wasted because he was locked up here. But it would be most preposterous of all to let his information loose to the other lunatics who aren't locked up because they're running governments!''

The Director sat down. The man from Washington said: ''Now, Dr. Braden—''

John Kingman spent days on end in scornful, triumphant glee. Braden watched him somberly. Meadeville Mental Hospital was an armed camp with sentries everywhere, and specially about the building in which John Kingman gloated. There were hordes of suitably certified scientists and psychiatrists about him, now, and he was filled with blazing satisfaction.

He sat in regal, triumphant aloofness. He was the greatest, the most important, the most consequential figure on this planet. The stupid creatures who inhabited it—they were only superficially like himself—had at last come to perceive his godliness. Now they clustered about him. In their stupid language which it was beneath his dignity to learn, they addressed him. But they did not grovel. Even groveling would not be sufficiently respectful for such inferior beings when addressing John Kingman. He very probably devised in his own mind the exact etiquette these stupid creatures must practice before he would condescend to notice them.

They made elaborate tests. He ignored their actions. They tried with transparent cunning to trick him into further revelations of the powers he held. Once, in malicious amusement, he drew a sketch of a certain reaction which such inferior minds could not possibly understand. They were vastly excited, and he was enormously amused. When they tried that reaction and square miles turned to incandescent vapor, the survivors would realize that they could not trick or force him into giving them the riches of his godlike mind. They must devise the proper etiquette to appease him. They must abjectly and humbly plead with him and placate him and sacrifice to him. They must deny all other gods but John Kingman. They would realize that he was all wisdom, all power, all greatness when the reaction he had sketched destroyed them by millions.

Braden prevented that from happening. When John Kingman gave a sketch of a new atomic reaction in response to an elaborate trick one of the newcomers had devised, Braden protested grimly.

''The patient,'' he said doggedly, ''is a paranoiac. Suspicion and trickiness are inherent in his mental processes. At any moment, to demonstrate his greatness, he may try to produce unholy destruction. You absolutely cannot trust him! Be careful!"

He hammered the fact home, arguing the sheer flat fact that a paranoiac will do absolutely anything to prove his grandeur.

The new reaction was tried with microscopic quantities of material, and it only destroyed everything within a fifty-yard radius. Which brought the final decision on John Kingman. He was insane. He knew more about one overwhelmingly important subject than all the generations of men. But it was not possible to obtain trustworthy data from him on that subject or any other while he was insane. It was worth while to take the calculated risk of attempting to cure him.

Braden protested again:

"I urged the attempt to cure him," he said firmly, "before I knew he had given the United States several centuries head-start in knowledge of atomic energy. I was thinking of him as a patient. For his own sake, any risk was proper. Since he is not human, I withdraw my urging. I do not know what will happen. Anything could happen."

His refusal held up treatment for a week. Then a Presidential executive order resolved the matter. The attempt was to be made as a calculated risk. Dr. Braden would make the attempt.

He did. He tested John Kingman for tolerance of euphoric drugs. No unfavorable reaction. He tested him for tolerance of drugs producing hallucination. No unfavorable reaction. Then—

He injected into one of John Kingman's veins a certain quantity of the combination of drugs which on human beings was most effective for euphoric shock, and whose separate constituents had been tested on John Kingman and found harmless. It was not a sufficient dose to produce the full required effect. Braden expected to have to make at least one and probably two additional injections before the requisite euphoria was produced. He was taking no single avoidable chance. He administered first a dosage which should have produced no more than a feeling of mild but definite exhilaration.

And John Kingman went into convulsions. Horrible ones.

There is such a thing as allergy and such a thing as synergy, and nobody understands either. Some patients collapse when given aspirin. Some break out in rashes from penicillin. Some drugs, taken alone, have one effect, and taken together quite another and drastic one. A drug producing euphoria was harmless to John Kingman. A drug producing hallucinations was harmless. But—synergy or allergy or whatever—the two taken together were deadly poison.

He was literally unconscious for three weeks, and in continuous convulsion for two days. He was kept alive by artificial nourishment, glucose, nasal feeding—everything. But his coma was extreme. Four separate times he was believed dead.

But after three weeks he opened his eyes vaguely. In another week he was able to talk. From the first his expression was bewildered. He was no longer proud. He began to learn English. He showed no paranoiac symptoms. He was wholly sane. In fact, his I.Q.—tested later—was ninety, which is well within the range of normal intelligence. He was not overbright, but adequate. And he did not remember who he was. He did not remember anything at all about his life before rousing from coma in the Meadeville Mental Hospital. Not anything at all. It was, apparently, either the price or the cause of his recovery.

Braden considered that it was the means. He urged his views on the frustrated scientists who wanted now to try hypnotism and "truth serum" and other devices for picking the lock of John Kingman's brain.

"As a diagnosis," said Braden, moved past the tendency to be technical, "the poor devil smashed up on something we can't even guess at. His normal personality couldn't take it, whatever it was, so he fled into delusions—into insanity. He lived in that retreat over a century and a half, and then we found him out. And we wouldn't let him keep his beautiful delusions that he was great and godlike and all-powerful. We were merciless. We forced ourselves upon him. We questioned him. We tricked him. In the end, we nearly poisoned him! And his delusions couldn't stand up. He couldn't admit that he was wrong, and he couldn't reconcile such experiences with his delusions. There was only one thing he could do—forget the whole thing in the most literal possible manner. What he's done is to go into what they used to call dementia praecox. Actually, it's infantilism. He's fled back to his childhood. That's why his I.Q. is only ninety, instead of the unholy figure it must have been when he was a normal adult of his race. He's mentally a child. He sleeps, right now, in the foetal position. Which is a warning! One more attempt to tamper with his brain, and he'll go into the only place that's left for him—into the absolute blankness that is the mind of the unborn child!"

He presented evidence. The evidence was overwhelming. In the end, reluctantly, John Kingman was left alone.

He gets along all right, though. He works in the records department of Meadeville Mental now, because there his six-fingered hands won't cause remark. He is remarkably accurate and perfectly happy.

But he is carefully watched. The one question he can answer now is—how long he's going to live. A hundred and sixty-two years is only part of his lifetime. But if you didn't know, you'd swear he wasn't more than fifty.

THAT ONLY A MOTHER

by Judith Merril (1923–   )

ASTOUNDING SCIENCE FICTION
June

Like Peter Phillips' story in this book, "That Only a Mother" is a famous first story. Unlike Phillips' however, this one caused a sensation and was recognized as one of the most important stories of 1948. "Judith Merril" (Josephine Grossman) was an active fan and personality in science fiction before she tried writing it, and she became an influential figure in the field through her work as an editor and anthologist. Her "Best of the Year" series, which appeared from 1956 to 1964, helped to expand the field by drawing attention to excellent stories that were appearing outside of the genre magazines. In addition, she was an influential advocate of the "New Wave" stories being produced in England during the mid-1960s, and her anthology England Swings SF *(1968) helped to change the direction of American science fiction.*

As a writer, she produced four novels and a brace of fine short stories, all, unfortunately, overshadowed by this powerful one.

(I always think of Judy with a certain amount of sadness. —No, she's alive and well and, as far as I know, happy. That's not it. The point is this—

Some science fiction writers are pertinacious and seemingly endless, to the delight of their readers. As an example, Bob Heinlein, Arthur Clarke, and I (the endlessly cited ''Big Three'') have been at it for forty years and more now, and show absolutely no signs of any loss in ability. We'll stop when we die, but not short of that, I'm sure. There are others I can name, too. And then there are some who, for several years, blaze across the heavens and then, for some reason, stop. *Judy is one of them. She was the morning star predecessor of the great women writers who now are the supernovas of the field; the first to write as well as any man without imitating the characteristic work of men. And then she stopped, which is calamitous. Think of the dozen great novels she might have written in the last thirty years—and did not.—I. A.)*

Margaret reached over to the other side of the bed where Hank should have been. Her hand patted the empty pillow, and then she came altogether awake, wondering that the old habit should remain after so many months. She tried to curl up, cat-style, to hoard her own warmth, found she couldn't do it anymore, and climbed out of bed with a pleased awareness of her increasingly clumsy bulkiness.

Morning motions were automatic. On the way through the kitchenette, she pressed the button that would start breakfast cooking—the doctor had said to eat as much breakfast as she could—and tore the paper out of the facsimile machine. She folded the long sheet carefully to the ''National News'' section, and propped it on the bathroom shelf to scan while she brushed her teeth.

No accidents. No direct hits. At least none that had been officially released for publication. *Now, Maggie, don't get started on that. No accidents. No hits. Take the nice newspaper's word for it.*

The three clear chimes from the kitchen announced that breakfast was ready. She set a bright napkin and cheerful colored dishes on the table in a futile attempt to appeal to a faulty morning appetite. Then, when there was nothing more to prepare, she went for the mail, allowing herself the full pleasure of prolonged anticipation, because today there would *surely* be a letter.

There was. There were. Two bills and a worried note from her mother: "Darling. Why didn't you write and tell me sooner? I'm thrilled, of course, but, well, one hates to mention these things, but are you *certain* the doctor was right? Hank's been around all that uranium or thorium or whatever it is all these years, and I know you say he's a designer, not a technician, and he doesn't get near anything that might be dangerous, but you know he used to, back at Oak Ridge. Don't you think . . . well, of course, I'm just being a foolish old woman, and I don't want you to get upset. You know much more about it than I do, and I'm sure your doctor was right. He *should* know . . ."

Margaret made a face over the excellent coffee, and caught herself refolding the paper to the medical news.

Stop it, Maggie, stop it! The radiologist said Hank's job couldn't have exposed him. And the bombed area we drove past . . . No, no. Stop it, now! Read the social notes or the recipes, Maggie girl.

A well-known geneticist, in the medical news, said that it was possible to tell with absolute certainty, at five months, whether the child would be normal, or at least whether the mutation was likely to produce anything freakish. The worst cases, at any rate, could be prevented. Minor mutations, of course, displacements in facial features, or changes in brain structure could not be detected. And there had been some cases recently, of normal embryos with atrophied limbs that did not develop beyond the seventh or eighth month. But, the doctor concluded cheerfully, the *worst* cases could now be predicted and prevented.

"Predicted and prevented." We predicted it, didn't we? Hank and the others, they predicted it. But we didn't prevent it. We could have stopped it in '46 and '47. Now . . .

Margaret decided against the breakfast. Coffee had been enough for her in the morning for ten years; it would have to do for today. She buttoned herself into interminable folds of material that, the salesgirl had assured her, was the *only* comfortable thing to wear during the last few months. With a surge of pure pleasure, the letter and newspaper forgotten, she realized she was on the next to the last button. It wouldn't be long now.

The city in the early morning had always been a special kind of excitement for her. Last night it had rained, and the sidewalks were still damp-gray instead of dusty. The air smelled the fresher, to a city-bred woman, for the occasional pungency of acrid factory smoke. She walked the six blocks to work, watching the lights go out in the all-night hamburger joints, where the plate-glass walls were already catching the sun, and the lights go on in the dim interiors of cigar stores and drycleaning establishments.

The office was in a new Government building. In the rolovator, on the way up, she felt, as always, like a frankfurter roll in the ascending half of an old-style rotary toasting machine. She abandoned the air-foam cushioning gratefully at the fourteenth floor, and settled down behind her desk, at the rear of a long row of identical desks.

Each morning the pile of papers that greeted her was a little higher. These were, as everyone knew, the decisive months. The war might be won or lost on these calculations as well as any others. The manpower office had switched her here when her old expediter's job got to be too strenuous. The computer was easy to operate, and the work was absorbing, if not as exciting as the old job. But you didn't just stop working these days. Everyone who could do anything at all was needed.

And—she remembered the interview with the psychologist—*I'm probably the unstable type. Wonder what sort of neurosis I'd get sitting home reading that sensational paper . . .*

She plunged into the work without pursuing the thought.

February 18.

Hank darling,

Just a note—from the hospital, no less. I had a dizzy spell at work, and the doctor took it to heart. Blessed if I know what I'll do with myself lying in bed for weeks, just waiting—but Dr. Boyer seems to think it may not be so long.

There are too many newspapers around here. More infanticides all the time, and they can't seem to get a jury to convict any of them. It's the fathers who did it. Lucky thing you're not around, in case—

Oh, darling, that wasn't a very *funny* joke, was it? Write as often as you can, will you? I have too much time to think. But there really isn't anything wrong, and nothing to worry about.

Write often, and remember I love you.

Maggie.

SPECIAL SERVICE TELEGRAM

FEBRUARY 21, 1953
22:04 LK37G

FROM: TECH. LIEUT. H. MARVELL
X47–016 GCNY
TO: MRS. H. MARVELL
WOMEN'S HOSPITAL
NEW YORK CITY

HAD DOCTOR'S GRAM STOP WILL ARRIVE FOUR OH TEN STOP SHORT LEAVE STOP YOU DID IT MAGGIE STOP LOVE HANK

February 25.

Hank dear,

So you didn't see the baby either? You'd think a place this size would at lease have visiplates on the incubators, so the fathers could get a look, even if the poor benighted mommas can't. They tell me I won't see her for another week, or maybe more—but of course, mother always warned me if I didn't slow my pace, I'd probably even have my babies too fast. Why must she *always* be right?

Did you meet that battle-ax of a nurse they put on here? I imagine they save her for people who've already had theirs, and don't let her get too near the prospectives—but a woman like that simply shouldn't be allowed in a maternity ward. She's obsessed with mutations, can't seem to talk about anything else. Oh, well, *ours* is all right, even if it was in an unholy hurry.

I'm tired. They warned me not to sit up so soon, but I *had* to write you. All my love, darling,

Maggie.

February 29.

Darling,

I finally got to see her! It's all true, what they say about new babies and the face that only a mother could love—but it's all there, darling, eyes, ears, and noses—no, only one!—all in the right places. We're so *lucky*, Hank.

I'm afraid I've been a rambunctious patient. I kept telling that hatchet-faced female with the mutation mania that I wanted to *see* the baby. Finally the doctor came in to "explain" everything to me, and talking a lot of nonsense, most of which I'm sure no one could have understood, any more than I did. The only thing I got out of it was that she didn't actually *have* to stay in the incubator; they just thought it was "wiser."

I think I got a little hysterical at that point. Guess I was more worried than I was willing to admit, but I threw a small fit about it. The whole business wound up with one of those hushed medical conferences outside the door, and finally the Woman in White said: "Well, we might as well. Maybe it'll work out better that way."

I'd heard about the way doctors and nurses in these places develop a God complex, and believe me it is as true figuratively as it is literally that a mother hasn't got a leg to stand on around here.

I *am* awfully weak, still. I'll write again soon. Love,

Maggie.

March 8.

Dearest Hank,

Well, the nurse was wrong if she told you that. She's an idiot anyhow. It's a girl. It's easier to tell with babies than with cats, and *I know*. How about Henrietta?

I'm home again, and busier than a betatron. They got *everything* mixed up at the hospital, and I had to teach myself how to bathe her and do just about everything else. She's getting prettier, too. When can you get a leave, a *real* leave?

Love,
Maggie.

May 26.

Hank dear,

You should see her now—and you shall. I'm sending along a reel of color movie. My mother sent her those nighties with drawstrings all over. I put one on, and right now she looks like a snow-white potato sack with that beautiful, beautiful flower-face blooming on top. Is that *me* talking? Am I a doting mother? But wait till you *see* her!

July 10.

. . . Believe it or not, as you like, but your daughter can talk, and I don't mean baby talk. Alice discovered it—she's a dental assistant in the WACs, you know—and when she heard the baby giving out what I thought was a string of gibberish, she said the kid knew words and sentences, but couldn't say them clearly because she has no teeth yet. I'm taking her to a speech specialist.

September 13.

. . . We have a prodigy for real! Now that all her front teeth are in, her speech is perfectly clear and—a new talent now—she can sing! I mean really carry a tune! At seven months! Darling, my world would be perfect if you could only get home.

November 19.

. . . At last. The little goon was so busy being clever, it took her all this time to learn to crawl. The doctor says development in these cases is always erratic . . .

SPECIAL SERVICE TELEGRAM

DECEMBER 1, 1953
08:47 LK59F

FROM: TECH. LIEUT. H. MARVELL
X47–016 GCNY
TO: MRS. H. MARVELL
APT. K-17
504 E. 19 St.
N.Y. N.Y.

WEEK'S LEAVE STARTS TOMORROW STOP WILL ARRIVE AIRPORT TEN OH FIVE STOP DON'T MEET ME STOP LOVE LOVE LOVE HANK

Margaret let the water run out of the bathinette until only a few inches were left, and then loosed her hold on the wriggling baby.

"I think it was better when you were retarded, young woman," she informed her daughter happily. "You *can't* crawl in a bathinette, you know."

"Then why can't I go in the bathtub?" Margaret was used to her child's volubility by now, but every now and then it caught her unawares. She swooped the resistant mass of pink flesh into a towel, and began to rub.

"Because you're too little, and your head is very soft, and bathtubs are very hard."

"Oh. Then when can I go in the bathtub?"

"When the outside of your head is as hard as the inside, brainchild." She reached toward a pile of fresh clothing. "I cannot understand," she added, pinning a square of cloth through the nightgown, "why a child of your intelligence can't learn to keep a diaper on the way other babies do. They've been used for centuries, you know, with perfectly satisfactory results."

The child disdained to reply; she had heard it too often. She waited patiently until she had been tucked, clean and sweet-smelling, into a white-painted crib. Then she favored her mother with a smile that inevitably made Margaret think of the first golden edge of the sun bursting into a rosy predawn. She remembered Hank's reaction to the color pictures of his beautiful daughter, and with the thought, realized how late it was.

"Go to sleep, puss. When you wake up, you know, your *daddy* will be here."

"Why?" asked the four-year-old mind, waging a losing battle to keep the ten-month-old body awake.

Margaret went into the kitchenette and set the timer for the roast. She examined the table, and got her clothes from the closet, new dress, new shoes, new slip, new everything, bought weeks before and saved for the day Hank's telegram came. She stopped to pull a paper from the facsimile, and, with clothes and news, went into the bathroom and lowered herself gingerly into the steaming luxury of a scented bath.

She glanced through the paper with indifferent interest. Today at least there was no need to read the national news. There was an article by a geneticist. The same geneticist. Mutations, he said, were increasing disproportionately. It was too soon for recessives; even the first mutants, born near Hiroshima and Nagasaki in 1946 and 1947 were not old enough yet to breed. *But my baby's all right.* Apparently, there was some degree of free radiation from atomic explosions causing the trouble. *My baby's fine. Precocious, but normal.* If more attention had been paid to the first Japanese mutations, he said . . .

There was that little notice in the paper in the spring of '47. That was when Hank quit at Oak Ridge. "Only 2 or 3 percent of those guilty of infanticide are being caught and punished in Japan today . . ." *But* MY BABY'S *all right.*

She was dressed, combed, and ready to the last light brush-on of lip paste, when the door chime sounded. She dashed for the door, and heard for the first time in eighteen months the almost-forgotten sound of a key turning in the lock before the chime had quite died away.

"Hank!"

"Maggie!"

And then there was nothing to say. So many days, so many months of small news piling up, so many things to tell him, and now she just stood there, staring at a khaki uniform and a stranger's pale face. She traced the features with the finger of memory. The same high-bridged nose, wide-set eyes, fine feathery brows; the same long jaw, the hair a little farther back now on the high forehead, the same tilted curve to his mouth. Pale . . . Of course, he'd been underground all this time. And strange, stranger because of lost familiarity than any newcomer's face could be.

She had time to think all that before his hand reached out to touch her, and spanned the gap of eighteen months. Now, again, there was nothing to say, because there was no need. They were together, and for the moment that was enough.

"Where's the baby?"

"Sleeping. She'll be up any minute."

No urgency. Their voices were as casual as though it were a daily exchange, as though war and separation did not exist. Margaret picked up the coat he'd thrown on the chair near the door, and hung it carefully in the hall closet. She went to check the roast, leaving him to wander through the rooms by himself, remembering and coming back. She found him, finally, standing over the baby's crib.

She couldn't see his face, but she had no need to.

"I think we can wake her just this once." Margaret pulled the covers down and lifted the white bundle from the bed. Sleepy lids pulled back heavily from smoky brown eyes.

"Hello." Hank's voice was tentative.

"Hello." The baby's assurance was more pronounced.

He had heard about it, of course, but that wasn't the same as hearing it. He turned eagerly to Margaret. "She really can—?"

"Of course she can, darling. But what's more important, she can even do nice normal things like other babies do, even stupid ones. Watch her crawl!" Margaret set the baby on the big bed.

For a moment young Henrietta lay and eyed her parents dubiously.

"Crawl?" she asked.

"That's the idea. Your daddy is new around here, you know. He wants to see you show off."

"Then put me on my tummy."

"Oh, of course." Margaret obligingly rolled the baby over.

"What's the matter?" Hank's voice was still casual, but an undercurrent in it began to charge the air of the room. "I thought they turned over first."

"This baby"—Margaret would not notice the tension—"*This* baby does things when she wants to."

This baby's father watched with softening eyes while the head advanced and the body hunched up propelling itself across the bed.

"Why, the little rascal." He burst into relieved laughter. "She looks like one of those potato-sack racers they used to have on picnics. Got her arms pulled out of the sleeves already." He reached over and grabbed the knot at the bottom of the long nightie.

"I'll do it, darling." Margaret tried to get there first.

"Don't be silly, Maggie. This may be *your* first baby, but *I* had five kid brothers." He laughed her away, and reached with his other hand for the string that closed one sleeve. He opened the sleeve bow, and groped for an arm.

"The way you wriggle," he addressed his child sternly, as his hand touched a moving knob of flesh at the shoulder, "anyone might think you are a worm, using your tummy to crawl on, instead of your hands and feet."

Margaret stood and watched, smiling. "Wait till you hear her sing, darling—"

His right hand traveled down from the shoulder to where he thought an arm would be, traveled down, and straight down, over firm small muscles that writhed in an attempt to move against the pressure of his hand. He let his fingers drift up again to the shoulder. With infinite care he opened the knot at the bottom of the nightgown. His wife was standing by the bed, saying, "She can do 'Jingle Bells,' and—"

His left hand felt along the soft knitted fabric of the gown, up toward the diaper that folded, flat and smooth, across the bottom end of his child. No wrinkles. No kicking. *No . . .*

"Maggie." He tried to pull his hands from the neat fold in the diaper, from the wriggling body. "Maggie." His throat was dry; words came hard, low and grating. He spoke very slowly, thinking the sound of each word to make himself say it. His head was spinning, but he had to *know* before he let it go. "Maggie, why . . . didn't you . . . tell me?"

"Tell you what, darling?" Margaret's poise was the immemorial patience of woman confronted with man's childish impetuosity.

Her sudden laugh sounded fantastically easy and natural in that room; it was all clear to her now. "Is she wet? I didn't know."

She didn't know. His hands, beyond control, ran up and down the soft-skinned baby body, the sinuous, limbless body. *Oh God, dear God*—his head shook and his muscles contracted in a bitter spasm of hysteria. His fingers tightened on his child— *Oh God, she didn't know . . .*

THE MONSTER

by A. E. van Vogt (1912–)

ASTOUNDING SCIENCE FICTION
August

1948 was aother banner year for A. E. van Vogt. In addition to the two selections in this book, the year saw the serialization of his The Players A, *a sequel (in many ways a better novel) to his very popular and controversial* The World of A, *and the publication of "The Rull," another installment of an interesting series.*

"The Monster" is a fresh look at a very old science fiction theme—the invaders of Earth story. Here van Vogt speculates on the effects of an invasion of an apparently *lifeless Earth.*

(One of the important corollaries of John Campbell's notion that "there are supermen against us," is that the supermen are human beings, or some human beings, or the descendants of human beings. In fact, I don't think John would consider any story in which human beings were pictured as inferior to other intelligences. This was something I found myself unable to accept, so that I tended to write stories about robots, or about interstellar travel that did not involve extraterrestrial intelligences. In fact, I invented the "all-human Galaxy"

in order to make an end-run around John Campbell's convictions. Just the same, by doing this I deprived myself of the sort of very dramatic situations that A. E. van Vogt develops in this story—I. A.)

The great ship poised a quarter of a mile above one of the cities. Below was a cosmic desolation. As he floated down in his energy bubble, Enash saw that the buildings were crumbling with age.

"No signs of war damage!" The bodiless voice touched his ears momentarily. Enash tuned it out.

On the ground he collapsed his bubble. He found himself in a walled enclosure overgrown with weeds. Several skeletons lay in the tall grass beside the rakish building. They were of long, two-legged, two-armed beings with skulls in each case mounted at the end of a thin spine. The skeletons, all of adults, seemed in excellent preservation, but when he bent down and touched one, a whole section of it crumbled into a fine powder. As he straightened, he saw that Yoal was floating down nearby. Enash waited until the historian had stepped out of his bubble, then he said:

"Do you think we ought to use our method of reviving the long dead?"

Yoal was thoughtful. "I have been asking questions of the various people who have landed, and there is something wrong here. This planet has no surviving life, not even insect life. We'll have to find out what happened before we risk any colonization."

Enash said nothing. A soft wind was blowing. It rustled through a clump of trees nearby. He motioned toward the trees. Yoal nodded and said, "Yes, the plant life has not been harmed, but plants after all are not affected in the same way as the active life forms."

There was an interruption. A voice spoke from Yoal's receiver: "A museum has been found at approximately the center of the city. A red light has been fixed on the roof."

Enash said, "I'll go with you, Yoal. There might be skeletons of animals and of the intelligent being in various stages of his evolution. You didn't answer my question. Are you going to revive these things?"

Yoal said slowly, "I intend to discuss the matter with the council, but I think there is no doubt. We must know the cause of this disaster." He waved one sucker vaguely to take in half the compass. He added as an afterthought, "We shall proceed cautiously, of course, beginning with an obviously early development. The absence of the skeletons of children indicates that the race had developed personal immortality."

The council came to look at the exhibits. It was, Enash knew, a formal preliminary only. The decision was made. There would be revivals. It was more than that. They were curious. Space was vast, the journeys through it long and lonely, landing always a stimulating experience, with its prospect of new life forms to be seen and studied.

The museum looked ordinary. High-domed ceilings, vast rooms. Plastic models of strange beasts, many artifacts—too many to see and comprehend in so short a time. The life span of a race was imprisoned here in a progressive array of relics. Enash looked with the others, and was glad when they came to the line of skeletons and preserved bodies. He seated himself behind the energy screen, and watched the biological experts take a preserved body out of a stone sarcophagus. It was wrapped in windings of cloth, many of them. The experts did not bother to unravel the rotted material. Their forceps reached through, pinched a piece of skull—that was the accepted procedure. Any part of the skeleton could be used, but the most perfect revivals, the most complete reconstructions resulted when a certain section of the skull was used.

Hamar, the chief biologist, explained the choice of body. "The chemicals used to preserve this mummy show a sketchy knowledge of chemistry. The carvings on the sarcophagus indicate a crude and unmechanical culture. In such a civilization there would not be much development of the potentialities of the nervous system. Our speech experts have been analyzing the recorded voice mechanism which is a part of each exhibit, and though many languages are involved—evidence that the ancient language spoken at the time the body was alive has been reproduced—they found no difficulty in translating the meanings. They have now adapted our universal speech machine, so that anyone who wishes to need only speak into his communicator, and so will have his words translated into the language of the revived person. The reverse, naturally, is also true. Ah, I see we are ready for the first body."

Enash watched intently with the others as the lid was clamped down on the plastic reconstructor, and the growth processes were started. He could feel himself becoming tense. For there was nothing haphazard about what was happening. In a few minutes a full-grown ancient inhabitant of this planet would sit up and stare at them. The science involved was simple and always fully effective.

. . . Out of the shadows of smallness, life grows. The level of beginning and ending, of life and—not life; in that dim region matter oscillates easily between old and new habits. The habit of organic, or the habit of inorganic. Electrons do not have life and un-life values. Atoms form into molecules, there is a step in the process, one tiny step, that is of life—if life begins at all. One step, and then darkness. Or aliveness.

A stone or a living cell. A grain of gold or a blade of grass, the sands of the sea or the equally numerous animalcules inhabiting the endless fishy waters—the difference is there in the twilight zone of matter. Each living cell has in it the whole form. The crab grows a new leg when the old one is torn from its flesh. Both ends of the planarian worm elongate, and soon there are two worms, two identities, two digestive systems, each as greedy as the original, each a whole, unwounded, unharmed by its experience. Each cell can be the whole. Each cell remembers in detail so intricate that no totality of words could ever describe the completeness achieved.

But—paradox—memory is not organic. An ordinary wax record remembers sounds. A wire recorder easily gives up a duplicate of the voice that spoke into it years before. Memory is a physiological impression, a mark on matter, a change in the shape of a molecule, so that when a reaction is desired the *shape* emits the same rhythm of response.

Out of the mummy's skull had come the multi-quadrillion memory shapes from which a response was now being evoked. As ever, the memory held true.

A man blinked, and opened his eyes.

"It is true, then," he said aloud, and the words were translated into the Ganae tongue as he spoke them. "Death is merely an opening into another life—but where are my attendants?" At the end, his voice took on a complaining tone.

He sat up, and climbed out of the case, which had automatically opened as he came to life. He saw his captors. He froze, but only for a moment. He had a pride and a very special arrogant courage, which served him now. Reluctantly, he sank to his knees and made obeisance, but doubt must have been strong in him. "Am I in the presence of the gods of Egypt?" He climbed to his feet. "What nonsense is this? I do not bow to nameless demons."

Captain Gorsid said, "Kill him!"

The two-legged monster dissolved, writhing in the beam of a ray gun.

The second revived man stood up, pale, and trembled with fear. "My God, I swear I won't touch the stuff again. Talk about pink elephants—"

Yoal was curious. "To what *stuff* do you refer, revived one?"

"The old hooch, the poison in the hip pocket flask, the juice they gave me at that speak . . . my lordie!"

Captain Gorsid looked questioningly at Yoal, "Need we linger?"

Yoal hesitated. "I am curious." He addressed the man. "If I were to tell you that we were visitors from another star, what would be your reaction?"

The man stared at him. He was obviously puzzled, but the fear was stronger. "Now, look," he said, "I was driving along, minding my own business. I admit I'd had a shot or two too many, but it's the liquor they serve these days. I swear I didn't see the other car—and if this is some new idea of punishing people who drink and drive, well, you've won. I won't touch another drop as long as I live, so help me."

Yoal said, "He drives a 'car' and thinks nothing of it. Yet we saw no cars. They didn't even bother to preserve them in the museums."

Enash noticed that everyone waited for everyone else to comment. He stirred as he realized the circle of silence would be complete unless he spoke. He said, "Ask him to describe the car. How does it work?"

"Now, you're talking," said the man. "Bring on your line of chalk, and I'll walk it, and ask any questions you please. I may be so tight that I can't see straight, but I can always drive. How does it work? You just put her in gear, and step on the gas."

"Gas," said engineering officer Veed. "The internal combustion engine. That places him."

Captain Gorsid motioned to the guard with the ray gun.

The third man sat up, and looked at them thoughtfully. "From the stars?" he said finally. "Have you a system, or was it blind chance?"

The Ganae councillors in that domed room stirred uneasily in their curved chairs. Enash caught Yoal's eye on him. The shock in the historian's eye alarmed the meteorologist. He thought:

"The two-legged one's adjustment to a new situation, his grasp of realities, was unnormally rapid. No Ganae could have equalled the swiftness of the reaction."

Hamar, the chief biologist, said, "Speed of thought is not necessarily a sign of superiority. The slow, careful thinker has his place in the hierarchy of intellect."

But Enash found himself thinking, it was not the speed; it was the accuracy of the response. He tried to imagine himself being revived from the dead, and understanding instantly the meaning of the presence of aliens from the stars. He couldn't have done it.

He forgot his thought, for the man was out of the case. As Enash watched with the others, he walked briskly over to the window and looked out. One glance, and then he turned back.

"Is it all like this?" he asked.

Once again, the speed of his understanding caused a sensation. It was Yoal who finally replied.

"Yes. Desolation. Death. Ruin. Have you any ideas as to what happened?"

The man came back and stood in front of the energy screen that guarded the Ganae. "May I look over the museum? I have to estimate what age I am in. We had certain possibilities of destruction when I was last alive, but which one was realized depends on the time elapsed."

The councillors looked at Captain Gorsid, who hesitated; then, "Watch him," he said to the guard with the ray gun. He faced the man. "We understand your aspirations fully. You would like to seize control of this situation and ensure your own safety. Let me reassure you. Make no false moves, and all will be well."

Whether or not the man believed the lie, he gave no sign. Nor did he show by a glance or a movement that he had seen the scarred floor where the ray gun had burned his two predecessors into nothingness. He walked curiously to the nearest doorway, studied the other guard who waited there for him, and then, gingerly, stepped through. The first guard followed him, then came the mobile energy screen, and finally, trailing one another, the councillors.

Enash was the third to pass through the doorway. The room contained skeletons and plastic models of animals. The room beyond that was what, for want of a better term, Enash called a culture room. It contained the artifacts from a single period of civilization. It looked very advanced. He had examined some of the machines when they first passed through it, and had thought:

Atomic energy. He was not alone in his recognition. From behind him, Captain Gorsid said to the man:

"You are forbidden to touch anything. A false move will be the signal for the guards to fire."

The man stood at ease in the center of the room. In spite of a curious anxiety, Enash had to admire his calmness. He must have known what his fate would be, but he stood there thoughtfully, and said finally, deliberately, "I do not need to go any farther. Perhaps you will be able to judge better than I of the time that has elapsed since I was born and these machines were built. I see over there an instrument which, according to the sign above it, counts atoms when they explode. As soon as the proper number have exploded it shuts off the power automatically, and for just the right length of time to prevent a chain explosion. In my time we had a thousand crude devices for limiting the size of an atomic reaction, but it required two thousand years to develop those devices from the early beginnings of atomic energy. Can you make a comparison?"

The councillors glanced at Veed. The engineering officer hesitated. At last, reluctantly, he said, "Nine thousand years ago we had a thousand methods of limiting atomic explosions." He paused, then even more slowly, "I have never heard of an instrument that counts out atoms for such a purpose."

"And yet," murmured Shuri, the astronomer, breathlessly, "the race was destroyed."

There was silence. It ended as Gorsid said to the nearest guard, "Kill the monster!"

But it was the guard who went down, bursting into flame. Not just one guard, but the guards! Simultaneously down, burning with a blue flame. The flame licked at the screen, recoiled, and licked more furiously, recoiled and burned brighter. Through a haze of fire, Enash saw that the man had retreated to the far door, and that the machine that counted atoms was glowing with a blue intensity.

Captain Gorsid shouted into his communicator, "Guard all exits with ray guns. Spaceships stand by to kill alien with heavy guns."

Somebody said, "Mental control. Some kind of mental control. What have we run into?"

They were retreating. The blue flame was at the ceiling, struggling to break through the screen. Enash had a last glimpse of the machine. It must still be counting atoms, for it was a hellish blue. Enash raced with the others to the room where the man had been resurrected. There, another energy screen crashed to their rescue. Safe now, they retreated into their separate bubbles and whisked through outer doors and up to the ship. As the great ship soared, an atomic bomb hurtled down from it. The mushroom of flame blotted out the museum and the city below.

"But we still don't know why the race died," Yoal whispered into Enash's ear, after the thunder had died from the heavens behind them.

The pale yellow sun crept over the horizon on the third morning after the bomb was dropped, the eighth day since the landing. Enash floated with the others down on a new city. He had come to argue against any further revival.

"As a meteorologist," he said, "I pronounce this planet safe for Ganae colonization. I cannot see the need for taking any risks. This race has discovered the secrets of its nervous system, and we cannot afford—"

He was interrupted. Hamar, the biologist, said dryly, "If they knew so much why didn't they migrate to other star systems and save themselves?"

"I will concede," said Enash, "that very possibly they had not discovered our system of locating stars with planetary families." He looked earnestly around the circle of his friends. "We have agreed that was a unique accidental discovery. We were lucky, not clever."

He saw by the expressions on their faces that they were mentally refuting his arguments. He felt a helpless sense of imminent catastrophe. For he could see that picture of a great race facing death. It must have come swiftly, but not so swiftly that they didn't know about it. There were too many skeletons in the open, lying in the gardens of magnificent homes, as if each man and his wife had come out to wait for the doom of his kind. He tried to picture it for the council, that last day long, long ago, when a race had calmly met its ending. But his visualization failed somehow, for the others shifted impatiently in the seats that had been set up behind the series of energy screens, and Captain Gorsid said, "Exactly what aroused this intense emotional reaction in you, Enash?"

The question gave Enash pause. He hadn't thought of it as emotional. He hadn't realized the nature of his obsession, so subtly had it stolen upon him. Abruptly now, he realized.

"It was the third one," he said slowly. "I saw him through the haze of energy fire, and he was standing there in the distant doorway watching us curiously, just before we turned to run. His bravery, his calm, the skilful way he had duped us—it all added up."

"Added up to his death!" said Hamar. And everybody laughed.

"Come now, Enash," said Vice-captain Mayad good-humouredly, "you're not going to pretend that this race is braver than our own, or that, with all the precautions we have now taken, we need fear one man?"

Enash was silent, feeling foolish. The discovery that he had had an emotional obsession abashed him. He did not want to appear unreasonable. He made a final protest, "I merely wish to point out," he said doggedly, "that this desire to discover what happened to a dead race does not seem absolutely essential to me."

Captain Gorsid waved at the biologist. "Proceed," he said, "with the revival."

To Enash, he said, "Do we dare return to Gana, and recommend mass migrations—and then admit that we did not actually complete our investigation here? It's impossible, my friend."

It was the old argument, but reluctantly now Enash admitted there was something to be said for that point of view. He forgot that, for the fourth man was stirring.

The man sat up. And vanished.

There was a blank, horrified silence. Then Captain Gorsid said harshly, "He can't get out of there. We know that. He's in there somewhere."

All around Enash, the Ganae were out of their chairs, peering into the energy shell. The guards stood with ray guns held limply in their suckers. Out of the corner of his eye, he saw one of the protective screen technicians beckon to Veed, who went over. He came back grim. He said, "I'm told the needles jumped ten points when he first disappeared. That's on the nucleonic level."

"By ancient Ganae!" Shuri whispered. "We've run into what we've always feared."

Gorsid was shouting into the communicator. "Destroy all the locators on the ship. Destroy them, do you hear!"

He turned with glaring eyes. "Shuri," he bellowed. "They don't seem to understand. Tell those subordinates of yours to act. All locators and reconstructors must be destroyed."

"Hurry, hurry!" said Shuri weakly.

When that was done they breathed more easily. There were grim smiles and a tensed satisfaction. "At least," said Vice-captain Mayad, "he cannot now ever discover Gana. Our great system of locating suns with planets remains our secret. There can be no retaliation for—'' He stopped, said slowly, ''What am I talking about? We haven't done anything. We're not responsible for the disaster that has befallen the inhabitants of this planet.''

But Enash knew what he had meant. The guilt feelings came to the surface at such moments as this—the ghosts of all the races destroyed by the Ganae, the remorseless will that had been in them, when they first landed, to annihilate whatever was here. The dark abyss of voiceless hate and terror that lay behind them; the days on end when they had mercilessly poured poisonous radiation down upon the unsuspecting inhabitants of peaceful planets—all that had been in Mayad's words.

''I still refuse to believe he has escaped.'' That was Captain Gorsid. ''He's in there. He's waiting for us to take down our screens, so he can escape. Well, we won't do it.''

There was silence again as they stared expectantly into the emptiness of the energy shell. The reconstructor rested on metal supports, a glittering affair. But there was nothing else. Not a flicker of unnatural light or shade. The yellow rays of the sun bathed the open spaces with a brilliance that left no room for concealment.

''Guards,'' said Gorsid, ''destroy the reconstructor. I thought he might come back to examine it, but we can't take a chance on that.''

It burned with a white fury. And Enash, who had hoped somehow that the deadly energy would force the two-legged thing into the open, felt his hopes sag within him.

''But where can he have gone?'' Yoal whispered.

Enash turned to discuss the matter. In the act of swinging around, he saw that the monster was standing under a tree a score of feet to one side, watching them. He must have arrived at *that* moment, for there was a collective gasp from the councillors. Everybody drew back. One of the screen technicians, using great presence of mind, jerked up an energy screen between the Ganae and the monster. The creature came forward slowly. He was slim of build, he held his head well back. His eyes shone as from an inner fire.

He stopped as he came to the screen, reached out and touched it with his fingers. It flared, blurred with changing colors. The colors grew brighter, and extended in an intricate pattern all the way from his head to the ground. The blur cleared. The pattern faded into invisibility. The man was through the screen.

He laughed, a soft curious sound; then sobered. "When I first awakened," he said, "I was curious about the situation. The question was, what should I do with you?"

The words had a fateful ring to Enash on the still morning air of that planet of the dead. A voice broke the silence, a voice so strained and unnatural that a moment passed before he recognized it as belonging to Captain Gorsid.

"*Kill him!*"

When the blasters ceased their effort, the unkillable thing remained standing. He walked slowly forward until he was only a half dozen feet from the nearest Ganae. Enash had a position well to the rear. The man said slowly:

"Two courses suggest themselves, one based on gratitude for reviving me, the other based on reality. I know you for what you are. Yes, *know* you—and that is unfortunate. It is hard to feel merciful. To begin with," he went on, "let us suppose you surrender the secret of the locator. Naturally, now that a system exists, we shall never again be caught as we were."

Enash had been intent, his mind so alive with the potentialities of the disaster that was here that it seemed impossible that he could think of anything else. And yet, a part of his attention was stirred now. "What did happen?" he asked.

The man changed color. The emotions of that far day thickened his voice. "A nucleonic storm. It swept in from outer space. It brushed this edge of our galaxy. It was about ninety light-years in diameter, beyond the farthest limit of our power. There was no escape from it. We had dispensed with spaceships, and had no time to construct any. Castor, the only star with planets ever discovered by us, was also in the path of the storm." He stopped. "The secret?" he said.

Around Enash, the councillors were breathing easier. The fear of race destruction that had come to them was lifting. Enash saw with pride that the first shock was over, and they were not even afraid for themselves.

"Ah," said Yoal softly, "you don't know the secret. In spite of all your great development, we alone can conquer the galaxy." He looked at the others, smiling confidently. "Gentlemen," he said, "our pride in a great Ganae achievement is justified. I suggest we return to our ship. We have no further business on this planet."

There was a confused moment while their bubbles formed, when Enash wondered if the two-legged one would try to stop their departure. But when he looked back, he saw that the man was walking in a leisurely fashion along a street.

That was the memory Enash carried with him, as the ship began to move. That and the fact that the three atomic bombs they dropped, one after the other, failed to explode.

"We will not," said Captain Gorsid, "give up a planet as easily as that. I propose another interview with the creature."

They were floating down again into the city, Enash and Yoal and Veed and the commander. Captain Gorsid's voice tuned in once more:

". . . As I visualize it"—through the mist Enash could see the transparent glint of the other three bubbles around him—"we jumped to conclusions about this creature, not justified by the evidence. For instance, when he awakened, he vanished. Why? Because he was afraid, of course. He wanted to size up the situation. *He* didn't believe he was omnipotent."

It was sound logic. Enash found himself taking heart from it. Suddenly, he was astonished that he had become panicky so easily. He began to see the danger in a new light. Only one man alive on a new planet. If they were determined enough, colonists could be moved in as if he did not exist. It had been done before, he recalled. On several planets, small groups of the original populations had survived the destroying radiation, and taken refuge in remote areas. In almost every case, the new colonists gradually hunted them down. In two instances, however, that Enash remembered, native races were still holding small sections of their planets. In each case, it had been found impractical to destroy them because it would have endangered the Ganae on the planet. So the survivors were tolerated. One man would not take up very much room.

When they found him, he was busily sweeping out the lower floor of a small bungalow. He put the broom aside and stepped on to the terrace outside. He had put on sandals, and he wore a loose-fitting robe made of very shiny material. He eyed them indolently but he said nothing.

It was Captain Gorsid who made the proposition. Enash had to admire the story he told into the language machine. The commander was very frank. That approach had been decided on. He pointed out that the Ganae could not be expected to revive the dead of this planet. Such altruism would be unnatural considering that the ever-growing Ganae hordes had a continual need for new worlds. Each vast new population increment was a problem that could be solved by one method only. In this instance, the colonists would gladly respect the rights of the sole survivor of this world.

It was at this point that the man interrupted. "But what is the purpose of this endless expansion?" He seemed genuinely curious. "What will happen when you finally occupy every planet in this galaxy?"

Captain Gorsid's puzzled eyes met Yoal's, then flashed to Veed, than Enash. Enash shrugged his torso negatively, and felt pity for the creature. The man didn't understand, possibly never could understand. It was the old story of two different viewpoints, the virile and the decadent, the race that aspired to the stars and the race that declined the call of destiny.

"Why not," urged the man, "control the breeding chambers?"

"And have the government overthrown!" said Yoal.

He spoke tolerantly, and Enash saw that the others were smiling at the man's naiveté. He felt the intellectual gulf between them widening. The creature had no comprehension of the natural life forces that were at work. The man spoke again.

"Well, if you don't control them, we will control them for you."

There was silence.

They began to stiffen. Enash felt it in himself, saw the signs of it in the others. His gaze flicked from face to face, then back to the creature in the doorway. Not for the first time, Enash had the thought that their enemy seemed helpless. "Why," he decided, "I could put my suckers around him and crush him."

He wondered if mental control of nucleonic, nuclear, and gravitonic energies included the ability to defend oneself from a macrocosmic attack. He had an idea it did. The exhibition of power two hours before might have had limitations, but if so, it was not apparent. Strength or weakness could make no difference. The threat of threats had been made: "If you don't control—we will."

The words echoed in Enash's brain, and, as the meaning penetrated deeper, his aloofness faded. He had always regarded himself as a spectator. Even when, earlier, he had argued against the revival, he had been aware of a detached part of himself watching the scene rather than being a part of it. He saw with a sharp clarity that that was why he had finally yielded to the conviction of the others. Going back beyond that to remoter days, he saw that he had never quite considered himself a participant in the seizure of the planets of other races. He was the one who looked on, and thought of reality, and speculated on a life that seemed to have no meaning. It was meaningless no longer. He was caught by a tide of irresistible emotion, and swept along. He felt himself sinking, merging with the Ganae mass being. All the strength and all the will of the race surged up in his veins.

He snarled, "Creature, if you have any hopes of reviving your dead race, abandon them now."

The man looked at him, but said nothing. Enash rushed on, "If you could destroy us, you would have done so already. But the truth is that you operate within limitations. Our ship is so built that no conceivable chain reaction could be started in it. For every plate of potential unstable material in it there is a counteracting plate, which prevents the development of a critical pile. You might be able to set off explosions in our engines, but they, too, would be limited, and would merely start the process for which they are intended—confined in their proper space."

He was aware of Yoal touching his arm. "Careful," warned the historian. "Do not in your just anger give away vital information."

Enash shook off the restraining sucker. "Let us not be unrealistic," he said harshly. "This thing has divined most of our racial secrets, apparently merely by looking at our bodies. We would be acting childishly if we assumed that he has not already realized the possibilities of the situation."

"*Enash!*" Captain Gorsid's voice was imperative.

As swiftly as it had come, Enash's rage subsided. He stepped back. "Yes, commander."

"I think I know what you intended to say," said Captain Gorsid. "I assure you I am in full accord, but I believe also that I, as the top Ganae official, should deliver the ultimatum."

He turned. His horny body towered above the man. "You have made the unforgivable threat. You have told us, in effect, that you will attempt to restrict the vaulting Ganae spirit."

"Not the spirit," said the man.

The commander ignored the interruption. "Accordingly, we have no alternative. We are assuming that, given time to locate the materials and develop the tools, you might be able to build a reconstructor. In our opinion it will be at least two years before you can complete it, *even if you know how*. It is an immensely intricate machine, not easily assembled by the lone survivor of a race that gave up its machines millennia before disaster struck.

"You did not have time to build a spaceship. We won't give you time to build a reconstructor.

"Within a few minutes our ship will start dropping bombs. It is possible you will be able to prevent explosions in your vicinity. We will start, accordingly, on the other side of the planet. If you stop us there, then we will assume we need help. In six months of travelling at top acceleration, we can reach a point where the nearest Ganae planet would hear our messages. They will send a fleet so vast that all your powers of resistance will be overcome. By dropping a hundred or a thousand bombs every minute, we will succeed in devastating every city so that not a grain of dust will remain of the skeletons of your people.

"That is our plan. So it shall be. Now, do your worst to us who are at your mercy."

The man shook his head. "I shall do nothing—now!" he said. He paused, then thoughtfully, "Your reasoning is fairly accurate. Fairly. Naturally, I am not all powerful, but it seems to me you have forgotten one little point. I won't tell you what it is. And now," he said, "good day to you. Get back to your ship, and be on your way. I have much to do."

Enash had been standing quietly, aware of the fury building up in him again. Now, with a hiss, he sprang forward, suckers outstretched. They were almost touching the smooth flesh—when something snatched at him.

He was back on the ship.

He had no memory of movement, no sense of being dazed or harmed. He was aware of Veed and Yoal and Captain Gorsid standing near him as astonished as he himself. Enash remained very still, thinking of what the man had said: ". . . *Forgotten one little point*." Forgotten? That meant they knew. What could it be? He was still pondering about it when Yoal said:

"We can be reasonably certain our bombs alone will not work."

They didn't.

Forty light-years out from Earth, Enash was summoned to the council chambers. Yoal greeted him wanly. "The monster is aboard."

The thunder of that poured through Enash, and with it came a sudden comprehension. "That was what he meant we had forgotten," he said finally, aloud and wonderingly. "That he can travel through space at will within a limit—what was the figure he once used—of ninety light-years."

He sighed. He was not surprised that the Ganae, who had to use ships, would not have thought immediately of such a possibility. Slowly, he began to retreat from the reality. Now that the shock had come, he felt old and weary, a sense of his mind withdrawing again to its earlier state of aloofness. It required a few minutes to get the story. A physicist's assistant, on his way to the storeroom, had caught a glimpse of a man in a lower corridor. In such a heavily manned ship, the wonder was that the intruder had escaped earlier observation. Enash had a thought.

"But after all we are not going all the way to one of our planets. How does he expect to make use of us to locate it if we only use the video—" he stopped. That was it, of course. Directional video beams would have to be used, and the man would travel in the right direction the instant contact was made.

Enash saw the decision in the eyes of his companions, the only possible decision under the circumstances. And yet, it seemed to him they were missing some vital point. He walked slowly to the great video plate at one end of the chamber. There was a picture on it, so sharp, so vivid, so majestic that the unaccustomed mind would have reeled as from a stunning blow. Even to him, who knew the scene, there came a constriction, a sense of unthinkable vastness. It was a video view of a section of the Milky Way. Four hundred *million* stars as seen through telescopes that could pick up the light of a red dwarf at thirty thousand light-years.

The video plate was twenty-five yards in diameter—a scene that had no parallel elsewhere in the plenum. Other galaxies simply did not have that many stars.

Only one in two hundred thousand of those glowing suns had planets.

That was the colossal fact that compelled them now to an irrevocable act. Wearily, Enash looked around him.

"The monster has been very clever," he said quietly. "If we go ahead, he goes with us, obtains a reconstructor, and returns by his method to his planet. If we use the directional beam, he flashes along it, obtains a reconstructor, and again reaches his planet first. In either event, by the time our fleets arrived back here, he would have revived enough of his kind to thwart any attack we could mount."

He shook his torso. The picture was accurate, he felt sure, but it still seemed incomplete. He said slowly, "We have one advantage now. Whatever decision we make, there is no language machine to enable him to learn what it is. We can carry out our plans without his knowing what they will be. He knows that neither he nor we can blow up the ship. That leaves us one real alternative."

It was Captain Gorsid who broke the silence that followed. "Well, gentlemen, I see we know our minds. We will set the engines, blow up the controls, and take him with us."

They looked at each other, race pride in their eyes. Enash touched suckers with each in turn.

An hour later, when the heat was already considerable, Enash had the thought that sent him staggering to the communicator, to call Shuri, the astronomer. "Shuri," he yelled, "when the monster first awakened—remember Captain Gorsid had difficulty getting your subordinates to destroy the locators. We never thought to ask them what the delay was. Ask them . . . ask them—"

There was a pause, then Shuri's voice came weakly over the roar of the static. "They . . . couldn't . . . get . . . into the . . . room. The door was locked."

Enash sagged to the floor. They had missed more than one point, he realized. The man had awakened, realized the situation; and, when he vanished, he had gone to the ship, and there discovered the secret of the locator and possibly the secret of the reconstructor—if he didn't know it previously. By the time he reappeared, he already had from them what he wanted. All the rest must have been designed to lead them to this act of desperation.

In a few moments, now, *he* would be leaving the ship, secure in the knowledge that shortly no alien mind would know his planet existed. Knowing, too, that his race would live again, and this time never die.

Enash staggered to his feet, clawed at the roaring communicator, and shouted his new understanding into it. There was no answer. It clattered with the static of uncontrollable and inconceivable energy. The heat was peeling his armoured hide as he struggled to the matter transmitter. It flashed at him with purple flame. Back to the communicator he ran shouting and screaming.

He was still whimpering into it a few minutes later when the mighty ship plunged into the heart of a blue-white sun.

DREAMS ARE SACRED

by Peter Phillips (1921–   )

ASTOUNDING SCIENCE FICTION
September

Peter Phillips is a British newspaperman who has written only a relatively small number of science fiction stories, all appearing in the 1948–1958 period. His best known story, in addition to the present selection, is the excellent "Lost Memory," which appeared in the May, 1952 issue of Galaxy Science Fiction. *As is the case with several other writers who have appeared in this series, we wish he had written more in the science fiction field.*

"Dreams are Sacred". is one of the very best first stories ever published, a stunning study in paranoia that anticipates the work of such writers as Phillip K. Dick. If you have never read this wonderful story, you are in for a treat.

(It occurs to me that there ought to be a collection of stories in which science fiction/fantasy writers are important characters. I wonder if such stories are ever written by writers who have not themselves written science fiction or fantasy. I can think offhand of one story I have written in which a fantasy writer was the hero. Generally, and this is not surprising, the writers

tend to be the hero; that was certainly the case in my own story. Here, however, is a story in which the science fiction writer is, after a fashion, the menace—very unusual. Let me point out, by the way, the first scene, in which people who put ghost stories into the hands of children are excoriated, while people who put deadly guns into their hands are pictured as wise and heroic. Well, I don't have to agree with everything in these stories that Marty and I select.—I.A.)

When I was seven, I read a ghost story and babbled of the consequent nightmare to my father.

"They were coming for me, Pop," I sobbed. "I couldn't run, and I couldn't stop 'em, great big things with teeth and claws like the pictures in the book, and I couldn't wake myself up, Pop, I couldn't come awake."

Pop had a few quiet cuss words for folks who left such things around for a kid to pick up and read; then he took my hand gently in his own great paw and led me into the six-acre pasture.

He was wise, with the canny insight into human motives that the soil gives to a man. He was close to Nature and the hearts and minds of men, for all men ultimately depend on the good earth for sustenance and life.

He sat down on a stump and showed me a big gun. I know now it was a heavy Service Colt .45. To my child eyes, it was enormous. I had seen shotguns and sporting rifles before, but this was to be held in one hand and fired. Gosh, it was heavy. It dragged my thin arm down with its sheer, grim weight when Pop showed me how to hold it.

Pop said: "It's a killer, Pete. There's nothing in the whole wide world or out of it that a slug from Billy here won't stop. It's killed lions and tigers and men. Why, if you aim right, it'll stop a charging elephant. Believe me, son, there's nothing you can meet in dreams that Billy here won't stop. And he'll come into your dreams with you from now on, so there's no call to be scared of anything."

He drove that deep into my receptive subconscious. At the end of half an hour, my wrist ached abominably from the kick of that Colt. But I'd seen heavy slugs tear through two-inch teakwood and mild steel plating. I'd looked along that barrel, pulled the trigger, felt the recoil rip up my arm and seen the fist-size hole blasted through a sack of wheat.

And that night, I slept with Billy under my pillow. Before I slipped into dreamland, I'd felt again the cool, reassuring butt.

When the Dark Things came again, I was almost glad. I was ready for them. Billy was there, lighter than in my waking hours—or maybe my dream-hand was bigger—but just as powerful. Two of the Dark Things crumpled and fell as Billy roared and kicked, then the others turned and fled.

Then I was chasing them, laughing, and firing from the hip.

Pop was no psychiatrist, but he'd found the perfect antidote to fear—the projection into the subconscious mind of a common-sense concept based on experience.

Twenty years later, the same principle was put into operation scientifically to save the sanity—and perhaps the life—of Marsham Craswell.

"Surely you've heard of him?" said Stephen Blakiston, a college friend of mine who'd majored in psychiatry.

"Vaguely," I said. "Science-fiction, fantasy . . . I've read a little. Screwy."

"Not so. Some good stuff." Steve waved a hand round the bookshelves of his private office in the new Pentagon Mental Therapy Hospital, New York State. I saw multicolored magazine backs, row on row of them. "I'm a fan," he said simply. "Would you call me screwy?"

I backed out of that one. I'm just a sports columnist, but I knew Blakiston was tops in two fields—the psycho stuff and electronic therapy.

Steve said: "Some of it's the old 'peroo, of course, but the level of writing is generally high and the ideas thought-provoking. For ten years, Marsham has been one of the most prolific and best-loved writers in the game.

"Two years ago, he had a serious illness, didn't give himself time to convalesce properly before he waded into writing again. He tried to reach his previous output, tending more and more toward pure fantasy. Beautiful in parts, sheer rubbish sometimes.

"He forced his imagination to work, set himself a wordage routine. The tension became too great. Something snapped. Now he's here."

Steve got up, ushered me out of his office. "I'll take you to see him. He won't see you. Because the thing that snapped was his conscious control over his imagination. It went into high gear, and now instead of writing his stories, he's living them—quite literally, for him.

"Far-off worlds, strange creatures, weird adventures—the detailed phantasmagoria of a brilliant mind driving itself into insanity through the sheer complexity of its own invention. He's escaped from the harsh reality of his strained existence into a dream world. But he may make it real enough to kill himself.

"He's the hero of course," Steve continued, opening the door into a private world. "But even heroes sometimes die. My fear is that his morbidly overactive imagination working through his subconscious mind will evoke in this dream world in which he is living a situation wherein the hero must die.

"You probably know that the sympathetic magic of witchcraft acts largely through the imagination. A person imagines he is being hexed to death—and dies. If Marsham Craswell imagines that one of his fantastic creations kills the hero—himself—then he just won't wake up again.

"Drugs won't touch him. Listen."

Steve looked at me across Marsham's bed. I leaned down to hear the mutterings from the writer's bloodless lips.

". . . . We must search the Plains of Istak for the Diamond. I, Multan, who now have the Sword, will lead thee; for the Snake must die and only in virtue of the Diamond can his death be encompassed. Come."

Craswell's right hand, lying limp on the coverlet, twitched. He was beckoning his followers.

"Still the Snake and the Diamond?" asked Steve. "He's been living that dream for two days. We only know what's happening when he speaks in his role of hero. Often it's quite unintelligible. Sometimes a spark of consciousness filters through, and he fights to wake up. It's pretty horrible to watch him squirming and trying to pull himself back into reality. Have you ever tried to pull yourself out of a nightmare and failed?"

It was then that I remembered Billy, the Colt .45. I told Steve about it, back in his office.

He said: "Sure. Your Pop had the right idea. In fact, I'm hoping to save Marsham by an application of the same principle. To do it, I need the cooperation of someone who combines a lively imagination with a severely practical streak, hoss-sense—and a sense of humor. Yes—you."

"Uh? How can I help? I don't even know the guy."

"You will," said Steve, and the significant way he said it sent a trickle of ice water down my back. "You're going to get closer to Marsham Craswell than one man has ever been to another.

"I'm going to project you—the essential you, that is, your mind and personality—into Craswell's tortured brain."

I made pop-eyes, then thumbed at the magazine-lined wall. "Too much of yonder, brother Steve," I said. "What you need is a drink."

Steve lit his pipe, draped his long legs over the arm of his chair. "Miracles and witchcraft are out. What I propose to do is basically no more miraculous than the way your Pop put that gun into your dreams so you weren't afraid anymore. It's merely more complex scientifically.

"You've heard of the encephalograph? You know it picks up the surface neural currents of the brain, amplifies and records them, showing the degree—or absence—of mental activity. It can't indicate the kind or quality of such activity save in very general terms. By using comparison-graphs and other statistical methods to analyze its data, we can sometimes diagnose incipient insanity, for instance. But that's all—until we started work on it, here at the Pentagon.

"We improved the penetration and induction pickup and needled the selectivity until we could probe any known portion of the brain. What we were looking for was a recognizable pattern among the millions of tiny electric currents that go to make up the imagery of thought, so that if the subject thought of something—a number, maybe—the instruments would react accordingly, give a pattern for it that would be repeated every time he thought of that number.

"We failed, of course. The major part of the brain acts as a unity, no one part being responsible for either simple or complex imagery, but the activity of one portion inducing activity in other portions—with the exception of those parts dealing with automatic impulses. So if we were to get a pattern we should need thousands of pickups—a practical impossibility. It was as if we were trying to divine the pattern of a colored sweater by putting one tiny stitch of it under a microscope.

"Paradoxically, our machine was too selective. We needed, not a probe, but an all-encompassing field, receptive simultaneously to the multitudinous currents that made up a thought pattern.

"We found such a field. But we were no further forward. In a sense, we were back where we started from—because to analyze what the field picked up would have entailed the use of thousands of complex instruments. We had amplified thought, but we could not analyze it.

"There was only one single instrument sufficiently sensitive and complex to do that—another human brain."

I waved for a pause. "I'm home," I said. "You've got a thought-reading machine."

"Much more than that. When we tested it the other day, one of my assistants stepped up the polarity-reversal of the field—that is, the frequency—by accident. I was acting as analyst and the subject was under narcosis.

"Instead of 'hearing' the dull incoherencies of his thoughts, I became part of them. I was inside that man's brain. It was a nightmare world. He wasn't a clear thinker. I was aware of my own individuality. . . . When he came round, he went for me bald-headed. Said I'd been trespassing inside his head.

"With Marsham, it'll be a different matter. The dream world of his coma is detailed, as real as he used to make dream worlds to his readers."

"Hold it," I said. "Why don't you take a peek?"

Steve Blakiston smiled and gave me a high-voltage shot from his big gray eyes. "Three good reasons: I've soaked in the sort of stuff he dreams up, and there's a danger that I would become identified too closely with him. What he needs is a salutary dose of common sense. You're the man for that, you cynical old whisky-hound.

"Secondly, if my mind gave way under the impress of his imagination, I wouldn't be around to treat myself; and thirdly, when—and if—he comes round, he'll want to kill the man who's been heterodyning his dreams. You can scram. But I want to stay and see the results."

"Sorting that out, I gather there's a possibility that I shall wake up as a candidate for a bed in the next ward?"

"Not unless you let your mind go under. And you won't. You've got a cast-iron non-gullibility complex. Just fool around in your usual iconoclastic manner. Your own imagination's pretty good, judging by some of your fight reports lately."

I got up, bowed politely, said: "Thank you, my friend. That reminds me—I'm covering the big fight at the Garden tomorrow night. And I need sleep. It's late. So long."

Steve unfolded and reached the door ahead of me.

"Please," he said, and argued. He can argue. And I couldn't duck those big eyes of his. And he is—or was—my pal. He said it wouldn't take long—(just like a dentist)—and he smacked down every "if" I thought up.

Ten minutes later, I was lying on a twin bed next to that occupied by a silent, white-faced Marsham Craswell. Steve was leaning over the writer adjusting a chrome-steel bowl like a hair-drier over the man's head. An assistant was fixing me up the same way.

Cables ran from the bowls to a movable arm overhead and thence to a wheeled machine that looked like something from the Whacky Science Section of the World's Fair, A.D. 2000.

I was bursting with questions, but the only ones that would come out seemed crazily irrelevant.

"What do I say to this guy? 'Good morning, and how are all your little complexes today?' Do I introduce myself?"

"Just say you're Pete Parnell, and play it off the cuff," said Steve. "You'll see what I mean when you get there."

Get there. That hit me—the idea of making a journey into some nut's nut. My stomach drew itself up to a softball size.

"What's the proper dress for a visit like this? Formal?" I asked. At least, I think I said that. It didn't sound like my voice.

"Wear what you like."

"Uh-huh. And how do I know when to draw my visit to a close?"

Steve came round to my side. "If you haven't snapped Craswell out of it within an hour, I'll turn off the current."

He stepped back to the machine. "Happy dreams."

I groaned.

It was hot. Two high summers rolled into one. No, two suns, blood-red, stark in a brazen sky. Should be cool underfoot—soft green turf, pool table smooth to the far horizon. But it wasn't grass. Dust. Burning green dust—

The gladiator stood ten feet away, eyes glaring in disbelief. All of six-four high, great bronzed arms and legs, knotted muscles, a long shining sword in his right hand.

But his face was unmistakable.

This was where I took a good hold of myself. I wanted to giggle.

"Boy!" I said. "Do you tan quickly! Couple of minutes ago, you were as white as the bed sheet."

The gladiator shaded his eyes from the twin suns. "Is this yet another guise of the magician Garor to drive me insane—an

Earthman here, on the Plains of Istak? Or am I already—mad?" His voice was deep, smoothly modulated.

My own was perfectly normal. Indeed, after the initial effort, I felt perfectly normal, except for the heat.

I said: "That's the growing idea where I've just come from—that you're going nuts."

You know those half-dreams, just on the verge of sleep, in which you can control your own imagery to some extent? That's how I felt. I knew intuitively what Steve was getting at when he said I could play it off the cuff. I looked down. Tweed suit, brogues—naturally. That's what I was wearing when I last looked at myself. I had no reason to think I was wearing—and therefore to be wearing—anything else. But something cooler was indicated in this heat, generated by Marsham Craswell's imagination.

Something like his own gladiator costume, perhaps.

Sandals—fine. There were my feet—in sandals.

Then I laughed. I had nearly fallen into the error of accepting his imagination.

"Do you mind if I switch off one of those suns?" I asked politely. "It's a little hot."

I gave one of the suns a very dirty look. It disappeared.

The gladiator raised his sword. "You are—Garor!" he cried. "But your witchery shall not avail you against the Sword!"

He rushed forward. The shining blade cleaved the air toward my skull.

I thought very, very fast.

The sword clanged, and streaked off at a sharp tangent from my G.I. brain-pan protector. I'd last worn that homely piece of hardware in the Argonne, and I knew it would stop a mere sword. I took it off.

"Now listen to me, Marsham Craswell," I said. "My name's Pete Parnell, of the Sunday *Star*, and—"

Craswell looked up from his sword, chest heaving, startled eyes bright as if with recognition. "Wait! I know now who you are—Nelpar Retrep, Man of the Seven Moons, come to fight with me against the Snake and his ungodly disciple, magician and sorceress, Garor. Welcome, my friend!"

He held out a huge bronzed hand. I shook it.

It was obvious that, unable to rationalize—or irrationalize—me, he was writing me into the plot of his dream! Right. It had been amusing so far. I'd string along for a while. My imagination hadn't taken a licking—yet.

Craswell said: "My followers, the great-hearted Dok-men of

the Blue Hills, have just been slain in a gory battle. We were about to brave the many perils of the Plains of Istak in our quest for the Diamond—but all this, of course, you know."

"Sure," I said. "What now?"

Craswell turned suddenly, pointed. "There," he muttered. "A sight that strikes terror even into my heart—Garor returns to the battle, at the head of her dread Legion of Lakros, beasts of the Overworld, drawn into evil symbiosis with alien intelligences—invulnerable to men, but not to the Sword, or to the mighty weapons of Nelpar of the Seven Moons. We shall fight them alone!"

Racing across the vast plain of green dust toward us was a horde of . . . er . . . creatures. My vocabulary can't cope fully with Craswell's imagination. Gigantic, shimmering things, drooling thick ichor, half-flying, half-lolloping. Enough to say I looked around for a washbasin to spit in. I found one, with soap and towels complete, but I pushed it over, looked at a patch of green dust and thought hard.

The outline of the phone booth wavered a little before I could fix it. I dashed inside, dialed "Police H.Q.? Riot squad here—and quick!"

I stepped outside the booth. Craswell was whirling the Sword round his head, yelling war cries as he faced the onrushing monsters.

From the other direction came the swelling scream of a police siren. Half a dozen good, solid patrol cars screeched to a dust-spurting stop outside the phone booth. I don't have to think hard to get a New York cop car fixed in my mind. These were just right. And the first man out, running to my side and patting his cap on firmly, was just right, too.

Michael O'Faolin, the biggest, toughest, nicest cop I know.

"Mike," I said, pointing. "Fix 'em."

"Shure, an' it's an aisy job f'the bhoys I've brought along," said Mike, hitching his belt.

He deployed his men.

Craswell looked at them fanning out to take the charge, then staggered back toward me, hand over his eyes. "Madness!" he shouted. "What madness is this? What are you doing?"

For a moment, the whole scene wavered. The lone red sun blinked out, the green desert became a murky transparency through which I caught a split-second glimpse of white beds with two figures lying on them. Then Craswell uncovered his eyes.

The monsters began to diminish some twenty yards from the

riot squad. By the time they got to the cops, they were man-size, and very amenable to discipline—enforced by raps over their horny noggins with nightsticks. They were bundled into the squad cars, which set off again over the plains.

Michael O'Faolin remained. I said: "Thanks, Mike. I may have a couple of spare tickets for the big fight tomorrow night. See you later."

"Just what I was wantin', Pete. 'Tis me day off. Now, how do I get home?"

I opened the door of the phone booth. "Right inside." He stepped in. I turned to Craswell.

"Mighty magic, O Nelpar!" he exclaimed. "To creatures of Garor's mind you opposed creatures of your own!"

He'd woven the whole incident into his plot already.

"We must go forward now, Nelpar of the Seven Moons—forward to the Citadel of the Snake, a thousand lokspans over the burning Plains of Istak."

"How about the Diamond?"

"The Diamond—?"

Evidently, he'd run so far ahead of himself getting me fixed into the landscape that he'd forgotten all about the Diamond that could kill the Snake. I didn't remind him.

However, a thousand lokspans over the burning plains sounded a little too far for walking, whatever a lokspan might be.

I said: "Why do you make things tough for yourself, Craswell?"

"The name," he said with tremendous dignity, "is Multan."

"Multan, Sultan, Shashlik, Dikkidam, Hammaneggs or whatever polysyllabic pooh-bah you wish to call yourself—I still ask, why make things tough for yourself when there's plenty of cabs around? Just whistle."

I whistled. The Purple Cab swung in, perfect to the last detail, including a hulking-backed, unshaven driver, dead ringer for the impolite gorilla who'd brought me out to Pentagon that evening.

There is nothing on earth quite so unutterably prosaic as a New York Purple Cab with that sort of driver. The sight upset Craswell, and the green plains wavered again while he struggled to fit the cab into his dream.

"What new magic is this! You are indeed mighty, Nelpar!"

He got in. But he was trembling with the effort to maintain the structure of this world into which he had escaped, against my deliberate attempts to bring it crashing round his ears and restore him to colorless—but sane—normality.

At this stage, I felt curiously sorry for him; but I realized that it might only be by permitting him to reach the heights of creative imagery before dousing him with the sponge from the cold bucket that I could jerk his drifting ego back out of dreamland.

It was dangerous thinking. Dangerous—for me.

Craswell's thousand lokspans appeared to be the equivalent of ten blocks. Or perhaps he wanted to gloss over the mundane near-reality of a cab ride. He pointed forward, past the driver's shoulder: "The Citadel of the Snake!"

To me, it looked remarkably like a wedding cake designed by Dali in red plastic: ten stories high, each story a platter half a mile thick, each platter diminishing in size and offset to the one beneath so that the edifice spiraled toward the glossy sky.

The cab rolled into its vast shadow, stopped beneath the sheer, blank precipice of the base platter, which might have been two miles in diameter. Or three. Or four. What's a mile or two among dreamers?

Craswell hopped out quickly. I got out on the driver's side.

The driver said: "Dollar-fifty."

Square, unshaven jar, low forehead, dirty-red hair straggling under his cap. I said: "Comes high for a short trip."

"Lookit the clock," he growled, squirming his shoulders. "Do I come out and get it?"

I said sweetly: "Go to hell."

Cab and driver shot downward through the green sand with the speed of an express elevator. The hole closed up. The times I've wanted to do just that—

Craswell was regarding me open-mouthed. I said: "Sorry. Now I'm being escapist, too. Get on with the plot."

He muttered something I didn't catch, strode across to the red wall in which a crack, meeting place of mighty gates, had appeared, and raised his sword.

"Open, Garor! Your doom is nigh. Multan and Nelpar are here to brave the terrors of this Citadel and free the world from the tyranny of the Snake!" He hammered at the crack with the sword-hilt.

"Not so loud," I murmured. "You'll wake the neighbors. Why not use the bell-push?" I put my thumb on the button and pressed. The towering gates swung slowly open.

"You . . . you have been here before—"

"Yes—after my last lobster supper." I bowed. "After you."

I followed him into a great, echoing tunnel with fluorescent walls. The gates closed behind us. He paused and looked at me with an odd gleam in his eyes. A gleam of—sanity. And there was anger in the set of his lips. Anger for me, not Garor or the Snake.

It's not nice to have someone trampling all over your ego. Pride is a tiger—even in dreams. The subconscious, as Steve had explained to me, is a function or state of the brain, not a small part of it. In thwarting Craswell, I was disparaging not merely his dream, but his very brain, sneering at his intellectual integrity, at his abilities as an imaginative writer.

In a brief moment of rationality, I believe he was strangely aware of this.

He said quietly: "You have limitations, Nelpar. Your outward-turning eyes are blind to the pain of creation; to you the crystal stars are spangles on the dress of a scarlet woman, and you mock the God-blessed unreason that would make life more than the crawling of an animal from womb to grave. In tearing the veil from mystery, you destroy not mystery—for there are many mysteries, a million veils, world within and beyond worlds—but beauty. And in destroying beauty, you destroy your soul."

These last words, quiet as they sounded, were caught up by the curving walls of the huge tunnel, amplified then diminished in pulsing repetition, loud then soft, a surging hypnotic echo: "Destroy your SOUL, DESTROY your soul. SOUL—"

Craswell pointed with his sword. His voice was exultant. "There is a Veil, Nelpar—and you must tear it lest it become your shroud! The Mist—the Sentient Mist of the Citadel!"

I'll admit that, for a few seconds, he'd had me a little groggy. I felt—subdued. And I understood for the first time his power as a word-spinner.

I knew that it was vital for me to reassert myself.

A thick, gray mist was rolling, wreathing slowly toward us, filling the tunnel to roof-height, puffing out thick, groping tentacles.

"It lives on Life itself," Craswell shouted. "It feeds, not on flesh, but on the vital principle that animates all flesh. I am safe, Nelpar, for I have the Sword. Can your magic save you?"

"Magic!" I said. "There's no gas invented yet that'll get through a Mark 8 mask."

Gas-drill—face-piece first, straps behind the ears. No, I hadn't forgotten the old routine.

I adjusted the mask comfortably. "And if it's not gas," I added, "this will fix it." I felt over my shoulder, unclipped a nozzle, brought it round into the "ready" position.

I had only used a one-man flame-thrower once—in training—but the experience was etched on my memory.

This was a de luxe model. At the first thirty-foot oily, searing blast, the Mist curled in on itself and rolled back the way it had come. Only quicker.

I shucked off the trappings. "You were in the Army for a while, Craswell. Remember?"

The shining translucency of the walls dimmed suddenly, and beyond them I glimpsed, as in a movie close-up through an unfocused projector, the square, intense face of Steve Blakiston.

Then the walls re-formed, and Craswell, still the bronzed, naked-limbed giant of his imagination, was looking at me again, frowning, worried. "Your words are strange, O Nelpar. It seems you are master of mysteries beyond even my knowing."

I put on the sort of face I use when the sports editor queries my expenses, aggrieved, pleading. "Your trouble, Craswell, is that you don't want to know. You just won't remember. That's why you're here. But life isn't bad if you oil it a little. Why not snap out of this and come with me for a drink?"

"I do not understand," he muttered. "But we have a mission to perform. Follow." And he strode off.

Mention of drink reminded me. There was nothing wrong with my memory. And that tunnel was as hot as the green desert. I remembered a very small pub just off the streetcar depot end of Sauchiehall Street, Glasgow, Scotland. A ginger-whiskered ancient, an exile from the Highlands, who'd listened to me enthusing over a certain brand of Scotch. "If ye think that's guid, mon, ye'll no' tasted the brew from ma own private deestillery. Smack yer lips ower this, laddie—" And he'd produced an antique silver flask and poured a generous measure of golden whisky into my glass. I had never tasted such mellow nectar before or since. Until I was walking down the tunnel behind Craswell.

I nearly envisaged the glass, but changed my mind in time to make it the antique flask. I raised it to my lips. Imagination's a wonderful thing.

Craswell was talking. I'd nearly forgotten him.

". . . near the Hall of Madness, where strange music assaults the brain, weird harmonies that enchant, then kill, rupturing the very cells by a mixture of subsonic and supersonic frequencies. Listen!"

We had reached the end of the tunnel and stood at the top of a slope which, broadening, ran gently downward, veiled by a blue haze, like the smoke from fifty million cigarettes, filling a vast circular hall. The haze eddied, moved by vagrant, sluggish currents of air, and revealed on the farther side, dwarfed by distance but obviously enormous, a complex structure of pipes and consoles.

A dozen Mighty Wurlitzers rolled into one would have appeared as a miniature piano at the foot of this towering music-machine.

At its many consoles which, even at that distance, I could see consisted of at least half a dozen manuals each, were multilimbed creatures—spiders or octopuses or Polilollipops—I didn't ask what Craswell called them—I was listening.

The opening bars were strange enough, but innocuous. Then the multiple tones and harmonies began to swell in volume. I picked out the curious, sweet harshness of oboes and bassoons, the eldritch, rising ululation of a thousand violins, the keen shrilling of a hundred demonic flutes, the sobbing of many cellos. That's enough. Music's my hobby, and I don't want to get carried away in describing how that crazy symphony nearly carried me away.

But if Craswell ever reads this, I'd like him to know that he missed his vocation. He should have been a musician. His dream-music showed an amazing intuitive grasp of orchestration and harmonic theory. If he could do anything like it consciously, he would be a great modern composer.

Yet not too much like it. Because it began to have the effects he had warned about. The insidious rhythm and wild melodies seemed to throb inside my head, setting up a vibration, a burning, in the brain tissue.

Imagine Puccini's "Recondita Armonia" re-orchestrated by Stravinsky then re-arranged by Honegger, played by fifty symphony orchestras in the Hollywood Bowl, and you might begin to get the idea.

I was getting too much of it. Did I say music was my hobby? Certainly—but the only instrument I play is the harmonica. Quite well, too. And with a microphone, I can make lots of nice noise.

A microphone—and plenty of amplifiers. I pulled the harmonica from my pocket, took a deep breath, and whooped into "Tiger Rag," my favorite party-piece.

The stunning blast-wave of jubilant jazz, riffs, tiger-growls and tremolo discords from the tiny mouth organ, crashed into the vast hall from the amplifiers, completely swamping Craswell's mad music.

I heard his agonized shout even above the din. His tastes in music were evidently not as catholic as mine. He didn't like jazz.

The music-machine quavered, the multi-limbed organists, ludicrous in their haste to escape from an unreal doom, shrank, withered to scuttling black beetles; the lighting effects that had sprayed a rich, unearthly effulgence over the consoles died away into pastel, blue gloom; then the great machine itself, caught in swirl upon wave of augmented chords complemented and reinforced by its own outpourings, shivered into fragments, poured in a chaotic stream over the floor of the hall.

I heard Craswll shout again, then the scene changed abruptly. I assumed that, in his desire to blot out the triumphant paean of jazz from his mind, and perhaps in an unconscious attempt to confuse me, he had skipped a part of his plot and, in the opposite of the flashback beloved of screen writers, shot himself forward. We were—somewhere else.

Perhaps it was the inferiority complex I was inducing, or in the transition he had forgotten how tall he was supposed to be, but he was now a mere six feet, nearer my own height.

He was so hoarse, I nearly suggested a gargle. "I . . . I left you in the Hall of Madness. Your magic caused the roof to collapse. I thought you were—killed."

So the flash-forward wasn't just an attempt to confuse me. He'd tried to lose me, write me out of the script altogether.

I shook my head. "Wishful thinking, Craswell old man," I said reproachfully. "You can't kill me off between chapters. You see, I'm not one of your characters at all. Haven't you grasped that yet? The only way you can get rid of me is by waking up."

"Again you speak in riddles," he said, but there was little confidence in his voice.

The place in which we stood was a great, high-vaulted chamber. The lighting effects—as I was coming to expect—were unusual and admirable—many colored shafts of radiance from unseen sources, slowly moving, meeting and merging at the farther end of the chamber in a white, circular blaze which seemed to be suspended over a thronelike structure.

Craswell's size-concepts were stupendous. He'd either studied the biggest cathedrals in Europe, or he was reared inside Grand Central Station. The throne was apparently a good half-mile away, over a completely bare but softly resilient floor. Yet it was coming nearer. We were not walking. I looked at the walls, realized that the floor itself, a gigantic endless belt, was carrying us along.

The slow, inexorable movement was impressive. I was aware

that Craswell was covertly glancing at me. He was anxious that I should be impressed. I replied by speeding up the belt a trifle. He didn't appear to notice.

He said: "We approach the Throne of the Snake, before which, his protector and disciple, stands the female magician and sorceress, Garor. Against her, we shall need all your strange skills, Nelpar, for she stands invulnerable within an invisible shield of pure force.

"You must destroy that barrier, that I may slay her with the Sword. Without her, the Snake, though her master and self-proclaimed master of this world, is powerless, and he will be at our mercy."

The belt came to a halt. We were at the foot of a broad stairway leading to the throne itself, a massive metal platform on which the Snake reposed beneath a brilliant ball of light.

The Snake was—a snake. Coil on coil of overgrown python, with an evil head the size of a football swaying slowly from side to side.

I spent little time looking at it. I've seen snakes before. And there was something worth much more prolonged study standing just below and slightly to one side of the throne.

Craswell's taste in feminine pulchritude was unimpeachable. I had half-expected an ancient, withered horror, but if Flo Ziegfeld had seen this baby, he'd have been scrambling up those steps waving a contract, force-shield or no force-shield, before you could get out the first glissando of a wolf-whistle.

She was a tall, oval-faced, green-eyed brunette, with everything just so, and nothing much in the way of covering—a scanty metal chest-protector and a knee-length, filmy green skirt. She had a tiny, delightful mole on her left cheek.

There was a curious touch of pride in Craswell's voice as he said, rather unnecessarily: "We are here, Garor," and looked at me expectantly.

The girl said: "Insolent fools—you are here to die."

Mm-m-m—that voice, as smooth and rich as a Piatigorski cello note. I was ready to give quite a lot of credit to Craswell's imagination, but I couldn't believe that he'd dreamed up this baby just like that. I guessed that she was modelled on life; someone he knew; someone I'd like to know—someone pulled out of the grab bag of memory in the same way as I had produced Mike O'Faolin and that grubby-chinned cab driver.

"A luscious dish," I said. "Remind me to ask you later for a phone number of the original, Craswell."

Then I said and did something that I have since regretted. It was not the behavior of a gentleman. I said: "But didn't you know they were wearing skirts longer, this season?"

I looked at the skirt. The hem line shot down to her ankles, evening-gown length.

Outraged, Craswell glared at his girlfriend. The skirt became knee-length. I made it fashionable again.

Then that skirt hem was bobbing up and down between her ankles and her knees like a crazy window blind. It was a contest of wills and imaginations, with a very pretty pair of well-covered tibiae as battleground. A fascinating sight, Garor's beautiful eyes blazed with fury. She seemed to be strangely aware of the misbecoming nature of the conflict.

Craswell suddenly uttered a ringing, petulant howl of anger and frustration—a score of lusty-lunged infants whose rattles had been simultaneously snatched from them couldn't have made more noise—and the intriguing scene was erased from view in an eruption of jet-black smoke.

When it cleared, Craswell was still in the same relative position but his sword was gone, his gladiator rig was torn and scorched, and thin trickles of blood streaked his muscular arms.

I didn't like the way he was looking at me. I'd booted his super-ego pretty hard that time.

I said: "So you couldn't take it. You've skipped a chapter again. Wise me up on what I've missed, will you?" Somehow it didn't sound as flippant as I intended.

He spoke incisively. "We have been captured and condemned to die, Nelpar. We are in the Pit of the Beast, and nothing can save us, for I have been deprived of the Sword and you of your magic.

"The ravening jaws of the Beast cannot be stayed. It is the end, Nelpar. The End—"

His eyes, large, faintly luminous, looked into mine. I tried to glance away, failed.

Irritated beyond bearing by my importunate clowning, his affronted ego had assumed the whole power of his brain, to assert itself through his will—to dominate me.

The volition may have been unconscious—he could not know why he hated me—but the effect was damnable.

And for the first time since my brash intrusion into the most private recesses of his mind, I began to doubt whether the whole business was quite—decent.

Sure, I was trying to help the guy, but . . . but dreams are sacred.

Doubt negates confidence. With confidence gone, the gateway is open to fear.

Another voice, sibilant. Steve Blakiston saying, ". . . unless you let your mind go under." My own voice, ". . . wake up as a candidate for a bed in the next ward—" No, not— ". . . not unless you let your mind go under—" And Steve had been scared to do it himself, hadn't he? I'd have something to say to that guy when I got out. If I got out . . . if—

The whole thing just wasn't amusing any more.

"Quit it, Craswell," I said harshly. "Quit making goo-goo eyes, or I'll bat you one—and you'll feel it, coma or no coma."

He said: "What foolish words are these, when we are both so near to death?"

Steve's voice: ". . . sympathetic magic . . . imagination. If he imagines that one of his fantastic creations kills the hero—himself—he just won't wake up again."

That was it. A situation in which the hero must die. And he wanted to envisage my death, too. But he couldn't kill me. Or could he? How could Blakiston know what powers might be unleashed by the concept of death during this ultramundane communion of minds?

Didn't psychiatrists say that the death-urge, the will to die, was buried deep, but potent, in the subconscious minds of men? It was not buried deep here. It was glaring, exultant, starkly displayed in the eyes of Marsham Craswell.

He had escaped from reality into a dream, but it was not far enough. Death was the only full escape—

Perhaps Craswell sensed the confusion of thought and speculation that laid my mind wide open to the suggestions of his rioting, perfervid, death-intent imagination. He waved an arm with the grandiloquent gesture of a Shakespearean Chorus introducing a last act, and brought on his monster.

In detail and vividness it excelled everything that he had dreamed up previously. It was his swan-song as a creator of fantastic forms, and he had wrought well.

I saw, briefly, that we were in the center of an enormous, steep-banked amphitheater. There were no spectators. No crowd scenes for Craswell. He preferred that strange, timeless emptiness which comes from using a minimum number of characters.

Just the two of us, under the blazing rays of great, red suns swinging in a molten sky. I couldn't count them.

I became visually aware only of the Beast.

An ant in the bottom of a washbowl with a dog snuffling at it might feel the same way. If the Beast had been anything like a dog. If it had been anything like *anything*.

It was a mass the size of several elephants. An obscene hulking gob of animated, semi-transparent purple flesh, with a gaping, circular mouth or vent, ringed inside with pointed beslimed tusks, and outside with—eyes.

As a static thing, it would have been a filthy envenomed horror, a thing of surpassing dread in its mere aspect; but the most fearsome thing was its nightmarish mode of progression.

Limbless, it jerked its prodigious bulk forward in a series of heaves—and lubricated its lath with a glaucous, viscid fluid which slopped from its mouth with every jerk.

It was heading for us at an incredible pace. Thirty yards—Twenty—

The rigidity of utter fear gripped my limbs. This was true nightmare. I tried desperately to think . . . flame-thrower . . . how . . . I couldn't remember . . . my mind was slipping away from me in face of the onward surging of that protoplasmic juggernaut . . . the slime first, then the mouth, closing . . . my thoughts were a screaming turmoil—

Another voice, a deep, drawling, kindly voice, from an unforgettable hour in childhood—"There's nothing in the whole wide world or out of it that a slug from Billy here won't stop. There's nothing you can meet in dreams that Billy here won't stop. He'll come into your dreams with you from now on. There's no call to be scared of anything." Then the cool, hard butt in my hand, the recoil, the whining irresistible chunk of hot, heavy metal—deep in my subconscious.

"Pop!" I gasped. "Thanks, Pop."

The Beast was looming over me. But Billy was in my hand, pointing into the mouth. I fired.

The Beast jerked back on its slimy trail, began to dwindle, fold in on itself. I fired again and again.

I became aware once more of Craswell beside me. He looked at the dying Beast, still huge, but rapidly diminishing, then at the dull metal of the old Colt in my hand, the wisp of blue smoke from its uptilted barrel.

And then he began to laugh.

Great, gusty laughter, but with a touch of hysteria.

And as he laughed, he began to fade from view. The red suns

sped away into the sky, became pin points; and the sky was white and clean and blank—like a ceiling.

In fact—what beautiful words are "In fact"—In fact, in sweet reality, it *was* a ceiling.

Then Steve Blakiston was peering down, easing the chromium bowl off the rubber pads round my head.

"Thanks, Pete," he said. "Half an hour to the minute. You worked on him quicker than an insulin shock."

I sat up, adjusting myself mentally. He pinched my arm. "Sure—you're awake. I'd like you to tell me just what you did—but not now. I'll ring you at your office."

I saw an assistant taking the bowl off Craswell's head.

Craswell blinked, turned his head, saw me. Half a dozen expressions, none of them pleasant, chased over his face.

He heaved upright, pushed aside the assistant.

"You lousy bum," he shouted. "I'll murder you!"

I just got clear before Steve and one of the others grabbed his arms.

"Let me get at him—I'll tear him open!"

"I warned you," Steve panted. "Get out, quick."

I was on my way. Marsham Craswell in a nightshirt may not have been quite so impressive physically as the bronzed gladiator of his dreams, but he was still passably muscular.

That was last night. Steve rang this morning.

"Cured," he said triumphantly. "Sane as you are. Said he realized he'd been overworking, and he's going to take things easier—give himself a rest from fantasy and write something else. He doesn't remember a thing about his dream-coma—but he had a curious feeling that he'd still like to do something unpleasant to a certain guy who was in the next bed to him when he woke up. He doesn't know why, and I haven't told him. But better keep clear."

"The feeling is mutual," I said. "I don't like his line in monsters. What's he going to write now—love stories?"

Steve laughed. "No. He's got a sudden craze for Westerns. Started talking this morning about the sociological and historical significance of the Colt revolver. He jotted down the title of his first yarn—'Six-Gun Rule.' Hey—is that based on something you pulled on him in his dream?"

I told him.

* * *

So Marsham Craswell's as sane as me, huh? I wouldn't take bets.

Three hours ago, I was on my way to the latest heavyweight match at Madison Square Garden when I was buttonholed by an off-duty policeman.

Michael O'Faolin, the biggest, toughest, nicest cop I know.

"Pete, m'boy," he said. "I had the strangest dream last night. I was helpin' yez out of a bit of a hole, and when it was all over, you said, in gratitude it may have been, that yez might have a couple of spare tickets f'the fight this very night, and I was wondering whether it could have been a sort of tellypathy like, and—"

I grabbed the corner of the bar doorway to steady myself. Mike was still jabbering on when I fumbled for my own tickets and said: "I'm not feeling too well, Mike. You go. I'll pick my stuff up from the other sheets. Don't think about it, Mike. Just put it down to the luck of the Irish."

I went back to the bar and thought hard into a large whisky, which is the next best thing to a crystal ball for providing a focus of concentration.

"Tellypathy, huh?"

No, said the whisky. Coincidence. Forget it.

Yet there's something in telepathy. Subconscious telepathy—two dreaming minds in rapport. But I wasn't dreaming. I was just tagging along in someone else's dream. Minds are particularly receptive in sleep. Premonitions and what-have-you. But I wasn't sleeping either. Six and four makes minus ten, strike three—you're out. You're nuts, said the whisky.

I decided to find myself a better quality crystal ball. A Scotch in a crystal glass at Cevali's club.

So I hailed a Purple Cab. There was something reminiscent about the back of the driver's head. I refused to think about it. Until the payoff.

"Dollar-fifty," he growled, then leaned out. "Say—ain't I seen you some place?"

"I'm around," I said, in a voice that squeezed with reluctance past my larynx. "Didn't you drive me out to Pentagon yesterday?"

"Yeah, that's it," he said. Square unshaven jaw, low forehead, dirty red hair straggling under his cap. "Yeah—but there's something else about your pan. I took a sleep between cruises last night and had a daffy dream. You seemed to come into it. And I got the screwiest idea you already owe me a dollar-fifty."

For a moment, I toyed with the idea of telling him to go to hell. But the roadway wasn't green sand. It looked too solid to open up. So I said, "Here's five," and staggered into Cevali's.

I looked into a whisky glass until my brain began to clear, then I phoned Steve Blakiston and talked. "It's the implications," I said finally. "I'm driving myself bats trying to figure out what would have happened if I'd conjured up a few score of my acquaintances. Would they all have dreamed the same dream if they'd been asleep?"

"Too diffuse," said Steve, apparently through a mouthful of sandwich. "That would be like trying to broadcast on dozens of wavelengths simultaneously with the same transmitter. Your brain was an integral part of that machine, occupying the same position in the circuit as a complexus of recording instruments, keyed in place with Craswell's brain—until the pick-up frequency was raised. What happened then I imagined purely as an induction process. It was—as far as the Craswell hook-up was concerned, but—"

I couldn't stand the juicy champing noises any longer, and said: "Swallow it before you choke." The guy lives on sandwiches.

His voice cleared. "Don't you see what we've got? During the amplification of the cerebral currents, there was a backsurge through the tubes and the machine became a transmitter. These two guys were sleeping, their unconscious minds wide open and acting as receivers; you'd seen them during the day, envisaged them vividly—and got tuned in, disturbing their minds and giving them dreams. Ever heard of sympathetic dreams? Ever dreamed of someone you haven't seen for years, and the next day he looks you up? Now we can do it deliberately—mechanically assisted dream telepathy, the waves reinforced and transmitted electronically! Come on over. We've got to experiment some more."

"Sometimes," I said, "I sleep. That's what I intend to do now—without mechanical assistance. So long."

A nightcap was indicated. I wandered back to the club bar. I should have gone home.

She hipped her way to the microphone in front of the band, five-foot ten of dream wrapped up in a white, glove-tight gown. An oval-faced, green-eyed brunette with a tiny, delightful mole on her left cheek. The gown was a little exiguous about the upper regions, perhaps, but not as whistle-worthy as the outfit Craswell had dreamed on her.

Backstage, I got a double shot of ice from those green eyes. Yes, she knew Mr. Craswell slightly. No, she wasn't asleep around midnight last night. And would I be so good as to inform her what business it was of mine? College type, ultra. How they do drift into the entertainment business. Not that I mind.

When I asked about the refrigeration, she said: "It's merely that I have no particular desire to know you, Mr. Parnell."

"Why?"

"I'm hardly accountable to you for my preferences." She frowned as if trying to recall something, added: "In any case—I don't know. I just don't like you. Now if you'll pardon me, I have another number to sing—"

"But, please . . . let me explain—"

"Explain what?"

She had me there. I stumble-tongued, and got a back view of the gown.

How can you apologize to a girl when she doesn't even know that you owe her an apology? She hadn't been asleep, so she couldn't have dreamed about the skirt incident. And if she had—she was Craswell's dream, not mine. But through some aberration a trickle of thought waves from Blakiston's machine had planted an unreasonable antipathy to me in her subconscious mind. And it would need a psychiatrist to dig it out. Or—

I phoned Steve from the club office. He was still chewing. I said: "I've got some intensive thinking to do—into that machine of yours. I'll be right over."

She was leaving the microphone as I passed the band on my way out. I looked at her as she came up, getting every detail fixed.

"What time do you go to bed?" I asked.

I saw the slap coming and ducked.

I said: "I can wait. I'll be seeing you. Happy dreams."

MARS IS HEAVEN!

by Ray Bradbury

PLANET STORIES
Fall

"Mars is Heaven" is one of the most famous stories that form a part of The Martian Chronicles, *one of the cornerstones of modern science fiction. Tremendously moving, it is at the same time a terrifying story, for it concerns people confronted by* shape-changers, *creatures that look like something they are not. The concept of the shape-changer seems to tap into the psyche of human beings—they (and their close relation the* possessor*) always seem to frighten us, as the commercial success of the movie* The Thing *(1982) testifies.*

Bradbury's skill is so great that the obvious impossibilities of his Martian landscape do not really bother us.

(It seems to me that when I was young, the stories I read were populated exclusively by people who either lived in small towns [preferably midwestern] or who lived in big cities and were spiritually lost and longed to return to the small towns from which they had come. That made me worry about myself. I was indeed born in a small town, but not in the United States, and I arrived in New York City at such a young age that I

remember nothing else. What's more, I love New York City and don't want to live in a small town. They make me feel rather an outsider. Even in science fiction, which we ordinarily think of as future-oriented and technophilic, we have the small-town syndrome with Ray Bradbury and Clifford Simak as the most skillful exploiters thereof. My favorite science-fictional small town, however, is by all odds the one in "Mars is Heaven!" That is how small towns ought to be [in my own prejudiced mind].—I.A.)

The ship came down from space. It came down from the stars and the black velocities, and the shining movements and the silent gulfs of space. It was a new ship, the only one of its kind, it had fire in its belly and men in its body, and it moved with clean silence, fiery and hot. In it were seventeen men, including a captain. A crowd had gathered at the New York tarmac and shouted and waved their hands up into the sunlight, and the rocket had jerked up, bloomed out great flowers of heat and color, and run away into space on the first voyage to Mars!

Now it was decelerating with metal efficiency in the upper zones of Martian atmosphere. It was still a thing of beauty and strength. It had shorn through meteor streams, it had moved in the majestic black midnight waters of space like a pale sea leviathan, it had passed the sickly, pocked mass of the ancient moon, and thrown itself onward into one nothingness following another. The men within it had been battered, thrown about, sickened, made well again, scarred, made pale, flushed, each in his turn. One man had died after a fall, but now, seventeen of the original eighteen with their eyes clear in their heads and their faces pressed to the thick glass ports of the rocket, were watching Mars swing up under them.

"Mars! Mars! Good old Mars, here we are!" cried Navigator Lustig.

"Good old Mars!" said Samuel Hinkston, archaeologist.

"Well," said Captain John Black.

The ship landed softly on a lawn of green grass. Outside, upon the lawn, stood an iron deer. Farther up the lawn, a tall brown Victorian house sat in the quiet sunlight, all covered with scrolls and rococo, its windows made of blue and pink and yellow and green colored glass. Upon the porch were hairy geraniums and an old swing which was hooked into the porch ceiling and which now swung back and forth, back and forth, in a little breeze. At the top of the house was a cupola with diamond, leaded-glass windows, and a dunce-cap roof! Through the front window you could see an ancient piano with yellow keys and a piece of music titled *Beautiful Ohio* sitting on the music rest.

Around the rocket in four directions spread the little town, green and motionless in the Martian spring. There were white houses and red brick ones, and tall elm trees blowing in the wind, and tall maples and horse chestnuts. And church steeples with golden bells silent in them.

The men in the rocket looked out and saw this. Then they looked at one another and then they looked out again. They held on to each other's elbows, suddenly unable to breathe, it seemed. Their faces grew pale and they blinked constantly, running from glass port to glass port of the ship.

"I'll be damned," whispered Lustig, rubbing his face with his numb fingers, his eyes wet. "I'll be damned, damned, damned."

"It can't be, it just can't be," said Samuel Hinkston.

"Lord," said Captain John Black.

There was a call from the chemist. "Sir, the atmosphere is fine for breathing, sir."

Black turned slowly. "Are you sure?"

"No doubt of it, sir."

"Then we'll go out," said Lustig.

"Lord, yes," said Samuel Hinkston.

"Hold on," said Captain John Black. "Just a moment. Nobody gave any orders."

"But, sir—"

"Sir, nothing. How do we know what this is?"

"We know what it is, sir," said the chemist. "It's a small town with good air in it, sir."

"And it's a small town the like of Earth towns," said Samuel Hinkston, the archaeologist. "Incredible. It can't be, but it is."

Captain John Black looked at him, idly. "Do you think that the civilizations of two planets can progress at the same rate and evolve in the same way, Hinkston?"

"I wouldn't have thought so, sir."

Captain Black stood by the port. "Look out there. The geraniums. A specialized plant. That specific variety has only been known on Earth for fifty years. Think of the thousands of years of time it takes to evolve plants. Then tell me if it is logical that the Martians should have: one, leaded glass windows; two, cupolas; three, porch swings; four, an instrument that looks like a piano and probably is a piano; and, five, if you look closely, if a Martian composer would have published a piece of music titled, strangely enough, *Beautiful Ohio*. All of which means that we have an Ohio River here on Mars!"

"It is quite strange, sir."

"Strange, hell, it's absolutely impossible, and I suspect the whole bloody shooting setup. Something's wrong here, and I'm not leaving the ship until I know what it is."

"Oh, sir," said Lustig.

"Darn it," said Samuel Hinkston. "Sir, I want to investigate this at first hand. It may be that there are similar patterns of thought, movement, civilization on *every* planet in our system. We may be on the threshold of the great psychological and metaphysical discovery in our time, sir, don't you think?"

"I'm willing to wait a moment," said Captain John Black.

"It may be, sir, that we are looking upon a phenomenon that, for the first time, would absolutely prove the existence of a God, sir."

"There are many people who are of good faith without such proof, Mr. Hinkston."

"I'm one myself, sir. But certainly a thing like this, out there," said Hinkston, "could not occur without divine intervention, sir. It fills me with such terror and elation I don't know whether to laugh or cry, sir."

"Do neither, then, until we know what we're up against."

"Up against, sir?" inquired Lustig. "I see that we're up against nothing. It's a good quiet, green town, much like the one I was born in, and I like the looks of it."

"When were you born, Lustig?"

"In 1910, sir."

"That makes you fifty years old now, doesn't it?"

"This being 1960, yes, sir."

"And you, Hinkston?"

"1920, sir. In Illinois. And this looks swell to me, sir."

"This couldn't be Heaven," said the captain, ironically. "Though, I must admit, it looks peaceful and cool, and pretty much like Green Bluff, where I was born, in 1915." He looked at the chemist. "The air's all right, is it?"

"Yes, sir."

"Well, then, tell you what we'll do. Lustig, you and Hinkston and I will fetch ourselves out to look this town over. The other 14 men will stay aboard ship. If anything untoward happens, lift the ship and get the hell out, do you hear what I say, Craner?"

"Yes, sir. The hell out we'll go, sir. Leaving *you*?"

"A loss of three men's better than a whole ship. If something bad happens get back to Earth and warn the next Rocket, that's Lingle's Rocket, I think, which will be completed and ready to take off some time around next Christmas, what he has to meet up with. If there's something hostile about Mars we certainly want the next expedition to be well armed."

"So are we, sir. We've got a regular arsenal with us."

"Tell the men to stand by the guns, then, as Lustig and Hinkston and I go out."

"Right, sir."

"Come along, Lustig, Hinkston."

The three men walked together, down through the levels of the ship.

It was a beautiful spring day. A robin sat on a blossoming apple tree and sang continuously. Showers of petal snow sifted down when the wind touched the apple tree, and the blossom smell drifted upon the air. Somewhere in the town, somebody was playing the piano and the music came and went, came and went, softly, drowsily. The song was *Beautiful Dreamer*. Somewhere else, a phonograph, scratchy and faded, was hissing out a record of *Roamin' In The Gloamin'*, sung by Harry Lauder.

The three men stood outside the ship. The port closed behind them. At every window, a face pressed, looking out. The large metal guns pointed this way and that, ready.

Now the phonograph record being played was:

"Oh give me a June night
The moonlight and you—"

Lustig began to tremble. Samuel Hinkston did likewise.

Hinkston's voice was so feeble and uneven that the captain had to ask him to repeat what he had said. "I said, sir, that I think I have solved this, all of this, sir!"

"And what is the solution, Hinkston?"

The soft wind blew. The sky was serene and quiet and somewhere a stream of water ran through the cool caverns and tree shadings of a ravine. Somewhere a horse and wagon trotted and rolled by, bumping.

"Sir, it must be, it has to be, this is the *only* solution! Rocket travel began to Mars in the years before the first World War, sir!"

The captain stared at his archaeologist. "No!"

"But, yes, sir! You must admit, look at all of this! How else explain it, the houses, the lawns, the iron deer, the flowers, the pianos, the music!"

"Hinkston, Hinkston, oh," and the captain put his hand to his face, shaking his head, his hand shaking now, his lips blue.

"Sir, listen to me." Hinkston took his elbow persuasively and looked up into the captain's face, pleading. "Say that there were some people in the year 1905, perhaps, who hated wars and wanted to get away from Earth and they got together, some scientists, in secret, and built a rocket and came out here to Mars."

"No, no, Hinkston."

"Why not? The world was a different place in 1905, they could have kept it a secret much more easily."

"But the work, Hinkston, the work of building a complex thing like a rocket, oh, no, no." The captain looked at his shoes, looked at his hands, looked at the houses, and then at Hinkston.

"And they came up here, and naturally the houses they built were similar to Earth houses because they brought the cultural architecture with them, and here it is!"

"And they've lived here all these years?" said the captain.

"In peace and quiet, sir, yes. Maybe they made a few trips, to bring enough people here for one small town, and then stopped, for fear of being discovered. That's why the town seems so old-fashioned. I don't see a thing, myself, that is older than the year 1927, do you?"

"No, frankly, I don't, Hinkston."

"These are *our* people, sir. This is an American city; it's definitely not European!"

"That—that's right, too, Hinkston."

"Or maybe, just maybe, sir, rocket travel is older than we think. Perhaps it started in some part of the world hundreds of years ago, was discovered and kept secret by a small number of men, and they came to Mars, with only occasional visits to Earth over the centuries."

"You make it sound almost reasonable."

"It is, sir. It has to be. We have the proof here before us, all we have to do now, is find some people and verify it!"

"You're right there, of course. We can't just stand here and talk. Did you bring your gun?"

"Yes, but we won't need it."

"We'll see about it. Come along, we'll ring that doorbell and see if anyone is home."

Their boots were deadened of all sound in the thick green grass. It smelled from a fresh mowing. In spite of himself, Captain John Black felt a great peace come over him. It had been thirty years since he had been in a small town, and the buzzing of spring bees on the air lulled and quieted him, and the fresh look of things was a balm to the soul.

Hollow echoes sounded from under the boards as they walked across the porch and stood before the screen door. Inside, they could see a bead curtain hung across the hall entry, and a crystal chandelier and a Maxfield Parrish painting framed on one wall over a comfortable Morris Chair. The house smelled old, and of the attic, and infinitely comfortable. You could hear the tinkle of ice rattling in a lemonade pitcher. In a distant kitchen, because of the heat of the day, someone was preparing a soft, lemon drink.

Captain John Black rang the bell.

Footsteps, dainty and thin, came along the hall and a kind-faced lady of some forty years, dressed in the sort of dress you might expect in the year 1909, peered out at them.

"Can I help you?" she asked.

"Beg your pardon," said Captain Black, uncertainly. "But we're looking for, that is, could you help us, I mean." He stopped. She looked out at him with dark wondering eyes.

"If you're selling something," she said. "I'm much too busy and I haven't time." She turned to go.

"No, *wait*," he cried, bewilderedly. "What town is this?"

She looked him up and down as if he were crazy. "What do you mean, what town is it? How could you be in a town and not know what town it was?"

The captain looked as if he wanted to go sit under a shady apple tree. "I beg your pardon," he said. "But we're strangers here. We're from Earth, and we want to know how this town got here and you got here."

"Are you census takers?" she asked.

"No," he said.

"What do you want then?" she demanded.

"Well," said the captain.

"Well?" she asked.

"How long has this town been here?" he wondered.

"It was built in 1868," she snapped at them. "Is this a game?"

"No, not a game," cried the captain. "Oh, God," he said. "Look here. We're from Earth!"

"From *where*?" she said.

"From Earth!" he said.

"Where's that?" she said.

"From Earth," he cried.

"Out of the ground, do you mean?"

"No, from the planet Earth!" he almost shouted. "Here," he insisted, "come out on the porch and I'll show you."

"No," she said, "I won't come out there, you are all evidently quite mad from the sun."

Lustig and Hinkston stood behind the captain. Hinkston now spoke up. "Mrs.," he said. "We came in a flying ship across space, among the stars. We came from the third planet from the sun, Earth, to this planet, which is Mars. *Now* do you understand, Mrs.?"

"Mad from the sun," she said, taking hold of the door. "Go away now, before I call my husband who's upstairs taking a nap, and he'll beat you all with his fists."

"But—" said Hinkston. "This is Mars, is it not?"

"This," explained the woman, as if she were addressing a child, "is Green Lake, Wisconsin, on the continent of America, surrounded by the Pacific and Atlantic Oceans, on a place called the world, or sometimes, the Earth. Go away now. Good-bye!"

She slammed the door.

The three men stood before the door with their hands up in the air toward it, as if pleading with her to open it once more.

They looked at one another.

"Let's knock the door down," said Lustig.

"We can't," sighed the captain.

"Why not?"

"She didn't do anything bad, did she? We're the strangers here. This is private property. Good God, Hinkston!" He went and sat down on the porchstep.

"What, sir?"

"Did it ever strike you, that maybe we got ourselves, somehow, some way, fouled up. And, by accident, came back and landed on Earth!''

''Oh, sir, oh, sir, oh oh, sir.'' And Hinkston sat down numbly and thought about it.

Lustig stood up in the sunlight. ''How could we have done that?''

''I don't know, just let me think.''

Hinkston said, ''But we checked every mile of the way, and we saw Mars and our chronometers said so many miles gone, and we went past the moon and out into space and here we are, on Mars. I'm sure we're on Mars, sir.''

Lustig said, ''But, suppose, just suppose that, by accident, in space, in time, or something, we landed on a planet in space, in another time. Suppose this is Earth, thirty or fifty years ago? Maybe we got lost in the dimensions, do you think?''

''Oh, go away, Lustig.''

''Are the men in the ship keeping an eye on us, Hinkston?''

''At their guns, sir.''

Lustig went to the door, rang the bell. When the door opened again, he asked, ''What year is this?''

''1926, of course!'' cried the woman, furiously, and slammed the door again.

''Did you hear that?'' Lustig ran back to them, wildly. ''She said 1926! We *have* gone back in time! This *is* Earth!''

Lustig sat down and the three men let the wonder and terror of the thought afflict them. Their hands stirred fitfully on their knees. The wind blew, nodding the locks of hair on their heads.

The captain stood up, brushing off his pants. ''I never thought it would be like this. It scares the hell out of me. How can a thing like this happen?''

''Will anybody in the whole town believe us?'' wondered Hinkston. ''Are we playing around with something dangerous? Time, I mean. Shouldn't we just take off and go home?''

''No. We'll try another house.''

They walked three houses down to a little white cottage under an oak tree. ''I like to be as logical as I can get,'' said the captain. He nodded at the town. ''How does this sound to you, Hinkston? Suppose, as you said originally, that rocket travel occurred years ago. And when the Earth people had lived here a number of years they began to get homesick for Earth. First a mild neurosis about it, then a full-fledged psychosis. Then, threatened insanity. What would you do, as a psychiatrist, if faced with such a problem?''

Hinkston thought. ''Well, I think I'd re-arrange the civilization on Mars so it resembled Earth more and more each day. If there was any way of reproducing every plant, every road and every lake, and even an ocean, I would do so. Then I would, by some vast crowd hypnosis, theoretically anyway, convince everyone in a town this size that this really *was* Earth, not Mars at all.''

''Good enough, Hinkston. I think we're on the right track now. That woman in that house back there, just *thinks* she's living on Earth. It protects her sanity. She and all the others in this town are the patients of the greatest experiment in migration and hypnosis you will ever lay your eyes on in your life.''

''That's it, sir!'' cried Lustig.

''Well,'' the captain sighed. ''Now we're getting somewhere. I feel better. It all sounds a bit more logical now. This talk about time and going back and forth and traveling in time turns my stomach upside down. But, *this* way—'' He actually smiled for the first time in a month. ''Well. It looks as if we'll be fairly welcome here.''

''Or, will we, sir?'' said Lustig. ''After all, like the Pilgrims, these people came here to escape Earth. Maybe they won't be too happy to see us, sir. Maybe they'll try to drive us out or kill us?''

''We have superior weapons if that should happen. Anyway, all we can do is try. This next house now. Up we go.''

But they had hardly crossed the lawn when Lustig stopped and looked off across the town, down the quiet, dreaming afternoon street. ''Sir,'' he said.

''What is it, Lustig?'' asked the captain.

''Oh, sir, *sir*, what I see, what I do see now before me, oh, oh—'' said Lustig, and he began to cry. His fingers came up, twisting and trembling, and his face was all wonder and joy and incredulity. He sounded as if any moment he might go quite insane with happiness. He looked down the street and he began to run, stumbling, awkwardly, falling, picking himself up, and running on. ''Oh, God, God, thank you, God! Thank you!''

''Don't let him get away!'' The captain broke into a run.

Now Lustig was running at full speed, shouting. He turned into a yard halfway down the little shady side street and leaped up upon the porch of a large green house with an iron rooster on the roof.

He was beating upon the door, shouting and hollering and crying when Hinkston and the captain ran up and stood in the yard.

The door opened. Lustig yanked the screen wide and in a high wail of discovery and happiness, cried out, "Grandma! Grandpa!"

Two old people stood in the doorway, their faces lighting up.

"Albert!" Their voices piped and they rushed out to embrace and pat him on the back and move around him. "Albert, oh, Albert, it's been so many years! How you've grown, boy, how big you are, boy, oh, Albert boy, how are you!"

"Grandma, Grandpa!" sobbed Albert Lustig. "Good to see you! You look fine, fine! Oh, fine!" He held them, turned them, kissed them, hugged them, cried on them, held them out again, blinked at the little old people. The sun was in the sky, the wind blew, the grass was green, the screen door stood open.

"Come in, lad, come in, there's lemonade for you, fresh, lots of it!"

"Grandma, Grandpa, good to see you! I've got friends down here! Here!" Lustig turned and waved wildly at the captain and Hinkston, who, all during the adventure on the porch, had stood in the shade of a tree, holding onto each other. "Captain, captain, come up, come up, I want you to meet my grandfolks!"

"Howdy," said the folks. "Any friend of Albert's is ours, too! Don't stand there with your mouth open! Come on!"

In the living room of the old house it was cool and a grandfather clock ticked high and long and bronzed in one corner. There were soft pillows on large couches and walls filled with books and a rug cut in a thick rose pattern and antimacassars pinned to furniture, and lemonade in the hand, sweating, and cool on the thirsty tongue.

"Here's to our health." Grandma tipped her glass to her porcelain teeth.

"How long you *been* here, Grandma?" said Lustig.

"A good many years," she said tartly. "Ever since we died."

"Ever since you what?" asked Captain John Black, putting his drink down.

"Oh, yes," Lustig looked at his captain. "They've been dead thirty years."

"And you *sit* there, calmly!" cried the captain.

"Tush," said the old woman, and winked glitteringly at John Black. "Who are we to question what happens? Here we are. What's life, anyways? Who does what for why and where? All we know is here we are, alive again, and no questions asked. A second chance." She toddled over and held out her thin wrist to Captain John Black. "Feel." He felt. "Solid, ain't I?" she asked. He nodded. "You hear my voice, don't you?" she inquired. Yes, he did. "Well, then," she said in triumph, "why go around questioning?"

"Well," said the captain, "it's simply that we never thought we'd find a thing like this on Mars."

"And now you've found it. I dare say there's lots on every planet that'll show you God's infinite ways."

"Is this Heaven?" asked Hinkston.

"Nonsense, no. It's a world and we get a second chance. Nobody told us why. But then nobody told us why we were on Earth, either. That *other* Earth, I mean. The one you came from. How do we know there wasn't *another* before *that* one?"

"A good question," said the captain.

The captain stood up and slapped his hand on his leg in an off-hand fashion. "We've got to be going. It's been nice. Thank you for the drinks."

He stopped. He turned and looked toward the door, startled.

Far away, in the sunlight, there was a sound of voices, a crowd, a shouting and a great hello.

"What's that?" asked Hinkston.

"We'll soon find out!" And Captain John Black was out the front door abruptly, jolting across the green lawn and into the street of the Martian town.

He stood looking at the ship. The ports were open and his crew were streaming out, waving their hands. A crowd of people had gathered and in and through and among these people the members of the crew were running, talking, laughing, shaking hands. People did little dances. People swarmed. The rocket lay empty and abandoned.

A brass band exploded in the sunlight, flinging off a gay tune from upraised tubas and trumpets. There was a bang of drums and a shrill of fifes. Little girls with golden hair jumped up and down. Little boys shouted, "Hooray!" And fat men passed around ten-cent cigars. The mayor of the town made a speech. Then, each member of the crew with a mother on one arm, a father or sister on the other, was spirited off down the street, into little cottages or big mansions and doors slammed shut.

The wind rose in the clear spring sky and all was silent. The brass band had banged off around a corner leaving the rocket to shine and dazzle alone in the sunlight.

''Abandoned!'' cried the captain. ''Abandoned the ship, they did! I'll have their skins, by God! They had orders!''

''Sir,'' said Lustig. ''Don't be too hard on them. Those were all old relatives and friends.''

''That's no excuse!''

''Think how they felt, captain, seeing familiar faces outside the ship!''

''I would have obeyed orders! I would have—'' The captain's mouth remained open.

Striding along the sidewalk under the Martian sun, tall, smiling, eyes blue, face tan, came a young man of some twenty-six years.

''John!'' the man cried, and broke into a run.

''What?'' said Captain John Black. He swayed.

''John, you old beggar, you!''

The man ran up and gripped his hand and slapped him on the back.

''It's you,'' said John Black.

''Of course, who'd you *think* it was!''

''Edward!'' The captain appealed now to Lustig and Hinkston, holding the stranger's hand. ''This is my brother Edward. Ed, meet my men, Lustig, Hinkston! My brother!''

They tugged at each other's hands and arms and then finally embraced. ''Ed!'' ''John, you old bum, you!'' ''You're looking fine, Ed, but, Ed, what is this? You haven't changed over the years. You died, I remember, when you were twenty-six, and I was nineteen, oh God, so many years ago, and here you are, and, Lord, what goes on, what goes on?''

Edward Black gave him a brotherly knock on the chin. ''Mom's waiting,'' he said.

''Mom?''

''And Dad, too.''

''And Dad?'' The captain almost fell to earth as if hit upon the chest with a mighty weapon. He walked stiffly and awkwardly, out of coordination. He stuttered and whispered and talked only one or two words at a time. ''Mom alive? Dad? Where?''

''At the old house on Oak Knoll Avenue.''

''The old house.'' The captain stared in delighted amazement. ''Did you *hear* that, Lustig, Hinkston?''

''I know it's hard for you to believe.''

''But alive. Real.''

''Don't I *feel* real?'' The strong arm, the firm grip, the white smile. The light, curling hair.

Hinkston was gone. He had seen his own house down the

street and was running for it. Lustig was grinning. "Now you understand, sir, what happened to everybody on the ship. They couldn't help themselves."

"Yes. Yes," said the captain, eyes shut. "Yes." He put out his hand. "When I open my eyes, you'll be gone." He opened his eyes. "You're still here. God, Edward, you look fine!"

"Come along, lunch is waiting for you. I told Mom."

Lustig said, "Sir, I'll be with my grandfolks if you want me."

"What? Oh fine, Lustig. Later, then."

Edward grabbed his arm and marched him. "You need support."

"I do. My knees, all funny. My stomach, loose. God."

"There's the house. Remember it?"

"Remember it? Hell! I bet I can beat you to the front porch!"

They ran. The wind roared over Captain John Black's ears. The earth roared under his feet. He saw the golden figure of Edward Black pull ahead of him in the amazing dream of reality. He saw the house rush forward, the door open, the screen swing back. "Beat you!" cried Edward, bounding up the steps. "I'm an old man," panted the captain, "and you're still young. But, then, you *always* beat me, I remember!"

In the doorway, Mom, pink and plump and bright. And behind her, pepper grey, Dad, with his pipe in his hand.

"Mom, Dad!"

He ran up the steps like a child, to meet them.

It was a fine long afternoon. They finished lunch and they sat in the living room and he told them all about his rocket and his being captain and they nodded and smiled upon him and Mother was just the same, and Dad bit the end off a cigar and lighted it in his old fashion. Mom brought in some iced tea in the middle of the afternoon. Then, there was a big turkey dinner at night and time flowing on. When the drumsticks were sucked clean and lay brittle upon the plates, the captain leaned back in his chair and exhaled his deep contentment. Dad poured him a small glass of dry sherry. It was seven-thirty in the evening. Night was in all the trees and coloring the sky, and the lamps were halos of dim light in the gentle house. From all the other houses down the streets came sounds of music, pianos playing, laughter.

Mom put a record on the victrola and she and Captain John Black had a dance. She was wearing the same perfume he remembered from the summer when she and Dad had been killed in the train accident. She was very real in his arms as they danced lightly to the music.

"I'll wake in the morning," said the captain. "And I'll be in my rocket in space, and all this will be gone."

"No, no, don't think that," she cried softly, pleadingly. "We're here. Don't question. God is good to us. Let's be happy."

The record ended with a circular hissing.

"You're tired, son," said Dad. He waved his pipe. "You and Ed go on upstairs. Your old bedroom is waiting for you."

"The old one?"

"The brass bed and all," laughed Edward.

"But I should report my men in."

"Why?" Mother was logical.

"Why? Well, I don't know. No reason, I guess. No, none at all. What's the difference?" He shook his head. "I'm not being very logical these days."

"Good night, son." She kissed his cheek.

" 'Night, Mom."

"Sleep tight, son." Dad shook his hand.

"Same to you, Pop."

"It's good to have you home."

"It's good to *be* home."

He left the land of cigar smoke and perfume and books and gentle light and ascended the stairs, talking, talking with Edward. Edward pushed a door open and there was the yellow brass bed and the old semaphore banners from college days and a very musty raccoon coat which he petted with strange, muted affection. "It's too much," he said faintly. "Like being in a thunder shower without an umbrella. I'm soaked to the skin with emotion. I'm numb. I'm tired."

"A night's sleep between cool clean sheets for you, my bucko." Edward slapped wide the snowy linens and flounced the pillows. Then he put up a window and let the night-blooming jasmine float in. There was moonlight and the sound of distant dancing and whispering.

"So this is Mars," said the captain undressing.

"So this is Mars." Edward undressed in idle, leisurely moves, drawing his shirt off over his head, revealing golden shoulders and the good muscular neck.

The lights were out, they were into bed, side by side, as in the days, how many decades ago? The captain lolled and was nourished by the night wind pushing the lace curtains out upon the dark room air. Among the trees, upon a lawn, someone had cranked up a portable phonograph and now it was playing softly, "I'll be loving you, always, with a love that's true, always."

The thought of Anna came to his mind. "Is Anna here?"

His brother, lying straight out in the moonlight from the window, waited and then said, "Yes. She's out of town. But she'll be here in the morning."

The captain shut his eyes. "I want to see Anna very much."

The room was square and quiet except for their breathing. "Good night, Ed."

A pause. "Good night, John."

He lay peacefully, letting his thoughts float. For the first time the stress of the day was moved aside, all of the excitement was calmed. He could think logically now. It had all been emotion. The bands playing, the sight of familiar faces, the sick pounding of your heart. But—now . . .

How? He thought. How was all this made? And why? For what purpose? Out of the goodness of some kind God? Was God, then, really that fine and thoughtful of His children? How and why and what for?

He thought of the various theories advanced in the first heat of the afternoon by Hinkston and Lustig. He let all kinds of new theories drop in lazy pebbles down through his mind, as through a dark water, now, turning, throwing out dull flashes of white light. Mars. Earth. Mom. Dad. Edward. Mars. Martians.

Who had lived here a thousand years ago on Mars? Martians? Or had this always been like this? Martians. He repeated the word quietly, inwardly.

He laughed out loud, almost. He had the most ridiculous theory, all of a sudden. It gave him a kind of chilled feeling. It was really nothing to think of, of course. Highly improbable. Silly. Forget it. Ridiculous.

But, he thought, just suppose. Just *suppose* now, that there were Martians living on Mars and they saw our ship coming and saw us inside our ship and hated us. Suppose, now, just for the hell of it, that they wanted to destroy us, as invaders, as unwanted ones, and they wanted to do it in a very clever way, so that we would be taken off guard. Well, what would the best weapon be that a Martian could use against Earthmen with atom weapons?

The answer was interesting. Telepathy, hypnosis, memory and imagination.

Suppose all these houses weren't real at all, this bed not real, but only figments of my own imagination, given substance by telepathy and hypnosis by the Martians.

Suppose these houses are really some other shape, a Martian shape, but, by playing on my desires and wants, these Martians have made this seem like my old home town, my old house, to lull me out of my suspicions? What better way to fool a man, than by his own emotions.

And suppose those two people in the next room, asleep, are not my mother and father at all. But two Martians, incredibly brilliant, with the ability to keep me under this dreaming hypnosis all of the time?

And that brass band, today? What a clever plan it would be. First, fool Lustig, then fool Hinkston, then gather a crowd around the rocket ship and wave. And all the men in the ship, seeing mothers, aunts, uncles, sweethearts dead ten, twenty years ago, naturally, disregarding orders, would rush out and abandon the ship. What more natural? What more unsuspecting? What more simple? A man doesn't ask too many questions when his mother is suddenly brought back to life; he's much too happy. And the brass band played and everybody was taken off to private homes. And here we all are, tonight, in various houses, in various beds, with no weapons to protect us, and the rocket lies in the moonlight, empty. And wouldn't it be horrible and terrifying to discover that all of this was part of some great clever plan by the Martians to divide and conquer us, and kill us. Some time during the night, perhaps, my brother here on this bed, will change form, melt, shift, and become a one-eyed, green-and-yellow-toothed Martian. It would be very simple for him just to turn over in bed and put a knife into my heart. And in all those other houses down the street a dozen other brothers or fathers suddenly melting away and taking out knives and doing things to the unsuspecting, sleeping men of Earth.

His hands were shaking under the covers. His body was cold. Suddenly it was not a theory. Suddenly he was very afraid. He lifted himself in bed and listened. The night was very quiet. The music had stopped. The wind had died. His brother (?) lay sleeping beside him.

Very carefully he lifted the sheets, rolled them back. He slipped from bed and was walking softly across the room when his brother's voice said, "Where are you going?"

"What?"

His brother's voice was quite cold. "I said, where do you think you're going?"

"For a drink of water."

"But you're not thirsty."

"Yes, yes, I am."

"No, you're not."

Captain John Black broke and ran across the room. He screamed. He screamed twice.

He never reached the door.

In the morning, the brass band played a mournful dirge. From every house in the street came little solemn processions bearing long boxes and along the sun-filled street, weeping and changing, came the grandmas and grandfathers and mothers and sisters and brothers, walking to the churchyard, where there were open holes dug freshly and new tombstones installed. Seventeen holes in all, and seventeen tombstones. Three of the tombstones said, CAPTAIN JOHN BLACK, ALBERT LUSTIG, and SAMUEL HINKSTON.

The mayor made a little sad speech, his face sometimes looking like the mayor, sometimes looking like something else.

Mother and Father Black were there, with Brother Edward, and they cried, their faces melting now from a familiar face into something else.

Grandpa and Grandma Lustig were there, weeping, their faces also shifting like wax, shivering as a thing does in waves of heat on a summer day.

The coffins were lowered. Somebody murmured about "the unexpected and sudden deaths of seventeen fine men during the night—"

Earth was shoveled in on the coffin tops.

After the funeral the brass band slammed and banged back into town and the crowd stood around and waved and shouted as the rocket was torn to pieces and strewn about and blown up.

THANG

by Martin Gardner (1914–)

COMMENT
Fall

Martin Gardner is an excellent science writer whose humorous and challenging puzzle stories appear regularly in Isaac Asimov's Science Fiction Magazine. *He is also the author of such outstanding books as* Fads and Fallacies in the Name of Science *(1957),* The Annotated Alice *(1960),* The Ambidextrous Universe *(1964), and many others. In addition, he has written the Mathematical Games feature in* Scientific American *for many years.*

"Thang" is the best of his too few science fiction stories.

(The first time I ever met Martin Gardner, I said to him, "Mr. Gardner, I've got every one of your books that I could find and I am such an admirer of your style that I do my best to imitate it." And he replied to me, "Isn't that strange? I do my best to imitate yours."

Some years later, I nominated him for membership in "The Trap Door Spiders," a small grouping of highly intelligent and articulate people who find no music more enticing and compelling than the sounds of each other's voices, and who each makes sense out of the cacophony by listening only to his own. Why Martin should enjoy the group when he is so quiet himself, I don't know, but enjoy it, he did, and we enjoyed him, until he decided to retire and move to North Carolina, something for which I will never forgive him. I miss him so *badly.—I.A.)*

The Earth had completed another turn about the sun, whirling slowly and silently as it always whirled. The East had experienced a record-breaking crop of yellow rice and yellow children, larger stockpiles of atomic weapons were accumulating in certain strategic centers, and the sages of the University of Chicago were uttering words of profound wisdom, when Thang reached down and picked up the Earth between his thumb and finger.

Thang had been sleeping. When he finally awoke and blinked his six opulent eyes at the blinding light (for the light of our stars when viewed in their totality is no thing of dimness) he had become uncomfortably aware of an empty feeling near the pit of his stomach. How long he had been sleeping even he did not know exactly, for in the mind of Thang time is a term of no significance. Although the ways of Thang are beyond the ways of men, and the thoughts of Thang scarcely conceivable by our thoughts; still—stating the matter roughly and in the language we know—the ways of Thang are this: When Thang is not asleep, he hungers.

After blinking his opulent eyes (in a specific consecutive order which had long been his habit) and stretching forth a long arm to sweep aside the closer suns, Thang squinted into the deep. The riper planets were near the center and usually could be recognized by surface texture; but frequently Thang had to thump them with his middle finger. It was some time until he found a piece that suited him. He picked it up with his right hand and shook off most of the adhering salty moisture. Other fingers scaled away thin flakes of bluish ice that had caked on opposite sides. Finally, he dried the ball completely by rubbing it on his chest.

He bit into it. It was soft and juicy, neither unpleasantly hot nor freezing to the tongue; and Thang, who always ate the entire planet, core and all, lay back contentedly, chewing slowly and permitting his thoughts to dwell idly on trivial matters, when he felt himself picked up suddenly by the back of the neck.

He was jerked upward and backward by an arm of tremendous bulk (an arm covered with greyish hair and exuding a foul smell). Then he was lowered even more rapidly. He looked down in time to see an enormous mouth—red and gaping and watering around the edges—then the blackness closed over him with a slurp like a clap of thunder.

For there are other gods than Thang.

BROOKLYN PROJECT

by William Tenn

PLANET STORIES
Fall

One of the most interesting of the several types of time travel story are those that suggest that a tiny change in some seeming minor aspect of the past might result in tremendous changes in the present. Perhaps the most famous story of this type is Ray Bradbury's "A Sound of Thunder" (1952). Here, the witty and urbane Professor Klass turns his attention to this concept, with entertaining and chilling effect.

(Every once in a while, I amuse myself with thoughts of the unknowable:

1) You know what your senses tell you; but how can you find out what other peoples' senses tell them? X and Y both agree that a rose is something each calls "red," but what does "red" look like to X and Y? The same?

2) Suppose the Universe is expanding steadily and rapidly, everything in it—everything including you and every part of you and all the atoms that make up you and everything else. Could you tell? Would it matter? Or suppose everything was contracting—or sometimes contracting or expanding?

3) Suppose the Earth and the Universe were created 6,000 years ago, with all the fossils in place, with the light from the stars en route to us, and all the evidence pointing to a big bang having taken place 15 billion years ago. How could we tell? For that matter, suppose it were all created one second ago, with each of us at our present age and created with all our present memories? How could we tell?

4) Suppose every once in a while, people traveled into the past and changed everything radically and that all of us exist now because such a change has just taken place———

Oh, well, you see what I mean.—I. A.)

The gleaming bowls of light set in the creamy ceiling dulled when the huge, circular door at the back of the booth opened. They returned to white brilliance as the chubby man in the severe black jumper swung the door shut behind him and dogged it down again.

Twelve reporters of both sexes exhaled very loudly as he sauntered to the front of the booth and turned his back to the semi-opaque screen stretching across it. Then they all rose in deference to the cheerful custom of standing whenever a security official of the government was in the room.

He smiled pleasantly, waved at them and scratched his nose with a wad of mimeographed papers. His nose was large and it seemed to give added presence to his person. "Sit down, ladies and gentlemen, do sit down. We have no official fol-de-rol in the Brooklyn Project. I am your guide, as you might say, for the duration of this experiment: the acting secretary to the executive assistant on press relations. My name is not important. Please pass these among you."

They each took one of the mimeographed sheets and passed the rest on. Leaning back in the metal bucket-seats, they tried to make themselves comfortable. Their host squinted through the heavy screen and up at the wall clock which had one slowly revolving hand. He patted his black garment jovially where it was tight around the middle.

"To business. In a few moments, man's first large-scale

excursion into time will begin. Not by humans, but with the aid of a photographic and recording device which will bring us incalculably rich data on the past. With this experiment, the Brooklyn Project justifies ten billion dollars and over eight years of scientific development; it shows the validity not merely of a new method of investigation, but of a weapon which will make our glorious country even more secure, a weapon which our enemies may justifiably dread.

"Let me caution you, first, not to attempt the taking of notes even if you have been able to smuggle pens and pencils through Security. Your stories will be written entirely from memory. You all have a copy of the Security Code with the latest additions as well as a pamphlet referring specifically to Brooklyn Project regulations. The sheets you have just received provide you with the required lead for your story; they also contain suggestions as to treatment and coloring. Beyond that—so long as you stay within the framework of the documents mentioned—you are entirely free to write your stories in your own variously original ways. The press, ladies and gentlemen, must remain untouched and uncontaminated by government control. Now, any questions?"

The twelve reporters looked at the floor. Five of them began reading from their sheets. The paper rustled noisily.

"What, no questions? Surely there must be more interest than this in a project which has broken the last possible frontier—the fourth dimension, Time. Come now, you are the representatives of the nation's curiosity—you must have questions. Bradley, you look doubtful. What's bothering you? I assure you, Bradley, that I don't bite."

They all laughed and grinned at each other.

Bradley half-rose and pointed at the screen. "Why does it have to be so thick? I'm not the slightest bit interested in finding out how chronar works, but all we can see from here is a greyed and blurry picture of men dragging apparatus around on the floor. And why does the clock only have one hand?"

"A good question," the acting secretary said. His large nose seemed to glow. "A very good question. First, the clock has but one hand, because, after all, Bradley, this is an experiment in Time, and Security feels that the time of the experiment itself may, through some unfortunate combination of information leakage and foreign correlation—in short, a clue might be needlessly exposed. It is sufficient to know that when the hand points to the red dot, the experiment will begin. The screen is translucent and the scene below somewhat blurry for the same reason: camouflage of detail and adjustment. I *am* empowered to inform you that the *details* of the apparatus are—uh, very significant. Any other questions? Culpepper? Culpepper of Consolidated, isn't it?''

''Yes, sir. Consolidated News Service. Our readers are very curious about that incident of the Federation of Chronar Scientists. Of course, they have no respect or pity for them—the way they acted and all—but just what did they mean by saying that this experiment was dangerous because of insufficient data? And that fellow, Dr. Shayson, their president, do you know if he'll be shot?''

The man in black pulled at his nose and paraded before them thoughtfully. ''I must confess that I find the views of the Federation of Chronar Scientists—or the federation of *chronic sighers*, as we at Pike's Peak prefer to call them—are a trifle too exotic for my tastes; I rarely bother with weighing the opinions of a traitor in any case. Shayson himself may or may not have incurred the death penalty for revealing the nature of the work with which he was entrusted. On the other hand, he—uh, *may not* or *may* have. That is all I can say about him for reasons of security.''

Reasons of security. At mention of the dread phrase, every reporter had straightened against the hard back of his chair. Culpepper's face had lost its pinkness in favor of a glossy white. They can't consider the part about Shayson a leading question, he thought desperately. But I shouldn't have cracked about that damned federation!

Culpepper lowered his eyes and tried to looked as ashamed of the vicious idiots as he possibly could. He hoped the acting secretary to the executive assistant on press relations would notice his horror.

The clock began ticking very loudly. Its hand was now only one-fourth of an arc from the red dot at the top. Down on the floor of the immense laboratory, activity had stopped. All of the seemingly tiny men were clustered around two great spheres of shining metal resting against each other. Most of them were watching dials and switchboards intently; a few, their tasks completed, chatted with the circle of black-jumpered Security guards.

''We are almost ready to begin Operation Periscope. Operation Periscope, of course, because we are, in a sense, extending a periscope into the past—a periscope which will take pictures and record events of various periods ranging from fifteen thousand years to four billion years ago. We felt that in view of the various critical circumstances attending this experiment—international, scientific—a more fitting title would be Operation Crossroads. Unfortunately, that title has been—uh, preempted."

Everyone tried to look as innocent of the nature of that other experiment as years of staring at locked library shelves would permit.

"No matter. I will now give you a brief background in chronar practice as cleared by Brooklyn Project Security. Yes, Bradley?"

Bradley again got partly out of his seat. "I was wondering—we know there has been a Manhattan Project, a Long Island Project, a Westchester Project and now a Brooklyn Project. Has there ever been a Bronx Project? I come from the Bronx; you know, civic pride."

"Quite. Very understandable. However, if there is a Bronx Project you may be assured that until its work has been successfully completed, the only individuals outside of it who will know of its existence are the President and the Secretary of Security. If—*if*, I say—there is such an institution, the world will learn of it with the same shattering suddenness that it learned of the Westchester Project. I don't think that the world will soon forget *that*."

He chuckled in recollection and Culpepper echoed him a bit louder than the rest. The clock's hand was close to the red mark.

"Yes, the Westchester Project and now this; our nation shall yet be secure! Do you realize what a magnificent weapon chronar places in our democratic hands? To examine only one aspect—consider what happened to the Coney Island and Flatbush Subprojects (the events are mentioned in those sheets you've received) before the uses of chronar were fully appreciated.

"It was not yet known in those first experiments that Newton's third law of motion—action equalling reaction—held for time as well as it did for the other three dimensions of space. When the first chronar was excited backwards into time for the length of a ninth of a second, the entire laboratory was propelled into the future for a like period and returned in an—uh, unrecognizable condition. That fact, by the by, has prevented excursions into the future: the equipment seems to suffer amazing alterations and no human could survive them. But do you realize what we could do to an enemy by virtue of that property alone? Sending an adequate mass of chronar into the past while it is adjacent to a hostile nation would force that nation into the future—all of it simultaneously—a future from which it would return populated only with corpses!"

He glanced down, placed his hands behind his back and teetered on his heels. "That is why you see two spheres on the floor. Only one of them, the ball on the right, is equipped with chronar. The other is a dummy, matching the other's mass perfectly and serving as a counterbalance. When the chronar is excited, it will plunge four billion years into our past and take photographs of an earth that was still a half-liquid, partly gaseous mass solidifying rapidly in a somewhat inchoate solar system.

"At the same time, the dummy will be propelled four billion years into the future, from whence it will return much changed but for reasons we don't completely understand. They will strike each other at what is to us *now* and bounce off again to approximately half the chronological distance of the first trip, where our chronar apparatus will record data of an almost solid planet, plagued by earthquakes and possibly holding forms of sub-life in the manner of certain complex molecules.

"After each collision, the chronar will return roughly half the number of years covered before, automatically gathering information each time. The geological and historical periods we expect it to touch are listed from I to XXV in your sheets; there will be more than twenty-five, naturally, before both balls come to rest, but scientists feel that all periods after that number will be touched for such a short while as to be unproductive of photographs and other material. Remember, at the end, the balls will be doing little more than throbbing in place before coming to rest, so that even though they still ricochet centuries on either side of the present, it will be almost unnoticeable. A question, I see."

The thin woman in gray tweeds beside Culpepper got to her feet. "I—I know this is irrelevant," she began, "but I haven't been able to introduce my question into the discussion at any pertinent moment. Mr. Secretary—"

"Acting secretary," the chubby little man in the black suit told her genially. "I'm only the acting secretary. Go on."

"Well, I want to say—Mr. Secretary, is there any way at all that our post-experimental examination time may be reduced? Two years is a very long time to spend inside Pike's Peak simply out of fear that one of us may have seen enough and be unpatriotic enough to be dangerous to the nation. Once our stories have passed the censors, it seems to me that we could be allowed to return to our homes after a safety period of say, three months. I have two small children and there are others here—''

''Speak for yourself, Mrs. Bryant!'' the man from Security roared. ''It *is* Mrs. Bryant, isn't it? Mrs. Bryant of the Women's Magazine Syndicate? Mrs. *Alexis* Bryant.'' He seemed to be making minute pencil notes across his brain.

Mrs. Bryant sat down beside Culpepper again, clutching her copy of the amended Security Code, the special pamphlet on the Brooklyn Project and the thin mimeographed sheet of paper very close to her breast. Culpepper moved hard against the opposite arm of his chair. Why did everything have to happen to him? Then, to make matters worse, the crazy woman looked tearfully at him as if expecting sympathy. Culpepper stared across the booth and crossed his legs.

''You must remain within the jurisdiction of the Brooklyn Project because that is the only way that Security can be *certain* that no important information leakage will occur before the apparatus has changed beyond your present recognition of it. You didn't have to come, Mrs. Bryant—you volunteered. You all volunteered. After your editors had designated you as their choices for covering this experiment, you all had the peculiarly democratic privilege of refusing. None of you did. You recognized that to refuse this unusual honor would have shown you incapable of thinking in terms of National Security, would have, in fact, implied a criticism of the Security Code itself from the standpoint of the usual two-year examination time. And now this! For someone who had hitherto been thought as able and trustworthy as yourself, Mrs. Bryant, to emerge at this late hour with such a request makes me, why it,'' the little man's voice dropped to a whisper, ''—it almost makes me doubt the effectiveness of our security screening methods.''

Culpepper nodded angry affirmation at Mrs. Bryant who was bitting her lips and trying to show a tremendous interest in the activities on the laboratory floor.

''The question *was* irrelevant. Highly irrelevant. It took up time which I had intended to devote to a more detailed discussion of the popular aspects of chronar and its possible uses in industry. But Mrs. Bryant must have her little feminine outburst: it makes no difference to Mrs. Bryant that our nation is daily surrounded by more and more hostility, more and more danger. These things matter not in the slightest to Mrs. Bryant. All she is concerned with are the two years of her life that her country asks her to surrender so that the future of her own children may be more secure."

The acting secretary smoothed his black jumper and became calmer. Tension in the booth decreased.

"Activation will occur at any moment now, so I will briefly touch upon those most interesting periods which the chronar will record for us and from which we expect the most useful data. I and II, of course, since they are the periods at which the earth was forming into its present shape. Then III, the Pre-Cambrian Period of the Proterozoic, one billion years ago, the first era in which we find distinct records of life—crustaceans and algae for the most part. VI, a hundred twenty-five million years in the past, covers the Middle Jurassic of the Mesozoic. This excursion into the so-called "Age of Reptiles" may provide us with photographs of dinosaurs and solve the old riddle of their coloring, as well as photographs, if we are fortunate, of the first appearance of mammals and birds. Finally, VIII and IX, the Oligocene and Miocene Epochs of the Tertiary Period, mark the emergence of man's earliest ancestors. Unfortunately, the chronar will be oscillating back and forth so rapidly by that time that the chance of any decent recording—"

A gong sounded. The hand of the clock touched the red mark. Five of the technicians below pulled switches and, almost before the journalists could lean forward, the two spheres were no longer visible through the heavy plastic screen. Their places were empty.

"The chronar has begun its journey to four billion years in the past! Ladies and gentlemen, an historic moment—a profoundly historic moment! It will not return for a little while; I shall use the time in pointing up and exposing the fallacies of the—ah, *federation of chronic sighers!*"

Nervous laughter rippled at the acting secretary to the executive assistant on press relations. The twelve journalists settled down to hearing the ridiculous ideas torn apart.

"As you know, one of the fears entertained about travel to the past was that the most innocent-seeming acts would cause cataclysmic changes in the present. You are probably familiar with the fantasy in its most currently popular form; if Hitler had been killed in 1930, he would not have forced scientists in Germany and later occupied countries to emigrate, this nation might not have had the atomic bomb, thus no third atomic war, and Australia would still be above the Pacific.

"The traitorous Shayson and his illegal federation extended

this hypothesis to include much more detailed and minor acts such as shifting a molecule of hydrogen that in our past really was never shifted.

"At the time of the first experiment at the Coney Island Sub-project, when the chronar was sent back for one-ninth of a second, a dozen different laboratories checked through every device imaginable, searched carefully for any conceivable change. There were none! Government officials concluded that the time stream was a rigid affair, past, present and future, and nothing in it could be altered. But Shayson and his cohorts were not satisfied, they—"

> *I. Four billion years ago. The chronar floated in a cloudlet of silicon dioxide above the boiling earth and languidly collected its data with automatically operating instruments. The vapor it had displaced condensed and fell in great, shining drops.*

"—insisted that we should do no further experimenting until we had checked the mathematical aspects of the problem yet again. They went so far as to state that it was possible that if changes occurred we would not notice them, that no instruments imaginable could detect them. They said that we would accept these changes as things that had always existed. Well! This at a time when our country—and theirs, ladies and gentlemen of the press, *theirs*, too—was in greater danger than ever. Can you—"

Words failed him. He walked up and down the booth, shaking his head. All the reporters on the long, wooden bench shook their heads with him in sympathy.

There was another gong. The two dull spheres appeared briefly, clanged against each other and ricocheted off into opposite chronological directions.

"There you are." The government official waved his arms at the transparent laboratory floor above them. "The first oscillation has been completed; has anything changed? Isn't everything the same? But the dissidents would maintain that alterations have occurred and we haven't noticed them. With such faith-based, unscientific viewpoints, there can be no argument. People like these—"

> *II. Two billion years ago. The great ball clicked its photographs of the fiery, erupting ground below. Some red-hot crusts rattled off its sides. Five or six thousand complex molecules lost their basic structure as they impinged against it. A hundred didn't.*

"—will labor thirty hours a day out of thirty-three to convince you that black isn't white, that we have seven moons instead of two. They are especially dangerous—"

A long, muted note as the apparatus collided with itself. The warm orange of the corner lights brightened as it started out again.

"—because of their learning, because they are looked to for guidance in better ways of vegetation." The government official was slithering up and down rapidly now, gesturing with all of his pseudopods. "We are faced with a very difficult problem, at present—"

> *III. One billion years ago. The primitive triple trilobite the machine had destroyed when it materialized began drifting down wetly.*

"—a *very* difficult problem. The question before us: should we *shllk* or shouldn't we *shllk*?" He was hardly speaking English now; in fact, for some time, he hadn't been speaking at all. He had been stating his thoughts by slapping one pseudopod against the other—as he always had. . . .

> *IV. A half-billion years ago. Many different kinds of bacteria died as the water changed temperature slightly.*

"This, then, is no time for half-measures. If we can reproduce well enough—"

> *V. Two hundred fifty million years ago. VI. One hundred twenty-five million years ago.*

"to satisfy the Five Who Spiral, we have—"

> *VII. Sixty-two million years. VIII. Thirty-one million.*
> *IX. Fifteen million. X. Seven and a half million.*

"—spared all attainable virtue. Then—"

> *XI. XII. XIII. XIV. XV. XVI. XVII. XVIII. XIX.*
> *Bong—bong—bong bongbongbongongongngngng . . .*

"—we are indeed ready for refraction. And that, I tell you is good enough for those who billow and those who snap. But those who billow will be proven wrong as always, for in the snapping is the rolling and in the rolling is only truth. There need be no change merely because of sodden cilia. The apparatus has rested at last in the fractional conveyance; shall we view it subtly?"

They all agreed, and their bloated purpled bodies dissolved into liquid and flowed up and around to the apparatus. When they reached its four square blocks, now no longer shrilling mechanically, they rose, solidified and regained their slime-washed forms.

"See," cried the thing that had been the acting secretary to the executive assistant on press relations. "See, no matter how subtly! Those who billow were wrong: we haven't changed." He extended fifteen purple blobs triumphantly. "Nothing has changed!"

RING AROUND THE REDHEAD

by John D. MacDonald (1916–)

STARTLING STORIES
November

*John D. MacDonald is the best-selling mystery and suspense writer whose novels starring Travis McGee are read all over the world. He began his writing career after service in World War II with a veritable flood of stories in almost all the pulp magazines still in existence, and he wrote in all genres: mystery, sports, fantasy, Western, and science fiction. His total output in sf was only some fifty stories and three novels—*Wine of the Dreamers *(1951),* Ballroom of the Skies *(1952), and* The Girl, The Gold Watch, and Everything *(1962). The best of his science fiction short stories can be found in* Other Times, Other Days *(1978). His success in other fields deprived sf of a great talent, as the two selections in this book demonstrate.*

(When things are new in science, they are grist for the science fiction writer's mill; they could be given all kinds of magical powers. I remember when heavy water was made magical in science fiction; and before my time, radium was.

In the first few years after Hiroshima, nuclear explosions could be held accountable for anything. They made it possible to reach into other dimensions or to travel in time. My first book, Pebble in the Sky, *began with precisely such a device, intended to get the plot going. Of course, although it was published in 1950, the first version of* Pebble *was written in 1947.*

"Ring Around the Redhead" also starts with the mysterious effect of a nuclear explosion—but you're allowed one assumption in a science fiction story. After that, the story moves along with inevitability.—I. A.)

The prosecuting attorney was a lean specimen named Amery Heater. The buildup given the murder trial by the newspapers had resulted in a welter of open-mouthed citizens who jammed the golden oak courtroom.

Bill Maloney, the defendant, was sleepy and bored. He knew he had no business being bored. Not with twelve righteous citizens who, under the spell of Amery Heater's quiet, confidential oratory were beginning to look at Maloney as though he were a fiend among fiends.

The August heat was intense and flies buzzed around the upper sashes of the dusty windows. The city sounds drifted in the open windows, making it necessary for Amery Heater to raise his voice now and again.

But though Bill Maloney was bored, he was also restless and worried. Mostly he was worried about Justin Marks, his own lawyer.

Marks cared but little for this case. But, being Bill Maloney's best friend, he couldn't very well refuse to handle it. Justin Marks was a proper young man with a Dewey mustache and frequent daydreams about Justice Marks of the Supreme Court. He somehow didn't feel that the Maloney case was going to help him very much.

Particularly with the very able Amery Heater intent on getting the death penalty.

The judge was a puffy old citizen with signs of many good years at the brandy bottle, the hundreds of gallons of which surprisingly had done nothing to dim the keenness of eye or brain.

Bill Maloney was a muscular young man with a round face, a

round chin and a look of sleepy skepticism. A sheaf of his coarse, corn-colored hair jutted out over his forehead. His eyes were clear, deep blue.

He stifled a yawn, remembering what Justin Marks had told him about making a good impression on the jury. He singled out a plump lady juror in the front row and winked solemnly at her. She lifted her chin with an audible sniff.

No dice there. Might as well listen to Amery Heater.

". . . and we, the prosecution, intend to prove that on the evening of July tenth, William Howard Maloney did murderously attack his neighbor, James Finch and did kill James Finch by crushing his skull. We intend to prove there was a serious dispute between these men, a dispute that had continued for some time. We further intend to prove that the cause of this dispute was the dissolute life being led by the defendant."

Amery Heater droned on and on. The room was too hot. Bill Maloney slouched in his chair and yawned. He jumped when Justin Marks hissed at him. Then he remembered that he had yawned and he smiled placatingly at the jury. Several of them looked away, hurriedly.

Fat little Doctor Koobie took the stand. He was sworn in and Amery Heater, polite and respectful, asked questions which established Koobie's name, profession and presence at the scene of the "murder" some fifty minutes after it had taken place.

"And now, Dr. Koobie, would you please describe in your own words exactly what you found."

Koobie hitched himself in his chair, pulled his trousers up a little over his chubby knees and said, "No need to make this technical. I was standing out by the hedge between the two houses. I was on Jim Finch's side of the hedge. There was a big smear of blood around. Some of it was spattered on the hedge. Barberry, I think. On the ground there was some hunks of brain tissue, none of them bigger than a dime. Also a piece of scalp maybe two inches square. Had Jim's hair on it all right. Proved that in the lab. Also found some pieces of bone. Not many." He smiled peacefully. "Guess old Jim is dead all right. No question of that. Blood was his and the hair was his."

Three jurors swallowed visibly and a fourth began to fan himself vigorously.

Koobie answered a few other questions and then Justin Marks took over the cross-examination.

"What would you say killed Jim Finch?"

Many people gasped at the question, having assumed that the defense would be that, lacking a body, there was no murder.

Koobie put a fat finger in the corner of his mouth, took it out again. "Couldn't rightly say."

"Could a blow from a club or similar weapon have done it?"

"Good Lord, no! Man's head is a pretty durable thing. You'd have to back him up against a solid concrete wall and bust him with a full swing with a baseball bat and you still wouldn't do that much hurt. Jim was standing right out in the open."

"Dr. Koobie, imagine a pair of pliers ten feet long and proportionately thick. If a pair of pliers like that were to have grabbed Mr. Finch by the head, smashing it like a nut in a nutcracker, could it have done that much damage?"

Koobie pulled his nose, tugged on his ear, frowned, and said, "Why, if it clamped down real sudden like, I imagine it could. But where'd Jim go?"

"That's all, thank you," Justin Marks said.

Amery Heater called other witnesses. One of them was Anita Hempflet.

Amery said, "You live across the road from the defendant?"

Miss Anita Hempflet was fiftyish, big-boned, and of the same general consistency as the dried beef recommended for Canadian canoe trips. Her voice sounded like fingernails on the third grade blackboard.

"Yes I do. I've lived there thirty-five years. That Maloney person, him sitting right over there, moved in two years ago, and I must say that I . . ."

"You are able to see Mr. Maloney's house from your windows?"

"Certainly!"

"Now tell the court when it was that you first saw the red-headed woman."

She licked her lips. "I first saw that . . . that woman in May. A right pleasant morning it was, too. Or it was until I saw her. About ten o'clock, I'd say. She was right there in Maloney's front yard, as bold as brass. Had on some sort of shiny silver thing. You couldn't call it a dress. Too short for that. Didn't half cover her the way a lady ought to be covered. Not by half. She was . . ."

"What was she doing?"

"Well, she come out of the house and she stopped and looked around as though she was surprised at where she was. My eyes are good. I could see her face. She looked all around. Then she sort of slouched, like she was going to keel over or something. She walked real slow down toward the gate. Mr. Maloney came running out of the house and I heard him yell to her. She stopped. Then he was making signs to her, for her to go back into the house. Just like she was deaf or something. After a while she went back in. I guessed she probably was made deaf by that awful bomb thing the government lost control of near town three days before that."

"You didn't see her again?"

"Oh, I saw her plenty of times. But after that she was always dressed more like a girl should be dressed. Far as I could figure out, Mr. Maloney was buying her clothes in town. It wasn't right that anything like that should be going on in a nice neighborhood. Mr. Finch didn't think it was right either. Runs down property values, you know."

"In your knowledge, Miss Hempflet, did Mr. Maloney and the deceased ever quarrel?"

"They started quarreling a few days after that woman showed up. Yelling at each other across the hedge. Mr. Finch was always scared of burglars. He had that house fixed up so nobody could get in if he didn't want them in. A couple of times I saw Bill Maloney pounding on his door and rapping on the windows. Jim wouldn't pay any attention."

Justin cross-examined.

"You say, Miss Hempflet, that the defendant was going down and shopping for this woman, buying her clothes. In your knowledge, did he buy her anything else?"

Anita Hempflet sniggered. "Say so! Guess she must of been feeble minded. I asked around and found out he bought a blackboard and chalk and some kids' books."

"Did you make any attempt to find out where this woman came from, this woman who was staying with Mr. Maloney?"

"Should say I did! I know for sure that she didn't come in on the train or Dave Wattle would've seen her. If she'd come by bus, Myrtle Gisco would have known it. Johnny Farness didn't drive her in from the airport. I figure that any woman who'd live openly with a man like Maloney must have hitchhiked into town. She didn't come any other way."

"That's all, thank you," Justin Marks said.

Maloney sighed. He couldn't understand why Justin was looking so worried. Everything was going fine. According to plan. He saw the black looks the jury was giving him, but he wasn't worried. Why, as soon as they found out what had actually happened, they'd be all for him. Justin Marks seemed to be sweating.

He came back to the table and whispered to Bill, "How about temporary insanity?"

"I guess it's okay if you like that sort of thing."

"No. I mean as a plea!"

Maloney stared at him. "Justy, old boy. Are you nuts? All we have to do is tell the truth."

Justin Marks rubbed his mustache with his knuckle and made a small bleating sound that acquired him a black look from the judge.

Amery Heater built his case up very cleverly and very thoroughly. In fact, the jury had Bill Maloney so definitely electrocuted that they were beginning to give him sad looks—full of pity.

It took Amery Heater two days to complete his case. When it was done, it was a solid and shining structure, every discrepancy explained—everything pinned down. Motive. Opportunity. Everything.

On the morning of the third day, the court was tense with expectancy. The defense was about to present its case. No one knew what the case was, except, of course, Bill Maloney, Justin Marks, and the unworldly redhead who called herself Rejapachalandakeena. Bill called her Keena. She hadn't appeared in court.

Justin Marks stood up and said to the hushed court, "Your Honor. Rather than summarize my defense at this point, I would like to put William Maloney on the stand first and let him tell the story in his own words."

The court buzzed. Putting Maloney on the stand would give Amery Heater a chance to cross-examine. Heater would rip Maloney to tiny shreds. The audience licked its collective chops.

"Your name?"

"William Maloney, 12 Braydon Road."

"And your occupation?"

"Tinkering. Research, if you want a fancy name."

"Where do you get your income?"

"I've got a few gimmicks patented. The royalties come in."

"Please tell the court all you know about this crime of which you are accused. Start at the beginning, please."

Bill Maloney shoved the blond hair back off his forehead with a square, mechanic's hand and smiled cheerfully at the jury. Some of them, before they realized it, had smiled back. They felt the smiles on their lips and sobered instantly. It wasn't good form to smile at a vicious murderer.

Bill slouched in the witness chair and laced his fingers across his stomach.

"It all started," he said, "the day the army let that rocket get out of hand on the seventh of May. I've got my shop in my cellar. Spend most of my time down there.

"That rocket had an atomic warhead, you know. I guess they've busted fifteen generals over that affair so far. It exploded in the hills forty miles from town. The jar upset some of my apparatus and stuff. Put it out of kilter. I was sore.

"I turned around, cussing away to myself, and where my coal bin used to be, there was a room. The arch leading into the room was wide and I could see in. I tell you, it really shook me up to see that room there. I wondered for a minute if the bomb hadn't given me delusions.

"The room I saw didn't have any furniture in it. Not like furniture we know. It had some big cubes of dull silvery metal, and some smaller cubes. I couldn't figure out the lighting.

"Being a curious cuss, I walked right through the arch and looked around. I'm a great one to handle things. The only thing in the room I could pick up was a gadget on top of the biggest cube. It hardly weighed a thing.

"In order to picture it, you've got to imagine a child's hoop made of silvery wire. Then right across the wire imagine the blackest night you've ever seen, rolled out into a thin sheet and stretched tight like a drumhead on that wire hoop.

"As I was looking at it I heard some sort of deep vibration and there I was, stumbling around in my coal bin. The room was gone. But I had that darn hoop in my hand. That hoop with the midnight stretched across it.

"I took it back across to my workbench where the light was better. I held it in one hand and poked a finger at that black stuff. My finger went right through. I didn't feel a thing. With my finger still sticking through it, I looked on the other side.

"It was right there that I named the darn thing. I said, 'Gawk!' And that's what I've called it ever since. The Gawk. My finger didn't come through on the other side. I stuck my whole arm through. No arm. I pulled it back out. Quick. Arm was okay. Somehow it seemed warm on the other side of the gawk.

"Well, you can imagine what it was like for me, a tinkerer, to get my hands on a thing like that. I forgot all about meals and so on. I had to find out what it was and why. I couldn't see my own hand on the other side of it. I put it right up in front of my face, reached through from the back and tried to touch my nose. I couldn't do it. I reached so deep that without the gawk there, my arm would have been halfway through my head . . ."

"Objection!" Amery Heater said. "All this has nothing to do with the fact . . ."

"My client," Justin said, "is giving the incidents leading up to the alleged murder."

"Overruled," the judge said.

Maloney said, "Thanks. I decided that my arm had to be someplace when I stuffed it through the gawk. And it wasn't in this dimension. Maybe not even in this time. But it had to be someplace. That meant that I had to find out what was on the other side of the gawk. I could use touch, sight. Maybe I could climb through. It intrigued me, you might say.

"I started with touch. I put my hand through, held it in front of me and walked. I walked five feet before my hand rammed up against something. I felt it. It seemed to be a smooth wall. There wasn't such a wall in my cellar.

"There has to be some caution in science. I didn't stuff my head through. I couldn't risk it. I had the hunch there might be something unfriendly on the other side of the gawk. I turned the thing around and stuck my hand through from the other side. No wall. There was a terrible pain. I yanked my hand back. A lot of little bloodvessels near the surface had broken. I dropped the gawk and jumped around for a while. Found out I had a bad case of frostbite. The broken blood vessels indicated that I had stuffed my hand into a vacuum. Frostbite in a fraction of a second indicated nearly absolute zero. It seemed that maybe I had put my hand into space. It made me glad it had been my hand instead of my head.

"I propped the thing up on my bench and shoved lots of things through, holding them a while and bringing them back out. Made a lot of notes on the effect of absolute zero on various materials.

"By that time I was bushed. I went up to bed. Next day I had some coffee and then built myself a little periscope. Shoved it through. Couldn't see a thing. I switched the gawk, tested with a thermometer, put my hand through. Warm enough. But the periscope didn't show me a thing. I wondered if maybe something happened to light rays when they went through that blackness. Turns out that I was right.

"By about noon I had found out another thing about it. Every time I turned it around I was able to reach through into a separate and distinct environment. I tested that with the thermometer. One of the environments I tested slammed the mercury right out through the top of the glass and broke the glass and burned my hand. I was glad I hadn't hit that one the first time. It would have burned my hand off at the wrist.

"I began to keep a journal of each turn of the gawk, and what seemed to be on the other side of it. I rigged up a jig on my workbench and began to grope through the gawk with my fireplace tongs.

"Once I jabbed something that seemed to be soft and alive. Those tongs were snatched right through the gawk. Completely gone. It gave me the shudders, believe me. If it had been my hand instead of the tongs, I wouldn't be here. I have a hunch that whatever snatched those tongs would have been glad to eat me.

"I rigged up some grappling hooks and went to work. Couldn't get anything. I put a lead weight on some cord and lowered it through. Had some grease on the end of the weight. When the cord slacked off, I pulled it back up. There was fine yellow sand on the bottom of the weight. And I had lowered it thirty-eight feet before I hit sand.

"On try number two hundred and eight, I brought an object back through the gawk. Justy has it right there in his bag. Show it to the people, Justy."

Justin looked annoyed at the informal request, but he unstrapped the bag and took out an object. He passed it up to the judge who looked at it with great interest. Then it was passed through the jury. It ended up on the table in front of the bench, tagged as an exhibit.

"You can see, folks, that such an object didn't come out of our civilization."

"Objection!" Heater yelled. "The defendant could have made it."

"Hush up!" the judge said.

"Thanks. As you can see that object is a big crystal. That thing in the crystal is a golden scorpion, about five times life size. The corner is sawed off there because Jim Finch sawed it off. You notice that he sawed off a big enough piece to get a hunk of the scorpion's leg. Jim told me that leg was solid gold. That whole bug is solid gold. I guess it was an ornament in some other civilization.

"Now that gets me around to Jim Finch. As you all know, Jim

retired from the jewelry business about five years ago. Jim was a pretty sharp trader. You know how he parlayed his savings across the board so that he owned a little hunk of just about everything in town. He was always after me to let him in on my next gimmick. I guess those royalty checks made his mouth water. We weren't what you'd call friends. I passed the time of day with him, but he wasn't a friendly man.

"Anyway, when I grabbed this bug out of the gawk, I thought of Jim Finch. I wanted to know if such a thing could be made by a jeweler. Jim was home and his eyes popped when he saw it. You know how he kept that little shop in his garage and made presents for people? Well, he cut off a section with a saw. Then he said that he'd never seen anything like it and he didn't know how on earth it was put together. I told him that it probably wasn't put together on earth. That teased him a little and he kept after me until I told him the whole story. He didn't believe it. That made me mad. I took him over into my cellar and showed him a few things. I set the gawk between two boxes so it was parallel to the floor, then dropped my grapples down into it. In about three minutes I caught something and brought it up. It seemed to be squirming."

Maloney drew a deep breath.

"That made me a shade cautious. I brought it up slow. The head of the thing came out. It was like a small bear—but more like a bear that had been made into a rug. Flat like a leech, and instead of front legs it just seemed to have a million little sucker disks around the flat edge. It screamed so hard, with such a high note, that it hurt my ears. I dropped it back through.

"When I looked around, old Jim was backed up against the cellar wall, mumbling. Then he got down on his hands and knees and patted the floor under the gawk. He kept right on mumbling. Pretty soon he asked me how that bear-leech and that golden bug could be in the same place. I explained how I had switched the gawk. We played around for a while and then came up with a bunch of stones. Jim handled them, and his eyes started to pop out again. He began to shake. He told me that one of the stones was an uncut ruby. You couldn't prove it by me. It would've made you sick to see the way old Jim started to drool. He talked so fast I could hardly understand him. Finally I got the drift. He wanted us to go in business and rig up some big machinery so we could dig through the gawk and come back with all kinds of things. He wanted bushels of rubies and a few tons of gold.

"I told him I wasn't interested. He got so mad he jumped up and down. I told him I was going to fool around with the thing for a while and then I was going to turn it over to some scientific foundation so the boys could go at it in the right way.

"He looked mad enough to kill me. He told me we could have castles and cars and yachts and a million bucks each. I told him that the money was coming in faster than I could spend it already and all I wanted was to stay in my cellar and tinker.

"I told him that I guessed the atomic explosion had dislocated something, and the end product belonged to science. I also told him very politely to get the devil home and stop bothering me.

"He did, but he sure hated to leave. Well, by the morning of the tenth, I had pretty well worn myself out. I was bushed and jittery from no sleep. I had made twenty spins in a row without getting anything, and I had begun to think I had run out of new worlds on the other side of the gawk.

"Like a darn fool, I yanked it off the jig, took it like a hoop and scaled it across the cellar. It went high, then dropped lightly, spinning.

"And right there in my cellar was this beautiful redhead. She was dressed in a shiny silver thing. Justy's got that silver thing in his bag. Show it to the people. You can see that it's made out of some sort of metal mesh, but it isn't cold like metal would be. It seems to hold heat and radiate it."

The metal garment was duly passed around. Everybody felt of it, exclaimed over it. This was better than a movie. Maloney could see from Amery Heater's face that the man wanted to claim the metal garment was also made in the Maloney cellar.

Bill winked at him. Amery Heater flushed a dull red.

"Well, she stood there, right in the middle of the gawk which was flat against the floor. She had a dazed look on her face. I asked her where she had come from. She gave me a blank look and a stream of her own language. She seemed mad about something. And pretty upset.

"Now what I should have done was pick up that gawk and lift it back up over her head. That would have put her back in her own world. But she stepped out of it, and like a darn fool, I stood and held it and spun it, nervous like. In spinning it, I spun her own world off into some mathematical equation I couldn't figure.

"It was by the worst or the best kind of luck, depending on how you look at it, that I made a ringer on her when I tossed the gawk across the cellar. Her makeup startled me a little. No lipstick. Tiny crimson beads on the end of each eyelash. Tiny emerald green triangles painted on each tooth in some sort of enamel. Nicely centered. Her hairdo wasn't any wackier than some you see every day.

"Well, she saw the gawk in my hands and she wasn't dumb at all. She came at me, her lips trembling, her eyes pleading, and tried to step into it. I shook my head, hard, and pushed her back and set it back in the jig. I shoved a steel rod through, holding it in asbestos mittens. The heat beyond the blackness turned the whole rod cherry red in seconds. I shoved it on through the rest of the way, then showed her the darkened mitten. She was quick. She got the most horrified look on her face.

"Then she ran upstairs, thinking it was some sort of joke, I guess. I noticed that she slammed right into the door, as though she expected it to open for her. By the time I got to her, she had figured out the knob. She went down the walk toward the gate.

"That's when nosy Anita must have seen her. I shouted and she turned around and the tears were running right down her face. I made soothing noises and she let me lead her back into the house. I've never seen a prettier girl or one stacked any . . . I mean her skin is translucent, sort of. Her eyes are enormous. And her hair is a shade of red that you never see.

"She had no place to go and she was my responsibility. I certainly didn't feel like turning her over to the welfare people. I fixed her up a place to sleep in my spare room and I had to show her everything. How to turn on a faucet. How to turn the lights off and on.

"She didn't do anything except cry for four days. I gave her food that she didn't eat. She was a mess. Worried me sick. I didn't have any idea how to find her world again. No idea at all. Of course, I could have popped her into any old world, but it didn't seem right.

"On the fourth day I came up out of the cellar and found her sitting in a chair looking at a copy of See Magazine. She seemed very much interested in the pictures of the women. She looked up at me and smiled. That was the day I went into town and came back with a mess of clothes for her. I had to show her how a zipper worked, and how to button a button."

He looked as if that might have been fun.

"After she got all dressed up, she smiled some more and that evening she ate well. I kept pointing to things and saying the right name for them.

"I tell you, once she heard the name for something, she didn't forget it. It stayed right with her. Nouns were easy. The other words were tough. About ten that night I finally caught her name. It was Rejapachalandakeena. She seemed to like to have me call her Keena. The first sentence she said was, 'Where is Keena?'

"That is one tough question. Where is here and now? Where is this world, anyway? On what side of what dimension? In which end of space? On what twisted convolution of the time stream? What good is it to say 'This is the world'? It just happens to be our world. Now I know that there are plenty of others.

"Writing came tougher for her than the sounds of the words. She showed me her writing. She took a piece of paper, held the pencil pointing straight up and put the paper on top of the rug. Then she worked that pencil like a pneumatic hammer, starting at the top right corner and going down the page. I couldn't figure it until she read it over, and made a correction by sticking in one extra hole in the paper. I saw then that the pattern of holes was very precise—like notes on a sheet of music.

"She went through the grade school readers like a flash. I was buying her some arithmetic books one day, and when I got back she said, 'Man here while Billy gone.' She was calling me Billy. 'Keena hide,' she said.

"Well, the only thing missing was the gawk, and with it, Keena's chance to make a return to her own people. I thought immediately of Jim Finch. I ran over and pounded on his door. He undid the chain so he could talk to me through a five-inch crack, but I couldn't get in. I asked him if he had stolen the little item. He told me that I'd better run to the police and tell them exactly what it was that I had lost, and then I could tell the police exactly how I got it. I could tell by the look of naked triumph in his eyes that he had it. And there wasn't a thing I could do about it.

"Keena's English improved by leaps and bounds and pretty soon she was dipping into my texts on chemistry and physics. She seemed puzzled. She told me that we were like her people a few thousand years back. Primitives. She told me a lot about her world. No cities. The houses are far apart. No work. Everyone is assigned to a certain cultural pursuit, depending on basic ability. She was a designer. In order to train herself, she had had to learn the composition of all fabricated materials used in her world.

"I took notes while she talked. When I get out of this jam,

I'm going to revolutionize the plastics industry. She seemed bright enough to be able to take in the story of how she suddenly appeared in my cellar. I gave it to her slow and easy.

"When I was through, she sat very still for a long time. Then she told me that some of the most brilliant men of her world had long ago found methods of seeing into other worlds beyond their own. They had borrowed things from worlds more advanced than their own, and had thus been able to avoid mistakes in the administration of their own world. She told me that it was impossible that her departure should go unnoticed. She said that probably at the moment of her disappearance, all the resources of a great people were being concentrated on that spot where she had been standing talking to some friends. She told me that some trace of the method would be found and that they would then scan this world, locate her and take her back.

"I asked her if it would be easier if we had the gawk, and she said that it wasn't necessary, and that if it was, she would merely go next door and see Jim Finch face to face. She said she had a way, once she looked into his eyes, of taking over the control of his involuntary muscles and stopping his heartbeat.

"I gasped, and she smiled sweetly and said that she had very nearly done it to me when I had kept her from climbing back through the gawk. She said that everybody in her world knew how to do that. She also said that most adults knew how to create, out of imagination, images that would respond to physical tests. To prove it she stared at the table. In a few seconds a little black box slowly appeared out of misty nothingness. She told me to look at it. I picked it up. It was latched. I opened it. Her picture smiled out at me. She was standing before the entrance of a white castle that seemed to reach to the clouds.

"Suddenly it was gone. She explained that when she stopped thinking of it, it naturally disappeared, because that was what had caused it. Her thinking. I asked her why she didn't think up a doorway to her own world and then step through it while she was still thinking about it. She said that she could only think up things by starting with their basic physical properties and working up from there, like a potter starts with clay.

"So I stopped heckling Jim Finch at about that time. I was sorry, because I wanted the gawk back. Best toy I'd ever had. Once I got a look in Jim's garage window. He'd forgot to pull the shade down all the way. He had the gawk rigged up on a stand, and had a big arm, like the bucket on a steam shovel rigged up, only just big enough to fit through the hoop. He wasn't working it when I saw him. He was digging up the concrete in the corner of his cellar. He was using a pick and he had a shovel handy. He was pale as death. I saw then that he had a human arm in there on the floor and blood all over. The bucket was rigged with jagged teeth. It didn't take much imagination to figure out what Jim had done.

"Some poor innocent character in one of those other worlds had had a massive contraption come out of nowhere and chaw his arm off. I thought of going to the police, and then I thought of how easy it would be for Jim Finch to get me stuck away in a padded cell, while he stayed on the outside, all set to pull more arms off more people."

Heater glanced uneasily at the jury. They were drinking it in.

"I told Keena about it and she smiled. She told me that Jim was digging into many worlds and that some of them were pretty advanced. I gradually got the idea that old Jim was engaging in as healthy an occupation as a small boy climbing between the bars and tickling the tigers. I began to worry about old Jim a little. You all know about that couple of bushels of precious stones that were found in his house. That's what made him tickle the tigers. But the cops didn't find that arm. I guess that after he got the hole dug, Jim got over his panic and realized that all he had to do was switch the gawk around and toss the arm through. Best place for old razor blades I ever heard of.

"Well, as May turned into June and June went by, Keena got more and more confident of her eventual rescue. As I learned more about her world, I got confident of it too. In a few thousand years we may be as bright as those people. I hope we are. No wars, no disease.

"And the longer she stayed with me, the more upset I got about her leaving me. But it was what she wanted. I guess it's what I'd want, if somebody shoved me back a thousand years B.C. I'd want to get home, but quick.

"On the tenth of July, I got a phone call from Jim Finch. His voice was all quavery like a little old lady. He said, 'Maloney, I want to give that thing back to you. Right away.' Anything Jim Finch gave anybody was a spavined gift horse. I guessed that the gobblies were after him like Keena had hinted.

"So I just laughed at him. Maybe I laughed to cover up the fact that I was a little scared, too. What if some world he messed with dropped a future type atomic bomb back through the gawk into his lap? I told him to burn it up if he was tired of it.

"I didn't know Jim could cuss like that. He said that it wouldn't burn and he couldn't break it or destroy it anyway. He said that he was coming out and throw it across the hedge into my yard right away.

"As I got to my front door, he came running out of his house. He carried the thing like it was going to blow up.

"Just as he got to the hedge, I saw a misty circle in the air over his head. Only it was about ten feet across. A pair of dark blue shiny pliers with jaws as big as the judge's desk there swooped down and caught him by the head. The jaws snapped shut so hard that I could hear sort of a thick, wet, popping sound as all the bones in old Jim's head gave way all at once.

"He dropped the gawk and hung limp in those closed jaws for a moment, then he was yanked up through that misty circle into nothingness. Gone. Right before my eyes. The misty circle drifted down to grass level, and then faded away. The gawk faded right away with it. You know what it made me think of? Of a picnic where you're trying to eat and a bug gets on your arm and bothers you. You pinch it between your thumb and forefinger, roll it once and throw it away. Old Jim was just about as important to those blue steel jaws as a hungry red ant is to you or me. You could call those gems he got crumbs, I guess.

"I was just getting over being sick in my own front yard when Timmy came running over, took one look at the blood and ran back. The police came next. That's all there is to tell. Keena is still around and Justy will bring her in to testify tomorrow."

Bill Maloney yawned and smiled at the jury.

Amery Heater got up, stuck his thumbs inside his belt and walked slowly and heavily over to Bill.

He stared into Bill's smiling face for ten long seconds. Bill shuffled his feet and began to look uncomfortable.

In a low bitter tone, Amery Heater said, "Gawks! Golden scorpions! Tangential worlds! Blue jaws!" He sighed heavily, pointed to the jury and said, "Those are intelligent people, Maloney. No questions!"

The judge had to pound with his gavel to quiet the court. As soon as the room was quiet, he called an adjournment until ten the following morning.

When Bill Maloney was brought out of his cell into court the next morning, the jurors gave each other wise looks. It was obvious that the young man had spent a bad night. There were puffy areas under his eyes. He scuffed his heels as he walked, sat down heavily and buried his face in his hands. They wondered why his shoulders seemed to shake.

Justin Marks looked just as bad. Or worse.

Bill was sunk in a dull lethargy, in an apathy so deep that he didn't know where he was, and cared less.

Justin Marks stood up and said, "Your Honor, we request an adjournment of the case for twenty-four hours."

"For what reason?"

"Your Honor, I intended to call the woman known as Keena to the stand this morning. She was in a room at the Hotel Hollyfield. Last night she went up to her room at eleven after I talked with her in the lounge. She hasn't been seen since. Her room is empty. All her possessions are there, but she is gone. I would like time to locate her, your Honor."

The judge looked extremely disappointed.

He pursed his lips and said, in a sweet tone, "You are sure that such a woman actually exists, counsellor?"

Justin Marks turned pale and Amery Heater chuckled.

"Of course, your Honor! Why, only last night . . ."

"Her people came and got her," Bill Maloney said heavily. He didn't look up. The jury shifted restlessly. They had expected to be entertained by a gorgeous redhead. Without her testimony, the story related by Maloney seemed even more absurd than it had seemed when they had heard it. Of course, it would be a shame to electrocute a nice clean young man like that, but really you can't have people going about killing their neighbors and then concocting such a fantasy about it . . .

"What's that?" the judge asked suddenly.

It began as a hum, so low as to be more of a vibration than a sound. A throb that seemed to come from the bowels of the earth. Slowly it increased in pitch and in violence, and if the judge had any more to say on the subject, no one heard him. He appeared to be trying to beat the top of his desk in with the gavel. But the noise couldn't be heard.

Slowly climbing up the audible range, it filled the court. As it passed the index of vibration of the windows, they shattered, but the falling glass couldn't be heard. A man who had been wearing glasses stared through empty frames.

The sound passed beyond the upper limits of the human ear, became hypersonic, and every person in the courtroom was suddenly afflicted with a blinding headache.

It stopped as abruptly as a scream in the night.

For a moment there was a misty arch in the solid wall. Beyond it was the startling vagueness of a line of blue hills. Hills that didn't belong there.

She came quickly through the arch. It faded. She was not tall, but gave the impression of tallness. Her hair was the startling red of port wine, her skin so translucent as to seem faintly bluish. Her eyes were halfway between sherry and honey. Tiny crimson beads were on the tip of each eyelash. Her warm full lips were parted, and they could all see the little green enameled triangles on her white teeth. Her single garment was like the silver metallic garment they had touched. But it was golden. Without any apparent means of support, it clung to her lovely body, following each line and curve.

She looked around the court. Maloney's eyes were warm blue fire. "Keena!" he gasped. She ran to him, threw herself on him, her arms around his neck, her face hidden in the line of jaw, throat and shoulder. He murmured things to her that the jury strained to hear.

Amery Heater, feeling his case fade away, was the first to recover.

"Hypnotism!" he roared.

It took the judge a full minute of steady pounding to silence the spectators. "One more disturbance like this, and I'll clear the court," he said.

Maloney had come to life. She sat on his lap and they could hear her say, "What are they trying to do to you?"

He smiled peacefully. "They want to kill me, honey. They say I killed Jim Finch."

She turned and her eyes shriveled the jury and the judge.

"Stupid!" she hissed.

There was a little difficulty swearing her in. Justin Marks, his confidence regained, thoroughly astonished at finding that Bill Maloney had been telling the truth all along, questioned Keena masterfully. She backed up Maloney's story in every particular. Maloney couldn't keep his eyes off her. Her accent was odd, and her voice had a peculiar husky and yet liquid quality.

Justin Marks knuckled his mustache proudly, bowed to Amery Heater and said, "Do you wish to cross-examine?"

Heater nodded, stood up, and walked slowly over. He gave Keena a long and careful look. "Young woman, I congratulate you on your acting ability. Where did you get your training? Surely you've been on the stage."

"Stage?"

"Oh, come now! All this has been very interesting, but now we must discard this dream world and get down to facts. What is your real name?"

"Rejapachalandakeena."

Heater sighed heavily. "I see that you are determined to maintain your silly little fiction. That entrance of yours was somehow engineered by the defendant, I am sure." He turned and smiled at the jury—the smile of a fellow conspirator.

"Miss So-and-so, the defense has all been based on the idea that you come from some other world, or some hidden corner of time, or out of the woodwork. I think that what you had better do is just prove to us that you do come from some other world." His voice dripped with sarcasm. "Just do one or two things for us that we common mortals can't do, please."

Keena frowned, propped her chin on her fist. After a few moments she said, "I do not know completely what you are able to do. Many primitive peoples have learned through a sort of intuition. Am I right in thinking that those people behind that little fence are the ones who decide whether my Billy is to be killed?"

"Correct."

She turned and stared at the jury for a long time. Her eyes passed from face to face, slowly. The jurors were oddly uncomfortable.

She said, "It is very odd. That woman in the second row. The second one from the left. It is odd that she should be there. Not very long ago she gave a poison, some sort of vegetable base poison, to her husband. He was sick for a long time and he died. Is that not against your silly laws?"

The woman in question turned pale green, put her hands to her throat, rolled her eyes up and slid quietly off the chair. No one made a move to help her. All eyes were on Keena.

Some woman back in the courtroom said shrilly, "I knew there was something funny about the way Dave died! I knew it! Arrest Mrs. Watson immediately!"

Keena's eyes turned toward the woman who had spoken. The woman sat down suddenly.

Keena said, "This man you call Dave. His wife killed him because of you. I can read that in your eyes."

Amery Heater chuckled. "A very good trick, but pure imagination. I rather guess you have been prepared for this situation, and my opponent has briefed you on what to do should I call on you in this way."

Keena's eyes flashed. She said, "You are a most offensive person."

She stared steadily at Amery Heater. He began to sweat. Suddenly he screamed and began to dance about. Smoke poured from his pockets. Blistering his fingers, he threw pocketknife, change, moneyclip on the floor. They glowed dull red, and the smell of scorching wood filled the air.

A wisp of smoke rose from his tie clip, and he tore that off, sucking his blistered fingers. The belt buckle was next. By then the silver coins had melted against the wooden floor. But there was one last thing he had to remove. His shoes. The eyelets were metal. They began to burn the leather.

At last, panting and moaning he stood, surrounded by the cherry red pieces of metal on the floor.

Keena smiled and said softly, "Ah, you have no more metal on you. Would you like to have further proof?"

Amery Heater swallowed hard. He looked up at the open-mouthed judge. He glanced at the jury.

"The prosecution withdraws," he said hoarsely.

The judge managed to close his mouth.

"Case dismissed," he said. "Young woman, I suggest you go back wherever you came from."

She smiled blandly up at him. "Oh, no! I can't go back. I went back once and found that my world was very empty. They laughed at my new clothes. I said I wanted Billy. They said they would transport him to my world. But Billy wouldn't be happy there. So I came back."

Maloney stood up, yawned and stretched. He smiled at the jury. Two men were helping the woman back up into her chair. She was still green.

He winked at Keena and said, "Come on home, honey."

They walked down the aisle together and out the golden oak doors. Nobody made a sound, or a move to stop them.

Anita Hempflet, extremely conscious of the fact that the man who had left her waiting at the altar thirty-one years before was buried just beyond the corn hills in her vegetable garden, forced her razor lips into a broad smile, beamed around at the people sitting near her and said, in her high, sharp voice:

"Well! That girl is going to make a lovely neighbor! If you folks will excuse me, I'm going to take her over some fresh strawberry preserves."

PERIOD PIECE

by J. J. "Coupling" (John R. Pierce; 1910–   )

ASTOUNDING SCIENCE FICTION
November

Dr. John R. Pierce was one of the most distinguished scientists to publish regularly in the science fiction magazines. Before becoming a Professor of Engineering at the California Institute of Technology, he served as an administrator and researcher with the Bell Telephone Laboratories. He is the author of many notable scientific works, including Theory and Design of Electron Beams. *His crisp short stories appeared mostly in* Astounding, *under his own name and as by "Coupling."*

"Period Piece" is an outstanding cyborg story, and one of the first to focus on the alienation of an individual who is part machine and part something else.

(Consider one clause in the story: "Eddington's idea that the known universe is merely what man is able to perceive and measure." It seems to me [with the clarity of hindsight] that this is an obvious tautology. The known universe is the knowable universe. We know about the universe only what we can know, and anything we can't know is not part of it. So what else is knew?

Are there things about the Universe that we cannot

know in the usual way of observing and measuring, but that we can know in some other way—intuition, revelation, mad insight? If so, how can you know that what you know in these non-knowing ways is really so. Anything you know without knowing, others can know only on your flat statement without any proof other than "I know!"

All this leads to such madness that I, for one, am content with the knowable. That is enough to know. And somehow all this, I think, has something to do with the story—I. A.)

It was at that particular party of Cordoban's that he began actually to have doubts—real doubts. Before, there had been puzzlement and some confusion. But now, among these splendid people, in this finely appointed apartment, he wondered who he was, and where he was.

After his friend—or, his keeper?—Gavin had introduced him to his host, there had been a brief conversation about the twentieth century. Cordoban, a graying man with both dignity and alertness, asked the usual questions, always addressing Smith with the antique title, Mister, which he seemed to relish as an oddity. To Smith it seemed that Cordoban received the answers with the sort of rapt attention a child might give to a clever mechanical toy.

"Tell me, Mr. Smith," Cordoban said, "some of the scientists of your day must have been philosophers as well, were they not?"

Smith could not remember having been asked just this question before. For a moment he could think of nothing. Then, suddenly, as always, the knowledge flooded into his mind. He found himself making a neat little three-minute speech almost automatically. The material seemed to arrange itself as he spoke, telling how Einstein forced an abandonment of the idea of simultaneity, of Eddington's idea that the known universe is merely what man is able to perceive and measure, of Milne's two time scales, and of the strange ideas of Rhine and Dunne concerning precognition. He had always been a clever speaker, ever since high school, he thought.

"Of course," he found himself concluding, "it was not until later in the century that Chandra Bhopal demonstrated the absurdity of time travel."

Cordoban stared at him queerly. For a moment Smith was scarcely conscious of what he had said. Then he formulated his thoughts.

"But time travel must be possible," he said, "for I'm a twentieth century man, and I'm here in the thirty-first century."

He looked about the pleasant room, softly lighted, with deep recesses of color, for assurance, and at the handsome people, grouped standing or sitting in glowing pools of pearly illumination.

"Of course you're here, fellow," Cordoban said, reassuringly.

The remark was so true and so banal that Smith scarcely heard it. His thoughts were groping. Slowly, he was piecing together an argument.

"But time travel *is* absurd," he said.

Cordoban looked a little annoyed and made a nod with his head which Smith did not quite follow.

"It was shown in the twentieth century to be absurd," Smith said.

But, had it been shown in his part of the twentieth century, he wondered?

Cordoban glanced to his left.

"We know very little about the twentieth century," he said.

Gavin knows about the twentieth century, Smith thought.

Then, following Cordoban's glance, he saw that a young woman had detached herself from a group and was moving toward them. A segment of the pearly illumination followed her, making her a radiant creature indeed.

"Myria," Cordoban said, smiling, "you particularly wanted to meet Mr. Smith."

Myria smiled at Smith.

"Indeed, yes," she said. "I've always been curious about the twentieth century. And you must tell me about your music."

Cordoban bowed slightly and withdrew, the light which had been playing on him, seemingly from nowhere, detaching itself from the pool about Myria and Smith. And Smith's doubts fled to the back of his mind, crowded out, almost, by a flood of thoughts about music. And Myria was an enchanting creature.

Smith felt very chipper the next morning as he rose and bathed. The twentieth century had nothing like this to offer, he reflected. He knit his brows for a moment, trying to remember just what his room had been like, but at that moment the cupboard softly buzzed and he withdrew the glass of bland liquid which was his breakfast. His mind wandered while he sipped it. It wasn't until he walked down the corridor and sat in the office opposite Gavin that his doubts at Cordoban's returned to his mind.

Gavin was droning out the schedule. "We have a pretty full day, Smith," he said. "First, a couple of hours at the Lollards' country estate. We can stop by the Primus's on the way back. Then, a full afternoon at a party given by the decorators' council. In the evening—"

"Gavin," Smith said, "why do we see all these people?"

"Why," Gavin answered, a little taken aback, "everyone wants to see a man from the twentieth century."

"But why these people?" Smith persisted. "They all ask the same questions. And I never see them again. I just go on repeating myself."

"Are we too frivolous by twentieth century standards?" Gavin asked, smiling and leaning back in his chair.

Smith smiled back. Then his thoughts troubled him again. Cordoban hadn't been frivolous.

"How much do *you* know about the twentieth century, Gavin?" he asked, keeping his tone light.

"Pretty much what you do," Gavin replied.

But this couldn't be! Gavin appeared to be a kind of social tutor and arranger of things. As far as Smith could remember, mostly, information had passed from Gavin to him, not from him to Gavin. He decided to pursue the matter further, and as Gavin leaned forward to glance at the schedule again, Smith spoke once more.

"By the way, Gavin," he asked, "who is Cordoban?"

"Director of the Historical Institute, of course. I told you before we went there," Gavin replied.

"Who is Myria?" Smith asked.

"One of his secretaries," Gavin said. "A man of his position always has one on call."

"Cordoban said that not much was known about the twentieth century," Smith remarked mildly.

Gavin started up as if he had been stung. Then he sank back and opened his mouth. It was a moment before he found the words.

"Directors—" he said, and waved his hand as if brushing

the matter aside. Smith was really puzzled now. "Gavin," he said, "is time travel possible?"

If Gavin had been startled, he was at his ease now.

"You're here," he said, "not in the twentieth century."

Gavin spoke in so charming and persuasive a manner that Smith felt like a fool for a moment. His thoughts were slipping back toward the schedule when he realized, that wasn't an answer. It wasn't even couched as one. But this was silly, too. If it wasn't an answer, it was just what one would say.

Still, he'd try again.

"Gavin," he said, "Cordoban—"

"Look," Gavin said with a smile, "you'll get used to us in time. We'll keep the Lollards and their guests waiting if we don't start now. It isn't asking too much of you to see them now, is it? And you'll like it. They have a lovely fifteenth-century Chinese garden, with a dragon in a cave."

After all, Smith thought, he did owe his collective hosts of the thirty-first century something. And it was amusing.

The Lollards' garden was amusing, and so was the dragon, which breathed out smoke and roared. Primus's was dull, but the decorators' council had a most unusual display of fabrics which tinkled when they were touched, and of individual lighting in color. The evening was equally diverting, and delightful but strange people asked the same frivolous questions. Smith was diverted enough so that his doubts did not return until late that night.

But when Gavin left him at the door, Smith did not go to his bed and his usual dreamless sleep. Instead, he sat down in a chair, closed his eyes, and thought.

What did these people know about the twentieth century? Gavin had said, what he, Smith, knew. But that must be a great deal. An adult man, he, for instance, had a huge store of memories, accumulated over all his years. The human brain, he found himself thinking, has around ten billion nerve cells. If these were used to store words on a binary basis, they would hold some four hundred million words—a prodigious amount of learning. Tokayuki had, in 2117—

Strange, but he didn't remember talking with Gavin or anyone else about Tokayuki! And he could not have remembered about a man who had lived a century after his. But he could pursue this later.

Getting back to the gist of the matter, Cordoban had said that he knew little about the twentieth century. Yet Cordoban had not seemed anxious to question him at length. A few words about the philosophy of science, a dry enough subject, and he had called his secretary Myria—yes, Smith now saw, Cordoban had called Myria to relieve himself of Smith's presence. Here was an obviously astute man, and an historian, foregoing an opportunity to learn about an era of which he professed ignorance.

Well, I suppose one untrained man doesn't know much about an era, even his own, Smith thought. That is, not by thirty-first century standards. But, then, how do they know what I know? he wondered. Nobody has asked me any very searching questions.

Gavin and his schedules, now! All the occasions were purely social. That was strange! Most of the people weren't those likely to have much detailed interest in another era. Decorators, some, like the Lollards, apparently entirely idle-retired, perhaps. Anyway, the conversation was so much social chitchat.

Cordoban, now, had been an historian, even though he hadn't been curious. But that, too, was a purely social occasion. And Gavin himself! Just a sort of guide to a man from another age. Certainly not a curious man. Why not? Were men of the twentieth century so common here? But certainly he would have been brought into contact with others. Besides, time traveling was absurd!

But that was getting off the track. He *was* here. He didn't need Cordoban or Gavin to assure him of that. Being here, he would expect serious questioning by a small group—not all these frivolous, if delightful, parties. Surely he could tell them a great deal they had not asked.

Well, for instance, what could he tell them? His own personal experiences. What had happened day by day. But what had happened day by day? His schooling, for one thiing. High school, in particular. As he thought about high schools, there quickly rose in his mind a sequence of facts about their organization and curriculum. It was as if he were reviewing a syllabus on the subject.

The three-minute talks were getting him, he decided. He was so used to these impersonal summaries that they came to his mind automatically. Right now, he must be tired. He would spend more time thinking in the morning.

So Smith went to bed, thought about the events of the day a little, including the Lollards' amusing fire-breathing dragon, and was quickly asleep.

* * *

The following morning Smith did not feel chipper. He rose and bathed out of a sense of duty and routine. But then he sat down and ignored the buzzing of the cupboard which announced his breakfast. A pattern had crystallized in his mind over night. His thoughts in their uncertainty had paved the way for this, no doubt. But what was in his mind was no uncertain conclusion.

He, Smith, was no man of the twentieth century! He had carefully implanted memories, factual theses concerning his past, summaries of twentieth century history. But no real past! The little details that made a past were missing. Time travel was absurd. He was a fraud! An impostor!

But whom was he fooling? Not Gavin, he saw now. Not men like Cordoban. Was he fooling anyone? All of the people seemed eager to talk with him. Cordoban himself had been eager to talk with him. Cordoban had not been feigning. Cordoban had not been fooled. It seemed likely that Smith himself was the only one fooled.

But why? It was a stupid trick for people so obviously intelligent. What did they get out of this silly game? It could hardly be any personal quality of his—any charm. They were all so charming themselves.

Myria, Cordoban's secretary, for instance. A lovely woman. Handsome, poised, beautifully dressed. Suddenly a little three-minute talk about women in the twentieth century formed in Smith's mind. In part of his mind, that is. In a way, he watched it unfold. And with surprise.

He had thought of Myria as merely handsome and handsomely dressed. But even across the centuries—no, he must remember that he was not from the twentieth century. Across whatever gulf there was, there could have been more than this. Just how did he, Smith, differ from other men?

Well, what did he know of mankind? He reviewed matters in his mind, and went through little summaries on psychology, anthropology, and physiology. It was in the midst of this last that he felt a horrible conviction which changed his course from thought to action.

His first action was to wind a small gold chain which was a part of his clothing tightly around the tip of his index finger. The tip remained smooth and brown.

Dropping the chain, he dug the sharp point of a writing

instrument into his fingertip, ignoring the pain. The point passed into the rubbery flesh. There was no blood! But there was a little flash and a puff of vapor, and the finger went numb.

He was a cleverly constructed period piece, like the Lollards' dragon! Like a clockwork nightingale! That was why these people admired him briefly, for what he was—a charming mechanical toy!

Smith scarcely thought. The little review of twentieth century psychology returned to his mind, and automatically he opened the door onto the balcony and stepped over the railing. Consistent to the last, he thought in dull pain as he fell toward the ground twenty stories below.

But it wasn't the last. There was a terrible wrenching shock, a clashing noise, and confusion. Afterwards, there were still vision and hearing. True, the world stood at an odd angle. He saw the building leaning crazily into the sky. From the brief synopsis of physiology he gleaned that his psycho-kinetic sense was gone. He no longer felt which way his head and eyes were turned. Other senses than sight and sound were gone as well, and when he tried he found that he could not move. Junk, lying here, he thought bitterly. Not even release! But now he could see Gavin bending over him, and another man who looked as if he might be a mechanic.

"Junk," the mechanic said. "It's lucky we couldn't put the brain in that, or it would be gone, too. Making a new body won't be so bad," he added.

"I suppose we'll have to turn off the brain and reform the patterns," Gavin mused.

"You'd have had to, anyway," the mechanic said. "You must have put in something inconsistent or we wouldn't have had this failure."

"It's a shame, though," Gavin said. "I got to like him. Silly, isn't it? But he seemed so nearly alive. We spent a lot of time together. Now everything that happened, everything he learned, will have to be wiped out."

"You know," the mechanic said, "it gives me the creeps, sometimes. I mean, thinking, if I were just a body, connected by a tight beam to a brain off somewhere. And if, when the body was destroyed, the brain—"

"Nonsense," said Gavin.

He gestured toward Smith's crumpled body, and then up toward the building where, presumably, was Smith's brain.

"You'll be thinking that that thing was conscious, next," he said. "Come on, let's turn the brain off."

Smith stared numbly at the crazily leaning building, waiting for them to turn off his brain.

DORMANT

by A. E. van Vogt

STARTLING STORIES
November

A. E. van Vogt's second contribution to the best of 1948 is one of the author's major themes—power and its uses—a subject that is a constant through his work, sometimes obliquely, sometimes overtly, as in his Weapons Shop stories. "Dormant" was chosen for inclusion in The Best From Startling Stories *(1953) by Samuel Mines, himself a most underrated and capable editor.*

(I've spent my life as a writer without looking too closely at what it was I did while I was writing. Since I didn't pay any attention to subtleties I gradually learned to write directly, and with as little elaboration as I could possibly manage.

For instance, I would simply never start a story with the sentence "Old was that island." If I wanted to start a story with that notion I would surely phrase it as follows: "The island was old." If emphasis were wanted, I might add an exclamation mark. The reason for my choice would be that it was the simplest way of expressing the thought. Van Vogt's way would seem to my ears to be a kind of psuedo-archaism; an attempt at poetic inversion when none was necessary.

However, "Old was that island," emphasizes "old." That is the first word of the story and, what do you know, it has significance. See what I miss by avoiding subtleties.—I. A.)

Old was that island. Even the thing that lay in the outer channel exposed to the rude wash of the open sea had never guessed, when it was alive a million years before, that here was a protuberance of primeval earth itself.

The island was roughly three miles long and, at its widest, half a mile across. It curved tensely around a blue lagoon and the thin shape of its rocky, foam-ridden arms and hands came down toward the toe of the island—like a gigantic man bending over, striving to reach his feet and not quite making it.

Through the channel made by that gap between the toes and the fingers came the sea.

The water resented the channel. With an endless patience it fought to break the wall of rock, and the tumult of the waters was a special sound—a blend of all that was raucous and unseemly in the eternal quarrel between resisting land and encroaching wave.

At the very hub of the screaming waters lay Iilah, dead now almost forever, forgotten by time and the universe.

Early in 1941 Japanese ships came and ran the gauntlet of dangerous waters into the quiet lagoon. From the deck of one of the ships a pair of curious eyes pondered the thing, where it lay in the path of the rushing sea. But the owner of those eyes was the servant of a government that frowned on extra-military ventures of its personnel.

And so engineer Taku Onilo merely noted in his report that, "At the mouth of this channel there lies a solid shape of glittery rocklike substance about four hundred feet long and ninety feet wide."

The little yellow men built their underground gas and oil tanks and departed toward the setting sun. The water rose and fell, rose and fell again. The days and the years drifted by, and the hand of time was heavy. The seasonal rains arrived on their rough schedule and washed away the marks of man. Green growth sprouted where machines had exposed the raw earth.

The war ended. The underground tanks sagged a little in their beds of earth and cracks appeared in several main pipes. Slowly the oil drained off and for years a yellow-green oil slick brightened the gleam of the lagoon waters.

In the reaches of Bikini Atoll, hundreds of miles away, first one explosion, then another, started in motion an intricate pattern of radioactivated waters. The first seepage of that potent energy reached the island in the early fall of 1946.

It was about six months later that a patient clerk, ransacking the records of the Imperial Japanese Navy in Tokyo, reported the existence of the oil tanks. In due time—1948—the destroyer *Coulson* set forth on its routine voyage of examination.

The time of the nightmare was come.

Lieutenant Keith Maynard, a masochist of long experience, peered gloomily through his binoculars at the island. He was prepared to find something wrong but he expected a distracting monotony of sameness, not something radically different.

"Usual undergrowth," he muttered, "and a backbone of semi-mountain, running like a framework the length of the island, trees—"

He stopped there.

A broad swath had been cut through the palms on the near shoreline. They were not just down—they were crushed deep into a furrow that was already alive with grass and small growth. The furrow, which looked about a hundred feet wide, led upward from the beach to the side of a hill, to where a large rock lay half buried near the top of the hill.

Puzzled, Maynard glanced down at the Japanese photographs of the island. Involuntarily, he turned toward his executive officer, Lieutenant Gerson.

"Good lord!" he said, "how did that rock get up *there?* It's not on any photographs."

The moment he had spoken he regretted it. Gerson looked at him, with his usual faint antagonism, shrugged and said, "Maybe we've got the wrong island."

Maynard did not answer that. He considered Gerson a queer character. The man's tongue dripped ceaselessly with irony.

"I'd say it weighs about two million tons. The Japs probably dragged it up there to confuse us."

Maynard said nothing. He was annoyed that he had ever made a comment—and particularly annoyed because, for a moment, he had actually thought of the Japs in connection with the rock. The weight estimate, which he instantly recognized as fairly accurate, ended all his wilder thoughts.

If the Japs could move a rock weighing two million tons they had also won the war. Still, it was very curious and deserved investigation—afterward.

They ran the channel without incident. It was wider and deeper than Maynard had understood from the Jap accounts, which made everything easy. Their midday meal was eaten in the shelter of the lagoon. Maynard noted the oil on the water and issued immediate warnings against throwing matches overboard. After a brief talk with the other officers, he decided that they would set fire to the oil as soon as they had accomplished their mission and were out of the lagoon.

About one-thirty boats were lowered and they made shore in quick order. In an hour, with the aid of transcribed Japanese blueprints, they located the four buried tanks. It took somewhat longer to assess the dimensions of the tanks and to discover that three of them were empty.

Only the smallest contained high-octane gasoline, not worth the attention of the larger navy tankers that were still cruising around, picking up odd lots of Japanese and American matériel.

Maynard presumed that a lighter would eventually be dispatched for the gasoline, but that was none of his business.

In spite of the speed with which his job had been accomplished, Maynard climbed wearily up to the deck just as darkness was falling.

He must have overdone it a little because Gerson said too loudly, "Worn out, sir?"

Maynard stiffened. And it was that comment rather than any inclination that decided him not to postpone his exploration of the rock. As soon as possible after the evening meal he called for volunteers.

It was pitch dark as the boat, with seven men and Bosun's Mate Yewell and himself, was beached on the sands under the towering palms.

The party headed inland.

There was no moon and the stars were scattered among remnant clouds of the rainy season just past. They walked in the furrow, where the trees had been literally plowed into the ground. In the pale light of the flashlights the spectacle of numerous trees, burned and planed into a smoothed levelness with the soil, was unnatural.

Maynard heard one of the men mumble, "Must have been some freak of a typhoon did that."

Not only a typhoon, Maynard decided, but a ravenous fire followed by a monstrous wind, so monstrous that—his brain paused. He couldn't imagine any storm big enough to lift a two-million-ton rock to the side of a hill a quarter of a mile long and four hundred feet above sea level.

From nearby, the rock looked like nothing more than rough granite. In the beam of the flashlights it glinted with innumerable streaks of pink. Maynard led his party alongside it and the vastness of it grew upon him as he climbed past its four hundred feet of length and peered up at gleaming walls, like cliffs looming above him.

The upper end, buried though it was deeper into the ground, rose at least fifty feet above his head.

The night had grown uncomfortably warm. Maynard was perspiring freely. He enjoyed a moment of weary pleasure in the thought that he was doing his duty under unpleasant circumstances. He stood uncertain, gloomily savoring the intense primitive silence of the night.

"Break off some samples here and there," he said finally. "Those pink streaks look interesting."

It was a few seconds later that a man's scream of agony broke through the thrall of darkness.

Flashlights blinked on. They showed Seaman Hicks twisting on the ground beside the rock. In the bright flame of the lights, the man's wrists showed as a smoldering, blackened husk with the entire hand completely burned off.

He had touched Iilah.

Maynard gave the miserable wretch morphine and they rushed him back to the ship. Radio contact was established with base and a consulting surgeon gave cut-by-cut instructions on the operation. It was agreed that a hospital plane would be dispatched for the patient.

There must have been some puzzlement at headquarters as to how the accident had occurred, because "further information" was requested about the "hot" rock. By morning the people at the other end were calling it a meteorite. Maynard, who did not normally question opinions offered by his superiors, frowned over the identification and pointed out that this meteorite weighed two million tons and rested on the surface of the island.

"I'll send the assistant engineer officer to take its temperature," he said.

An engine-room thermometer registered the rock's surface temperature at eight-hundred-odd degrees Fahrenheit. The answer to that was a question that shocked Maynard.

"Why, yes," he replied, "we're getting mild radioactive reactions from the water but nothing else. And nothing serious. Under the circumstances we'll withdraw from the lagoon at once and await the ships with the scientists."

He ended that conversation, pale and shaken. Nine men, including himself, had walked along within a few yards of the rock, well within the deadly danger zone. In fact, even the *Coulson*, more than half a mile away, would have been affected.

But the gold leaves of the electroscope stood out stiff and the Geiger-Mueller counter clucked only when placed in the water and then only at long intervals.

Relieved, Maynard went down to have another look at Seaman Hicks. The injured man slept uneasily but he was not dead, which was a good sign. When the hospital plane arrived there was a doctor aboard, who attended Hicks and then gave everyone on the destroyer a blood-count test. He came up on deck, a cheerful young man, and reported to Maynard.

"Well, it can't be what they suspect," he said. "Everybody's okay, even Hicks, except for his hand. That burned awfully quick, if you ask me, for a temperature of only eight hundred."

"I think his hand stuck," said Maynard. And he shuddered. In his fashion he had mentally experienced the entire accident.

"So that's the rock," said Dr. Clason. "Does seem odd how it got there."

They were still standing there five minutes later when a hideous screaming from below deck made a discordant sound on the still air of that remote island lagoon.

Something stirred in the depths of Iilah's awareness of himself, something that he had intended to do—he couldn't remember what.

That was the first real thought he had in late 1946, when he felt the impact of outside energy. And stirred with returning life.

The outside flow waxed and waned. It was abnormally, abysmally dim. The crust of the planet that he knew had palpitated with the ebbing but potent energies of a world not yet cooled from its sun state.

It was only slowly that Iilah realized the extent of the disaster that was his environment. At first he was inwardly inclined, too pallidly alive to be interested in externals.

He forced himself to become more conscious of his environment. He looked forth with his radar vision out upon a strange world.

He was lying on a shallow plateau near the top of a mountain. The scene was desolate beyond his memory. There was not a glint nor pressure of atomic fire—not a bubble of boiling rock nor a swirl of energy heaved skyward by some vast interior explosion.

He did not think of what he saw as an island surrounded by an apparently limitless ocean. He saw the land below the water as well as above it.

His vision, based as it was on ultra-ultra short waves, could not see water.

He recognized that he was on an old and dying planet, where life had long since become extinct.

Alone and dying on a forgotten planet—if he could only find the source of the energy that had revived him.

By a process of simple logic he started down the mountain in the direction from which the current of atomic energy seemed to be coming. Somehow he found himself below it and had to levitate himself heavily, back up. Once started upward, he headed for the nearest peak, with the intention of seeing what was on the other side.

As he propelled himself out of the invisible, unsensed waters of the lagoon, two diametrically opposite phenomena affected him. He lost all contact with the water-borne current of atomic energy. And, simultaneously, the water ceased to inhibit the neutron and deuteron activity of his body.

His life took on an increased intensity. The tendency to slow stiflement ended. His great form became a self-sustaining pile, capable of surviving for the normal radioactive lifespan of the elements that composed it—still on an immensely less-than-normal activity level for him.

Iilah thought, "There was something I was going to do."

The flow of electrons through a score of gigantic cells as he strained to remember increased, then slowed gradually when no memory came.

The fractional increase of his life energy brought with it a wider, more exact understanding of his situation. Wave on wave of perceptive radaric forces flowed from him to the Moon, to Mars, to all the planets of the solar system—and the echoes that came back were examined with an alarmed awareness that out there, too, were dead bodies.

He was caught in the confines of a dead system, prisoned until the relentless exhaustion of his material structure brought him once more to rapport with the dead mass of the planet on which he was marooned.

He realized now that he had been dead. Just how it had happened he could not recall, except that explosively violent, frustrating substance had belched around him, buried him, and snuffed out his life processes. The atomic chemistry involved must eventually have converted the stuff into a harmless form, no longer capable of hindering him. But he was dead by then.

Now he was alive again, but in so dim a fashion that there was nothing to do but wait for the end. He waited. . . .

In 1948 he watched the destroyer float toward him through the sky. Long before it slowed and stopped just below him, he had discovered that it was not a life form related to him. It manufactured a dull internal heat and, through its exterior walls, he could see the vague glow of fires.

All that first day Iilah waited for the creature to show awareness of him. But not a wave of life emanated from it. And yet it floated in the sky above the plateau, an impossible phenomenon, utterly outside all his experience.

To Iilah, who had no means of sensing water, who could not even imagine air, and whose ultra waves passed through human beings as if they did not exist, the reaction could only mean one thing—here was an alien life form that had adapted itself to the dead world around him.

Gradually Iilah grew excited. The thing could move freely above the surface of the planet. It would know if any source of atomic energy remained anywhere. The problem was to get into communication with it.

The sun was high on the meridian of another day when Iilah directed the first questioning pattern of thought toward the destroyer. He aimed straight at the vaguely glowing fires in the engine room, where, he reasoned, would be the intelligence of the alien creature.

The thirty-four men who died in the spaces in and around the engine room and the fire room were buried on shore. Their surviving comrades, including all officers, moved half a mile up the east coast. And at first they expected to stay there until the abandoned *Coulson* ceased to give off dangerous radioactive energies.

On the seventh day, when transport planes were already dumping scientific equipment and personnel, three of the men fell sick and their blood count showed a fateful decrease in the number of red corpuscles. Although no orders had arrived, Maynard took alarm and ordered the entire crew shipped for observation to Hawaii.

He allowed the officers to make their own choice, but advised the second engineer officer, the first gunnery officer, and several ensigns who had helped hoist the dead men up to deck, to take no chances, but to grab space on the first planes.

Although all were ordered to leave, several crew members asked permission to remain. And, after a careful questioning by Gerson, a dozen men who could prove that they had not been near the affected area were finally permitted to stay.

Maynard would have preferred to see Gerson himself depart, but in this he was disappointed. Of the officers who had been aboard the destroyer at the time of the disaster, Lieutenants Gerson, Lausson, and Haury, the latter two being gunnery officers, and Ensigns McPelty, Roberts, and Manchioff, remained on the beach.

Among the higher ratings remaining behind were the chief commissary steward, Jenkins, and chief bosun's mate Yewell.

The navy group was ignored except that several times requests were made that they move their tents out of the way. Finally, when it seemed evident that they would be crowded out once more, Maynard in annoyance ordered the canvas moved well down the coast, where the palms opened up to form a grassy meadow.

Maynard grew puzzled, then grim, as the weeks passed and no orders arrived concerning the disposal of his command. In one of the Stateside papers that began to follow the scientists, the bulldozers and cement mixers onto the island he read an item in an "inside" column that gave him his first inkling.

According to the columnist, there had been a squabble between navy bigwigs and the civilian members of the Atomic Control Board over control of the investigation. With the result that the navy had been ordered to "stay out."

Maynard read the account with mixed feelings and a dawning understanding that he was *the* navy representative on the island. The realization included a thrilling mental visualization of himself rising to the rank of admiral—if he handled the situation right. Just what would be right, aside from keeping a sharp eye on everything, he couldn't decide.

It was an especially exquisite form of self-torture.

He couldn't sleep. He spent his days wandering as unobtrusively as possible through the ever vaster encampment of the army of scientists and their assistants. At night he had several hiding places from which he watched the brilliantly lighted beach.

It was a fabulous oasis of brightness in the dark vaulting vastness of a Pacific night. For a full mile string upon string of lights spread along the whispering waters. They silhouetted and spotlighted the long, thick, back-curving, cement-like walls that reared up eerily, starting at the rim of the hill. Protective walls were already soaring up around the rock itself, striving to block it off from all outside contact.

Always, at midnight, the bulldozers ceased their roarings, the cement-mixing trucks dumped their last loads and scurried down the makeshift beach road and so to silence. The entire, already intricate organization settled into an uneasy slumber—and Maynard waited with the painful patience of a man doing more than his duty, usually until around one o'clock, when he, too, would make his way to his bed.

The secret habit paid off. He was the only man who actually witnessed the rock climb to the top of the hill.

It was a stupendous event. The time was about a quarter to one and Maynard was on the point of calling it a day when he heard the sound. It was like a truck emptying a load of gravel. For a bare moment he thought of it entirely in relation to his hiding place.

His night-spying activities were going to be found out.

An instant after that the rock reared up into the brilliance of the lights.

There was a roaring now of cement barriers, crumbling before that irresistible movement. Fifty, sixty, then ninety feet of monster rock loomed up above the hill and slid with a heavy power over the crown.

And stopped.

For two months Iilah had watched the freighters breast the channel. Just why they followed that route interested him. And he wondered if there was some limitation on them, that kept them at such an exact level.

What was more interesting by far, however, was that in every case the aliens would slide around the island and disappear behind a high promontory that was the beginning of the east shore. In every case, after they had been gone for a few days, they would slide into view again, glide through the channel, and gradually move off through the sky.

During those months Iilah caught tantalizing glimpses of small but much faster winged ships that shot down from a great height—and disappeared behind the crest of the hill to the east.

Always to the east. His curiosity grew enormous, but he was reluctant to waste energy. And it was not until he grew aware of a nighttime haze of lights that brightened the eastern sky at night, that he finally set off the more violent explosions on his lower surface that made directive motion possible.

He climbed the last seventy or so feet to the top of the hill. And regretted it immediately.

One ship lay a short distance offshore. The haze of light along the eastern slope seemed to have no source. As he watched, scores of trucks and bulldozers raced around, some of them coming quite close to him.

Just what they wanted, or what they were doing he could not make out. He sent several questioning thought waves at various of the objects, but there was no response.

He gave it up as a bad job.

The rock was still resting on the top of the hill the next morning, poised so that both sides of the island were threatened by the stray bursts of energy which it gave off so erratically.

Maynard heard his first account of the damage done from Jenkins, the chief commissary steward. Seven truck-drivers and two bulldozer men dead, a dozen men suffering from glancing burns—and two months' labor wrecked.

There must have been a conference among the scientists, for, shortly after noon, trucks and bulldozers, loaded with equipment, began to stream past the navy camp. A seaman, dispatched to follow them, reported that they were setting up camp on the point at the lower end of the island.

Just before dark a notable event took place in the social history of the island. The director of the project, together with four executive scientists, walked into the lighted area and asked for Maynard.

The group was smiling and friendly. There was handshaking all around. Maynard introduced Gerson, who unfortunately (so far as Maynard was concerned) was in the camp at the moment. And then the visiting delegation got down to business.

"As you know," said the director, "the *Coulson* is only partially radioactive. The rear gun turret is quite unaffected, and we accordingly request that you cooperate with us and fire on the rock until it is broken into sections."

"Huh!" said Maynard.

It took only a moment for him to recover from his astonishment and to know what he would answer to that.

At no time, during the next few days, did Maynard question the belief of the scientists that the rock should be broken up and so rendered harmless. He refused their request and then doggedly continued to refuse it.

It was not until the third day that he thought of a reason.

"Your precautions, gentlemen," he said, "are not sufficient. I do not consider that moving the camp out to the point is a sufficient safeguard in the event that the rock should blow up. Now, of course, if I should receive a command from a naval authority to do as you wish. . . ."

He left that sentence dangling—and saw from their disappointed faces that there must have been a feverish exchange of radio messages with their own headquarters. The arrival of a Kwajalein paper on the fourth day quoted a "high" Washington naval officer as saying that, "any such decisions must be left to the judgment of the naval commander on the island."

And that, if a properly channeled request was made, the navy would be glad to send an atomic expert of its own to the scene.

It was obvious to Maynard that he was handling the situation exactly as his superiors desired. The only thing was that, even as he finished reading the account, the silence was broken by the unmistakable bark of a destroyer's five-inch guns, that sharpest of all gunfire sounds.

Unsteadily Maynard climbed to his feet. An awful suspicion was on him. A swift glance around the camp showed that Gerson and his crony, gunnery officer Haury, were nowhere in sight.

His anger was instantly personal. He began to climb to the nearest height. Before he reached it the second shattering roar came from the other side of the lagoon, and once again an ear-splitting explosion echoed from the vicinity of the rock.

Maynard reached his vantage point and, through his binoculars, saw about a dozen men scurrying over the aft deck in and about the rear gun turret. It was impossible to make out if Gerson and Haury were among those aboard. There seemed to be no uniforms.

His first terrible suspicion faded. A new and grimmer fury came, this time against the camp director, and a determination to assure himself that every man assisting on the destroyer was arrested for malicious and dangerous trespass.

A vague thought came that it was a sorry day indeed when interbureau squabbles could cause such open defiance of the armed forces, as if nothing more were involved than a struggle for power. But that thought faded as swiftly as it came.

He waited for the third firing, then hurried down the hill to his camp. Swift commands to the men and officers sent eight of them to positions along the shore of the island, where they could watch boats trying to land.

With the rest Maynard headed toward the nearest navy boat. He had to take the long way around, by way of the point, and there must have been radio communication between the point and those on the ship, for a motor boat was just disappearing around the far end of the island when Maynard approached the now silent and deserted *Coulson*.

He hesitated. Should he give chase? A careful study of the rock proved it to be apparently unbroken. The failure cheered him, but it also made him cautious. It wouldn't do for his superiors to discover that he had not taken the necessary precautions to prevent the destroyer being boarded.

He was still pondering the problem when Iilah started down the hill, straight toward the destroyer.

Iilah saw the first bright puff from the destroyer's guns. And then he had a moment during which he observed an object flash toward him. In the old, old times he had developed defenses against hurtling objects. Quite automatically now, he tensed for the blow of this one.

The object, instead of merely striking him with its hardness, exploded. The impact was stupendous. His protective crust cracked. The concussion blurred and distorted the flow from every electronic plate in his great mass.

Instantly the automatic stabilizing "tubes" sent off balancing impulses. The hot, internal, partly rigid, partly fluid matter that made up the greater portion of his body, grew hotter, more fluidic.

The weaknesses induced by that tremendous concussion accepted the natural union of a liquid—and hardened instantly under enormous pressure.

Sane again, Iilah considered what had happened. An attempt at communication?

The possibility excited him. Instead of closing the gap in his outer wall he hardened the matter immediately behind it, thus cutting off wasteful radiation.

He waited.

Again the hurtling object and the enormously potent blow, as it struck him. . . . After a dozen blows, each with its resulting disaster to his protective shell, Iilah writhed with doubts.

If these were messages he could not receive them or understand. He began reluctantly to allow the chemical reactions that sealed the protective barrier. Faster than he could seal the holes, the hurtling objects breached his defenses.

And still he did not think of what had happened as an attack.

In all his previous existence he had never been attacked in such a fashion. Just what methods had been used against him, Iilah could not remember. But certainly nothing so purely molecular.

The conviction that it was an attack came reluctantly and he felt no anger. The reflex of defense in him was logical, not emotional. He studied the destroyer and it seemed to him that his purpose must be to drive it away.

And he must drive away every similar creature that tried to come near him. All the scurrying objects he had seen when he mounted the crest of the hill—all that must depart. Everything eventually, but first the destroyer.

He started down the hill.

The creature floating above the plateau had ceased exuding flame. As Iilah eased himself near it, the only sign of life was a smaller object that darted alongside it.

There was a moment then when Iilah entered the water. That was a shock. He had almost forgotten that there was a level of this desolate mountain below which his life forces were affected.

He hesitated.

Then, slowly, he slid farther down the depressing area, conscious that he had attained a level of strength that he could maintain against such a purely negative pressure.

The destroyer began to fire at him. The shells, delivered at point-blank range, poked deep holes into the ninety-foot cliff with which Iilah faced his enemy.

As that wall of rock touched the destroyer the firing stopped. (Maynard and his men, having defended the *Coulson* as long as possible, tumbled over the far side into their boat and raced away as fast as possible.)

Iilah shoved. The pain that he felt from those titanic blows was the pain that comes to all living creatures experiencing partial dissolution.

Laboriously his body repaired itself. And with anger and hatred and fear now he shoved. In a few minutes he had tangled the curiously unwieldy structure in the rocks that rose up to form the edge of the plateau. Beyond was the sharp declining slope of the mountain.

A curious thing happened. Once among the rocks the creature started to shudder and shake, as if caught by some inner destructive force. It fell over on its side and lay there like some wounded thing, quivering and breaking up.

It was an amazing spectacle. Iilah withdrew from the water, reclimbed the mountain, and plunged down into the sea on the other side, where a freighter was just getting under way. It swung around the promontory and successfully floated through the channel and out, coasting along high above the bleak valley that fell away beyond the breakers. It moved along for several miles, then slowed and stopped.

Iilah would have liked to chase it further, but he was limited to ground movement. And so, the moment the freighter had stopped, he turned and headed toward the point, where all the small objects were cluttered.

He did not notice the men who plunged into the shallows near the shore and from that comparative safety watched the destruction of their equipment. Iilah left a wake of burning and crushed vehicles. The few drivers who tried to get their machines away became splotches of flesh and blood inside and on the metal of their machines.

There was a fantastic amount of stupidity and panic. Iilah moved at a speed of about eight miles an hour. Three hundred and seventeen men were caught in scores of individual traps and crushed by a monster that did not even know they existed.

Each man must have felt himself personally pursued.

Afterward Iilah climbed to the nearest peak and studied the sky for further interlopers.

Only the freighter remained, a shadowy threat some four miles away.

Darkness cloaked the island, slowly. Maynard moved cautiously through the grass, flashing his flashlight directly in front of him on a sharp downward slant.

Every little while he called out, "Anybody around?"

It had been like that four hours now. Through the fading day they had searched for survivors, each time loading them aboard their boat and ferrying them through the channel and out to where the freighter waited.

The orders had come through by radio. They had forty-eight hours to get clear of the island. After that the bomb run would be made by a drone plane.

Maynard pictured himself walking along on this monster-inhabited, night-enveloped island. And the shuddery thrill that came was almost pure unadulterated pleasure. He felt himself pale with a joyous terror.

It was like the time when his ship had been among those shelling a Jap-held beach. He had been gloomy until, suddenly, he had pictured himself out there on the beach at the receiving end of the shells.

He began to torture himself with the possibility that, somehow, he might be left behind when the freighter finally withdrew.

A moan from the near darkness ended that thought. In the glow of the flashlight Maynard saw a vaguely familiar face. The man had been smashed by a falling tree.

As Executive Officer Gerson came forward and administered morphine, Maynard bent closer to the injured man and peered at him anxiously.

It was one of the world-famous scientists on the island. Ever since the disaster the radio messages had been asking for him. There was not a scientific body on the globe that cared to commit itself to the navy bombing plan until he had given his opinion.

"Sir," began Maynard, "what do you think about—"

He stopped. He settled mentally back on his heels.

Just for a moment he had forgotten that the naval authorities had already ordered the atomic bomb dropped, after being given governmental authority to do as they saw fit.

The scientist stirred. "Maynard," he croaked, "there's something funny about that creature. Don't let them do any—"

His eyes grew bright with pain. His voice trailed.

It was time to push questions. The great man would soon be deep in a doped sleep and he would be kept that way. In a moment it would be too late.

The moment passed.

Lieutenant Gerson climbed to his feet. "There, that ought to do it, Captain." He turned to the seamen carrying the stretchers. "Two of you take this man back to the boat. Careful. I've put him to sleep."

Maynard followed the stretcher without a word. He had a sense of having been saved from the necessity of making a decision rather than of having made one.

The night dragged on.

The morning dawned grayly. Shortly after the sun came up a tropical shower stormed across the island and rushed off eastward.

The sky grew amazingly blue and the world of water all around seemed motionless, so calm did the sea become.

Out of the blue distance, casting a swiftly moving shadow on that still ocean, flew the drone plane.

Long before it came in sight, Iilah sensed the load it carried. He quivered through his mass. Enormous electron tubes waxed and waned with expectancy and, for a brief while, he thought it was one of his own kind coming near.

As the plane drew closer he sent cautious thoughts toward it. Several planes, to which he had directed his thought waves, had twisted jerkily in midair and tumbled down out of control.

This one did not deviate from its course. When it was almost directly overhead a large object dropped from it, turned lazily over and over as it curved toward Iilah. It was set to explode about a hundred feet above the target.

The timing was perfect, the explosion titanic.

As soon as the blurring effects of so much new energy had passed, the now fully alive Iilah thought in a quiet though rather startled comprehension, "Why, of course, that's what I was trying to remember. That's what I was supposed to do."

He was puzzled that he could have forgotten. He had been sent during the course of an interstellar war—which apparently was still going on. He had been dropped on the planet under enormous difficulties and had been instantly snuffed out by enemy frustrators.

Now, he was ready to do his job.

He took test sightings on the sun and on the planets that were within reach of his radar signals. Then he set in motion an orderly process that would dissolve all the shields inside his own body.

He gathered his pressure forces for the final thrust that would bring the vital elements hard together at exactly the calculated moment.

The explosion that knocked a planet out of its orbit was recorded on every seismograph on the globe.

It would be some time, however, before astronomers would discover that earth was falling into the sun.

And no man would live to see Sol flare into nova brightness and burn up the solar system before gradually sinking back into a dim G state.

Even if Iilah had known that it was not the same war that had raged ten thousand million centuries before, he would have had no choice but to do as he did.

Robot atom bombs do not make up their own minds.

IN HIDING

by Wilmar H. Shiras (1908–   )

ASTOUNDING SCIENCE FICTION
November

It is safe to say that this story caught the science fiction readership of the time by surprise. Readers had not heard of the author, and few knew that she was a woman. The story made a tremendous impact, led to four other connecting novelettes, and was finally published in book form as Children of the Atom *(1953). The central idea is an old one in science fiction, dating back at least to Stapledon's* Odd John *and somewhat reminiscent of A. E. van Vogt's* Slain. *The mutated, exceptional child was and still is popular; perhaps some of the science fiction readership see themselves in this way or would like to think so.*

In any event, "In Hiding" is an excellent story, in spite of the fact that we now know that the type and cause of the mutation is impossible. Ms. Shiras is still writing and still publishing in the science fiction field, although her output over the years has been small.

("There are supermen among us," remember? They could be our children. —Except that I never believed it. That's not the way mutations take place. Besides, I was a bright child once, and I made people uneasy. My

father was convinced there was something odd about me, and John Campbell actually tried to tell me once that I might be a mutation. [I shouldn't have laughed.] The trouble was that I was quite sure that my brightness was well within the normal variation of the human species and was balanced by an abysmal capacity for various kinds of stupidities that were also [thank goodness] within the normal variation of the species. I've known lots of bright people who had, in their time, been frighteningly bright children [some of them, I reluctantly admit, manifestly brighter than I am, or was] and all of them show plenty of capacity for non-brightness too. To expect anything else is to expect a chimpanzee to give birth to a young chimpanzee which, for some reason, is as bright as an ordinary human child. —But who cares about that. Read the story, and please don't bother to remind me that I, too, in some of my stories have used mutations to good effect. I know!—I.A.)

Peter Welles, psychiatrist, eyed the boy thoughtfully. Why had Timothy Paul's teacher sent him for examination?

"I don't know, myself, that there's really anything wrong with Tim," Miss Page had told Dr. Welles. "He seems perfectly normal. He's rather quiet as a rule, doesn't volunteer answers in class or anything of that sort. He gets along well enough with other boys and seems reasonably popular, although he has no special friends. His grades are satisfactory—he gets B faithfully in all his work. But when you've been teaching as long as I have, Peter, you get a feeling about certain ones. There is a tension about him—a look in his eyes sometimes—and he is very absentminded."

"What would your guess be?" Welles had asked. Sometimes these hunches were very valuable. Miss Page had taught school for thirty-odd years; she had been Peter's teacher in the past, and he thought highly of her opinion.

"I ought not to say," she answered. "There's nothing to go on—yet. But he might be starting something, and if it could be headed off—"

"Physicians are often called before the symptoms are sufficiently marked for the doctor to be able to see them," said Welles. "A patient, or the mother of a child, or any practiced observer, can often see that something is going to be wrong. But it's hard for the doctor in such cases. Tell me what you think I should look for."

"You won't pay too much attention to me? It's just what occurred to me, Peter; I know I'm not a trained psychiatrist. But it could be delusions of grandeur. Or it could be a withdrawing from the society of others. I always have to speak to him twice to get his attention in class—and he has no real chums."

Welles had agreed to see what he could find, and promised not to be too much influenced by what Miss Page herself called "an old woman's notions."

Timothy, when he presented himself for examination, seemed like an ordinary boy. He was perhaps a little small for his age, he had big dark eyes and close-cropped dark curls, thin sensitive fingers and—yes, a decided air of tension. But many boys were nervous on their first visit to the—psychiatrist. Peter often wished that he was able to concentrate on one or two schools, and spend a day a week or so getting acquainted with all the youngsters.

In response to Welles' preliminary questioning, Tim replied in a clear, low voice, politely and without wasting words. He was thirteen years old, and lived with his grandparents. His mother and father had died when he was a baby, and he did not remember them. He said that he was happy at home, and that he liked school "pretty well," that he liked to play with other boys. He named several boys when asked who his friends were.

"What lessons do you like at school?"

Tim hesitated, then said: "English, and arithmetic . . . and history . . . and geography," he finished thoughtfully. Then he looked up, and there was something odd in the glance.

"What do you like to do for fun?"

"Read, and play games."

"What games?"

"Ball games . . . and marbles . . . and things like that. I like to play with other boys," he added, after a barely perceptible pause, "anything they play."

"Do they play at your house?"

"No; we play on the school grounds. My grandmother doesn't like noise."

Was that the reason? When a quiet boy offers explanations, they may not be the right ones.

"What do you like to read?"

But about his reading Timothy was vague. He liked, he said, to read "boys' books," but could not name any.

Welles gave the boy the usual intelligence tests. Tim seemed willing, but his replies were slow in coming. *Perhaps,* Welles thought, I'm imagining this, but he is too careful—too *cautious.* Without taking time to figure exactly, Welles knew what Tim's I.Q. would be—about 120.

"What do you do outside of school?" asked the psychiatrist.

"I play with the other boys. After supper, I study my lessons."

"What did you do yesterday?"

"We played ball on the school playground."

Welles waited a while to see whether Tim would say anything of his own accord. The seconds stretched into minutes.

"Is that all?" said the boy finally. "May I go now?"

"No; there's one more test I'd like to give you today. A game, really. How's your imagination?"

"I don't know."

"Cracks on the ceiling—like those over there—do they look like anything to you? Faces, animals, or anything?"

Tim looked.

"Sometimes. And clouds, too. Bob saw a cloud last week that was like a hippo." Again the last sentence sounded like something tacked on at the last moment, a careful addition made for a reason.

Welles got out the Rorschach cards. But at the sight of them, his patient's tension increased, his wariness became unmistakably evident. The first time they went through the cards, the boy could scarcely be persuaded to say anything but, "I don't know."

"You can do better than this," said Welles. "We're going through them again. If you don't see anything in these pictures, I'll have to mark you a failure," he explained. "That won't do. You did all right on the other things. And maybe next time we'll do a game you'll like better."

"I don't feel like playing this game now. Can't we do it again next time?"

"May as well get it done now. It's not only a game, you know, Tim; it's a test. Try harder, and be a good sport."

So Tim, this time, told what he saw in the ink blots. They went through the cards slowly, and the test showed Tim's fear, and that there was something he was hiding; it showed his caution, a lack of trust, and an unnaturally high emotional self-control.

Miss Page had been right; the boy needed help.

"Now," said Welles cheerfully, "that's all over. We'll just run through them again quickly and I'll tell you what other people have seen in them."

A flash of genuine interest appeared on the boy's face for a moment.

Welles went through the cards slowly, seeing that Tim was attentive to every word. When he first said, "And some see what you saw here," the boy's relief was evident. Tim began to relax, and even to volunteer some remarks. When they had finished he ventured to ask a question.

"Dr. Welles, could you tell me the name of this test?"

"It's sometimes called the Rorschach test, after the man who worked it out."

"Would you mind spelling that?"

Welles spelled it, and added: "Sometimes it's called the ink-blot test."

Tim gave a start of surprise, and then relaxed again with a visible effort.

"What's the matter? You jumped."

"Nothing."

"Oh, come on! Let's have it," and Welles waited.

"Only that I thought about the ink-pool in the Kipling stories," said Tim, after a minute's reflection. "This is different."

"Yes, very different," laughed Welles. "I've never tried that. Would you like to?"

"Oh, no, sir," cried Tim earnestly.

"You're a little jumpy today," said Welles. "We've time for some more talk, if you are not too tired."

"No, I'm not very tired," said the boy warily.

Welles went to a drawer and chose a hypodermic needle. It wasn't usual, but perhaps—"I'll just give you a little shot to relax your nerves, shall I? Then we'd get on better."

When he turned around, the stark terror on the child's face stopped Welles in his tracks.

"Oh, no! Don't! Please, please, don't!"

Welles replaced the needle and shut the drawer before he said a word.

"I won't," he said, quietly. "I didn't know you didn't like shots. I won't give you any, Tim."

The boy, fighting for self-control, gulped and said nothing.

"It's all right," said Welles, lighting a cigarette and pretending to watch the smoke rise. Anything rather than appear to be watching the badly shaken small boy shivering in the chair opposite him. "Sorry. You didn't tell me about the things you don't like, the things you're afraid of."

The words hung in the silence.

"Yes," said Timothy slowly. "I'm afraid of shots. I hate needles. It's just one of those things." He tried to smile.

"We'll do without them, then. You've passed all the tests, Tim, and I'd like to walk home with you and tell your grandmother about it. Is that all right with you?"

"Yes, sir."

"We'll stop for something to eat," Welles went on, opening the door for his patient. "Ice cream, or a hot dog."

They went out together.

Timothy Paul's grandparents, Mr. and Mrs. Herbert Davis, lived in a large old-fashioned house that spelled money and position. The grounds were large, fenced, and bordered with shrubbery. Inside the house there was little that was new, everything was well-kept. Timothy led the psychiatrist to Mr. Davis's library, and then went in search of his grandmother.

When Welles saw Mrs. Davis, he thought he had some of the explanation. Some grandmothers are easy-going, jolly, comparatively young. This grandmother was, as it soon became apparent, quite different.

"Yes, Timothy is a pretty good boy," she said, smiling on her grandson. "We have always been strict with him, Dr. Welles, but I believe it pays. Even when he was a mere baby, we tried to teach him right ways. For example, when he was barely three I read him some little stories. And a few days later he was trying to tell us, if you will believe it, that he could read! Perhaps he was too young to know the nature of a lie, but I felt it my duty to make him understand. When he insisted, I spanked him. The child had a remarkable memory, and perhaps he thought that was all there was to reading. Well! I don't mean to brag of my brutality," said Mrs. Davis, with a charming smile. "I assure you, Dr. Welles, it was a painful experience for me. We've had very little occasion for punishments. Timothy is a good boy."

Welles murmured that he was sure of it.

"Timothy, you may deliver your papers now," said Mrs. Davis. "I am sure Dr. Welles will excuse you." And she settled herself for a good long talk about her grandson.

Timothy, it seemed, was the apple of her eye. He was a quiet boy, an obedient boy, and a bright boy.

"We have our rules, of course. I have never allowed Timothy

to forget that children should be seen and not heard, as the good old-fashioned saying is. When he first learned to turn somersaults, when he was three or four years old, he kept coming to me and saying, 'Grandmother, see me!' I simply had to be firm with him. 'Timothy,' I said, 'let us have no more of this! It is simply showing off. If it amuses you to turn somersaults, well and good. But it doesn't amuse me to watch you endlessly doing it. Play if you like, but do not demand admiration.' "

"Did you never play with him?"

"Certainly I played with him. And it was a pleasure to me also. We—Mr. Davis and I—taught him a great many games, and many kinds of handicraft. We read stories to him and taught him rhymes and songs. I took a special course in kindergarten craft, to amuse the child—and I must admit that it amused me also!" added Tim's grandmother, smiling reminiscently. "We made houses of toothpicks, with balls of clay at the corners. His grandfather took him for walks and drives. We no longer have a car, since my husband's sight has begun to fail him slightly, so now the garage is Timothy's workshop. We had windows cut in it, and a door, and nailed the large doors shut."

It soon became clear that Tim's life was not all strictures by any means. He had a workshop of his own, and upstairs beside his bedroom was his own library and study.

"He keeps his books and treasures there," said his grandmother, "his own little radio, and his schoolbooks, and his typewriter. When he was only seven years old, he asked us for a typewriter. But he is a careful child, Dr. Welles, not at all destructive, and I had read that in many schools they make use of typewriters in teaching young children to read and write and to spell. The words look the same as in printed books, you see; and less muscular effort is involved. So his grandfather got him a very nice noiseless typewriter, and he loved it dearly. I often hear it purring away as I pass through the hall. Timothy keeps his own rooms in good order, and his shop also. It is his own wish. You know how boys are—they do not wish others to meddle with their belongings. 'Very well, Timothy,' I told him, 'if a glance shows me that you can do it yourself properly, nobody will go into your rooms; but they must be kept neat.' And he has done so for several years. A very neat boy, Timothy."

"Timothy didn't mention his paper route," remarked Welles. "He said only that he plays with other boys after school."

"Oh, but he does," said Mrs. Davis. "He plays until five o'clock, and then he delivers his papers. If he is late, his grandfather walks down and calls him. The school is not very far from here, and Mr. Davis frequently walks down and watches the boys at their play. The paper route is Timothy's way of earning money to feed his cats. Do you care for cats, Dr. Welles?"

"Yes, I like cats very much," said the psychiatrist. "Many boys like dogs better."

"Timothy had a dog when he was a baby—a collie." Her eyes grew moist. "We all loved Ruff dearly. But I am no longer young, and the care and training of a dog is difficult. Timothy is at school or at the Boy Scout camp or something of the sort a great part of the time, and I thought it best that he should not have another dog. But you wanted to know about our cats, Dr. Welles. I raise Siamese cats."

"Interesting pets," said Welles cordially. "My aunt raised them at one time."

"Timothy is very fond of them. But three years ago he asked me if he could have a pair of black Persians. At first I thought not; but we like to please the child, and he promised to build their cages himself. He had taken a course in carpentry at vacation school. So he was allowed to have a pair of beautiful black Persians. But the very first litter turned out to be short-haired, and Timothy confessed that he had mated his queen to my Siamese tom, to see what would happen. Worse yet, he had mated his tom to one of my Siamese queens. I really was tempted to punish him. But, after all, I could see that he was curious as to the outcome of such crossbreeding. Of course I said the kittens must be destroyed. The second litter was exactly like the first—all black, with short hair. But you know what children are. Timothy begged me to let them live, and they were his first kittens. Three in one litter, two in the other. He might keep them, I said, if he would take full care of them and be responsible for all the expense. He mowed lawns and ran errands and made little footstools and bookcases to sell, and did all sorts of things, and probably used his allowance, too. But he kept the kittens and has a whole row of cages in the yard beside his workshop."

"And their offspring?" inquired Welles, who could not see what all this had to do with the main question, but was willing to listen to anything that might lead to information.

"Some of the kittens appear to be pure Persian, and others pure Siamese. These he insisted on keeping, although, as I have explained to him, it would be dishonest to sell them, since they are not pure-bred. A good many of the kittens are black short-haired and these we destroy. But enough of cats, Dr. Welles. And I am afraid I am talking too much about my grandson."

"I can understand that you are very proud of him," said Welles.

"I must confess that we are. And he is a bright boy. When he and his grandfather talk together, and with me also, he asks very intelligent questions. We do not encourage him to voice his opinions—I detest the smart-Aleck type of small boy—and yet I believe they would be quite good opinions for a child of his age."

"Has his health always been good?" asked Welles.

"On the whole, very good. I have taught him the value of exercise, play, wholesome food and suitable rest. He has had a few of the usual childish ailments, not seriously. And he never has colds. But, of course, he takes his cold shots twice a year when we do."

"Does he mind the shots?" asked Welles, as casually as he could.

"Not at all. I always say that he, though so young, sets an example I find hard to follow. I still flinch, and really rather dread the ordeal."

Welles looked toward the door at a sudden, slight sound.

Timothy stood there, and he had heard. Again, fear was stamped on his face and terror looked out of his eyes.

"Timothy," said his grandmother, "don't stare."

"Sorry, sir," the boy managed to say.

"Are your papers all delivered? I did not realize we had been talking for an hour, Dr. Welles. Would you like to see Timothy's cats?" Mrs. Davis inquired graciously. "Timothy, take Dr. Welles to see your pets. We have had quite a talk about them."

Welles got Tim out of the room as fast as he could. The boy led the way around the house and into the side yard where the former garage stood.

There the man stopped.

"Tim," he said, "you don't have to show me the cats if you don't want to."

"Oh, that's all right."

"Is that part of what you are hiding? If it is, I don't want to see it until you are ready to show me."

Tim looked up at him then.

"Thanks," he said. "I don't mind about the cats. Not if you like cats really."

"I really do. But, Tim, this I would like to know: You're not afraid of the needle. Could you tell me why you were afraid . . . why you said you were afraid . . . of my shot? The one I promised not to give you after all?"

Their eyes met.

"You won't tell?" asked Tim.

"I won't tell."

"Because it was pentothal. Wasn't it?"

Welles gave himself a slight pinch. Yes, he was awake. Yes, this was a little boy asking him about pentothal. A boy who—yes, certainly, a boy who knew about it.

"Yes, it was," said Welles. "A very small dose. You know what it is?"

"Yes, sir. I . . . I read about it somewhere. In the papers."

"Never mind that. You have a secret—something you want to hide. That's what you are afraid about, isn't it?"

The boy nodded dumbly.

"If it's anything wrong, or that might be wrong, perhaps I could help you. You'll want to know me better, first. You'll want to be sure you can trust me. But I'll be glad to help, any time you say the word, Tim. Or I might stumble on to things the way I did just now. One thing though—I never tell secrets."

"Never?"

"Never. Doctors and priests don't betray secrets. Doctors seldom, priests never. I guess I am more like a priest, because of the kind of doctoring I do."

He looked down at the boy's bowed head.

"Helping fellows who are scared sick," said the psychiatrist very gently. "Helping fellows in trouble, getting things straight again, fixing things up, unsnarling tangles. When I can, that's what I do. And I don't tell anything to anybody. It's just between that one fellow and me."

But, he added to himself, *I'll have to find out. I'll have to find out what ails this child. Miss Page is right—he needs me.*

They went to see the cats.

There were the Siamese in their cages, and the Persians in their cages, and there, in several small cages, the short-haired black cats and their hybrid offspring. "We take them into the house, or let them into this big cage, for exercise," explained Tim. "I take mine into my shop sometimes. These are all mine. Grandmother keeps hers on the sun porch."

"You'd never know these were not all pure-bred," observed Welles. "Which did you say were the full Persians? Any of their kittens here?"

"No; I sold them."

"I'd like to buy one. But these look just the same—it wouldn't make any difference to me. I want a pet, and wouldn't use it for breeding stock. Would you sell me one of these?"

Timothy shook his head.

"I'm sorry. I never sell any but the pure-breds."

It was then that Welles began to see what problem he faced. Very dimly he saw it, with joy, relief, hope and wild enthusiasm.

"Why not?" urged Welles. "I can wait for a pure-bred, if you'd rather, but why not one of these? They look just the same. Perhaps they'd be more interesting."

Tim looked at Welles for a long, long minute.

"I'll show you," he said. "Promise to wait here? No, I'll let you come into the workroom. Wait a minute, please."

The boy drew a key from under his blouse, where it had hung suspended from a chain, and unlocked the door of his shop. He went inside, closed the door, and Welles could hear him moving about for a few moments. Then he came to the door and beckoned.

"Don't tell grandmother," said Tim. "I haven't told her yet. If it lives, I'll tell her next week."

In the corner of the shop under a table there was a box, and in the box there was a Siamese cat. When she saw a stranger she tried to hide her kittens; but Tim lifted her gently, and then Welles saw. Two of the kittens looked like little white rats with stringy tails and smudgy paws, ears and noses. But the third—yes, it was going to be a different sight. It was going to be a beautiful cat if it lived. It had long, silky white hair like the finest Persian, and the Siamese markings were showing up plainly.

Welles caught his breath.

"Congratulations, old man! Haven't you told anyone yet?"

"She's not ready to show. She's not a week old."

"But you're going to show her?"

"Oh, yes, grandmother will be thrilled. She'll love her. Maybe there'll be more."

"You knew this would happen. You made it happen. You planned it all from the start," accused Welles.

"Yes," admitted the boy.

"How did you know?"

The boy turned away.

"I read it somewhere," said Tim.

The cat jumped back into the box and began to nurse her babies. Welles felt as if he could endure no more. Without a glance at anything else in the room—and everything else was hidden under tarpaulins and newspapers—he went to the door.

"Thanks for showing me, Tim," he said. "And when you have any to sell, remember me. I'll wait. I want one like that."

The boy followed him out and locked the door carefully.

"But Tim," said the psychiatrist, "that's not what you were afraid I'd find out. I wouldn't need a drug to get you to tell me this, would I?"

Tim replied carefully, "I didn't want to tell this until I was ready. Grandmother really ought to know first. But you made me tell you."

"Tim," said Peter Welles earnestly, "I'll see you again. Whatever you are afraid of, don't be afraid of me. I often guess secrets. I'm on the way to guessing yours already. But nobody else need ever know."

He walked rapidly home, whistling to himself from time to time. Perhaps he, Peter Welles, was the luckiest man in the world.

He had scarcely begun to talk to Timothy on the boy's next appearance at the office, when the phone in the hall rang. On his return, when he opened the door he saw a book in Tim's hands. The boy made a move as if to hide it, and thought better of it.

Welles took the book and looked at it.

"Want to know more about Rorschach, eh?" he asked.

"I saw it on the shelf. I—"

"Oh, that's all right," said Welles, who had purposely left the book near the chair Tim would occupy. "But what's the matter with the library?"

"They've got some books about it, but they're on the closed shelves. I couldn't get them." Tim spoke without thinking first, and then caught his breath.

But Welles replied calmly: "I'll get it out for you. I'll have it next time you come. Take this one along today when you go. Tim, I mean it—you can trust me."

"I can't tell you anything," said the boy. "You've found out some things. I wish . . . oh, I don't know what I wish! But I'd rather be let alone. I don't need help. Maybe I never will. If I do, can't I come to you then?"

Welles pulled out his chair and sat down slowly.

"Perhaps that would be the best way, Tim. But why wait for the ax to fall? I might be able to help you ward it off—what you're afraid of. You can kid people along about the cats; tell them you were fooling around to see what would happen. But you can't fool all of the people all of the time, they tell me. Maybe with me to help, you could. Or with me to back you up, the blowup would be easier. Easier on your grandparents, too."

"I haven't done anything wrong!"

"I'm beginning to be sure of that. But things you try to keep hidden may come to light. The kitten—you could hide it, but you don't want to. You've got to risk something to show it."

"I'll tell them I read it somewhere."

"That wasn't true, then. I thought not. You figured it out."

There was silence.

Then Timothy Paul said: "Yes, I figured it out. But that's my secret."

"It's safe with me."

But the boy did not trust him yet. Welles soon learned that he had been tested. Tim took the book home, and returned it, took the library books which Welles got for him, and in due course returned them also. But he talked little and was still wary. Welles could talk all he liked, but he got little or nothing out of Tim. Tim had told all he was going to tell. He would talk about nothing except what any boy would talk about.

After two months of this, during which Welles saw Tim officially once a week and unofficially several times—showing up at the school playground to watch games, or meeting Tim on the paper route and treating him to a soda after it was finished—Welles had learned very little more. He tried again. He had probed no more during the two months, respected the boy's silence, trying to give him time to get to know and trust him.

But one day he asked: "What are you going to do when you grow up, Tim? Breed cats?"

Tim laughed a denial.

"I don't know what, yet. Sometimes I think one thing, sometimes another."

This was a typical boy answer. Welles disregarded it.

"What would you like to do best of all?" he asked.

Tim leaned forward eagerly. "What you do!" he cried.

"You've been reading up on it, I suppose," said Welles, as casually as he could. "Then you know, perhaps, that before anyone can do what I do, he must go through it himself, like a patient. He must also study medicine and be a full-fledged doctor, of course. You can't do that yet. But you can have the works now, like a patient."

"Why? For the experience?"

"Yes. And for the cure. You'll have to face that fear and lick it. You'll have to straighten out a lot of other things, or at least face them."

"My fear will be gone when I'm grown up," said Timothy. "I think it will. I hope it will."

"Can you be sure?"

"No," admitted the boy. "I don't know exactly why I'm afraid. I just know I *must* hide things. Is that bad, too?"

"Dangerous, perhaps."

Timothy thought a while in silence. Welles smoked three cigarettes and yearned to pace the floor, but dared not move.

"What would it be like?" asked Tim finally.

"You'd tell me about yourself. What you remember. Your childhood—the way your grandmother runs on when she talks about you."

"She sent me out of the room. I'm not supposed to think I'm bright," said Tim, with one of his rare grins.

"And you're not supposed to know how well she reared you?"

"She did fine," said Tim. "She taught me all the wisest things I ever knew."

"Such as what?"

"Such as shutting up. Not telling all you know. Not showing off."

"I see what you mean," said Welles. "Have you heard the story of St. Thomas Aquinas?"

"No."

"When he was a student in Paris, he never spoke out in class, and the others thought him stupid. One of them kindly offered to help him, and went over all the work very patiently to make him understand it. And then one day they came to a place where the other student got all mixed up and had to admit he didn't understand. Then Thomas suggested a solution and it was the right one. He knew more than any of the others all the time; but they called him the Dumb Ox."

Tim nodded gravely.

"And when he grew up?" asked the boy.

"He was the greatest thinker of all time," said Welles. "A

fourteenth-century super-brain. He did more original work than any other ten great men; and he died young."

After that, it was easier.

"How do I begin?" asked Timothy.

"You'd better begin at the beginning. Tell me all you can remember about your early childhood, before you went to school."

Tim gave this his consideration.

"I'll have to go forward and backward a lot," he said. "I couldn't put it all in order."

"That's all right. Just tell me today all you can remember about that time of your life. By next week you'll have remembered more. As we go on to later periods of your life, you may remember things that belonged to an earlier time; tell them then. We'll make some sort of order out of it."

Welles listened to the boy's revelations with growing excitement. He found it difficult to keep outwardly calm.

"When did you begin to read?" Welles asked.

"I don't know when it was. My grandmother read me some stories, and somehow I got the idea about the words. But when I tried to tell her I could read, she spanked me. She kept saying I couldn't, and I kept saying I could, until she spanked me. For a while I had a dreadful time, because I didn't know any word she hadn't read to me—I guess I sat beside her and watched, or else I remembered and then went over it by myself right after. I must have learned as soon as I got the idea that each group of letters on the page was a word."

"The word-unit method," Welles commented. "Most self-taught readers learned like that."

"Yes. I have read about it since. And Macaulay could read when he was three, but only upside-down, because of standing opposite when his father read the Bible to the family."

"There are many cases of children who learned to read as you did, and surprised their parents. Well? How did you get on?"

"One day I noticed that two words looked almost alike and sounded almost alike. They were 'can' and 'man.' I remember staring at them and then it was like something beautiful boiling up in me. I began to look carefully at the words, but in a crazy excitement. I was a long while at it, because when I put down the book and tried to stand up I was stiff all over. But I had the idea, and after that it wasn't hard to figure out almost any words. The really hard words are the common ones that you get all the time in easy books. Other words are pronounced the way they are spelled."

"And nobody knew you could read?"

"No. Grandmother told me not to say I could, so I didn't. She read to me often, and that helped. We had a great many books, of course. I liked those with pictures. Once or twice they caught me with a book that had no pictures, and then they'd take it away and say, 'I'll find a book for a little boy.' "

"Do you remember what books you liked then?"

"Books about animals, I remember. And geographies. It was funny about animals—"

Once you got Timothy started, thought Welles, it wasn't hard to get him to go on talking.

"One day I was at the Zoo," said Tim, "and by the cages alone. Grandmother was resting on a bench and she let me walk along by myself. People were talking about the animals and I began to tell them all I knew. It must have been funny in a way, because I had read a lot of words I couldn't pronounce correctly, words I had never heard spoken. They listened and asked me questions and I thought I was just like grandfather, teaching them the way he sometimes taught me. And then they called another man to come, and said, 'Listen to this kid; he's a scream!' and I saw they were all laughing at me."

Timothy's face was redder than usual, but he tried to smile as he added, "I can see now how it must have sounded funny. And unexpected, too; that's a big point in humor. But my little feelings were so dreadfully hurt that I ran back to my grandmother crying, and she couldn't find out why. But it served me right for disobeying her. She always told me not to tell people things; she said a child had nothing to teach its elders."

"Not in that way, perhaps—at that age."

"But, honestly, some grown people don't know very much," said Tim. "When we went on the train last year, a woman came up and sat beside me and started to tell me things a little boy should know about California. I told her I'd lived here all my life, but I guess she didn't even know we are taught things in school, and she tried to tell me things, and almost everything was wrong."

"Such as what?" asked Welles, who had also suffered from tourists.

"We . . . she said so many things . . . but I thought this was the funniest: She said all the Missions were so old and interesting, and I said yes, and she said, 'You know, they were all built long before Columbus discovered America,' and I thought she meant it for a joke, so I laughed. She looked very serious and said, 'Yes, those people all come up here from Mexico.' I suppose she thought they were Aztec temples."

Welles, shaking with laughter, could not but agree that many adults were sadly lacking in the rudiments of knowledge.

"After that Zoo experience, and a few others like it, I began to get wise to myself," continued Tim. "People who knew things didn't want to hear me repeating them, and people who didn't know, wouldn't be taught by a four-year-old baby. I guess I was four when I began to write."

"How?"

"Oh, I just thought if I couldn't say anything to anybody at any time, I'd burst. So I began to put it down—in printing, like in books. Then I found out about writing, and we had some old-fashioned schoolbooks that taught how to write. I'm left-handed. When I went to school, I had to use my right hand. But by then I had learned how to pretend that I didn't know things. I watched the others and did as they did. My grandmother told me to do that."

"I wonder why she said that," marveled Welles.

"She knew I wasn't used to other children, she said, and it was the first time she had left me to anyone else's care. So, she told me to do what the others did and what my teacher said," explained Tim simply, "and I followed her advice literally. I pretended I didn't know anything, until the others began to know it, too. Lucky I was so shy. But there were things to learn, all right. Do you know, when I was first sent to school, I was disappointed because the teacher dressed like other women. The only picture of teachers I had noticed were those in an old Mother Goose book, and I thought that all teachers wore hoop skirts. But as soon as I saw her, after the little shock of surprise, I knew it was silly, and I never told."

The psychiatrist and the boy laughed together.

"We played games. I had to learn to play with children, and not be surprised when they slapped or pushed me. I just couldn't figure out why they'd do that, or what good it did them. But if it was to surprise me, I'd say 'Boo' and surprise them some time later; and if they were mad because I had taken a ball or something they wanted, I'd play with them."

"Anybody ever try to beat you up?"

"Oh, yes. But I had a book about boxing—with pictures. You

can't learn much from pictures, but I got some practice too, and that helped. I didn't want to win, anyway. That's what I like about games of strength or skill—I'm fairly matched, and I don't have to be always watching in case I might show off or try to boss somebody around."

"You must have tried bossing sometimes."

"In books, they all cluster around the boy who can teach new games and think up new things to play. But I found out that doesn't work. They just want to do the same thing all the time—like hide and seek. It's no fun if the first one to be caught is 'it' next time. The rest just walk in any old way and don't try to hide or even to run, because it doesn't matter whether they are caught. But you can't get the boys to see that, and play right, so the last one caught is 'it'."

Timothy looked at his watch.

"Time to go," he said. "I've enjoyed talking to you, Dr. Welles. I hope I haven't bored you too much."

Welles recognized the echo and smiled appreciatively at the small boy.

"You didn't tell me about the writing. Did you start to keep a diary?"

"No. It was a newspaper. One page a day, no more and no less. I still keep it," confided Tim. "But I get more on the page now. I type it."

"And you write with either hand now?"

"My left hand is my own secret writing. For school and things like that I use my right hand."

When Timothy had left, Welles congratulated himself. But for the next month he got no more. Tim would not reveal a single significant fact. He talked about ball-playing, he described his grandmother's astonished delight over the beautiful kitten, he told of its growth and the tricks it played. He gravely related such enthralling facts as that he liked to ride on trains, that his favorite wild animal was the lion, and that he greatly desired to see snow falling. But not a word of what Welles wanted to hear. The psychiatrist, knowing that he was again being tested, waited patiently.

Then one afternoon when Welles, fortunately unoccupied with a patient, was smoking a pipe on his front porch, Timothy Paul strode into the yard.

"Yesterday Miss Page asked me if I was seeing you and I said yes. She said she hoped my grandparents didn't find it too expensive, because you had told her I was all right and didn't need to have her worrying about me. And then I said to grandma, was it expensive for you to talk to me, and she said, 'Oh no, dear; the school pays for that. It was your teacher's idea that you have a few talks with Dr. Welles.' "

"I'm glad you came to me, Tim, and I'm sure you didn't give me away to either of them. Nobody's paying me. The school pays for my services if a child is in a bad way and his parents are poor. It's a new service, since 1956. Many maladjusted children can be helped—much more cheaply to the state than the cost of having them go crazy or become criminals or something. You understand all that. But—sit down, Tim!—I can't charge the state for you, and I can't charge your grandparents. You're adjusted marvelously well in every way, as far as I can see; and when I see the rest, I'll be even more sure of it."

"Well—gosh! I wouldn't have come—" Tim was stammering in confusion. "You ought to be paid. I take up so much of your time. Maybe I'd better not come any more."

"I think you'd better. Don't you?"

"Why are you doing it for nothing, Dr. Welles?"

"I think you know why."

The boy sat down in the glider and pushed himself meditatively back and forth. The glider squeaked.

"You're interested. You're curious," he said.

"That's not all, Tim."

Squeak-squeak. Squeak-squeak.

"I know," said Timothy. "I believe it. Look, is it all right if I call you Peter? Since we're friends."

At their next meeting, Timothy went into details about his newspaper. He had kept all the copies, from the first smudged, awkwardly printed pencil issues to the very latest neatly typed ones. But he would not show Welles any of them.

"I just put down every day the things I most wanted to say, the news or information or opinion I had to swallow unsaid. So it's a wild medley. The earlier copies are awfully funny. Sometimes I guess what they were all about, what made me write them. Sometimes I remember. I put down the books I read too, and mark them like school grades, on two points—how I liked the book, and whether it was good. And whether I had read it before, too."

"How many books do you read? What's your reading speed?"

It proved that Timothy's reading speed on new books of adult level varied from eight hundred to nine hundred fifty words a minute. The average murder mystery—he loved them—took him a little less than an hour. A year's homework in history Tim performed easily by reading his textbook through three or four times during the year. He apologized for that, but explained that he had to know what was in the book so as not to reveal in examinations too much that he had learned from other sources. Evenings, when his grandparents believed him to be doing homework he spent his time reading other books, or writing his newspaper, "or something." As Welles had already guessed, Tim had read everything in his grandfather's library, everything of interest in the public library that was not on the closed shelves, and everything he could order from the state library.

"What do the librarians say?"

"They think the books are for my grandfather. I tell them that, if they ask what a little boy wants with such a big book. Peter, telling so many lies is what gets me down. I have to do it, don't I?"

"As far as I can see, you do," agreed Welles. "But here's material for a while in my library. There'll have to be a closed shelf here, too, though, Tim."

"Could you tell me why? I know about the library books. Some of them might scare people, and some are—"

"Some of my books might scare you too, Tim. I'll tell you a little about abnormal psychology if you like, one of these days, and then I think you'll see that until you're actually trained to deal with such cases, you'd be better off not knowing too much about them."

"I don't want to be morbid," agreed Tim. "All right. I'll read only what you give me. And from now on I'll tell you things. There was more than the newspaper, you know."

"I thought as much. Do you want to go on with your tale?"

"It started when I first wrote a letter to a newspaper—of course, under a pen name. They printed it. For a while I had a high old time of it—a letter almost every day, using all sorts of pen names. Then I branched out to magazines, letters to the editor again. And stories—I tried stories."

He looked a little doubtfully at Welles, who said only: "How old were you when you sold the first story?"

"Eight," said Timothy. "And when the check came, with my name on it, 'T. Paul,' I didn't know what in the world to do."

"That's a thought. What did you do?"

"There was a sign in the window of the bank. I always read

signs, and that one came back to my mind. 'Banking By Mail.' You can see I was pretty desperate. So I got the name of a bank across the Bay and I wrote them—on my typewriter—and said I wanted to start an account, and here was a check to start it with. Oh, I was scared stiff, and had to keep saying to myself that, after all, nobody could do much to me. It was my own money. But you don't know what it's like to be only a small boy! They sent the check back to me and I died ten deaths when I saw it. But the letter explained. I hadn't endorsed it. They sent me a blank to fill out about myself. I didn't know how many lies I dared to tell. But it was my money and I had to get it. If I could get it into the bank, then some day I could get it out. I gave my business as 'author' and I gave my age as twenty-four. I thought that was awfully old."

"I'd like to see the story. Do you have a copy of the magazine around?"

"Yes," said Tim. "But nobody noticed it—I mean, 'T. Paul' could be anybody. And when I saw magazines for writers on the newsstands and bought them, I got on to the way to use a pen name on the story and my own name and address up in the corner. Before that I used a pen name and sometimes never got the things back or heard about them. Sometimes I did, though."

"What then?"

"Oh, then I'd endorse the check payable to me and sign the pen name, and then sign my own name under it. Was I scared to do that! But it was my money."

"Only stories?"

"Articles, too. And things. That's enough of that for today. Only—I just wanted to say—a while ago, T. Paul told the bank he wanted to switch some of the money over to a checking account. To buy books by mail, and such. So, I could pay you, Dr. Welles—" with sudden formality.

"No, Tim," said Peter Welles firmly. "The pleasure is all mine. What I want is to see the story that was published when you were eight. And some of the other things that made T. Paul rich enough to keep a consulting psychiatrist on the payroll. And, for the love of Pete, will you tell me how all this goes on without your grandparents' knowing a thing about it?"

"Grandmother thinks I send in box tops and fill out coupons," said Tim. "She doesn't bring in the mail. She says her little boy gets such a big bang out of that little chore. Anyway that's what she said when I was eight. I played mailman. And there were box tops—I showed them to her, until she said, about the third time, that really she wasn't greatly interested in such matters. By now she has the habit of waiting for me to bring in the mail."

Peter Welles thought that was quite a day of revelation. He spent a quiet evening at home, holding his head and groaning, trying to take it all in.

And that I.Q.—120, nonsense! The boy had been holding out on him. Tim's reading had obviously included enough about I. Q. tests, enough puzzles and oddments in magazines and such, to enable him to stall successfully. What could he do if he would cooperate?

Welles made up his mind to find out.

He didn't find out. Timothy Paul went swiftly through the whole range of Superior Adult tests without a failure of any sort. There were no tests yet devised that could measure his intelligence. While he was still writing his age with one figure, Timothy Paul had faced alone, and solved alone, problems that would have baffled the average adult. He had adjusted to the hardest task of all—that of appearing to be a fairly normal, B-average small boy.

And it must be that there was more to find out about him. What did he write? And what did he do besides read and write, learn carpentry and breed cats and magnificently fool his whole world?

When Peter Welles had read some of Tim's writings, he was surprised to find that the stories the boy had written were vividly human, the product of close observation of human nature. The articles, on the other hand, were closely reasoned and showed thorough study and research. Apparently Tim read every word of several newspapers and a score or more of periodicals.

"Oh, sure," said Tim, when questioned. "I read everything. I go back once in a while and review old ones, too."

"If you can write like this," demanded Welles, indicating a magazine in which a staid and scholarly article had appeared, "and this"—this was a man-to-man political article giving the arguments for and against a change in the whole Congressional system—"then why do you always talk to me in the language of an ordinary stupid schoolboy?"

"Because I'm only a boy," replied Timothy. "What would happen if I went around talking like that?"

"You might risk it with me. You've showed me these things."

"I'd never dare to risk talking like that. I might forget and do it again before others. Besides, I can't pronounce half the words."

"What!"

"I never look up a pronunciation," explained Timothy. "In case I do slip and use a word beyond the average, I can anyway hope I didn't say it right."

Welles shouted with laughter, but was sober again as he realized the implications back of that thoughtfulness.

"You're just like an explorer living among savages," said the psychiatrist. "You have studied the savages carefully and tried to imitate them so they won't know there are differences."

"Something like that," acknowledged Tim.

"That's why your stories are so human," said Welles. "That one about the awful little girl—"

They both chuckled.

"Yes, that was my first story," said Tim. "I was almost eight, and there was a boy in my class who had a brother, and the boy next door was the other one, the one who was picked on."

"How much of the story was true?"

"The first part. I used to see, when I went over there, how that girl picked on Bill's brother's friend, Steve. She wanted to play with Steve all the time herself and whenever he had boys over, she'd do something awful. And Steve's folks were like I said—they wouldn't let Steve do anything to a girl. When she threw all the watermelon rinds over the fence into his yard, he just had to pick them all up and say nothing back; and she'd laugh at him over the fence. She got him blamed for things he never did, and when he had work to do in the yard she'd hang out of her window and scream at him and make fun. I thought first, what made her act like that, and then I made up a way for him to get even with her, and wrote it out the way it might have happened."

"Didn't you pass the idea on to Steve and let him try it?"

"Gosh, no! I was only a little boy. Kids seven don't give ideas to kids ten. That's the first thing I had to learn—to be always the one that kept quiet, especially if there was any older boy or girl around, even only a year or two older. I had to learn to look blank and let my mouth hang open and say, 'I don't get it,' to almost everything."

"And Miss Page thought it was odd that you had no close friends of your own age," said Welles. "You must be the loneliest boy that ever walked this earth, Tim. You've lived in hiding like a criminal. But tell me, what are you afraid of?"

"I'm afraid of being found out, of course. The only way I can live in this world is in disguise—until I'm grown up, at any rate. At first it was just my grandparents' scolding me and telling me not to show off, and the way people laughed if I tried to talk to them. Then I saw how people hate anyone who is better or brighter or luckier. Some people sort of trade off; if you're bad at one thing you're good at another, but they'll forgive you for being good at some things, if you're not good at others so they can balance it off. They can beat you at something. You have to strike a balance. A child has no chance at all. No grownup can stand it to have a child know anything he doesn't. Oh, a little thing if it amuses them. But not much of anything. There's an old story about a man who found himself in a country where everyone else was blind. I'm like that—but they shan't put out my eyes. I'll never let them know I can see anything."

"Do you see things that no grown person can see?"

Tim waved his hand towards the magazines.

"Only like that, I meant. I hear people talking in street cars and stores, and while they work, and around. I read about the way they act—in the news. I'm like them, just like them, only I seem about a hundred years older—more matured."

"Do you mean that none of them have much sense?"

"I don't mean that exactly. I mean that so few of them have any, or show it if they do have. They don't even seem to want to. They're good people in their way, but what could they make of me? Even when I was seven, I could understand their motives, but they couldn't understand their own motives. And they're so lazy—they don't seem to want to know or to understand. When I first went to the library for books, the books I learned from were seldom touched by any of the grown people. But they were meant for ordinary grown people. But the grown people didn't want to know things—they only wanted to fool around. I feel about most people the way my grandmother feels about babies and puppies. Only she doesn't have to pretend to be a puppy all the time," Tim added, with a little bitterness.

"You have a friend now, in me."

"Yes, Peter," said Tim, brightening up. "And I have pen friends, too. People like what I write, because they can't see I'm only a little boy. When I grow up—"

Tim did not finish that sentence. Welles understood, now, some of the fears that Tim had not dared to put into words at all. When he grew up, would he be as far beyond all other grownups as he had, all his life, been above his contemporaries? The adult friends whom he now met on fairly equal terms—would they then, too, seem like babies or puppies?

Peter did not dare to voice the thought, either. Still less did he venture to hint at another thought. Tim, so far, had no great interest in girls; they existed for him as part of the human race, but there would come a time when Tim would be a grown man and would wish to marry. And where among the puppies could he find a mate?

"When you're grown up, we'll still be friends," said Peter. "And who are the others?"

It turned out that Tim had pen friends all over the world. He played chess by correspondence—a game he never dared to play in person, except when he forced himself to move the pieces about idly and let his opponent win at least half the time. He had, also, many friends who had read something he had written, and had written to him about it, thus starting a correspondence-friendship. After the first two or three of these, he had started some on his own account, always with people who lived at a great distance. To most of these he gave a name which, although not false, looked it. That was Paul T. Lawrence. Lawrence was his middle name; and with a comma after the Paul, it was actually his own name. He had a post office box under that name, for which T. Paul of the large bank account was his reference.

"Pen friends abroad? Do you know languages?"

Yes, Tim did. He had studied by correspondence, also; many universities gave extension courses in that manner, and lent the student records to play so that he could learn the correct pronunciation. Tim had taken several such courses, and learned other languages from books. He kept all these languages in practice by means of the letters to other lands and the replies which came to him.

"I'd buy a dictionary, and then I'd write to the mayor of some town, or to a foreign newspaper, and ask them to advertise for some pen friends to help me learn the language. We'd exchange souvenirs and things."

Nor was Welles in the least surprised to find that Timothy had also taken other courses by correspondence. He had completed, within three years, more than half the subjects offered by four separate universities, and several other courses, the most recent being Architecture. The boy, not yet fourteen, had completed a full course in that subject, and had he been able to disguise himself as a full-grown man, could have gone out at once and built almost anything you'd like to name, for he also knew much of the trades involved.

"It always said how long an average student took, and I'd take that long," said Tim, "so, of course, I had to be working several schools at the same time."

"And carpentry at the playground summer school?"

"Oh, yes. But there I couldn't do too much, because people could see me. But I learned how, and it made a good coverup, so I could make cages for the cats, and all that sort of thing. And many boys are good with their hands. I like to work with my hands. I built my own radio, too—it gets all the foreign stations, and that helps me with my languages."

"How did you figure it out about the cats?" said Welles.

"Oh, there had to be recessives, that's all. The Siamese coloring was a recessive, and it had to be mated with another recessive. Black was one possibility, and white was another, but I started with black because I liked it better. I might try white too, but I have so much else on my mind—"

He broke off suddenly and would say no more.

Their next meeting was by prearrangement at Tim's workshop. Welles met the boy after school and they walked to Tim's home together; there the boy unlocked his door and snapped on the lights.

Welles looked around with interest. There was a bench, a tool chest. Cabinets, padlocked. A radio, clearly not store-purchased. A file cabinet, locked. Something on a table, covered with a cloth. A box in the corner—no, two boxes in two corners. In each of them was a mother cat with kittens. Both mothers were black Persians.

"This one must be all black Persian," Tim explained. "Her third litter and never a Siamese marking. But this one carries both recessives in her. Last time she had a Siamese short-haired kitten. This morning—I had to go to school. Let's see."

They bent over the box where the newborn kittens lay. One kitten was like the mother. The other two were Siamese-Persian; a male and a female.

"You've done it again, Tim!" shouted Welles. "Congratulations!"

They shook hands in jubilation.

"I'll write it in the record," said the boy blissfully.

In a nickel book marked "compositions" Tim's left hand

added the entries. He had used the correct symbols—F_1, F_2, F_3; Ss, Bl.

"The dominants in capitals," he explained, "B for black, and S for short hair; the recessives in small letters—s for Siamese, l for long hair. Wonderful to write ll or ss again, Peter! Twice more. And the other kitten is carrying the Siamese marking as a recessive."

He closed the book in triumph.

"Now," and he marched to the covered thing on the table, "my latest big secret."

Tim lifted the cloth carefully and displayed a beautifully built doll house. No, a model house—Welles corrected himself swiftly. A beautiful model, and—yes, built to scale.

"The roof comes off. See, it has a big storage room and a room for a play room or a maid or something. Then I lift off the attic—"

"Good heavens!" cried Peter Welles. "Any little girl would give her soul for this!"

"I used fancy wrapping papers for the wallpapers. I wove the rugs on a little hand loom," gloated Timothy. "The furniture's just like real, isn't it? Some I bought; that's plastic. Some I made of construction paper and things. The curtains were the hardest; but I couldn't ask grandmother to sew them—"

"Why not?" the amazed doctor managed to ask.

"She might recognize this afterwards," said Tim, and he lifted off the upstairs floor.

"Recognize it? You haven't showed it to her? Then when would she see it?"

"She might not," admitted Tim. "But I don't like to take some risks."

"That's a very livable floor plan you've used," said Welles, bending closer to examine the house in detail.

"Yes, I thought so. It's awful how many house plans leave no clear wall space for books or pictures. Some of them have doors placed so you have to detour around the dining room table every time you go from the living room to the kitchen, or so that a whole corner of a room is good for nothing, with doors at all angles. Now, I designed this house to—"

"You designed it, Tim!"

"Why, sure. Oh, I see—you thought I built it from blueprints I'd bought. My first model home, I did, but the architecture courses gave me so many ideas that I wanted to see how they would look. Now, the cellar and game room—"

* * *

Welles came to himself an hour later, and gasped when he looked at his watch.

"It's too late. My patient has gone home again by this time. I may as well stay—how about the paper route?"

"I gave that up. Grandmother offered to feed the cats as soon as I gave her the kitten. And I wanted the time for this. Here are the pictures of the house."

The color prints were very good.

"I'm sending them and an article to the magazines," said Tim. "This time I'm T. L. Paul. Sometimes I used to pretend all the different people I am were talking together—but now I talk to you instead, Peter."

"Will it bother the cats if I smoke? Thanks. Nothing I'm likely to set on fire, I hope? Put the house together and let me sit here and look at it. I want to look in through the windows. Put its lights on. There."

The young architect beamed, and snapped on the little lights.

"Nobody can see in here. I got Venetian blinds; and when I work in here, I even shut them sometimes."

"If I'm to know all about you, I'll have to go through the alphabet from A to Z," said Peter Welles. "This is Architecture. What else in the A's?"

"Astronomy. I showed you those articles. My calculations proved correct. Astrophysics—I got A in the course, but haven't done anything original so far. Art, no. I can't paint or draw very well, except mechanical drawing. I've done all the Merit Badge work in scouting, all through the alphabet."

"Darned if I can see you as a Boy Scout," protested Welles.

"I'm a very good Scout. I have almost as many badges as any other boy my age in the troop. And at camp I do as well as most city boys."

"Do you do a good turn every day?"

"Yes," said Timothy. "Started that when I first read about Scouting—I was a Scout at heart before I was old enough to be a Cub. You know, Peter, when you're very young, you take all that seriously about the good deed every day, and the good habits and ideals and all that. And then you get older and it begins to seem funny and childish and posed and artificial, and you smile in a superior way and make jokes. But there is a third step, too, when you take it all seriously again. People who make fun of the Scout Law are doing the boys a lot of harm; but those who believe in things like that don't know how to say so, without sounding priggish and platitudinous. I'm going to do an article on it before long."

"Is the Scout Law your religion—if I may put it that way?"

"No," said Timothy. "But 'a Scout is Reverent.' Once I tried to study the churches and find out what was the truth. I wrote letters to pastors of all denominations—all those in the phone book and the newspaper—when I was on a vacation in the East, I got the names, and then wrote after I got back. I couldn't write to people here in the city. I said I wanted to know which church was true, and expected them to write to me and tell me about theirs, and argue with me, you know. I could read library books, and all they had to do was recommend some, I told them, and then correspond with me a little about them."

"Did they?"

"Some of them answered," said Tim, "but nearly all of them told me to go to somebody near me. Several said they were very busy men. Some gave me the name of a few books, but none of them told me to write again, and . . . and I was only a little boy. Nine years old, so I couldn't talk to anybody. When I thought it over, I knew that I couldn't very well join any church so young, unless it was my grandparents' church. I keep on going there—it is a good church and it teaches a great deal of truth, I am sure. I'm reading all I can find, so when I am old enough I'll know what I must do. How old would you say I should be, Peter?"

"College age," replied Welles. "You are going to college? By then, any of the pastors would talk to you—except those that are too busy!"

"It's a moral problem, really. Have I the right to wait? But I have to wait. It's like telling lies—I have to tell some lies, but I hate to. If I have a moral obligation to join the true church as soon as I find it, well, what then? I can't until I'm eighteen or twenty?"

"If you can't, you can't. I should think that settles it. You are legally a minor, under the control of your grandparents, and while you might claim the right to go where your conscience leads you, it would be impossible to justify and explain your choice without giving yourself away entirely—just as you are obliged to go to school until you are at least eighteen, even though you know more than most Ph.D's. It's all part of the game, and He who made you must understand that."

"I'll never tell you any lies," said Tim. "I was getting so desperately lonely—my pen pals didn't know anything about me really. I told them only what was right for them to know. Little kids are satisfied to be with other people, but when you get a little older you have to make friends, really."

"Yes, that's a part of growing up. You have to reach out to others and share thoughts with them. You've kept to yourself too long as it is."

"It wasn't that I wanted to. But without a real friend, it was only pretense, and I never could let my playmates know anything about me. I studied them and wrote stories about them and it was all of them, but it was only a tiny part of me."

"I'm proud to be your friend, Tim. Every man needs a friend. I'm proud that you trust me."

Tim patted the cat a moment in silence and then looked up with a grin.

"How would you like to hear my favorite joke?" he asked.

"Very much," said the psychiatrist, bracing himself for almost any major shock.

"It's records. I recorded this from a radio program."

Welles listened. He knew little of music, but the symphony which he heard pleased him. The announcer praised it highly in little speeches before and after each movement. Timothy giggled.

"Like it?"

"Very much. I don't see the joke."

"I wrote it."

"Tim, you're beyond me! But I still don't get the joke."

"The joke is that I did it by mathematics. I calculated what ought to sound like joy, grief, hope, triumph, and all the rest, and—it was just after I had studied harmony; you know how mathematical that is."

Speechless, Welles nodded.

"I worked out the rhythms from different metabolisms—the way you function when under the influences of these emotions; the way your metabolic rate varies, your heartbeats and respiration and things. I sent it to the director of that orchestra, and he didn't get the idea that it was a joke—of course I didn't explain—he produced the music. I get nice royalties from it, too."

"You'll be the death of me yet," said Welles in deep sincerity. "Don't tell me anything more today; I couldn't take it. I'm going home. Maybe by tomorrow I'll see the joke and come back to laugh. Tim, did you ever fail at anything?"

"There are two cabinets full of articles and stories that didn't sell. Some of them I feel bad about. There was the chess story. You know, in 'Through the Looking Glass,' it wasn't a very good game, and you couldn't see the relation of the moves to the story very well."

"I never could see it at all."

"I thought it would be fun to take a championship game and write a fantasy about it, as if it were a war between two little old countries, with knights and foot-soldiers, and fortified walls in charge of captains, and the bishops couldn't fight like warriors, and, of course, the queens were women—people don't kill them, not in hand-to-hand fighting and . . . well, you see? I wanted to make up the attacks and captures, and keep the people alive, a fairytale war you see, and make the strategy of the game and the strategy of the war coincide, and have everything fit. It took me ever so long to work it out and write it. To understand the game as a chess game and then to translate it into human actions and motives, and put speeches to it to fit different kinds of people. I'll show it to you. I loved it. But nobody would print it. Chess players don't like fantasy, and nobody else likes chess. You have to have a very special kind of mind to like both. But it was a disappointment. I hoped it would be published, because the few people who like that sort of thing would like it *very* much."

"I'm sure I'll like it."

"Well, if you do like that sort of thing, it's what you've been waiting all your life in vain for. Nobody else has done it." Tim stopped, and blushed as red as a beet. "I see what grandmother means. Once you get started bragging, there's no end to it. I'm sorry, Peter."

"Give me the story. I don't mind, Tim—brag all you like to me; I understand. You might blow up if you never expressed any of your legitimate pride and pleasure in such achievements. What I don't understand is how you have kept it all under for so long."

"I had to," said Tim.

The story was all its young author had claimed. Welles chuckled as he read it, that evening. He read it again, and checked all the moves and the strategy of them. It was really a fine piece of work. Then he thought of the symphony, and this time he was able to laugh. He sat up until after midnight, thinking about the boy. Then he took a sleeping pill and went to bed.

The next day he went to see Tim's grandmother. Mrs. Davis received him graciously.

"Your grandson is a very interesting boy," said Peter Welles carefully. "I'm asking a favor of you. I am making a study of various boys and girls in this district, their abilities and backgrounds and environment and character traits and things like that. No names will ever be mentioned, of course, but a statistical report will be kept, for ten years or longer, and some case histories might later be published. Could Timothy be included?"

"Timothy is such a good, normal little boy, I fail to see what would be the purpose of including him in such a survey."

"That is just the point. We are not interested in maladjusted persons in this study. We eliminate all psychotic boys and girls. We are interested in boys and girls who succeed in facing their youthful problems and making satisfactory adjustments to life. If we could study a selected group of such children, and follow their progress for the next ten years at least—and then publish a summary of the findings, with no names used—"

"In that case, I see no objection," said Mrs. Davis.

"If you'd tell me, then, something about Timothy's parents—their history?"

Mrs. Davis settled herself for a good long talk.

"Timothy's mother, my only daughter, Emily," she began, "was a lovely girl. So talented. She played the violin charmingly. Timothy is like her, in the face, but has his father's dark hair and eyes. Edwin had very fine eyes."

"Edwin was Timothy's father?"

"Yes. The young people met while Emily was at college in the East. Edwin was studying atomics there."

"Your daughter was studying music?"

"No; Emily was taking the regular liberal arts course. I can tell you little about Edwin's work, but after their marriage he returned to it and . . . you understand, it is painful for me to recall this, but their deaths were such a blow to me. They were so young."

Welles held his pencil ready to write.

"Timothy has never been told. After all, he must grow up in this world, and how dreadfully the world has changed in the past thirty years, Dr. Welles! But you would not remember the day before 1945. You have heard, no doubt, of the terrible explosion in the atomic plant, when they were trying to make a new type of bomb? At the time, none of the workers seemed to be injured. They believed the protection was adequate. But two years later they were all dead or dying."

Mrs. Davis shook her head sadly. Welles held his breath, bent his head, scribbled.

"Tim was born just fourteen months after the explosion, fourteen months to the day. Everyone still thought that no harm had been done. But the radiation had some effect which was very slow—I do not understand such things—Edwin died, and then Emily came home to us with the boy. In a few months she, too, was gone.

"Oh, but we do not sorrow as those who have no hope. It is hard to have lost her, Dr. Welles, but Mr. Davis and I have reached the time of life when we can look forward to seeing her again. Our hope is to live until Timothy is old enough to fend for himself. We were so anxious about him; but you see he is perfectly normal in every way."

"Yes."

"The specialists made all sorts of tests. But nothing is wrong with Timothy."

The psychiatrist stayed a little longer, took a few more notes, and made his escape as soon as he could. Going straight to the school, he had a few words with Miss Page and then took Tim to his office, where he told him what he had learned.

"You mean—I'm a mutation?"

"A mutant. Yes, very likely you are. I don't know. But I had to tell you at once."

"Must be a dominant, too," said Tim, "coming out this way in the first generation. You mean—there may be more? I'm not the only one?" he added in great excitement. "Oh, Peter, even if I grow up past you I won't have to be lonely?"

There. He had said it.

"It could be, Tim. There's nothing else in your family that could account for you."

"But I have never found anyone at all like me. I would have known. Another boy or girl my age—like me—I would have known."

"You came West with your mother. Where did the others go, if they existed? The parents must have scattered everywhere, back to their homes all over the country, all over the world. We can trace them, though. And, Tim, haven't you thought it's just a little bit strange that with all your pen names and various contacts, people don't insist more on meeting you? Everything gets done by mail? It's almost as if the editors are used to people who hide. It's almost as if people are used to architects and astronomers and composers whom nobody ever sees, who are only names in care of other names at post office boxes. There's a chance—just a chance, mind you—that there are others. If there are, we'll find them."

"I'll work out a code they will understand," said Tim, his

face screwed up in concentration. "In articles—I'll do it—several magazines and in letters I can enclose copies—some of my pen friends may be the ones—"

"I'll hunt up the records—they must be on file somewhere—psychologists and psychiatrists know all kinds of tricks—we can make some excuse to trace them all—the birth records—"

Both of them were talking at once, but all the while Peter Welles was thinking sadly, perhaps he had lost Tim now. If they did find those others, those to whom Tim rightfully belonged, where would poor Peter be? Outside, among the puppies—

Timothy Paul looked up and saw Peter Welles's eyes on him. He smiled.

"You were my first friend, Peter, and you shall be forever," said Tim. "No matter what, no matter who."

"But we must look for the others," said Peter.

"I'll never forget who helped me," said Tim.

An ordinary boy of thirteen may say such a thing sincerely, and a week later have forgotten all about it. But Peter Welles was content. Tim would never forget. Tim would be his friend always. Even when Timothy Paul and those like him should unite in a maturity undreamed of, to control the world if they chose, Peter Welles would be Tim's friend—not a puppy, but a beloved friend—as a loyal dog loved by a good master, is never cast out.

KNOCK

by Fredric Brown (1906–1972)

THRILLING WONDER STORIES
December

Fredric Brown, an old friend of this series, returns with one of his best and most famous stories. Its subject matter, the last man on Earth, has become somewhat of a cliché in science fiction since it is one of the oldest themes, going back (at least) to Mary Shelley's The Last Man *in the early 19th century. However, in the capable hands of Fredric Brown a simple idea becomes an ironic masterpiece of sf.*

(This is one of those stories that once read is never forgotten. Or, perhaps I ought to say, more cautiously, it is one of those stories that, once I read it, I never forget. I would, however, like to make a point about the story that I've never seen made. It illuminates with absolute clarity the sexist nature of our language. Ask yourself: What does "man" mean?

Now ask yourself: If you didn't think of "man" in a peculiarly unfair way, would that two-sentence horror story at the beginning be a horror story and would you need Fred to point it out to you?—I.A.)

There is a sweet little horror story that is only two sentences long:

"The last man on Earth sat alone in a room. There was a knock on the door . . ."

Two sentences and an ellipsis of three dots. The horror, of course, isn't in the two sentences at all; it's in the ellipsis, the implication: *what* knocked at the door? Faced with the unknown, the human mind supplies something vaguely horrible.

But it wasn't horrible, really.

The last man on Earth—or in the universe, for that matter—*sat alone in a room.* It was a rather peculiar room. He'd just noticed how peculiar it was and he'd been studying out the reason for its peculiarity. His conclusion didn't horrify him, but it annoyed him.

Walter Phelan, who had been associate professor of anthropology at Nathan University up until the time two days ago when Nathan University had ceased to exist, was not a man who horrified easily. Not that Walter Phelan was a heroic figure, by any wild stretch of the imagination. He was slight of stature and mild of disposition. He wasn't much to look at, and he knew it.

Not that his appearance worried him now. Right now, in fact, there wasn't much feeling in him. Abstractedly, he knew that two days ago, within the space of an hour, the human race had been destroyed, except for him and, somewhere, a woman—one woman. And that was a fact which didn't concern Walter Phelan in the slightest degree. He'd probably never see her and didn't care too much if he didn't.

Women just hadn't been a factor in Walter's life since Martha had died a year and a half ago. Not that Martha hadn't been a good wife—albeit a bit on the bossy side. Yes, he'd loved Martha, in a deep, quiet way. He was only forty now, and he'd been only thirty-eight when Martha had died, but—well—he just hadn't thought about women since then. His life had been his books, the ones he read and the ones he wrote. Now there wasn't any point in writing books, but he had the rest of his life to spend in reading them.

True, company would be nice, but he'd get along without it. Maybe after a while, he'd get so he'd enjoy the occasional company of one of the Zan, although that was a bit difficult to imagine. Their thinking was so alien to his that there seemed no common ground for discussion, intelligent though they were, in a way.

An ant is intelligent, in a way, but no man ever established communication with an ant. He thought of the Zan, somehow, as super-ants, although they didn't look like ants, and he had a hunch that the Zan regarded the human race as the human race had regarded ordinary ants. Certainly what they'd done to Earth had been what men did to ant hills—and it had been done much more efficiently.

But they had given him plenty of books. They'd been nice about that, as soon as he had told them what he wanted, and he had told them that the moment he had learned that he was destined to spend the rest of his life alone in this room. The rest of his life, or as the Zan had quaintly expressed it, for-ev-er. Even a brilliant mind—and the Zan obviously had brilliant minds—has its idiosyncrasies. The Zan had learned to speak Terrestrial English in a matter of hours but they persisted in separating syllables. But we digress.

There was a knock on the door.

You've got it all now, except the three dots, the ellipsis, and I'm going to fill that in and show you that it wasn't horrible at all.

Walter Phelan called out, "Come in," and the door opened. It was, of course, only a Zan. It looked exactly like the other Zan; if there was any way of telling one of them from another, Walter hadn't found it. It was about four feet tall and it looked like nothing on Earth—nothing, that is, that had been on Earth until the Zan came there.

Walter said, "Hello, George." When he'd learned that none of them had names he decided to call them all George, and the Zan didn't seem to mind.

This one said, "Hel-lo, Wal-ter." That was ritual; the knock on the door and the greetings. Walter waited.

"Point one," said the Zan. "You will please henceforth sit with your chair turned the other way."

Walter said, "I thought so, George. That plain wall is transparent from the other side, isn't it?"

"It is trans-par-ent."

"Just what I thought. I'm in a zoo. Right?"

"That is right."

Walter sighed. "I knew it. That plain, blank wall, without a single piece of furniture against it. And made of something different from the other walls. If I persist in sitting with my back to it, what then? You will kill me? I ask hopefully."

"We will take a-way your books."

"You've got me there, George. All right, I'll face the other way when I sit and read. How many other animals besides me are in this zoo of yours?"

"Two hun-dred and six-teen."

Walter shook his head. "Not complete, George. Even a bush league zoo can beat that—*could* beat that, I mean, if there were any bush league zoos left. Did you just pick at random?"

"Ran-dom sam-ples, yes. All spe-cies would have been too many. Male and fe-male each of one hun-dred and eight kinds."

"What do you feed them? The carnivorous ones, I mean."

"We make food. Syn-thet-ic."

"Smart," said Walter. "And the flora? You got a collection of that, too?"

"Flo-ra was not hurt by vi-bra-tions. It is all still grow-ing."

"Nice for the flora," said Walter. "You weren't as hard on it, then, as you were on the fauna. Well, George, you started out with 'point one'. I deduce there is a point two kicking around somewhere. What is it?"

"Some-thing we do not un-der-stand. Two of the o-ther a-ni-mals sleep and do not wake? They are cold."

"It happens in the best regulated zoos, George," Walter Phelan said. "Probably not a thing wrong with them except that they're dead."

"Dead? That means stopped. But noth-ing stopped them. Each was a-lone."

Walter stared at the Zan. "Do you mean, George, you don't know what natural death is?"

"Death is when a be-ing is killed, stopped from liv-ing."

Walter Phelan blinked. "How old are you, George?" he asked.

"Six-teen—you would not know the word. Your pla-net went a-round your sun a-bout sev-en thou-sand times. I am still young."

Walter whistled softly. "A babe in arms," he said. He thought hard a moment. "Look, George," he said, "you've got something to learn about this planet you're on. There's a guy here who doesn't hang around where you come from. An old man with a beard and a scythe and an hourglass. Your vibrations didn't kill him."

"What is he?"

"Call him the Grim Reaper, George. Old Man Death. Our people and animals live until somebody—Old Man Death—*stops* them ticking."

"He stopped the two crea-tures? He will stop more?"

* * *

Walter opened his mouth to answer, and then closed it again. Something in the Zan's voice indicated that there would be a worried frown on his face, if he had had a face recognizable as such.

"How about taking me to these animals who won't wake up?" Walter asked. "Is that against the rules?"

"Come," said the Zan.

That had been the afternoon of the second day. It was the next morning that the Zan came back, several of them. They began to move Walter Phelan's books and furniture. When they'd finished that, they moved him. He found himself in a much larger room a hundred yards away.

He sat and waited and this time, too, when there was a knock on the door, he knew what was coming and politely stood up. A Zan opened the door and stood aside. A woman entered.

Walter bowed slightly. "Walter Phelan," he said, "in case George didn't tell you my name. George tries to be polite, but he doesn't know all of our ways."

The woman seemed calm; he was glad to notice that. She said, "My name is Grace Evans, Mr. Phelan. What's this all about? Why did they bring me here?"

Walter was studying her as she talked. She was tall, fully as tall as he, and well-proportioned. She looked to be somewhere in her early thirties, about the age Martha had been. She had the same calm confidence about her that he'd always liked about Martha, even though it had contrasted with his own easy-going informality. In fact, he thought she looked quite a bit like Martha.

"I think I know why they brought you here, but let's go back a bit," he said. "Do you know just what has happened otherwise?"

"You mean that they've—killed everyone?"

"Yes. Please sit down. You know how they accomplished it?"

She sank into a comfortable chair nearby. "No," she said. "I don't know just how. Not that it matters, does it?"

"Not a lot. But here's the story—what I know of it, from getting one of them to talk, and from piecing things together. There isn't a great number of them—here, anyway. I don't know how numerous a race they are where they came from and I don't know where that is, but I'd guess it's outside the Solar System. You've seen the space ship they came in?"

"Yes. It's as big as a mountain."

"Almost. Well, it has equipment for emitting some sort of a

vibration—they call it that, in our language, but I imagine it's more like a radio wave than a sound vibration—that destroys all animal life. It—the ship itself—is insulated against the vibration. I don't know whether its range is big enough to kill off the whole planet at once, or whether they flew in circles around the earth, sending out the vibratory waves. But it killed everybody and everything instantly and, I hope, painlessly. The only reason we, and the other two-hundred-odd animals in this zoo, weren't killed was because we were inside the ship. We'd been picked up as specimens. You do know this is a zoo, don't you?"

"I—I suspected it."

"The front walls are transparent from the outside. The Zan were pretty clever at fixing up the inside of each cubicle to match the natural habitat of the creature it contains. These cubicles, such as the one we're in, are of plastic, and they've got a machine that makes one in about ten minutes. If Earth had had a machine and a process like that, there wouldn't have been any housing shortage. Well, there isn't any housing shortage now, anyway. And I imagine that the human race—specifically you and I—can stop worrying about the A-bomb and the next war. The Zan certainly solved a lot of problems for us."

Grace Evans smiled faintly. "Another case where the operation was successful, but the patient died. Things *were* in an awful mess. Do you remember being captured? I don't. I went to sleep one night and woke up in a cage on the space ship."

"I don't remember either," Walter said. "My hunch is that they used the vibratory waves at low intensity first, just enough to knock us all out. Then they cruised around, picking up samples more or less at random for their zoo. After they had as many as they wanted, or as many as they had space in the ship to hold, they turned on the juice all the way. And that was that. It wasn't until yesterday they knew they'd made a mistake and had underestimated us. They thought we were immortal, as they are."

"That we were—what?"

"They can be killed, but they don't know what natural death is. They didn't, anyway, until yesterday. Two of us died yesterday."

"Two of—Oh!"

"Yes, two of us animals in their zoo. One was a snake and one was a duck. Two species gone irrevocably. And by the Zan's way of figuring time, the remaining member of each species is going to live only a few minutes, anyway. They figured they had permanent specimens."

"You mean they didn't realize what short-lived creatures we are?"

"That's right," Walter said. "One of them is young at seven thousand years, he told me. They're bisexual themselves, incidentally, but they probably breed once every ten thousand years or thereabouts. When they learned yesterday how ridiculously short a life expectancy we terrestrial animals have, they were probably shocked to the core—if they have cores. At any rate they decided to reorganize their zoo—two by two instead of one by one. They figure we'll last longer collectively if not individually."

"Oh!" Grace Evans stood up, and there was a faint flush on her face. "If you think—if they think—" She turned toward the door.

"It'll be locked," Walter Phelan said calmly. "But don't worry. Maybe they think, but I *don't* think. You needn't even tell me you wouldn't have me if I were the last man on Earth; it would be corny under the circumstances."

"But are they going to keep us locked up together in this one little room?"

"It isn't so little; we'll get by. I can sleep quite comfortably in one of these overstuffed chairs. And don't think I don't agree with you perfectly, my dear. All personal considerations aside, the least favor we can do the human race is to let it end with us and not be perpetuated for exhibition in a zoo."

She said, "Thank you," almost inaudibly, and the flush receded from her cheeks. There was anger in her eyes, but Walter knew that it wasn't anger at him. With her eyes sparkling like that, she looked a lot like Martha, he thought.

He smiled at her and said, "Otherwise—"

She started out of her chair, and for an instant he thought she was going to come over and slap him. Then she sank back wearily. "If you were a *man,* you'd be thinking of some way to—They can be killed, you said?" Her voice was bitter.

"Oh, certainly. I've been studying them. They look horribly different from us, but I think they have about the same metabolism we have, the same type of circulatory system, and probably the same type of digestive system. I think that anything that would kill one of us would kill one of them."

"But you said—"

"Oh, there are differences, of course. Whatever factor it is in man that ages him, they don't have. Or else they have some gland that man doesn't have, something that renews cells."

She had forgotten her anger now. She leaned forward eagerly. She said, "I think that's right. And I don't think they feel pain."

"I was hoping that. But what makes you think so, my dear?"

"I stretched a piece of wire that I found in the desk on my cubicle across the door so my Zan would fall over it. He did, and the wire cut his leg."

"Did he bleed red?"

"Yes, but it didn't seem to annoy him. He didn't get mad about it; didn't even mention it. When he came back the next time, a few hours later, the cut was gone. Well, almost gone. I could see just enough of a trace of it to be sure it was the same Zan."

Walter Phelan nodded slowly.

"He wouldn't get angry, of course," he said. "They're emotionless. Maybe, if we killed one, they wouldn't even punish us. But it wouldn't do any good. They'd just give us our food through a trap door and treat us as men would have treated a zoo animal that had killed a keeper. They'd just see that he didn't have a crack at any more keepers."

"How many of them are there?" she asked.

"About two hundred, I think, in this particular space ship. But undoubtedly there are many more where they came from. I have a hunch this is just an advance guard, sent to clear off this planet and make it safe for Zan occupancy."

"They did a good—"

There was a knock at the door, and Walter Phelan called out, "Come in." A Zan stood in the doorway.

"Hello, George," said Walter.

"Hel-lo, Wal-ter," said the Zan.

It may or may not have been the same Zan, but it was always the same ritual.

"What's on your mind?" Walter asked.

"An-oth-er crea-ture sleeps and will not wake. A small fur-ry one called a wea-sel."

Walter shrugged.

"It happens, George. Old Man Death. I told you about him."

"And worse. A Zan has died. This morning."

"Is that worse?" Walter looked at him blandly. "Well, George, you'll have to get used to it, if you're going to stay around here."

The Zan said nothing. It stood there.

Finally Walter said, "Well?"

"About wea-sel. You ad-vise the same?"

Walter shrugged again. "Probably won't do any good. But sure, why not?"

The Zan left.

Walter could hear his footsteps dying away outside. He grinned. "It might work, Martha," he said.

"Mar—My name is Grace, Mr. Phelan. What might work?"

"My name is Walter, Grace. You might as well get used to it. You know, Grace, you do remind me a lot of Martha. She was my wife. She died a couple of years ago."

"I'm sorry," said Grace. "But what might work? What were you talking about to the Zan?"

"We'll know tomorrow," Walter said. And she couldn't get another word out of him.

That was the fourth day of the stay of the Zan.

The next was the last.

It was nearly noon when one of the Zan came. After the ritual, he stood in the doorway, looking more alien than ever. It would be interesting to describe him for you, but there aren't words.

He said, "We go. Our coun-cil met and de-ci-ded."

"Another of you died?"

"Last night. This is a pla-net of death."

Walter nodded. "You did your share. You're leaving two hundred and thirteen creatures alive, out of quite a few billion. Don't hurry back."

"Is there a-ny-thing we can do?"

"Yes. You can hurry. And you can leave our door unlocked, but not the others. We'll take care of the others."

Something clicked on the door; the Zan left.

Grace Evans was standing, her eyes shining.

She asked, "What—? How—?"

"Wait," cautioned Walter. "Let's hear them blast off. It's a sound I want to remember."

The sound came within minutes, and Walter Phelan, realizing how rigidly he'd been holding himself, relaxed in his chair.

"There was a snake in the Garden of Eden, too, Grace, and it got us in trouble," he said musingly. "But this one made up for it. I mean the mate of the snake that died day before yesterday. It was a rattlesnake."

"You mean it killed the two Zan who died? But—"

Walter nodded. "They were babes in the woods here. When they took me to look at the first creatures who 'were asleep and wouldn't wake up,' and I saw that one of them was a rattler, I had an idea, Grace. Just maybe, I thought, poison creatures were a development peculiar to Earth and the Zan wouldn't know about them. And, too, maybe their metabolism was enough like ours so that the poison would kill them. Anyway, I had nothing to lose trying. And both maybes turned out to be right."

"How did you get the snake to—"

Walter Phelan grinned. He said, "I told them what affection was. They didn't know. They were interested, I found, in preserving the remaining one of each species as long as possible, to study the picture and record it before it died. I told them it would die immediately because of the loss of its mate, unless it had affection and petting—constantly. I showed them how with the duck. Luckily it was a tame one, and I held it against my chest and petted it a while to show them. Then I let them take over with it—and the rattlesnake."

He stood up and stretched, and then sat down again more comfortably.

"Well, we've got a world to plan," he said. "We'll have to let the animals out of the ark, and that will take some thinking and deciding. The herbivorous wild ones we can let go right away. The domestic ones, we'll do better to keep and take charge of; we'll need them. But the carnivora—Well, we'll have to decide. But I'm afraid it's got to be thumbs down."

He looked at her. "And the human race. We've got to make a decision about that. A pretty important one."

Her face was getting a little pink again, as it had yesterday; she sat rigidly in her chair.

"*No!*" she said.

He didn't seem to have heard her. "It's been a nice race, even if nobody won it," he said. "It'll be starting over again now, and it may go backward for a while until it gets its breath, but we can gather books for it and keep most of its knowledge intact, the important things anyway. We can—"

He broke off as she got up and started for the door. Just the way his Martha would have acted, he thought, back in the days when he was courting her, before they were married.

He said, "Think it over, my dear, and take your time. But come back."

The door slammed. He sat waiting, thinking out all the things there were to do, once he started, but in no hurry to start them; and after a while he heard her hesitant footsteps coming back.

He smiled a little. See? It wasn't horrible, really.

The last man on Earth sat alone in a room. There was a knock on the door . . .

A CHILD IS CRYING

by John D. MacDonald

THRILLING WONDER STORIES
December

John D. MacDonald's second contribution to the best of 1948 is a moving story that can best be described as a "pre-holocaust" tale. The effects of Hiroshima on science fiction writers and their work were still being felt in 1948 (indeed, are still being felt today), and "A Child is Crying" is one of the finest stories of its kind.

This story is also the fifth and last in this book that first appeared in Thrilling Wonder Stories *or its sister magazine,* Startling Stories, *and points up the fact that John Campbell and his* Astounding Science Fiction *did not have a death grip on the sf market in the second half of the 1940s.*

(One value of this series of volumes, by the way, is that we are able to look over the work of a given year with the perspective of a generation's advance. This is the fifth story in this volume which deals with one aspect or another of the influence of the nuclear bomb. There were simply dozens of stories published in the late 1940s that were not [in our opinion] good enough to include in these volumes. We see, though, that they

were all wrong. The nuclear bomb had no mysterious, science-fictional consequences as far as we can tell. The only thing it does is what we knew all along it would do—destroy! It can smash civilization, kill billions of people, damage the Earth to the point where it might not recover for millions of years, if at all—but the scientists who witnessed the Alamogordo explosion knew that, and many tried to prevent Hiroshima for that reason. Science fiction has not accurately predicted anything beyond this.—I. A.)

His mother, who was brought to New York with him, said, at the press conference, "Billy is a very bright boy. There isn't anything else we can teach him."

The school teacher, back in Albuquerque, shuddered delicately, looking at the distant stars, her head on the broad shoulder of the manual training teacher. She said, "I'm sorry, Joe, if I talk about him too much. It seems as if everywhere I go and everything I do, I can feel those eyes of his watching me."

Bain, the notorious pseudo-psychiatrist, wrote an article loaded with clichés in which he said, "Obviously the child is a mutation. It remains to be seen whether or not his peculiar talents are inheritable." Bain mentioned the proximity of Billy's birthplace to atomic experimentation.

Emanuel Gardensteen was enticed out of his New Jersey study where he was putting on paper his newest theories in symbolic logic and mathematical physics. Gardensteen spent five hours in a locked room with Billy. At the end of the interview Gardensteen emerged, biting his thin lips. He returned to New Jersey, locked his house, and took a job as a section hand repairing track on the Pennsy Railroad. He refused to make a statement to the press.

John Folmer spent four days getting permission to go ninety feet down the corridor of the Pentagon Building to talk to a man who was entitled to wear five stars on his uniform.

"Sit down, Folmer," the general said. "All this is slightly irregular."

"It's an irregular situation," Folmer retorted. "I couldn't trust Garrity and Hoskins to relay my idea to you in its original form."

The lean little man behind the mammoth desk licked his lips slowly. "You infer that my subordinates are either stupid or self-seeking?"

Folmer lit a cigarette, keeping his movements slow and unhurried. He grinned at the little gray man. "Sir, suppose you let me tell you what I'm thinking, and after you have the story, then you can assess any blame you feel is due."

"Go ahead."

"You have read about Billy Massner, General?"

The gray man snorted. "Read about him! I've read about him, listened to newscasts about him, watched his monstrous little face in the newsreels. The devil with him! A confounded freak."

"But is he?" Folmer queried, his eyes fixed on the general's face.

"What do you mean, Folmer. Get to the point."

"Certainly. It is of no interest to you or to me, General, to determine the reason for the kid's talents. What do we know about those talents? Just this. The kid could read and write and carry on a conversation when he was thirteen months old. At two and a half he was doing quadratic equations. At four, completely on his own, he worked out theories regarding non-Euclidian geometry and theories of relativity that parallel the work of Einstein. Now he is seven. You read the Beach Report after the psychologists got through with him. He can carry a conversation on mathematical concepts right on over the heads of our best men who have given their life to such things.

"The thing that happened to Gardensteen is an example. The Beach Report states that William Massner, age 7, is the most completely rational being ever tested. The factor of imagination is so small as not to respond to any known test. The kid gets his results by taking known and observed data and extrapolating from that point, proving his theories by exhaustive cross checks."

"So what, Folmer? So what?" the general snapped.

"What is our weapon of war, General? The top weapon?" Folmer asked meaningly.

"The atom bomb, of course!"

"And the atom bomb was made possible by the work of physicists in the realm of pure theory. The men who made the first bomb compare to Billy Massner the way you and I compare to those men."

"What are you getting at?" The general's tone showed curiosity and a little uneasiness.

"Just this, General. Billy Massner is a national resource. He is our primary weapon of offense and defense. As soon as our enemy realize what we have in this kid, I have a hunch they'll have him killed. Inside that head of his is our success in the war that's coming up one of these days."

The general placed his small hard palm on a yellow octagonal pencil and rolled it back and forth on the surface of his huge desk. The wrinkles between his eyebrows deepened. He said gently, "Folmer, I'm sort of out of my depth on this atomic business. To me it's just a new explosive—more effective than those in use up to this time."

"And it will be continually improved," Folmer asserted. "You know what a very small portion of the available energy is released right now. I'll bet you this kid can point out the way to release all the potential energy."

"Why haven't you talked this over with the head physicist?"

"But I have! He sneered at the kid at first. I managed to get him an interview with Billy. Now he's on my side. He's too impressed to be envious. The kid fed him a production shortcut."

The general shrugged in a tired way. "What do we have to do?"

"I've talked to the boy's mother and last week I flew out and saw the father. They only pretend to love the kid. He isn't exactly the sort of person you can love. They'll be willing to let me adopt him. They'll sign him over. It will cost enough dough out of the special fund to give them a life income of a thousand a month."

"And then what?" the general wanted to know.

"The kid is rational. I explain to him what we want. If he does what we want him to do, he gets anything in the world *he* wants. Simple."

The general straightened his shoulders. "Okay, Folmer," he snapped. "Get under way. And make sure this monster of yours is protected until we can get him behind wire."

Folmer stood up and smiled. "I took the liberty of putting a guard on him, sir."

"Good work! I'll be available to iron out any trouble you run into. I'll have a copy disc of this conversation cut for your file. . . ."

In spite of the general's choice of words, William Massner was not a monster. He was slightly smaller than average for his age, fine-boned and with dark hair and fair skin. His knuckles had the usual grubby childhood look about them. At casual glance he seemed a normal, decent-looking youngster. The difference was in the absolute immobility of his face. His eyes were gray and level. He had never been known, since the age of six months, to show fear, anger, surprise or joy.

After the brief ten minutes in court, John Folmer brought Billy Massner to his hotel room. Folmer sat on the bed and Billy sat on a chair by the windows. John Folmer was a slightly florid man of thirty, with pale thinning hair and a soft bulge at the waistline. His hands were pink and well-kept. Though he had conducted all manner of odd negotiations with the confidence of an imaginative and thorough-going bureaucrat, the quiet gray-eyed child gave him a feeling of awe.

"Bill," he said, "are you disappointed in your parents for signing you away?"

"I made them uncomfortable. Their affection was a pretense. It was an obvious move for them to trade me for financial security." The boy's voice had the flat precision of a slide rule.

Folmer tried to smile warmly. "Well, Bill, at least the sideshow is over. We've gotten you away from all the publicity agents. You must have been getting sick of that."

"If you hadn't stopped it, I would have," the boy stated.

Folmer stared. "How would you do that?"

"I have observed average children. I would become an average child. They would no longer be interested."

"You could fake possessing their mentality?"

"It wouldn't be difficult," the boy said. "At the present time I am faking an intelligence level as much lower than my true level as the deviation between a normal child and the level I am faking."

Folmer uncomfortably avoided the level gray eyes. He said heartily, "We'll admit you're pretty . . . unusual, Bill. All the head doctors have been trying to find out why and how. But nobody has ever asked you for your opinion. Why are you such a . . . deviation from the norm, Bill?"

The boy looked at him for several motionless seconds. "There is nothing to be gained by giving you that information, Folmer."

Folmer stood up and walked over to the boy. He glared down at him, his arm half lifted. "Don't get snippy with me, you little freak!"

The level gray eyes met his. Folmer took three jerky steps backward and sat down awkwardly on the bed. "How did you do that?" he gasped.

"I suggested it to you."

"But—"

"I could just as well have suggested that you open the window and step out." And the child added tonelessly, "We're on the twenty-first floor."

Folmer got out a cigarette with shaking hands and lit it, sucking the smoke deep into his lungs. He tried to laugh. "Then why didn't you?"

"I don't like unnecessary effort. I have made a series of time-rhythm extrapolations. Even though you are an unimportant man, your death now would upset the rhythm of one of the current inevitabilities, changing the end result. With your death I would be forced to isolate once again all variables and re-establish the new time-rhythm to determine one segment of the future."

Folmer's eyes bulged. "You can tell what will happen in the future?"

"Of course. A variation of the statement that the end pre-exists in the means. The future pre-exists in the present, with all variables subject to their own cyclical rhythm."

"And my going out the window would change the future?"

"One segment of it," the boy replied.

Folmer's hands shook. He looked down at them. "Do—do you know when I'm supposed to die?"

"If I tell you, the fact of your knowledge will make as serious an upset in time-rhythm as the fact of your stepping out the window. Your probable future actions would be conditioned by your knowledge."

Folmer smiled tightly. "You're hedging. You don't know the future."

"You called me up here to tell me that we are taking a plane today or tomorrow to a secret research laboratory in Texas. We will take that plane. In Texas the head physicist at the laboratory will set up a morning conference system whereby each staff member will bring current research problems to a roundtable meeting. I will answer the questions they put to me. No more than that. I will not indicate any original line of research, even though I will be asked to do so."

"And why not?"

"For the same reason that you are not now dead on the pavement two hundred feet below that window. Any interference with time-rhythm means laborious re-calculations. Since by a process of extrapolation I can determine the future, my efforts would be conditioned by my knowledge of that future."

Folmer tried to keep his voice steady as he asked, "You could foresee military attacks?"

"Of course," the child said.

"Do you know of any?"

"I do."

"You will advise us of them so that we can prepare, so that we can strike first?" In spite of himself Folmer sounded eager.

"I will not. . . ."

Folmer took William Massner to Texas. They landed at San Antonio where an army light plane took them a hundred miles northwest to the underground laboratories of the government where able men kept themselves from thinking of the probable results of their work. They were keen and sensitive men, the best that the civilized world had yet produced—but they worked with death, with the musty odor of the grave like a gentle touch against their lips. And they didn't stop to think. It was impossible to think of consequences. Think of the job at hand. Think of CM. Think in terms of unbelievable temperatures, of the grotesque silhouette of a man baked into the asphalt of Hiroshima. . . .

Billy was given a private suite, his needs attended to by two WAC corporals who had been given extensive security checks. The two girls were frightened of the small boy. They were frightened because he spent one full hour each day doing a series of odd physical exercises which he had worked out for himself. But that didn't frighten them as much as the fact that during the rest of his free time he sat absolutely motionless in a chair, his eyes half closed, gazing at a blank wall a few feet in front of him. At times he seemed to be watching something, some image against the flat white wall.

Folmer was unable to sleep. He didn't eat properly. He had told no one of his talk with Billy at the New York hotel. His knowledge ate at him. As his cheeks sagged and turned sallow, as his plump body seemed to wither, the fear in his eyes became deeper and more set.

The research staff made more progress during the first month of roundtable meetings than they had during the entire previous year. The younger men went about with an air of excitement thinly covered by a rigid control. The older men seemed to sink more deeply into fortified battlements of the mind. William Massner's slow and deliberate answers to involved questions resulted in the scrapping of two complete lines of research and a tremendous spurt of progress in other lines.

Folmer could not forget the attack which Billy had spoken of and, moreover, could not forget the fact that Billy knew when the attack would occur. As Folmer lay rigid and unsleeping during the long hours of night, he felt that the silver snouts of mighty rockets were screaming through the stratosphere, arching and falling toward him, reaching out to explode each separate molecule of his body into a hot whiteness.

On the twenty-third of October, after William Massner had been at the Research Center for almost seven weeks, Folmer, made bold by stiff drinks, sought out Burton Janks, the Security Control Officer. They went together to a small soundproofed storeroom and closed the door behind them. Janks was a slim, tanned man with pale milky eyes, dry brown hair and muscular hands. He listened to Folmer's story without any change in expression.

When Folmer had finished, Janks said, "I'm turning you over to Robertson for a psycho."

"Don't be a fool, Burt! Give me a chance to prove it first!" Folmer pleaded.

"Prove that nonsense! How?"

"Will you grant that if any part of my story is true, all of it is true?"

Janks shrugged. "Sure."

"Then do this one thing, Burt. The kid'll be coming out of conference in about ten minutes. He'll go along the big corridor and take the elevator up to his apartment level. Meet him in the corridor, walk up to him and pretend that you are going to slap him. Your guards will be with you. You're the only man who could try such a thing and get away with it."

Janks stretched lazily. "I'd enjoy batting the little jerk's ears back. Maybe I won't pretend."

Ten minutes later Janks stood beside Folmer. They leaned against the wall of the corridor. The door at the end opened and Billy came out, closely followed by the two young guards who were always with him whenever he was out of his apartment. Billy walked slowly and steadily, no expression on his small-boy face, no glint of light in his ancient gray eyes.

Janks said, "Here goes," and walked out to intercept them. He nodded at the guards, drew one hand back as though to strike the boy. For a second Janks stood motionless. Then he went backward with odd, wooden steps, his back slamming against the corridor wall with a force that nearly knocked him off his feet. Billy stared at him for a moment without expression before continuing toward his apartment. The two guards stood with their mouths open, staring at Janks, and then hurried to their proper position a few feet behind William Massner.

Janks was pale. He looked toward the small figure of Billy, turned to Folmer and said, "Come on. We'll report to W. W. Gates."

Gates was an unhappy man. He had been a reasonably competent physicist, blessed with a charming personality and an ability to handle administrative details. As a consequence, he was no longer permitted to do research, but had become the buffer between the military and the research staff. His nominal position was head of research, but his time was spent on reports in quadruplicate and in soothing the battered sensibilities of the research staff. Gates loved his profession and continually told himself that he was helping it more by staying out of it. His rationalization didn't make him feel any better. He looked like a bald John L. Lewis without the eyebrows. And without the voice. Gates talked in a plaintive squeak.

He sat very still and listened while Folmer told the complete story and Janks substantiated it. Little beads of sweat appeared on Gates' upper lip in spite of the air-conditioning.

He said slowly, "If I had never sat in on the conferences, I wouldn't believe it. Science has believed that the future is the result of an infinite progression of possibilities and probabilities with a factor of complete randomness. If you quoted him properly, Folmer, this time-rhythm he spoke of indicates some kind of a pattern in the randomness, so that if you can isolate all the possibilities and probabilities and determine the past rhythm, you can extend that pattern. It's sort of a statistical approach to metaphysics and quite beyond our current science. I wish you hadn't told me."

"I've got an idea, sir," Folmer said. Both men looked at him. "I've spent a long time watching the kid. This reading the future is okay for big stuff, but little things fool him. Once he stumbled and fell against a door. Another time one of the men accidentally tramped on his foot. It hurt the kid."

"What does that mean?" Janks said.

"It means that the kid can avoid big stuff if he wants to, but not minor accidents. I don't think we can carry this much further. The three of us right here are carrying the ball. It's up to us. The future is locked up in the kid's mind. Now, here's what we do. . . ."

Corporal Alice Dentro was nervous. She knew that she had to forget her personal fears and carry out her orders. An order was an order, wasn't it? She was in the army, wasn't she? After all, her superiors must know what they're doing.

She aimlessly dusted the furniture and glanced toward the chair where William Massner sat motionless, staring at a blank wall. Her lips were tight, and little droplets of cold sweat trickled down her body. She moved constantly closer to the boy. Five feet from him, she reached into her blouse pocket and pulled out the hypodermic. It slid easily out of the aseptic plastic case. Quickly she held it up to the light, depressed the plunger until a drop of the clear liquid appeared at the needly tip.

A few feet closer. Now she could reach out and touch him. He didn't move. She held herself very still, the needle poised. A quick thrust. The boy jumped as the needle slid through the fabric of his sleeve and penetrated the smooth skin. She pushed the plunger before he twisted away. She backed across the room, dropping the hypodermic. It glistened against the thick pile of the rug. She stood with her back against the door. Billy tried to stand, but slumped back. In a few seconds his chin dropped on his chest, and he began to snore softly.

She glanced at her watch. With a trembling hand she unlocked the door. Gates, Janks and Folmer came in quickly and quietly. With them was Dr. Badloe from the infirmary. He carried a small black case. Janks nodded at Alice Dentro. She slipped out into the corridor and walked quickly away, her shoulders squared. Behind her she heard the click of the lock on the steel door.

As the results of the first drug went away, Billy was given small increments of a derivative of scopolamine. They had turned his chair around, loosened his clothing. Only one light shone in the apartment. It was directed at his face. Dr. Badloe sat near him, fingers on the boy's pulse. Janks, Gates and Folmer stood just outside the circle of light.

"He's ready now," Badloe said. "Just one of you ask the questions."

Both Janks and Folmer looked at Gates. He nodded. In his thin, high voice he said, "Billy, is it true that you can read the future?"

The small lips twitched. In a small, sleepy voice Billy said, "Yes. Not every aspect of the future. Merely those segments of it which interest me. The method is subject to a standard margin of error.''

''Can you explain that margin of error?'' Gates asked.

''Yes. One segment of the future concerns my relationship with this organization. My study of the future indicated that Folmer, knowing my ability to read the future, would interest others and that a successful attempt would be made to render me powerless to keep my readings to myself.''

The three men stared at each other in sudden shock. Gates, with a quaver in his voice said, ''Then you knew that we would—do this thing?''

''Yes?''

''Why didn't you anticipate it and avoid it?''

''To do so would have been to alter the future,'' the sleepy voice responded.

''Are you a mutation caused by atomic radiation?''

''No.''

''What are you?''

''A direct evolutionary product. There are precedents in history. The man who devised the bow and arrow is a case in point. He was necessary to humanity because otherwise humanity would not have survived. He was more capable than his fellows.'' The boy's droning voice halted.

''Are we to assume then that your existence is necessary to the survival of humanity?'' Gates questioned.

''Yes. The factor missing from man's intellect is the ability to read the future. To do so requires a more lucid mind than has hitherto existed. The use of atomic energy makes a knowledge of the future indispensable to survival. Thus evolution has provided humanity with a new species of man able to anticipate the results of his own actions.''

''Will we be attacked?''

''Of course. And you will counterattack again and again. As a result of this plan of yours, you hope to be able to attack first, but your military won't credit my ability to see into the future.''

''When will the attack come?'' Gates prodded.

''No less than forty, not more than fifty-two days from today. Minor variables that cannot be properly estimated give that margin for error.''

''Who will win?''

''Win? There will be no victory. That is the essential point. In the past the wars between city states ceased because the city states became too small as social units in a shrinking world.

Today a country is too small a social unit. This war will be the terminal point for inter-country warfare, as it will dissolve all financial, linguistic and religious barriers."

"What will the population of the world be when this war is over?" was Gates' next question.

"Between fifty and a hundred and fifty millions. There will be an additional fifty per cent shrinkage due to disease before population begins to climb again."

There was silence in the darkened room. The boy sat motionless, awaiting the next query. Badloe had taken his fingers from the boy's pulse and sat with his face in his hands.

Gates said slowly, "I don't understand. You spoke as though your type of individual has come into the world as an evolutionary answer to atomics. If this war will happen, in what sense are you saving mankind?"

"My influence is zero at this point," was the boy's answer. "I will be ready when the war is over. I will survive it, because I can anticipate the precautions to be taken. After it is over the ability to read the future will keep mankind from branching off into a repetition of militarism and fear. I have no part in this conflict."

"But you have improved our techniques!" Gates protested.

"I have increased your ability to destroy," Billy corrected him. "Were I to increase it further, you would be enabled to make the earth completely uninhabitable."

"Then your work is through?"

"Obviously. The result of the drug you have administered to me will be to impair the use of my intellect. I will be sent away. My abilities will return in sufficient time to enable me to survive."

Gates' voice became a whisper. "Are there others like you?"

"I estimate that there are at least twenty in the world today. Obviously many have managed to conceal their gifts. The oldest should be not more than nine. They are scattered all over the earth. They all have an excellent chance of survival. Thirty years from now there will be more than a thousand of us."

Gates glanced over at Janks, saw the fear and the obvious question. Folmer had the same expression on his face. With a voice that had in it a small touch of madness, Gates said, "What is the future of those of us in this room? Will we survive?"

"I have not explored the related probabilities. I knew in New York that it was necessary for Folmer to survive to bring me here and to tell you of my abilities. It can be calculated."

"Now?"

"Give me thirty seconds."

Again the room the room was silent. Badloe had lifted his face, his eyes naked with fear. Janks shifted uneasily. Folmer stood, barely breathing. Gates twisted his fingers together. The seconds ticked by. Four men waited for the word of death or life.

Billy Massner licked his lips. "Not one of you will live more than three months from this date." It was a flat, calm statement. Badloe made a sound in his throat.

"He's crazy!" Janks snarled.

They wanted to believe Janks. They had to believe the boy.

Gates whispered, "How will we die?"

They watched the small-boy face. Slowly the impassivity of it melted away. The gray eyes opened and they were not the dead gray eyes the men had grown accustomed to. They were the frightened eyes of boyhood. There was fear on the small face. Fear and indecision.

The voice had lost its flat and deadly calm.

"Who are you?" the boy asked, close to tears. "What do you want? What are you doing to me? I want to go home!"

In the darkened room four men stood and watched a small boy cry.

LATE NIGHT FINAL

by Eric Frank Russell

ASTOUNDING SCIENCE FICTION
December

Eric Frank Russell returns with his third appearance in this series (see Volumes 5 and 9) and with one of his best stories. "Late Night Final" is a culture confrontation story, a type that has a long and honorable history in science fiction. Russell here posits rigidity vs. flexibility and force vs. seeming passivity in a story that anticipates his wonderful "And Then There Were None" of 1951, which is the much better known story.

Isaac, the more I reread Russell the more convinced I am that he was one of the finest sf writers of his time. And although he was reasonably well known (he won a Hugo Award in 1955), it is sad that his work is almost entirely out of print. Publishers, please take note—there is a gold mine of wonderful writing waiting to come back into print.

(Campbell always enjoyed stories in which apparently superior aliens were beaten by the apparently weak people they were trying to conquer. That is, he enjoyed them when the apparently weak people were Earthpeople—and no one wrote this kind of story more plausibly than Russell. Of course, if we restrict it to

Earthpeople as a whole then it is the apparently weak Americans who cannot be conquered by apparently superior foreigners [''Hogan's Heroes'' on television is the best-known example of this.]

Somehow, I feel that Campbell would no longer enjoy this kind of story nor encourage it to be written for his magazine, if he were still alive. You see, a very powerful army came to this backward nation inhabited by primitive, inferior people and fought them for ten years and lost, and with the Vietnam War this whole notion has been stood on its head. Maybe we should all of us forget this business of conquest altogether. Where's the fun? This is exactly what Russell implies, I think. —I.A.)

Commander Cruin went down the extending metal ladder, paused a rung from the bottom, placed one important foot on the new territory, and then the other. That made him the first of his kind on an unknown world.

He posed there in the sunlight, a big bull of a man meticulously attired for the occasion. Not a spot marred his faultlessly cut uniform of gray-green on which jeweled orders of merit sparkled and flashed. His jack boots glistened as they had never done since the day of launching from the home planet. The golden bells of his rank tinkled on his heelhooks as he shifted his feet slightly. In the deep shadow beneath the visor of his ornate helmet his hard eyes held a glow of self-satisfaction.

A microphone came swinging down to him from the air lock he'd just left. Taking it in a huge left hand, he looked straight ahead with the blank intentness of one who sees long visions of the past and longer visions of the future. Indeed, this was as visionary a moment as any there had been in his world's history.

''In the name of Huld and the people of Huld,'' he enunciated officiously, ''I take this planet.'' Then he saluted swiftly, slickly, like an automaton.

Facing him, twenty-two long, black spaceships simultaneously thrust from their forward ports their glorypoles ringed with the red-black-gold colors of Huld. Inside the vessels twenty-two crews of seventy men apiece stood rigidly erect, saluted, broke into well-drilled song, "Oh, heavenly fatherland of Huld."

When they had finished, Commander Cruin saluted again. The crews repeated their salute. The glorypoles were drawn in. Cruin mounted the ladder, entered his flagship. All locks were closed. Along the valley the twenty-two invaders lay in military formation, spaced equidistantly, noses and tails dead in line.

On a low hill a mile to the east a fire sent up a column of thick smoke. It spat and blazed amid the remnants of what had been the twenty-third vessel—and the eighth successive loss since the fleet had set forth three years ago. Thirty then. Twenty-two now.

The price of empire.

Reaching his cabin, Commander Cruin lowered his bulk into the seat behind his desk, took off his heavy helmet, adjusted an order of merit which was hiding modestly behind its neighbor.

"Step four," he commented with satisfaction.

Second Commander Jusik nodded respectfully. He handed the other a book. Opening it, Cruin meditated aloud.

"Step one: Check planet's certain suitability for our form of life." He rubbed his big jowls. "We know it's suitable."

"Yes, sir. This is a great triumph for you."

"Thank you, Jusik." A craggy smile played momentarily on one side of Cruin's broad face. "Step two: Remain in planetary shadow at distance of not less than one diameter while scout boats survey world for evidence of superior life forms. Three: Select landing place far from largest sources of possible resistance but adjacent to a source small enough to be mastered. Four: Declare Huld's claim ceremoniously, as prescribed in manual on procedure and discipline." He worked his jowls again. "We've done all that."

The smile returned, and he glanced with satisfaction out of the small port near his chair. The port framed the smoke column on the hill. His expression changed to a scowl, and his jaw muscles lumped.

"Fully trained and completely qualified," he growled sardonically. "Yet he had to smash up. Another ship and crew lost in the very moment we reach our goal. The eighth such loss. There will be a purge in the astronautical training center when I return."

"Yes, sir," approved Jusik, dutifully. "There is no excuse for it."

"There are no excuses for anything," Cruin retorted.

"No, sir."

Snorting his contempt, Cruin looked at his book. "Step five: Make all protective preparations as detailed in defense manual." He glanced up into Jusik's lean, clearcut features. "Every captain has been issued with a defense manual. Are they carrying out its orders?"

"Yes, sir. They have started already."

"They better had! I shall arrange a demotion of the slowest." Wetting a large thumb, he flipped a page over. "Step six: If planet does hold life forms of suspected intelligence, obtain specimens." Lying back in his seat he mused a moment, then barked: "Well, for what are you waiting?"

"I beg your pardon, sir?"

"Get some examples," roared Cruin.

"Very well, sir." Without blinking, Jusik saluted, marched out.

The self-closer swung the door behind him. Cruin surveyed it with a jaundiced eye.

"Curse the training center," he rumbled. "It has deteriorated since I was there."

Putting his feet on the desk, he waggled his heels to make the bells tinkle while he waited for the examples.

Three specimens turned up of their own accord. They were seen standing wide-eyed in a row near the prow of number twenty-two, the endmost ship of the line. Captain Somir brought them along personally.

"Step six calls for specimens, sir," he explained to Commander Cruin. "I know that you require ones better than these, but I found these under our nose."

"Under your nose? You land and within short time other life forms are sightseeing around your vessel? What about your protective precautions?"

"They are not completed yet, sir. They take some time."

"What were your lookouts doing—sleeping?"

"No, sir," assured Somir desperately. "They did not think it necessary to sound a general alarm for such as these."

Reluctantly, Cruin granted the point. His gaze ran contemptuously over the trio. Three kids. One was a boy, knee-high, snubnosed, chewing at a chubby fist. The next, a skinny-legged, pigtailed girl obviously older than the boy. The third was another girl almost as tall as Somir, somewhat skinny, but with a hint of coming shapeliness hiding in her thin attire. All three were freckled, all had violently red hair.

The tall girl said to Cruin: "I'm Marva—Marva Meredith." She indicated her companions. "This is Sue and this is Sam. We live over there, in Williamsville." She smiled at him and suddenly he noticed that her eyes were a rich and startling green. "We were looking for blueberries when we saw you come down."

Cruin grunted, rested his hands on his paunch. The fact that this planet's life manifestly was of his own shape and form impressed him not at all. It had never occurred to him that it could have proved otherwise. In Huldian thought, all superior life must be humanoid and no exploration had yet provided evidence to the contrary.

"I don't understand her alien gabble and she doesn't understand Huldian," he complained to Somir. "She must be dull-witted to waste her breath thus."

"Yes, sir," agreed Somir. "Do you wish me to hand them over to the tutors?"

"No. They're not worth it." He eyed the small boy's freckles with distaste, never having seen such a phenomenon before. "They are badly spotted and may be diseased. *Pfaugh*!" He grimaced with disgust. "Did they pass through the ray-sterilizing chamber as they came in?"

"Certainly, sir. I was most careful about that."

"Be equally careful about any more you may encounter." Slowly, his authoritative stare went from the boy to the pigtailed girl and finally to the tall one. He didn't want to look at her, yet knew that he was going to. Her cool green eyes held something that made him vaguely uncomfortable. Unwillingly he met those eyes. She smiled again, with little dimples. "Kick 'em out!" he rapped at Somir.

"As you order, sir."

Nudging them, Somir gestured toward the door. The three took hold of each other's hands, filed out.

"Bye!" chirped the boy, solemnly.

"Bye!" said pigtails, shyly.

The tall girl turned in the doorway. "Good-bye!"

Gazing at her uncomprehendingly, Cruin fidgeted in his chair. She dimpled at him, then the door swung to.

"Good-bye." He mouthed the strange word to himself. Considering the circumstances in which it had been uttered, evidently it meant farewell. Already he had picked up one word of their language.

"Step seven: Gain communication by tutoring specimens until they are proficient in Huldian."

Teach them. Do not let them teach you—teach *them*. The slaves must learn from the masters, not the masters from the slaves.

"Good-bye." He repeated it with savage self-accusation. A minor matter, but still an infringement of the book of rules. There are no excuses for anything.

Teach them.

The slaves—

Rockets rumbled and blasted deafeningly as ships maneuvered themselves into the positions laid down in the manual of defense. Several hours of careful belly-edging were required for this. In the end, the line had reshaped itself into two groups of eleven-pointed stars, noses at the centers, tails outward. Ash of blast-destroyed grasses, shrubs and trees covered a wide area beyond the two menacing rings of main propulsion tubes which could incinerate anything within one mile.

This done, perspiring, dirt-coated crews lugged out their forward armaments, remounted them pointing outward in the spaces between the vessels' splayed tails. Rear armaments still aboard already were directed upward and outward. Armaments plus tubes now provided a formidable field of fire completely surrounding the double encampment. It was the Huldian master plan conceived by Huldian master planners. In other more alien estimation, it was the old covered-wagon technique, so incredibly ancient that it had been forgotten by all but most earnest students of the past. But none of the invaders knew that.

Around the perimeter they stacked the small, fast, well-armed scouts of which there were two per ship. Noses outward, tails inward, in readiness for quick take-off, they were paired just beyond the parent vessels, below the propulsion tubes, and out of line of the remounted batteries. There was a lot of moving around to get the scouts positioned at precisely the same distances apart and making precisely the same angles. The whole arrangement had that geometrical exactness beloved of the military mind.

Pacing the narrow catwalk running along the top surface of his flagship, Commander Cruin observed his toiling crews with satisfaction. Organization, discipline, energy, unquestioning obedience—those were the prime essentials of efficiency. On such had Huld grown great. On such would Huld grow greater.

Reaching the tail-end, he leaned on the stop-rail, gazed down upon the concentric rings of wide, stubby venturis. His own crew were checking the angles of their two scouts already positioned. Four guards, heavily armed, came marching through the ash with Jusik in the lead. They had six prisoners.

Seeing him, Jusik bawled: "Halt!" Guard and guarded stopped with a thud of boots and a rise of dust. Looking up, Jusik saluted.

"Six specimens, sir."

Cruin eyed them indifferently. Half a dozen middle-aged men in drab, sloppily fitting clothes. He would not have given a snap of the fingers for six thousand of them.

The biggest of the captives, the one second from the left, had red hair and was sucking something that gave off smoke. His shoulders were wider than Cruin's own though he didn't look half the weight. Idly, the commander wondered whether the fellow had green eyes; he couldn't tell that from where he was standing.

Calmly surveying Cruin, this prisoner took the smoke-thing from his mouth and said, tonelessly: "By hokey, a brasshat!" Then he shoved the thing back between his lips and dribbled blue vapor.

The others looked doubtful, as if either they did not comprehend or found it past belief.

"Jeepers, *no*!" said the one on the right, a gaunt individual with thin, saturnine features.

"I'm telling you," assured Redhead in the same flat voice.

"Shall I take them to the tutors, sir?" asked Jusik.

"Yes." Unleaning from the rail, Cruin carefully adjusted his white gloves. "Don't bother me with them again until they are certified as competent to talk." Answering the other's salute, he paraded back along the catwalk.

"See?" said Redhead, picking up his feet in time with the guard. He seemed to take an obscure pleasure in keeping in step with the guard. Winking at the nearest prisoner, he let a curl of aromatic smoke trickle from the side of his mouth.

Tutors Fane and Parth sought an interview the following evening. Jusik ushered them in, and Cruin looked up irritably from the report he was writing.

"Well?"

Fane said: "Sir, these prisoners suggest that we share their homes for a while and teach them to converse there."

"How did they suggest that?"

"Mostly by signs," explained Fane.

"And what made you think that so nonsensical a plan had sufficient merit to make it worthy of my attention?"

"There are aspects about which you should be consulted," Fane continued stubbornly. "The manual of procedure and discipline declares that such matters must be placed before the commanding officer whose decision is final."

"Quite right, quite right." He regarded Fane with a little more favor. "What are these matters?"

"Time is important to us, and the quicker these prisoners learn our language the better it will be. Here, their minds are occupied by their predicament. They think too much of their friends and families. In their own homes it would be different, and they could learn at great speed."

"A weak pretext," scoffed Cruin.

"That is not all. By nature they are naive and friendly. I feel that we have little to fear from them. Had they been hostile they would have attacked by now."

"Not necessarily. It is wise to be cautious. The manual of defense emphasizes that fact repeatedly. These creatures may wish first to gain the measure of us before they try to deal with us."

Fane was prompt to snatch the opportunity. "Your point, sir, is also my final one. Here, they are six pairs of eyes and six pairs of ears in the middle of us, and their absence is likely to give cause for alarm in their home town. Were they there, complacency would replace that alarm—and *we* would be the eyes and ears!"

"Well put," commented Jusik, momentarily forgetting himself.

"Be silent!" Cruin glared at him. "I do not recall any ruling in the manual pertaining to such a suggestion as this. Let me check up." Grabbing his books, he sought through them. He took a long time about it, gave up, and said: "The only pertinent rule appears to be that in circumstances not specified in the manual the decision is wholly mine, to be made in light of said circumstances providing that they do not conflict with the rulings of any other manual which may be applicable to the situation, and providing that my decision does not effectively countermand that or those of any senior ranking officer whose authority extends to the same area." He took a deep breath.

"Yes, sir," said Fane.

"Quite, sir," said Parth.

Cruin frowned heavily. "How far away are these prisoners' homes?"

"One hour's walk." Fane made a persuasive gesture. "If anything did happen to us—which I consider extremely unlikely—one scout could wipe out their little town before they'd time to realize what had happened. One scout, one bomb, one minute!" Dexterously, he added, "At your order, sir."

Cruin preened himself visibly. "I see no reason why we should not take advantage of their stupidity." His eyes asked Jusik what he thought, but that person failed to notice. "Since you two tutors have brought this plan to me, I hereby approve it, and I appoint you to carry it through." He consulted a list which he extracted from a drawer. "Take two psychologists with you—Kalma and Hefni."

"Very well, sir." Impassively, Fane saluted and went out, Parth following.

Staring absently at his half-written report, Cruin fiddled with his pen for a while, glanced up at Jusik, and spat: "At what are you smiling?"

Jusik wiped it from his face, looked solemn.

"Come on. Out with it!"

"I was thinking, sir," replied Jusik, slowly, "that three years in a ship is a very long time."

Slamming his pen on the desk, Cruin stood up. "Has it been any longer for others than for me?"

"For you," said Jusik, daringly but respectfully, "I think it has been longest of all."

"Get out!" shouted Cruin.

He watched the other go, watched the self-closer push the door, waited for its last click. He shifted his gaze to the port, stared hard-eyed into the gathering dusk. His heelbells were silent as he stood unmoving and saw the invisible sun sucking its last rays from the sky.

In short time, ten figures strolled through the twilight toward the distant, tree-topped hill. Four were uniformed; six in drab, shapeless clothes. They went by conversing with many gestures, and one of them laughed. He gnawed his bottom lip as his gaze followed them until they were gone.

The price of rank.

"Step eight: Repel initial attacks in accordance with techniques detailed in manual of defense." Cruin snorted, put up one hand, tidied his orders of merit.

"There have been no attacks," said Jusik.

"I am not unaware of the fact." The commander glowered at him. "I'd have preferred an onslaught. We are ready for them. The sooner they match their strength against ours the sooner they'll learn who's boss now!" He hooked big thumbs in his silver-braided belt. "And besides, it would give the men something to do. I cannot have them everlastingly repeating their drills of procedure. We've been here nine days and nothing has happened." His attention returned to the book. "Step nine: Follow defeat of initial attacks by taking aggressive action as detailed in manual of defense." He gave another snort. "How can one follow something that has not occurred?"

"It is impossible," Jusik ventured.

"Nothing is impossible," Cruin contradicted, harshly. "Step ten: In the unlikely event that intelligent life displays indifference or amity, remain in protective formation while specimens are being tutored, meanwhile employing scout vessels to survey surrounding area to the limit of their flight-duration, using no more than one-fifth of the numbers available at any time."

"That allows us eight or nine scouts on survey," observed Jusik, thoughtfully. "What is our authorized step if they fail to return?"

"Why d'you ask that?"

"Those eight scouts I sent out on your orders forty periods ago are overdue."

Viciously, Commander Cruin thrust away his book. His broad, heavy face was dark red.

"Second Commander Jusik, it was your duty to report this fact to me the moment those vessels became overdue."

"Which I have," said Jusik, imperturbably. "They have a flight-duration of forty periods, as you know. That, sir, made them due a short time ago. They are now late."

Cruin tramped twice across the room, medals clinking, heel-bells jangling. "The answer to nonappearance is immediately to obliterate the areas in which they are held. No half-measures. A salutary lesson."

"Which areas, sir?"

Stopping in mid-stride, Cruin bawled: "*You* ought to know that. Those scouts had properly formulated route orders, didn't they? It's a simple matter to—"

He ceased as a shrill whine passed overhead, lowered to a dull moan in the distance, curved back on a rising note again.

"Number one." Jusik looked at the little timemeter on the wall. "Late, but here. Maybe the others will turn up now."

"Somebody's going to get a sharp lesson if they don't!"

"I'll see what he has to report." Saluting, Jusik hurried through the doorway.

Gazing out of his port, Cruin observed the delinquent scout belly-sliding up to the nearest formation. He chewed steadily at his bottom lip, a slow, persistent chew which showed his thoughts to be wandering around in labyrinths of their own.

Beyond the fringe of dank, dead ash were golden buttercups in the grasses, and a hum of bees, and the gentle rustle of leaves on trees. Four engine-room wranglers of ship number seventeen had found this sanctuary and sprawled flat on their backs in the shade of a big-leafed and blossom-ornamented growth. With eyes closed, their hands plucked idly at surrounding grasses while they maintained a lazy, desultory conversation through which they failed to hear the ring of Cruin's approaching bells.

Standing before them, his complexion florid, he roared: "Get up!"

Shooting to their feet, they stood stiffly shoulder to shoulder, faces expressionless, eyes level, hands at their sides.

"Your names?" He wrote them in his notebook while obediently they repeated them in precise, unemotional voices. "I'll deal with you later," he promised. "March!"

Together, they saluted, marched off with a rhythmic pounding of boots, one-two-three-hup! His angry stare followed them until they reached the shadow of their ship. Not until then did he turn and proceed. Mounting the hill, one cautious hand continually on the cold butt of his gun, he reached the crest, gazed down into the valley he'd just left. In neat, exact positioning, the two star-formations of the ships of Huld were silent and ominous.

His hard, authoritative eyes turned to the other side of the hill. There, the landscape was pastoral. A wooded slope ran down to a little river which meandered into the hazy distance, and on its farther side was a broad patchwork of cultivated fields in which three houses were visible.

Seating himself on a large rock, Cruin loosened his gun in its holster, took a wary look around, extracted a small wad of reports from his pocket and glanced over them for the twentieth time. A faint smell of herbs and resin came to his nostrils as he read.

"I circled this landing place at low altitude and recorded it photographically, taking care to include all the machines standing thereon. Two other machines which were in the air went on their way without attempting to interfere. It then occurred to me that the signals they were making from the ground might be an invitation to land, and I decided to utilize opportunism as recommended in the manual of procedure. Therefore I landed. They conducted my scout vessel to a dispersal point off the runway and made me welcome."

Something fluted liquidly in a nearby tree. Cruin looked up, his hand automatically seeking his holster. It was only a bird. Skipping parts of the report, he frowned over the concluding words.

". . . lack of common speech made it difficult for me to refuse, and after the sixth drink during my tour of the town I was suddenly afflicted with a strange paralysis in the legs and collapsed into the arms of my companions. Believing that they had poisoned me by guile, I prepared for death . . . tickled my throat while making jocular remarks . . . I was a little sick." Cruin rubbed his chin in puzzlement. "Not until they were satisfied about my recovery did they take me back to my vessel. They waved their hands at me as I took off. I apologize to my captain for overdue return and plead that it was because of factors beyond my control."

The fluter came down to Cruin's feet, piped at him plaintively. It cocked its head sidewise as it examined him with bright, beady eyes.

Shifting the sheet he'd been reading, he scanned the next one. It was neatly typewritten, and signed jointly by Parth, Fane, Kalma and Hefni.

"Do not appear fully to appreciate what has occurred . . . seem to view the arrival of a Huldian fleet as just another incident. They have a remarkable self-assurance which is incomprehensible inasmuch as we can find nothing to justify such an attitude. Mastery of them should be so easy that if our homing vessel does not leave too soon it should be possible for it to bear tidings of conquest as well as of mere discovery."

"Conquest," he murmured. It had a mighty imposing sound. A word like that would send a tremendous thrill of excitement throughout the entire world of Huld.

Five before him had sent back ships telling of discovery, but none had gone so far as he, none had traveled so long and wearily, none had been rewarded with a planet so big, lush, desirable—and none had reported the subjection of their finds. One cannot conquer a rocky waste. But this—

In peculiarly accented Huldian, a voice behind him said, brightly: "Good morning!"

He came up fast, his hand sliding to his side, his face hard with authority.

She was laughing at him with her clear green eyes. "Remember me—Marva Meredith?" Her flaming hair was windblown. "You see," she went on, in slow, awkward tones. "I know a little Huldian already. Just a few words."

"Who taught you?" he asked, bluntly.

"Fane and Parth."

"It is your house to which they have gone?"

"Oh, yes. Kalma and Hefni are guesting with Bill Gleeson; Fane and Parth with us. Father brought them to us. They share the welcome room."

"Welcome room?"

"Of course." Perching herself on his rock, she drew up her slender legs, rested her chin on her knees. He noticed that the legs, like her face, were freckled. "Of course. Everyone has a welcome room, haven't they?"

Cruin said nothing.

"Haven't you a welcome room in your home?"

"Home?" His eyes strayed away from hers, sought the fluting bird. It wasn't there. Somehow, his hand had left his holster without realizing it. He was holding his hands together, each nursing the other, clinging, finding company, soothing each other.

Her gaze was on his hands as she said, softly and hesitantly, "You have got a home . . . somewhere . . . haven't you?"

"No."

Lowering her legs, she stood up. "I'm so sorry."

"*You* are sorry for *me*?" His gaze switched back to her. It held incredulity, amazement, a mite of anger. His voice was harsh. "You must be singularly stupid."

"Am I?" she asked, humbly.

"No member of my expedition has a home," he went on. "Every man was carefully selected. Every man passed through a screen, suffered the most exacting tests. Intelligence and technical competence were not enough; each had also to be young, healthy, without ties of any sort. They were chosen for ability to concentrate on the task in hand without indulging morale-lowering sentimentalities about people left behind."

"I don't understand some of your long words," she complained. "And you are speaking far too fast."

He repeated it more slowly and with added emphasis, finishing, "Spaceships undertaking long absence from base cannot be handicapped by homesick crews. We picked men without homes because they can leave Huld and not care a hoot. They are pioneers!"

" 'Young, healthy, without ties,' " she quoted. "That makes them strong?"

"Definitely," he asserted.

"Men especially selected for space. Strong men." Her lashes hid her eyes as she looked down at her narrow feet. "But now they are not in space. They are here, on firm ground."

"What of it," he demanded.

"Nothing." Stretching her arms wide, she took a deep breath, then dimpled at him. "Nothing at all."

"You're only a child," he reminded scornfully. "When you grow older—"

"You'll have more sense," she finished for him, chanting it in a high, sweet voice. "You'll have more sense, you'll have more sense. When you grow older you'll have more sense, tra-la-la-lala!"

Gnawing irritatedly at his lip, he walked past her, started down the hill toward the ships.

"Where are you going?"

"Back!" he snapped.

"Do you like it down there?" Her eyebrows arched in surprise.

Stopping ten paces away, he scowled at her. "Is it any of your business?"

"I didn't mean to be inquisitive," she apologized. "I asked because . . . because—"

"Because what?"

"I was wondering whether you would care to visit my house."

"Nonsense! Impossible!" He turned to continue downhill.

"Father suggested it. He thought you might like to share a meal. A fresh one. A change of diet. Something to break the monotony of your supplies." The wind lifted her crimson hair and played with it as she regarded him speculatively. "He consulted Fane and Parth. They said it was an excellent idea."

"They did, did they?" His features seemed molded in iron. "Tell Fane and Parth they are to report to me at sunset." He paused, added, "Without fail!"

Resuming her seat on the rock, she watched him stride heavily down the slope toward the double star-formation. Her hands were together in her lap, much as he had held his. But hers sought nothing of each other. In complete repose, they merely rested with the ineffable patience of hands as old as time.

Seeing at a glance that he was liverish, Jusik promptly postponed certain suggestions that he had in mind.

"Summon captains Drek and Belthan," Cruin ordered. When the other had gone, he flung his helmet onto the desk, surveyed himself in a mirror. He was still smoothing the tired lines on his face when approaching footsteps sent him officiously behind his desk.

Entering, the two captains saluted, remained rigidly at attention. Cruin studied them irefully while they preserved wooden expressions.

Eventually, he said: "I found four men lounging like undisciplined hoboes outside the safety zone." He stared at Drek. "They were from your vessel." The stare shifted to Belthan. "You are today's commander of the guard. Have either of you anything to say?"

"They were off-duty and free to leave the ship," exclaimed Drek. "They had been warned not to go beyond the perimeter of ash."

"I don't know how they slipped through," said Belthan, in official monotone. "Obviously the guards were lax. The fault is mine."

"It will count against you in your promotion records," Cruin promised. "Punish these four, and the responsible guards, as laid down in the manual of procedure and discipline." He leaned across the desk to survey them more closely. "A repetition will bring ceremonial demotion!"

"Yes, sir," they chorused.

Dismissing them, he glanced at Jusik. "When tutors Fane and Parth report here, send them in to me without delay."

"As you order, sir."

Cruin dropped the glance momentarily, brought it back. "What's the matter with you?"

"Me?" Jusik became self-conscious. "Nothing, sir."

"You lie! One has to live with a person to know him. I've lived on your neck for three years. I know you too well to be deceived. You have something on your mind."

"It's the men," admitted Jusik, resignedly.

"What of them?"

"They are restless."

"Are they? Well, I can devise a cure for that! What's making them restless?"

"Several things, sir."

Cruin waited while Jusik stayed dumb, then roared: "Do I have to prompt you?"

"No, sir," Jusik protested, unwillingly. "It's many things. Inactivity. The substitution of tedious routine. The constant waiting, waiting, waiting right on top of three years of close incarceration. They wait—and nothing happens."

"What else?"

"The sight and knowledge of familiar life just beyond the ash. The realization that Fane and Parth and the others are enjoying it with your consent. The stories told by the scouts about their experiences on landing." His gaze was steady as he went on. "We've now sent out five squadrons of scouts, a total of forty vessels. Only six came back on time. All the rest were late on one plausible pretext or another. The pilots have talked, and shown the men various souvenir photographs and a few gifts. One of them is undergoing punishment for bringing back some bottles of paralysis-mixture. But the damage has been done. Their stories have unsettled the men."

"Anything more?"

"Begging your pardon, sir, there was also the sight of you taking a stroll to the top of the hill. They envied you even that!" He looked squarely at Cruin. "I envied you myself."

"I am the commander," said Cruin.

"Yes, sir." Jusik kept his gaze on him but added nothing more.

If the second commander expected a delayed outburst, he was disappointed. A complicated series of emotions chased each other across his superior's broad, beefy features. Laying back in his chair, Cruin's eyes looked absently through the port while his mind juggled with Jusik's words.

Suddenly, he rasped: "I have observed more, anticipated more and given matters more thought then perhaps you realize. I can see something which you may have failed to perceive. It has caused me some anxiety. Briefly, if we don't keep pace with the march of time we're going to find ourselves in a fix."

"Indeed, sir?"

"I don't wish you to mention this to anyone else: I suspect that we are trapped in a situation bearing no resemblance to any dealt with in the manuals."

"Really, sir?" Jusik licked his lips. felt that his own outspokenness was leading into unexpected paths.

"Consider our present circumstances," Cruin went on. "We are established here and in possession of power sufficient to enslave this planet. Any one of our supply of bombs could blast a portion of this earth stretching from horizon to horizon. But they're of no use unless we apply them effectively. We can't drop them anywhere, haphazardly. If parting with them in so improvident a manner proved unconvincing to our opponents, and failed to smash the hard core of their resistance, we would find ourselves unarmed in a hostile world. No more bombs. None nearer than six long years away, three there and three back. Therefore we must apply our power where it will do the most good." He began to massage his heavy chin. "We don't know where to apply it."

"No, sir," agreed Jusik, pointlessly.

"We've got to determine which cities are the key points of their civilization, which persons are this planet's acknowledged leaders, and where they're located. When we strike, it must be at the nerve-centers. That means we're impotent until we get the necessary information. In turn, that means we've got to establish communication with the aid of tutors." He started plucking at his jaw muscles. "And that takes time!"

"Quite, sir, but—"

"But while time crawls past the men's morale evaporates. This is our twelfth day and already the crews are restless. Tomorrow they'll be more so."

"I have a solution to that, sir, if you will forgive me for offering it," said Jusik, eagerly. "On Huld everyone gets one day's rest in five. They are free to do as they like, go where they like. Now if you promulgated an order permitting the men say one day's liberty in ten, it would mean that no more than ten percent of our strength would be lost on any one day. We could stand that reduction considering our power, especially if more of the others are on protective duty."

"So at last I get what was occupying your mind. It comes out in a swift flow of words." He smiled grimly as the other flushed. "I have thought of it. I am not quite so unimaginative as you may consider me."

"I don't look upon you that way, sir," Jusik protested.

"Never mind. We'll let that pass. To return to this subject of liberty—there lies the trap! There is the very quandary with which no manual deals, the situation for which I can find no officially prescribed formula." Putting a hand on his desk he tapped the polished surface impatiently. "If I refuse these men a little freedom, they will become increasingly restless—naturally. If I permit them the liberty they desire, they will experience contact with life more normal even though alien, and again become more restless—naturally!"

"Permit me to doubt the latter, sir. Our crews are loyal to Huld. Blackest space forbid that it should be otherwise!"

"They were loyal. Probably they are still loyal." Cruin's face quirked as his memory brought forward the words that followed. "They are young, healthy, without ties. In space, that means one thing. Here, another." He came slowly to his feet, big, bulky and imposing. "I *know*!"

Looking at him, Jusik felt that indeed he did know. "Yes, sir," he parroted, obediently.

"Therefore the onus of what to do for the best falls squarely upon me. I must use my initiative. As second commander it is for you to see that my orders are carried out to the letter."

"I know my duty, sir." Jusik's thinly drawn features registered growing uneasiness.

"And it is my final decision that the men must be restrained from contact with our opponents, with no exceptions other than the four technicians operating under my orders. The crews are to be permitted no liberty, no freedom to go beyond the ash. Any form of resentment on their part must be countered immediately and ruthlessly. You will instruct the captains to watch for murmurers in their respective crews and take appropriate action to silence them as soon as found." His jowls lumped, and his eyes were cold as he regarded the other. "All scout-flights are canceled as from now, and all scout-vessels remain grounded. None moves without my personal instructions."

"That is going to deprive us of a lot of information," Jusik observed. "The last flight to the south reported discovery of ten cities completely deserted, and that's got some significance which we ought to—"

"I said the flights are canceled!" Cruin shouted. "If I say the scout-vessels are to be painted pale pink, they will be painted pale pink, thoroughly, completely, from end to end. I am the commander!"

"As you order, sir."

"Finally, you may instruct the captains that their vessels are to be prepared for my inspection at midday tomorrow. That will give the crews something to do."

"Very well, sir."

With a worried salute, Jusik opened the door, glanced out and said: "Here are Fane, Kalma, Parth and Hefni, sir."

"Show them in."

After Cruin had given forcible expression to his views, Fane said: "We appreciate the urgency, sir, and we are doing our best, but it is doubtful whether they will be fluent before another four weeks have passed. They are slow to learn."

"I don't want fluency," Cruin growled. "All they need are enough words to tell us the things we want to know, the things we *must* know before we can get anywhere."

"I said sufficient fluency," Fane reminded. "They communicate mostly by signs even now."

"That flame-headed girl didn't."

"She has been quick," admitted Fane. "Possibly she has an above-normal aptitude for languages. Unfortunately she knows the least in any military sense and therefore is of little use to us."

Cruin's gaze ran over him balefully. His voice became low and menacing. "You have lived with these people many days. I look upon your features and find them different. Why is that?"

"Different?" The four exchanged wondering looks.

"Your faces have lost their lines, their space-gauntness. Your cheeks have become plump, well-colored. Your eyes are no longer tired. They are bright. They hold the self-satisfied expression of a fat *skodar* wallowing in its trough. It is obvious that you have done well for yourselves." He bent forward, his mouth ugly. "Can it be that you are in no great hurry to complete your task?"

They were suitably shocked.

"We have eaten well and slept regularly," Fane said. "We feel better for it. Our physical improvement has enabled us to work so much the harder. In our view, the foe is supporting us unwittingly with his own hospitality, and since the manual of—"

"Hospitality?" Cruin cut in, sharply.

Fane went mentally off-balance as vainly he sought for a less complimentary synonym.

"I give you another week," the commander harshed. "No more. Not one day more. At this time, one week from today, you will report here with the six prisoners adequately tutored to understand my questions and answer them."

"It will be difficult, sir."

"Nothing is difficult. Nothing is impossible. There are no excuses for anything." He studied Fane from beneath forbidding brows. "You have my orders—obey them!"

"Yes, sir."

His hard stare shifted to Kalma and Hefni. "So much for the tutors; now *you*. What have you to tell me? How much have you discovered?"

Blinking nervously, Hefni said: "It is not a lot. The language trouble is—"

"May the Giant Sun burn up and perish the language trouble! How much have you learned while enjoyably larding your bellies?"

Glancing down at his uniform-belt as if suddenly and painfully conscious of its tightness, Hefni recited: "They are exceedingly strange in so far as they appear to be highly civilized in a purely domestic sense but quite primitive in all others. This Meredith family lives in a substantial, well-equipped house. They have every comfort, including a color-television receiver."

"You're dreaming! We are still seeking the secrets of plain television even on Huld. Color is unthinkable."

Kalma chipped in with: "Nevertheless, sir, they have it. We have seen it for ourselves."

"That is so," confirmed Fane.

"Shut up!" Cruin burned him with a glare. "I have finished with you. I am now dealing with these two." His attention returned to the quaking Hefni: "Carry on."

"There is something decidedly queer about them which we've not yet been able to understand. They have no medium of exchange. They barter goods for goods without any regard for the relative values of either. They work when they feel like it. If they don't feel like it, they don't work. Yet, in spite of this, they work most of the time."

"Why?" demanded Cruin, incredulously.

"We asked them. They said that one works to avoid boredom. We cannot comprehend that viewpoint." Hefni made a defeated gesture. "In many places they have small factories which, with their strange, perverted logic, they use as amusement centers. These plants operate only when people turn up to work."

"Eh?" Cruin looked baffled.

"For example, in Williamsville, a small town an hour's walk

beyond the Meredith home, there is a shoe factory. It operates every day. Some days there may be only ten workers there, other days fifty or a hundred, but nobody can remember a time when the place stood idle for lack of one voluntary worker. Meredith's elder daughter, Marva, has worked there three days during our stay with them. We asked her the reason."

"What did she say?"

"For fun."

"Fun . . . fun . . . fun?" Cruin struggled with the concept. "What does that mean?"

"We don't know," Hefni confessed. "The barrier of speech—"

"Red flames lick up the barrier of speech!" Cruin bawled. "Was her attendance compulsory?"

"No, sir."

"You are certain of that?"

"We are positive. One works in a factory for no other reason than because one feels like it."

"For what reward?" topped Cruin, shrewdly.

"Anything or nothing." Hefni uttered it like one in a dream. "One day she brought back a pair of shoes for her mother. We asked if they were her reward for the work she had done. She said they were not, and that someone named George had made them and given them to her. Apparently the rest of the factory's output for that week was shipped to another town where shoes were required. This other town is going to send back a supply of leather, nobody knows how much—and nobody seems to care."

"Senseless," defined Cruin. "It is downright imbecility." He examined Hefni as if suspecting him of inventing confusing data. "It is impossible for even the most primitive of organizations to operate so haphazardly. Obviously you have seen only part of the picture; the rest has been concealed from you, or you have been too dull-witted to perceive it."

"I assure you, sir," began Hefni.

"Let it pass," Cruin cut in. "Why should I care how they function economically? In the end, they'll work the way *we* want them to!" He rested his heavy jaw in one hand. "There are other matters which interest me more. For instance, our scouts have brought in reports of many cities. Some are organized but grossly underpopulated; others are completely deserted. The former have well-constructed landing places with air-machines making use of them. How is it that people so primitive have air-machines?"

"Some make shoes, some make air-machines, some play with

television. They work according to their aptitudes as well as their inclinations.''

''Has this Meredith got an air-machine?''

''No.'' The look of defeat was etched more deeply on Hefni's face. ''If he wanted one he would have his desire inserted in the television supply-and-demand program.''

''Then what?''

''Sooner or later, he'd get one, new or secondhand, either in exchange for something or as a gift.''

''Just by asking for it?''

''Yes.''

Getting up, Cruin strode to and fro across his office. The steel heelplates on his boots clanked on the metal floor in rhythm with the bells. He was ireful, impatient, dissatisfied.

''In all this madness is nothing which tells us anything of their true character or their organization.'' Stopping his stride, he faced Hefni. ''You boasted that *you* were to be the eyes and ears.'' He released a loud snort. ''Blind eyes and deaf ears! Not one word about their numerical strength, not one—''

''Pardon me, sir,'' said Hefni, quickly, ''there are twenty-seven millions of them.''

''Ah!'' Cruin registered sharp interest. ''Only twenty-seven millions? Why, there's a hundred times that number on Huld which has no greater area of land surface.'' He mused a moment. ''Greatly underpopulated. Many cities devoid of a living soul. They have air-machines and other items suggestive of a civilization greater than the one they now enjoy. They operate the remnants of an economic system. You realize what all this means?''

Hefni blinked, made no reply. Kalma looked thoughtful. Fane and Parth remained blank-faced and tight-lipped.

''It means two things,'' Cruin pursued. ''War or disease. One or the other, or perhaps both—and on a large scale. I want information on that. I've got to learn what sort of weapons they employed in their war, how many of them remain available, and where. Or, alternatively, what disease ravished their numbers, its source, and its cure.'' He tapped Hefni's chest to emphasize his words. ''I want to know what they've got hidden away, what they're trying to keep from your knowledge against the time when they can bring it out and use it against us. Above all, I want to know which people will issue orders for their general offensive and where they are located.''

"I understand, sir," said Hefni, doubtfully.

"That's the sort of information I need from your six specimens. I want information, not invitations to meals!" His grin was ugly as he noted Hefni's wince. "If you can get it out of them before they're due here, I shall enter the fact on the credit side of your records. But if I, your commander, have to do your job by extracting it from them myself—" Ominously, he left the sentence unfinished.

Hefni opened his mouth, closed it, glanced nervously at Kalma who stood stiff and dumb at his side.

"You may go," Cruin snapped at the four of them. "You have one week. If you fail me, I shall deem it a front-line offense and deal with it in accordance with the active-service section of the manual of procedure and discipline."

They were pale as they saluted. He watched them file out, his lips curling contemptuously. Going to the port, he gazed into the gathering darkness, saw a pale star winking in the east. Low and far it was—but not so far as Huld.

In the mid-period of the sixteenth day, Commander Cruin strode forth polished and bemedaled, directed his bell-jangling feet toward the hill. A sour-faced guard saluted him at the edge of the ash and made a slovenly job of it.

"Is that the best you can do?" He glared into the other's surly eyes. "Repeat it!"

The guard saluted a fraction more swiftly.

"You're out of practice," Cruin informed. "Probably all the crews are out of practice. We'll find a remedy for that. We'll have a period of saluting drill every day." His glare went slowly up and down the guard's face. "Are you dumb?"

"No, sir."

"Shut up!" roared Cruin. He expanded his chest. "Continue with your patrol."

The guard's optics burned with resentment as he saluted for the third time, turned with the regulation heel-click and marched along the perimeter.

Mounting the hill, Cruin sat on the stone at the top. Alternately he viewed the ships lying in the valley and the opposite scene with its trees, fields and distant houses. The metal helmet with its ornamental wings was heavy upon his head but he did not remove it. In the shadow beneath the projecting visor, his cold eyes brooded over the landscape to one side and the other.

She came eventually. He had been sitting there for one and a half periods when she came as he had known she would—without knowing what weird instinct had made him certain of this. Certainly, he had no desire to see her—no desire at all.

Through the trees she tripped light-footed, with Sue and Sam and three other girls of her own age. The newcomers had large, dark, humorous eyes, their hair was dark, and they were leggy.

"Oh, hello!" She paused as she saw him.

"Hello!" echoed Sue, swinging her pigtails.

" 'Lo!" piped Sam, determined not to be left out.

Cruin frowned at them. There was a high gloss on his jack boots, and his helmet glittered in the sun.

"These are my friends," said Marva, in her alien-accented Huldian. "Becky, Rita and Joyce."

The three smiled at him.

"I brought them to see the ships."

Cruin said nothing.

"You don't mind them looking at the ships, do you?"

"No," he growled with reluctance.

Lankily but gracefully she seated herself on the grass. The others followed suit with the exception of Sam who stood with fat legs braced apart sucking his thumb, and solemnly studying Cruin's decorated jacket.

"Father was disappointed because you could not visit us."

Cruin made no reply.

"Mother was sorry, too. She's a wonderful cook. She loves a guest."

No reply.

"Would you care to come this evening?"

"No."

"Some other evening?"

"Young lady," he harshed, severely, "I do not pay visits. Nobody pays visits."

She translated this to the others. They laughed so heartily that Cruin reddened and stood up.

"What's funny about that?" he demanded.

"Nothing, nothing." Marva was embarrassed. "If I told you, I fear that you would not understand."

"I would not understand." His grim eyes became alert, calculating as they went over her three friends. "I do not think, somehow, that they were laughing at me. Therefore they were laughing at what I do not know. They were laughing at something I ought to know but which you do not wish to tell me." He bent over her, huge and muscular, while she looked up at him with her great green eyes. "And what remark of mine revealed my amusing ignorance?"

Her steady gaze remained on him while she made no answer. A faint but sweet scent exuded from her hair.

"I said that nobody pays visits," he repeated. "That was the amusing remark—nobody pays visits. And I am not a fool!" Straightening, he turned away. "So I am going to call the rolls!"

He could feel their eyes upon him as he started down the valley. They were silent except for Sam's high-pitched, childish, "Bye!" which he ignored.

Without once looking back, he gained his flagship, mounted its metal ladder, made his way to the office and summoned Jusik.

"Order the captains to call their rolls at once."

"Is something wrong, sir?" inquired Jusik, anxiously.

"Call the rolls!" Cruin bellowed, whipping off his helmet. "Then we'll know whether anything is wrong." Savagely, he flung the helmet onto a wall hook, sat down, mopped his forehead.

Jusik was gone for most of a period. In the end he returned, set-faced, grave.

"I regret to report that eighteen men are absent, sir."

"They laughed," said Cruin, bitterly. "They laughed—because they *knew*!" His knuckles were white as his hands gripped the arms of his chair.

"I beg your pardon, sir?" Jusik's eyebrows lifted.

"How long have they been absent?"

"Eleven of them were on duty this morning."

"That means the other seven have been missing since yesterday?"

"I'm afraid so, sir."

"But no one saw fit to inform me of this fact?"

Jusik fidgeted. "No, sir."

"Have you discovered anything else of which I have not been informed?"

The other fidgeted again, looked pained.

"Out with it, man!"

"It is not the absentees' first offense," Jusik said with difficulty. "Nor their second. Perhaps not their sixth."

"How long has this been going on?" Cruin waited awhile, then bawled: "Come on! You are capable of speech!"

"About ten days, sir."

"How many captains were aware of this and failed to report it?"

"Nine, sir. Four of them await your bidding outside."

"And what of the other five?"

"They . . . they—" Jusik licked his lips.

Cruin arose, his expression dangerous. "You cannot conceal the truth by delaying it."

"They are among the absentees, sir."

"I see!" Cruin stamped to the door, stood by it. "We can take it for granted that others have absented themselves without permission, but were fortunate enough to be here when the rolls were called. That is their good luck. The real total of the disobedient cannot be discovered. They have sneaked away like nocturnal animals, and in the same manner they sneak back. All are guilty of desertion in the face of the enemy. There is one penalty for that."

"Surely, sir, considering the circ—"

"Considering nothing!" Cruin's voice shot up to an enraged shout. "Death! The penalty is death!" Striding to the table, he hammered the books lying upon it. "Summary execution as laid down in the manual of procedure and discipline. Desertion, mutinous conduct, defiance of a superior officer, conspiracy to thwart regulations and defy my orders—all punishable by death!" His voice lowered as swiftly as it had gone up. "Besides, my dear Jusik, if we fail through disintegration attributable to our own deliberate disregard of the manuals, what will be the penalty payable by *us*? What will it be, eh?"

"Death," admitted Jusik. He looked at Cruin. "On Huld, anyway."

"We are on Huld! *This* is Huld! I have claimed this planet in the name of Huld and therefore it is part of it."

"A mere claim, sir, if I may say—"

"Jusik, are *you* with these conspirators in opposing my authority?" Cruin's eyes glinted. His hand lay over his gun.

"Oh, no, sir!" The second commander's features mirrored the emotions conflicting within him. "But permit me to point out, sir, that we are a brotherly band who've been cooped together a long, long time and already have suffered losses getting here as we shall do getting back. One can hardly expect the men to—"

"I expect obedience!" Cruin's hand remained on the gun. "I expect iron discipline and immediate, willing, unquestionable obedience. With those, we conquer. Without them, we fail." He gestured to the door. "Are those captains properly prepared for examination as directed in the manuals?"

"Yes, sir. They are disarmed and under guard."

"Parade them in." Leaning on the edge of his desk, Cruin prepared to pass judgment on his fellows. The minute he waited for them was long, long as any minute he had ever known.

There had been scent in her hair.
And her eyes were cool and green.
Iron discipline must be maintained.
The price of power.

The manual provided an escape. Facing the four captains, he found himself taking advantage of the legal loophole to substitute demotion for the more drastic and final penalty.

Tramping the room before them while they stood in a row, pale-faced and rigid, their tunics unbuttoned, their ceremonial belts missing, the guards impassive on either side of them, he rampaged and swore and sprinkled them with verbal vitriol while his right fist hammered steadily into the palm of his left hand.

"But since you were present at the roll call, and therefore are not technically guilty of desertion, and since you surrendered yourself to my judgment immediately you were called upon to do so, I hereby sentence you to be demoted to the basic rank, the circumstances attending this sentence to be entered in your records." He dismissed them with a curt flourish of his white-gloved hand. "That is all."

They filed out silently.

He looked at Jusik. "Inform the respective lieutenant captains that they are promoted to full captains and now must enter recommendations for their vacated positions. These must be received by me before nightfall."

"As you order, sir."

"Also warn them to prepare to attend a commanding officer's court which will deal with the lower-ranking absentees as and when they reappear. Inform Captain Somir that he is appointed commander of the firing squad which will carry out the decisions of the court immediately they are pronounced."

"Yes, sir." Gaunt and hollow-eyed, Jusik turned with a click of heels and departed.

When the closer had shut the door, Cruin sat at his desk, placed his elbows on its surface, held his face in his hands. If the deserters did not return, they could not be punished. No power, no authority could vent its wrath upon an absent body. The law was impotent if its subjects lacked the essential feature of being present. All the laws of Huld could not put memories of lost men before a firing squad.

It was imperative that he make an example of the offenders. Their sly, furtive trips into the enemy's camp, he suspected, had been repeated often enough to have become a habit. Doubtless by now they were settled wherever they were visiting, sharing homes—welcome rooms—sharing food, company, laughter. Doubtless they had started to regain weight, to lose the space lines on their cheeks and foreheads, and the light in their eyes had begun to burn anew; and they had talked with signs and pictures, played games, tried to suck smoke things, and strolled with girls through the fields and the glades.

A pulse was beating steadily in the thickness of his neck as he stared through the port and waited for some sign that the tripled ring of guards had caught the first on his way in. Down, down, deep down inside him at a depth too great for him to admit that it was there, lay the disloyal hope that none would return.

One deserter would mean the slow, shuffling tread of the squad, the hoarse calls of "Aim!" and "Fire!" and the stepping forward of Somir, gun in hand, to administer the mercy shot.

Damn the manuals.

At the end of the first period after nightfall Jusik burst into the office, saluted, breathed heavily. The glare of the ceiling illumination deepened the lines on his thin features, magnified the bristles on his unshaven chin.

"Sir, I have to report that the men are getting out of control."

"What d'you mean?" Cruin's heavy brows came down as he stared fiercely at the other.

"They know of the recent demotions, of course. They know also that a court will assemble to deal with the absentees." He took another long-drawn breath. "And they also know the penalty these absentees must face."

"So?"

"So more of them have deserted—they've gone to warn the others not to return."

"Ah!" Cruin smiled lopsidedly. "The guards let them walk out, eh? Just like that?"

"Ten of the guards went with them," said Jusik.

"Ten?" Coming up fast, Cruin moved near to the other, studied him searchingly. "How many went altogether?"

"Ninety-seven."

Grabbing his helmet, Cruin slammed it on, pulled the metal

chin strap over his jaw muscles. "More than one complete crew." He examined his gun, shoved it back, strapped on a second one. "At that rate they'll all be gone by morning." He eyed Jusik. "Don't you think so?"

"That's what I'm afraid of, sir."

Cruin patted his shoulder. "The answer, Jusik, is an easy one—we take off immediately."

"Take off?"

"Most certainly. The whole fleet. We'll strike a balanced orbit where it will be impossible for any man to leave. I will then give the situation more thought. Probably we'll make a new landing in some locality where none will be tempted to sneak away because there'll be nowhere to go. A scout can pick up Fane and his party in due course."

"I doubt whether they'll obey orders for departure, sir."

"We'll see, we'll see." He smiled again, hard and craggy. "As you would know if you'd studied the manuals properly, it is not difficult to smash incipient mutiny. All one has to do is remove the ringleaders. No mob is composed of men, as such. It is made up of a few ringleaders and a horde of stupid followers." He patted his guns. "You can always tell a ringleader—invariably he is the first to open his mouth!"

"Yes, sir," mouthed Jusik, with misgivings.

"Sound the call for general assembly."

The flagship's siren wailed dismally in the night. Lights flashed from ship to ship, and startled birds woke up and squawked in the trees beyond the ash.

Slowly, deliberately, impressively, Cruin came down the ladder, faced the audience whose features were a mass of white blobs in the glare of the ships' beams. The captains and lieutenant captains ranged themselves behind him and to either side. Each carried an extra gun.

"After three years of devoted service to Huld," he enunciated pompously, "some men have failed me. It seems that we have weaklings among us, weaklings unable to stand the strain of a few extra days before our triumph. Careless of their duty they disobey orders, fraternize with the enemy, consort with our opponents' females, and try to snatch a few creature comforts at the expense of the many." His hard, accusing eyes went over them. "In due time they will be punished with the utmost severity."

They stared back at him expressionlessly. He could shoot the ears off a running man at twenty-five yards, and he was waiting for his target to name itself. So were those at his side.

None spoke.

"Among you may be others equally guilty but not discovered. They need not congratulate themselves, for they are about to be deprived of further opportunities to exercise their disloyalty." His stare kept flickering over them while his hand remained ready at his side. "We are going to trim the ships and take off, seeking a balanced orbit. That means lost sleep and plenty of hard work for which you have your treacherous comrades to thank." He paused a moment, finished with: "Has anyone anything to say?"

One man holding a thousand.

Silence.

"Prepare for departure," he snapped, and turned his back upon them.

Captain Somir, now facing him, yelped: "Look out, commander!" and whipped up his gun to fire over Cruin's shoulder.

Cruin made to turn, conscious of a roar behind him, his guns coming out as he twisted around. He heard no crack from Somir's weapon, saw no more of his men as their roar cut off abruptly. There seemed to be an intolerable weight upon his skull, the grass came up to meet him, he let go his guns and put out his hands to save himself. Then the hazily dancing lights faded from his eyesight and all was black.

Deep in his sleep he heard vaguely and uneasily a prolonged stamping of feet, many dull, elusive sounds as of people shouting far, far away. This went on for a considerable time, and ended with a series of violent reports that shook the ground beneath his body.

Someone splashed water over his face.

Sitting up, he held his throbbing head, saw pale fingers of dawn feeling through the sky to one side. Blinking his aching eyes to clear them, he perceived Jusik, Somir and eight others. All were smothered in dirt, their faces bruised, their uniforms torn and bedraggled.

"They rushed us the moment you turned away from them," explained Jusik, morbidly. "A hundred of them in the front. They rushed us in one united frenzy, and the rest followed. There were too many for us." He regarded his superior with red-rimmed optics. "You have been flat all night."

Unsteadily, Cruin got to his feet, teetered to and fro. "How many were killed?"

"None. We fired over their heads. After that—it was too late."

"Over their heads?" Squaring his massive shoulders, Cruin felt a sharp pain in the middle of his back, ignored it. "What are guns for if not to kill?"

"It isn't easy," said Jusik, with the faintest touch of defiance. "Not when they're one's own comrades."

"Do you agree?" The commander's glare challenged the others.

They nodded miserably, and Somir said: "There was little time, sir, and if one hesitates, as we did, it becomes—"

"There are no excuses for anything. You had your orders; it was for you to obey them." His hot gaze burned one, then the other. "You are incompetent for your rank. You are both demoted!" His jaw came forward, ugly, aggressive, as he roared: "Get out of my sight!"

They mooched away. Savagely, he climbed the ladder, entered his ship, explored it from end to end. There was not a soul on board. His lips were tight as he reached the tail, found the cause of the earth-rocking detonations. The fuel tanks had been exploded, wrecking the engines and reducing the whole vessel to a useless mass of metal.

Leaving, he inspected the rest of his fleet. Every ship was the same, empty and wrecked beyond possibility of repair. At least the mutineers had been thorough and logical in their sabotage. Until a report-vessel arrived, the home world of Huld had no means of knowing where the expedition had landed. Despite even a systematic and wide-scale search it might well be a thousand years before Huldians found this particular planet again. Effectively the rebels had marooned themselves for the rest of their natural lives and placed themselves beyond reach of Huldian retribution.

Tasting to the full the bitterness of defeat, he squatted on the bottom rung of the twenty-second vessel's ladder, surveyed the double star-formations that represented his ruined armada. Futilely, their guns pointed over surrounding terrain. Twelve of the scouts, he noted, had gone. The others had been rendered as useless as their parent vessels.

Raising his gaze to the hill, he perceived silhouettes against the dawn where Jusik, Somir and the others were walking over the crest, walking away from him, making for the farther valley he had viewed so often. Four children joined them at the top, romped beside them as they proceeded. Slowly the whole group sank from sight under the rising sun.

Returning to the flagship, Cruin packed a patrol sack with personal possessions, strapped it on his shoulders. Without a final glance at the remains of his once-mighty command he set forth away from the sun, in the direction opposite to that taken by the last of his men.

His jack boots were dull, dirty. His orders of merit hung lopsidedly and had a gap where one had been torn off in the fracas. The bell was missing from his right boot; he endured the pad-*ding*, pad-*ding* of its fellow for twenty steps before he unscrewed it and slung it away.

The sack on his back was heavy, but not so heavy as the immense burden upon his mind. Grimly, stubbornly he plodded on, away from the ships, far, far into the morning mists—facing the new world alone.

Three and a half years had bitten deep into the ships of Huld. Still they lay in the valley, arranged with mathematical precision, noses in, tails out, as only authority could place them. But the rust had eaten a quarter of the way through the thickness of their tough shells, and their metal ladders were rotten and treacherous. The field mice and the voles had found refuge beneath them; the birds and spiders had sought sanctuary within them. A lush growth had sprung from encompassing ash, hiding the perimeter for all time.

The man who came by them in the midafternoon rested his pack and studied them silently, from a distance. He was big, burly, with a skin the color of old leather. His deep gray eyes were calm, thoughtful as they observed the thick ivy climbing over the flagship's tail.

Having looked at them for a musing half hour he hoisted his pack and went on, up the hill, over the crest and into the farther valley. Moving easily in his plain, loose-fitting clothes, his pace was deliberate, methodical.

Presently he struck a road, followed it to a stone-built cottage in the garden of which a lithe, dark-haired woman was cutting flowers. Leaning on the gate, he spoke to her. His speech was fluent but strangely accented. His tones were gruff but pleasant.

"Good afternoon."

She stood up, her arms full of gaudy blooms, looked at him with rich, black eyes. "Good afternoon." Her full lips parted with pleasure. "Are you touring? Would you care to guest with us? I am sure that Jusik—my husband—would be delighted to have you. Our welcome room has not been occupied for—"

"I am sorry," he chipped in. "I am seeking the Merediths. Could you direct me?"

"The next house up the lane." Deftly, she caught a falling bloom, held it to her breast. "If their welcome room has a guest, please remember us."

"I will remember," he promised. Eyeing her approvingly, his broad, muscular face lit up with a smile. "Thank you so much."

Shouldering his pack he marched on, conscious of her eyes following him. He reached the gate of the next place, a long, rambling, picturesque house fronted by a flowering garden. A boy was playing by the gate.

Glancing up as the other stopped near him, the boy said: "Are you touring, sir?"

"Sir?" echoed the man. "*Sir?*" His face quirked. "Yes, sonny, I am touring. I'm looking for the Merediths."

"Why, I'm Sam Meredith!" The boy's face flushed with sudden excitement. "You wish to guest with us?"

"If I may."

"Yow-ee!" He fled frantically along the garden path, shrieking at the top of his voice, "Mom, Pop, Marva, Sue—we've got a guest!"

A tall, red-headed man came to the door, pipe in mouth. Coolly, calmly, he surveyed the visitor.

After a little while, the man removed the pipe and said: "I'm Jake Meredith. Please come in." Standing aside, he let the other enter, then called, "Mary, Mary, can you get a meal for a guest?"

"Right away," assured a cheerful voice from the back.

"Come with me." Meredith led the other to the veranda, found him an easy-chair. "Might as well rest while you're waiting. Mary takes time. She isn't satisfied until the legs of the table are near to collapse—and woe betide you if you leave anything."

"It is good of you." Seating himself, the visitor drew a long breath, gazed over the pastoral scene before him.

Taking another chair, Meredith applied a light to his pipe. "Have you seen the mail ship?"

"Yes, it arrived early yesterday. I was lucky enough to view it as it passed overhead."

"You certainly were lucky considering that it comes only once in four years. I've seen it only twice, myself. It came right over this house. An imposing sight."

"Very!" endorsed the visitor, with unusual emphasis. "It looked to me about five miles long, a tremendous creation. Its mass must be many times greater than that of all those alien ships in the valley."

"Many times," agreed Meredith.

The other leaned forward, watching his host. "I often wonder whether those aliens attributed smallness of numbers to war or disease, not thinking of large-scale emigration, nor realizing what it means."

"I doubt whether they cared very much seeing that they burned their boats and settled among us." He pointed with the stem of his pipe. "One of them lives in that cottage down there. Jusik's his name. Nice fellow. He married a local girl eventually. They are very happy."

"I'm sure they are."

They were quiet a long time, then Meredith spoke absently, as if thinking aloud. "They brought with them weapons of considerable might, not knowing that we have a weapon truly invincible." Waving one hand, he indicated the world at large. "It took us thousands of years to learn about the sheer invincibility of an idea. That's what we've got—a way of life, an idea. Nothing can blast that to shreds. Nothing can defeat an idea—except a better one." He put the pipe back in his mouth. "So far, we have failed to find a better one.

"They came at the wrong time," Meredith went on. "Ten thousand years too late." He glanced sidewise at his listener. "Our history covers a long, long day. It was so lurid that it came out in a new edition every minute. But this one's the late night final."

"You philosophize, eh?"

Meredith smiled. "I often sit here to enjoy my silences. I sit here and think. Invariably I end up with the same conclusion."

"What may that be?"

"That if I, personally, were in complete possession of all the visible stars and their multitude of planets I would still be subject to one fundamental limitation"—bending, he tapped his pipe on his heel—"in this respect—that no man can eat more than his belly can hold." He stood up, tall, wide-chested. "Here comes my daughter, Marva. Would you like her to show you your room?"

* * *

Standing inside the welcome room, the visitor surveyed it appreciatively. The comfortable bed, the bright furnishings.

"Like it?" Marva asked.

"Yes, indeed." Facing her, his gray eyes examined her. She was tall, red-haired, green-eyed, and her figure was ripe with the beauty of young womanhood. Pulling slowly at his jaw muscles, he asked: "Do you think that I resemble Cruin?"

"Cruin?" Her finely curved brows crinkled in puzzlement.

"The commander of that alien expedition."

"Oh, him!" Her eyes laughed, and the dimples came into her cheeks. "How absurd! You don't look the least bit like him. He was old and severe. You are *young*—and far more handsome."

"It is kind of you to say so," he murmured. His hands moved aimlessly around in obvious embarrassment. He fidgeted a little under her frank, self-possessed gaze. Finally, he went to his pack, opened it. "It is conventional for the guest to bring his hosts a present." A tinge of pride crept into his voice. "So I have brought one. I made it myself. It took me a long time to learn . . . a long time . . . with these clumsy hands. About three years."

Marva looked at it, raced through the doorway, leaned over the balustrade and called excitedly down the stairs. "Pop, Mom, our guest has a wonderful present for us. A clock. A clock with a little metal bird that calls the time."

Beneath her, feet bustled along the passage and Mary's voice came up saying: "May I see it? Please let me see it." Eagerly, she mounted the stairs.

As he waited for them within the welcome room, his shoulders squared, body erect as if on parade, the clock whirred in Cruin's hands and its little bird solemnly fluted twice.

The hour of triumph.

ABOUT THE EDITORS

ISAAC ASIMOV is the author of numerous volumes of science fiction (among countless other books), as well as scores of science fiction stories.

MARTIN H. GREENBERG has edited more than two dozen science fiction anthologies and has published extensively in the field.